STEVE VEALE, who lives in Toronto, is a free-lance contributor of travel articles to many Canadian and U.S. newspapers and magazines. A member of the Society of American Travel Writers, he is the editorial consultant for this guidebook.

SHERRY BOECKH has more than 20 years of experience writing on travel for CBC Television and TV Ontario as well as for Canada's major newspapers and magazines.

GEORGE BRYANT was until recently the travel editor for the *Toronto Star,* Canada's largest newspaper. Since 1949 he has covered places and events in every province and territory in Canada.

ASHOK CHANDWANI, with 12 years of experience as a senior writer and editor at Montreal daily newspapers, was the travel editor at Montreal's *The Gazette* and is now the lifestyle editor. He also reviews restaurants and writes an occasional cooking column for the newspaper.

JEAN DANARD, a long-time author of travel articles at Canada's *Financial Post,* is now a free-lance writer in Ontario.

NAN DROSDICK, a staff and free-lance newspaper and magazine writer, editor, and photographer for the past 17 years, has covered Atlantic Canada since 1979.

DAVID DUNBAR, formerly an editor at Reader's Digest books, contributed to *Heritage of Canada, Atlas of Canada,* and *Canadian Book of the Road.*

CHARMAINE GAUDET, who was born on Prince Edward Island and now lives in Nova Scotia, has for 11 years written about her native province for magazines in the U.S. and Canada.

MAURA GIULIANI has spent the last nine years in the Ottawa area working as a free-lance writer and editor.

JOHN GODDARD, after travelling through the Yukon and Northwest Territories as a reporter and photographer, opened a bureau for the Canadian news agency there in 1982. He is currently writing a book on the Lubicon Lake Cree of northern Alberta.

JOSEPH HOARE, a fifth-generation Canadian, has been a staff researcher and food editor at *Toronto Life* since 1978.

HAROLD HORWOOD is the author of *Newfoundland* as well as many other books on travel, biography, and popular history. A native Newfoundlander, he now lives in Nova Scotia.

MARY KELLY, a communications consultant in Montreal, is the author of a guide to the city as well as a contributor to several guidebooks about the province of Quebec.

HAZEL LOWE was the associate travel editor for *The Gazette* and travel editor of *The Montreal Star*. She now writes a syndicated weekly column on family travel for Southam News in Montreal.

GARRY MARCHANT, the winner of many international travel writing awards, writes monthly travel articles for *Vancouver Magazine* and other magazines in North America.

MARNIE MITCHELL, a native of Vancouver, writes a monthly column for *Key to Vancouver* magazine.

LEE SCHACTER, who has lived in Manitoba all her life, has been a free-lance writer for the *Winnipeg Free Press* and the *Tribune*.

DAVID SCOTT, a native of Quebec, is the travel editor of the *London Free Press* of Ontario.

DAVID STARRE, a resident of Saskatchewan since 1975, has been writing about the province for 11 years.

COLLEEN THOMPSON, a lifelong resident of New Brunswick, has written extensively about the province in various publications. She is the author of the best-selling *New Brunswick Inside Out,* and a travel columnist for the *Saint John Telegraph Journal.*

ROBERTA WALKER founded *Real Travel,* a magazine for adventuresome travellers. She now writes freelance articles for several magazines in North America.

THE PENGUIN TRAVEL GUIDES

THE PENGUIN GUIDE TO CANADA 1990

ALAN TUCKER
General Editor

PENGUIN BOOKS

PENGUIN BOOKS

Published by the Penguin Group
Viking Penguin a division of Penguin Books USA Inc.,
40 West 23rd Street, New York, New York 10010, U.S.A.
Penguin Books Ltd, 27 Wrights Lane,
London W8 5TZ, England
Penguin Books Australia Ltd, Ringwood,
Victoria, Australia
Penguin Books Canada Ltd, 2801 John Street,
Markham, Ontario, Canada L3R 1B4
Penguin Books (N.Z.) Ltd, 182-190 Wairau Road,
Auckland 10, New Zealand

Penguin Books Ltd, Registered Offices:
Harmondsworth, Middlesex, England

First published in Penguin Books 1989
This revised edition published 1990

1   3   5   7   9   10   8   6   4   2

ISBN 0 14 019.918 7
ISSN 0897-6872

Printed in the United States of America

Set in ITC Garamond Light
Designed by Beth Tondreau Design
Maps by Bette Duke
Illustrations by Bill Russell
Editorial services by Stephen Brewer Associates

THIS GUIDEBOOK

The Penguin Travel Guides are designed for people who are experienced travellers in search of exceptional information to help them sharpen and deepen their enjoyment of the trips they take.

Where, for example, are the interesting, isolated, fun, charming, or romantic places within your budget to stay? The hotels described by our writers (each of whom is an experienced travel writer who either lives in or regularly tours the city or region of Canada he or she covers) are some of the special places, in all price ranges except for the lowest—not the run-of-the-mill, heavily marketed places on every travel agent's CRT display and in advertised airline and travel-agency packages. We indicate the approximate price level of each accommodation in our descriptions of it (no indication means it is moderate), and at the end of every chapter we supply contact information so that you can get precise, up-to-the-minute rates and make reservations.

The Penguin Guide to Canada 1990 highlights the more rewarding parts of the country so that you can quickly and efficiently home in on a good itinerary.

Of course, the guides do far more than just help you choose a hotel and plan your trip. *The Penguin Guide to Canada 1990* is designed for use *in* Canada. Our Penguin Canada writers tell you what you really need to know, what you can't find out so easily on your own. They identify and describe the truly out-of-the-ordinary restaurants, shops, activities, and sights, and tell you the best way to "do" your destination.

Our writers are highly selective. They bring out the significance of the places they cover, capturing the personality and the underlying cultural and historical resonances of a city or region—making clear its special appeal. For exhaustive detailed coverage of activities and attractions, we suggest that you also use a supplementary reference-type guidebook, probably obtained locally.

The Penguin Guide to Canada 1990 is full of reliable and timely information, revised each year. We would like to know if you think we've left out some very special place.

ALAN TUCKER
General Editor
Penguin Travel Guides

40 West 23rd Street
New York, New York 10010
or
27 Wrights Lane
London   W8 5TZ

CONTENTS

MAPS

THE
PENGUIN
GUIDE
TO
CANADA
1990

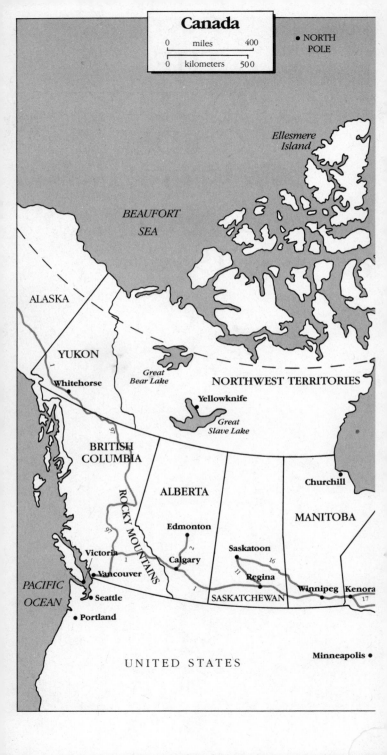

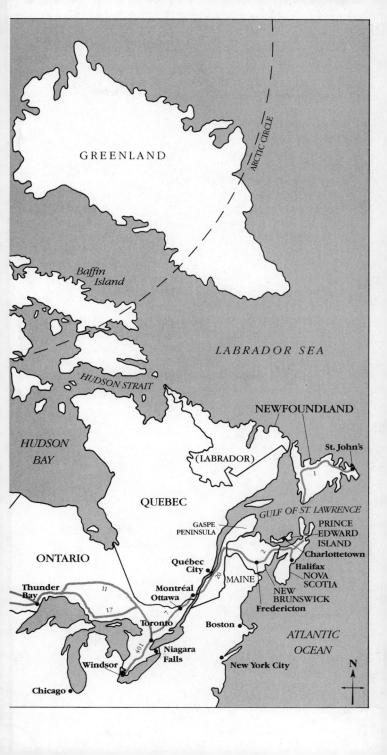

OVERVIEW

By George Bryant

George Bryant, until recently the travel editor of the Toronto Star, *Canada's largest newspaper, has been a reporter, columnist, correspondent, and editor since 1949. He has travelled more than one million miles for the* Star, *covering places and events in every province and territory of Canada as well as around the world.*

Canada has urban delights to please any visitor: Sophisticated cities with downtown cores that are alive with people, with infinitesimal crime rates, and with tree-shaded thoroughfares, fine restaurants, theaters, and museums.

It has historic forts, a European settlement that predates Columbus by 500 years, and a province that offers not only a Continental flavor but the only walled city north of Mexico.

It has sports palaces, ski runs that reach the clouds, and fine hotels—and 25 million inhabitants who exhibit a small-town friendliness even on the subways of the largest cities.

But when all that is said, the major lure of Canada remains the wonders of its endless outdoors, the magnificent prospects to be found from ocean to ocean, the mountains, waterfalls and fjords, the glaciers, lakes, animals, beaches, and rock-bound coasts.

And that outdoors does seem endless, as prospective visitors soon discover, because the land is not just huge, it's immense, sprawling nearly 5,000 miles across the top of the North American continent and encompassing all the land, water, and ice between Buffalo, New York, and the North Pole.

That's a mind-boggling 3,845,774 square miles, and it

offers one problem along with a lot of bonuses: You have to know what you want to do and see and where to find it.

As to the bonuses, size is not an attraction in itself, but at these dimensions it does provide room for infinite variety, which is why Canada can offer just about anything a traveller would want short of hula skirts and coral reefs; everything from a simulated journey through space to a walk on a glacier or close-up encounters with migrating polar bears.

A visitor can run television cameras or count radioactive ants at Toronto's Ontario Science Centre, stand right beneath the plunging, thundering waters of Niagara Falls, drive Alberta's Icefield Parkway and watch mountain rams battle at the highway's edge, take afternoon tea in Victoria's Empress Hotel, visit Lake Louise in the Canadian Rockies to experience the unforgettable dawn beauty of the lake and trees and reflected glacier, explore the narrow alleys and superb restaurants of Quebec City's walled acres, go whale watching in the Gulf of St. Lawrence, or admire the genius of Alexander Graham Bell at a museum near his summer home in Baddeck, Nova Scotia.

You can do all that and just be touching the surface, just starting to explore this land. And then you can visit the spot in Newfoundland where Vikings built a settlement long before William the Conqueror won England, and another place, near Wood Mountain, Saskatchewan, where 4,000 Sioux under Chief Sitting Bull, fresh from their annihilation of General George Armstrong Custer and his men, settled peacefully into camp at the behest of a few North West Mounted Police officers.

And after that you can go on to ski the steepest slopes in North America at Whistler/Blackcomb in British Columbia, look out over Lake Ontario from the 150-story observation deck of Toronto's CN Tower, shop the miles of underground malls beneath Montreal's streets, and then head for Cape Breton to explore the magnificently restored Fortress of Louisbourg. It cost more to rebuild than France's Louis XV spent on it in the first place, although he grumbled at the time that he was paying so much he awoke every morning expecting to see its towers rising over the western horizon.

And still that is a mere beginning, just a sampling. There are ten provinces standing shoulder to shoulder just above the U.S. border, and north of them two vast regions: the Yukon and Northwest Territories—the latter so huge it forms one third of the country—and every one of them has its own attractions, man-made and natural. So the choices are many.

As a result there is no one tourist route that everybody follows, no London or Paris where most visitors land. Rather, there are several major gateways: Montreal, Toronto, or Vancouver on the main tourist routes, particularly for visitors from overseas; St. John's (Newfoundland), Saint John (New Brunswick), Halifax, Quebec City, Ottawa, Winnipeg, Edmonton, or Calgary on the secondary routes. The one you will use will depend on which Canada you want to visit. (We'll help you with that choice a bit further on.)

And then there are scores of highway crossing points all along the Canada/U.S. border from Maine to Washington, including a busy bridge at Niagara Falls, and ferries and passenger ships on both sides of the continent. So there's no lack of entry points or transport once you've made your decision to visit.

The Canadians are friendly, if a little reserved and a bit shy, a sober inheritance from the Scottish Presbyterians who flocked to the land when the Highland clearances took place in the last century. They're fun-loving enough but not as exuberant in it as citizens might be south of the border or, indeed, in the province of Quebec, where the tongue is French and the residents add a Gallic flair and color to everything they do.

That reserve sometimes makes English-speaking Canadians slow in proffering help or advice, but if asked they'll overwhelm with information and/or aid. And mostly— except for Newfoundland's Irish Outport lilt and a bit of a burr in the Ottawa Valley—in the same accent, a neutral sort of North American English with the Scottish heritage coming through on words such as "out" and "about," which have an "oot" and "aboot" sound to English-speaking visitors, particularly those from the United States.

Why so few regional accents? Because the railway moved west with settlers in the last century and there was constant passenger traffic back and forth between the new settlements and the old. The result: No isolated pockets of residents to develop regional speech patterns.

These English-speaking Canadians may look and sound much like Americans, but they are different. They shared a common history with their neighbors to the south up to the American Revolution, but then everything turned upside down, as a look at any Canadian history book will show. U.S. Revolutionary heroes are villains or traitors (Benedict Arnold was one who came to his senses), and the War of 1812 was a naked attempt by the U.S. to swallow the infant colony to the north—all of which gives Canadians a somewhat different perspective on the world.

In the East, from the Maritimes through to Ontario, the United Empire Loyalists (the Canadian name for the Tory landowners, doctors, lawyers, businessmen, and farmers who fled the American Revolution) are revered as founding fathers, with annual celebrations to honor their memory. U.S. visitors are welcomed, of course.

In the West there was one short war of rebellion against the Crown but no cowboy and Indian shootouts, no gunslingers or gunfighters at the O.K. Corral. It was a West that wasn't so wild, a West where several thousand Sioux would peacefully obey one Mountie who spoke for the Queen.

The measure of this West, perhaps, lies in a little grave-yard near the old headquarters of the North West Mounted Police at Fort Walsh, in southern Saskatchewan. In this northern Boot Hill there are more than a dozen gravestones, but only one records the death of a Mountie by violence. Constable Marmaduke Graeburn, 19, whose very name proclaims that this was not Dodge City or Tombstone, was mysteriously shot from ambush on November 17, 1879. All the others died of natural causes.

So Canadians retain more of the British heritage than their continental neighbors, in speech, in folklore, in attitude, even in humor. Quebec is an exception, of course, and Canadians in Newfoundland, which was a British colony until as late as 1949, have that Irish lilt in their speech and ways.

Newfoundland is the most easterly province and a good place to start a quick crosscountry rundown of major sights and points of interest. It is a place of cliffs, pounding seas, fishermen, wilderness parks, and little ports with such ingenuous names as Joe Batt's Arm, Bumble Bee Bight, Witless Bay, Heart's Content, Sap's Arm, and Dating Cove, a place where the speech, the shanties, and the songs have a wonderfully vital humor—if you can decipher the accent. As well it's the place where the Vikings landed 1,000 years ago and planted a colony, recording the event in their Sagas. They were later driven away by hostile Indians, but the remains of their settlement—six low, sodded burrows, a smithy, cooking pits, and, of course, a sauna—have been found at L'Anse-Aux-Meadows at the north end of the island. The spot, low-lying by a gray sea, is now a World Heritage Site; the Vikings' spartan way of life can be studied, without envy, at a re-created village nearby.

Southwest of the island, across the Cabot Strait, lies **Nova Scotia**, where it's a good idea to leave extra time for the Fortress of Louisbourg and the Bell Museum. At the former costumed attendants whisk you back to 1774, a hard year to leave, and at the latter there are so many examples of Alexander Graham Bell's genius in fact or photograph, everything from airplanes to iron lungs, that a day can pass like a dream.

Drive the Cabot Trail, too, while you're on Cape Breton, and also try the Lighthouse Route south from Halifax along a coast that's indented and furrowed and rocky. Don't forget Peggy's Cove, a picture-postcard-perfect bay that's now one of the most photographed spots on earth—but still worth a look.

Tories fleeing the Revolution helped build Nova Scotia—one year three quarters of all the Harvard graduates in the world were wintering there—but it's across the Bay of Fundy to the northwest in **New Brunswick** that United Empire Loyalist Days are celebrated in a big way, with costumes, speeches, parades, and re-created military units of the time.

If New Brunswick gained with the Loyalists, it lost with the Acadians, for it was from this province that the people who became Louisiana's Cajuns were expelled. Their relatives can be found along the Acadian coast by the Bay of Chaleur. It's a region of stories and songs delivered in French accents, of sand dunes and beaches and winds and the rumbling, accentless sea.

Prince Edward Island, just across Northumberland Strait to the north from New Brunswick, is the smallest province, a summertime attraction for its lobsters and wide, warm-water beaches, and the home of Lucy Maud Montgomery, author of *Anne of Green Gables*.

North and west across the Gulf of St. Lawrence lies **Quebec City**, where the city within the walls dates back to 1608 and the Château Frontenac Hotel towers like a turreted castle above the St. Lawrence River. If you can't stay at the Château visit it for its magnificent view, and be sure to wander the Old Town with its fine restaurants, strolling minstrels, and its joie de vivre.

West of the city the resorts of the **Laurentians**, old round-topped mountains, are full of song and après-ski parties in winter and nature lovers in summer. And in

Montreal, a city second only to Paris in French speakers, there's an underground city to roam, a rapids to run, some of the world's best food, and a major-league baseball team, the Expos, to cheer. Or boo.

Canada's capital, **Ottawa**, in Ontario at the juncture of the Ottawa River and the Rideau Canal, has a small-town feel, a Parliament to watch, museums to visit, and in winter a canal skating rink that runs for miles.

In **Ontario**, there is Niagara Falls—where there *is* some schlock, but more majesty—and one of the world's unique trains: The Polar Bear Express (a misleading name—it shows riders nary a bear) travels from Cochrane north through the wilderness to Indian country at Moosonee and Moose Factory on James Bay. Another train, worth the trip for the woodland scenery, runs from Sault Ste. Marie through the forests to Agawa Canyon, north of Lake Huron, well away from the works of man.

Toronto, like Montreal, has superb restaurants and a major league baseball team, the Blue Jays, who play under a SkyDome that rolls open on sunny days. Visit in summer and Toronto's Ontario Place offers a complex of theaters, pubs, and entertainment built out over the waters of Lake Ontario; ferries chug off to the parks on Toronto Island, and Harbourfront beckons with folk singers, poets, dancers, and shows of every sort.

To the west is **Manitoba**, where you can take a train that really does offer a sight of polar bears. Operated by VIA Rail, the national passenger service, it runs from Winnipeg to Churchill, where the great white giants lumber out onto the pack ice of Hudson Bay every autumn. Farther west is **Saskatchewan**, a place of wheat and endless sky, of Fort Walsh and Wood Mountain Post and the Sioux encampment, and of the battlefields of the short-lived North West Rebellion.

West again is **Alberta**, with two of the continent's most magnificent parks, Banff and Jasper, sprawling over hills, lakes, and valleys in the heart of the Rockies and connected by the Icefield Parkway, 230 km (143 miles) of sheer beauty.

Icefield Parkway runs between the main range of the Rockies, with mountains and glaciers and waterfalls on every side, and every turn of the wheel brings new vistas, changing always as the light changes so that no scene is ever the same from minute to minute. And, since it runs through national parks, on any trip visitors may see bear, elk, wolf, moose, deer, or mountain sheep (males often use its level pavement as jousting fields) against the majesty of the mountains.

There are campsites and lodges and resorts in and around the parks, and Banff is a good place to stay overnight, at Château Lake Louise—if only to see the lake, backed by the Victoria Glacier, in the mist of a summer dawn. Then drive the Parkway both ways, staying overnight in Jasper and stopping to walk on the Athabasca Glacier, part of the huge Columbia Icefield that parallels the road, the largest sheet of glacial ice in North America south of the Arctic.

This is a country, too, of badlands, and dinosaur bones, and is a good spot to try trail riding or to learn about horses at places such as Homeplace Ranch in Priddis, among the foothills of the Rockies.

You can take a train from Banff to Vancouver and roll through the passes with the mountains dark against a sunset sky, then rise at dawn to see the bulk of the coastal ranges in **British Columbia**: a memorable experience.

Vancouver has one of the world's most beautiful settings between the mountains and the sea, and the provincial capital, **Victoria**, on Vancouver Island, is the most British of North American cities, in climate, in gardens, in accent and attitude. Most visitors stroll Vancouver's Stanley Park and ride the ferries to the Gulf Islands; tour Victoria's outstanding Provincial Museum with its evocative sounds and smells; admire the bright blooms of Butchart Gardens and take a Victorian tea in the Empress Hotel lobby, where time seems to stand still.

North from the capital is Pacific Rim Park, where waves from the Pacific beat on a long, lone shore. Canada ends there in an appropriately wild setting.

North again along the mainland coast behind the barrier islands lies the Inside Passage of fjords and glaciers, a spectacular area for cruise ships. In the interior are ghost towns and mining camps, relics of the days when gold was the travel lure.

It was the lure, too, on the Trail of '98, when the world flocked to the **Yukon** "clean mad for that muck called gold," and the trail can be followed at Whitehorse and Dawson, where the poems of Robert Service and the entertainment of the gold fields find their place.

There's a road down to the Arctic Ocean now, the Dempster Highway, which runs from the Yukon through the **Northwest Territories** to Tuktoyaktuk, an Inuit settlement on the Beaufort Sea. But most visitors to the Territories, which encompass all of northern Canada east of the Yukon, fly in to remote lakes or camps for fishing or for nature studies. Or they visit Wood Buffalo Park, which lies across the border of Alberta and the Territories far to the south of Tuktoyaktuk.

These are only a few of the pleasures to be discovered in Canada. Details on them and hundreds of others can be found in the following chapters.

USEFUL FACTS

When To Go

Most visitors prefer the warm weather between May and Canadian Thanksgiving, the second weekend of October, unless they choose to ski the Rockies of Alberta or the Laurentians in Quebec. Summer weather can range from a muggy 90 degrees F (about 30 degrees C) in Toronto to a dry prairie heat of 80 degrees F (about 25 degrees C). It is also the season when sandy beaches bloom in the mild Maritimes and the sun shines for about 20 hours a day in the balmy Northwest Territories sunshine.

Winter temperatures, however, can often descend to a chilly 15 degrees F (about −10 degrees C) in windy Montreal or a mind-numbing −20 degrees F (about −30 degrees C) in northern Saskatchewan. Best to plan a summer visit.

Entry Documents

This is likely the easiest border crossing that a U.S. citizen can make; not even a passport is required (though certainly beneficial), but simply some proof of citizenship, such as a birth certificate or Social Security card. And with a few standard questions (where you were born, where you live, purpose of visit, length of stay) you can be on your way. Anyone from the United Kingdom or any of its dependent territories (from Hong Kong to the Turks and Caicos Islands) does not need a visa to enter Canada, but should hold a valid passport.

Hunters may bring "long guns" (defined as hunting rifles or shotguns) without a gun permit, although they must have a valid hunting license.

Motorists entering Canada should render all radar-detecting devices inoperative and note that some provinces (e.g., Ontario) do not allow studded tires; other provinces permit them only in winter.

Household pets may be imported from the U.S. and parts of Europe (some restrictions may apply for certain countries; check with Customs in advance), provided each animal has a veterinarian's certificate of vaccination against rabies. More exotic animals, such as birds from South America, are subject to quarantine or may even be refused an entry permit. Again, check in advance with Customs.

Getting There

By Plane. Canada is a huge country, second only to the U.S.S.R. in land mass, although the plethora of flights to its major air terminals and the daily connections of its intracity services (for example, there are hourly flights between Toronto and Ottawa) somehow make it seem manageable. International terminals with flights from both the U.S. and Europe arrive daily at the following major destination cities: Vancouver, Calgary, Edmonton, Winnipeg, Toronto, Montreal, and Halifax.

Canadian carriers that service the international market include Air Canada, the government-operated airline, and the ever-growing Canadian Airlines, which recently purchased the country's third major airline, Wardair, which will continue to operate under its own name. U.S. carriers such as American, Eastern, and United also provide direct service to the various international terminals, as do national European carriers.

By Car. Again, this is the easiest border crossing for an American citizen (see Entry Documents), especially along busy corridors such as Detroit–Windsor, or Niagara Falls, U.S.A. and Canada, where citizens of both nationalities make daily crossings for their jobs, an afternoon of shopping, or perhaps an evening meal in a foreign country.

Normally, a verbal declaration of citizenship, place of residence, and proposed length of stay is all that is required to drive across a U.S.–Canada border. The question-and-answer session may take less than a minute but the wait—especially with all the summer vacationing traffic of camper trailers and mobile homes—could take well over an hour at the more popular entry points, not only at the Niagara Falls Peace Bridge but at such little northern crossings as the one linking Fort Francis and International Falls.

Motorists on the East Coast can enter the Maritime provinces through New Brunswick only from two border points in Maine: along Highway 95 from Houlton and

Highway 3 from Calais. From here you can drive into Nova Scotia and Cape Breton Island on the Trans-Canada Highway, although to reach Prince Edward Island or Newfoundland you must take a car ferry. Check with local tourist information for varying times and prices.

On the West Coast, you can reach Vancouver by ship/car ferry daily from Seattle. All passengers pass through the standard customs check prior to leaving the ship at the port of Vancouver following the approximately two-hour ferry ride along the coast. There are also ferries daily between Vancouver Island and Port Angeles, Washington.

Road signs are posted in metric (kmh) instead of miles per hour. (100 km is approximately 60 miles per hour; 300 km is a mere 188 miles. Gasoline and oil are measured in liters; one U.S. gallon is 3.78 liters.)

Seat belts for drivers and passengers are compulsory in most provinces (except Alberta, Prince Edward Island, the Yukon, and the Northwest Territories), as is proof of automobile liability insurance. A caution: Most Montreal drivers seem to have taken the New York cab drivers' training course. Also, the Canadian Automobile Association (CAA) will provide full service to any AAA member as well as a member of any other automobile affiliate group. (Note: Visiting motorists are advised to obtain a Canadian Non-Resident Inter-Provincial Motor Vehicle Liability Card, available through U.S. insurance companies.)

Car Rentals

It is a relatively simple matter to arrange a car rental in Canada; a visitor must produce identification (listing permanent address) and a valid driver's license (or international license) and should be over 25 years of age.

Rates are comparable to the U.S., and most companies offer special weekend rates or weekly discounts; you may also leave the vehicle at a corresponding office in another province, although there may be a drop-off charge applied to your bill. Rental agencies can be found in all major cities and airports. The standard rental firms operate in Canada—Avis, Budget, Hertz—or you can request information from Tilden, the largest Canadian-owned agency: Tilden Rent-A-Car (National in the U.S.), 250 Bloor Street East, Suite 1300, Toronto, Ontario M4W 1E6; in Canada, Tel: (416) 922-2000 or (800) 268-7133; in U.S., Tel: (800) 387-4747 (Tilden) or (800) 227-7368 (National).

Getting Around

Airplanes are used almost like taxicabs by most professional people in Canada; the population requires hourly flights between major political and business centers such as the Toronto-Ottawa-Montreal-Quebec City power corridor. Also, there are numerous daily flights linking the major cities of the entire country on major carriers, Air Canada and Canadian Airlines.

Since Canada is so vast, there are numerous regional "feeder" airline companies that connect urban centers and service the far reaches of each province. For example, City Express uses Toronto's Island Airport to connect several times daily with Ottawa, Montreal, and New York, while QuebecAir flies to the northern tip of the province at Deception Bay and other outposts served by no other commercial airline. Airlines from Bearskin to Voyageur, plus innumerable private bush pilots for hire, will enable you to reach any spot in the Great White North.

For complete information on all available airlines, routes, and flying services, contact Aeronautical Information Services, Transport Canada, Ottawa, Ontario K1A 0N8; Tel: (613) 995-0197.

Rail. Crossing the country by rail, from Halifax to Vancouver, takes about four days and $400 CDN, from Toronto to Vancouver, a mere $302; these are base prices, of course, and a sleeper or roomette (well advised for this long trip) will cost slightly more. Prices depend on advance purchase, age (i.e., youth, regular, senior citizen), family or group rates, etc. There is only one passenger line in Canada, VIA Rail, since both CP and CN (Canadian Pacific and Canadian National, respectively) terminated passenger service and now concentrate on hauling freight. As with the airlines, there are regional feeder rail lines, such as from Labrador Railroad to Ontario's Algoma Central, that will take you off the beaten path and into the far reaches of each province (except for the Yukon and Northwest Territories, which do not have rail service). A coast-to-coast rail adventure, usually booked solid all summer, features amenities from white-glove, four-fork dining to fast-food snack bars, parlor cars, smoking lounges, drawing rooms, and private roomettes. For complete information on prices and rail timetables, check with a travel agent or your local railroad (i.e., Amtrak, British Rail, etc.) or write directly to VIA Rail Canada, 2 Place Ville Marie, Suite 400, Montreal, Quebec H3B 2G6; Tel: (514) 871-1331/9395 or (800) 361-3677.

Telephones

A local telephone call can last one minute or one hour; the rate will be the same. Only long-distance connections are subject to per-minute charges. You can dial direct to any point in the U.S., Europe, or most areas of the world. And if they are not on strike the operators of Bell Canada will assist with difficult overseas connections.

To call Canada from the U.S., just dial the long distance "1," then the area code and telephone number. From overseas, dial the overseas operator code, then the country code, "1," area code, and number. (Check the Accommodations Reference section of each area for complete listing of all local area codes.)

Local Time

Canada uses time zones similar to those in the United States, but claiming six different regions from coast to coast; so when it is noon in Vancouver (or Los Angeles), it is, respectively, 1:00 P.M. in Calgary; 2:00 P.M. in Winnipeg; 3:00 P.M. in Montreal and Toronto; 4:00 P.M. in Halifax—yet only 4:30 P.M. in Newfoundland (one of the mysteries of the time zone system). Unfortunately, the time zones don't follow neat provincial boundaries. With the aforementioned exception of Newfoundland, the Maritimes—Labrador, Prince Edward Island, Nova Scotia, New Brunswick—are on Atlantic Standard Time, one hour ahead of the Eastern Standard Time of New York and Toronto (and so only four hours behind GMT).

Most of Canada uses Daylight Saving Time (DST) from the end of April to the end of October, gaining an hour of summer's sun.

Electric Current

The same electrical system is used in Canada as in the United States: 110 volts, 60 amps AC. There is no need for adaptors or converters for any electrical appliance brought from the U.S.

Currency

The colorful Canadian money, plus the new gold $1 Canadian coin known affectionately as the "loonie" (so named after the loon imprinted on the thick coin), is the legal tender. American money is certainly accepted, but it is best to have this converted at a bank to get the full rate of exchange, which fluctuates daily. In the past few years the American dollar has been much higher than its Canadian counterpart, somewhere between 20 and 25 percent (at the time of updating $1 U.S. equals $1.25 CDN, while £1 U.K. is $2.40 CDN and one Aus. dollar is $0.95 CDN). As of May 1989 the Canadian Mint ceased printing the green $1 bills.

Business Hours

The general business day in Canada parallels the standard nine-to-five, Monday through Friday routine of the United States. Banks are open from 10:00 A.M. to 3:00 P.M., although some branches of major banks and various trust companies have been extending their hours in both directions to make them more appealing to customers.

Most department stores and shopping malls are open until 6:00 P.M. with extended hours—usually until 10:00 P.M.—on Thursdays and Fridays; convenience outlets and drugstores are often open until 11:00 P.M.; and many in major centers (as well as some supermarkets) are open for complete 24-hour service.

Canada has always maintained its famous religious-based "blue laws" where everything shuts down for the Sabbath. (Or, as W.C. Fields once remarked, "I went to Toronto last Sunday; it was closed.") However, more and more the law is being challenged in the courts as unconstitutional, and various shops—especially those in populated tourist areas—are now open for Sunday business.

Holidays

Certain holidays are celebrated by the entire country (i.e., Christmas, New Year's, etc.), while some occasions (such as St-Jean-Baptiste Day in Quebec) only affect an individual province. If travelling in the fall season, remember that Canada sets aside the second weekend in October (with the Monday as the official holiday) for its annual Thanksgiving turkey feast.

The following holidays are observed throughout the country (banks, schools, government buildings, and most shops will likely be closed): New Year's Day; Good Friday; Easter Monday; Victoria Day (a "moveable" holiday to mark Queen Victoria's birthday, always celebrated on the Monday preceding May 25, to make a three-day weekend); Canada Day (always July 1, corresponding to the U.S. Independence Day); Labour Day, the first Monday of every September; Thanksgiving (the second Monday of every October); Remembrance Day (every November 11; based initially on the armistice of 1918—signed the eleventh month, eleventh day at 11:00 A.M.—it now commemorates the sacrifices from both World Wars and Korea); Christmas and Boxing Day (December 26; shopping sales usually take place now on December 27).

Provincial holidays include British Columbia Day, the first Monday of August; while Manitoba, New Brunswick, the Northwest Territories, and Ontario all celebrate a similar Civic Holiday the first Monday of August, another moveable celebration to provide a three-day work holiday.

Quebec has its separate St-Jean-Baptiste festivities every June 24, while both the Yukon and Newfoundland romp through a Discovery Day celebration: the third Monday of every August for the Yukon and the second to last Monday in June for the Maritime island province.

Further Information
Tourist offices for Canada and the separate provinces and territories can provide specific information regarding each region—the sights and sites, various types of accommodation and dining establishments, tourism literature—and can answer your practical questions.

Canada
Tourism Canada
    235 Queen Street
    Ottawa, Ontario K1A 0H6
    (613) 996-4610

Provinces
British Columbia: Tourism B.C.
    1117 Wharf Street
    Victoria, B.C. V8W 2Z2
    (604) 387-1642
Alberta: Travel Alberta
    Box 2500
    Edmonton, Alberta T5J 2Z4
    (403) 427-4321
Saskatchewan: Tourism Saskatchewan
    2103 11th Avenue
    Regina, Saskatchewan S4P 3V7
    (305) 787-2300
Manitoba: Travel Manitoba
    155 Carlton Street/7th floor
    Winnipeg, Manitoba R3C 3H8
    (204) 945-3777
Ontario: Ontario Travel
    Queen's Park

Toronto, Ontario M7A 2E5
(416) 965-4008 or (800) 268-3735 toll free from U.S.
Quebec: Tourism Quebec
P.O. Box 20000
Quebec City, Quebec G1K 7X2
(800) 443-7000 toll free from Eastern U.S.
Nova Scotia: Dept. of Tourism
Box 456
Halifax, Nova Scotia B3J 2R5
(902) 425-5781
New Brunswick: Tourism New Brunswick
Box 12345
Fredericton, New Brunswick E3B 5C3
(800) 561-0123 toll free from U.S.
Prince Edward Island: Visitors Service Division
Box 940
Charlottetown, P.E.I. C1A 7M5
(902) 892-2457
Newfoundland: Dept. of Development and Tourism
Box 2016
St. John's, Newfoundland A1C 7M5
(709) 576-2830
Yukon: Tourism Yukon
P.O. Box 2703
Whitehorse, Yukon Y1A 2C6
(403) 667-5340
Northwest Territories: Travel Arctic
Govt. of N.W.T.
P.O. Box 1320
Yellowknife, N.W.T. X1A 2L9
(403) 873-7200

—*Steve Veale*

BIBLIOGRAPHY

One of the best sources of travel books in Canada is Open
Air Books & Maps, 25 Toronto Street, Toronto, Ont. M5C
2R1; Tel: (416) 363-0719.

General

DAVID J. BERCUSON AND J.L. GRANATSTEIN, *Collins Dictionary
of Canadian History, 1867 to the Present*. Among other
items, it gives some background leading to the Canada-
U.S. Free Trade Agreement.

PIERRE BERTON, *The National Dream* (covering 1871–1881) and *The Last Spike* (1881–1885). History of the planning and building of the transcontinental railways and the people and adventures involved.

MICHAEL BLISS, *Years of Change: 1967–1985*. A provocative review with questions for discussion. Includes Constitution Act of 1982. Century of Canada series.

HUGH BRODY, *The Living Arctic*. An experienced northern anthropologist talks about the Inuit and their dependence on the land.

STEPHEN BROOK, *Maple Leaf Rag: Travels Across Canada*. British writer Brook is seldom off base in this light and often humorous look at countryside and people. Now in paperback.

CRAIG BROWN, ED., *Illustrated History of Canada*. Six historians and geographers tell how Canada and Canadians developed.

HAROLD CARDINAL, *The Rebirth of Canada's Indians*. A leading spokesman provides the Indian's perspective on today's relations with government.

BILL COO, *Scenic Rail Guide to Western Canada* and to *Central & Atlantic Canada*. Mile-by-mile guides to 12,600 miles of train trips and connecting roads from a 30-year rail veteran.

DONALD CREIGHTON, *Dominion of the North*. Good, basic history through the end of World War II.

ROBERTSON DAVIES, *The Lyre of Orpheus*. Third in a trilogy (*Rebel Angels, What's Bred in the Bone*) in which Davies, a distinguished writer, essayist, and dramatist, depicts some of the geography of Canadian society over the past century.

RICHARD GWYN, *The Northern Magus*. The best of many biographies about Pierre Elliott Trudeau when he was Canada's Prime Minister.

PETER GZOWSKI, *The New Morningside Papers*. Highlights from and comments on Gzowski's weekday morning national radio programs reveal the lives and loves of everyday Canadians.

J. RUSSELL HARPER, *Painting in Canada: A History*. Listing only major artists, he starts with Abbe Pommier in 1663 and ends in the 1980s.

COLE HARRIS, ED., AND GEOFFREY MATTHEWS, CARTOGRAPHER, *Historical Atlas of Canada*. The story of Canada from ice sheets of 18,000 B.C. to the 18th century, told in graphs, pictures, maps, and essays. Two more volumes to come.

ROBERT F. LEGGET, *Railways of Canada*. History to 1987.

A. R. M. LOWER, *Colony to Nation, a History of Canada*. Easily read history to 1945. Lower explains why things happened, with minimal attention to dates and details.

KENNETH MCNAUGHT, *The Penguin History of Canada*. A general history of Canada, revised and updated in 1988.

ANDREW MALCOLM, *The Canadians*. An American who lived in Canada analyzes the differences between the two cultures.

Michelin Tourist Guide to Canada. For motorists.

ALBERT AND THERA MORITZ, *Oxford Illustrated Literary Guide to Canada*. Biographies of today's writers.

PETER NEWMAN, *The Canadian Establishment* and *The Acquisitors*. Interconnections and use and abuse of power of business people who, in the author's opinion, run the country.

PETER NEWMAN, ED., *Debrett's Illustrated Guide to the Canadian Establishment*. Portraits in text and photographs of the country's trendsetters in business and the arts; includes 21 dynasties and over 600 individuals.

PENNY PETRONE, ED., *First People, First Voices*. Collection of Indian writing—speeches, letters, diaries, prayers, songs, and stories—from the 1630s to 1980s.

Quick Canadian Facts. A pocket encyclopedia with answers to 1,000 questions, including history.

The West

MARK ABLEY, *Beyond Forget: Rediscovering the Prairies*. A wonderful mixture of travelog, oral history, politics, and environmental study.

DORIS ANDERSEN, *Evergreen Islands*. History of the islands between the north end of Vancouver Island and the mainland.

LAURA BEATRICE BERTON, *I Married the Klondike*. An Edwardian Toronto schoolteacher's life in the Yukon, 1904–1932.

PIERRE BERTON, *Klondike: The Last Great Gold Rush*. Gripping history, rich in human details of the 1897–1898 Klondike frenzy.

PIERRE BERTON, *The Promised Land: Settling the West 1896–1914*. Historical but written in Berton's usual provocative dramatic style.

JAMES R. BUTLER AND ROLAND R. MAW, *Fishing: Canada's Mountain Parks*. Where and what to fish. One in the series on outdoor pleasures by Lone Pine Publishing.

MARJORIE WILKINS CAMPBELL, *The Saskatchewan*. History around the great river that rises in the Rockies and empties into Manitoba's Lake Winnipeg.

BEN GADD, *Handbook of the Canadian Rockies*. Encyclopedic detail covers geology, history, recreation, plants, animals, even butterflies.

RENIE GROSS, *Dinosaur Country*. Text and many illustrations on the Alberta Badlands, where dinosaurs used to roam.

RICK KUNELIUS, *Animals of the Rockies*. A 71-page pamphlet with text and illustrations.

CHAUNCEY LOOMIS, *Weird and Tragic Shores*. One of the best books on the search for the Northwest Passage.

ERNIE LYALL, *An Arctic Man*. Lyall recounts his 65 years of practicing the Inuit way of life.

J. W. GRANT MACEWAN, *West to the Sea*. A history of western Canada from early man to postwar industry.

BRUCE OBEE, *The Gulf Islands*. A guide more than a history of the better-known islands at the south end of Vancouver Island.

GREY OWL, *Tales of an Empty Cabin* (1936) and *Men of the Last Frontier* (1931). The real name of this Englishman, undoubtedly one of the first environmentalists, was Archie Belaney, but he adopted Indian customs, worked as a trapper in Northern Saskatchewan, and wrote about Indian friends and animal companions.

ARCHIE SATTERFIELD, *Chilkoot Pass*. The most famous pass in the Rockies, used by the goldseekers.

ROBERT SERVICE, *Songs of a Sourdough* and *The Best of Robert Service*. Includes Service's best-known Klondike poem, *Cremation of Sam McGee*.

Ontario

ERIC ARTHUR, *Toronto: No Mean City*. Guide to Toronto's architectural history and architects.

MARGARET ATWOOD, *Cat's Eye*. Mainly set in Toronto, a nostalgic yet incisive look at the maturing of a woman artist. Atwood at her best.

JAMES BARRY, *Georgian Bay*. A narrative-style history with plenty of anecdotes.

ROBERT BOTHWELL, *A Short History of Ontario*. A quick read.

BARBARANNE BOYER, *Muskoka's Grand Hotels*. Text and illustrations on dozens of past and present properties.

WILLIAM S. FOX, *The Bruce Beckons: Story of Lake Huron's Great Peninsula*. With facts and folklore, the author tells why the little-known Bruce is such a special place.

EDWIN C. GUILLET, *Early Life in Upper Canada*. Details and stories give the past vivid reality.

MARJORIE HARRIS, *Toronto: City of Neighborhoods*. A very readable account of the hows and whys of Toronto's ethnicity.

ROBERT LEGGET, *Rideau Waterway*. Definitive history and guide with photos of this Ontario canal system.

JACK MINER, *Wild Goose Jack*. Autobiography of the naturalist who turned his Kingsville, Ontario, farm into a now renowned sanctuary for wild geese and ducks.

SUSANNA MOODIE, *Roughing It in the Bush*. Life in Upper Canada (Ontario), 1830–1850, described by an English gentlewoman.

Toronto: Celebrate Our City. Mainly a photo collection of buildings and people published by the *Toronto Sun* newspaper and City TV for the city's sesquicentennial in 1984.

Quebec

GORDON DONALDSON, *Battle for a Continent: Quebec 1759*. A lively account of the British conquest.

DAVID FENNARIO, *Balconville*. A powerful play—half-English, half-French—about life in a contemporary blue-collar Montreal neighborhood.

KATHLEEN JENKINS, *Montreal: Island City of the St. Lawrence*. The standard popular history of the city, somewhat dated but entertaining. Only found in libraries and second-hand book stores.

WILLIAM KIRBY, *The Golden Dog*. A romance set in old Quebec, 1748–1777.

ROGER LEMELIN (translated by Mary Finch), *The Plouffe Family*. Story of a large, lovable French-Canadian family, which became a popular TV series.

RENE LEVESQUE, *Memoirs of René Lévesque*. Autobiography of the late *premier ministre* who brought separatism to the fore in Quebec.

HUGH MACLENNAN, *Two Solitudes*. The first popular novel to examine the gulf between the French and English in Montreal. A Canadian classic.

MIA AND KLAUS, with commentary by Hugh MacLennan, *Quebec*. An imaginative photographic impression of the land and its four seasons.

DESMOND MORTON, *Sieges of Quebec: 1759–60*. Both sides of the background, strategies, and personal conflicts that caused France's loss of Quebec City—and thus New France—to the English.

HILDA NEATBY, *Quebec: The Revolutionary Age 1760–1791*. Historical roots of the unrest in modern Quebec. One of the 18-volume Canadian Centenary series.

Atlantic Provinces

DAVID BELL, *Early Loyalists of Saint John*. A good look at Loyalist life as the New Brunswick city flourished.

WILL R. BIRD, *Off Trail in Nova Scotia*. Anecdotes, local characters, and local history off the beaten track.

F. W. P. BOLGER, ED., *Canada's Smallest Province*. Though academic in style, a definitive history of Prince Edward Island.

WILLIAM C. BORRETT, *Historic Halifax: Tales in the Old Town Clock*. Compilation of radio broadcasts about events and people in the city's first 200 years.

HAROLD HORWOOD, *Dancing on the Shore: A Celebration of Life at Annapolis Basin*. Mainly about birds, squirrels, and other animal life.

DON MACGILLVRAY AND BRIAN TENNYSON, EDS., *Cape Breton Historical Essays*. Insightful and feisty comment, with maps, on high and low points in history of this very Scottish extremity of Nova Scotia.

NEIL MACKINNON, *This Unfriendly Soil: The Loyalist Experience in Nova Scotia*. The heartbreaks and adjustments that had to be made.

W. S. MACNUTT, *New Brunswick: A History 1784–1867*. A good general history of the province from the time of the Loyalists to Confederation.

PETER L. MCCREATH AND JOHN G. LEEFE, *History of Early Nova Scotia*. How the province was involved in New World and European turmoil from the Edict of Nantes in 1598 (which gave French people freedom of worship) to 1782.

LUCY MAUD MONTGOMERY, *Anne of Green Gables*. The children's classic, with many sequels, now known world-wide.

CLAIRE MOWAT, *The Outport People*. Warm fictional memoir of life in a Newfoundland outport where access is only by sea.

PETER NEARY AND PATRICK O'FLAHERTY, EDS., *By Great Waters: A Newfoundland and Labrador Anthology*. Selections, many told as narratives, from 1003 to the present, that portray the province's boisterous history and culture.

IRENE L. ROGERS, *Charlottetown: The Life in Its Buildings*. History of Prince Edward Island's capital city and its architecture.

STUART TRUEMAN, *An Intimate History of New Brunswick*. Stories about the Acadians and other ethnic groups who make up this friendly province.

Food and Accommodation
MARGARET ROSS CHANDLER, *Great Little Country Inns of Southern Ontario*. Selective list of 53 inns starting in Bayfield on Lake Huron and going to Gananoque on the St. Lawrence River.

MARVIN FREMES, *Historic Inns of Ontario*.

PAULINE GUETTA, *Inns and Manoirs of Quebec*.

ANNE HARDY, *Where to Eat in Canada*. Straightforward guide for lovers of good food.

MECHTILD HOPPENRATH AND CHARLES OBERDORF, *First-Class Canada*. Coverage of the top restaurants, hotels, shopping, and diversions—as seen by the authors—in eight cities.

GERDA PANTEL, *Canadian Bed & Breakfast Guide*. Has 1,000 entries.

PAULINE SCOTEN AND HELEN BURICH, *Town & Country Bed & Breakfast in B.C.*

PATRICIA WILSON, *Canadian Bed & Breakfast Book* and *Ontario Bed & Breakfast Book, with a Quebec supplement*.

—Jean Danard

NOVA SCOTIA

By Nan Drosdick

Nan Drosdick is an award-winning travel writer who wrote Travel & Leisure's 1989 Independent Traveler's Guide to Canada. Her work appears in major Canadian and U.S. publications and she is contributing editor at ASTA (American Society of Travel Agents), Agency Management (formerly ASTA Travel News), and a member of the Society of American Travel Writers and American Society of Journalists & Authors.

Nova Scotians like to describe their province as "Canada's ocean playground." As the center of Maritime Canada, the province seems more island than peninsula; it juts out far into the Atlantic, with the Gulf of St. Lawrence, Northumberland Strait, and the Bay of Fundy surrounding it—except for a few miles where it is connected by land to New Brunswick.

Nova Scotia is large, and so spread out that it defies cubbyholing. Each coast is a region in itself, and the focus or busiest place in each is often a separate gateway by which visitors enter and leave that particular part of the province.

Halifax is, for example, the central focus on the Atlantic coast, and most visitors to the province arriving by air come through the international airport near the capital. Along the Bay of Fundy, Yarmouth and Digby are gateways for visitors arriving from Maine or New Brunswick by ferry. Northumberland Strait's gateways are Amherst (by highway from New Brunswick) and Pictou (with its ferry

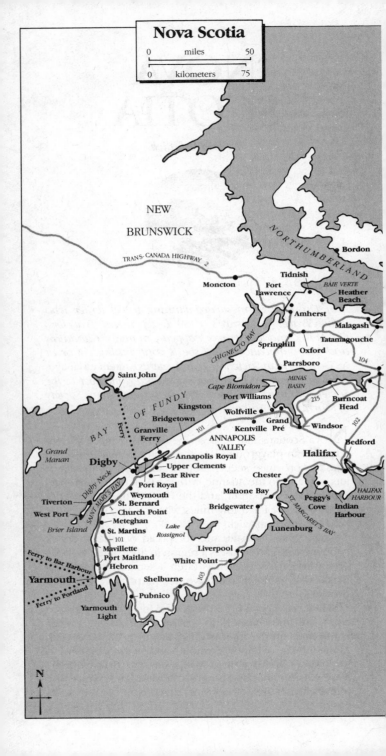

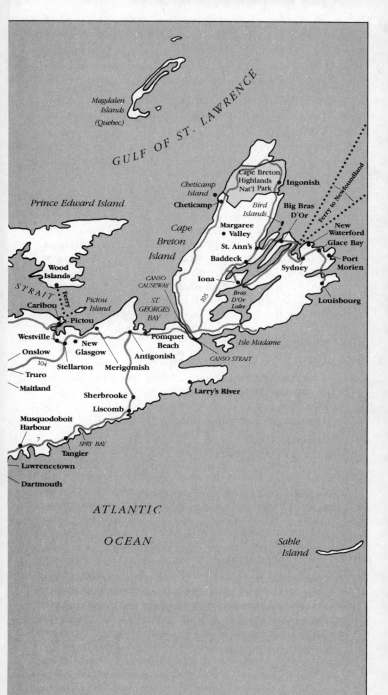

connections to nearby Prince Edward Island). Cape Breton has the Gulf of St. Lawrence along one coast and the Atlantic on the other, and its link is to Newfoundland, at North Sydney near Sydney, the area's largest city. The province's interior is mostly undeveloped; towns and attractions are mainly on the coasts.

Some visitors come to Nova Scotia to trace ancestral roots. Festivals are another strong lure, and the plethora of events range from province-wide lobster suppers, to regattas and military muster at Halifax's Citadel, to ethnic shows such as the annual Festival of the Tartans at New Glasgow and the once-every-four-years Gathering of the Clans, held alternately between Scotland and Nova Scotia and scheduled for the province in 1991. The strongest draw of all are the idyllic seacoasts, ribboned with two-lane roads and dotted with picture-book villages, and altogether perfect for exploring. The province is the best known in Atlantic Canada for beaches, seafood dining, local wines, the arts scene, and crafts shopping.

MAJOR INTEREST

Tranquil, small, unspoiled towns
British, Loyalist, French, Acadian, and especially
  Scottish heritages
Beaches
Seacoast scenery and dining

Halifax
Halifax Citadel National Historic Park
Harbor front for sight-seeing, shopping, dining,
  nightlife
Maritime Museum of the Atlantic
Historic Properties' restored period buildings

Elsewhere along the Atlantic
Peggy's Cove
Sherbrooke Village

Bay of Fundy
Port Royal National Historic Park
Fort Anne National Historic Park, Annapolis Royal
Annapolis Valley scenic beauty
Grand Pré National Historic Park
The Evangeline Trail

Northumberland Strait Coast
Joggins Fossil Cliffs, upper Chignecto Bay
Pictou Scots heritage

Sydney Area of Cape Breton
Fortress Louisbourg National Historic Park

Elsewhere on Cape Breton
Cabot Trail, Cape Breton Highlands National Park
Alexander Graham Bell National Historic Park,
   Baddeck

THE ATLANTIC SEACOAST

Nova Scotia has its Atlantic seacoast in mind when it claims the province has "so much to sea." It is a great stretch of coast, 400 miles from Yarmouth in the southwest to the Strait of Canso in the northeast, a series of alternating low cliffs and beaches backed by deep bays, dunes, and marshes—and marked all along with lighthouses. (Sable Island, an uninhabited and deserted sandspit with wrecked ships and lighthouses, lies 177 miles offshore to the southeast.)

The Atlantic seacoast is a paradox, both the most developed and least developed part of the provincial coastline. The capital city of Halifax lies at its midpoint on a densely developed peninsula along Halifax Harbour, one of Canada's major seaports. Its affluence overflows southwest to the select Mahone Bay settlements, yet the coast northeast of Halifax is a slice of the province as it once was, good roads notwithstanding. There's a dual mood along the Atlantic, a sense of Canada at its spit-and-polished best along a coastline nonetheless reminiscent of old England before piers lined its shores.

HALIFAX

Halifax is the focal point of the Atlantic coast. The province is served by expressways, of which three major ones converge at metropolitan Halifax. Locals understand how one highway feeds into another with route number changes, but it may be confusing to visitors, so study it first on a map. Route 103 links Halifax to Yarmouth on the South Shore facing Portland, Maine, while meandering

Route 7's two lanes run along the East Shore. Route 102 feeds in from the northeast, from the direction of Amherst and Pictou. By all means, take alternate coastal roads when possible, as they're far more scenic and reveal more of the local flavor.

Anglophone Atlantic settlements began on Nova Scotia when Cornwallis brought English settlers in 1749 to develop Halifax and counteract France's strong colonial presence at Louisbourg on Cape Breton. Simultaneously, Lunenburg, on the coast southwest of Halifax, began as the English Crown's effort to settle German Protestants to counterbalance French Roman Catholicism in the New World.

Eastern Seaboard unrest and then the American Revolution fueled Loyalist immigration to the area; in 1783 ships from New York brought pro-Crown settlers to Shelburne on the South Shore, whose population swelled to 16,000. Acadians from France date farther back, to 1653 at the Pubnicos near Yarmouth, but the Acadian influence, and then the effect of the 1755 expulsion, were greater along the Bay of Fundy and on Cape Breton.

Halifax has always been a city propelled by strongwilled people. Government House owes its splendid design to Royal Governor John Wentworth, a Loyalist and the luxury-loving former New Hampshire governor who in 1800 demanded and got a residence to equal his expectations of Halifax. The city is also proud of its privateers, who harried the Eastern seaboard during the American Revolution, and were blockade runners during the United States Civil War—on the South's side.

Halifax has always been a sentimental city, too, and its people treasure its landmark, the oversize Old Town Clock, gift of Prince Edward, duke of Kent, who sojourned in Halifax during Wentworth's time. The splendid Halifax Public Gardens are a tribute to Edward's daughter, Queen Victoria; the ornate, red-roofed bandstand was built to mark the Queen's Golden Jubilee. And as Queen Victoria esteemed the Scots, so has Halifax, modeling its Dalhousie University after the University of Edinburgh.

Founded for Crown defense with a ring of formidable forts, the city never fired a gun in anger, and now the forts are all parks, many—like Halifax Citadel—of national historic significance. Her Majesty's Royal Navy (after 1910 the Royal Canadian Navy) has been based here for centuries, Halifax Harbour being Atlantic Canada's major port. Her Majesty's Canadian Dockyard is part of the harbor complex, and sloops and brigantines have given way to aircraft carriers, hydrofoils, submarines, destroyers, and supply-ship convoys.

Halifax is very Canadian but in a British sort of way, and has a sophistication that dates from its having been designated capital by the Crown in 1749, and chosen the main New World seaport for Her Majesty's Royal Navy. Through the centuries, Haligonians have wined and dined with visiting royalty, and to this day no one has forgotten King George III's illustrious son Prince Edward, who flaunted local propriety with his French mistress, Julie St. Laurent. Generous Governor Wentworth loaned the lovers his Hemloch Ravine estate along Bedford Basin (northwest of Halifax), and the couple lived there from 1794 to 1800. Once back in London the prince married a proper German princess who gave birth to Victoria in 1819. Julie St. Laurent returned to France to live out a secluded life.

Halifax's past also includes privateers who unloaded booty into warehouses along Water Street. The Cunard steamship empire started here along the waterfront, too. In the 1970s, when the harbor front was more dilapidated than functional, and some Haligonians thought the heart of the city was aged beyond repair, an infusion of research, historical restoration, and new construction backed by federal and provincial investment brought back all that the centuries had hidden. Halifax is, consequently, both very old and very new.

A bon-vivant sense of tradition is bound up in Halifax, and it is a city of casual propriety whose pace seems both leisurely and measured. Halifax is, most of all, a city that exists to be enjoyed, with Atlantic Canada's most abundantly available music, theater, performing arts, and art. It is known for sociability and willingness to find any good reason to create an event. Its greatest annual event is the **Nova Scotia Tattoo**, the celebration of the province's military history. For a week in late June/early July, military bands, pipe bands, choirs, and various other pomp attract around 50,000 spectators to the Metro Centre.

Like the rest of the province, Halifax works Monday to Friday, parties Friday and Saturday, and closes up tight as a drum on Sunday. Also like the rest of the province, it shares Canada's unspoken feeling that nothing of any great accomplishment happens in summer, when it re-

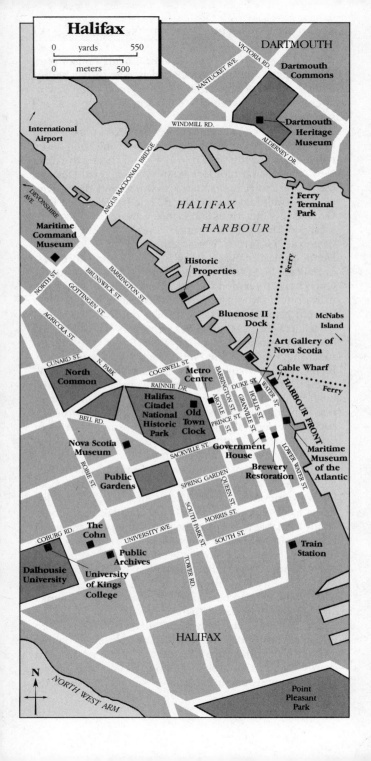

signs itself quite graciously to welcoming visitors. Autumn's balmy foliage months (through October) are becoming an extension of the traditional tourist season.

Exploring the City

Halifax is worth a visit of three to five days, more if excursions are planned. The **harbor front**, however, is *the* reason to visit Halifax. The main summertime happenings (like the Cable Wharf outdoor concerts) center along promenades on Water Street and the adjacent streets and up the steep hill to the Halifax Citadel and nearby.

The re-created harbor front runs along eight city blocks of the angled seven-mile-long peninsula. The harbor-front setting is picturesque, but it is a Haligonian domain, too, as locals by the thousands use the ferry terminal for Dartmouth across the harbor to the northeast—a ten-minute sail. From the harbor front Halifax overlooks her sister city across a fast-moving array of oceangoing vessels, small sailing craft, and usually several oil rigs parked improbably in the middle of the harbor.

Choices for getting out on the water run to all manner of Nova Scotian craft, including a paddle-wheeler and deep-sea-fishing charters; the costs for all are reasonable. The ferry to **McNabs Island** at Halifax Harbour entrance, with historic defense batteries, walking trails, and a beach, costs $7.

The other sight-seeing operations are lined up one after another on the harbor front, from Historic Properties, a national historic site, to **Brewery Market**, a cavernous place on Hollis Street where Alexander Keith's beer company brewed and bottled India Pale Ale from the early 1800s to 1971, and which is now a complex of shops, bars, and restaurants with a farmers' market on Friday and Saturday mornings in the central courtyard.

Historic Properties is the core of the harbor front. It starts near **Clipper Cay** and **Privateers' Warehouse**—both boast restaurants with sublime harbor views—and extends up the hillside to Granville Street, which is lined with shops. In all, it is an enclave of ten restored old Halifax buildings—colorful, scrubbed, stone-and-shingled structures that are remarkably well kept and clean, considering the crowds. The nearby **Art Gallery of Nova Scotia** has changing exhibits of top-notch provincial paintings, sculpture, and crafts—ranging from the traditional to the avant garde—in its quarters in the 1867 post office on Hollis Street.

Having seen the harbor, head directly for the **Maritime Museum of the Atlantic**. Some of the province's most interesting seafaring craft, plus Queen Victoria's royal barge, are displayed on the exhibit hall's main floor. The only star missing is *Bluenose,* whose image is on the Canadian dime. The Lunenburg-built schooner of 1921 sank off Haiti in 1946; its replica, *Bluenose II,* does summer duty as harbor sight-seeing schooner and is berthed next to the waterfront Halifax Sheraton. In *Bluenose's* place is a smaller same-class sloop from East Chester, one of 12 such originals, providing a closeup look at the craftsmanship that produced some of the world's fastest schooners and sloops.

Halifax, contained on its own peninsula, is easy to handle on foot. It spreads out in three directions from the Old Town Clock, the city landmark on the Citadel grounds overlooking the harbor front.

The Citadel area above the harbor front is worth a full day. **Halifax Citadel National Historic Park** is an island of grass whose interior fortress has summer tours and military drills. The Public Gardens lie adjacent, with Victorian gardens in many parts. The **Nova Scotia Museum** is a block north of the Gardens devoting its lower floor to natural-history exhibits.

The domain below the Citadel belongs to the harbor front. Beyond the Citadel, where the peninsula flattens out, is residential. The southern area is where the rich folks live, and is the home of several of Halifax's universities, among them Dalhousie. The cream of provincial performing arts is at the Cohn, Dalhousie's cultural center, though it shares the spotlight with the Metro Centre's ongoing programs in front of the Old Town Clock. Working-class neighborhoods are farther north, and rim the shipyards. The Maritime Command Museum, ensconced there off Gottigen Street, has a stunning display of naval history and ship portraits in an old mansion.

Halifax is at its commercial best along here in the hillside area from the harbor front up to the Old Town Clock: Sight-seeing vans, taxis, rickshaws, and a double-decker bus wheel along Water Street, offering a number of ways to see the city.

Nightlife is dense in the area; spend an entertaining Friday or Saturday night strolling from pub to pub. Young people tend to gather in the hillside clubs with disco music and strobe lights or country music. Among the best are **Lawrence of Oregano** and **My Apartment**, both on Argyle Street above Grand Parade. More reserved night people stay along the waterfront at places like **Privateers Warehouse Lower Deck**, with jazz and sometimes sing-alongs.

This is the domain of restaurants, too, especially up along Spring Garden Road, which starts west of the harbor at Barrington Street. Lobster and other crustaceans may be what visitors want most when dining in the province and are on every menu, but more sophisticated fare can also be found. Seafood is plentiful—fried, broiled, sauced, or in a Wellington pastry, and the same goes for meat dishes with an emphasis on beef. Halifax is a wine-drinking city, doting on imports, but varieties of local Grand Pré and Jost whites and reds are abundant too. The dining scene's downside is space, as these restaurants in historic buildings are picturesque but small, so in season be content with any table, reservations notwithstanding. For old-time ambience, **Fat Frank's** is probably the best. The **Silver Spoon** and **O'Carroll's** are similar. For a harbor view, the Halifax Sheraton's **Café Maritime** or the hotel's waterside and often breezy **Boardwalk Grill** do the job nicely.

Added to all this is a wide range of galleries and shops. Surprisingly, Haligonians see their gorgeous provincial craft goods as exports for tourists, and themselves wear high-priced imports from Korea and elsewhere, so check labels if you want local products. Genuine provincial crafts are found at **Jennifer's** on Spring Garden Road, where shelves overflow with homespuns and knits. Smaller shops are more specialized and draw on local talents.

Staying in Halifax

Waterfront proximity means hotel prestige. The view is what's important here, and it makes sense too to be in the midst of everything. The **Halifax Sheraton** is one of the two top-grade hotels in the province (the other is The Pines at Digby), and is laid out in a horseshoe shape abutting both the harbor front and the Historic Properties. There are rooms on all levels overlooking Nova Scotia's most spectacular views—and they are among the most expensive in the province. **Chateau Halifax**, farther up on Barrington Street, has similar vistas from upper-floor tower rooms, and is a bit less expensive.

The **Citadel Inn** farther up the hillside is still within

walking distance of the action and includes free parking (the Sheraton and Chateau Halifax charge extra for guests' cars), a huge asset in car-clogged Halifax; rooms with a view cost less than at the other two, but are still pricey. **Lord Nelson Hotel** near the Public Gardens overlooks that Victorian park, but is quite a hike from the harbor front; the upper-floor rooms are simply furnished (its guests are usually scholars from local universities who don't need tourist pizzazz) and a good buy. Nearer to the harbor front, **Halliburton House** on Morris Street is a series of town houses charmingly furnished with antiques. Rates are quite reasonable for a back room, while sumptuous quarters with a fireplace can be expensive; there is car parking in back.

THE HALIFAX METROPOLITAN AREA

The metropolitan Halifax-Dartmouth area, with almost 300,000 inhabitants, is a contrast to the contained harbor front and Citadel area, covering as it does a 25-mile radius of harbors and inlets, lake slivers and rivers, over to the seacoast. The metro area comprises Halifax (the center) with the bedroom communities of Dartmouth (its Heritage Museum and its Black Cultural Centre, both with genealogical records, are interesting), Bedford, and the Sackvilles.

Peggy's Cove, the famous protected seacoast village, is also in metro's domain, on St. Margaret's Bay, 40 minutes southwest of Halifax along winding, two-lane roads. Signs for Lighthouse Route (a sight-seeing drive) mark the way from Halifax. The fishing village is one of Canada's most photographed places, with its seacoast lighthouse—used in summer as a post office—perched above acres of granite boulders left from the Ice Age. The 100-foot-long monument to Canadian fisherfolk that William deGarthe carved on the face of a granite outcropping is marked as a provincial park in the village's midst (two deGarthe murals are in nearby St. John's Anglican Church). The boulder-wrapped cove can be blissfully peaceful, but is usually packed with visitors and tour buses.

Sou'wester Restaurant, Peggy Cove's only commercial dining room, is handy for a quick snack, as dining choices hereabouts are limited. It's just as easy to drive on to **Candleriggs** dining room and craft shop at Indian Harbour, five minutes northwest along the bay, and seacoast views here are pleasant. If you take the Lighthouse Route you will see several off-road signs advertising lobster suppers—and lunches, too—that are worth following up for plain but hearty seafood meals. Otherwise, plan to be in Halifax for dinner.

Back in Halifax, on Bedford Highway along the basin to Bedford, is Hemloch Ravine, the former haunt of Prince Edward and Julie St. Laurent, now a city park. Remnants of the former estate include the round Music House—separated from the rest of the estate by the highway—a heart-shaped pool, and miles of walking paths beneath hemlocks, some 100 feet high (parking lots are marked inside the ravine).

Across Halifax Harbour, Dartmouth describes itself as the City of Lakes; especially nice ones are at Shuben-acadie Grand Lake's Laurie and Oakfield, both with beaches. Here and everywhere in the province Nova Scotia's provincial parks provide picnic tables, drinking water, and toilets, and if there's a beach there will be changing rooms, all open late May to early October. Most of the provincial parks are unsupervised and without lifeguards, except where seaside tides are strong.

ELSEWHERE ON THE ATLANTIC COAST

East of Dartmouth, the surf angles just right for surfing and sail-boarding; several outfits in Halifax rent equip-ment. **Crystal Crescent Beach**, 18 miles directly south of Halifax at Cape Sambro, is a favorite with local surfers, as are Eastern Shore's Lawrencetown, Martinique, and Clam Harbour beaches.

Otherwise, departing Halifax—whether to head south-west on the South Shore's expressway or scenic coastal Lighthouse Route, or northeast on Marine Drive along the Eastern Shore—calls for an immediate directional choice. Beaches lie along both routes; the sea is cold, but warms in pools between sandbars, and the many salt marshes make good seabird-watching sites.

On the South Shore, Haligonians go as far as the Chester–Mahone Bay–Lunenburg triangle. These are the getaway towns facing the Atlantic across sheltered harbors and coves, all in all three of the province's most charming silk-stocking enclaves of good living, with select shops and restaurants. In museums, the pièce de résistance is **Lunenburg**'s Fisheries Museum of the Atlantic on the waterfront, which documents the trials and triumphs of seafaring centuries. DesBrisay Museum at **Bridgewater** (the area's expressway gateway) is another delightful setting, with displays on early Lunenburg County's Micmac Indian and German settlements; outside, tables under the trees are ideal for picnicking.

In the **Mahone Bay** area, if it looks good, it is—high prices notwithstanding. At Chester, **The Galley**'s wall of windows overlooks sailboats and yachts from the dimly lit dining room; **The Rope Loft**, on the harbor farther around the bend, sets small tables at windows, with a spacious outside deck for drinks and light meals. **Zwicker's Inn** is Mahone Bay's dining treasure, and needs reservations (Tel: 624-8045). Lunenburg's luminary is **Boscawen Inn** on Cumberland Street—no views from its ground-floor dining room in town, but expert cuisine more than makes up for it, and guest rooms on the floors above make the most of the 1888 Victorian mansion setting. **Compass Rose** is smaller, but just as picturesque, with period guest rooms and dining room and a few front windows overlooking busy King Street.

Shop wares seem more plentiful here than even in Halifax; **Suttles and Seawinds**, featuring designer calicos superbly fashioned into women's and children's apparel, is based at New Germany near Bridgewater, and there's an outlet at Mahone Bay. More provincial arts and crafts than can be fully comprehended are at **Chester's Warp and Woof** on Water Street, and if you are short on time for shopping, this is the place for exquisitely crafted hooked rugs from Cheticamp on Cape Breton.

Nothing else along the South Shore can equal this trio of towns for creature comforts and pleasure. If and when town interests pale, head for the **Oak Island Inn & Marina** (exit 9 or 10 off Route 103) to sign up for a place on a fishing trip, or, if you prefer, you will find that beaches are plentiful—the best is at **Sand Hills** farther southwest beyond Shelburne near Barrington.

The opposite directional choice from Halifax, Marine Drive, the Eastern Shore's seacoast sight-seeing route northeast, is quite different. Settlements here are sparse and rustic. At Tangier, about 50 miles east of Dartmouth, **W.J. Krauch** is a major provincial exporter of smoked fish, and Danish-style salted eel, salmon, and mackerel are sold retail; if it's not too busy, visitors can tour the smokehouse.

Fifty miles farther northeast, where Route 7 turns north, the remote **Liscombe Lodge** at Liscomb Mills is spread along Liscombe River. The lodge's rustic but toney trappings include the main lodge with a spacious dining room overlooking river rapids, a new hotel, and nicely furnished chalets, some with fireplaces, set here and there. The place is secluded and romantic; Atlantic Canadians like it for honeymoons.

Farther north along Route 7 lie new and old Sherbrooke. The modern village is a four-corners settlement, best known for **Bright House**, with airy dining quarters and a back bakery esconced in a historic setting along the highway. **Sherbrooke Village**, one of Nova Scotia's regional museums, has 30 remarkably preserved buildings, reclaimed from the mid-1800s when the village prospered with gold mining and lumbering. The village's working water-powered sawmill is a wonder to behold, re-created from memory by a local Micmac Indian craftsman.

What remote Marine Drive lacks in development it more than makes up for in long beaches; **Martinique**, two miles of fine sand, is south of Musquodoboit, and other popular sand stretches are **Taylors Head** east of Spry Bay and **Tor Bay** south of Larrys River.

THE BAY OF FUNDY COAST

The Bay of Fundy—one of the world's great natural wonders—and its coast are the province's leading attractions after Halifax.

The Fundy and its Nova Scotia seacoast, facing New Brunswick across the bay, coexist like the proverbial lion and the lamb. About 100 billion gallons of tidal seawater push into the funnel-shaped estuary twice a day. Tides at Yarmouth, at the southwest end of the province, rise 12 feet. Tides can reach 54 feet at Burncoat Head on Minas Basin, near Windsor, where the estuary narrows. All along the Fundy's upper reaches the enormous surge spills over into rivers, led by the tidal bore—the advance wave sometimes up to three feet high. Then the tide pulls back, laying bare red, glistening mud flats and stranding boats that will be buoyant again in a few hours.

The Fundy coast's best-known feature is the corridor northeast of Digby, stretching up to Windsor. Along here, Ice Age glaciers scoured a wide band of terrain and retreated between high, protective ridges known as the North and South Mountains. This created the exquisite, picture-book Annapolis Valley, with fruit orchards rooted in rich alluvial soil, warmed by sunshine and nourished by moisture from the sea.

In summer, sight-seeing boats from **Brier Island,** at the end of Digby Neck southwest of Digby, cruise the Fundy on the watch for the whales, porpoises, and dolphins that come in on the tides. The fishermen's catch (in season) brings in Digby scallops, among Atlantic Canada's best. Herring fillets are transformed into restaurant appetizers: marinated as salmagundi, or smoked as Digby chicks.

Like much of the province, the Fundy shore's road system follows the coast rather than the sparsely settled interior. Route 101 traces the curve of the shoreline from Yarmouth to Windsor, a five-hour drive. The highways from Windsor and Truro that meet in a V near Halifax are the exceptions; their inland route runs along former stagecoach roads. The more picturesque secondary roads along the Minas Basin coast are less travelled but provide unforgettable glimpses of the tempestuous tides. Be careful walking the Minas Basin bay floor, as tides pour in at eight to ten feet per hour.

Political development of the area began very early during the British and French wars for dominance in Europe and the New World. (United States historians label the power struggles from 1689 to 1763 in the New World the French and Indian Wars.) Port Royal, a French fur-trading post here in 1605, was Canada's first settlement. By the start of Queen Anne's War in 1701 England had demolished Port Royal, and France moved the settlement to what is now Annapolis Royal. The Peace of Utrecht, which ended the War of the Spanish Succession (and the corresponding Queen Anne's War), awarded French Acadia to the British, who renamed it Nova Scotia, a name that originated in the 1621 land grant given by King James VI, Scottish king (and later England's James I). Annapolis Royal, northeast of Digby, was the capital until 1749, when Halifax emerged on the scene.

Then the great turnover of people began. French Acadian farm families claimed neutrality, but England demanded unqualified allegiance oaths, and most of Nova Scotia's 8,000 Acadians who had not hidden were deported in the Acadian expulsion of 1755. British subjects, first New England planters, then, during the American Revolution, Loyalists, lured by the promise of free land, settled along the coast from Yarmouth to Truro—most often on the productive land formerly worked by the Acadians.

Returning Acadians were left with parts of the rocky seacoast known as **French Shore**, the municipality of Clare which consists of 27 villages along the lower reaches of St. Mary's Bay southwest of Digby, and a region so distinct from the rest of the province that the provincial highway narrows and is posted with many speed limit warnings between St. Martin and St. Bernard, becoming a 25-mile-long span of Acadian two-lane roads. Along here, Acadian houses are large and plain, sometimes gabled, in contrast to Quebec Province's brightly painted, decorative houses with mansard roofs. Acadians are fishermen and mink and fox ranchers, rather than the tillers of the soil they had been in Grand Pré's halcyon farming years. **Meteghan** is the busiest French Shore port; visitors can buy fresh lobster and scallops on the busy wharves. Restaurants—particularly **La Rapure Acadienne** and Université Ste-Anne's **Le Casse-Croûte**, both in Church Point—serve the province's most authentic deep-dish rappie pie, an Acadian entrée of potatoes with meat or chicken. All along the narrow roads of this region, where only the Acadian tricolor flag flies, oversize churches are grand tributes to Roman Catholicism. Church Point's St. Mary's Church has a 185-foot-high steeple anchored with 40 tons of ballast to keep it from swaying in Fundy winds.

The sea is of course firmly entrenched in the Fundy's past. In Canada's Great Age of Sail in the early 1800s, the coast from Yarmouth to Maitland became the site of ports and shipyards. Later, St. Mary's Bay was among the rum-running ports during the United States Prohibition years.

YARMOUTH

Yarmouth is Nova Scotia's southwesternmost major town and the province's largest port west of Halifax. It lies on the coastal curve that juts into the Atlantic, and is Nova

Scotia's closest link to United States ports in Maine, where ferry crossings from Bar Harbor take 6½ hours (11 hours from Portland).

Entering the province in Yarmouth, the visitor has an immediate choice to make. One route out of town (Route 101) goes northeast along the Bay of Fundy to Digby (two hours by car) and then farther up along the lush Annapolis Valley. The other choice is Route 103, which loops along the southern coast of the Atlantic past resort towns like White Point, Lunenburg, Mahone Bay, and Chester (see the Atlantic Coast section above) to Halifax in five hours. Tantalizing choices notwithstanding, a third option is to stop in Yarmouth before moving on. The province's Great Age of Sail port has enough interests for a full day, and more if its subtle, easygoing pace captures you.

Thanks to the lay of the land the Yarmouth area is sublime biking terrain, and a bike (rentals are $6 a day from the **Rodd Grand Hotel** outlet on Main Street) is a ticket to old Yarmouth and environs.

One of the best routes goes north on Main Street and turns left onto Cape Forchu, a peninsula ending at Yarmouth Light. Along here is the picture-postcard view of Yarmouth, so bring your camera. Cape Forchu was sighted and named by Champlain as he sailed the Bay of Fundy to establish French presence at Port Royal Habitation in 1605. This area may also be the site of Leif Eriksson's Vinland; a large inscribed runic stone, now on exhibit at Yarmouth County Museum in town, was found hereabouts in 1812. Another charming bike route goes south from Yarmouth to Chebogue Point, where pink and purple lupines line back roads, and long-legged willets wade along the coast from May to August.

The **Yarmouth County Museum** is, though, the real reason to visit Yarmouth. Set in a granite former church, the main floor's collection of ship portraits is one of Canada's largest, each vessel directly associated with the port. It is a magnificent collection representing barks, schooners, and brigantines from the period when Yarmouth was Canada's second-largest port of registry in tonnage. The museum has all the local memorabilia that makes such a place interesting, and it is skillfully documented and presented.

Local historian James Farish described Yarmouth as "solid, substantial, nothing luxurious"—still a fitting description. The town's layout is simple: Main Street runs along the harbor front, with cross streets intersecting it.

The ferry terminal is at Forest Street's end. Collins Street has the county museum. The Arts Centre on Parade Street has summer events, so check the playbill. From June to October there is a farmers' market at Centre Square on Saturday mornings. Seafest, in mid- to late July, is for boat races, theater, and seafood.

Yarmouth Wool Shoppe near the ferry is the place to buy Nova Scotian tartan—by the yard or as kilts and such. The local bar scene unfolds until 11:00 P.M. at **Clipper Ship**, with a large selection of beers, a band, and dancing. More upscale drinkers may prefer **Rodd Haleys Grand Lounge**, which has the sentimental harmonies of the 1950s and 1960s.

If watching ferry arrivals and departures sounds interesting, stay at the **Rodd Colony Harbour Inn**, with 24 of its 65 rooms overlooking the scene, but be sure to book ahead. Otherwise, any motel will do and there's a choice of about a dozen in the area, each much the same as the next.

Near Yarmouth

Around on the Atlantic coast, Shelburne, with Loyalist-period buildings, is a nice day's outing, a two-hour-plus drive on backcountry coastal roads, passing interesting Acadian settlements at the Pubnicos on the way.

For dining, the best places are outside Yarmouth. **Manor Inn** in Hebron, northeast of Yarmouth, sets a fine table in period surroundings. **Harris' Seafood**, along the road to Manor Inn, is the place locals go for dining, its plain exterior notwithstanding.

DIGBY

Digby is the province's smallest gateway town, the ferry port for Saint John, New Brunswick, across the Bay of Fundy.

It's best to think of Digby as one of about 150 coastal towns that together form Nova Scotia's premier sightseeing region, aside from Halifax. The 169-mile-long coastline on the Fundy coast from Yarmouth to Windsor is known as the **Evangeline Trail**. Longfellow's poem "Evangeline," drawn from parts of this region, eloquently depicts the 1755 Acadian expulsion. What happened afterwards is, however, what makes the contemporary route so interesting. Returning Acadians (many, including those who became the Louisiana Cajuns, didn't return) settled along the previously mentioned French Shore southwest of Digby, while Loyalists fleeing the American Revolution homed in on Digby, Annapolis Royal, and elsewhere along the coast northeast of Digby. Resulting differences in architecture and lifestyle are striking, as the Acadian tricolor flag coexists with English-like towns.

This coastal route is like a long main street, with Digby conveniently situated at its midpoint. The seaport can work as a day-tripping base for swings up and down the coast; it works equally well to drive through Digby, stay overnight farther up the Annapolis Valley, and return to the town for a day. Digby's **Pines Resort Hotel**, one of the two higher-grade hotels in the province, with rates to match (though some rooms are moderate), gives reason to stay longer. Unquestionably the province's most splendid resort estate, the Norman-style mansion and clusters of chalets are outshone only by the setting on the prow of a hill overlooking Digby. The golf course sweeps across the terrain and hiking trails cut across the hillsides. The total flavor is Canadian at its toney best, while the Pines' cuisine is French under chef Bernard Meyer's direction. This is a retreat untarnished by commercialism or by any hint of the outside world.

What Digby is known for, aside from its famed scallop fleet, is the **Admiral Digby Museum** at the harbor front. The place is brimming with local historical tidbits—to get a more cohesive picture of the port's past walk the harbor front and *then* browse through the exhibits in the 1840 house.

The town was founded by Admiral Robert Digby, a British naval officer who in 1783 led a convoy of 1,000 Loyalists, some of whom brought doors, windows, and other valuables from New York and New England homes, up the tempestuous Fundy to settle the town.

Digby hugs the southwestern corner of the protected Annapolis Basin off Fundy, and lies along the basin's harbor front. A sightseer's walk starts at Cannon Banks, which was once used for fortification against United States privateers. Fishermen's Wharf juts into the harbor here and one of Canada's largest fleets of scallop draggers lies just beyond when in port (particularly photogenic at sunset). Their catch is Digby's fame, for sale at the wharf's **Royal Fundy Market** or succulently prepared at small restaurants. **Captain's Cabin** is probably the best; a table at the back overlooks the harbor, and there is outdoor dining in good weather.

The port's local stores line Water Street, interrupted in parts by passageways once used to haul fish from the beach, or to haul hay in the other direction. Thistle Down Inn rents bikes at $10 a day.

A rousing Digby bar scene can be found at **Club 98** along here. Out of town, **Porky's Pub** does a brisk business serving locals and tourists with basic cooking, and has weekend folk, rock, and other zesty shows ($5 to get in) in Quonset-hut quarters. The other extreme is at **The Pines**, 3 km (2 miles) from town, where dinner is quite expensive (keeps away browsers), Château Latour heads a mostly French wine list, and the evening merriment consists of organ music, dancing, and Singapore slings.

THE ANNAPOLIS VALLEY AND THE FUNDY COAST

What lies along the Fundy is, simply put, a major cut above most North American sightseeing regions, stretched-out distances notwithstanding. Thirty minutes southwest of Digby on the narrow **Digby Neck Peninsula**, whale-watching excursions depart from Westport. Also to the southwest but on the mainland, the Bay of Fundy (too cold for swimming in most places) warms up in the tidal flats of Mavillette Beach near the town of the same name. Heading back toward Digby, you will drive along Highway 101 through the French Shore seacoast villages that extend as far north as the Weymouth area.

Centuries ago the village of **Weymouth** on the northern edge of the Acadian region was a bitter territorial bone of contention between Loyalists from New Jersey, who carved the town from the forests, and the Acadians, intent on resettling after the 1755 deportation by the British drove them from the Gran Pré region. Low-profile Weymouth has been a study in reconciliation ever since. Its northern area is centered around the former St. Thomas Anglican Church, where the historical society serves English-inspired afternoon tea and pastries on summer Thursdays, while the commercial beat of the village is now dominated by Acadian names. One such Acadian enterprise is the **Goodwin Hotel**, the village's century-old country inn. The Comeaus, she from New Brunswick and he of the ubiquitous Comeau clan of Nova Scotia's French shore, create some of the heartiest down-home cooking that you will find in the Maritimes. Try the roasted chicken with sweetly spiced stuffing or the fluffy lemon pies in the back dining room, which is usually filled with Acadians and tourists.

Twenty minutes inland and southeast of Digby, **Bear River** has evolved as an artists' colony with the studios of provincial names such as painter Charles Couper and silk-fashion designers Diane Axent and Louise Williams. The **Flight of Fancy** co-op stocks other local arts and crafts.

Annapolis Royal, 40 minutes northeast of Digby on Highway 1, is the center of several attractions. The town itself is worth a stop, for its Historic Gardens, Fort Anne's swooping grassy defensive shoulders set at the edge of the Annapolis River, and shops such as the **Market House Gallery**, which stocks wares from local crafts people, among them Roman Bartkiw, a ceramicist and glassblower. Port Royal Habitation, the re-created Norman-style fort based on Champlain's 1605 plans, is a ten-minute drive on a looping road across the Annapolis River. **Upper Clements Family Theme Park** is in the town of the same name ten minutes southwest of Annapolis Royal. The area's newest attraction, the park was conceived as a lure to boost the region's economy. Nonetheless, the park gets across an educational message of Nova Scotia's legends, history, and geography in an array of amusement park rides, as well as providing a showcase for local crafts.

The heart of the Annapolis Valley lies in a 50-mile expanse to the northwest of Annapolis Royal up to Windsor. Here you will find a string of pretty towns and the nearby drama of the Fundy tides. Plan a day or two to wander the main streets of Bridgetown, Kentville, and Wolfville. Although you can drive to Windsor from Annapolis Royal in about two hours, plan on at least double that, as you will be lulled by the peaceful prosperity of these towns. The influence of the planters and Loyalists who settled along here is strong—the aura of richness hangs on still. It is more lovely and fragrant still during the Apple Blossom Festival during late May; Kentville is the center of parades and concerts. Bridgetown, on Highway 101 between Annapolis and Kentville, is especially worth a stop for the **Tolmie Gallery** on Granville Street East, which exhibits Ken Tolmie's paintings, including some from his Bridgetown Series of the local townspeople.

The civilized sensibilities of these towns may make you forget the fierce Fundy, just minutes from tree-shaded main streets. It is understandable—from Digby to Wolfville is an almost two hour drive and you will not catch sight of the Fundy once. The Fundy at its fiercest is in the Minas Basin, the bay's upper reaches east of Wolfville, formed by the jutting of the Cape Blomidon peninsula into the bay. A nature trail walk to Cape Split at Cape Blomidon's tip will take you along the cliffs for spectacular views of the Fundy. You can see Parrsboro on the opposite shore, basking in the fame brought by *National Geographic*'s periodic visits to cover the nearby site of the world's largest fossil find ever. The Fundy also erodes the Parrsboro coast, and the village's tourist office sponsors summer rock-hound trips for agate and amethyst. A Cape Blomidon expedition can easily fill a day. While you can reach it in about two hours from Digby, it is even more enjoyable to spend the night in any of the towns in the Annapolis Valley.

As near as Parrsboro may appear from Cape Blomidon, it is too far for day trips from the Annapolis Valley; Truro makes an excellent base. The city's **Best Western Glengarry** lies just off the highway arterial and is a notch above the other local hotels. By all means take the Minas Basin southern seacoast road (Highway 215) on your way up from the Annapolis Valley to Truro and allow for a leisurely half day. The road wends past Burncoat Head, where the world's highest tides peak at 54 feet, and farther on is the Lawrence House at Maitland, where Canada's largest ever full-rigged wooden ship was launched in 1874. All along here the sea seems to boil twice a day; it is so fierce that it pushes tidal bores or upright waves into the rivers to mark high tides. This is a time to watch the sea, but not to wade.

Yet another reason to explore this area is the abundance of local festivals. There are the Digby Scallop Days for four days in August, and the Festival Acadien de Clare, with its Evangeline pageant, for six days in early July in Clare, just for starters.

Staying on the Fundy Coast

The Fundy region has a long swath of interesting places to stay, from Annapolis Royal to Port Williams. Small inns range from vintage mansions like **Planters' Barracks**, one of the province's Heritage Properties, at Port Williams near Wolfville, to stylish historic farmhouses, such

as **Auberge Sieur de Monts** in Granville Ferry outside
Annapolis Royal, to Victorian-style manor houses like
Bread and Roses Country Inn in Annapolis Royal. Rates
are moderate, seldom more than $70. The carriage trade
seems to like this area of Nova Scotia, and there are
Lincolns among the Nissans at **Aurora Inn**, halfway up
the valley in Kingston, a well-appointed motel gaining a
local reputation for evening buffets.

That may explain why there are so few restaurants per
se, as most every inn has a cozy public dining room as
well as renting out rooms upstairs to spend the night.
Worth a meal strictly on its restaurant's merits is **Newman's** in Annapolis Royal, where the nicely inexpensive
rappie pie is among the local dishes, and after November's black-bear hunting season bear dishes are available
until the quantity runs out. **Old Orchard Inn** (a motel),
Wolfville, deserves special mention. Its dining room with
sweeping Fundy Bay views is tonier than many restaurants in Halifax, and its service and presentation are
among the best in the province. Try seafood and linguine
in the main dining room for a memorable upscale meal.
Lobster, scallops, and shrimp meld together lusciously in
a delicately spiced sauce on a bed of homemade pasta,
made even more mellow by a dry Italian white and
finished off with a milk chocolate rum mousse. Seafood
reigns here, and basic lobster dinner is the fare at the
historic barn also on the grounds.

THE NORTHUMBERLAND STRAIT COAST

Nova Scotia has Northumberland Strait's coastline in
mind when it calls itself "Canada's ocean playground."
From Baie Verte at the New Brunswick border to Canso
Causeway, the narrow strip of water that separates mainland Nova Scotia from Cape Breton, there is mile after
mile of angled seacoast spliced with bays, a domain of 35
beaches on Gulf Stream-warmed shallow waters with
wind-surfing, sailing, swimming, and clamming.

Nova Scotians know this coast, facing Prince Edward

Island across the strait, as the North Shore, and it has always been an escape from summertime Halifax to a simpler, easygoing life in a region as old as Amherst, founded as the long French and Indian Wars wound down, and as sentimental as Pictou, birthplace of New Scotland—both now gateways to New Brunswick and Prince Edward Island.

The coastal sight-seeing route is called the Sunrise Trail—well marked with road signs of the rising sun above rippling waters—and it follows the strait on two-lane, backcountry roads through a hundred four-corner villages, bypassed by time for decades. The route's meanderings take some patience—it follows Route 6 along the seacoast's western half to Pictou; between Pictou and New Glasgow it becomes part of the Trans-Canada Highway; from there it follows Route 245 to Malignant Cove, and continues around St. Georges Bay's coastal hook on Route 337 to Antigonish where it is the Trans-Canada again to Auld Cove.

The Trans-Canada Highway, which runs inland beneath the Sunrise Trail, hits all the bigger towns. It enters the province from New Brunswick at Amherst, dips down to Truro at the Fundy Bay's eastern end, and then goes east to New Glasgow and Antigonish. Use the Trans-Canada Highway for making time, but if time is not an issue opt for sight-seeing on the Sunrise Trail; the road lopes along the undulating coast for 200-plus miles in a far better, more leisurely way.

The province's official road map is the only guide you will need for the strait's seacoast. The large tourist information centers at entry points in Amherst and Pictou and in Antigonish stock free descriptive literature and the map; such towns as Springhill, Tatamagouche, and Truro have summertime tourist bureaus with regional information.

In these parts, local folks celebrate the summer season for *themselves,* while at the same time properly welcoming visitors as guests at lobster suppers, festivals, and church socials.

The North Shore is mainly British in ancestry, one of the Crown's most successful efforts to transform French Acadia into Anglo–Nova Scotia. After the 1755 Acadian expulsion, Loyalist New Englanders settled Amherst, Onslow Township, and Merigomish, while Scottish immigration spread through Pictou and Antigonish counties.

Work-hungry immigrants and the discovery of Pictou County's 48-foot-thick coal seam at Stellarton meshed during Canada's industrial revolution. Canada's first successful steel ingots were poured in Trenton, near Pictou. Riches opened architecture's door, particularly at Pictou; 20 early 19th-century buildings there are now designated historic properties.

Some heavy industry remains, but the frenzied development of the 1800s has given way to more serene scenes: fields of strawberries and blueberries, rose greenhouses at Oxford, and the once-fledgling Jost Vineyards, at Malagash, now producing award-winning wines. There have been decades of partiality for golf at, for example, Amherst Golf and Country Club, started in 1912, and a strong reverence for the area's Scottish heritage, now marked memorably at the Hall of Clans at St. Francis Xavier University in Antigonish, east along the coast from Pictou.

The strait in summer is lushly warm at 70 to 75 degrees F at the coast's edge, perfect for dips and lazy floating among the sandbar fingers. It's so serene some days, a seaside stroll with a bucket for clams is the perfect way to go. Among the nicest beaches are **Northport Beach**, northeast of Amherst; **Gulf Shore**, which lies three miles north of Pugwash; and **Rushton's Beach**, tranquilly protected by Tatamagouche Bay. (Red-sand beaches are picturesque, but the red stains, so it's wise to use seaside boulders for sitting. If you prefer white-sand beaches they extend east from the Antigonish area, while those from the New Brunswick border to Antigonish are strictly the red oxide type.)

Lobster fanciers will relish the sight of pounds (holding tanks) brimming with fresh lobster along Northumberland Strait's seaport wharves; Northport Beach has a nearby lobster pound, and Port Howe, west of Pugwash, has a whole string of pounds with the fresh catch from the afternoon fishing boats. Here and everywhere along the province's seacoast, lobster harvesting is strictly limited according to the different seasons; for example, western Northumberland Strait's time of bounty is May and June. Not to worry. Seaport fish stores *always* stock the delicacy, and lobster is on every provincial menu. The Strait's eastern end is the game fish realm; a 678-pound bluefin tuna took the hook at Auld Cove on St. Georges Bay in 1979. Charters operate out of Havre Boucher, northeast of Auld Cove.

AMHERST

It's a matter of minutes to New Brunswick from Amherst on Nova Scotia's northwestern edge on the Trans-Canada Highway, which loops around town. Amherst is a long, seven-hour drive from Digby, almost nine from Yarmouth, and four from Halifax. All of which explains why remotely located Amherst is a story unto itself, and definitely worth a stopover of several hours, or a leisurely day for the area.

The **Cumberland County Museum**, a top-notch regional museum, tells the story best. Amherst started in 1760, named for the British major general who won control of Canada that year for the English Crown and two years earlier defeated the French at Louisbourg, Cape Breton. It is now a county shire town, the second-largest settlement in the Northumberland Strait region, and boasts some of the province's best Victorian Canadiana along its main streets.

In its early heyday the region contributed four Fathers of the Confederation, one of whom was Robert Dickey, whose white 1831 Victorian manor house on Church Street off Victoria now houses the museum. Amherst was so rich then that conspicuous consumption became the art of understatement, and Dickey's modest mansion began as Grove Cottage, resplendent with almost two dozen windows across the façade, and fireplace chimneys across the rear roof line—all set atop a spacious hilltop lawn.

Exhibits at the museum trace cultivation of the diked Tantramar Marshes, first by French Acadians from 1672, then by Yorkshire immigrants from 1772. Textile and shoe manufacturing from the 1800s through World War I made Amherst rich, and the resultant wealth built stately mansions along Victoria and the cross streets, still the best part of town, and financed the street's impressive local red-sandstone commercial buildings.

The town seems drenched in quietness. Whatever's happening is along the northern rim on Victoria Street, which crosses the Trans-Canada Highway. Any noise there originates from **Teazers Pub** near the railroad station, where a wine and draft-beer crowd packs the place late Friday and Saturday nights for live music. Farther up Victoria, **Touch of Country** stocks provincial crafts; strictly local buys are at the Thursday late-afternoon Market Fair at the parking lot behind **Cecil's Bakery and Restaurant**,

the favorite local meal stop (inexpensive). New ownership at Cecil's has redesigned the restaurant's rear and
now offers outdoor patio dining.

For lodgings, the Amherst area offers only a half-dozen
motels designed for visitors driving through from New
Brunswick; **Auberge Wandlyn Inn** in town, plus **Chignecto Motel** and **Fundy Winds Family Motel** at the Fort
Lawrence crossing do a good job with an overnight stay.

Around Amherst

Outside town, two-lane roads wander across tidy farmland; many of the farms are open in season with pick-
your-own berry fields and produce stands. The Amherst
area and all of Cumberland County are known for summer blueberries, and the season peaks with culinary festivals at restaurants and at advertised church socials for a
week in August.

Three-hundred-million-year-old upright fossil trees are
embedded in cliffs at Joggins, southwest of Amherst. Fundy
tides churn up the beaches beneath the cliffs to expose
some amethyst (north of the wharf on upper Chignecto
Bay; looking is legal, taking what's attached to bedrock
isn't). Nearer Amherst, Victoria Street leads across the
Trans-Canada into the Amherst Point Migratory Bird Sanctuary, with 200 species, such as Virginia rail and black tern,
on 1,225 acres of Tantramar Marshes (with trails). **Heather
Beach**, 40 km (25 miles) northeast on Gulf Stream-
warmed shallow strait waters, makes a bucolic place for
swimming, clamming, and, in May and June, buying lobster fresh off the boats.

PICTOU

Three hours east of Amherst on the Sunrise Trail sight-
seeing route, 15 minutes north of New Glasgow, or 10
minutes from Caribou, where ferries connect to Prince
Edward Island's **Wood Islands**, is Pictou: not only old, but
of great provincial significance.

Nova Scotia's beloved Scottish heritage originated at
Pictou, when Highlanders aboard the *Hector* landed in
1773; the event is deeply revered here. Sanctity brings its
own rewards: Aside from some industrial development,
garish commercialism has bypassed the town. Pictou merits an overnight stop; stay longer if you want to explore.

The town in its oldest part along Pictou Harbour is a pretty place with an unusual assortment of different architectural styles; there's Scottish stone domestic from the early Scottish settlement years, Second Empire (a rare style in Nova Scotia), Victorian, and Canadian eclectic. The oldest structure in Pictou is the 1806 **McCulloch House** overlooking the harbor.

Pictou's pulse is along Water Street, a diminutive slice through an Old World town. But it's the thoroughly modern DeCoste Entertainment Centre that's the draw here these days, with national and local live theater, dance, and music in one of the province's best concert halls.

A special setting for dinner is **New Consulate**, whose raison d'être is formal dining (expensive) in an 1810 stone house, once the American consulate.

Local color and culinary goodies characterize the Pictou Lobster Carnival during July. Scottish tributes fill five days in July at nearby New Glasgow's Festival of the Tartans. The Antigonish Highland Games, to the east of Pictou on the coast, are in mid-July, at which time there are absolutely no rooms anywhere in the area. (**The Best Western Claymore Inn** at Antigonish is a better-than-average motel with inexpensive rates, and is a short distance from the Highland Games, but you need to make arrangements beforehand.)

Around Pictou

Pictou's strait shore is for relaxing, maybe wind-sailing at **Little Harbour**, and certainly for resort trappings at **Pictou Lodge**, a historic lodge and cottages on Shore Road, where live music takes over on summer weekends, and a bucolic luncheon is served on the screened porch for locals and visitors in the know. Nearby Wharf Road leads to the **Pictou Island** ferry, nice for a picnic lunch and solitary island hikes. Carefree Cruises is at **Caribou Wharf** (north of Pictou) June to October; a fishing charter with gear supplied for 10 people runs $75 an hour when the fiberglass *Special K* is not otherwise running morning Pictou Harbour tours ($10) and Pictou Island afternoon sailings and island tours ($15).

On the way to Cape Breton, the **Pictou County Historical Museum** in New Glasgow is well worth a stop, particularly if you are a railroad buff, since the *Samson,* one of Canada's earliest steam locomotives, is on exhibit near the museum. Farther east and almost at Cape Breton, **Pomquet Beach** at St. Georges Bay is a beach spread with dunes (unusual for this area) and laced with boardwalks to the water. Stay on the walks, as poison ivy flourishes hereabouts, but the beach is sandy and the water fine for swimming.

CAPE BRETON ISLAND

Cape Breton is the definitive Nova Scotia for many visitors. The island rises from sea level at Canso Causeway at its southwestern end to the northern Cape Breton Highlands, the wild and almost inaccessible tableland plateau spliced by hiking trails and rimmed by **Cabot Trail**, the spectacular sight-seeing route. On one side Acadian villages lie along the Gulf of Saint Lawrence, plied in summer by whale-watching boats from the town of Grand Etang. Just inland, there is salmon fishing in the Margarees area. The Atlantic boasts the offshore **Bird Islands** with gray seals and puffin and other seabird colonies, reached by cruises from Big Bras d'Or.

Cape Breton has a distinctness about it, being actually two islands meshed together by **Bras d'Or**, an inland sea as deep as 900 feet in some places, with marinas tucked along the fjord coastline. The western island is Cape Breton's scenic beauty half, and has Scottish and Acadian settlements. Sydney lies on the smaller eastern island, the domain's industrial pulse and once capital of Cape Breton when it was a colony independent of Nova Scotia. The double island is one of North America's most interesting for idyllic vacation retreats. Alexander Graham Bell, the inventor who was born in Scotland and made his fortune in the United States, spent summers on Cape Breton at Baddeck on Bras d'Or, and his descendants still summer at the Bell estate.

Aside from Sydney, Cape Breton lacks a central focus, so allow extra time to see it. The island's routes tend to run southwest to northeast; sight-seeing is best done by selecting the destination and any peripheral sights on the way, planning the individuated routes with a map, and using the Trans-Canada Highway whenever possible.

Cape Breton is most closely associated with Scottish Highlanders, the province's largest culture base. Yet it is a thorough mix of different people, starting with Micmac Indians, now 2,000 of the island's 175,000 inhabitants.

England's claim to North America was based on John Cabot's sighting of Cape Breton in 1497. Cape Breton was known as New France's Isle Royale, with the French settled in—but ultimately deported from—Louisbourg on the east coast. Acadians still live along the coast from Cheticamp to Isle Madame. The first Anglo infusion came, as usual, with Loyalists fleeing the American Revolution, who settled Sydney. The next arrived with the Scots aboard *Northern Friends* at Sydney Harbour in 1802, and by the 1850s there were 50,000 Scots on Cape Breton. Not all stayed; Rev. Norman MacLeod and his flock of South Gut St. Ann's went on to Australia in 1851, for example. The mix became more cosmopolitan from the late 1800s, as the coal and steel industries here lured Greeks, Chinese, West Indians, Eastern Europeans, Lebanese, Syrians, and Italians (from Boston and from Italy), all told, a total of 23 ethnic groups.

Cape Breton's earlier lures had been fur trading and fishing; the coal frenzy, in contrast, brought illusions of riches and new city dreams, illusions finally dispelled during the post–World War II steel slump, and when oil replaced coal as an energy source.

For visitors, the scenic beauty of the land and the coast has a powerful impact, yet Cape Bretoners are the real lure. They are courteous in a most civil way, never intruding but very willing to assist if needed.

SYDNEY

Sydney is Cape Breton's largest city, third largest in the province, a five-hour drive from Pictou or seven-plus hours from Halifax by car. The Trans-Canada Highway is the most efficient land route into the area. (Flying in from Halifax is quicker and easier.) The expressway slices through central Cape Breton, along the west side of Bras d'Or, the inland sea, and over to the eastern island, where it ends at North Sydney's ferry terminal (which connects Nova Scotia with Newfoundland). Sydney lies farther southeast on the highway's continuation around Sydney's Atlantic harbor.

The city is best known as Nova Scotia's steel town; Sydney is also the hub of coal towns like Glace Bay and Sydney Mines. It is coal rather than steel that undergirds so much of Sydney's history. As early as 1719 French troops dug coal from Port Morien cliffs for fuel for **Louisbourg Fortress**, New France's premier settlement in this part of Canada, a half hour southeast of Sydney on the coast. Centuries later, when metropolitan Sydney's economy floundered due to diminished steel and coal demand, the federal government rebuilt a fifth of the fortress town. This time Louisbourg's purpose was, and still is, to bolster Cape Breton's economy with tourism. Louisbourg is a magnificent re-creation of a walled town, with 50 perfectly duplicated buildings, costumed guides for visitors, and a strong sense of authenticity.

The Louisbourg **Craft Workshops**, initially government funded, is now on its own, designing, making, and marketing a fine line of distinctive Cape Breton crafts and wares. Stoneware is another good Cape Breton product.

France's plan for colonial Isle Royale, as Cape Breton was known, ended when Louisbourg fell to the British in 1758. By 1760, England demolished it so it would never rise again as a threat to the Crown. England's plan to strengthen its own hand started 24 years later when Loyalists fleeing the American Revolution founded Sydney. Cape Breton became a colony in 1785, with Sydney as capital. In 1820 the realm was annexed by Nova Scotia.

Cape Breton's former status as a colony also explains Sydney's very strong identity as the region's major base and gateway, notwithstanding its location off to one side of the island. As a base for day trips Sydney offers tantalizing proximity to Cape Breton's grandeur and interesting sites.

Exploring Sydney

Sydney lies along Sydney Harbour's eastern side with its historic, residential North End a narrow peninsula jutting into the harbor. Piers along here are now used for cruise ships from June to October. Industrial Sydney is farther northwest along the harbor front and is known as Whitney Pier. Sydney's influx of immigrants from all over the world settled around that area's coke oven, and the ethnic churches there—Polish, African Orthodox, and Ukrainian—are now historic properties.

The Sydney that visitors see stretches from North End along Esplanade to Kings Road (Sydney's old whipping post is on Esplanade). All hotels and motels (a third of Cape Breton's lodgings) are along the harbor front, essentially a hotel row, making lodgings easy to find and size up. Most are basic motels at moderate to expensive rates, and are usually filled with tour groups, so it's wise to make advance reservations.

The best for years has been **Holiday Inn Sydney** on three sprawling floors; the corner mini-suites have expansive harbor views. The new **Ramada Mariner Hotel** is a worthy competitor, as *all* of its rooms overlook the water. **Best Western Cape Bretoner** is set back from the road, seems most secluded, and has pleasant, basic amenities.

The blocks up from Esplanade are full of interest. Crafts, a vital part of the recovering economy, have found a sizable niche in the upper floors of the **Lyceum**, once Sydney's performing-arts center. (The Cape Breton Centre for Heritage and Science uses the first floor for exhibits.) Concerts and so forth have moved over to the new **Centre 200**, the focus of early August's Action Week festivals. The city also has a thriving farmers' market on Saturday mornings in summer, a good place to browse for more crafts as well as fresh produce and baked goods. **Island Crafts** on Charlotte Street is another interesting place. The shop is the local outlet for 300 crafts people, whose wares are not cheap but are unusual, with an emphasis on Cape Breton specialties.

Along the same byways are good to excellent restaurants, but unfortunately there are not enough to serve the crowds. **Le Petit Jean** is the upscale place, especially the red front room with fireplace. **Joe's Warehouse & Food Emporium** lures no-jacket, no-tie diners for prime ribs. Along the harbor, with views, are Holiday Inn's **Alexander** dining room and the **Cromarty** restaurant, ensconced in the part of the Auberge Wandlyn Inn motel that had once been an estate.

Some of the province's most outstanding nightlife is here along Charlotte Street and its cross streets. Among the best is **Smooth Herman's** live bands, where younger locals and yuppie types imbibe Singapore slings and beer. The over-30 people go to **Ivory's** at Keddy's Motel on Kings Road.

The Cape Outside Sydney

The Miners' Museum at Glace Bay on the Atlantic has a mine tour, and a re-created village with hearty dining at reasonable costs. There's also dining at Louisbourg (see above for a discussion of Louisbourg Fortress).

Baddeck, site of the **Alexander Graham Bell Museum,** lies 48 km (30 miles) west on the Trans-Canada Highway; at its wharfs and marinas you can rent a canoe or sailboat for enjoying Bras d'Or's pleasures. The resort's main street runs off the Trans-Canada along the lake, and the area's attractions follow one after another. Lobster is always on menus—try the **Inverary Inn Resort** (ask for a table on the back porch overlooking Bras d'Or; Tel: 902-295-2674) and **Telegraph House**'s Victorian-style dining room, or plain lobster fixings at **Baddeck Lobster Suppers** from 4:00 to 9:00 P.M. in the former legion hall. The town has lodgings galore, mostly motels as it is on the Cabot Trail bus circuit; major cuts above the ordinary are the above-mentioned Inverary Inn, with a lakeside motel and cottages behind the main lodge, and **MacNeil House,** a vintage mansion offering suites on the grounds of the Silver Dart Lodge.

Nova Scotia Highland Village Museum at Iona is another worthwhile stop, as its historic buildings are an example of early Scottish settlement hereabouts. The adjacent **Highland Heights Inn** is a neat-as-a-pin motel, whose window-walled restaurant overlooks the lake coast. The drive from Baddeck to Iona will teach you a lesson in patience—a virtue for driving on Cape Breton—as you drive an hour on the Trans-Canada and winding Route 223, to cover a distance of only 16 km (ten miles), as the crow flies.

The **Cabot Trail** is what Cape Breton is all about—181 miles of some of North America's finest scenic beauty, with more than a few scary ascents and descents, and 32 kmh (20 mph) is not an unreasonable speed. The highway, like Cape Breton Highlands National Park that borders Cabot Trail on three sides, is open year-round. With no stops the drive takes about six hours; mid-June through September are the best months, when the weather is mostly clear, and shops and restaurants are open.

There are several ways to do Cabot Trail. As quickly as possible is one way, and you will see sight-seeing buses on Nova Scotia or Atlantic Canada tours from United States and Canadian cities lumbering up and down the gracefully curved route. Much better is the easy-does-it car drive, poking through seaports and exploring side roads with stops at marked lookouts. The best mile-by-mile description is found in the province's travel guide, free from Nova Scotia Tourism, P.O. Box 130, Halifax, Nova Scotia B3J 2M7. (This guide also gives detailed descriptions of other Nova Scotia scenic drives, and is an invaluable source of history and practical information.) Parts of the trail bordering the national park are detailed in literature from Cape Breton Highlands National Park, Ingonish Beach, Nova Scotia B0C 1L0; Tel: (902) 285-2535. The information center at the Port Hastings end of the Canso Causeway also stocks Cabot Trail details, and the area's map entitled "Cape Breton Island" makes a fine highway guide. Another good local source is the Cape Breton Tourism Association at 220 Keltic Drive, Sydney River, Nova Scotia B1S 1P5; Tel: (902) 539-9876.

Driving Cabot Trail works best by sizing it up first on a map. Like other provincial sight-seeing roads, it is marked with signs (but no route number), in this case a mountain peak over the sea. Cabot Trail is shaped like an irregular oval with the Trans-Canada Highway on its southwest-to-northeast base line. The seaport of Pleasant Bay, with the stone picnic shelter known as the Lone Sheiling, marks the route's halfway point and is located at the park's northwestern corner on the Gulf of Saint Lawrence.

You will encounter some memorable places along the route. Going in a clockwise direction from the Baddeck area, you will come upon the lush glens of the Margarees, some 30 minutes north and slightly west of Hunters Mountain—the circular route off Cabot Trail into the valley will take you to the village of Margaree Valley. The **Normaway Inn** resort lodge at the end of a tree-lined lane wins raves for its home-cooked meals in the rustic but very adequate lodge that also serves as a salmon-fishing outfitter center hereabouts; if you stay the night ask for one of the nine lodge rooms rather than a cabin. The village's **Salmon Museum** is dedicated to the art of salmon fishing and local lore. From here, **Cheticamp**, the main Acadian seaport on the gulf, is another half hour; interesting stops are the Acadian Museum, also known as Les Trois Pignons, with genealogy and history, and nearby **LeFort Gallery** with examples of Elizabeth LeFort's hooked tapestries that hang in halls of state around the world. The **Cape Breton Highlands National Park**'s entrance lies three miles beyond Cheticamp; its May to October tourist center has literature handouts, while its bookstore is well stocked with volumes about the province and Atlantic Canada (the park's other center at Ingonish Beach has similar offerings).

Mountainous ups and downs begin here and continue across the park's northern border to the Atlantic and then south on the winding seacoast to the Ingonish Ferry area. The highway tops French Mountain at 1,492 feet above sea level, dips to 1,222 feet at MacKenzie Mountain, and then takes you down on 10- to 12-percent grade switchbacks. The biggest thrill is at Cape Smokey just outside the park limits at Ingonish Ferry, where Cabot Trail descends 1,200 feet in two miles in swooping switchbacks. Mountain majesties notwithstanding, some interesting places lie along the way—a park with picnic tables and beach marks Cabot's Landing, 10 km (6 miles) off the route at Cape North, and Neil Harbour at the park's eastern corner on the Atlantic has fresh fish and lobster for sale at the wharf.

Keltic Lodge at **Ingonish Beach** is the prime place to stop for a meal, a manorial lodging set on a peninsula slim as a finger. Fine facilities range from an indoor pool, tennis courts, and nearby Highlands Golf Links (18 holes, open June to mid-October) to skiing (the ski season runs from January to March). Ingonish Beach, as the name implies, also has beaches—one on the Atlantic, another on a lake.

Another long pocket of interests lies near the end of Cabot Trail around **St. Ann's Bay and Harbour**. North Shore's Plaster Park overlooks the bay along a forest and has sinkhole ponds. Below Indian Brook the road divides, with Route 312 joining the Trans-Canada in the direction of Sydney, while the trail road goes inland, then along St. Ann's Harbour to South Gut St. Ann's, where it joins up again with the Trans-Canada.

Plan an hour at Gaelic College at **South Gut St. Ann's**— more if the spirit of the place gets to you. At North America's only Gaelic college there are six-week summer language classes, as well as facilities for Highland dancing, piping, and weaving. Its Celtic Arts Centre sells clan tartans by the yard and also the Nova Scotian tartan in kilts and apparel. The college's Great Hall of the Clans makes much of local Scottish ancestries with exhibits.

From here it is 20 minutes on the Trans-Canada to Baddeck. The whole Cabot Trail makes for a long, long day—it makes more sense to break up the drive with an overnight stay or perhaps several leisurely days, making the most of Keltic Lodge's creature comforts. Normaway Inn, also mentioned above, is another option; the lodging is also an outfitter for Atlantic salmon fly-fishing on the

Margaree River. June to September is open season, and a nonresident fishing license is easy to obtain.

Midsummer is the time to be on Cape Breton for a variety of events. Gaelic Mod at Gaelic College runs for a week in early August with Scottish piping, drumming, and Highland dancing. Festival on the Bay at Glace Bay spans the last half of July, and more grassroots doings are at New Waterford's Coal Dust Days in mid-July, while Action Week in early August is Sydney's summer festival.

GETTING AROUND

Halifax

Halifax International Airport lies 35 miles northeast of the city and is a spacious easy-in, easy-out complex. It serves as the hub for provincial, Maritime, domestic, and several international nonstop flights.

The main airlines serving Halifax are Air Canada and its local affiliated airline Air Nova, and Canadian Airlines International, whose local airline is Air Atlantic. Ticket counters for the four airlines are separate at the Halifax Airport and also at Yarmouth and Sydney airports, but the relationships are worth noting, as reservations may be made through the larger airlines for their smaller affiliates. Arriving in Halifax are Air Canada's nonstop flights from Montreal, Ottawa, or Toronto, and international nonstop flights from Boston, Newark Airport (New York City area; summers and fall only), London, and Glasgow, Scotland. Canadian Airlines International also has domestic and international service, and flies nonstop from Toronto, Ottawa, Montreal, and Portland, Maine, and transatlantic from Amsterdam. Other carriers are Air St. Pierre from Iles de la Madeleine in Quebec and new air service from the Netherlands with KLM Royal Dutch Airlines.

Car rentals are near the baggage pickup area: There is an Avis counter (Avis also has rental cars at Yarmouth and Sydney), as well as Budget, Hertz, Tilden, and Thrifty. Cars are beyond the terminal, so take along a luggage cart. A shuttle to Halifax/Dartmouth hotels meets flights; $10. Taxis are outside, at about $23 to downtown.

Driving in Halifax is no problem September to May, aside from rush hours. Parking is extremely difficult, though most major hotels have room enough for guests' cars. The local bus ($1) runs everywhere. The bus terminal houses Acadian Lines, with routes throughout the province, and smaller lines like Zinck's to the Eastern

Shore's Sherbrooke; Acadian Bus provides area sight-seeing. VIA Rail is near the waterfront, with routes to provincial gateways. Service cuts have been discussed recently, but for now the trains are still chugging along.

Yarmouth

Plan ahead: 200,000 people, on foot or in cars and buses, arrive in Yarmouth annually on ferry connections from Maine ports.

By Sea. Prince of Fundy Cruises *Scotia Prince* maintains early May through October, 11-hour crossings, which depart daily from Yarmouth at 10:00 A.M. and from Portland, Maine, at 9:00 P.M. The one-way costs are $65, per person, $90 for the car, and if you want a cabin in addition, it costs $32 to $95; the foregoing prices are in U.S. dollars, and the cruise line wants payment in U.S. currency—the provincial information center near the ferry terminal will convert currency, as will banks in Yarmouth. The cruise line has headquarters at Box 4216, Station A, Portland, Maine 04101; Tel: (207) 775-5616 locally; (800) 341-7540 from U.S. points; (800) 482-0955 in Maine; (800) 565-7900 from Nova Scotia, Prince Edward Island, and New Brunswick; and (902) 742-5164 for the rest of Canada.

Marine Atlantic's *Bluenose* operates daily mid-June to mid-September, and two or three times a week the rest of the year, with six-hour crossings, leaving Bar Harbor, Maine, at 8:00 A.M. and Yarmouth at 4:30 P.M. One-way passage costs $34 per person, and $63 for the car. Marine Atlantic is based at Box 250, North Sydney, Nova Scotia B2A 3M3; Tel: (902) 794-7203 locally; (800) 565-9470 handles the Maritimes; (800) 563-7701 from Newfoundland and Labrador; and (800) 565-9411 from Quebec and Ontario. The United States office is at Marine Atlantic in care of the Terminal Supervisor at Bar Harbor, Maine 04609; Tel: (800) 341-7981 for the United States except for Maine, which is (800) 432-7344.

Visitors in the know make advance reservations as far ahead as possible. Marine Atlantic tickets have to be picked up an hour before sailing here and from Digby to New Brunswick and two hours beforehand from North Sydney to Newfoundland, or the reservations are canceled automatically.

By Air. Air Canada and Canadian affiliated airlines fly in to Yarmouth from Halifax, and Air Canada also has non-stop flights from Boston. If Cape Breton is on your itinerary, it is worthwhile to fly from here via Halifax to Sydney, as the trip will take about 13 hours by car. Rail is daily, except Sunday, to Halifax; VIA Rail's route goes from Yarmouth to Digby and then east to Halifax; beyond Halifax the route is then north and slightly east to Truro, from where you can travel farther east to New Glasgow and then up to Cape Breton's Sydney or go west through Amherst and on to Moncton, New Brunswick.

Public transit is excellent in the Yarmouth area, and local buses stop everywhere. Taxis, and shuttles to Rodd Grand Hotel, wait outside the ferry terminal. Avis and Budget rental cars are available at the ferry terminal, as well as the airport 5 km (3 miles) from town. Acadian Lines shares the same terminal as the train station and has daily bus routes to Digby and elsewhere.

Digby

Princess of Acadia is another Marine Atlantic ferry service—see the Yarmouth Getting Around section for details on addresses, phones, and reservations. The 2½-hour crossing on the sometimes turbulent Bay of Fundy to Saint John, New Brunswick, is year-round and costs $14.25 per person and $44 for the car. From Digby, the ferry sails at 5:00 A.M., 1:00 P.M., and 8:15 P.M.; from Saint John departures are at 12:30 A.M., 9:30 A.M., and 4:55 P.M.— there are fewer departures on Sundays.

At the ferry terminal there are wall phones to call a taxi, The Pines' shuttle service, or an Avis car. The local airport, 8 km (5 miles) from Digby, has limited air service, mainly charter flights to **Grand Manan** in the Bay of Fundy. Yarmouth-to-Halifax rail service stops daily in Digby; Acadian Lines maintains a daily bus route along the coast that covers most towns.

With no local or county bus, Digby is a place where wheels are a necessity of life. Car drivers will find the sight-seeing Evangeline Trail works as a skein of back-country roads, roughly parallel to the expressway (Route 101).

Amherst

Nova Scotia's only land connection to mainland Canada is through Amherst via New Brunswick. The major crossing is at Fort Lawrence, five minutes northwest of town, and the route leads to Moncton, New Brunswick, on the Trans-Canada Highway. Fort Lawrence's information complex stocks visitor literature about Nova Scotia in general, with an emphasis on the Amherst area, and a kilt-clad piper plays the bagpipes on the half hour, daily, from May to August, adding a nice touch. The second area border crossing is at Tidnish, 24 km (15 miles) northeast of Amherst on Route 366, and that route leads to Cape Tormentine in New Brunswick, for the ferry connection to Borden, Prince Edward Island. Acadian Lines connects daily with the SMT bus line that runs to the ferry terminal for Prince Edward Island as well.

Rail goes twice daily from Amherst to provincial points via Truro, and to Moncton out of the province into New Brunswick. Acadian Lines has service to provincial points, and also connects with New Brunswick's SMT bus line at Moncton across the border, which in turn connects with Greyhound from the United States and Voyageur from Montreal. Local bus service links Springhill, Oxford, and Parrsboro. Otherwise, there is no local service, so be prepared to walk or drive, and taxis are on call. Rent-A-Wreck (better than the name implies) and Budget have rental cars in Amherst.

Pictou

Four ferries connect Caribou, 15 minutes north of Pictou, with Wood Islands, Prince Edward Island, across Northumberland Strait. Service operates May to mid-December, daily, and during summer peak season 19 departures per day from 6:00 A.M. to 9:50 P.M. from each ferry gateway are scheduled; car waiting lines can be horrendous, but ease from 6:00 P.M. to 10:00 A.M. The cost for the 1¼-hour crossing is $3.30 per person, and $10.60 for the vehicle, one way. Contact Northumberland Ferries at the Caribou or Wood Islands terminals for details at (800) 565-0201 in Nova Scotia, Prince Edward Island, and New Brunswick, or (902) 485-6580/962-2016 locally. The ferry company has offices at Box 634, Charlottetown, Prince Edward Island C1A 7L3.

Pictou slipped off the well-worn tourist route decades ago, which makes it nice for discovering, but tough for getting around—wheels are a must for visiting. Pictou County Transit connects the town with New Glasgow, 20 minutes southeast, plus area villages. If you want to get to Halifax or other provincial points, take the above Pictou County bus to New Glasgow, where there are rail and bus connections. Avis has rental cars in New Glasgow and Stellarton; Budget, Tilden, and Rent-A-Wreck have area rental-car locations also.

Sydney

Flying into Sydney from Halifax is easy with Air Canada or Canadian affiliated airlines; there are no hotel shuttles, but Avis and others rent cars, and taxis are available; 15 minutes to town. Rail from Sydney to the mainland goes through New Glasgow and Truro to Halifax and other points twice daily. Acadian Lines has frequent bus departures to various destinations in Nova Scotia.

Ferry service to two Newfoundland ports is based in North Sydney; Marine Atlantic handles the service—specifics detailed in the foregoing Yarmouth Getting Around coverage are the same here. The ferry terminal lies on the northern side of Sydney Harbour; road access is from the Trans-Canada Highway, which moves fast along here, so watch for the signs.

One-way passage costs $13.25 per person, and $41 for the car from North Sydney to Port-aux-Basques, Newfoundland. The new *Caribou* makes the crossing in five hours, the *John Hamilton Gray* in seven. The service is twice daily, year-round, more frequent July through September; departure times vary, usually about 9:30 A.M. and midnight from North Sydney, and 11 A.M. and 11:30 P.M. from Port-aux-Basques.

The North Sydney-to-Argentia, Newfoundland, ferry crossing runs from mid-June to early September at $36.25 per person, and $88 for the vehicle. The *Ambrose Shea* has scheduled 11:30 A.M. sailings on Monday, Wednesday, and Friday from North Sydney, and 1:30 P.M. departures on Tuesday, Thursday, and Saturday from Argentia. Cabins ($40 to $80) on the 19-hour service need reservations the winter or spring before arrival.

In Sydney, the local bus service covers the town and also goes to Glace Bay and North Sydney and area. For sight-seeing, ask at the hotel desk for touring company phone numbers; Briands Cab goes around the Cabot Trail in taxis; each of three passengers pays about $35.

Further Information

The province's official Nova Scotia museums are open mid-May to mid-October. Privately owned museums are not as dependable and, aside from the summer months, hours vary from place to place. The province puts out a thick, full-sized Nova Scotia travel guide, free from Nova Scotia Tourism and Culture, PO Box 130, Halifax, Nova

Scotia B3J 2M7; it has details on what's open when and how to get there.

ACCOMMODATIONS REFERENCE

Check In is a service that will make reservations for you throughout Nova Scotia. Call (800) 341-6096 in the U.S.; (800) 492-0643 in Maine; (800) 565-7105 in the Maritimes; (800) 565-7180 in Newfoundland and Quebec; (800) 565-7140 in central and southern Ontario; and (800) 565-7166 in northern Ontario, Manitoba, Saskatchewan, Alberta, British Columbia, Northwest Territories, and Yukon. The local phone in Halifax and Dartmouth is (902) 425-5781.

▶ **Auberge Sieur de Monts.** Box 2055 R.R. 2, **Granville Ferry,** N.S. B0S 1K0. Tel: (902) 532-7883.

▶ **Auberge Wandlyn Inn.** Box 275, Route 104/Victoria Street, **Amherst,** N.S. B4H 3Z2. Tel: (902) 667-3331; in U.S., (800) 561-0006; in Canada, (800) 561-0000; Telex: 019-23517.

▶ **Best Western Aurora Inn.** Box 609, 338 Main Street, **Kingston,** N.S. B0P 1R0. Tel: (902) 765-3306; in U.S. and Canada, (800) 528-1234.

▶ **Best Western Cape Bretoner.** 560 Kings Road, **Sydney,** N.S. B1S 1B8. Tel: (902) 539-8101; in U.S. and Canada, (800) 528-1234.

▶ **Best Western Claymore Inn.** Box 1720, Church Street, **Antigonish,** N.S. B2G 2M5. Tel: (902) 863-1050; in U.S. and Canada, (800) 528-1234; Telex: 019-36567.

▶ **Best Western Glengarry.** 150 Willow Street, **Truro,** N.S. B2N 4Z6. Tel: (902) 893-4311; in U.S. and Canada, (800) 528-1234.

▶ **Boscawen Inn.** 150 Cumberland Street, Box 1343, **Lunenburg,** N.S. B0J 2C0. Tel: (902) 634-3325.

▶ **Bread and Roses Country Inn.** 82 Victoria Street, Box 177, **Annapolis Royal,** N.S. B0S 1A0. Tel: (902) 532-5727.

▶ **Chateau Halifax.** 1990 Barrington Street, **Halifax,** N.S. B3J 1P2. Tel: (902) 425-6700; in U.S., (800) 828-7447; in Canada, (800) 268-9411; in Ontario and Quebec, (800) 268-9420. Reservations worldwide may also be made through any Canadian Airlines International sales office. Telex: 019-21802; Fax: (902) 429-6672.

▶ **Chignecto Motel & Dining Room.** Box 144, LaPlanche Street, **Amherst at Fort Lawrence,** N.S. B4H 3Y6. Tel: (906) 667-3865/66.

▶ **Citadel Inn.** 1960 Brunswick Street, **Halifax,** N.S. B3J

2G7. Tel: (902) 422-1391; in Canada, (800) 565-7162; Telex: 019-21802.

▶ **Compass Rose Bed and Breakfast.** Box 1267, 15 King Street, **Lunenburg**, N.S. B0J 2C0. Tel: (902) 634-8509.

▶ **Fundy Winds Family Motel.** Box 1136, LaPlanche Street, **Amherst at Fort Lawrence**, N.S. B4H 3Y6. Tel: (902) 667-3881.

▶ **Goodwin Hotel.** Box 15, Route 1, **Weymouth**, N.S. B0W 3T0. Tel: (902) 837-5120.

▶ **Halifax Sheraton.** 1919 Upper Water, **Halifax**, N.S. B3J 3J5. Tel: (902) 421-1700; in U.S. and Canada, (800) 325-3535; in U.K., (0800) 35-35-35; in Australia, (008) 22-22-29; Telex: 019-21773.

▶ **Halliburton House Inn.** 5184 Morris, **Halifax**, N.S. B3J 1B3. Tel: (902) 420-0658.

▶ **Highland Heights Inn.** Box 19, **Iona**, N.S. B0A 1L0. Tel: (902) 622-2360.

▶ **Holiday Inn Sydney.** Box 1326, 480 Kings Road, **Sydney**, N.S. B1S 1A8. Tel: (902) 539-6750; in U.S. and Canada, (800) HOLIDAY; Telex: 019-35278; Fax: (902) 539-2773.

▶ **Inverary Inn Resort.** Box 190, Shore Road, **Baddeck**, N.S. B0E 1B0. Tel: (902) 295-2674; Fax: (902) 295-2427.

▶ **Keltic Lodge.** Box 70, **Ingonish Beach**, N.S. B0C 1L0. Tel: (902) 285-2880; Telex: 019-35117; Fax: (902) 285-2859.

▶ **Liscombe Lodge.** Route 7, **Liscomb Mills**, N.S. B0J 2A0. Tel: (902) 779-2307; Fax: (902) 779-2700.

▶ **Lord Nelson Hotel.** Box 700, 1515 South Park Street, **Halifax**, N.S. B3J 2T3. Tel: (902) 423-6331; Telex: 019-21866.

▶ **MacNeil House.** c/o Silver Dart Lodge, Box 399, Shore Road, **Baddeck**, N.S. B0E 1B0. Tel: (902) 295-2340; Telex: 019-35234.

▶ **Normaway Inn.** Box 101, Egypt Road, **Margaree Valley**, N.S. B0E 2C0. Tel: (902) 248-2987.

▶ **Oak Island Inn and Marina.** **Western Shore**, N.S. B0J 3M0. Tel: (902) 627-2600.

▶ **Old Orchard Inn.** Box 1090, **Wolfville**, N.S. B0P 1X0. Tel: (902) 542-5751; Telex: 019-32176.

▶ **Pictou Lodge.** Braeshore Road, P.O. Box 1539, **Pictou**, N.S. B0K 1H0. Tel: (902) 485-4322.

▶ **Pines Resort Hotel.** Box 70, Shore Road, **Digby**, N.S. B0V 1A0. Tel: (902) 245-2511; Telex 019-32186; Fax: (902) 245-6133.

▶ **Planters' Barracks.** Starrs Point Road, R.R. 1, **Port Williams**, N.S. B0P 1T0. Tel: (902) 542-7879.

▶ **Ramada Mariner Hotel.** 300 Esplanade, **Sydney**, N.S.

B1P 1A7. Tel: (902) 562-7500; in U.S., (800) 2-RAMADA; Fax: (902) 562-3023.

▶ **Rodd Colony Harbour Inn.** 6 Ferry Street, **Yarmouth,** N.S. B5A 3K7. Tel: (902) 742-9194; in Eastern U.S., (800) 565-9077; in Maritime Canada, (800) 565-0207; in Ontario, Quebec, Newfoundland, (800) 565-0241; Telex: 019-38546; Fax: (902) 742-4645.

▶ **Rodd Grand Hotel.** 417 Main Street, Box 220, **Yarmouth,** N.S. B5A 4B2. Tel: (902) 742-2446; in Eastern U.S., (800) 565-9077; in Maritime Canada, (800) 565-0207; in Ontario, Quebec, Newfoundland, (800) 565-0241; Telex: 019-38546; Fax: (902) 742-4645.

NEW BRUNSWICK

By Colleen Thompson

Colleen Thompson is a regular contributor to the Atlantic Advocate *magazine and a columnist for the* Saint John Telegraph-Journal *and for* Atlantic Insight *magazine. She is also the author of* New Brunswick Inside Out, *a guidebook, and* The Very Best, *a* Country Restaurants of New Brunswick Guide. *A contributor to newspapers and magazines throughout Canada and the United States (*Newsday, *the* Toronto Star, *and others), she is a native New Brunswicker.*

If there's a miniaturized version of Canada, New Brunswick might well be it. With a 35 percent French-Acadian population, mostly in the northeastern section, and the rest generally of British descent, New Brunswick provides a look at two cultures that sometimes blend, and often differ completely.

Jacques Cartier explored its shores in 1534. Seventy years later, Samuel de Champlain sailed into Saint John harbor on the feast day of Saint John the Baptist, hence its name. Other explorers named the coastland area Utopia, one saying "the country is as pleasing as the good cheer."

Already settled by scattered handfuls of Acadians who defied the British order to leave (Acadia was the name for the area when it was largely a French colony—before the British expelled the French inhabitants in the mid-1700s), New Brunswick became overwhelmingly British Loyalist after the American Revolution: American refugees who remained loyal to the king arrived by the thousands. At

71

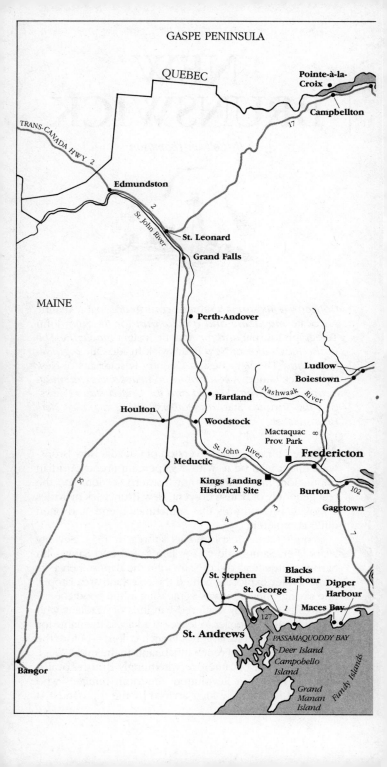

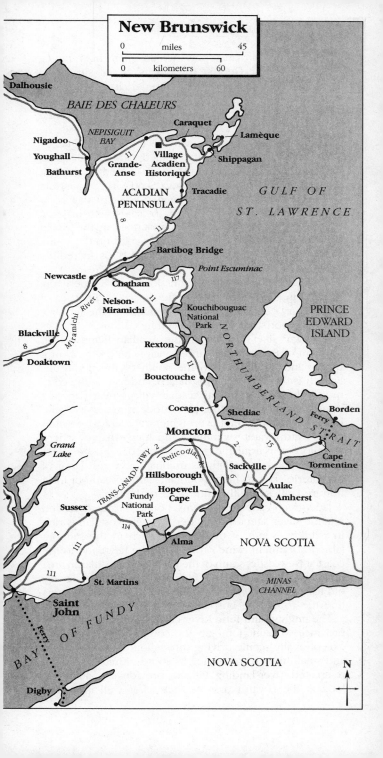

that time the province was named after the reigning British monarch, George III, and its capital city called Fredericton after his second son, Frederick.

For generations Acadians have clung to the province's north shores. Their heritage has, in many ways, remained unchanged.

The coffeepot-shaped province is tucked into Quebec at its northern perimeter and joined to Maine all along its western boundary; a narrow neck of land on the east connects New Brunswick to Nova Scotia. Three-quarters of the province glories in a rugged seacoast that combines 700 miles of warm, sandy beaches with majestic rocky headlands where the highest tides in the world are found. Scattered about the Fundy coast on the south, facing Nova Scotia, are escapist islands of incredible serenity.

Mainland cities such as Saint John and Fredericton, steeped in a British heritage, offer nostalgic glimpses of the country's Loyalist past, good restaurants, theater, professional sports, and modern accommodations.

In towns like Caraquet in the **Acadian Peninsula** on the Gulf of St. Lawrence, and Bouctouche on the Northumberland Strait coast to the south of the peninsula, French is the language most heard, and fishing the common industry. A historical Acadian village near Caraquet draws visitors to view the past. Modern motels vie with historical inns to tempt overnighters, and craggy beaches afford warm-water swimming and long wharves where fresh lobster is available right off the boats.

The rugged and relatively uninhabited forest lands of the interior rise to high mountains and spread out for a hundred miles on either side of scenic highways.

Jade green canoeing streams, home of trout, bass, and Atlantic silver salmon, meander through woodlands rich in wildlife. Some of these rivers, such as the salmon-fabled **Miramichi**, wind on through the heartland to the coast at Newcastle, south of the Acadian Peninsula, an area noted for the "come all ye" ballads of lumbermen. Lovely old towns with the sturdy homes of early lumber barons line the route; the hospitality of the region is sincere.

The mighty **Saint John River** cuts a blue path across the province to Saint John on the south shore, providing exceptionally scenic driving throughout its valley. Cities and small historic towns hug its shores. Kings Landing, a re-created river-landing village, provides an authentic look at the Loyalist past. Marinas offer well-appointed havens for yachts and small craft. Free car ferries criss-cross the river.

New Brunswick craftspeople are responsible for the resurgence of old-time quality crafts, such as weaving and glassblowing, in the Maritime provinces, and outlets are plentiful. Pewter items, including jewelry, are of the highest quality here, especially those of **Aitkin's Pewter** in Fredericton. Potters such as Tom Smith of St. Andrews and Peter Powning of Markhamville (near Sussex) have reached the status of artist rather than artisan. Weavers such as **Madawaska Weavers** in St. Leonard and **Loomcrafters** in Gagetown sometimes outfit royalty.

For warm-water swimming, the shores of Northumberland Strait across from Prince Edward Island, from Shediac to Kouchibouquac National Park, offer long sandbars. Above that are the excellent **Baie des Chaleurs beaches**.

Hardier souls brave the cool **Fundy coast** waves at the bottom of the province, where spectacular tides have carved cliffs and rocks that adorn no less inviting beaches. Just off the Fundy Isles, Right whales (so-named by ancient whalers as these were the whales they were looking for) frolic for the benefit of sight-seeing expeditions to the breeding ground of these mammoth creatures.

With four major areas—the Fundy coast, the Saint John Valley, the Acadian Peninsula, and the Miramichi region—each distinct in scenery and character, New Brunswick is ideal for touring. Its historic background, convenient network of roads, endless outdoor activities, local festivals, surprisingly cosmopolitan art scene, as well as excellent examples of local, European, and Acadian cuisine, make it both enjoyable and interesting.

What makes it all the more enticing is the fact that the residents have not yet lost their old-fashioned sense of hospitality and laid-back lifestyle. There's a ditty sometimes sung by the residents that sums up the New Brunswick attitude.

> Take it easy, take it easy,
> You're in the maritimes,
> Where the livin' is slow. . . .

It makes sense to hum along.

MAJOR INTEREST

Saint John
The Reversing Falls Rapids

Market Slip Loyalist Landing Place: shops, historic
    buildings, restaurants
The Old City Market
Loyalist Days celebration
Festival by the Sea
Historical walks

The Fundy Coast
Fundy Isles
The 1700s town of St. Andrews-by-the-Sea
Whale watching from Deer Island or Grand Manan
Roosevelt Home on Campobello
Scenic St. Martins area
Fundy National Park
Salem and Hillsborough Railroad steam-engine
    rides and sunset dinner trips
Moncton's Tidal Bore and Magnetic Hill
University of Moncton Acadian Museum and Art
    Gallery

Fredericton
The Legislative Library, copy of Domesday Book
    and Audubon prints
The Changing of the Guard, Officer's Square
Pioneer Princess Riverboat tours
River Jubilee celebration
Boyce Farmer's Market
Christ Church Cathedral
Mactaquac Craft Festival

Along the Saint John River Valley
Madawaska Weavers
Kings Landing Historical Village

The Acadian Peninsula
Beaches, park, and lobster festival at Shediac
Kouchibouquac National Park and beaches
Acadian Historical Village in Grand Anse
Acadian Festival at Caraquet
Fishing charters from Dalhousie
Campbellton Salmon Festival

The Miramichi
Fishing
Canada's International Irish Festival in Chatham
Miramichi Atlantic Salmon Museum at Doaktown
Woodmen's Museum in Boiestown

Food in New Brunswick

An edible fern called the fiddlehead is a particularly favorite spring food in New Brunswick. It is available frozen year-round, and some restaurants feature it. Dulse, a dried purple seaweed, is another popular snack of the residents.

Fish and shellfish, although readily available on the coast, are not always prepared with finesse, except for lobster, which is usually boiled to perfection. Deep frying is, alas, the usual method, but steaming, poaching, and broiling are catching on. Local lamb and pork can be delicious, and Acadian specialties such as chicken *fricot* (a stew), *poutine rapé* (a potato ball with a core of pork), or a delicious dessert pastry, *poutine à trou,* are served in the Acadian area.

THE FUNDY COAST

One of the most popular areas is the Fundy shore, dotted with small islands and tiny fishing villages, tide-carved rocks drenched with awesomely high tides, and encompassing a large national park as well as the cosmopolitan but historic old city of Saint John.

Saint John

As far as North American cities go, Saint John is ancient. The oldest incorporated city in Canada, with the oldest police force in the country (established in 1826 even before the British bobbies), it has the oldest city market charter in North America.

It's also noted for its native sons. Movie greats such as Louis B. Mayer (who used to ride on the back of his father's junk wagon), Walter Pidgeon (who began here as a baritone singer), and Donald Sutherland played childhood games (although not all at the same time) among the ancient stones of Loyalist Burying Grounds. Benedict Arnold carried on a business near the harbor and Harry Houdini and Ethel Barrymore graced the stage at the ornate Old Capital Theatre—which is now, like everything else in Saint John, being restored.

The harbor is Saint John's focal point and the site of its

most historic event, the landing of the Loyalists in 1783. On that day 3,000 refugees from the American Revolution landed on the rocky banks, quickly followed by thousands more who wished to live "under the King."

Aided by the Micmac and Maliseet Indians of the area, who showed them how to survive the winters, they soon created a thriving port city with an elegant lifestyle. Much of that gracious era survives in the city today.

Saint John sprawls up from the year-round port, with red-bricked and lantern-lined **King Street** its main pathway from restored Market Slip and Market Square on the waterfront to King Square and the **Loyalist Burying Grounds** in the town center. Shops, historic sites, excellent restaurants, and some fine hotels are spread out in every direction. Walking is the best way to explore this city; several walking-tour maps are available through the tourist offices at City Hall and Sydney Street, or at the Tugboat Information Center at Market Slip. Costumed guides lead historical walks from Barbour's General Store at Market Slip.

Market Slip at the foot of King Street is a perfect place to begin an exploration of Saint John. There's a complex of small historic buildings set up as museums, and plenty of shops, restaurants, and promenades in the restored complex of old warehouses now known as **Market Square**. Devouring seafood under the outside umbrellas at **Grannan's** is like having a front and center seat at "What's going on in Saint John."

This is where the festivities that mark **Loyalist Days** begin in late July, when costumed residents come ashore in small boats, guided by Indians in a reenactment of that first arrival. During August's **Festival by the Sea**, the folk dancing of cultural groups from across Canada is presented here also.

A sky walk leads from Market Square to the extensive facilities of the Aquatic Center, Saint John's legacy from the 1985 Canada Games.

Part of the Market Square complex includes Hilton's smallest hotel, the **Hilton International**, with most rooms decorated in Loyalist style and many providing an excellent view of the Loyalist Days pageant. Both the Hilton and the ultra-modern **Delta Brunswick Hotel** have lots of parking. The Delta overlooks restored King Street and is connected to the **Brunswick Square** shopping complex, a two-tier center with chic boutiques, antiques markets, and occasional amateur theater.

The historic core of the city is concentrated near the harbor. **Old Loyalist House**, a gracious 1817 home that remained in the same family for five generations, reflects the well-to-do Loyalist way of life. The **Old City Market** (two blocks up from the harbor, with entrances on Charlotte and Germaine streets), built in 1876, extends for a full block. Under its arched roof, built with hand-hewn timbers by early ship carpenters, vendors display red lobster, yellow wheels of cheese, barrels of purple dulse (the dried seaweed residents eat like potato chips), preserves, pies, flowers, and crafts. A couple of snack bars cater to light appetites (the best hot dogs in town are here), and outdoor cafés offer lunch in the sun.

Antiques stores and craft shops, such as **Windrush Galleries**, where Inuit and Indian arts are featured, string along Prince William Street and its offshoot lanes.

There are some good restaurants in this area. The chef's light hand at **Incredible Edibles**, 42 Princess Street, makes for pleasant terrace dining in an old building that also houses craft and antiques shops. **Café Creole**, at the corner of King Square, specializes in peppery New Orleans dishes. Traditional dining is excellent in the Delta Brunswick Hotel's quiet **Mallard Room** or the Hilton's more elegant, Loyalist style **Turn of the Tide** restaurant.

Two of the city's major attractions are a bit far for walking but a short trip by taxi. The **New Brunswick Museum**, 277 Douglas Avenue (opened in 1842 as the first public museum in Canada), deserves an hour or two for an overview of the province's past and present. The collection includes Indian artifacts, early shipbuilding relics, Loyalist rooms, and a modern-art gallery.

A bit farther on, the **Reversing Falls Rapids** puts on a show twice every 24 hours when the strong Fundy tide (40 or more feet) tries to push up the Saint John River. Because the river is so powerful, the tides are turned around and the result is a series of boiling whirlpools and angry rippling rapids. There is one drawback. If the pulp mill across the stream is emitting fumes that day, you may want to skip the viewing. Luckily the odor doesn't seem to permeate downtown Saint John.

Moncton

Moncton, the second city of the Fundy area, was founded by Acadians and Pennsylvania Dutch and Germans, who came here to farm and build ships. It sits on the southeastern coast near the mouth of the Petitcodiac River, near the eastern end of the Fundy coast and at the beginning of the Acadian section of New Brunswick. Some residents call this city the "gateway to Acadia," and much of its population is bilingual. Once an important railway center, its rail role has dwindled in late years, although you'll still see mementos of the age of steam in Centennial Park, where an old locomotive is enshrined, and in the Moncton Museum. Just outside Moncton, on the Fundy shore, the town of **Hillsborough** has refurbished an old engine and some passenger cars, providing daily trips to a small community called Salem. Dinner is available on board for steam nostalgia buffs.

The Acadian Museum on the campus of the University of Moncton (New Brunswick's only French-language university) has a large collection of artifacts, but Moncton's main claim to fame has always been two phenomena of nature, the Tidal Bore and the Magnetic Hill. Some say they are highly overrated. Others consider them fascinating.

The **Tidal Bore** happens twice every 24 hours; you can see it at Bore View Park on Main Street in Moncton. Because the entrance to the Petitcodiac River is narrow, the tide is funneled and surges up all at once, creating a low tidal wave that covers red mud riverbanks in the wink of an eye and creates a wide river out of what was a trickle seconds before.

Magnetic Hill, just off the Trans-Canada Highway at Mountain Road, Moncton, seems to be an uphill grade when it is actually downhill. Startled motorists, who sometimes turn off the ignition and put the car in neutral, find themselves coasting "uphill" at an ever-increasing rate. There is a large water theme park, called Magic Mountain, at the hill.

Moncton's top and most expensive hotel, the **Beausejour**, is central, decorated in an Acadian theme, and has a good restaurant. For excellent seafood try the noted **Cy's** and for fine French crepes it's **Le Mascaret**; both on Main Street near Bore Park.

Shopping here is probably some of the best in the province. Downtown Moncton, where red-brick courtyards curve between store fronts, is particularly attractive in the summer, when hanging baskets adorn its lamp posts and benches and cafés provide summertime people-watching areas.

The Fundy Shore

West on Passamaquoddy Bay, via Routes 1 and 127, the lovely old town of **St. Andrews-by-the-Sea** spreads its mellow homes and streets back from the shore in perfect harmony. More than half the buildings in town were erected before 1900, 14 of them in the 1700s. The best way to explore the town is by bicycle, available for rent at the venerable old **Algonquin Hotel**, where kilted bell-hops speed your luggage to large modernized rooms, and dining on the wide veranda is de rigueur; tennis and golf are available.

The shops on Water Street in St. Andrews are full of British woolens, china, local crafts, and works of well-known local artists. A lobster roll or a bowl of chowder at **A Whale of a Café** (in the same building as the Baleine crafts shop) is a Fundy tradition, and dinner or a room at the atmospheric old **Shiretown Inn** on Water Street is part of the St. Andrews experience. Another enjoyable way to experience St. Andrews is a stay at the beautiful **Victorian Rossmount Inn**, just outside of town, where the elegant decor includes antiques and scenic views.

Be sure to visit the **Huntsman Marine Laboratory and Aquarium** and the **Pansy Patch**, a gingerbread fairy-tale house which is part rare-book and antiques shop, part bed and breakfast in totally charming quarters. Also don't miss the **Tara Manor**, a former Canadian politician's summer home, now turned into a resort noted for its **Evening Star** dining room and lovely setting. The **Algonquin Golf Course**, said to be one of the most beautiful in Canada, runs along the Passamaquoddy Bay.

A free ferry at Letete, on the Fundy shore near St. George (Route 1), takes cars and passengers to **Deer Island** in about ten minutes. This small landfall is ringed by serene harbors and scattered with small villages. Friendly fishermen will point out Old Sow Whirlpool, offshore at Deer Point, and direct you to the best lobster outlets. Guest rooms are available at **West Isles World**, a bed and breakfast that offers private accommodations and where the Cline family can provide whale-, bird-, and seal-watching cruises.

Campobello Island is reached by ferry from Deer Island or by bridge from Maine. Although there is a pretty shoreside golf course, the big attraction is the **Roosevelt Summer Home**, unchanged since FDR's last visit. The movie "Sunrise at Campobello" was filmed here and

Greer Garson, its star, stayed in historic **Owen House**, a bed-and-breakfast inn with fireplaces in the bedrooms and reeking of island history.

Grand Manan Island is almost two hours farther out to sea by a car-carrying ferry from Black's Harbour, Route 776 on the New Brunswick mainland. On the way whales are sometimes sighted on the horizon. Seals occasionally follow and sea lions grump from rocks.

This Atlantic gem, raised by high rocky cliffs, is topped by lighthouses at each end. The old **Marathon Inn**, which sits on a hill above the ferry landing, offers old-fashioned comfort (some rooms with bathroom down the hall) along with a heated pool. The smaller—but no less atmospheric—**Compass Rose** is just up the road, a friendly, well-run inn serving wonderful chowder and afternoon tea.

Whale-watching expeditions leave from the Marathon, where bicycles are also available. Nature walks extend throughout the island, although a car is needed for sites such as Dark Harbour, where dulse is harvested and photographers gather each evening for spectacular sunsets. Once darkness descends, the islanders say the sound of a phantom rower is often heard. He's believed to be the ghost of one of Captain Morgan's men, doomed to guard the old pirate's treasure forever. Old legends are believable here.

In the other direction from Saint John, northeast of the city about 20 miles on Route 111, the town of **St. Martins** nestles on the coast, a cozy, perfect example of a Fundy fishing village. Stately old homes with widow's walks are backed against the forest. Two covered bridges, two long wharves—where lobster boats are usually tied up—and a Fundy lighthouse set against the sea are their views. The high Fundy tides have scoured rocks into mushroomlike shapes and polished a hole right through one of the red cliffs that guards the sheltered harbor and the long crescent of beach. St. Martins is a find and should be savored; the best way to do that is to stay at the **Quaco Inn**, in an old mansion, where some rooms face the sea and dinner is only by reservation, unless you are a guest. Rooms are sunny and comfortable with fine old furnishing. The town is still unspoiled, as are **Mace's Bay** and **Dipper Harbour** on the southwestern side of Saint John.

Also at the eastern end of the Fundy coast, between Saint John and Moncton, the magnificent **Fundy National Park** stretches along the shore and pushes into game-filled woodlands. A golf course runs along a rocky ridge overlooking the bay, and deer come into the meadows in such numbers that they sometimes dot them at twilight. Driving at night here can be hazardous if speed signs aren't heeded, since the area abounds in moose, which often take exception to anyone but themselves on the wooded roads.

The **Fundy Park Chalets** and the **Caledonia Highlands Inn and Chalets**, both within the park, offer modern, comfortable accommodations (good for families) in a secluded area where wildlife often wanders near at night. The park also offers a good restaurant, and many activities including hiking, canoeing, fishing, swimming (in a heated pool), and beachcombing. (See Accommodations Reference at the end of the chapter.)

Look for terrific sticky buns, lobster, and crafts at the park gate village of Alma. Farther on, at **Hopewell Cape**, it's possible to walk among giant rock sculptures and explore caves in the cliff face, all carved by the tides.

About 56 km (35 miles) past Moncton on Route 2 toward Nova Scotia, the town of **Sackville** is noted for its English atmosphere, the lovely campus of Mount Allison University (where the excellent collection of the Owens Art Gallery is found), and the **Marshlands Inn**, an antiques-filled mansion with a dignified dining room serving many local products (even homemade ice cream with fresh berries).

SAINT JOHN RIVER VALLEY

The Saint John River flows a 250-mile scenic course throughout the province, occasionally forming the border between Maine and New Brunswick, wandering through rolling farmlands, rushing over a high ledge to create a dazzling waterfall, and brushing against some historic towns and three major cities along its winding route.

Kings Landing, a re-created river-landing village of the late 1700s, is found along this valley 37 km (23 miles) west of Fredericton, and so is **Mactaquac Provincial Park**, on Route 105, 24 km (14 miles) west of Fredericton, with excellent camping facilities, a beach, and championship 18-hole golf course. Water slides and zoos, an exceptional art gallery, a lovely capital city, plenty of craftspeople, and

crisscrossing river ferries make this route exceptionally
rewarding.

Fredericton

Fredericton's 44,000 residents claim it is the loveliest of
Canada's Atlantic cities, and that boast is usually not disputed. Part of the capital's charm is in its setting on the
banks of the broad Saint John River, where lush green
slopes and drooping willows provide an Old English
tranquility.

Fredericton's British background is further empha-
sized by the graceful spire of Christ Church Cathedral
pushing from beneath the feathery blanket of maples and
elms which, along with complacent homes and Victorian
mansions, line its neatly laid out streets.

The British established a military base here in 1785.
Loyalists founded the University of New Brunswick with
Kings College in 1785. When the cathedral foundation
was laid in 1845, Queen Victoria made Fredericton a city.

A gracious and social place from the beginning, Fredericton's upper-crust young people, immortalized in
prints by 1800s artists, were known as "the fashionables."

Even today, Governor's levees and Beaux-Arts balls,
riverboat cruises, rowing shells, band concerts in the park,
and a profusion of old-time craft activities keep part of
Fredericton's spirit gently clasped in a bygone time. But
bustling shopping malls now compete with the traditional
Queen Street shops by the river. Glass office buildings and
modern bridges have replaced old iron structures and
some pockets of the past.

It's a walking city, with much of its history in the
downtown area and "up the hill" at the University of New
Brunswick. A quick lesson on its past can be pleasantly
learned by taking a free walking tour with a costumed
guide, available at City Hall during the summer.

There's an odd cornucopia of treasures among Fredericton's downtown attractions. At the Beaverbrook Art
Gallery, one whole wall is hung with a gigantic Salvador
Dali painting. The collection includes the works of major
British painters such as Thomas Gainsborough, Sir Joshua
Reynolds, and Joseph Mallord William Turner, a Gobelins
tapestry, and an excellent representation of Canadian and
regional artists. The **Legislative Building Library** displays
a rare copy of the 1087 Domesday Book. Also on view are
435 hand-colored copper engravings by John James Audu-

bon. Christ Church Cathedral's stained glass is best seen from inside, where you'll also find another of those Fredericton surprises: the original model for London's Big Ben. In late May the cathedral hosts a colorful **Festival of the Arts**, which includes crafts and musical entertainment.

The **York Sunbury Historical Museum** in Officer's Square, Queen Street, would like to be known for its Indian artifacts and accurately restored rooms of the Loyalist and Acadian periods. But it's the stuffed body of a mammoth 42-pound frog, said to have been caught in a nearby lake, that remains a top drawing card, cherished by the residents.

The museum, part of the original restored British Military Compound, encompasses two blocks and includes a guardhouse and officers' and enlisted men's quarters, all open to the public. Every day but Sunday during the summer a band of red-coated soldiers is piped into the compound for the changing-of-the-guard ceremony. *Pioneer Princess,* which pretends to be a paddle-wheeler, offers short water tours and dinner theater on board; you'll find it downtown, at the wharf at the base of Regent Street. It's worth a walk around the streets near Officer's Square for the fine craft shops such as **Aitkin's Pewter**, the **Regent Craft Gallery**, and **Table for Two**. The work of highly acclaimed local artists can be purchased at outlets such as **Gallery 78**.

The University of New Brunswick, established in 1785, is one of the oldest institutions of education in North America; the building that housed the first astronomical observatory in North America is still extant.

About three times a year regional craftspeople and artists hold mammoth markets in the city. Times and locations vary, but the best-known one is always held throughout the Labour Day weekend (the first weekend in September) at nearby Mactaquac Park (MAC-ta-quack).

Harness racing made its debut in Fredericton in 1863. Drivers and sulkies still zip around the **Fredericton Raceway**. (Curling is the residents' game in winter.) Racing sculls set out from the Aquatic Center on the shore, and at the beginning of July everything centers around the water for **River Jubilee** celebrations.

To be complete, a visit to Fredericton should take in the **Boyce Farmer's Market**, which happens every Saturday from 6:00 A.M. to noon. Although local products are ostensibly the draw, it is the gathering place for residents, visitors, politicians, artists, musicians, writers, actors, and any VIP who happens to be in town. Chances are, they'll be breakfasting at **Goofy Roofy's** lunch counter.

The **Lord Beaverbrook Hotel**, situated on the riverbank downtown, next to the Beaverbrook Art Gallery, is the only hotel in town, although there are plenty of motels, including a large Howard Johnson's. It's handy for sight-seeing and shopping in the downtown core and close to government offices. The rooms are adequate, modern, and there's a major hot pool and swimming area within the complex. Its **River Room** is a popular lounge/bar and the main dining room, **The Terrace**, overlooks the river. Steaks are well prepared in the hotel's **Maverick Room**; have drinks on its terrace, which also overlooks the river.

Restaurants are scattered around town. **Eighty Eight Ferry Restaurant**, at 88 Ferry Street in North Fredericton, provides atmosphere, with food served on a greenery-hung sun porch overlooking lawns, gardens, and a stream. Fredericton's finest dining is found at **Benoit's**, a small French restaurant on Queen Street across from the post office. Reservations are a must; Tel: 459-3666.

Out in the Valley

The upper section of the Saint John River valley is French in character, noted for its regional specialties and independent nature. Because of this spirit, it's often called the Republic of Madawaska. **Edmundston**, located in the heart of Madawaska County, is its undisputed capital. It's a happy little city, where you can sit on the veranda of **La Tulipe Blanche Restaurant**, sipping a glass of wine or nibbling at *les ployes avec creton* (a local type of pancake with the area's special coarse pork pâté). Surprisingly, there is also fine dining at **La Chaumière**, in the Howard Johnson's hotel in downtown Edmundston.

At **St. Leonard** to the south, the studios of renowned **Madawaska Weavers** are worth a stop for skirts, scarves, ties, or place mats, and farther on at Grand Falls a park and footpath follow along the falls and magnificent gorge created by the Saint John River as it forces through a narrow rocky channel.

Anyone who cares to sample typical New Brunswick country cooking would do well to take the side trip into Perth-Andover, where **York's**, a noted restaurant, serves gargantuan quantities of nostalgic dishes.

At Hartland, farther south, the longest covered bridge in the world is visible as you drive along Route 2. Nearby to the south, on Route 2, outside the sleepy town of Woodstock, **Heino and Monika's Restaurant**, in the pleasant **John Gyles Motel**, serves authentic, delicious German food. The motel offers spanking clean rooms and views of the valley.

One of the province's major attractions is also a great way to forget about highway driving for a while. Cars are not allowed in **Kings Landing**, a re-created historical village of the late 1700s to mid-1800s, about 34 km (21 miles) west of Fredericton on the river. This showcase of early Loyalist living has a costumed staff working on the farms, in the lumber mill, or cooking over the fireplaces of the old homes. Wagons rumble along, taking foot-weary visitors to the far end of the village or to the **Kings Head Inn**, where traditional meals are served and there's cold beer or cider at the old Tap Room. For nearby accommodation, try the **Olde Road Bed & Breakfast**, almost at the village gate (wonderful breakfasts and homey rooms) or the **Chickadee Lodge Bed & Breakfast**, a rustic fishing lodge-type of accommodation, but with all the modern conveniences.

Below Fredericton, toward Saint John, Route 102 is far prettier and more interesting than the straight-through Route 7. At Burton, **Goan's On—The Muffin Shop**, in an old general store, makes an exceptional stop for tea or lunch. **Old Orchard Crafts**, about 5 km (3 miles) west of Goan's On on Route 102, provides quantities of artisans' wares, and antiques are for sale along the highway.

At **Gagetown**, a sleepy town on the Saint John River (the city once dreamed of becoming the province's capital), nothing has changed much in generations. There's a general store (with ice cream) at Colpitt's Marina, where you can rent sailboats and houseboats. The river is broad and varied. From Gagetown you can also sail into Grand Lake where there is a provincial park. Yachts and sailboats from all along the eastern seaboard tie up at Colpitt's Marina, making it a busy and fun-filled area during summer weekends.

The Queen's County Museum in Gagetown was once the gracious home of one of Canada's Fathers of the Confederation. A 200-year-old blockhouse is inhabited by **Loomcrafters**, noted designers and weavers of tartans and plaids. **Flo Grieg's** pottery studio, located in an old store on Front Street, and **Claremont Crafts** on Tilley Road, whose artists create enamelware and batik items in a distinctive old home, are also good stops in Gagetown.

On the river, the **Steamers Stop Inn**, is one of the province's most enchanting old-fashioned hostelries. Each room is decorated in a specific turn of the century style and the charming dining room is intimate and pleasant for lingering. There's also a craft shop with local arts.

All along this route car ferries cross the river to pastoral and historic peninsulas with alternate routes to Saint John.

THE ACADIAN PENINSULA

The Acadian area in northeastern New Brunswick includes sandy shores warmed by the Gulf Stream, several cities, a major national park, and scores of fishing communities where, in some ways, life has changed little in generations. A curious history enfolds the traveller in a friendly French environment that can almost be mistaken for a land across the sea.

In 1755 the British victors of the French and English wars for possession of the land and the lucrative fur trade expelled the French settlers from the maritime area. Scattering in many directions, such as Louisiana (where they are known as Cajuns), they attempted to build new lives. But small bands of Acadians refused to leave the land where they had lived for generations and hid in the woods of New Brunswick, biding their time until the British relented and once more allowed them to build permanent residences.

The Acadians had the good sense to settle along the moderate shores of Northumberland Strait and the **Baie des Chaleurs**. Not only are the waters warmer here because of the wash of the Gulf Stream, but the mainland is protected by both Prince Edward Island and the Gaspé Peninsula coast of Quebec.

Nowhere is the Acadian area more typically represented than in the Acadian Peninsula, a part of the northeast shore from Escuminac to Dalhousie that juts out into the Gulf of St. Lawrence like a giant lobster claw.

Meadows sweet with wild strawberries and wildflowers stretch inland here. Rich marshlands have been reclaimed from the sea and ethereal mists often hang over lonely peat bogs. By the sea, long, lively wharves, colorful with lobster traps and buoys, embrace sturdy little lobster boats. Lighthouses and church spires soar against incomparable summer skies. Old customs, such as the Blessing of the Fleet, where the local priest blesses the outgoing boats, are still observed and Sunday Mass fills churches to overflowing.

Old crafts, such as rug hooking, quilting, and wooden ship building are still part of life on the Acadian Peninsula, and, although day-to-day life is as modern as anywhere else in the province, there is a certain Acadian joie de vivre that bubbles up in singalongs, bonfires and lobster parties on the beach or simply over a good meal in a restaurant. Although French is the common language of the area, English is so widespread that an Anglophone at the next table can easily understand the conversation as it switches rapidly from French to English in an unconscious blending of the languages.

At **Shediac**, northeast of Moncton, shallow water over soft sandbars is often heated to bathtub temperature, and lobster suppers are a normal way of life. They're available at places like **Fisherman's Paradise**, **Paturel's Restaurant** (where there's also a fresh lobster outlet), and at **Chez Françoise**, which serves gourmet dishes in an old mansion turned inn. Cut glass sparkles, antiques glow, and tiled fireplaces warm summer-by-the-sea evenings in this jolly inn with comfortable rooms and a fine dining room. Parades, lobster feeds, sports competitions, and pageants are part and parcel of the mid-July **Shediac Lobster Festival**.

Signs become French here, and roadside outlets advertise "homard" and "coquille" as you drive on into Acadian country and through small seaside towns such as Cocagne (where an international hydroplane regatta is held in early August) and Bouctouche (buck-TOOSH), with miles of deserted sandy beaches.

Just past Bouctouche and across a little bridge, the **Bouctouche Bay Inn** sprawls along the shore, offering comfortable accommodation, good seafood, and German specialty desserts (German cheesecake, German strawberry cake). Richibucto, north up the coast, holds a scallop festival July 3–10, and there are more lobster dinners at **Bon Accueil Restaurant** in **Kouchibouquac Park** (kooch-ee-boo-QUACK), noted for its sensational beaches, warm water, and 16 miles of sand dunes.

Following Route 11 along the shore means easy access to numerous beaches and a look at timeless fishing villages. It's worth a side trip on Route 117 to **Pointe Escuminac**, where a long wharf stretches out into the water, hugging lobster boats to its sides.

At **Shippegan**, at the end of the Acadian Peninsula, a marine museum provides a look at sea creatures. The nearby Lameque area, where the major industry comes from peat bogs, may seem an unlikely place for a Baroque music festival, but every summer international choirs, ensembles, and famous conductors gather here in the innovatively decorated Ste-Cecile church.

The prosperous fishing town of **Caraquet** sits on the peninsula's rocky cliffs above lovely beaches and looks across the Baie des Chaleurs toward the Gaspé coast of Quebec. Each year during the annual Acadian Festival de Caraquet (centered around August 15) there's a Blessing of the Fleet ceremony, when flag-bedecked boats set traps. The equally noisy Foire Brayonne in Edmundston is the first week in August. At the busy wharf, a market provides fish and shellfish right out of the ocean.

One of the best restaurants in Caraquet in which to find a fresh shore dinner is the old inn, **Hotel Paulin**. The tiny dining room is noted for its fish preparation and, with notice, an authentic Acadian feast can be arranged by owner Gerard Paulin. Once a restaurant for railroad passengers, the Paulin retains a bit of nostalgia for that era. There are also small, uniquely decorated rooms available for overnight stays, although some share a bathroom down the hall. For those with more luxurious or private tastes, accommodations are available in Caraquet and environs—the modern **Motel du Village** is at the gate of the Acadian village, Route 11, and has all the modern amenities—but for an authentic peek into the community take a room at the Paulin; it's much like visiting relatives.

Just beyond Caraquet, on Route 11 toward Bathurst, the **Village Acadien Historique**, a re-created Acadian village of 1780–1890, provides a look at Acadian history after the expulsion in 1755. Horses whinny, wagon wheels creak, bells toll from the little chapel, and the smells of fresh wood shavings, salt cod, and baking bread emerge from various buildings. The happy little village has created a tremendous pride in the Acadian background and is well worth a visit by anyone who is curious about this culture.

Bathurst, a busy pulp-mill town, can greet you with the overpowering fragrance of sulfur as you drive across the bridge, but the odor doesn't seem to hover over the downtown area, the marina, or the pleasant golf course that winds around the bay. **Youghall Beach** is a favored spot for swimming here, and there are several good motels in the area, among them the **Atlantic Host Inn**, a large motel with pool, good dining room, bar, and pleasant rooms, and the **Fundy Line Motel**, in an old seminary with long corridors and an excellent dining room. Both motels' restaurants specialize in fresh local seafood.

But for special dining, most people who travel this area head for the small town of Nigadoo on the shore of Nipisiquit Bay, on Route 134, 20 km (15 miles) north of Bathurst, where the restaurant **La Fine Grobe** turns out gourmet meals in a rustic lodge hung with gaily colored quilts and paintings and decorated with the pottery of local artisans. The elegant menu includes interesting local specialties such as rabbit in creamy mustard sauce as well as plenty of seafood.

Deep-sea-fishing charters and scenic cruises aboard such boats as the *Chaleur Phantom* are available in the small town of **Dalhousie**, Route 11 northwest of Bathurst. You'll find the vessel at the ferry wharf at the bottom of Renfrew Street (Tel: 506-684-4722).

At **Campbellton**, near the Quebec border 28 km (14 miles) northwest of Dalhousie, there's an English turn to the population again. Campbellton celebrates a Salmon Festival in late June. Just across the bridge, in Quebec, a museum contains artifacts brought up from the water between the towns pertaining to the 1760 Battle of the Restigouche, which marked the end of the wars between the English and the French.

MIRAMICHI AREA

The Miramichi section across the center of the province, mainly settled by Scots, Irish, and English, is the mecca of sportsmen who come to hunt and fish at outfitters' camps. Roads wind past streams and rivers where avid anglers fly-cast in hip-deep water and canoes glide over the surface. Legends, great men, folklore, folk festivals, and heritage museums are all part and parcel of a Miramichi visit.

It's hard to say where the Miramichi (mirry-ma-SHEE) region begins. Its natives begin to refer to it as soon as they leave Fredericton going north on Route 8, travelling along the scenic Nashwaak River. At Boiestown, where you hit the main Miramichi River, the feel of the Miramichi begins to seep in. Giant statues of woodsmen stand by the road and a Woodmen's Museum provides an excellent look at the area's background. One prosperous-appearing town almost runs into the next on this road. **Doaktown** and **Blackville** are meccas for anglers who stand in the streams for hours, like pilgrims who reach the Ganges. Conservationists have been instrumental in establishing the Atlantic Salmon Museum in Doaktown. It honors this silvery fighting fish, which is making a comeback after almost becoming extinct because of excessive commercial fishing practices. The **Inn By the Pond**, in Doaktown, is a pleasant spot for overnighting in a restored old home in peaceful surroundings. **Pond's Chalet Resort** in Ludlow, near Boiestown, is the perfect spot for some rustic resting in log cabins or in the main lodge overlooking the salmon anglers in the river. The lodge also houses a public dining room full of interesting old mementos of the area and is lumbering history.

Newcastle, at the mouth of the Miramichi River, is another pulp-mill town and port, but its past claim to fame has been its association with the Cunard empire. At one time the Cunards employed almost everyone in the area, either in cutting trees for building ships or in the shipyards. When the steam engine came along the industry declined, but the homes of wealthy lumbermen and shipbuilders still grace the streets of Newcastle and nearby Chatham.

Here, Max Aitkin, who became British peer Lord Beaverbrook, grew up. His family home, the Old Manse, is now a well-stocked library with many books on the area. Beaverbrook's ashes rest in the base of his statue in the town square, a piece of land he gave to the city.

The Wharf Inn, a large motel in Newcastle, offers comfortable accommodations. With 70 rooms, 6 of them housekeeping, The Wharf Inn makes a good stopping place for families and has a restaurant and indoor pool. Across the river, in Nelson-Miramichi, **The Governor's Mansion**, formerly the home of one of New Brunswick's Lieutenant Governors, has bed-and-breakfast rooms of lumber-baron elegance. The home baking at **Le Portage Restaurant** in **Chatham**, also across the river from Newcastle, is well known. In early August Newcastle hosts a folk-song festival open to all comers. Its performers are usually old-timers who sing the "come all ye" ballads of the original settlers. It seems to be the Irish who made the most lasting impression here; not only do the inhabitants speak with a touch of brogue, but Chatham hosts the biggest Irish festival in Canada (in mid-July).

The **Miramichi Natural History Museum** in Chatham, or the **MacDonald Farm Historic Park** in Bartibog Bridge, just outside town, provide information and historic background on the area. The ledgers of Cunard and the old stones of the MacDonald farm whisper of a time when life was rich, even opulent, in a bounteous land.

GETTING AROUND

July and August are busy tourist months when the temperature here can climb over 90 degrees F (30 degrees C). It's wise to book accommodations ahead for then. June and September are excellent months for touring, with all but empty roads, fine days, and cooler nights. Brilliant foliage begins in late September through mid-October. Casual clothing is the rule, although some of the better restaurants will expect reasonable dress. Winter temperatures can sink to many degrees below zero, so warm clothing is a must then.

New Brunswick's highways are good and continually being upgraded and facilities numerous along major tourist routes. The only map you'll need is the free one available at tourist information centers. The Department of Tourism, Recreation and Heritage, P.O. Box 12345, Fredericton, N.B., Canada E3B 5C3 (Tel: 800-561-0123), has plenty of other helpful information. Major entry points are at St. Stephen, Houlton, Edmundston, and Cape Tormentine from Prince Edward Island, and Aulac from Nova Scotia. A Marine Atlantic ferry brings cars and passengers from Digby, Nova Scotia, to Saint John. The 2½-hour trip costs $14.25 per person, $44 per car, one way. For reservations, in U.S. call (800) 341-7981; in Maine call (800) 432-7344; and in the Maritimes call (800) 565-9470.

Canadian Air and Air Canada service the province through the three major airports at Saint John, Fredericton, and Moncton. Air Atlantic flies directly to Saint John from Boston daily.

SMT bus line connects with major bus lines throughout Canada and the United States; VIA Rail connects with Amtrak.

ACCOMMODATIONS REFERENCE

▶ **Algonquin Hotel. St. Andrews**, N.B. E0G 2X0. Tel: (506) 529-8823; in Canada, (800) 268-9411; in Ontario and Quebec, (800) 268-9421.

▶ **Atlantic Host Inn**. Box 910, Vanier Boulevard, **Bathurst**, N.B. E2A 4H7. Tel: (506) 548-3335.

▶ **Hotel Beausejour**. 750 Main Street, P.O. Box 906, **Moncton**, N.B. E1C 1E6. Tel: (506) 854-4344; in U.S. and Canada, (800) 268-9143.

► **Bouctouche Bay Inn**. Box 455, **Bouctouche**, N.B. E0A 1G0. Tel: (506) 743-2726.

► **Caledonia Highlands Inn and Chalets**. Fundy National Park, P.O. Box 99, **Alma**, Albert County, N.B. E0A 1B0. Tel: (506) 887-2930.

► **Chez Françoise**. 93 Main Street, **Shediac**, N.B. E0A 3G0. Tel: (506) 532-4233.

► **Chickadee Lodge Bed & Breakfast**. Route 2, **Prince William**, N.B. E0H 1S0. Tel: (506) 363-2759.

► **Compass Rose**. North Head, **Grand Manan**, N.B. E0G 2M0. Tel: (506) 662-8570.

► **Delta Brunswick Hotel**. 39 King Street, **Saint John**, N.B. E2L 4W3. Tel: (506) 648-1981; in U.S. and Canada, (800) 268-1133.

► **Fundy Line Motel**. 855 Saint Anne's Street, **Bathurst**, N.B. E2A 2Y6. Tel: (506) 548-8803.

► **Fundy Park Chalets**. Fundy National Park, **Alma**, N.B. E0A 1B0. Tel: (506) 887-2808 or 433-2084.

► **The Governor's Mansion**. **Nelson-Miramichi**, N.B. E06 1T0. Tel: (506) 622-3036.

► **Hilton International.** One Market Square, **Saint John**, N.B. E2L 1Z1. Tel: (506) 693-8484; in Canada, (800) 268-9275; in U.S., (800) 654-2000.

► **Inn by the Pond**. P.O. Box 114, **Doaktown**, N.B. E0C 1G0. Tel: (506) 365-7492.

► **John Gyles Motor Inn**. R.R. #1, **Woodstock**, N.B. E0J 2B0. Tel: (506) 328-6622.

► **Lakeside Lodge and Resort**. Box 2350, **Grand Falls**, N.B. E0J 1M0. Tel: (506) 473-6252 or, in Canada, (800) 561-9687.

► **Lord Beaverbrook Hotel**. 659 Queen Street, **Fredericton**, N.B. E3B 5A6. Tel: (506) 455-3371.

► **Marathon Inn**. North Head, **Grand Manan**, N.B. E0G 2M0. Tel: (506) 662-8144.

► **Marshlands Inn**. 73 Bridge Street, P.O. Box 1440, **Sackville**, N.B. E0A 3C0. Tel: (506) 536-0170.

► **Olde Road Bed & Breakfast**. R.R. #2, **Prince William**, N.B. E0H 1S0. Tel: (506) 363-2758.

► **Owen House**. Welshpool, **Campobello**, N.B. E0G 3H0. Tel: (506) 752-2977.

► **Pansy Patch**. 59 Carleton Street, **St. Andrews**, N.B. E0G 2X0. Tel: (506) 529-3834.

► **Hotel Paulin**. 143 Boulevard St. Pierre West, R.R. 2, **Caraquet**, N.B. E0B 1K0. Tel: (506) 727-9981.

► **Pond's Chalet Resort**. Keith Pond, **Ludlow**, N.B. E0C 1N0. Tel: (506) 369-2612.

▶ **Quaco Inn. St. Martins**, N.B. E0G 2Z0. Tel: (506) 833-4772.

▶ **Rossmount Inn**. R.R. 2, **St. Andrews**, N.B. E0G 2X0. Tel: (506) 529-3351.

▶ **Shiretown Inn**. Box 145, Water Street, **St. Andrews**, N.B. E0G 2X0. Tel: (506) 529-8877.

▶ **Steamers Stop Inn**. Front Street, Box 155, **Gagetown**, N.B. E0G 1V0. Tel: (506) 488-2903.

▶ **Tara Manor**. 559 Mowatt Drive, **St. Andrews**, N.B. E0G 2X0. Tel: (506) 529-2304.

▶ **Motel du Village**. P.O. Box 1116, **Caraquet**, N.B. E0B 1K0. Tel: (506) 727-4447.

▶ **West Isles World**. **Lambert's Cove**, Deer Island, N.B. E0G 2E0. Tel: (506) 747-2946.

▶ **The Wharf Inn**. Box 474, Jane Street, **Newcastle**, N.B. E1V 3M6. Tel: (506) 622-0302.

PRINCE EDWARD ISLAND

By Charmaine Gaudet

Charmaine Gaudet, born in Prince Edward Island, regularly contributes articles on travel, food, and lifestyle to national magazines in the United States and Canada, and has written guidebooks to cities in New Brunswick and to Prince Edward Island.

Prince Edward Island is a crescent carved in brick red sandstone—gently rolling, carpeted in green fields, and edged in wide, powdery beaches. The island, stretching above the north coasts of New Brunswick and, to the east, Nova Scotia, has charmed visitors since ancient times. As early as 2,000 years ago, mainland Micmac Indians revered it as the sacred summer residence of the Great Spirit. Abegweit, they called it, meaning "cradled on the waves," and they crossed the Northumberland Strait each summer to fish on the island, which they eventually made their year-round home. French explorer Jacques Cartier, the first known European visitor, was similarly smitten and, upon seeing the island in 1534, immediately declared it "the fairest land 'tis possible to see."

Since the time of the Micmac Indians and Jacques Cartier, the tranquility of the countryside has taken on the patchwork pattern of farmland and the snug neatness of rural villages, with a smattering of pretty fishing ports. Besides that charm, the island has some of eastern Canada's best beaches, temperate ocean water, a vibrant summer musical-theater festival, the storybook Anne of Green Gables farmhouse at Cavendish, tuna fishing, golfing, and fresh seafood. Canada's smallest province is a mecca for modern-day tourists, who each summer outnumber by four times the island's permanent population of 123,000. At the same time, the island's essentially rural character—evident in the deep green sea of potato fields, the ever-present drone of tractors, and the sight of grazing milk cows—spares it from most of the usual commercialism of a tourist destination.

This compact island—140 miles long and from 4 to 40 miles across—is crisscrossed with an intricate system of paved roads. Major attractions tend to be focused in central Prince Edward Island, within a 25-mile radius of Charlottetown (population 15,000), the capital and the island's only city. The popular north-shore beaches of the Prince Edward Island National Park, which is also the site of the Green Gables farmhouse, are just 12 miles north of the city. The south shore's less spectacular beaches attract islanders and knowledgeable visitors to warmer swimming waters only a few minutes from Charlottetown.

In recent years the quality and quantity of the island's handcrafts have made them a legitimate attraction in themselves. While you will no doubt run across the usual selection of crocheted baby booties and salt-glazed honey pots, many island craft shops carry outstanding work, both traditional and contemporary. The best of island crafts include handmade quilts, braided rugs, pottery, wooden furniture, toys, hand-knit sweaters, and stained glass.

Avoid the common mistake of trying to "do" Prince Edward Island in a day. Instead, plan on three to five days—time enough to relax on the beaches, take in a stage performance at the Charlottetown Summer Festival, have a "feed" of lobster, browse through the numerous craft and antiques shops, and explore at a leisurely pace in tune with the laid-back island way of life.

MAJOR INTEREST

Charlottetown
Province House national historic site
The Charlottetown Summer Festival
Old Charlottetown's shops, cafés, and waterfront

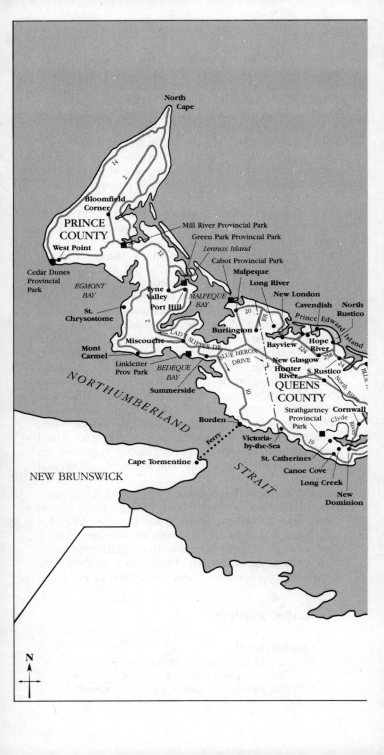

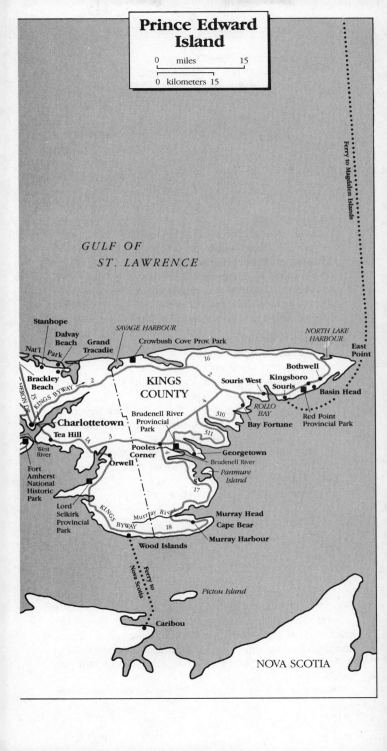

Elsewhere in Queens County

Prince Edward Island National Park's beaches
Green Gables Farmhouse and Golf Course
Lucy Maud Montgomery's birthplace in New
  London
Anne of Green Gables Museum at Silver Bush, in
  Park Corner
Traditional lobster suppers
Victoria-by-the-Sea scenic fishing village
Tea Hill Provincial Park beaches
Orwell Corner historic village

Kings County

The village of Murray River
Panmure Island beaches
Brudenell River Provincial Park
Scenic Bay Fortune area
Red Point, Basin Head, and Bothwell beaches
Tuna–fishing charters at North Lake
Crowbush Cove Provincial Park beach

Prince County

The town of Summerside
The Acadian Museum at Miscouche
Traditional Acadian handcrafts at the Abrams
  Village Handcraft Co-op
Malpeque area and Cabot Provincial Park beach
Mill River Provincial Park's resort, golf course,
  camping, water sports
Re-created shipyard and restored shipbuilder's
  home at Green Park Provincial Park
The village of Tyne Valley
Indian arts and crafts on Lennox Island

Prince Edward Island is divided into three counties of approximately equal area.

The central county, **Queens County**, draws by far the most visitors because it includes Charlottetown, much of the north-shore resort area, and coastal scenery typified by beautiful beaches, bays, and fishing ports. Queens County is also the most commercialized area, particularly around Cavendish on the north shore, where tourist operators have capitalized on Green Gables and the national park as a premise for innumerable attractions, from children's theme parks to a string of souvenir and fast-food shops.

While the easternmost county, **Kings County**, has fewer

commercial tourist attractions, its bay-notched coast offers scenery as pretty and beaches as powdery as those in Queens County. It also boasts a port known as the "Tuna Fishing Capital of the World" and an outstanding 18-hole golf course at Brudenell River.

Windswept sandstone cliffs, remote beaches, and a rich sense of history provide **Prince County** in western Prince Edward Island with a timeless quality. The south shore is home to Acadians, many of whom still speak the ancient French dialect brought over by their 18th-century ancestors. A hundred years ago the area spawned shipbuilding empires, now recalled by a re-created shipyard at Green Park. Prince County also offers one of eastern Canada's best golf courses, at Mill River.

QUEENS COUNTY
Charlottetown

You can easily explore the small area of downtown Charlottetown on foot. Combine sight-seeing and shopping with a walking tour, like those described in the book *Walks in Charlotte Town,* available at local bookstores.

Named for Queen Charlotte, wife of George III, Charlottetown, in the middle of the south coast, has been the capital of Prince Edward Island since 1763, when the island was ceded to Britain.

The center of historic Charlottetown is dominated by the 1964 **Confederation Centre of the Arts**, a massive, modern, and arguably inappropriate concrete structure plunked down amid brick and wooden 19th-century storefronts. The center was built as a national memorial to the birth of Canadian nationhood set in motion at the Charlottetown Conference a hundred years before. It houses an 1,100-seat theater, an art gallery, a library, and a gift shop with an eclectic collection of Canadian crafts.

Province House next door, the site of the conference, still houses the Prince Edward Island legislature, and visitors are welcome to tour much of the Georgian-style building, including the restored Confederation Chamber.

From May 1 to September 30 the **Charlottetown Summer Festival** kindles excitement in the normally quiet city. Tourists flock to see *Anne of Green Gables* (Canada's longest-running musical) and other alternating performances that have given the festival a deserved reputation as the country's major musical-theater showcase. (It's best to reserve tickets in advance; Tel: 902-566-1267.) The David Mackenzie Theatre across the street provides an intimate atmosphere for the festival's Cameo Cabaret, a lineup of plays and revues more suited to the small stage.

Harness racing is Prince Edward Island's favorite sport, and in mid-August islanders go to the Charlottetown Driving Park in droves for the annual Gold Cup and Saucer Race—the biggest racing event of the season. The evening race is preceded by a late-morning parade of floats, marching bands, and clowns through downtown Charlottetown.

Several Charlottetown restaurants are good dinner choices. The **Claddagh Room Restaurant** on Sydney Street specializes in superbly prepared local seafood and the dining room in the **Dundee Arms Inn** on Pownal Street offers a cozy Victorian atmosphere and reliably good food. A bright new dinner spot is the **Queen Street Café**, with a small but eclectic menu that mixes traditional and nouvelle-style dishes. **Cedars Eatery** on University Avenue specializes in Middle Eastern food—their steak sandwich made with Lebanese bread is a favorite with regulars—or opt for pizza and people watching at **Pat's Rose and Grey Room**, a wide-open eatery lined with knickknacks and nostalgia, in a former drug store across the Confederation Centre stage door on Richmond Street. Pat's is a busy after-the-theater spot, as is the **Off Broadway Café** on nearby Sydney Street, which specializes in dessert crepes.

The Confederation Court Mall defines the downtown core with a square block of shops offering such specialties as Maritime-made pine furniture, local and imported woolen knits, and high-quality Paderno stainless-steel cookware. (There's a Paderno factory on the island.)

A few short blocks away on the waterfront **Old Charlottetown**'s 19th-century architecture, craft shops, and food emporiums invite exploring for an hour or two.

Victoria Park, a 40-acre, pine-studded green belt, overlooks Charlottetown Harbour. The park's seaside walk will lead you past the elegant residence of the province's lieutenant governor and the six-gun battery remaining from Fort Edward, built in 1805 to defend the harbor mouth. Beaconsfield, the handsome yellow Victorian mansion near the park entrance, houses the offices of the Prince Edward Island Museum and Heritage Foundation, the Centre for Genealogical Research, and a bookstore with a large selection of books about island history.

Accommodations are plentiful in downtown Charlottetown. The **Prince Edward Hotel and Convention Centre** on the waterfront has all the amenities that you might expect of the city's most luxurious, and expensive, hotel. Less expensive and luxurious is the stately **Charlottetown Hotel**, a landmark. The Dundee Arms Inn (containing the aforementioned restaurant) and the **Duchess of Kent Inn** offer Victorian charm and antiques-filled guest rooms. There are several other hotels and motels that are on a par and all modern and comfortable: **Best Western MacLauchlan's Motel**, the **Inn on the Hill**, the **Kirkwood Motor Hotel**, **Rodd's Confederation Inn**, and **Rodd's Royalty Inn**. Any one of these is about as good as any of the others.

The North Shore

Brackley Beach, 18 km (11 miles) northeast of Charlottetown via Route 15, is one of five gateways to the Prince Edward Island National Park. (The other four are at Stanhope and Dalvay to the east and Cavendish and North Rustico to the west.) At the **Dunes Studio Gallery**, a modern glass-and-wood building set against the backdrop of Brackley Bay and the national park sand dunes, one-of-a-kind sculptural and functional ceramics vie for attention with hand-blown glass, stained-glass hangings, painted-silk clothing and banners, and exquisite hand-knit sweaters.

Neighboring **Shaw's Hotel** has two claims to fame: Established in 1860, it is the island's oldest family-operated summer resort, and there are few island restaurants that serve better home cooking. The hotel's restaurant is open daily, but the Sunday buffet is the star attraction: an opulent array of fresh fish and shellfish, hot meats, salads, and homemade breads and desserts.

The **Prince Edward Island National Park** is a ribbon of white-sand beaches 40 km (25 miles) long. While most people flock to Cavendish and Brackley beaches, those at Rustico Island and Dalvay are relatively uncrowded, inviting long, quiet walks.

Dalvay-by-the-Sea, at the eastern end of the national park, was built in 1896 as a summer home by onetime Standard Oil president Alexander MacDonald. Today the sprawling mansion is a comfortable lodge and resort operated by the park. The dining room, which is open to visitors, specializes in fresh seafood, including perfectly poached salmon, and homegrown vegetables.

The nearby **Stanhope Golf and Country Club** features one of the island's longest and most challenging golf courses. Ranging along beautiful Covehead Bay, it is also one of the most scenic.

Watts' in Tracadie Harbour is a hidden gem of a restaurant worth seeking out (just past Grand Tracadie on Highway 6; look for signs and a side road leading to Watts'). An unpretentious little place with a panoramic view of Tracadie Bay, Watts' serves up some of the best, simply prepared seafood (haddock, sole, scallops, and lobster) to be had in the province. The vegetables are also excellent, as are the fresh-daily pies and carrot cake.

South Rustico, on Route 243 just west of Brackley Beach, is like a toy village, with a small collection of Victorian buildings clustered around an ornate church, the whole perched on a peninsula on Rustico Bay. The pretty community is the site of one of Canada's first cooperative banks—now a national historic site and museum. The lovely **Barachois Inn,** a restored Victorian home with six guest rooms, combines historic charm with a peaceful setting in the middle of the tucked-away village.

Take a quick jaunt along the pretty Hunter River via routes 258 and 224 to the village of New Glasgow and the **P.E.I. Preserve Company.** Located in the former village dairy, the factory makes delicious liqueur-spiked preserves from island fruit, plus specialty mustards, vinegars, and honey—all for sale in the sunny bakeshop/tearoom that serves fresh pastries, tea, and coffee.

The simple white **Green Gables Farmhouse** near the **Cavendish** entrance to the national park draws visitors from around the world, thanks to a red-haired, freckle-faced orphan and the book that made her and her island-born author-creator an overnight sensation. The orphan Anne Shirley, whom Mark Twain called "the dearest and most loveable child in fiction since the immortal Alice," made her debut in the 1908 novel *Anne of Green Gables,* written by Cavendish native Lucy Maud Montgomery. The novel has been translated into 16 languages and inspired worldwide stage and screen productions, including the Charlottetown festival musical and two recent award-winning TV movies aired in Canada and the United States. The 18-hole **Green Gables Golf Course** overlooking the house and its surrounding nature walks is beautiful and challenging.

The hub of the island's tourist trade, modern-day Cavendish bears little resemblance to the sleepy farming community of Avonlea, its fictional counterpart described in Montgomery's novels. Montgomery's pristine island is more recognizable elsewhere on the north shore: along the powdery beaches, below the steep, red bluffs of Orby Head, in pretty ports like North Rustico Harbour and New London, and in meadows knee-deep in wild flowers—all places where the author loved to roam.

If you want to make Cavendish your base, both the **Shining Waters Lodge and Cottages** and the **Ingleside Lodge** are a short walk from the national park beaches. The rustic Shining Waters Lodge has ten pretty guest rooms and a dining room that serves a Continental breakfast, while Ingleside Lodge offers a spectacular view of Cavendish Beach and has a good dining room. The **Marco Polo Inn**, 2 km (1½ miles) from Cavendish on Route 13, has two heated swimming pools and a full-service dining room.

At the **New London Village** crossroads, the tiny white cottage where Montgomery was born in 1874 is now a museum chock-full of Montgomery memorabilia, including the author's wedding dress and original editions of her books. Silver Bush, the Park Corner farmhouse home of her favorite cousins, has also been converted into a museum. Overlooking the real "Lake of Shining Waters" that figures prominently in the Anne books, Silver Bush is still owned by relatives of Montgomery.

This is Lobster Supper country, and several area community halls and restaurants serve up the most traditional of Prince Edward Island feasts—or "feeds," as the locals say: typically, boiled lobster in the half shell, preceded by clam chowder, and served with heaping helpings of potato salad, coleslaw, homemade pickles, and fresh-baked rolls, bread, pies, cakes, and strawberry shortcake. Reliably good are the **St. Ann's Church Suppers** in Hope River, the **New London Lions Club Lobster Suppers**, the **New Glasgow Lobster Suppers**, and the lobster suppers served at the **Fisherman's Wharf Restaurant** in North Rustico and the **Fiddles 'n Vittles Restaurant** in Bayview.

By contrast, **Woodleigh Replicas** on Route 234 east of Burlington lends a distinctly foreign flavor to Prince Edward Island. Dunvegan Castle, the Tower of London, St. Paul's Cathedral, and nearly 20 other famous architectural landmarks of the British Isles are accurately detailed in large-scale models. Begun 40 years ago by a retired World War I colonel who wanted to transplant some part of his ancestral overseas homeland to Prince Edward Island, Woodleigh has grown into one of the island's most-visited attractions.

For lunch stop at the nearby **Kitchen Witch**, also on Route 234, at Long River. Located in an old schoolhouse, this simple little restaurant specializes in hearty sandwiches, soups, and pies, and they also have a nice selection of teas and coffees.

The South Shore

Victoria-by-the-Sea is a storybook village tucked just within the boundary of Queens County. This tiny fishing port has some good antiques and handcraft shops, live summer theater in the historic **Victoria Playhouse**, and a tearoom (in the blue converted harness shop across from the playhouse) that serves real high teas and mouthwatering desserts. Another sweet attraction is the recently opened **Island Chocolates**, which makes and sells confections made with pure Belgian chocolate. The tiny factory has afternoon tours Wednesdays through Sundays.

Prince Edward Island's rivers are winding, lazy streams banked by cultivated fields, and the Clyde and West rivers, with their rural valleys, are typical. The hilltops of Strathgartney Provincial Park provide a nice overview of the area, which you can explore close up by following the secondary routes through pretty communities like St. Catherines, Long Creek, and New Dominion. (If you're on Highway 1, for example, leave it at Clyde River, following Routes 247, 9, and 19A to Canoe Cove, then 19 east along the coast to Fort Amherst Historic Park.)

Just across the harbor from Charlottetown, **Fort Amherst Historic Park** is located on the site of Port Lajoie, the first capital of the island under the French regime of the early 1700s. The British Fort Amherst replaced it in 1758, and today an interpretive center and rolling lawns cover the collapsed earthworks of the long-abandoned fortress.

One of the island's most popular restaurants is located in the bedroom community of Cornwall, a few miles west of Charlottetown. The **Bonnie Brae** has an eclectic menu ranging from traditional island favorites (lobster, fish, steaks, and roast beef) to schnitzels and other Swiss-German specialties (the owner-chefs are Swiss). The all-you-can-eat lobster buffet offered every evening is outstanding, as are the featherlight European desserts.

At the Island Market Village on the North River cause-way, shops offering island-made handcrafts and sports-wear are housed in log cabins.

Smooth red sand and warmer water characterize the beaches of the south shore. While less spectacular than those in the north, the south shore beaches often offer better swimming and fewer crowds. **Tea Hill Provincial Park**, at the base of scenic Tea Hill, is one of the best, and it's also a prime clam-digging spot.

A visit to **Orwell Corner Historic Village** will make you feel as if you've stepped into the 1800s. Operated by the P.E.I. (Prince Edward Island) Museum and Heritage Foundation, the re-created rural crossroads village is a working farming community. In summer, Orwell Corner holds weekly *ceilidhs,* or Scottish programs of musical entertainment (usually with fiddle music and step danc-ing), and two popular annual events: in mid-July, the annual strawberry social—an old-fashioned strawber-ries-and-ice-cream affair with games, historic costumes, and foot-stompin', oldtime music—and in late August, the Scottish Festival and Highland Games that feature kilt-clad Highland pipe bands and dancers, storytellers, and traditional athletic competitions like tossing the caber (not unlike heaving a telephone pole), throwing the hammer, and putting the stone.

Nearby, **Lord Selkirk Provincial Park** throws a similar Highland games celebration every year in early August. The park overlooks the cove where in 1803 three ships landed with 800 Highlanders from the Isle of Skye—constituting the island's largest Scottish migration.

The **Netherstone Inn**, a few miles west of the ferry terminal at Wood Islands (to Pictou in Nova Scotia), serves good, simple food—a bouillabaisse, made with smoked mackerel, is a specialty—and offers overnight and housekeeping units.

KINGS COUNTY

The bay-notched shoreline of eastern Prince Edward Is-land, particularly the eastern shore, is a sightseer's de-light. You'll find some of the best scenery here off the beaten track; for example, the road to Cape Bear and Murray Head offers a view from the high bluffs that is well worth the short side trip.

Murray River, just west of the picturesque port of

Murray Harbour, was once a shipbuilding center. Today the cozy village is a center for crafts. One of the most interesting shops is Shumate's Toy Factory, where the proprietor, a Santa Claus look-alike, makes old-fashioned, handmade wooden pull-cars, animals, and other toys. Murray River is also home to **Terrace Heights**, a new restaurant that has already established itself as one of the island's best. Fresh seafood is a specialty, and everything is homemade, including the bread and the sumptuous desserts.

Nearby, the long, narrow isthmus connecting **Panmure Island** to the mainland is edged in powdery beaches, making it a popular spot in summer. The Panmure Island lighthouse is one of the island's most photographed.

The Kings Byway Visitor Information Centre at Poole's Corner contains a wealth of information on the history, sights, and attractions of eastern Prince Edward Island. Plan a lunch stop at the dining room of the **Kingsway Motel** at Poole Corner; the food is plain but good. The beautiful 1,400-acre **Brudenell River Provincial Park** nearby boasts an outstanding, 6,500-yard, par-72, 18-hole golf course. Offering a variety of narrow and open fairways, tricky water plays, and a scenic river view, the course is considered one of eastern Canada's finest. The park's self-guided wildflower walk through the forest is another pleasant way to stretch your legs. A short causeway in the park takes you to tiny Brudenell Island and the early 18th-century burial ground for the area's first Scottish settlers. The island looks across the river mouth to Brudenell Point, where a simple cairn marks the site of a 16th-century Acadian fishing settlement. **Rodd's Brudenell River Resort**, overlooking the golf course, offers simple but comfortable accommodations in 50 chalet-style cabins. In neighboring Georgetown, the King's Playhouse produces live summer theater.

The Platter House in Souris West, perched right on the beach, is an informal, cafeteria-style eatery where the cook knows how to deep-fry fresh island fish. The huge seafood platter, not surprisingly, is probably your best choice.

Swimming, bicycling, wind-surfing, seafood, and scenery draw thousands of visitors to the **Magdalen Islands** each year. The 62-mile-long, hook-shaped archipelago belonging to Quebec is five hours by sea from **Souris**, where a car ferry service makes daily crossings to and from the islands. Most of the 14,000 inhabitants live on the largest islands: Cap aux Meules, Havre aux Maisons, Havre Aubert, Grosse Ile, and Ile de l'Est, which are all connected by highway over long sandspits, and Ile d'Entree, which is connected by boat from the other main islands. (See also the Quebec Province chapter below.)

If you want to visit the Magdalens set aside at least four days because the better part of two days will be spent travelling. Once you're there, the best places to stay include the **Hotel Château Madelinot** in Cap aux Meules, the **Motel Thériault** in Havre aux Maisons, and the **Motel des Iles**, also in Havre aux Maisons. The last has the islands' best restaurant. While French is the main language spoken by islanders, service in hotels, motels, and restaurants is bilingual.

The beauty of P.E.I.'s **Bay Fortune** area makes it a popular summer resort. The charm of the riverside cottages along Route 310, for example, contrasts with the brooding spruce forest.

Beautiful beaches are a trademark of eastern Prince Edward Island, and three of the best are at **Red Point Provincial Park** (the beach is a five-minute walk from the park), Basin Head, and Bothwell. **Basin Head** and **Bothwell** are part of a sand dune system that stretches 20 km (12 miles) eastward, to East Point. The Basin Head Fisheries Museum, right beside Basin Head beach, comprises re-created boat and tackle sheds, a canning factory, a fish-box factory, and a smokehouse. The museum hosts a giant seafood barbecue as part of its annual Harvest of the Sea celebration in early August.

The **Sea Breeze Motel Restaurant**, near the entrance to Basin Head, serves good, simple fare, on the order of club sandwiches, roast chicken, and pan-fried fish.

The waters around Prince Edward Island are among the world's best tuna-fishing grounds. You can charter a tuna boat from several ports, including North Rustico in Queens County, and Red Head Harbour and North Lake Harbour in Kings County. **North Lake Harbour** prides itself as the "Tuna Fishing Capital of the World," and indeed charters out of North Lake have hooked several world-record-breaking bluefin. Giant Bluefin Tuna Charters (Tel: 902-357-2785/2480), Captain Merrill MacDonald (Tel: 902-357-2599 or 583-2214), and North Lake Tuna Charters (Tel: 902-357-2055) operate the Harbour's main charters, which should be booked at least a day ahead. The boats leave around 10:00 A.M., returning at 6:00 P.M.—unless there's a feisty bluefin hooked on the end of the line, in which case a fisherman might do battle many hours longer.

There's a beautiful white-sand beach at **Crowbush Cove Provincial Park**, and Routes 350 and 218 to the pretty port of Savage Harbour are a worthwhile side trip.

PRINCE COUNTY
The South Shore

Stop at the Lady Slipper Visitor Information Centre, just east of Summerside, for information on places of interest in western Prince Edward Island. In **Summerside** (population 10,000), the island's second-largest center, the **Class of '61 Feast** at the Brother's Two Restaurant combines music from the Buddy Holly era, skits, and seafood in a lively dinner-theater format. The **Silver Fox Inn** downtown offers plenty of historic charm in one of the town's loveliest 19th-century homes. The whole house, including its six guest rooms, is decorated with handsome antiques, and while the inn doesn't have a dining room, it does serve a Continental breakfast. Both the **Best Western Linkletter Inn** and the **Quality Inn** offer good motel accommodations. The Linkletter's dining room is one of the best in town. Nearby **Linkletter Provincial Park** has a very good red-sand beach, but tends to be crowded on weekends.

The Acadian Shore

Miscouche is the gateway to the Acadian Shore, which extends to St. Chrysostome on the west coast of Egmont Bay, an area where most of the Prince Edward Islanders of French descent, the Acadians, are concentrated. Acadia was a territory made up of present-day Prince Edward Island, New Brunswick, Nova Scotia, southeastern Quebec, and eastern Maine. From the early 1600s to the mid-1700s Acadia changed hands several times between France and England, until it came into English possession for good in 1713. Through the 18th century tensions between the two nations intensified, and between 1755 and 1763 the English exiled some 10,000 of the area's French-speaking settlers to France or to the then French colony of Louisiana—where their modern-day descendants are known as Cajuns.

Some of Prince Edward Island's Acadians escaped into the woods, while others fled to the mainland and returned later. Today, many of their descendants who live on the island's Acadian Shore still speak a variation of their forefathers' Old French, which predates the modern French language as established in the 17th century by the French Academy. The Acadian Museum in Miscouche has a collection of Acadian artifacts dating to the early 1700s.

While the Acadian Pioneer Village at Mont Carmel is a somewhat generic collection of re-created historic buildings, its **Etoile de Mer** restaurant is the island's only restaurant specializing in authentic Acadian food. The **Abrams Village Handcraft Co-op** is the best place to shop for braided and hooked rugs, quilts, woven wear, wooden toys, and other traditional Acadian crafts.

The **West Point Lighthouse** (1874) is now an inn—the island's only lighthouse inn, in fact—with seven antiques-furnished double rooms and a luxurious room in the tower that comes complete with whirlpool and Champagne breakfast. The lighthouse overlooks the white-sand beach of **Cedar Dunes Provincial Park**. The lighthouse also contains displays and artifacts from the days when West Point was a working light, and there's a small dining room downstairs that serves seafood chowder and home-baked goods.

North Shore

Succulent Malpeque oysters are prized around the world for their superior flavor, and these famous Prince Edward Island natives take their name from **Malpeque Bay**, where they were originally found. Today Malpeque oysters are cultivated in sheltered coves around the island's coast, and because they're so plentiful they're readily available in most restaurants.

But Malpeque Bay has more to brag about than oysters; this big body of water that nearly severs the island in two is bordered by some of the province's prettiest scenery—and one of its finest sandy beaches, at **Cabot Provincial Park**. The park is near Malpeque, the site of a long-ago Micmac Indian camp and an early 18th-century Acadian settlement. Malpeque almost became the capital of Prince Edward Island on the recommendation of the chief surveyor sent by the British in 1765. Shortly after, Malpeque received a sizable contingent of Scottish settlers, many of whom have descendants living in the area today.

Malpeque Gardens is a treat for flower fanciers, with hundreds of varieties of dahlias and splendid rose gardens, old-fashioned gardens, and decorations of all kinds. **Cabot's Reach**, a family-owned and run restaurant in Malpeque, is a good place to sample the native oysters, as well as the broiled mackerel, a delectable staple of island home kitchens but unfortunately rare on the menus of island restaurants.

Prince Edward Island was an important shipbuilding center during the last century, and **Green Park Provincial Park** is located on the former estate of one of the island's wealthiest shipbuilders. The historic family home is restored, and a shipbuilding interpretive center and recreated shipyard are added incentives to spend some time at this pretty provincial park. In mid-August, the park hosts its annual old-fashioned Blueberry Social, carrying on a tradition begun by the estate's former owner.

The **Senator's House**, a charming six-bedroom inn in Port Hill, was the home of a prominent island politician of the same shipbuilding family. The restaurant, which is open to visitors, specializes in Malpeque oysters and other fresh seafood, and fresh fruit pies.

In the heart of **Tyne Valley**, a village of Victorian gingerbread homes, the tiny **Studio Tea Room** serves such treats as whole-wheat cinnamon rolls, apple crisp, wild blueberry pie, home-pressed cider, and wild-flower honey. The adjoining craft shop carries a variety of well-made local handcrafts, including pottery and quilts. In early August Tyne Valley's annual four-day Oyster Festival celebrates the region's famous bivalve with oyster suppers and an oyster-shucking competition.

The arts-and-crafts shop on the nearby **Lennox Island Micmac Indian Reservation** on Route 163 carries beautiful traditional Micmac woven baskets, as well as jewelry, ceremonial masks, and many one-of-a-kind items by artists belonging to other Indian nations.

Another good stop for handcrafted souvenirs in this area is **MacAusland's Woollen Mills** in Bloomfield Corner on Route 2. The old-fashioned mill washes, cards, spins, dyes, and weaves raw wool into handsome, durable blankets, which, because they're made of 100 percent pure virgin wool, last virtually a lifetime. Very reasonably priced, MacAusland's blankets are among the best buys on the island. The mill carries a good selection of woolen yarns, too, which are also manufactured on the premises.

Many golfers consider the challenging and scenic **Mill River Provincial Golf Course** on Route 136 to be the island's finest. Certainly it rates among the top in eastern

Canada. The golf course is part of a 1,200-acre recreational park that includes the modern, 80-room **Rodd's Mill River Resort** hotel.

GETTING AROUND

By Sea. The ferry ride across the Northumberland Strait is a highlight for thousands of tourists visiting Prince Edward Island. Marine Atlantic operates a year-round car ferry service to and from Cape Tormentine, New Brunswick, and Borden, Prince Edward Island, with hourly crossings in summer between 6:30 A.M. and 8:30 P.M. Northumberland Ferries operates a second car ferry service from May through December between Caribou, Nova Scotia, and Wood Islands, Prince Edward Island, with hourly summer crossings. The ferry rides take 45 minutes from New Brunswick (about $2.50 per person, $6.75 for the car) and 90 minutes from Nova Scotia ($3.30 per person, $10.60 for a car). You can't make reservations with either service, and in the peak of summer long lines can mean two- and three-hour waits. So plan on arriving at the terminals early in the day or late in the evening when traffic is lightest.

By Air. Charlottetown's brand-new airport is serviced by five airlines—Air Canada, Air Nova, Canadian Airlines International, Air Atlantic, and Inter-Canadian—with direct daily flights to and from Halifax, Toronto, Ottawa, and Montreal. At present there are no direct flights into Charlottetown from the U.S. or England.

Prince Edward Island has a very good highway system, with paved roads leading to all major centers and communities, attractions, and points of interest. The official Prince Edward Island Visitors Map, available free at any visitor information center, is the only map you'll need. One note of caution: While traffic generally moves at a steady pace and at the speed limit, watch for slow-moving tractors, harvesters, and other farm vehicles, particularly on secondary roads.

There are three coastal sight-seeing routes around the province: the 190-km (120-mile) Blue Heron Drive (named for the huge, migratory water birds that visit the island by the thousands each summer) in central Prince Edward Island; the 375-km (234-mile) Kings Byway in the east; and the 288-km (180-mile) Lady Slipper Drive (named for the wild Lady Slipper orchid, the island's floral emblem) in the west. All three scenic drives lead to, or near, major attractions, and are marked clearly and frequently with roadside symbols. The drives are also color-coded on the Prince Edward Island Visitors Map.

ACCOMMODATIONS REFERENCE

▶ **Barachois Inn.** P.O. Box 1022, **Charlottetown,** P.E.I. C1A 7M4. Tel: (902) 963-2194.

▶ **Best Western Linkletter Inn.** 311 Market Street, **Summerside,** P.E.I. C1N 1K8. Tel: (902) 436-2157.

▶ **Best Western MacLauchlan's Motel.** 238 Grafton Street, **Charlottetown,** P.E.I. C1A 1L5. Tel: (902) 892-2461; in U.S. and Canada, (800) 528-1234; Telex: 014-44149.

▶ **Charlottetown Hotel.** Corner Kent and Pownal Streets, P.O. Box 159, **Charlottetown,** P.E.I. C1A 7K4. Tel: (902) 894-7371; in eastern U.S., (800) 565-9077; in the Maritimes, (800) 565-0207; Telex: 014-44239.

▶ **Dalvay-by-the-Sea Hotel.** P.O. Box 8, **Little York,** P.E.I. C0A 1P0. Tel: (902) 672-2048.

▶ **Duchess of Kent Inn.** 218 Kent Street, **Charlottetown,** P.E.I. C1A 1P2. Tel: (902) 566-5826.

▶ **Dundee Arms Inn and Motel.** 200 Pownal Street, **Charlottetown,** P.E.I. C1A 3W8. Tel: (902) 892-2496.

▶ **Hotel Château Madelinot.** Route 199, **Cap aux Meules,** Que. G0B 1B0. Tel: (418) 986-3695.

▶ **Ingleside Lodge.** R.R. 2, **Hunter River,** P.E.I. C0A 1N0. Tel: (902) 963-2431.

▶ **Inn on the Hill.** 150 Euston Street, P.O. Box 1720, **Charlottetown,** P.E.I. C1A 7N4. Tel: (902) 894-8572; Telex: 014-44108.

▶ **Kingsway Motel.** Junction of Routes 3 and 4, at **Poole's Corners,** P.O. Box 907, Montague, P.E.I. C0A 1R0. Tel: (902) 838-2112.

▶ **Kirkwood Motor Hotel.** 455 University Avenue, **Charlottetown,** P.E.I. C1A 4N8. Tel: (902) 892-4206; Telex: 014-44155.

▶ **Marco Polo Inn.** Route 13, P.O. Box 9, **Cavendish Beach,** Hunter River, P.E.I. C0A 1N0. Tel: (902) 963-2352.

▶ **Motel des Iles. Havre aux Maisons,** Que. G0B 1K0. Tel: (418) 969-2931.

▶ **Motel Thériault.** Dune du Sud, **Havre aux Maisons,** Que. J0B 1K0. Tel: (418) 969-2955.

▶ **Netherstone Inn.** P.O. Box 1053, **Montague,** P.E.I. C0A 1R0. Tel: (902) 962-3200; in winter, (902) 962-3188.

▶ **Prince Edward Hotel and Convention Centre.** 18 Queen Street, **Charlottetown,** P.E.I. C1A 8B9. Tel: (902) 566-2222; Telex: 014-44122.

▶ **Quality Inn.** 618 Water Street East, **Summerside,** P.E.I. C1N 2V5. Tel: (902) 436-2295; Telex: 014-2622.

▶ **Rodd's Brudenell River Resort.** Brudenell River Provincial Park, P.O. Box 67, **Cardigan,** P.E.I. C0A 1G0. Tel: (902) 652-2332; in eastern U.S., (800) 565-9077; in the Maritimes, (800) 565-0207; Telex: 014-44251.

▶ **Rodd's Confederation Inn.** Trans-Canada Highway, Junction of Routes 1 and 2 west, P.O. Box 651, **Charlottetown,** P.E.I. C1A 7L3. Tel: (902) 892-2481; in eastern U.S., (800) 565-9077, in the Maritimes, (800) 565-0207; Telex: 014-44145.

▶ **Rodd's Mill River Resort.** Off Route 2 in **Mill River Provincial Park,** P.O. Box 399, O'Leary, P.E.I. C0B 1V0. Tel: (902) 859-3555; in eastern U.S., (800) 565-9077; in the Maritimes, (800) 565-0207; Telex: 014-44251.

▶ **Rodd's Royalty Inn.** Trans-Canada Highway, Junction of Routes 1 and 2 west, P.O. Box 2499, **Charlottetown,** P.E.I. C1A 8C2. Tel: (902) 894-8566; in eastern U.S., (800) 565-9077; in the Maritimes, (800) 565-0207; Telex: 014-44157.

▶ **Sea Breeze Motel.** Route 16, **Souris,** RR2, P.E.I. C0A 2B0. Tel: (902) 357-2371.

▶ **The Senator's House.** Route 12, **Port Hill,** P.O. Box 63, Tyne Valley, P.E.I. C0B 2C0. Tel: (902) 831-2071.

▶ **Shaw's Hotel and Cottages.** Route 15, **Brackley Beach,** P.E.I. C0A 2H0. Tel: (902) 672-2022.

▶ **Shining Waters Lodge and Cottages.** Route 13, **Cavendish,** P.E.I. C0A 1N0. Tel: (902) 963-2251.

▶ **Silver Fox Inn.** 61 Granville Street, **Summerside,** P.E.I. C1N 2Z3. Tel: (902) 436-4033.

▶ **West Point Lighthouse.** Route 14, adjacent to **Cedar Dunes Provincial Park,** R.R. 2, O'Leary, P.E.I. C0B 1V0. Tel: (902) 859-3605 or 859-3117.

NEWFOUND-LAND
AND LABRADOR
By Harold Horwood

Harold Horwood is the author of Newfoundland *and many other books of travel, popular history, fiction, and biography. He is a native Newfoundlander who now lives in Nova Scotia.*

Newfoundland is a place apart, essentially separate from the melting pot of the Canadian mainland—less North American than European, a blend of England and Ireland as they were in the last century. Newfoundlanders, who joined the Canadian union only in 1949, still think of themselves as a separate nation, with their own traditions and customs.

Summer visitors can tour the oldest European settlement in North America, dine on cod tongues and seal flippers, see performances of unique folk theater and music, or jig fish from a trap boat. You can take a ferry from Fortune, Newfoundland, to the French islands of St. Pierre and Miquelon—the only remaining bit of New France in North America—or drive (via car ferry) into subarctic Labrador, the only part of the true north that can be reached in a one-day trip from a southern city. In St. Pierre there are excellent pensions; reservations are not necessary, just check the tourist information center upon arrival.

Except for big-game hunters seeking moose or caribou (of which Newfoundland has the most accessible herds on the continent), the best time to visit is July and August, when you stand at least a reasonable chance of sunshine and the summer festivals are in progress. Earlier than that, even in June, there may be week-long fogs and bone-chilling rainstorms. September is sunny but cool, a good time for motoring and sight-seeing, though the arts and folk festivals are over by the end of August.

MAJOR INTEREST

Experiencing nature and the sea
Salmon fishing and nature in Labrador
Gros Morne National Park
Port au Choix prehistoric site
St. Anthony's Grenfell Mission parkas and crafts
L'Anse aux Meadows ancient Norse settlement site
The Road to the Isles for scenery, seafood, and
    icebergs
Trinity for whale watching
St. John's shopping and dining
Early French fortifications at Placentia
The south coast's isolated fishing villages

Northern Newfoundland

Corner Brook, a third of the way northward along Newfoundland's west coast from Port aux Basques (the terminal for the ferry from Nova Scotia), has the best hotel in the region—the **Glynmill Inn**. A golf course overlooks the Bay of Islands with a view that makes it difficult to keep your eye on the ball, and it also has the best downhill skiing in Newfoundland (December to April). At Corner Brook in August you may catch the Hangashore Folk Festival, with modern versions of Newfoundland music—a rich tradition, much of it brought from Europe centuries ago.

From either Corner Brook or Deer Lake (Corner Brook's airport town) it is an easy one-day trip by car to the Viking settlement of L'Anse aux Meadows on Newfoundland's northern tip. On the way you pass through **Gros Morne National Park**, a scenic, mountain-and-seashore park with ice-carved fjords, and hiking trails to the 2,000-foot-high plateau, where, with moderate effort, you can see herds of woodland caribou and small groups of arctic hares. You can also take a boat tour to the headwaters of one of the great fjords, St. Paul's Inlet.

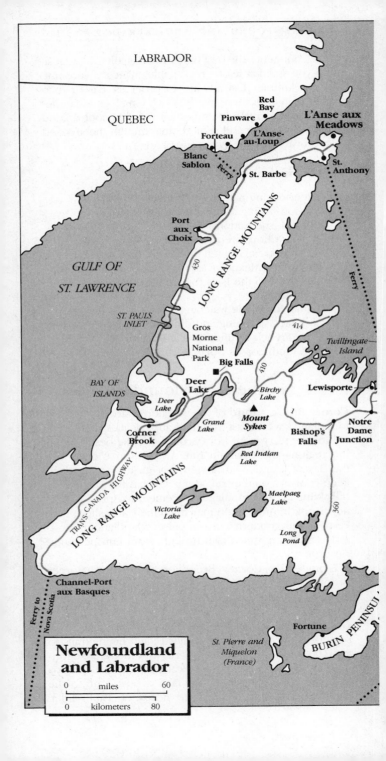

Newfoundland and Labrador

0   miles   60

0   kilometers   80

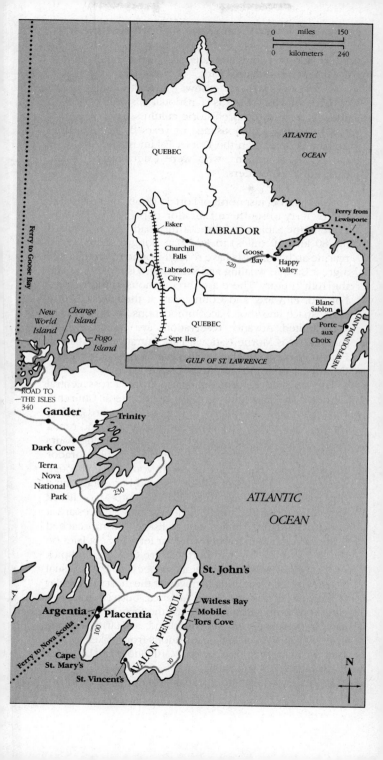

Information on times and rates is available at the entrance to Gros Morne National Park.

At **Port au Choix** (Port-a-shwa), 80 km (50 miles) north of Gros Morne, there is a national historic park with artifacts from three prehistoric cultures. This little cove was inhabited for thousands of years by the Maritime Archaic People, then the Dorset Eskimos, and finally by the Beothuck Indians, who were exterminated by the early European settlers.

From **St. Barbe,** just north of Port au Choix, there is a side trip by ferry to **southern Labrador**, departing twice daily. From **Blanc Sablon** in Labrador the road runs northward for 80 km (50 miles) to Red Bay along a shore where marine archaeologists have recently found the remains of a great Basque whaling and sealing industry dating from the 16th century. There are three famous salmon rivers, Forteau, Pinware, and County Cat, at their best in July. Ferry space and motel accommodations on this trip are very limited. Advance reservations are essential; make them at Gros Morne National Park entrance. For fishing Forteau there is the **Harvey Sheppard** lodge; Pinware and County Cat offer **Pinware River Lodge.**

The truly adventurous can also drive across central Labrador to the world's greatest hydro site at **Churchill Falls.** You must take a ferry at Lewisporte (near Gander) for the 33-hour trip to Goose Bay in Labrador and rent a car at the Goose Bay Airport if you didn't bring yours over on the ferry. After you stay the night at the **Labrador Inn** in Goose Bay you can begin your drive through three hundred miles of wilderness and barrenness on a dirt road to Churchill Falls and the outpost of Esker. Except for those in Churchill Falls, the only services are at **Lobstick Lodge,** 60 miles east of Esker. Having reached Esker, you can then travel by rail-car ferry to Sept Isles on the St. Lawrence River in northeastern Quebec, and pick up the Trans-Canada Highway at Quebec City. This unusual journey by ferry, car, and rail traverses the most spectacular wilderness in eastern North America, but requires very careful planning. Reservations for the ferry to Goose Bay can be made only in Newfoundland, at Marine Atlantic (Tel: 800-563-7701), and reservations from Esker to Sept Isles are made with the Quebec North Shore and Labrador Railway (Tel: 709-944-8205).

It is expected that the road from Esker to **Labrador City** will be completed by January 1990. This will be another worthwhile route to follow in exploring Labrador. The city itself has much to offer, including tours of its mines, which are highly automated and of interest to high-tech fans, and several comfortable lodges.

Back on Newfoundland, **St. Anthony**, the Grenfell Mission "capital," is at the end of the road, 136 km (85 miles) beyond St. Barbe, and 27 km (17 miles) south of the L'Anse aux Meadows site. St. Anthony, the northernmost active settlement on the island, includes the gravesite of the famous missionary-doctor, Sir Wilfred Thomason Grenfell, the hospitals, schools, and other public buildings that he founded, and his craft workshop, where the visitor can buy beautiful knitted, sewn, woven, and carved articles made from designs unique to the region. Among the best are the Grenfell cloth parkas—strong, warm, well made, and hand embroidered by Labrador natives.

L'Anse aux Meadows, on the coast above St. Anthony, is a well-restored settlement dating from A.D. 1005 to 1025, the oldest European settlement yet discovered in North America, and the only fully authenticated Norse site south or west of Greenland. It is believed to have been founded by Icelandic settlers under Thorfinn Karlsefni, who followed close on the heels of Leif the Lucky, an earlier discoverer who may have voyaged much farther south. L'Anse aux Meadows includes a typical small Norse farm complex like those in western Greenland, and a smithy where bog iron was smelted nearly a thousand years ago.

From St. Anthony the choice is either to fly to Gander or to drive back to Deer Lake and take the road east across Newfoundland to St. John's. The motor trip from St. Anthony to Gander includes some of the most beautiful and striking areas in Newfoundland and can easily be accomplished in a day. East of Deer Lake you pass directly below stark Mount Sykes and the Teapot Dome along the shore of Birchy Lake as you travel through Newfoundland's finest inland scenery. At Sir Richard Squires Memorial Park, on this same route, you can see Atlantic salmon attempting to leap Big Falls almost any day in mid summer. The pool below the falls has some of the finest fishing on the island. An enjoyable side trip is along the south shore of Bonne Bay, perhaps Newfoundland's most beautiful spot.

Farther east is another interesting side trip: the **Road to the Isles**, which leaves the Trans-Canada Highway at Notre-Dame junction and skips north by bridge and causeway over the islands to **Twillingate** through the most scenic part of Newfoundland's northeast coast. Here you can buy lobsters fresh from the pot, or gather blue mussels from beds right beside the road. On New World Island and Twillingate Island you are in the track of icebergs, where dozens of great ice islands are often visible at once. The compressed ice in the bergs can be thousands of years old, and is often colored sky blue or jade green, with spires that may rise hundreds of feet into the air.

If you fly into central Newfoundland by way of **Gander**, and have a few minutes to spare, visit the small museum devoted to the history of flight. In the early days of commercial aviation the town was carved out of the forest to provide a large airport as close to Europe as possible, and was headquarters of the Atlantic Ferry Command in World War II.

Trinity—72 km (45 miles) from the Trans-Canada, exiting past Gander at Dark Cove—is one of the oldest settlements in North America, with restored forts, merchant houses, historic markers, and a small museum. The first vice-admiralty court in the New World was held here in 1615, but it was an established fishery center long before that. Trinity has specialized in the building of wooden fishing ships for at least the past 300 years. It is also one of the best places on the East Coast for whale watching, with pods of the great mammals cruising past its headlands almost every day in summer.

St. John's

St. John's, on the northeast horn of the Avalon Peninsula, has been the center of commerce in Newfoundland (though not always the capital) since the 1500s. It was already a major trading center when Jacques Cartier, the discoverer of the St. Lawrence River, first called here in 1534 to resupply and repair his ships. Repeatedly destroyed by fire, downtown St. John's has nonetheless retained its European character.

The best places to stay in St. John's are **Hotel Newfoundland** (just a few blocks from the shops) or the **Stel Battery**, half a mile farther from the center of things, but with a panoramic view of the city and harbor. Both hotels have widely patronized dining rooms. Cod au gratin, a locally famous combination of fish and cheddar cheese, was invented at Hotel Newfoundland. The new **Radisson**

Plaza Hotel is at the west end of downtown St. John's. It offers luxurious rooms and suites at the highest prices.

Adventurous diners will certainly look for cod tongues—a delicacy in such demand here that some are even imported from Europe—and seal flippers. The so-called flipper is not a paw, but a shoulder, like a shoulder of lamb. It is dark, gamey meat resembling sea duck, highly recommended to visitors. The best place to eat flipper pie is **Woodstock Colonial Inn**, 8 km (5 miles) west of St. John's. It takes several hours to prepare—so order it by phone in the morning, and enjoy it with Burgundy by candlelight; Tel: (709) 722-6933. The **Stone House Restaurant**, a few minutes' walk from Hotel Newfoundland, offers excellent seafood and a choice of French wines. Various other places nearby specialize in French, Italian, Mexican, Indian, and Cajun cuisine and several English and Irish pubs serve food, beer, and porter.

The specialty shops are on a mile-long stretch of Duckworth and Water streets, parallel to the waterfront. These include **Nonia**, selling products of outport (any place in Newfoundland outside St. John's) cottage industries—weaving, knitting, carving, and sewing—and the **Cod Jigger**, a craft shop offering many local products. **Melendy's**, in addition, has model ships made by hobbyists, and handmade copper kettles. In any of these stores, ask about "double-knit" mitts—a traditional Newfoundland specialty. **Mary Jane's Specialty Foods**, near the west end of Duckworth Street, caters to the ethnic palate, and offers imported craft items.

On Water Street, a block south of Mary Jane's, is the **Murry Premises**, a beautifully preserved and restored merchant house on a site that has been occupied since the 16th century, when cargoes of fish and trayne oil were bought and sold on this spot and shipped to trading centers in Europe. It now includes restaurants, cafés, and shops specializing in European imports.

Major entertainment in St. John's is at the Arts and Culture Centre, adjoining Memorial University campus on the north side of the city. There is a summer-long festival of music and drama in its large and small theaters, the latter often including experimental work. On the lawn in front of the center small musical groups perform at lunch hour throughout the summer. Some of the troupes presenting their own dramatic works (Codco, the Mummers, Sheila's Brush) have enjoyed enormous success in Newfoundland and across the country. They often perform at the L.S.P.U. hall in downtown St. John's as well as at the center.

The annual **Regatta Day** on Quidi Vidi lake (pronounced Kiddy-Viddy), held on the first fine Wednesday in August, is a combination sporting event and carnival that attracts crowds of up to 50,000 to the mile-long lake inside the city. The races are in six-oared shells, and continue all day, with a "championship" race at the end. But the real attractions are the bands, sideshows, food booths, and small gambling games such as wheels of fortune. Regatta Day is a provincial holiday and draws visitors from afar. The queen, the governor general, and the prime minister have all attended the regatta at one time or another.

North of the university campus lies **Pippy Park**, 4,000 acres of woodland, lake, and hill, with a golf course, trailer park, pool, animal display, and **Memorial University Botanic Gardens** at Oxen Pond. The latter, created by an enthusiastic botanist, contains dozens of exotic species of flowering plants not seen elsewhere in Atlantic Canada, as well as most native wild plants.

Southern Newfoundland

The easily accessible seabird sanctuaries at **Cape St. Mary**'s and **Witless Bay** are an unforgettable experience for the casual visitor as well as the devoted naturalist. You can hire a boat to visit the islands (about 48 km/30 miles south of St. John's) at Witless Bay, Tors Cove, or Mobile. Thousands of petrels, murres, razor-billed auks, puffins, terns, and gulls nest there. Cape St. Mary's has a rare gannet colony that can be reached without a boat from the highway south of Placentia. Murres nest among the gannets, and kittiwakes occupy narrow ledges on the cliff below. It is a wild and barren region, with cliffs that are steep and dangerous.

Placentia is the one place south of St. John's that demands a visit. The former French capital of Newfoundland, it is built on a bar between two river estuaries, overlooked by fortified hills. Basque privateers sailed from here against the English in Newfoundland and Nova Scotia. The principal fort has been excavated and restored, and there is an interpretation center, with artifacts from the fort and what is perhaps the oldest gravestone on the island, that of the famous privateer Captain John Svigaricipi, who was buried at Placentia in 1694.

There are ferry and passenger-ship services to many parts of Newfoundland and Labrador that cannot be reached by car. Labrador services are heavily booked in summer, and reservations should be made as many months in advance as possible (reservations can be made at Marine Atlantic; see the Getting Around section below). The **Labrador** voyage is a subarctic experience with icebergs, seals, whales, and—in calm, sunny weather—the far-famed northern mirages in which islands appear to be floating in the sky.

The **Newfoundland south coast**, between the ferry terminal of Argentia, just north of Placentia on the southwestern side of the Avalon Peninsula, and the ferry terminal of Port aux Basques, the southwesternmost town on Newfoundland, is easier to visit, on small, fast, passenger ships that resemble seagoing tour buses. You can catch these boats daily in Argentia; contact Marine Atlantic (Tel: 800-563-7701) for schedules. Ports of call include fishing villages to which roads have never penetrated, where Newfoundland outport life remains much as it was in the 19th century. It can be foggy in this area, but if you are lucky enough to be there on a clear day you will discover the south coast's essential charm: It is one of the very few places where you can almost literally voyage into the past.

GETTING AROUND

Scheduled airlines fly to many places in Newfoundland and Labrador: St. John's, Deer Lake (for Corner Brook), Gander, St. Anthony, Goose Bay, and Labrador City. The best connection is a direct Toronto–St. John's flight. All bookings, including connecting flights, may be made through Air Canada and Canadian Airlines at any major city. Their subsidiaries Air Nova and Air Atlantic fly to every major point in the province. Small local airlines give connections to coastal communities, and to interior hunting and fishing. The best way to travel, however, is by car or camper.

Ferries run several times daily between North Sydney in Nova Scotia and Port aux Basques in Newfoundland (the trip takes four and a half hours) and in summer also between North Sydney and Argentia, which is just an hour and a half by car from St. John's. The Argentia run takes 20 hours, and is usually booked a month in advance. A week or less is all the booking needed for the ferry to Port aux Basques. Reservations for all ferries can be made at Marine Atlantic; Tel: in U.S., (800) 341-7981; in Maine, (800) 432-7344; in Ontario and Quebec, (800) 565-9411; in Newfoundland, (800) 563-7701; in Nova Scotia, New Brunswick, and Prince Edward Island, (800) 565-9470. There are car-rental services at all major ferry terminals and airports, including those in Labrador.

Remember that the time for Newfoundland Island is a *half hour* ahead of the rest of the Atlantic provinces—including Labrador.

ACCOMMODATIONS REFERENCE

▶ **Glynmill Inn.** P.O. Box 550, **Corner Brook**, Nfld. A2H 6E6. Tel: (709) 634-5181 or, in Canada, (800) 563-4894.

▶ **Hotel Newfoundland.** P.O. Box 5637, Duckworth Street, **St. John's**, Nfld. A1C 5W8. Tel. (709) 726-4980.

▶ **Labrador Inn.** P.O. Box 58, Station C, **Goose Bay**, Labrador, Nfld. A0P 1C0. Tel: (709) 896-3351.

▶ **Lobstick Lodge.** P.O. Box 86, **Churchill Falls**, Labrador, Nfld. A0R 1A0. Tel: (709) 925-3235.

▶ **Pinware River Lodge. L'Anse-au-Loupe**, Labrador, Nfld. A0K 3L0. Tel: (709) 925-5789.

▶ **Radisson Plaza Hotel.** 120 New Gower Street, **St. John's**, Nfld. A1C 1J3. Tel: (709) 739-6404.

▶ **Harvey Sheppard.** P.O. Box 307, **Corner Brook**, Nfld. A2H 6E3. Tel: (709) 639-9651.

▶ **Stel Battery Hotel.** 100 Signal Hill Road, **St. John's**, Nfld. A1A 1B3. Tel: (709) 576-0040 or (800) 267-STEL.

MONTREAL

By David Dunbar and Mary Kelly

David Dunbar, a native of Saskatchewan, lived in Montreal from 1975 to 1986—some of the most turbulent and interesting years in the city's history—and returns to the city frequently. He has written articles for the Montreal Gazette, Travel & Leisure *magazine, and many other publications. Mary Kelly is a communications consultant in Montreal. She is the author of a guidebook to the city as well as a contributor to several books about the province of Quebec. She has also published articles in several Canadian periodicals.*

Wedged between Mont Royal and the St. Lawrence River, Montreal attracts five million visitors annually with a vigorous mixture of French and English cultures, food, fashion, international film and jazz festivals, and spirited conviviality. Two-thirds of Montreal's 2.8 million inhabitants claim French as their mother tongue; English-speaking Canadians and more than a hundred other ethnic minorities (*les autres* to Francophones) make up the other third. This unusual combination of sensibilities and speech makes the city unlike any other in North America.

Montreal is richly endowed with distinctive *quartiers:* Vieux-Montréal, where the city was born in 1642; the Golden Square Mile, cradle of Canada's 19th-century commercial aristocracy; Plateau Mont-Royal, traditional first address of the city's immigrants; and half a dozen other less-storied but equally interesting neighborhoods. Besides its neighborhoods, Quebec's largest city abounds in many other singular attractions.

MAJOR INTEREST

Dining and cafés
Vieux-Montréal
Terre des Hommes (Man and His World)
Musée des beaux-arts de Montréal
— Parc Mont Royal
— Parc Olympique
Montreal Botanical Gardens
Château Dufresne museum of decorative arts
St. Joseph's Oratory
International Fireworks Competition
International Jazz Festival
World Film Festival
Lachine Rapids
Shopping in the Underground City

The most dramatic way to discover firsthand why Montreal was established where it was—on the south shore of an anvil-shaped island in the St. Lawrence River—is to sign up with Lachine Rapids Tours, a company that takes passengers nine miles upstream for jet boating among the angry whitecaps of the Lachine Rapids. With luck, the day will be sunny and warm, and Joe Kowalski, an ebullient Pennsylvanian and one of the company's owners, will be on board to provide an irreverent and amusing commentary, in English and French, on the city and its river.

The excursion is a reminder that Quebec's largest metropolis is not only a river city like London, Paris, and Vienna but also one of the world's great island cities, comfortably seated in the first row of the second rank (to paraphrase Somerset Maugham) behind New York, Hong Kong, Singapore, and Venice—but well ahead of Miami Beach.

Kowalski's aluminum-hulled vessel, named *Saute-Mouton* (leapfrog), slips away from **Victoria Pier** in Montreal Harbor and glides upstream on the swiftly flowing St. Lawrence. At first, its course is crowded with wharves, jetties, and islands, but soon the river bellies out to lake-size proportions.

Downstream at Quebec City, the 750-mile-long St. Lawrence broadens into an estuary, a mighty, tide-tugged arm of the sea that beckoned Jacques Cartier in 1535 with its promise of a waterway to the Orient. From there the French explorer navigated the river inland to an island

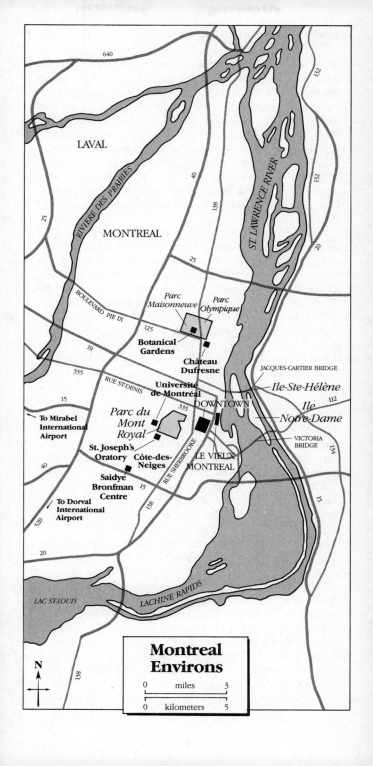

Montreal
Environs

crowned by a wooded mountain and stepped in broad terraces, one of which was the site of a palisaded Iroquois village called Hochelaga. The hospitable Indians welcomed Cartier with dancing and a feast. Later they led him to the summit, which he named for the cardinal of the Medicis, once Bishop of Monreale in Sicily (Monreale became Mont Royal in French). The navigator planted a wooden cross on the ridgetop and caught his first glimpse of the rapids to the west. Beyond, said the Iroquois, lay a freshwater sea. And beyond that, Cartier might have speculated, his mind dazzled by visions of pearls, spices, and silks, lay China.

Alas, between the dream and the destination flashed dangerous white water—the rapids—and Cartier reluctantly turned back. He had unknowingly reached the head of deepwater navigation on the St. Lawrence, where journeys by oceangoing vessels had to be continued by rivercraft. At that terminus, the settlement of Montreal would rise a century later.

Back aboard the *Saute-Mouton,* the same impediment faced by Cartier looms into view. Passengers hunker down under slickers and sou'westers as the skipper regales all hands with tales of other daredevils who challenged the rapids: first, Etienne Brûlé, Canada's original *coureur de bois;* next, Cartier's successor, Samuel de Champlain, the "Father of New France"; and, much later, during the age of Victorian tourism, the 18-year-old Prince of Wales (later Edward VII), who enjoyed a rollicking ride in 1860 on a steamboat piloted by a Kahnawake Indian in full traditional dress.

Within seconds the jet boat plunges into a maelstrom, bucking and churning in water that boils over sedan-sized boulders, only the first skirmish in a 30-minute battle as the boat slaloms back and forth through the rapids on a route designed to generate maximum thrills. The St. Lawrence regularly sweeps over the windshield in great sheets.

The half-hour return trip to Victoria Pier provides an opportunity to dry out and admire the Montreal skyline, set against the green ridge of Mont Royal with the vast dome of St. Joseph's Oratory peering over the upland's western shoulder. To the right, freighters ease through the St. Lambert Lock on the St. Lawrence Seaway (the modern 2,300-mile waterway that would have enabled Cartier to bypass the rapids).

The *Saute-Mouton* slips beneath Route 112's Victoria

Bridge, the longest in the world at the time of its completion in 1859 and the first to span the St. Lawrence. The boat then eases past the Cubist modules of Moishe Safdie's Habitat apartment complex, stacked on the riverbank to the left like a child's building blocks. Habitat was built as an "experiment in urban living" for Expo 67, Montreal's vastly successful world's fair. The skeletal frame of Buckminster Fuller's geodesic dome, another vestige of the fair, peeks above the foliage of Ile Ste-Hélène, one of a dozen islets strewn like stepping stones along the length of the city. Finally, the passengers are deposited back at Victoria Pier.

On first impression, Montreal seems foreign to the North American continent, a European city somehow run aground on alien shores. In the past decade or so, this aesthetic aspect (combined with an exceptionally favorable exchange rate) has made the metropolis a bustling backlot for American filmmakers looking for the streets of Rome or Paris only six hours away from Hollywood. For any European visitor, strolling through Place Jacques-Cartier or Square Dorchester is an oddly familiar experience. Surely, the City Hall is a copy of the Hôtel de Ville in Paris, and the Mary Queen of the World Basilica a miniature of St. Peter's in Rome?

Yet to North Americans, there's no mistaking Montreal for any other city on the continent: raffish, risqué, carefree, a wide-open town, nightclubs packed till all hours. Certifiably French, foreign. An exotic place, romantic, sensual, its past filled with adventure and colorful characters.

Montreal is a city of diversity and complexity, with a non-French ethnic population that is a mixture of English and a hundred other minorities. Greeks, Italians, Portuguese, and Jews each have a community 100,000-strong. There are Asians and Haitians too. Montreal is also cosmopolitan, fashionable, intellectual, a political hotbed, a university town, bohemian, a mecca for artists and nonconformists who gather here to slip the stifling bonds of provincialism. And it is a cultured city that supports fine-arts museums, two symphonies, ballet companies, an opera company, and French and English theater. Not to mention the Festivale de Théâtre des Amériques biennial, which takes over the city every odd year and has established an international reputation for presenting superior avant-garde and over-the-edge theater.

As in France, dining out in Montreal tends to be a ritual:

The best meals are evening-long affairs with a late start, uncounted courses, unrestrained conversation, uninhibited conviviality. The city's café society, perhaps the largest on the continent, thrives on Bishop, Crescent, Laurier, St-Denis, St-Laurent (the Main), St-Paul, and half a dozen other lively thoroughfares. In summer, these cafés *en plein air*—more than 400 at last count—may be the quintessential Montreal social forum. Striped awnings are unrolled; bright umbrellas bloom above sidewalk tables. A jug of *sangría,* a carafe of wine, a mug of beer, and spirited companions combine with a comfortable setting for watching the world go by and savoring the precious days and evenings of the few warm months. Montreal is indeed theatrical, extroverted, and gregarious.

This vivacious city is on a roll, the long winter of separatism finally yielding to an uncertain spring of peaceful cooperation between the French and *les autres.* The Parti Québecois of the late René Lévesque was a painful but necessary instrument for asserting the primacy of French language and culture in the province of its North American birth. But that party is now obsolete, the only plank in its platform knocked out from under it with the resounding *Non, merci* of the 1981 Quebec referendum on sovereignty as opposed to association with the rest of Canada, as well as the ascendancy of a well-educated, bilingual Québecois business class that has displaced priests, politicians, lawyers, and bureaucrats as the province's elite.

This new generation of Québecois has shattered longtime Anglophone domination of the province, even elbowing into *le haute monde.* A society-page roster of a recent Hunt Club soirée at the Ritz (what could be more Anglo?) reads like a *Who's Who* of Francophone high society, with a sprinkling of WASPs for old time's sake. Culturally and economically, the Québecois are confidently *maîtres chez nous.*

For the most part, the province and the city have turned from cultural affairs to economic ones. The FOR SALE/A VENDRE signs that sprouted like mushrooms on front lawns in predominantly English-speaking neighborhoods during the threatening days of separatism have been replaced with the signs of a vigorous economy flexing its muscles after a decade of political confinement—soaring property values, gentrification of run-down neighborhoods, new Metro (subway) lines, a new symphony hall, new museums, a downtown construction boom. Montreal, *en forme encore.*

The Montreal street grid is actually oriented on a northeast-southwest axis, but no one in the city follows that. The convention is that rue Sherbrooke runs east-west, and boulevard St-Laurent (The Main) runs north-south. So, for example, McGill University is west of St-Laurent, and Vieux-Montréal and the river are at the southern end of town.

Vieux-Montréal
(Old Montreal)

From Victoria Pier, the patinated spires and gleaming domes in Vieux-Montréal present an essentially antique picture; the eye willingly overlooks the dissonant details of modernity. At the district's eastern extremity, a copper statue of the Virgin Mary stands behind the tiny **Notre-Dame-de-Bonsecours chapel**. Known also as the sailors' chapel, its roofline is cluttered with steeple and tower. This is the 1773 Our Lady of the Harbour, celebrated in the song "Suzanne" by Montrealer Leonard Cohen. Beside the church shines the silver dome of Bonsecours Market, Canada's Parliament in 1849–1852 and, for decades following, Montreal's principal market (it now houses municipal offices). On a slight elevation behind Bonsecours' classical façade rises the Second Empire roof of City Hall, where, on a third-floor balcony in 1967, Charles de Gaulle fanned the flames of separatism with his disruptive exhortation, "*Vive le Québec libre!*" Farther west, sunlight gleams off the white cupola of the former Palais de Justice. Still farther west, twin Gothic spires nicknamed Temperance and Perseverance soar above the nave of Notre-Dame Basilica, cynosure of the Roman-Catholic faithful since 1829.

Behind these archaisms, the more familiar North American cityscape to the north and northwest reaffirms itself in concrete apartment buildings and office high-rises, undistinguished except for the anodized elegance of the Bourse de Montréal (Stock Exchange Tower) and the cruciform mass of Place Ville-Marie. Then the eye looks deeper into the scene and alights on another of Montreal's unique views: Behind the downtown spires, Mont

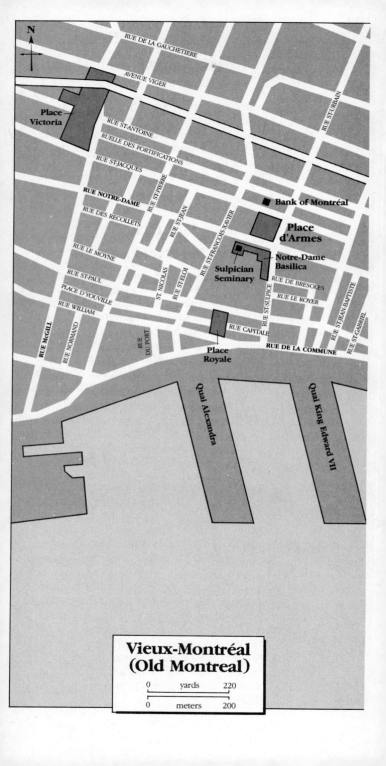

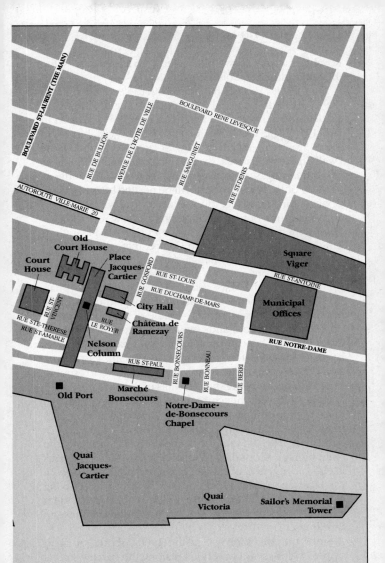

ST. LAWRENCE RIVER

Royal lifts a leafy crown bejeweled with a metal cross, the thematic antecedent of Place Ville-Marie.

But this view is fast-changing: Both the expanded Palais des Congrès de Montréal convention center and the World Trade Centre office-retail and hotel complex will open in late 1990. The latter will occupy several city blocks in Vieux-Montréal, including rue St-Jacques, formerly the "Wall Street" of Canada. By 1991, the area will be home to two other megascale commercial projects: A $250-million, 51-story office tower project will be nestled between Place Bonaventure and Place du Canada with a winter garden and year-round outdoor skating rink à la New York's Rockefeller Center. Rivalling it will be the 45-story IBM-Marathon building, facing the Sheraton Centre, that will feature an adjoining eight-story winter garden.

The waterfront area has also undergone critical development in the past six years, critical because the harborside and rue de la Commune form the southern boundary of Vieux-Montréal—cradle of the city, its greatest tourist attraction, and, second only to Quebec City's Place Royale, a repository of the nation's past. The 95-acre historic district extends west to rue McGill, east to rue Berri, and north to rue St-Antoine—roughly corresponding to the perimeter of the old walls of the city.

Most of the architecture here is Victorian, although there remain enough crooked alleys and cockeyed houses from earlier eras to proclaim the district's 350 years of habitation. The old quarter is enclosed and intimate, the scale human. Around every corner a new scene presents itself—a confusion of ancient masonry and fire escapes, a carriageway leading to an enclosed courtyard, a curving row of century-old gray-stone buildings (no two of them alike), a blue sliver of the St. Lawrence glimpsed between dwellings.

Since the area's revival in the 1960s, scores of fieldstone dwellings and warehouses along the narrow streets have been scrubbed down and renovated; they are now occupied by shops, restaurants, clubs, businesses, studios, museums, and private homes. The venerable *quartier* has become a vibrant place in which to live, work, eat, and play.

There's little danger that Vieux-Montréal will turn into a touristy museum piece like New York City's South Street Seaport or Boston's Faneuil Hall–Quincy Market. Even when it was down at the heels, this was still a working neighborhood, with banks along rue St-Jacques, law offices and courthouses on rue Notre-Dame, and, along lesser thoroughfares, import-export companies, shipping firms, photography studios, book publishers, printers, nightclubs, and restaurants, even a costume emporium.

After its revival, Vieux-Montréal was still cut off from the river—its lifeline since the 17th century—by fenced dockyards, railroad tracks, and a phalanx of five grain elevators that seemed to crush the old city with their mass. Then, in the late 1970s, the bulk of the dockyard operations shifted several miles east. Down came the fences and the elevators. What remained were the railroad tracks, several hangars, and four empty piers as broad as aircraft-carrier decks: Alexandra, King Edward, Jacques-Cartier, and Victoria. The river had been "returned" to the city, and a great debate began: What to do with this wonderful new resource?

Fortunately, the city spurned the usual pressure to construct a megaproject and instead chose a modest, step-by-step plan. Two phases have thus far produced grassy, landscaped expanses, ponds, and flower-filled planters on both sides of the tracks; grade crossings for pedestrians; cycling paths; and renovation of the 1922 Sailor's Memorial Tower at the tip of Victoria Pier.

People drift down from Place Jacques-Cartier, the heart of Vieux-Montréal, to stroll around the piers or rent bicycles and quadricycles. Clowns, jugglers, musicians, balloon sculptors, and food vendors add to the festive air as a once moribund part of town comes alive with activity. Concerts take place on summer nights beneath a big-top tent on Jacques-Cartier Pier; later in the evening, the musical torch is passed to Québecois *chanteurs* performing on a beer-garden boat docked at the end of the pier.

A flea market occupies part of former Hangar No. 8. The hangar's upper level is devoted to one of the Vieux-Port's two major annual summer exhibitions, Images du Futur. This international showcase highlights the latest technological advances in the visual arts: laser and video displays, computer graphics, holography, sound-and-light-wave sculptures, computer-synthesized soundscapes, and multi-sensory, multi-media installations. Each year the exhibition presents a different country's artists, cultural organizations, and corporations involved in pioneering technological developments in the visual arts. Next door in Hangar No. 9 is Expotec, an equally popular exhibition presenting interactive displays about the latest scientific research and technological developments of interest to the general public. The 1989 exhibition was about communication of every kind. Also here is the IMAX Super Cinema 7-story-high, 70-foot-wide screen, which presents films year-round.

Those who would like to see Canada at work can tour the Great Lakes freighter *Maplecliffe Hall,* which carries grain from Thunder Bay to a deep-sea transfer terminal at Baie-Comeau on the north shore of the Gulf of St. Lawrence; from late June to early September, business is slow, so the owners dock the *Maplecliffe* at the Vieux-Port and welcome visitors on board.

Until the 1960s, **Place Jacques-Cartier**, a cobbled rectangle sloping down from the ornate City Hall to rue de la Commune, was the city's busiest open-air market (the only reminders of this function are flower stands on a narrow median). Today the plaza justifiably remains the focal point of Vieux-Montréal. Place Jacques-Cartier can be magical, especially on a warm summer night, with the splashing Vauquelin fountain, the shadowy columns on the City Hall's floodlit façade, the sidewalk vendors and street musicians, the *calèches* drawn by stoic nags snuffling battered oat bags. The caricaturists and Titians of the tourist trade sketch furiously along tiny rue St-Amable, outdoor cafés democratically mix boisterous visitor and resident alike beneath their colorful awnings, and beyond the Vieux-Port cruise boats glittering with strings of lights beat against the dark current.

At the top of the square stands the controversial Nelson Column, erected in 1808 as the first commemorative anywhere in the world to honor the victor of the Battle of Trafalgar. Anglophones didn't like it because it faced away from the river; Francophones hated it because it honored a British admiral who had defeated the French. During the *séparatiste* 1970s, it was a provocative and convenient target for sloganeers.

Just east of the square and opposite City Hall stands the **Château de Ramezay**, one of a handful of structures in Montreal that date from the French regime. Now a museum furnished in 18th-century style, this robust fieldstone dwelling was built in 1705 for the 11th governor of Montreal, Claude de Ramezay. The château was commandeered by the Continental Army in 1775 during the American occupation of Montreal. Among the invaders who were billeted here while trying to rally Canada to the Revolutionary cause were an old and tired Benjamin

Franklin, Benedict Arnold, General Richard Montgomery, and John Carroll, a Marylander who became the first Roman-Catholic bishop of the United States. It was Carroll's unenviable task to convince the staunchly Catholic *habitants* that their religion could accommodate both Rome and the new republic. He failed. (Many Americans do not know that the Continental Army invaded Canada and occupied Montreal during the War of Independence. Is this a testament to the two countries' generally friendly relations since 1812, which make such an infringement seem so unlikely, or is this indicative of Canada's traditionally obscure role in American affairs?)

The old quarter's most delightful thoroughfare is the east-west **rue St-Paul**, one of Montreal's original streets and the first to be lighted with oil lamps (in 1815). Now paved with bricks and brightened with Victorian lampposts, St-Paul is lined with late-19th-century stone commercial buildings that have been pleasingly reborn as airy, gracious restaurants, boutiques, craft shops, artists' lofts and studios, even specialty stores for flags and kites.

Vieux-Montréal's other principal square, **Place d'Armes**, in the northwest part of the area, has a more serious demeanor than Place Jacques-Cartier, despite the tourist buses and *calèches* that congregate here. In its center a ten-foot-high statue of Paul de Chomedey, Sieur de Maisonneuve, stands near the site where in 1644 the city's founder and a tiny band of men successfully defended Montreal (then a missionary outpost called Ville-Marie) against an attack by 200 Iroquois warriors. A statue of one of the vanquished natives kneels at the base of the monument, which is crowded with other historical figures, including Jeanne Mance, who established Montreal's first hospital; Charles LeMoyne, whose sons founded New Orleans and Mobile, Alabama; and the vigilant mastiff Pilote, whose barking alerted the settlement to the impending danger of an Iroquois attack.

Dominating the south side of the square is **Notre-Dame Basilica**, one of the largest examples of the Gothic Revival style in North America. Its twin spires reach a height just two and a half feet short of those of Notre-Dame in Paris. The history of the church, which was completed in 1829, is rife with anomalies. Montreal's Protestants and Jews contributed to its construction. Notre-Dame's architect, James O'Donnell, was not only Protestant and Irish but a New Yorker as well. His work on the church inspired his conversion, and after his death his body was entombed beneath the first pillar to the right of the altar, with an entire church as his eloquent epitaph.

The dazzling interior is gilt and soaring polychromatic blue, similar to Sainte Chapelle in Paris. Three rose windows in the roof contribute much-needed light to the vast nave. Fourteen stained-glass windows designed in Limoges present a historical frieze relating the founding of Montreal. The extraordinarily detailed altar and pulpit are ornamented with wooden statues of the prophets.

Adjacent to Notre-Dame behind a tall fieldstone wall and a wrought-iron gate is the **Sulpician Seminary**, constructed in 1685 and generally considered to be Montreal's oldest building. The appearance of the squat Medieval-looking structure is lightened by a charming classical portal with Ionic pilasters and the lacy seminary clock, reputedly the oldest public timepiece in North America (1710).

For more than 300 years the seminary has served as a residence and headquarters for the Sulpicians, who bought the island of Montreal in 1668 from de Maisonneuve and La Société de Notre-Dame de Montréal for 130,000 livres (about $260,000). The Sulpicians administered the legal and religious life of the settlement, kept its records (still in the seminary's subterranean barrel vaults), and granted concessions to prospective landowners.

Confronting Notre-Dame on Place d'Armes, physically and spiritually, is the nation's oldest bank, the **Bank of Montreal**, which was founded in 1817. One of the most elegant monuments in the metropolis, the Greek Revival structure with its solid portico and Corinthian pillars anchors rue St-Jacques, once the Wall Street of Canada. (Like its New York City counterpart, it too ran inside a rampart that fortified the early city.) The bank's interior is stunning. Wealth is apotheosized by McKim, Mead and White's row of 40 black-marble columns and a magnificent 90-foot dome. The original bronze lamps, marble counters, and brass gates gleam with loving care and heavy use.

Surrounding the square are other temples of finance and insurance, the business legacy of Montreal's conservative Scottish-Canadian ruling class. An eight-story sandstone structure on the southeast corner, vigorously gargoyled and grilled, is Montreal's first skyscraper, built in 1818.

Central Business District

To get from Vieux-Montréal to the central business district take rue McGill at the western end of the *vieux quartier* heading north. You'll pass **Square-Victoria**, a windswept expanse overwhelmed by the Bourse de Montréal and the twin aluminum façades of the Bell-Banque Canadien Nationale complex. Here rue McGill becomes Côte du Beaver-Hall, named after the 19th-century estate of fur trader Joseph Frobisher, which at the time was out in the country, beyond the city walls.

The twisting street climbs a modest escarpment and intersects a narrow east-west thoroughfare called de la Gauchetière. A few blocks east, Montreal's tiny **Chinatown**, which is home to about 300 residents, is squeezed between two massive public works projects, Complexe Guy-Favreau to the north (home of federal offices in Montreal) and the Palais des Congrès (convention center) to the south. On Sundays, though, these narrow streets fill with life as Chinese families from more affluent addresses visit relatives and patronize the old neighborhood's restaurants, shops, and specialty stores.

Return to Côte du Beaver-Hall and continue north to boulevard René Lévesque (formerly boulevard Dorchester), an east-west commercial canyon hemmed in by such tall landmarks as the Hydro-Quebec Building, Place Félix Martin's twin granite and marble towers, the C-I-L House, the La Reine Elizabeth Hotel, and Place Ville-Marie.

The Underground City

Montreal's celebrated underground city, **la ville souterraine**, began at **Place Ville-Marie** in the late 1950s, when architect I. M. Pei and developer William Zeckendorf decided to build a shopping concourse beneath the trio of office towers Pei designed. The all-weather arcade was such a hit that other developers plugged into the system and the underground network spread. (Part of the network is actually above ground—city officials prefer the term "weatherproof city"—but the underground designation has stuck.) It gives Montrealers coatless access to six hotels, ten shopping plazas, two train stations, a dozen commercial buildings, residential highrises, 25 movie theaters, more than 1,000 shops, and hundreds of restaurants and bars. Some building clusters are within walking

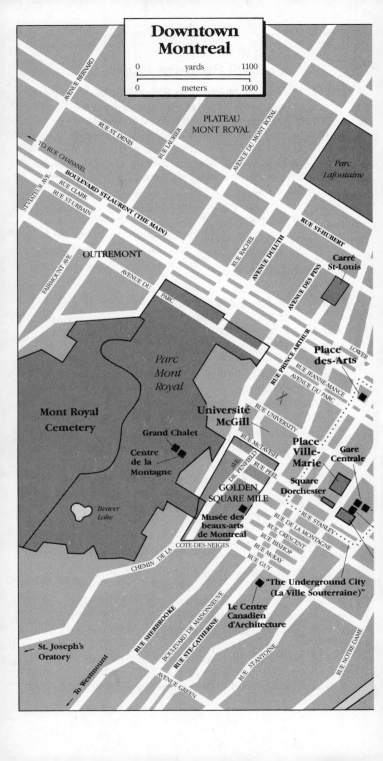

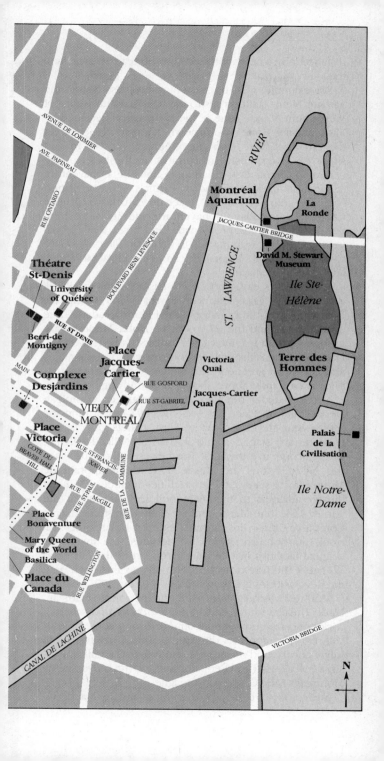

distance; other neighborhoods can be reached by taking the Metro.

For example, west of the central business district the Atwater Metro station runs to the haute couture shops of **Westmount Square** (one of the last projects designed by Mies van der Rohe), well-known as Anglophone turf in the old days, and **Plaza Alexis-Nihon**, with its myriad shops and inexpensive restaurants. In the heart of the central business district, tunnels link the Bonaventure subway station with Canadian Pacific's Windsor Station (used for commuter trains), **Place du Canada**, Le Château Champlain, and **Place Bonaventure**, with its vast exhibition halls, shopping promenade, and hotel. Place Bonaventure, in turn, is connected to Canadian National's Gare Centrale (Central Station), the La Reine Elizabeth Hotel, and Place Ville-Marie.

A few blocks east, north-south passages link the Palais des Congrès, Complexe Guy-Favreau, and **Complexe Desjardins**, most impressive of the indoor arcades. Three office towers and the 601-room **Le Hotel Meridien** are grouped around a multilevel galleria called **La Place**. Daylight streams through seven-story windows; fountains and islands of greenery defy winter, and enormous mobiles twist gently above shoppers bound for boutiques.

A tunnel under rue Ste-Catherine connects Complexe Desjardins with **Place des Arts**, the city's performing-arts center near McGill University. Plays, ballets, operas, and concerts are staged at the Port-Royal, Wilfrid-Pelletier, and Maisonneuve theaters. The newest kid on the Place des Arts block is the **Musée d'Art Contemporain de Montréal**. Its state-of-the-art facilities include a 350-seat theater adjacent to the main building. Located at the corner of Jeanne Mance and Ste-Catherine streets facing Complexe Desjardins, it was designed by architect Gabriel Charbonneau, who also designed the museum's original facilities in Cité du Havre, part of the old Expo '67 site. (The Cité du Havre location remains open until the new facilities are inaugurated in spring 1991.)

Montreal's other venues for the performing arts include Théâtre Saint-Denis in the *quartier Latin,* scene of rock concerts year-round, comedy during comedy festivals, and jazz concerts during the annual jazz festival in July. Concerts and recitals are also given at McGill University's Pollack Hall and Redpath Hall, and the Université de Montréal's Salle Claude-Champagne.

Newcomers are Théâtre Outremont and the Rialto Cinema in the now very trendy Outremont area (about a 10-minute drive north of downtown). They present more alternate or avant-garde music, dance, and theater productions, while the Saidye Bronfman Centre—a long-time performing and visual arts mecca for Montrealers—presents dance, music, film, theater, and spoken word programs in English, French, and Yiddish. This is the home of North America's only permanent Yiddish Theatre troupe, founded some 32 years ago by Dora Wasserman.

The Centaur Theatre, home of Montreal's only major English-language theater, is housed in the Neo-classical former stock-exchange building in Vieux-Montréal. Three major French-language theaters are Théâtre de Quat'Sous on avenue des Pins, Théâtre du Nouveau Monde on rue Ste-Catherine just south of Place des Arts, and Théâtre du Rideau Vert on upper St-Denis.

Montreal is considered the dance capital of Canada, so it is not surprising that several dance groups perform year-round. Among the best-known are Ballets Classiques de Montréal, Les Grands Ballets Canadiens, Les Ballets Eddy Toussaint, Montréal Danse, LaLaLa Human Steps, Les Ballets Jazz de Montréal, Michael Montanaro Dance Company, Margie Gillis, and Tangente—the last a nucleus for many of the city's more avant-garde dance troupes. Most have established international reputations and can be seen at Place des Arts or any of the Maisons de la Culture performance spaces around town. As of September 1990, these groups will have a brand-new downtown performance and rehearsal space, the Agora Dance Theatre, affiliated with the Université de Montréal dance faculty. Every other September (the next will be in 1991) the Festival International de Nouvelle Danse presents the hottest and most avant-garde dance troupes and soloists from the international scene. Be forewarned: Tickets for this event always go quickly—such is the caliber of the companies and the fanaticism of Montreal dance fans.

East of the central business district, the Berri-UQAM subway station tunnels beneath several office towers, the Voyageur bus terminal, and the Université du Québec à Montréal. Light streams into the seven-story **Les Atriums**, a shopping mall also connected to the cluster; down the atrium's sides, waterfalls cascade from balcony to balcony into reflecting pools and tropical garden below street level.

New to the underground city are three major complexes—all opened in 1988. One block north of

Place Ville-Marie, at the corner of McGill College and Ste-Catherine is **Place Montreal Trust**. This gigantic complex has a five-story central atrium and courtyard complete with fountain—all topped off by huge skylights. Some 120 trendy boutiques offer virtually something for everyone in taste and price range. Abercrombie & Fitch is just one of the "outfitters" found here. The glass wall at street level alongside the McGill College Promenade makes an ideal people-watching spot. Popular eateries here include **Le Notre de Paris**'s divine patisserie and chocolatier, as well as **Les Palmes** "Californian" courtyard restaurant.

Place Montreal Trust, which connects underground to the former Simpson department store on its western side, connects on its eastern side to the long-standing **Eaton** department store—one of the Big Three retailers doing business on Ste-Catherine since the turn of the century. Eaton and **Les Terrasses** (which are being transformed into Le Centre Eaton à la Toronto's major shopping emporium) have long been part of the underground city, as has **La Baie**, just one block east. These three now have a new neighbor and a rather unusual one at that.

Set between Eaton and La Baie (each of which occupy a city block on Ste-Catherine), is **La Promenade de la Cathedrale**, a major new retail and office complex. Some say it symbolizes an "open marriage" between commerce and religion: Its office tower looms above the venerable Christ Church Cathedral, with a 150-store retail mall located directly beneath. The redevelopment of this Montreal landmark drew some criticism when it first opened in the fall of 1988. However, this only piqued Montrealers' penchant for the new and unusual, resulting in its becoming a favorite shopping spot, as well as a retreat from the bustle of Ste-Catherine commerce. The complex's latest addition, **Le Parchemin**, opened to gastronomic fanfare in spring 1989. Aside from being the first major French restaurant to open downtown in some years, it is notable for its unusual venue—the 1876 Christ Church Cathedral rectory and parish house.

Les Cours Mont-Royal is the third—and most grandiose—of the new underground city tie-ins: The once-renowned Sheraton Mont Royal Hotel, whose halcyon days are still fondly recalled by Montreal's elite, had fallen into disrepair and disrepute in recent years. Now it has been reborn as a luxury condominium, office, and retail complex. A beauty to behold—inside and out—with many of the original hotel's architectural high-lights and treasures triumphantly restored, Les Cours Mont-Royal has become a mecca for Montrealers seeking elegance in their daily lives. Boutiques, restaurants (including the fabled Hediard's of Paris and Montreal's homage to Harry's New York Bar), a magnificently chandeliered vaulted lobby, atriums, sweeping staircases, fountained courtyards featuring live entertainment and mini exhibitions, as well as a cinema with Egyptian decor and a thriving marketplace have restored this landmark to its former glory.

Back at Place Ville-Marie, continue west along boulevard René Lévesque to the western end of the downtown office towers. Here, the thin frame of the Canadian Imperial Bank of Commerce building rises over **Square Dorchester**, for more than a century one of the loveliest spaces in the city. Square Dorchester, with Place du Canada to its south, might be considered the "center" of the center. Now it is the locale for the Art Deco–inspired Info-Touriste headquarters in the Dominion Square Building. Situated at street level on the north side of the Square, it's run by the Greater Montreal Convention and Tourism Bureau and the Maison du Tourisme Quebec—the first pit-stop for first-time visitors to the city.

Public squares are the finest legacy of the Victorian era in Montreal. Indeed, it would be difficult to imagine the city without these pocket-size oases, some gifts of philanthropists (Beaver Hall, Viger, Phillips), others vacant land that was almost miraculously preserved (St-Louis). Square Dorchester itself was expropriated from a Catholic cemetery. Around it was erected the largest collection of eclectic, notable buildings produced by Victorian architecture anywhere in the city.

Mary Queen of the World Basilica, at the southeast corner of the square, was started in 1875 by Bishop Ignace Bourget as a reminder to English Montreal that the Church of Rome still ruled in what was then Canada's largest city. A wonderful historical curiosity, the Neo-Baroque confection is (perhaps fortunately) the world's only one-quarter-size replica of St. Peter's in Rome—and the very embodiment of cultural colonialism.

The former Windsor Hotel, gutted and reborn on the west side of the square as shops and offices, began life as luxurious accommodations for wealthy bourgeoisie nostalgic for the cosmopolitan Second Empire of Napoléon

III ("salons frescoed and furnished in strictly Egyptian style," noted early promotional literature). The Dominion Square Building and the massive Sun Life Building are rich mixtures of Classical, Renaissance, and Baroque elements: in sum, "Beaux Arts." Although the square has lost some of its glamour and spatial balance, it remains one of the most harmonious environments in Montreal.

By 1910 **rue Ste-Catherine**, running parallel to and north of boulevard René Lévesque, was the city's main commercial thoroughfare, and it is still a busy shopping area, set today between the central business district and the restaurants and nightclubs of rue Crescent. Montreal's large department stores—La Baie, Eaton, and Ogilvy— and an unbroken stretch of retail shops line the street. To the north is rue Sherbrooke, the southern boundary of the famous Golden Square Mile, and home to some of Montreal's most elegant boutiques.

The Golden Square Mile

The British conquest of New France in 1759 unleashed on Montreal a commercial class of shrewd, tough-minded Scotsmen, many of them refugees from the brutal Highland Clearances. Within a generation, the McTavishes, the McGills, and the Frasers dominated the city's fur trade, then its financial institutions, then its politics. These "Caesars of the Wilderness" built grand country estates north of the city, where they entertained on an imperial scale. (This tradition, along with the historic congeniality of the French population, may represent the twin streams that nourish Montreal's enduring reputation for lavish hospitality and joie de vivre.)

Industrialization followed, with sugar mills, breweries, factories, and railroads; the tireless Scots dominated those too. Ogilvies, Cantlies, McDougalls, Molsons, Macdonalds, Strathconas, McIntyres, Drummonds, and Rosses—famous names in the annals of Montreal—continued the relentless residential climb up Mont Royal.

From the late 1800s to World War II, 70 percent of Canada's wealth was concentrated in the hands of some 25,000 residents of what was called the Golden Square Mile, bounded by Sherbrooke on the south, avenue des Pins (angling along the ridges of Mont Royal) to the north, rue McTavish to the east, and chemin de la Côte des Neiges to the west. It was the cradle of Canada's commercial aristocracy, the men who built Canada: the wealthy merchants, founders of international steamship lines, bankers, railroad barons, all the kings of capitalism in an illustrious, audacious age.

Determined to proclaim their power and prosperity, they hired Stanford White from New York City and the Maxwell brothers from Boston to design Italianate palaces on the wooded slopes. They trumpeted the external signs of *nouveaux riches* with automobiles, race horses, gardens, and greenhouses to perpetuate their day in the sun as the Empire of the North.

These prosperous Victorians exercised at the Montreal Amateur Athletic Association clubhouse on rue Peel, took high tea at the Ritz-Carlton, sent their towheaded scions to McGill (founded by fur trader James McGill just to the east of the Golden Square Mile), and indulged in culture at the Musée des beaux-arts de Montréal, also within the Golden Square Mile, whose galleries were hung with Rembrandts, Constables, and Renoirs from their own private collections.

Much of the glory has since crumbled beneath the wrecker's ball. More fortunate structures became alumni offices and faculty clubs for McGill; others were enlisted for diplomatic duty along avenue McGregor (now Docteur Penfield) and avenue des Pins, Montreal's Consulate Row. Echoes of this gilded age continue to reverberate in the art galleries and elegant shops along Sherbrooke that cater to a diminished carriage trade. Still, a brief look around the Golden Square Mile conveys some sense of the awesome concentration of power and wealth, unlike anything Canada had ever seen—or is likely to ever see again.

Down on Sherbrooke, still occasionally referred to as Montreal's Fifth Avenue, the Ritz-Carlton Hotel, gracious monarch of the street, has been the favorite watering hole of Square Milers since 1912. Holt Renfrew, one block west, supplied fur coats to four generations of British royalty. Some blocks east, facing the Roddick Gates of McGill, the **McCord Museum of Canadian History** and its famed Notman Photography Archives is presently undergoing a $20-million renovation and expansion. The McCord will reopen in 1992, the year of Montreal's 350th anniversary.

Its cultural neighbor to the west, the **Musée des beaux-arts de Montréal**, was designed by the Maxwell brothers. Canada's oldest art institution (which dates from a distressingly recent 1860), it was moribund for years, seemingly irrelevant to much of the community. It finally closed in 1973 for a badly needed renovation and expansion, which doubled the museum's size with the addition of a modern wing.

In 1976 the bronze front doors behind the Ionic portico were flung open, and Montreal responded. Splashy major exhibits of works by Bouguereau, Picasso, and Leonardo have boosted attendance.

Rue Crescent Area

The museum was so invigorated by its success that a second expansion plan was devised, calling for an extension south of Sherbrooke along rue Crescent, a street of wall-to-wall restaurants, cafés, bars, and boutiques. This cultural incursion might have elevated the tone of Montreal's liveliest west-end street scene, which spills over onto the parallel streets of Bishop, de la Montagne, and Mackay, but the proposal was shouted down because it would have meant eviscerating one of Canada's largest concentrations of Victorian homes, all splendidly renovated. A new proposal that incorporates the façade of the landmark New Sherbrooke Apartments has been adopted, but for now the night along Crescent still belongs to music, laughter, and frivolous conversation and the day to shopping, noshing, and gallery-hopping.

The area is an Anglo counterpart to the clubs and bars along the predominantly Francophone St-Denis, east of the central business district. Young professionals congregate at the **Winston Churchill Pub** (known locally as "Winnie's"), one of the most long-lived of the bars here. Other upwardly mobile types congregate at **Thursday's**, connected by a passageway—Montreal is a veritable rabbit warren of underground corridors—to a basement disco and the **Hôtel de la Montagne**, an upscale hostelry with a good restaurant, intimate bar, and splendid Art Nouveau lobby.

Not far from Crescent—and not to be missed—is **Le Faubourg Ste-Catherine**. This lively market emporium has revitalized the neighborhood around Guy and Ste-Catherine streets, attracting throngs of sightseers and Montreal bon vivants since it opened in 1986. International cuisine of the finger-food type can be enjoyed on the spot or as take-out fare for picnic noshes. It boasts a liquor store, flower stall, boutiques with handicraft and artisan wares from Quebec and Central and South America, and a cinema, a discotheque, and the **Le Faubourg**

Ste-Honoré grill/restaurant/bar housed in the historic fieldstone mansion hidden behind the main complex.

Le Faubourg's newest neighbor is **Le Centre Canadien d'Architecture**. Located at St-Marc on rue Baile, and just opened in the spring of 1989, this museum is a veritable showcase of architecture past, present, and future. The magnificently restored Shanghnessy House mansion is its centerpiece, flanked on either side by two connecting wings designed by project architect Peter Rose. Le Centre Canadien d'Architecture is the only museum in the world dedicated solely to architecture: It houses one of the world's most important and most extensive collections of prints, drawings, maquettes, models, and books, all relating to the subject. As well, the CCA has exhibition halls, a bookstore, and an auditorium for public use. There are regular tours of the museum and its grounds, which occupy the city block from rue Baile to boulevard René Lévesque Ouest and St-Marc to du Fort. Its public face is particularly evident in the sculpture gardens on boulevard René Lévesque.

Parc Mont Royal

For more than a century, Montreal's mountain, a swayback ridge whose twin summits rise some 750 feet above the island, has been a place of refuge in the heart of the city, a reassuring presence, a retreat for recreation, seclusion, contemplation.

The upland's spiritual role was its earliest. In 1535, as we have seen, Cartier named the mountain for a cardinal and planted a wooden cross on the summit. De Maisonneuve duplicated this pious act in 1643 as thanksgiving to God for sparing his year-old mission from a flood. This religious theme was continued in the 1850s, when farms on the mountain's north slope were turned into two cemeteries, one Catholic, one Protestant—"the most romantic and secluded burying grounds in the world," according to an 1856 guidebook. In 1924, to commemorate de Maisonneuve's long-vanished cross, the St. Jean-Baptiste Society raised a 100-foot iron cross illuminated by 150 lightbulbs—a homely beacon proclaiming Quebec's Catholic roots for 50 miles on a clear night.

A brief secular intrusion occurred when wealthy landowners partitioned the mountain into private estates. With unusual foresight, the city stepped in to expropriate the land for a park—at least that half of the mountain not occupied by sprawling necropolises. In 1874 a similar astuteness guided the councillors in their choice of landscape architect: Frederick Law Olmsted, the celebrated genius behind Manhattan's Central Park and the Capitol grounds in Washington. Seventeen years of experience had instilled in Olmsted the conviction that a park should serve the subtle purpose of restoring city dwellers spiritually—a tenet in keeping with the mountain's early function.

Olmsted interfered with Mont Royal's natural attributes as little as possible: "If it is to be cut up with roads and walks, spotted with shelters and streaked with staircases it is likely to lose whatever natural charm you first saw in it. Your mountain of less than a thousand feet is royal in name only by courtesy, and if you attempt to deal with it as if it had the impregnable majesty of an alpine monarch, you only make it ridiculous."

The park is still largely as Olmsted envisioned, an urban sanctuary, nature untrammeled by zoos and amphitheaters, undiminished by muggers, oversize portable radios, or boardwalks, untainted by what Olmsted called "insipid picturesqueness." Thick stands of maple and oak, spruce and chestnut, floriated meadows and secluded glades are the haunts of squirrels fattened on baguette crumbs; woodchucks, red foxes, snowshoe hares, pheasants, and broad-wing hawks are plentiful; and herring gulls, up from the docks, can also be seen.

The animals share their leafy domain with joggers and cyclists, elderly strollers, and mothers with babies. On summer Sundays especially, the mountain echoes with the conversation of picnicking families. Hikers leave on nature walks from the **Grand Chalet**, a seigneurial-style hall built in the center of the park in 1931 as a blatant compromise of Olmsted's original plan. More sedentary types buy snacks from a bustling concession stand inside the chalet, and eat beneath the historic scenes and heraldic crests of Quebec, Canada, and England that decorate the walls. The royal blue of France highlights the heavy beams of the buttressed ceiling. A terrace in front of the chalet offers fine views of the city below; on clear days you can see the Green Mountains of Vermont.

At Beaver Lake, a 15-minute walk west of the chalet, junior yachtsmen sail their toy sloops and schooners while sunworshippers bronze on the sloping lawns. Here, in the winter, downhill skiers will grasp a short tow rope to take up a nearby incline's modest challenge, cross-country skiers will set off along five miles of mountaintop trails, snowshoers will galumph through the woods, and skaters will pirouette on the frozen lake.

Plateau Mont-Royal

This old commercial and residential district stretches about 20 blocks north of rue Sherbrooke and about the same distance east of avenue du Parc, on the eastern side of Mont Royal. The plateau is Montreal at its most intensely ethnic, most urban: densely populated, extravagantly Victorian. Three main commercial thoroughfares—du Parc, St-Laurent, and St-Denis—run north to south through it. Lining the narrow side streets are brick- and limestone-faced duplexes and triplexes with distinctive balconies and spiralling exterior staircases, ornate trademarks of Montreal's architectural landscape.

The staircases, a feature imported from rural Quebec of the 1880s, saved space by eliminating interior stairs, and doubled as fire escapes. (Considered unsafe, they were banned in new construction by a 1940s city ordinance, but existing ones were exempted.) Montreal's *balconville* is a counterpart to New York City's brownstone stoop, a refuge from summer heat, a perch from which to gab with neighbors, a sentry post for watching children at play on the sidewalks below.

These days **avenue du Parc** is the most ethnically diverse street in Montreal. When the area was first developed in the 1880s, it was predominantly Jewish, and traditional Orthodox garb is still a frequent sight along the busy, scrabbling avenue. Subsequently, Greeks settled here, then Portuguese, and most recently Latin Americans from Guatemala, Nicaragua, and Mexico.

Like nearby St-Laurent, avenue du Parc is a microcosm of the city and the diversity of its inhabitants that becomes more gentrified the farther north you go. The avenue cuts through the area known as **Outremont**, the Francophone counterpart of toney Westmount. Outremont is considered to be the neighborhood roughly bordered by avenue du Mont Royal and Mont Royal itself to the south and west, Chemin de la Côte Ste-Catherine and avenue Van Horne to the north, and abutting the Plateau Mont-Royal area to the east. The French elite, including Quebec premier Robert Bourassa, live in this enclave, often in stately mansions on the lower reaches of Mont Royal. Quiet tree-lined streets and many small public parks exist alongside chic boutiques and bistros. Shopping is big business here, and Laurier and Bernard avenues in particular cater to the carriage trade. The area is also increasingly the haunt of adventurous Anglophones, drawn by the promise of oh-so-French ambiance, reliably fine food, and lively, informal café society. The ethnic hubbub of Plateau Mont-Royal is right next door, and the harmonious coexistence of the two neighborhoods is yet another example of the cosmopolitan nature of Montreal.

Rue St-Denis is Montreal's boulevard St-Michel, the *quartier Latin,* a Francophone student ghetto of bookstores, cafés, boutiques, restaurants, smoky jazz clubs, cinemas, and theaters. The action centers on the Montreal campus of the Université du Québec, at Ste-Catherine and St-Denis, which has an enrollment of 12,800.

Every July, the **Montreal International Jazz Festival** and the **Just Pour Rire** (Just For Laughs) **Festival** turn St-Denis between Sherbrooke and boulevard René Lévesque into one big block party. Some groups give free concerts at outdoor bandstands to thousands of music lovers, who mill about the sidewalks until late into the warm summer evenings; others perform at such venues as Théâtre St-Denis, one of the largest cinemas in North America when it was built in 1908.

North of Sherbrooke, St-Denis loses much of its student character and becomes a wide avenue lined with graystone town houses occupied by splashy boutiques, salons, and cafés. Carré St-Louis, just north of Sherbrooke, St-Denis's apogee and the loveliest residential square in the city, is crowned with trees and bordered on three sides by elegant Victorian houses inhabited by some of Quebec's brightest cultural lights. The turn-of-the-century graystone mansions almost vibrate with a profusion of ornamental details—arched porches, lacy balconies, frilly rooftop ironwork, turrets, dormer windows, bulging cornices—all conspiring to evoke the image of gracious Victorian city life. **Rue Prince-Arthur**, at the square's western end, is a pedestrian mall lined with dozens of inexpensive, bring-your-own-bottle restaurants, mostly Greek.

Boulevard St-Laurent, popularly known as the Main, has long been a sociological isobar, a de facto demarcation between the English west end of the city and the French east end; in between lies a wide buffer zone of immigrants. Tradition has it that newcomers got off the boat at the docks in Vieux-Montréal and just walked north along the Main, a moniker that comes from the street's former name, rue Principale du Faubourg St-Laurent, or St. Lawrence Main Street.

The Lower Main, between René Lévesque and Sherbrooke, and along Ste-Catherine between Jeanne-Mance and St-Denis, is a mild-mannered Tenderloin of taverns, strip joints, porno theaters, and tattoo parlors. These are mixed with more reputable business landmarks like Main Importing, S. Enkin & Sons, and the Montreal Pool Room, famed for its "steamies" (steamed hot dogs slathered with chopped onion, mustard, and coleslaw—former mayor Jean Drapeau's favorite junk food). At night the Tenderloin's bikers, hookers, and pushers are like snakes: they won't bother you if you don't bother them.

The Main and its side streets are most strongly associated with the Jewish immigrants who crowded into the neighborhood during the czarist pogroms of the 1880s. One reason for the continuing connection may be that their descendants enriched Canadian culture with a remarkable outpouring—musician Alexander Brott, artist Stanley Lewis, sociologist Lionel Tiger, actor William Shatner, and, most especially, such literary luminaries as poets Irving Layton, A. M. Klein, and Leonard Cohen (Westmounter by birth, Plateau Mont-Royal resident by choice).

Certainly the funniest voice from the streets belongs to Mordecai Richler, whose stinging satires—*Son of a Smaller Hero, The Apprenticeship of Duddy Kravitz, St. Urbain's Horseman, Joshua Then and Now*—have become indelibly linked to the Jewish quarter. Remnants of Duddy's world remain: Richler's boyhood home at 5257 St-Urbain; Wilensky's Light Lunch (established in 1931) on the corner of Clark and Fairmount; the rococo Rialto Cinema on Parc, where Duddy and his pals ogled the cupids and nymphs in diaphanous robes—painted on the ceiling in 1920 by Emmanuel Briffa; the Fairmount Bagel Factory on Fairmount, of course, and its arch-rival the Bagel Shop on St-Viateur. (Montreal bagels are lighter, thinner, and believed by residents to be far superior in taste to their more celebrated New York cousins.)

North of Sherbrooke, the Main has taken on another character in recent years. Yes, there are still the delis, luncheonettes, and cheap but hearty restaurants, junk stores, wholesalers, and clothing stores that have proved a boon to many a bargain hunter or impoverished soul throughout the Main's history. But they have been joined by fashionable boutiques featuring clothes, jewelry and accessories by Québeçois and avant-garde designers (one of international superstars Harry Parnass and Nicola Pelly's Parachute boutiques is here). And every day seems to herald the arrival of yet another bistro, café, bar, night-club, bookstore, or gallery representing the latest wave of "immigrants" to the area—up-and-coming artists and en-trepreneurial gentrifiers.

The Main north of Prince Arthur, once solidly Jewish, is now an olio of more Greek restaurants, Jewish tailors, Portuguese bakeries, German meat markets, and Hungar-ian social clubs. The Banque Laurentienne at avenue des Pins has window signs in French, English, Spanish, Portu-guese, Italian, Greek, Ukrainian, and Hebrew. Just east of the Main at Dellixo Waldman fish market on rue Roy, a Montreal institution since 1928, restaurateurs and wealthy matrons trade elbowing infractions with Vietnamese and Moroccan shoppers to get at Gaspé salmon, red snapper, live lobster, and octopus. Farther north, sidestreets like Duluth, Rachel, Mont-Royal, and Laurier have also been gentrified with fern-hung *brocheteries,* bars, and bou-tiques. This has been wrought by *la petite bourgeoisie décapant*—the paint-stripping, middle-class progeny of immigrants who hoisted themselves into upscale neigh-borhoods after World War II (much to the dismay of longtime, low-income residents).

Still farther north on St-Laurent, up around rue Lau-rier, is one of Montreal's hottest new neighborhoods, where run-down storefronts have been stripped, sand-blasted, and renovated beyond Duddy's recognition into industrial-chic clothing stores and nouvelle restaurants. The needle trade has been augmented (but not sup-planted) by designer boutiques like Le Château and Robert Krief; bagels have yielded to sophisticated bean-eries like Berlin, Prego, Chez Better, and Lux.

The most influential institution on the Main (at the cor-ner of rue Napoléon) remains the humble Montreal He-brew Delicatessen (established in 1927), usually called Schwartz's after its original owners, Maurice and Reuben Schwartz. A single, narrow room with ancient waiters, For-mica tables, and what may be original decor, Schwartz's is famed far and wide for its Montreal smoked meat, the tender, aromatic result of a secret Romanian recipe.

Like Swann contemplating a *madeleine,* far-flung ex-Montrealers of all ethnic persuasions become misty-eyed just thinking about Schwartz's smoked-meat sandwiches, which seem to embody all their longings for and associations with the old hometown. Emotions intensified by the imagined injustice of their economic exile at the hands of the *séparatistes,* they sit over drinks at the roof bar of the Park Plaza Hotel in Toronto and similar watering holes in Calgary, Vancouver, and Miami, and itemize a sentimental list of what they've left behind: the Montreal Canadiens, the mountain, the bars along Crescent, the Expos, the Ritz-Carlton's garden restaurant, the clubs of Vieux-Montréal, Montreal bagels, "and this little hole in the wall on the Main where you can get the best smoked meat in the world. . . ."

Other Attractions

Parc Olympique. One of the world's most ambitious, controversial, and expensive sports complexes, the facilities for the two-week 1976 Summer Olympics cost an absurd $1-billion-plus to build. Surrounded by sterile, futuristic concrete plazas, the seven-story Olympic Stadium resembles a vast, ribbed mollusk. It is the home of the Expos, as well as the site of Pope John Paul II's last Montreal pilgrimage. A 37-story mast inclining over the stadium houses a bright orange retractable roof; At the base of the mast are the Olympic pool and diving area while a nearby low-slung trilobite houses the Vélodrome cycling track. Guided tours in French and English are interesting but fail to explain where all the money went. The latest attraction here is the mast's funicular cable car, which rockets visitors to the tower's observation deck in seconds flat, and offers a spectacular view of Montreal, the St. Lawrence River, and the South Shore. The Parc is located at the corner of boulevard Pie-IX and Sherbrooke Est.

Situated near the Olympic site in Parc Maisonneuve, but light-years away in spirit, Montreal's highly rated **botanical gardens** are the third largest in the world (after those in Berlin and London). More than two million people a year admire the flowers and other plants that flourish in ten interconnected greenhouses and 30 outdoor gardens. The gardens' star attraction is the largest bonsai collection outside Asia. Visitors enter the peaceful bonsai greenhouse through a moon gate, symbol of perfection and fertility. A recent addition is a Japanese tea ceremony pavilion, where even more elaborate Japanese gardens proliferate. A highlight is the daily enactment of the Japanese tea brewing and drinking ritual. For a foreign encounter of another kind, the botanical garden's newest addition is the Montreal Insectarium, housing more than 130,000 specimens from 88 countries. A worthwhile minitrain tour provides an overview of the gardens.

Château Dufresne is one of the loveliest small museums in Canada. Housed in a restored Beaux Arts mansion that faces the Olympic complex, this museum of decorative arts features ground-floor period rooms (an Oriental smoking room, a cluttered dining room) furnished in Victorian and Edwardian styles.

The world's largest shrine to Saint Joseph, Canada's patron saint, **St. Joseph's Oratory** was the last architectural gasp of monolithic Catholicism in an increasingly secular society. Founded by a lay member of the Congregation of the Holy Cross named Brother André, the oratory evolved from a simple wooden chapel into an internationally known shrine that welcomes more than three million visitors a year—some pious, some merely curious, some racked by disease or deformity, all hoping for help by praying to Brother André and Saint Joseph. The former doorman, who died in 1931, was beatified in 1982 by Pope John Paul II.

The oratory and its grounds cover six acres of landscaped terraces at the western end of Mont Royal in the Côte des Neiges area, near the Université de Montréal. At the head of a 99-step staircase—the central concrete steps are flanked by wooden ones for pilgrims ascending on their knees, a practice not so common as it was 20 or 30 years ago but still seen occasionally—stands the solid, low mass of the Crypt Church.

Looming above is an immense Renaissance-style basilica, begun in 1924 and not finished until 1967. Its great green, copper-sheathed dome is second in size only to St. Peter's in Rome. The oratory is most impressive when a colorful light show illuminates the basilica and the carillon chimes with music produced by bells originally intended for the Eiffel Tower.

The city tried to maintain a permanent exhibition at the Expo 67 site on Ile Notre-Dame and Ile Ste-Hélène in the St. Lawrence River, but lack of funds and commitment led to the deterioration of the pavilions and a drop in attendance. Recently, though, **Terre des Hommes** (Man and His World) has made a comeback, and the islands can provide a pleasant, parklike, warm-weather outing within minutes of downtown. Ferries, including a converted school bus, shuttle an increasing number of visitors from Jacques-Cartier Quai in the Vieux-Port. (Terre des Hommes can also be reached via Jacques Cartier Bridge, and by Metro.)

On **Ile Notre-Dame**, the Palais de la Civilisation, the French pavilion during Expo 67, is host to major art exhibitions (Gold of the Thracian Horsemen in 1987, Cités-Cinés homage to Hollywood in 1989). Concerts, both formal and impromptu, are staged in manicured floral gardens maintained on the island since an international flower show in 1980. The Olympic rowing basin does duty in winter as a skating rink and every June the Gilles-Villeneuve Race Track hosts the Grand Prix Molson du Canada.

Ile Ste-Hélène, which Champlain named for the patron saint of his 12-year-old bride, is home to La Ronde amusement park—Coney Island by the river. Nearby, L'Aquaparc's 20 water slides are great fun on a hot summer day, but only the truly brave attempt the near-vertical chute. The Montreal Aquarium is small, but don't overlook the 20,000-gallon coral-reef tank with its brilliantly colored tropical fish.

At the **David M. Stewart Museum** on the Ile Ste-Hélène, students dressed in 18th-century uniforms and representing members of Fraser Highlanders and Compagnie Franche de la Marine drill within the stone walls of an 1824 fort. But Canadiana is not all this museum presents, though it has an impressive permanent collection. It is the venue for exhibitions exploring the history and culture of many of the world's great civilizations, arts, and artifacts. In 1990 the museum will collaborate with Montreal's Jewish Public Library—the only one in North America with extensive and priceless archives and collections of Judaica, Hebrew, and Yiddish documents and artifacts—to mount "Hebraica Scientifica: Six Centuries of Hebrew Scientific Writings." Culled from the Library's own collection as well as from international private and public collections, this exhibition celebrating the Library's 75th anniversary will also feature an 18th-century gentleman's library. Artifacts from the Museum's own collections will animate the mathematical, astronomical, astrological, palmistry, calendation, geographical, travel, and navigational documents from all places and periods of Hebrew printing. A special highlight will be a fragment of the Dead Sea Scrolls.

Just two blocks west of Victoria and the Metro Côte Ste-Catherine station is the nationally renowned **Saidye**

Bronfman Centre, long recognized as a central force of cultural activity within the Jewish community, in particular, and Montreal as a whole. Accessible by car (just one block east of the Decarie Expressway, four blocks north of Queen Mary Road), the Centre is open year-round, with many of its activities free to the public. In particular, the Centre's gallery is recognized in national and international art circles for the excellence of its contemporary art exhibitions. It is also home to the Yiddish Theatre group, the only permanent Yiddish company performing today in North America.

GETTING AROUND

Some 60 airlines serve Montreal's two main airports. **Dorval Airport**, on the island and west of downtown, handles flights from North America (including other points in Canada); **Mirabel Airport**, about 65 km (40 miles) northwest of the city, is used for charters and flights arriving from other continents.

A bus service called Aerocar leaves every 20 minutes from Dorval for downtown Montreal, with stops at the Sheraton Centre, Château Champlain, Le Grand Hôtel, and Le Reine Elizabeth Hotel. The final destination is the Voyageur bus terminal at Berri-UQAM, a Metro station. The trip takes about 20 minutes and costs $7. A metered cab from Dorval to downtown is about $20 before tip; private limousines cost slightly more, depending on destination but regardless of the number of passengers. Cab fare from Mirabel is at least $50; Aerocar service to Le Reine Elizabeth Hotel costs $9 one way, and the trip takes about an hour, stopping at the Voyageur bus terminal. Aerocar also runs a shuttle between the two airports.

Visitors travelling by car from the west and east arrive in Montreal via Highway 20 or Highway 40 (via the Trans-Canada Highway). Three major expressways link Montreal with the United States: Interstate 87 in New York, and either 87 or 91 in Vermont. Buses from Quebec City and the United States—Voyageur, Voyageur-Colonial, and Greyhound—arrive at the centrally located Voyageur terminal.

Both VIA Rail Canada and Amtrak from the United States arrive in downtown Montreal at **Gare Centrale** Central Station, at the south side of Le Reine Elizabeth Hotel facing Place Bonaventure on de la Gauchetière, across boulevard René Lévesque from Place Ville-Marie.

The station is also connected to the Metro via the Bonaventure Station.

Montreal's bus and subway systems are, for the most part, clean, safe, and efficient. Each Metro station is decorated differently with specially commissioned murals, ceramics, and stained glass and there are five lines connecting 65 stations. The Metro runs from 5:30 A.M. to 12:30 A.M. (except for the Blue Line, which stops at 11:00 P.M.). The fare for bus and subway is $1.05 for any length trip (exact change is required for buses). Passengers can transfer between bus and Metro at no extra charge.

Car rental is expensive, with occasional discounting on weekend rates. Most companies charge for mileage. Try Tilden Rent-a-Car (Tel: 878-2771) or Budget (Tel: 937-9121).

The major sight-seeing bus-tour companies are Gray Line of Montreal (Tel: 280-5327) and Murray Hill (Tel: 937-5311). Save Montreal (Tel: 282-2069), an architectural conservationist group, and les Montréalistes (Tel: 744–3009), a tour company, organize daily bus and walking tours through many neighborhoods. Guidatour (Tel: 844-4021) provides licensed guides and escort services for traditional and specialized tours for individuals and groups around the city and surrounding areas in several languages.

Calèches offer rides year round from starting points at Square Dorchester and on Mont Royal. *Calèches* can also be hailed in Vieux-Montréal around Place Jacques-Cartier and Place d'Armes, and on Bonsecours, Gosford, and de la Commune streets. The hourly cost is about $30.

Montreal Harbor Cruises (Tel: 842-3871) operates three vessels and offers a variety of tours of the St. Lawrence River from early May to mid-October. **Lachine Rapids Tours** (Tel: 284-9607) offers jet-boat excursions through the Lachine Rapids.

Montreal's seasonal events include the Benson & Hedges International Fireworks Competition, with spectacular shows presented by entrants from a dozen countries. Some six million people watch the kaleidoscopic aerial productions during several weeks in June. The same month brings the outstanding **International Jazz Festival**, with 1,000 musicians from 15 countries participating in a ten-day series of indoor and outdoor shows. Also in June is the **Tour de l'Île de Montréal** amateur cycling event. Now in its fifth year, the event attracts over

30,000 cycling enthusiasts of all ages. Starting at the Vélodrome in Parc Olympique, cyclists follow a course that takes them along most of the major streets throughout the island of Montreal. Another event this month is the **Juste Pour Rire** comedy festival.

The **World Film Festival** in August, arguably the best in North America, screens hundreds of international films at venues all over town. Attendance at this tremendously popular event now tops a quarter of a million.

ACCOMMODATIONS

Montreal underwent hotel construction booms prior to Expo 67 and the 1976 Summer Olympics. Several hotels that date from those special events have undergone much-needed face-lifts to enable them to keep up with the cutthroat competition in a crowded market. Despite overcapacity, prices remain high, even with a reasonable Canadian dollar (worth about $0.83 U.S.) and the repeal of a provincial room tax. Many large downtown hotels, including Hôtel Méridien and Le Shangrila, which rely on Monday–Thursday business clientele, offer greatly reduced weekend rates to keep rooms filled. Even the elegant Ritz-Carlton promotes weekend deals. Travellers may have to stay a minimum of two nights, but often included are such incentives as a welcoming cocktail, Continental breakfast, or a free city tour.

These accommodations in downtown Montreal have been selected for their location, service, amenities, and value for money. (The telephone area code for Montreal is 514.)

Le Baccarat. Less expensive than big downtown luxury hotels, this establishment just east of the McGill University campus is popular with bus-tour groups. Completely renovated in 1988, it now boasts a spa with whirlpool, sauna, and exercise machines. The lobby has been spiffed up, as has the hotel's restaurant, which now has lots of brass and marble Italianate-style. Bay windows overlook Sherbrooke, and there's a summer terrace for outdoor dining.

475 rue Sherbrooke Ouest, Montreal, Quebec H3A 2L9. Tel: 842-3961 or (800) 361-4973; Telex: 055 61216.

Bonaventure Hilton International. The Bonaventure has the most unusual location of the midtown luxury hotels: the top six floors of Place Bonaventure (west of Square Victoria and just south of the city's business center), a massive, six-acre building housing retail shops, offices, and a vast exhibition hall. The hotel has 400 rooms distributed around an inner courtyard. Guests stroll through a rooftop Japanese garden and swim year-round in the heated outdoor pool. The attempt to create privacy and quiet seclusion has been so successful that surrounding skyscrapers are the only reminders that these lodgings are in the heart of a metropolis. Its **Le Castillon** restaurant has been widely acclaimed for its excellent French cuisine.

1 Place Bonaventure, Montreal, Quebec H5A 1E4. Tel: 878-2332; in Canada, (800) 455-8667; in U.S., (800) 268-9275.

Le Centre Sheraton. Elegantly understated appointments and an excellent restaurant are the hallmarks of this expensive hotel, located near Gare Centrale and west of Square Dorchester. One end of the lobby is a plant-filled atrium, with cocktails served at tables tucked amid the plants and palms. Executive suites are on the top five floors—the popular "hotel within a hotel" concept for pampered guests and entertainment celebrities.

1201 boulevard René Lévesque Ouest, Montreal, Quebec H3B 2L7. Tel: 878-2000 or (800) 325-3535.

Château Champlain. This Canadian Pacific hotel, just across the street from the corporation's historic sandstone downtown headquarters, is a 38-story luxury property whose arched windows make the structure look like a giant cheese grater. The Bar Gauguin on the 36th floor has outstanding views of midtown and Mont Royal in the distance. According to some reports, the window in the women's washroom of the bar presents the best panorama of downtown and the mountain.

1 Place du Canada, Montreal, Quebec H3B 4C9. Tel: 878-9000; in Canada, (800) 828-7477; in U.S., (800) 269-9411.

Hôtel La Citadelle. A Quality Inn hotel just east of the McGill campus, La Citadelle has been done over as a European-style hotel, heavy on the marble and burgundy and mauve decor. The staff is friendly and efficient; the jazz piano lounge is as comfortable as a living room. **Le Châtelet Restaurant** offers French cuisine. Large double rooms, about 20 percent less than they would be in midtown luxury hotels, are popular with business travellers. Ask for a north-facing room for wonderful views of Mont Royal.

410 rue Sherbrooke Ouest, Montreal, Quebec H3A 1B3. Tel: 844-8851 or, in Canada, (800) 361-1616; in New England, (800) 361-7545.

Hôtel Delta Montréal. One of Montreal's newest hotels, the French-style Delta is a best buy in an excellent midtown location east of McGill, near La Citadelle and Le Baccarat. Due to special low rates, rooms cost one-third less than those in the Ritz-Carlton and Le Quatre Saisons. A fireplace warms the lobby, and most rooms have balconies. Other amenities include a business center, day-care services, and a health club with indoor and outdoor pools. Mesquite-grilled meat and fish are the house specialties at Delta's **Le Bouquet,** one of the city's most attractive hotel dining rooms. There is also jazz nightly in the hotel's bar, which attracts many Montreal fans. Guests are greeted by a doorman in breeches, waistcoat, and tricorne hat, although the reasons for the colonial American costume are not readily apparent.

450 rue Sherbrooke Ouest, Montreal, Quebec H3A 2T4. Tel: 286-1986 or, in Canada and the U.S., (800) 268-1133.

Le Grand Hôtel. The location is not promising: The serrated V-shaped building on the south side of Place Victoria is just north of expressway ramps and east of elevated train tracks. Still, after extensive renovations, the former Hyatt Regency is glassy elegance in isolation, with windowed elevators, the city's only revolving rooftop restaurant, pool, and atrium lobby. The new **Chez Antoine** bistro, decked out in Art Nouveau–style, is known for its grilled meat specialities and its hot jazz. This pricey hotel is adjacent to the Bourse de Montréal and within walking distance of Vieux-Montréal.

777 rue University, Montreal, Quebec H3C 3Z7. Tel: 879-1370 or, in Canada, (800) 361-8155.

Hôtel Château Versailles. Montreal's most charming European-style hotel inspires Bermudian loyalty: Guests keep coming back and wouldn't think of staying anywhere else. To construct the hotel, which is just west of where chemin de la Côte des Neiges descends into Sherbrooke and becomes rue Guy, French-born André Villeneuve and his Canadian wife, Marie-Louise, connected four gray-stone mansions built between 1911 and 1913, restored plaster moldings and fireplaces, and scoured the province for antique furnishings. The rooms are simple, clean, and functional. Some overlook a courtyard garden. The service is courteous and professional. There is no bar, and only breakfast is served in the 12-table dining room, although afternoon tea is available from room service. A ten-minute walk away, though, are the boutiques, bars, and restaurants of Bishop, Crescent, and de la Montagne streets.

1659 rue Sherbrooke Ouest, Montreal, Quebec H3H 1E3. Tel: 933-3611 or, in Canada, (800) 361-7199; in the U.S., (800) 361-3664.

Hôtel de la Montagne. One of Montreal's smaller hotels, the de la Montagne is favored by affluent business and pleasure travellers in their 30s and 40s who frequent places like the Morgan in Manhattan. The hotel is right in the downtown street scene. Owner Bernard Ragueneau manages the lodgings, restaurants, bars, and discotheque. The foyer is nearly overwhelmed by a rococo fountain, but the bar is intimate, with a jazz duo of piano and double bass. Other amenities include a rooftop summer pool (with open-air restaurant and bar), connection to the disco one flight down from the lobby, and access to the back of one of Crescent's busiest singles bars by the same route.

1430 rue de la Montagne, Montreal, Quebec H3G 1Z5. Tel: 288-5656 or (800) 361-6262.

Le Hôtel Méridien. Another luxury hotel in an unusual location, Air France's Méridien anchors one corner of Complexe Desjardins, a multilevel glassed-in plaza bounded by three office towers and the hotel, a vast and dynamic space. The hotel's **Café Fleuris** is one of the city's best, and so are the swimming pool, sundeck, and garden terrace. The Méridien is slightly away from downtown, but it is convenient via all-weather corridors to Place des Arts, Chinatown, and the convention center. Vieux-Montréal is a short, above-ground walk away. The hotel is popular with movie people during the August film festival. In recent years, it has also become the official headquarters for musicians and organizers of the Montreal International Jazz Festival, with many concerts taking place on its outdoor terraces.

4 Complexe Desjardins, C.P. 130, Montreal, Quebec H5B 1E5. Tel: 285-1450 or, in Canada, (800) 543-4300.

L'Hôtel Ritz-Carlton. The grande dame of Montreal hotels, the Ritz has been dispensing Old World hospitality to silver-haired tycoons and svelte beauties since 1912. Guests have included Mary Pickford and Douglas Fairbanks, Edward VIII and Queen Marie of Rumania, and Dick and Liz, who were married here in 1964—again. It is also Prime Minister Brian Mulroney's favorite hotel when he is in town. Designed by Stanford White, the Ritz encapsulates this starchy stretch of rue Sherbrooke: elegance and grace, wealth and power, understatement and tradition, and, occasionally, stuffy pretension. Jackets and ties are mandatory for men, even at the **Café de Paris** bar (portly maître d' John Dominique once denied entrance to a jeans-clad Mick Jagger). *The* hotel for Montreal's power brokers and socialites, its outdoor garden terrace with a duck pond is a favorite power-breakfast and brunch spot in summer. Executive chef Jean Saliou is a regular member of Canada's medal-winning team that competes at the World Culinary Olympics in Frankfurt. When booking, ask for a room facing Mont Royal.

1228 rue Sherbrooke Ouest, Montreal, Quebec H3G 1H6. Tel: 842-4212 or, through the Inter-Continental Hotels reservation service, (800) 327-0200 or (800) 223-9868.

Lord Berri. This no-frills establishment south of boulevard René Lévesque in the Latin quartier offers moderate prices and adequate rooms with simple furnishings. There is no bellman or room service, only a café-bistro. Minibars and non-smoking floors are also featured.

1199 rue Berri, Montreal, Quebec H2L 4C6. Tel: 845-9236 or (800) 363-0363.

Le Quatre Saisons. The best (the hotel has racked up several awards recently)—and most expensive—of Montreal's modern hotels is a favorite with international expense-account executives. The large rooms in the 31-story tower at rue Peel, at the southern end of the Golden Square Mile, are attractively furnished with Georgian-style writing desks and decorated with pastel chintz. Facilities include a Gymtech health club and a year-round outdoor heated pool. The ground-floor piano lounge is restful. The hotel's attractive dining room, **Pierre de Coubertin**, has an outstanding wine cellar.

1050 rue Sherbrooke Ouest, Montreal, Quebec H3A 2R6. Tel: 284-1110 or (800) 332-3422.

Le Reine Elizabeth. The city's largest midtown luxury hotel, a monotonous concrete slab atop Gare Centrale and opposite Place Ville-Marie, recently underwent a badly needed renovation. The result is a much brighter and more welcoming lobby and rooms that are modern and spacious. There is also an executive floor, which is even more elegant and features office services. Some old favorites are also still compelling, like the **Beaver Club**, the domain of chef Edouard Mirard, a member of the Académie Culinaire de France. The restaurant, which is the only one in town to list cigars on its menu, is named for a 19th-century fraternity of fur-trade barons that counted New Yorker John Jacob Astor as an honorary member. There's also a new bistro, **Le Montrealais**, that offers Continental cuisine. Tour groups and local conventions are mainstays of the hotel, which has a convenient downtown location with connections to the Metro.

900 boulevard René Lévesque Ouest, Montreal, Quebec H3B 4A5. Tel: 861-3511.

Le Shangrila. An establishment with a Hong Kong owner, Le Shangrila has a central location at Sherbrooke near the McGill campus, and excellent weekend rates. Every floor of this refurbished hostelry has a distinct theme from Asian folklore; the doorman sports a six-piece blue Mongolian warrior's suit with silver bangles. There is a Continental-style restaurant, a piano bar, and a Korean dining room in which each table is equipped with its own grill: The chef prepares the raw ingredients, and the guest cooks them. For those tired of eggs Benedict and mimosas, try the hotel's Sunday buffet brunch in **Le Jardinier Restaurant**. The offerings include sushi, sashimi, and stir-fried Napoleon chicken, as well as more predictable North American fare.

3407 rue Peel, Montreal, Quebec H3A 1W7. Tel: 288-4141 or (800) 361-7791.

—David Dunbar and Mary Kelly

DINING

Montreal loves to eat and party. There are more than 5,000 restaurants to choose from that offer dozens of cuisines—the city rivals New York as the gastronomic capital of the continent. We've selected just *some* of the good ones—or most interesting ones. In a predominantly French-speaking city, it is French cuisine that dominates. But Montrealers seem to be obsessed with Italian, Chinese, Japanese, and Indian as well. Then there are the cuisines of the many other nations the city's residents hail from.

Montrealers generally eat late, though not as late as people in Spain. Peak dining time is 8:00 P.M. Unless you have a reservation, try to arrive for dinner at 7:00 P.M. or 9:30 P.M. to ensure a table. At lunch, if you're not in at a popular spot by 12:15 don't bother going until 2:00 P.M.. This is the city with the highest percentage of two-hour lunches in the country.

Montrealers also stay out late, irrespective of the day of the week. Bars in the province of Quebec can serve liquor up to 3:00 A.M. seven days a week. On most nights, they finally close at 4:00 A.M.

Lunch is always a bargain. All restaurants offer three-course meals at low, prix fixe rates. This means that you can lunch at expensive restaurants for a quarter to half of what it might cost at night. And remember that provincial law requires all restaurants to post their menus outside.

Liquor and wine are heavily taxed in Quebec, and markups are high in restaurants and bars. A premium cognac in a bar can cost you $5 CDN and up. A good bottle of wine is rarely below $25 in a restaurant, although you can find acceptable table wines in the $15 to $20 range. A sales tax of ten percent applies to all food and liquor sales. To that, you are expected to add up to 15 percent as a tip.

French and Continental

Bistro Bagatelle. This new bistro at 4806 avenue du Parc east of Mont Royal is notable for its reasonably priced, quasi-nouvelle French cuisine. There are always five or more kinds of fresh fish on the menu, along with meat, poultry, and veal. Often you can find a fish consommé or a gratin of mussels with crayfish bisque sauce. When available, fresh leg of lamb with garlic confit is terrific. Vegetables, served crisp but in very small quantities, are perfectly cooked.

Boulevards. 3435 boulevard St. Laurent. Mussels and sweetbreads are just two of the many enticing dishes served at this noisy but lively bistro-bar. It's very crowded into the early hours and there are long line-ups on weekends. A good taste of trendy, bilingual Montreal. Tel: 499-9944.

Chez La Mère Michel. If you go to this downtown spot (1209 Guy Street) for lunch, you'll leave with your wallet practically undented—and you're bound to return at dinner to empty it. The French cuisine here is as memorable as the setting: a romantic old stone house with lots of stained glass. The cooks do some pretty impressive things with tournedos, sweetbreads, and lamb, as well as with seafood. Service is courteous, and you must have a drink in the bar downstairs before dinner, if only to admire its coziness.

Citrus. Dinner at Citrus (5282 boulevard St. Laurent) is a blissful immersion in sunny California flavors and aromas married to memorable French cuisine. The distinctive flavors of oranges, limes, clementines, fresh herbs, and flowers permeate the nouvelle, inventive cooking.

Everything in the market-oriented menu is beguiling. Some suggestions: spinach fettucine and scallops in a grapefruit and basil butter, grilled loin of lamb with truffles and goat cheese, or a mille-feuille of sweetbreads and lobster in an orange and Port sauce. Tel: 276-2353.

La Marée. Step back 100 years or more in this romantic 18th-century gray stone in Vieux-Montréal that specializes in fresh fish and seafood, some with exquisite sauces. Try a pâté of turbot or fresh halibut in a lobster cream sauce. The fish are all flown in fresh from France. 404 Place Jacques-Cartier; Tel: 861-9794.

Laloux. Another in a new generation of French bistros, this one, a block from carré St. Louis at 250 Pine Avenue East, is rather austere and less lively than its rivals. The cuisine has definite nouvelle touches, with a hint of California. Ginger, sesame, and lemon are some of the the innovative flavorings. Try the crab bisque or any of the fish dishes; Tel: 287-9127.

La Rapiere. A venerable downtown institution where they believe sculpted vegetables belong in a museum; the cuisine is hearty and bourgeois French. Old World service (spotless linen, full-size heavy cutlery, warmed plates) complements dishes such as boudin noir (black or blood pudding), veal liver, and fresh fish. 1490 Stanley Street.

Le Castillon. On the 17th floor of the massive Place Bonaventure complex and part of the downtown Hilton, this roof-garden restaurant comes complete with lush vegetation, flowing water, and ducklings. The ducklings disappear in winter, but the garden stays. Indoors, the decor is somewhat imperial with plush chairs. Best bets here are the seasonal specials. Tel: 878-2332.

L'Express. Lines are the norm at this most popular of Montreal bistros at 3927 rue St-Denis. The ambience— noisy conversations, much flailing of arms—competes with reasonably priced bistro fare. Portions are hearty; try the soups or steak tartare. Call 24 hours in advance for reservations; Tel: 845-5333.

Le St. Amable. In this romantic and expensive Vieux-Montréal haunt (188 St-Amable), classic versions of kidneys, sweetbreads, and sole are served. Try to eat downstairs; it's ultra cozy and transports you to an old-fashioned time. Tel: 866-3471.

Le Tricolore. The menu in this warm basement restaurant (downtown at 2065 rue Bishop) is small but enticing. The chef-owner always uses fresh fish; an extremely generous fillet of fresh Atlantic salmon, exquisitely light and tender, might be served in a flawless sauce of white shallot butter and tingly pink peppercorns. Other delicious dishes have been a mousseline of rabbit followed by veal with foie gras. Prices are very reasonable, particularly for the five-course *table d'hôte*.

The decor is homey—a large, antique armoire dominates one wall; a grandfather clock hugs another wall near the entrance; there are fresh flowers on linen-covered tables; the chairs are highbacked and comfy. Add soft classical music and subdued lighting, and you could be sitting in your own dining room.

For dessert try poire royale—a decadent offering of a poached pear, ice cream, a liqueur, strawberry purée, and English cream. Tel: 843-7745.

Les Halles. In the heart of the rue Crescent bar-and-boutique jungle downtown, this is one of the best French restaurants in Montreal.

Ambience in the lower of its two floors is that of an upscale Parisian bistro. If you'd rather avoid the noise and bustle downstairs, book upstairs in the romantic dining room. The menu frequently offers specials and is always innovative. If you're up for a big splurge, ask for a dinner planned by the chef. From the regular menu, try quail mousse or tart of duck, veal, and foie gras flavored with truffle juices, rosemary, Port, and Cognac. Or try any of the fish dishes, and, if you have a taste for them, calf sweetbreads. 1450 rue Crescent; Tel: 844-2328.

Les Mignardises. Muted decor and an intriguing menu distinguish this highly nouvelle and very expensive French restaurant at 2035 rue St-Denis. You'll swoon over the lobster soup and marvel at the artistry of dishes like salad of scallops and turbot in a pimento sauce. Tel: 842-1151.

Partz. This innocuously situated restaurant is easy to miss on rue Stanley. People who do find it, at number 1422, are rewarded with innovative French cuisine. Tables are comfortably spaced, and the decor—soothing shades of brown—quickly makes you forget its basement location.

Sauces are simple and delicate, and there is a constantly changing list of daily seasonal specials based on what's fresh in the market. Thus, you might find white asparagus flown in from France or fresh girolle mushrooms. It's almost worth ignoring the regular menu for the daily specials, but try their eggs scrambled to creamy perfection with Roquefort cheese, slices of duck breast, pears, and green ginger. Tel: 842-6515.

Ritz Garden. The perfect place for relaxed afternoon tea or a leisurely dinner in summer is here at the luxurious Ritz-Carlton Hotel at 1228 Sherbrooke Ouest. You'll pay for it but won't regret the setting—ducklings on a pond, lush lawns, and umbrellas. Splurge on caviar or lobster, sole or smoked salmon. Altogether, very decadent and memorable. Tel: 842-4212.

Seafood

Chez Delmo. Not much has changed in the last 25 years in this Vieux-Montréal fish restaurant. Two long, polished-wood oyster bars line a pathway to a modest dining room where longtime waitresses politely and competently serve an unchanging menu of fish and seafood.

In season, Chez Delmo has the best raw oysters in town, and it's usually more fun to sit at the long bars than in the simple dining room. Order the fresh fish of the day, and skip any sauces that might be suggested with it unless you like old-fashioned, heavier sauces—the fish here is best just grilled or sautéed. 211 Notre Dame Ouest; Tel: 849-4061.

Etoile d'Ocean. An unpretentious entrance at 101 rue Rachel Est leads to a large, cozy dining room connected by a short passage at the back to a bar next door. Blue-and-white ceramic tiles with Moorish motifs, dark wood beams, a ceiling of red roof tiles, Algarve pottery, fishing nets, and lampshades made from seashells all conspire to transport you to Portugal.

Try clams in coriander sauce, fried squid, or carne Alentejano, a traditional dish from Alentejo province that consists of generous cubes of succulent fried pork tossed with clams in their shells and served in a tomato, garlic, and fresh coriander sauce.

French-Canadian

Les Filles du Roi. A must for first-time visitors if only to sample traditional *tourtière*—French-Canadian meat pie—and to be served by waitresses in authentic early Quebec dresses. The Vieux-Montréal setting (415 Bonsecours Street) has thick stone walls, spinning wheels, and antique pine. Other traditional favorites here are *cipaille* (a kind of layered pie with assorted meats that can include chicken, pork, veal, elk, and hare), and maple-syrup pie. The menu also features steaks and seafood, which, like the traditional dishes, are not as appealing as the ambience. There is a no smoking section. Tel: 849-3535.

Italian

Baci. The setting is ultramodern in this multilevel Italian restaurant downtown. There's a variety of seating choices, from the lush conservatory near the front to the cozy, sunken dining rooms. Some of the best Italian food in Montreal can be found here. Sauces for pasta are creative, and classical dishes like risotto are executed with finesse. The fish and veal dishes are good too. 2095 McGill College Avenue; Tel: 284-7901.

Bocca d'Oro. Superbly designed and decorated, this downtown Italian restaurant (1448 rue St-Mathieu) has an excellent kitchen. Its daily fresh arrivals, announced by the waiters, are your best bet. Try a plate of pasta with three different sauces. Tel: 933-8414.

Il Gentile Rico. This is a discreet little place that tends to be overlooked on the rejuvenated strip of boulevard St-Laurent. The cuisine is not in the award-winning bracket, but it is good value for the money. Add friendly, prompt service, pleasant, unobtrusive decor, and comfortable seating and it's all very satisfying.

Cream, garlic, parsley, and easy on the tomatoes seem to be the formula here, creating an effect that's perhaps more French than Italian in some dishes. Try the homemade spinach-and-ricotta cannelloni, served in a cream-rich sauce of white wine, tomatoes, and parsley that'll stick to your ribs. Shrimp and veal are also good here. 5308 boulevard St-Laurent.

La Sila. One of the best Italian restaurants in town, La Sila is in the heart of the Latin Quarter at 2040 rue St-Denis. Veal and homemade pastas are excellent here; the secret is homegrown herbs used fresh. Cream, tomato, and basil are used with great imagination. The scampi cardinale is worth the splurge—ten plump devils sautéed with Cognac and served in a rich cream sauce. It's the sort of place where they only turn over the tables once a night, so reserve and plan on a long, leisurely dinner. Tel: 844-5083.

Café Modigliani. Paintings by the owner and discarded props from plays dominate the decor at this eclectic

Italian hideaway on the Plateau Mont-Royal. Cozy, café-spaced tables are separated by plants.

Ledges along the front glass walls sport angled mirrors, birdcages, and cactuses. On weekends, jammed into a small corner, a piano player entertains diners with soft jazz. It's a totally relaxed, unhurried restaurant. Stay one or ten hours, the owners don't mind. The cooking is home-style. Pastas and veal are the norm in predictable, unpretentious sauces, but the food is reasonably priced and satisfying. 1251 Gilford.

Pizzeria Napoletana. Known mostly for its superb pizzas, this crowded family-operated restaurant in the Little Italy district of the city also serves outstanding made-on-the-premises gnocchi, tortellini, cannelloni, and lasagna.

The fettucine and spaghetti are the dried, packaged kind but served to order and properly *al dente*. The home-style sauces used with the pizzas and pasta immerse you in the lusty pleasures of Southern Italian cooking: ripe tomatoes, garlic, olive oil, onions, oregano, basil, and sharp peppers. Be prepared for lines at supper time, especially on weekends. And don't forget to bring your own wine. 189 Dante Street; no credit cards, no reservations.

Trois Marie. The floors have two-tone beige-and-brown tiles. The walls have white tiles with an orange motif, though not all the way up to the ceiling. Add chrome-and-black stacking chairs, checked tablecloths, Mevon No. 11 industrial hand cleanser in the washrooms, and you have one of the best places in town for home-style Southern Italian cooking. Three motherly women run the kitchen at this Little Italy restaurant much the same way they would at home—with affection, authority, and an uncompromising attachment to routine.

Most of the goodies go by the day of the week. On Mondays, you're guaranteed cotoletta (veal cutlet) Parmigiana or Milanese, roast beef, and spezzatino (veal). Thursdays, it's chicken cacciatore and tripe among five specials. Fridays, there's sole, cod, and clam sauce, in keeping with the former Roman-Catholic tradition of no meat on this day. And so on.

The regular menu is short but holds such favorites as spaghetti with oil and garlic. A mound of pasta arrives bathed in olive oil and garlic; *slices* of the latter, singed golden, decorate the top—no skimping on garlic here. 6934 Clark Street; no credit cards. Tel: 277-9859.

Villa Orlando. Don't be daunted by the suburban location of this Italian restaurant—there are handsome rewards waiting at the end of the 20-minute drive or cab ride from downtown. (Call for directions.) The Calabrese chef is a wizard with pasta sauces, traditional as well as innovative. His veal and fish dishes are made from market-fresh ingredients and his longtime buddy and maitre d' ensures attentive service in a comfortable environment. Tel: 634-9219.

Hispanic

Fiesta Tapas. The menu of Spanish snack-size dishes changes weekly but there's generally a good assortment of fish, mushroom, potato, squid, quail, shrimp, and sausage dishes. Graze on a few to make your meal or gorge on the paella for two. In Vieux-Montréal. Tel: 287-7482.

La Hacienda. Soft Mariachi music, a terrace, tropical colors, and arches all add to the illusion that you're in sunny Mexico at La Hacienda. It's the closest thing Montreal has to a true Mexican restaurant, as opposed to TexMex or CalMex or—dare we say it—CanMex. La Hacienda makes liberal use of cilantro (fresh coriander) in dishes that feature fresh ingredients. There's a good selection of meat and chicken dishes and several kinds of burritos and enchiladas. 1148 Van Horne Avenue. Open for dinner only; Tel: 270-3043.

La Selva. You can bring your own wine to this Peruvian restaurant on the Plateau Mont-Royal. The small menu is dominated by fish and shrimp, but a few meat dishes are also offered, notably cubed heart of beef. It's a small place, but pretty, with huge glass windows offering interesting glimpses of city life. The portions are generous. Try chupe de camarones, a rich and filling soup of cream, tomatoes, corn, and six medium-size fresh shrimp. Or the aforementioned heart—served en brochette. If you haven't tried beef heart, it tastes like a cross between liver and kidney. 862 Marie-Anne. Open for dinner only; Tel: 525-1798.

Le Pavillon Espagnol. Try the paellas and garlic chicken at this long-established, cozy Spanish restaurant on the Plateau Mont-Royal (127 Mont Royal Ouest). Good, grilled fresh sardines and chorizo (sausage) are available, and it also has a separate bar section with a snack menu. Tel: 843-8088.

Pappacitos. The menu is as straightforward as the trappings—self-service trays and disposable dishes—but there is a lot of love in the popular Mexican food cooked here. Dollar for cheap dollar this weekday (7:00 A.M. to 5:00 P.M.) breakfast and lunch restaurant in the Bell Canada building downtown offers superlative value and quality. The cheese used with burritos, for example, is genuine Monterey Jack. The coriander is fresh and the spicing authentic and honest. And when they ask if you want a medium hot salsa or the "dangerous stuff" they're not kidding about the latter. Be warned.

Greek

Faros. Everything is tops at this Greek psarotaverna off avenue du Parc—from fresh fish to the pikilia. Service is polished, and the decor comfortable. Don't miss the soft-shell crabs, if they have them; they're memorable, as is the grilled octopus. 362 Fairmount Ouest; Tel: 270-8437.

  Milos. Quite simply the best (and most expensive) Greek psarotaverna in town. If you can, go here for lunch; it's far less crowded then, and the service less harried. Whatever time you go, you'll have a perplexing choice of the freshest of fish flown in from all corners of the world. It's prepared the traditional Greek-islands way—a whole fish grilled on charcoal, served boned, with a brushing of olive oil and oregano. For the big splurge, try truly jumbo shrimp in garlic, or lobster. 5357 avenue du Parc; Tel: 272-3522.

  Molivos. A cheerful, comfortable Greek fish restaurant at 4859 avenue du Parc, a street that has the best of this species of Greek restaurant, with blue and white accents on everything from tablecloths to walls, as well as fishing nets, photos and paintings of Greek islands, fresh fish, and friendly service.

  The Molivos menu is compact and simple. A selection of pikilia—hot or cold hors d'oeuvres that include tzatziki and tarama—is offered. Octopus, squid, and shrimp are offered, or you can choose from a basket of fresh fish brought to your table. You can't go wrong—everything is good here; Tel: 271-5354.

Middle Eastern

Daou. One of the best Lebanese restaurants in the city, Daou has a service staff that leaves a lot to be desired. If you can cope with indifference and confusion that is occasionally tempered by friendliness, you'll enjoy top-quality, home-style Middle Eastern dishes in a simple, unpretentious north-end setting. These include kababs and kibbehs; tabbouleh; baba ghannouj; falafel; and meat, spinach, and thyme pies. 519 Faillon Est; Tel: 276-8310.

La Medina. The absence of the traditional belly dancer and musicians makes this rue St-Denis establishment an unusually quiet and soothing Moroccan restaurant. Here the music mingles gently with the soothing sound of running water in a mini-fountain, setting the tone for a relaxed sampling of the restaurant's North African Arabic cuisine.

The restaurant is divided into two sections, one with conventional Western tables and chairs, the other with low Moroccan divans and sofas. Delicate brass and glass lamps cast a warm, intimate glow on walls adorned with Moroccan rugs. Antique guns and daggers are displayed in the front (Western) section, while the Moroccan section has a genuine desert chieftain's tent that forms an exotic canopy over the richly brocaded sofas.

Harira soup is outstanding here, a rich, filling creation of chick peas, green lentils, and fresh coriander. If you feel like splurging, go for the couscous royale. This princely offering arrives in a large, deep, Moroccan clay dish ringed with a thick layer of perfectly cooked couscous that covers chunks of tender chicken and lamb and is topped with turnips, carrots, chick peas, and Merguez (sausages). The whole is crowned with four skewers of grilled lamb and veal, and an entire orange nestles in the middle of the couscous. The grilled meats, marinated for a day in garlic, olive oil, cumin, red peppers, and parsley, are succulent. 3464 rue St-Denis. Call ahead to reserve if you want to sit in the Moroccan section; Tel: 282-0359.

Indian

Le Taj. The most elegant (and expensive) Indian restaurant in town, Le Taj has decor that makes clever and imaginative use of traditional Indian carvings and handcrafts.

A glassed-in area holds two tandoors, the traditional brick-and-clay ovens used in northern India to grill marinated chicken, meats, and fish. The same tandoors are used to bake fresh breads as you watch.

Try the tandoori chicken and lamb chops. The latter, a generous serving of five, are marinated overnight, grilled and served on a sizzle platter. The breads here—nans and roti—are exceptional, as are the vegetable dishes like spinach and *paneer,* an Indian form of Italian ricotta. For a treat, try nans stuffed with potatoes or minced meat. 2077 Stanley Street; Tel: 845-9015.

New Delhi. The place to go if you have curry cravings is the New Delhi restaurant. The cuisine at this informal restaurant at 5014 avenue du Parc isn't consistent, but they can be relied upon to produce London-style vinda-loos and Madras curries in varying degrees of spiciness. Tandoori chicken and other grilled meats are also avail-able, and the vegetable curries are noted for the fresh-ness of ingredients used.

Woodlands. Woodlands is the city's best restaurant for southern Indian cuisine. Masala dosas—lacy, golden len-til-rice crêpes stuffed with spicy potatoes—are always outstanding. Fresh coconut, black mustard seeds, ginger, asafoetida, turmeric, and fresh coriander dominate the sauces accompanying the dosas and other southern In-dian dishes such as idlies (steamed, lentil-rice cakes), vadai (deep-fried lentil doughnuts), and upma (spicy semolina).

This downtown restaurant also has a full range of north-ern Indian tandoori dishes, breads, and curries, but their quality has yet to match that of the dishes from the south. This doesn't mean you should ignore them—some of them, particularly chicken tikka, are very good. 1241 Guy Street; Tel: 933-1553.

Chinese and Southeast Asian

Tong Wa, **Cathay**, and **Kam Fung** are three excellent restaurants for Hong Kong–style dim sum—a bewilder-ing variety of "heart's delight" snacks are served between noon and 3:00 P.M. Each restaurant has a battery of dim sum chefs from Hong Kong and Great Hall of the People type decor and seating. All three restaurants have impres-sive à la carte Cantonese menus as well. Tong Wa is at 1059 boulevard St. Laurent in Chinatown, Cathay is at 73 La Gauchetière Ouest, and Kam Fung is at 1008 Clark Street.

Chao Praya. Wade warily into the spicy delights at this Thai restaurant on trendy Laurier Avenue—they can turn out to be fiery surprises. Fish, duck, pork, chicken, beef, and seafood here wear the enticing flavors of lemon grass, fresh coriander, coconut milk, sweet basil, and those deadly "bird's eye" chilis. Satays come with seduc-tive peanut sauces and the portions are generous.

Hong Kong. This no-frills Chinatown restaurant at 25 La Gauchetière Est offers good Cantonese cuisine at bargain prices. Service is rapid, the bare tables are adorned only with sauces, and seating is bare-bones cafeteria-style.

Choose from a wide range of duck, pork, lobster, fish, chicken, beef, noodles, rice, and vegetables. A few favorites you might like to try: barbecued pork and duck on rice; lobster Cantonese-style or with fresh ginger and shallots; beef with fresh lotus root; crispy chicken; watercress in oyster sauce; steamed jumbo shrimp; and Singapore noodles.

Le Chrysanthème. The place to go for superior northern Chinese cuisine in a superchic town-house setting downtown (1208 rue Crescent). Steamed or sautéed dumplings are particularly good here, as are the lamb, beef, and seafood dishes; Tel: 397-1408.

L'Orchidée de Chine. Owned by the same people who run Le Chrysanthème, this is one of the classier Sichuan restaurants in town. Waiters wear black ties at this 2017 rue Peel establishment with its Art Deco dining rooms spread over three levels.

Particularly interesting dishes here are eggplant in garlic, five-flavored boned crispy pork spareribs, squid sautéed with red bell peppers, chicken with Sichuan pepper, greens, and sautéed beef in a spicy garlic sauce. Call to reserve; Tel: 287-1878.

Luong Huu. The music in this Chinatown restaurant is disco-and-schmaltz in Vietnamese and Chinese, the tables are cafeteria-style, and the menu is supplemented by a numbering system and color photos. But don't be discouraged—the Luong Huu is not as tacky as it sounds. It has some of the most exotic Vietnamese food and Chinese pastries you're likely to find in Montreal.

The pastries—some in rather gaudy shades of pink, green, and white—are flavored with lotus and sesame seeds and coconut. They are on display in a large glass case to one side of the entrance, a section that also has a selection of freshly baked buns, some topped with green onions, others stuffed with barbecued pork or curried beef.

Luong Huu is also big on fresh-fruit shakes (fruit and crushed ice) and iced drinks. Red beans and pickled lemon are among the unusual flavorings for the latter, while the fresh fruit includes mangos, pineapples, kiwis, and melons.

The photo menu, which has color pictures of some of the dishes on the printed menu, is your best bet on a first visit. Try goi cuon—cold spring rolls of rice paper stuffed with fresh mint leaves, bean sprouts, onion greens, shrimp, shredded pork, and vermicelli. Or banh yeo, a large, golden, bean-and-green-onion crêpe stuffed with sprouts, thin slices of beef, and a couple of shrimp. You must experiment with the assorted sauces on the table; they can improve or alter your meal dramatically. 84 La Gauchetière Ouest; no credit cards.

Palais d'Ivoire. Sprawling, elegant Sichuan restaurant with very reasonable prices. Especially good deals at lunchtime when complete meals can be had for under $10. Service is as upscale as the decor and the cuisine fresh—even the spring rolls are made on the premises. Slightly west of downtown in Westmount. 1232 Greene Avenue; Tel: 932-1244.

Palais Impérial de Chine. Unlike the city's other trendy, chic Sichuan restaurants, at the Impérial you are never in doubt that you're in a Chinese restaurant, perhaps overpoweringly so. Red, green, and gold are dominant on the pillars, the tiles on the ceiling, and the tall carved vases with dragons on them. The seating is comfortable and well-spaced, though the lighting is a bit bright. The service is prompt and efficient.

For those who like their Sichuan food really spicy, the good news is that you may have to ask them to tone it down. Ask for medium, and you're set. Try the shrimp Sichuan style, shredded lamb in spicy sauce, and the subgum vegetables—ordinary, down-to-earth assorted Chinese vegetables. Dumplings in hot sauce here come with a gingery and extremely peppery sauce. The stuffing of minced pork and green onions is exceptionally fresh and spicy. You can also try other dishes here, like moo shu pork with four pancakes, and spicy ma bo bean curd. 2080 de la Montagne Street.

Pattaya. One of the city's only exclusively Thai restaurant serves good fish, crab, squid, and meat dishes flavored with fresh coriander, lemon grass, basil, coconut milk, and, where called for, fiery peppers.

Try a mixed-seafood po tak soup—firm white fish, shrimp, and a crab claw in a broth whose peppery lemongrass and citrus-leaf flavor leaves a fiery, eye-popping afterburn.

The same fire is present in the spicy sauce covering a whole, deep-fried fish, pla lad plik, and in the chili-fried crab claws. Milder dishes include some salads with squid or beef, mixed noodles, and boneless chicken in a sauce of coconut milk, green peas, fresh bamboo shoots, and basil. 1235 Guy Street; Tel: 933-9949.

Peninsula. Good Cantonese cuisine is served at Peninsula (1108 Clark Street) in a typical Chinatown setting—lots of dragons, lanterns, and red colors. Ignore the numbered, preset dinners and exotic drinks, and choose from the regular menu. Fish and seafood are good here, particularly seafood nests and whole pickerel in a black-bean sauce; good quail and noodles too.

Tong Nam. Almost next door to the Hong Kong sits the Tong Nam, which claims to be the only Montreal restaurant serving Chu-chou and Chaozhou dishes. These are similar to but not the same as Cantonese dishes. Each table is also equipped with several interesting and spicy sauces. There's a fish-soy sauce similar to that used in Vietnamese and Thai cooking; there's a hot garlic and chili sauce; and there's a peppery satay sauce made on the premises from crushed peanuts, soya, and chile peppers. You also have crushed red peppers and two kinds of soy sauce.

Try the duck, fried egg noodles with seafood, and the pickerel Chaozhou-style. The last is a large fish—at least three pounds—that's lightly floured and crisply deep-fried to a light golden color, topped with a sweet-and-sour hot sauce that includes carrots, onions, Chinese greens, pineapple chunks, slices of orange, scallions, and green peppers. 1017 boulevard St-Laurent.

Japanese

Azuma. Try the whole fried fish at this east-end restaurant (901 Sherbrooke Est; Tel: 525-5262)—it's something you won't find at the other Japanese restaurants in town. The place is informal but generally crowded, so reservations are in order. Sushi, served at night only, is fresh and somewhat cheaper than the competitions'.

Osaka. An unpretentious, family-run downtown restaurant at 2137 Bleury, Osaka has no sushi, but the soups, sukiyaki, tempura, and teriyaki dishes are very good. The ambience is casual, and the friendly staff will cheerfully tailor a meal to your whims.

Sushibar. Sit at the long bar at this striking restaurant at 3711 boulevard St-Laurent and nibble away at the fresh morsels of raw fish. Dozens of varieties are bought or flown in fresh; you can go the sushi way—vinegared rice and all—or eat your fish straight, the sashimi way; Tel: 845-2881.

Tokyo Sukiyaki. The oldest and most consistently packed Japanese restaurant in Montreal can only be found with the aid of a map because of its location in a semi-industrial neighborhood.

From the outside, it looks little different from the garages and warehouses nearby. Inside, it's a warm and intimate sukiyaki house where all guests sit in raised tatami rooms after taking their shoes off. The rooms are built around streams and tiny bridges, giving an exotic air.

Reservations are a must, and the place is open only for dinner. There's a full range of standard Japanese dishes—sukiyaki, shabu-shabu, and tempura among them. 7355 Mountain Sights; Tel: 737-7245.

Yamabuki. In Japan, they call it Genghis Khan cooking. At the Yamabuki, it's called yakiniku dome cooking. This is how it works: You place a cast-iron dome over gas or electric heat, smear the dome with soya oil, and then leisurely grill marinated slices of sirloin, vegetables, or seafood on it, dip them in a ginger sauce, and eat them with rice.

At the Yamabuki, you can eat your yakiniku in the privacy of bamboo-and-parchment "huts" built village-style on two floors of a renovated town house. The decor, as in most Japanese restaurants, is soft, muted, soothing, and in impeccable taste.

The seating is Western-style, on regular chairs around square tables. Each table is equipped with an electric ring with temperature controls. Soft Japanese music mingles with the chatter from adjoining huts to create a relaxed ambience, with some help from warm sake, of course.

Try one of the multi-course, fixed-price yakiniku special-ties like the seafood special or the the beef-and-vegetable yakiniku. Miso soup, salads, and assorted appetizers are of average quality and quickly forgotten as you choose mor-sels to grill from platters of marinated jumbo shrimp, scallops, sirloin, and thinly sliced eggplant, carrots, green peppers, and onions.

Working quickly but carefully, a kimono-clad waitress will deftly cook your meat and vegetables on one side of the heated dome and the seafood on the other. Within seconds, everything on the dome sizzles pleasantly in a cloud of steam scented by the soya-ginger-shallot-sake marinade. 1184 Bishop Street.

Other

Bagel-Etc. An all-night restaurant, Bagel-Etc is in the old diner style of New York City and Montreal: lots of taped late-night jazz, and a menu that has everything from caviar and Champagne to bagels and blintzes. You can also g half-decent Hungarian-style goulash, East European sausage and cabbage, schnitzels, herring, and smoked salmon. Bagel-Etc also serves a range of elaborate burgers. 4320 boulevard St-Laurent.

Café Mozart. Elegant, somewhat whimsical, decor creates a delightful other-world ambience at this postcard-pretty Austro-Hungarian downtown restaurant. Cold cherry soup, blini with caviar, and pork with gnocchi are only a few of the traditional dishes on the menu. And yes, the desserts are as rich and chocolaty as they are in Vienna and Budapest. 2090 rue de la Montagne.

Café Santropol. The Sixties have yet to end for this eclectic café-restaurant on the Plateau Mont-Royal. The colors are only slightly short of psychedelic and the mismatched banquettes, chairs and tables come in assorted shapes, sizes, and shades. In the summer the treed backyard offers more tables, wind chimes, a birdhouse, a pond with goldfish, and sometimes Chaucer, a canine neighbor from upstairs. Santropol's passion for color spills over into the gigantic sandwiches served here with names such as Sisters of Jeanne Mance and Yelapa Moon. Fresh grapefruit, orange, kiwi, watermelon, cantaloupe, cucumber, alfalfa sprouts, and red cabbage accompany thick slices of brown bread filled with lobster and cheese spreads, ham, or salamis. They also serve more than 50 kinds of tea and excellent coffees.

Futenbulle. Beer, on tap and in bottles, from all over the world—including more than 20 from Belgium—is supplemented by a menu that features such items as terrine of smoked salmon, caribou burgers, quiche of the day, and bagel and lox (smoked salmon). This bistro-like beer parlor at 273 Bernard Avenue Ouest also has mussels, pasta, and sausage, all at reasonable prices.

If you get bored drinking or eating, you can play chess or Scrabble or read one of the many magazines lying around. These include *Paris Match*, *Fortune*, *Robb Report*, *Art and Auction*, and *Entrepreneur*. They also have a giant TV screen on which music videos and sports telecasts are screened.

La Mer Rouge. A simple place at 256 Roy Street near carré St-Louis, La Mer Rouge has frayed carpets, plastic tablecloths, rickety folding chairs, and grocery-store white napkins—and good, honest, spicy Ethiopian cuisine. Turmeric, red chili powder, garlic, onions (lots), and ginger in varying proportions and strength are the backbone of such dishes here as doro wot, siga wot, atekelt wot, misir wot, and yesimir kik wot. Or, translated: chicken, beef, vegetables, and lentils, all in sauces that remind you of Indian cuisine, and all served with injera, a large, white, crêpe-like Ethiopian bread.

Lola's Paradise Café. If paradise is sipping wine as you loll on oversize sofas or gaze at ceramic miniatures under the lighted glass top of a 35-foot bar, then Lola's is the perfect place for you.

Lola's is for nocturnal types; no lunches with Perrier here. The place opens at 5:00 P.M. and stays open until 6:00 A.M. There are two menus, one for dinner until midnight, the other for lighter meals until 6:00 A.M. The post-midnight menu has reasonably priced soups, salads, croques, and sandwiches. The main menu focuses on chicken, veal, and fish dishes. The dishes here sound more impressive than they actually are; you're better off just drinking or snacking.

It's a totally informal place. You're just as likely to find a young woman in shorts with a motorcycle helmet here as you might a party of four in tuxes and evening dresses.

Patterned after a 1930s ballroom, Lola's has turquoise walls, swag draperies, and everything from low, comfy sofas to armchairs to formal dining furniture. The music is best after midnight, when a deejay plays jazz, some light classics, and Brazilian samba, and if you get bored you can go to the bar upstairs, **Talullah Darling**. 3604 boulevard St-Laurent.

Moishe's. It's worth a short wait for a table at this steakhouse at 3961 boulevard St-Laurent, where at least four waiters are guaranteed to fuss mightily, plying you with water, liquor, pickles, and trimmings. The steaks are perfect and expensive; the decor is plush. Call to reserve; Tel: 845-3509.

Schwartz's Montreal Hebrew Delicatessen. The tables are narrow and shared, Schwartz's doesn't sell liquor, and service can be brusque, but you'll forget all that when you taste what people come from all over the world to this boulevard St-Laurent deli for: Montreal smoked meat.

Not to be confused with pastrami, Montreal smoked meat is juicy beef cured in spices according to assorted secret recipes passed down to their successors by Romanian Jews who emigrated to Montreal.

No one in Montreal has a better recipe than Schwartz's. You must order the smoked meat hot, on rye bread, with an order of Schwartz's french fries—thick, greasy, and a legend in their own right. 3895 boulevard St-Laurent; no credit cards.

Troika. An established Russian restaurant downtown (2171 rue Crescent), Troika is done in czarist decor: lots of velvet and red plush. There is live music every night—some of it at your table—and expensive caviar, of course. Traditional dishes like chicken Kiev are your best bet if you're not in a decadent mood. Tel: 849-9333.

Rue Prince-Arthur

Rue Prince-Arthur is a phenomenon unique in Canada—a street converted into a pedestrian mall lined by restaurants, many of which allow you to bring your own wine (there are several grocery stores handily situated to pick up a couple of bottles if you haven't remembered to buy them at the government liquor stores).

In summer this year-round mall also attracts buskers and other street performers, giving it a festive air. Many of the restaurants here are Greek, specializing in brochettes, but there are also Vietnamese, Japanese, Indian, and Italian restaurants. The quality of cuisine is average; the ambience and lower prices are the main reason to eat on this street. It's fun to stroll around, compare menus, and experiment.

Try **Vivaldi**, which has reasonably satisfying Italian food and striking decor, or the **Mazurka**, a cheap and excellent Polish restaurant that was on the street long before it acquired its present character. Also, try the **Akita** for good sushi, or **Place Balkan** for Yugoslavian cuisine.

A few blocks north a similar street is taking shape, although **rue Duluth** is not a pedestrian mall yet. Restaurants similar to those on rue Prince-Arthur have sprung up here, and the same rules apply. Try **Jardin de Panos**, a Greek restaurant with a charming garden and terrace, and **Bellini**, which serves acceptable Italian cuisine.

—*Ashok Chandwani*

NIGHTLIFE

There are scores of bars and cafés to choose from in Montreal, but unless you're famous or happen to know a regular, be prepared to wait in line at some of the more popular ones.

Most bars or restaurants aren't fussy about clothes, even in the posh hotels. However, blue jeans are the most frequent cause of denied entry. Ambience in bars in Montreal is relaxed and casual; it's easy to strike up a conversation, even make friends.

You're expected to pay for a drink at the time you receive it unless you have an honest face—or a credit card you're willing to surrender, in which case the place will run a tab for you. Almost every bar has a happy hour on weekdays, when drinks are discounted or you get two for the price of one. This "hour" is generally between 5:00 and 7:00 P.M. but can sometimes start as early as 4:00 P.M. and end at 9:00 P.M.

French is Montreal's principal language, but English is widely understood. Nevertheless, there are clear-cut Anglo and French bar areas, with a trend lately toward a cluster of cosmopolitan bars that otherwise defy labeling.

Mackay, Bishop, Crescent, and de la Montagne are four main downtown streets crammed with bars where you'll hear more English than French. The opposite is true of St-Denis and Ontario, and Vieux-Montréal.

Avenue du Parc and boulevard St-Laurent are late bloomers on the bar scene. Some of the trendiest locales can be found on these streets, all in the cosmo class. You'll also find many low-life bars here, if you feel like slumming.

For conventional nightlife of the leg-kicking variety, your best bet is at the larger hotels. Each has some sort of nightclub with singing or dancing acts that change frequently.

Outside the hotels, there is a lively music scene: Montreal is on the tour circuit of many major international performers. The city also has a good selection of clubs that feature jazz, having had a long association with that genre of music. Pianist Oscar Peterson is from Montreal, as is Oliver Jones. In summer the city is host to one of the largest jazz festivals in the world, when more than 1,000 musicians perform over a ten-day period.

Au Cepage. Favored by journalists, shipping executives, and theatergoers, this is a one-of-a-kind bar/bistro/restaurant at 482 rue St-François Xavier in Vieux-Montréal, with a super-friendly staff. There are a couple of cozy dining rooms. Au Cepage is a perfect spot for Sunday brunch, particularly if you're seated in the courtyard café in the summer. Sit here in the sun or under a chestnut tree beside an old wall and listen to the cries of the falcons that nest high up in the buildings nearby as you munch on bagels or croissants, and perhaps sip Champagne and freshly squeezed orange juice, or, hold the orange juice.

Biddles. Downtown, at 2060 Alymer, with good live jazz. You can also dine here on ribs, chicken wings, or potato skins. More fun after 11:00 P.M.

Blue Angel. Downtown at 1228 Drummond; old-fashioned country-music bar, Stetsons and all. Small dance floor, frayed banquettes, and waiters from the 1950s. Amateur night on Monday is entertaining; drinks are cheap.

Charles Darwin. Comfortable bar at 1187 Bishop Street with pleasant courtyard terrace in warm weather. Quiet except when an important hockey game is on.

Club Jazz 2080. Between downtown and rue St-Denis at 2080 Clark Street. Good live jazz.

Club Soda. Avenue du Parc bar-cum-concert-stage. Touring music shows. Check newspaper listings for what's on. 5240 rue du Parc.

Déjà Vu. Downtown, at 1224 Bishop. A great place if you like crowds and are with a group. It spreads over two-and-a-half floors, and there is good live music, usually from the sixties.

Faubourg St. Denis. In the heart of the bar and restaurant strip at 1660 St-Denis. Lots of tables open to the outdoors in summer, and a cozy bar in the basement.

Grumpy's. Downtown, at 1242 Bishop. A friendly staff, and many regulars. For an older crowd; no dance floor, but people still shuffle around anyway late at night. Grumpy's is a good place for conversation; the music here is softer, the bar augmented by comfortable sofas.

L'Air du Temps. In Vieux-Montréal at 191 rue St-Paul Ouest. Lots of plants, and live jazz.

Le Bijou. An ultra-chic bar with live jazz, and a place to watch people and be watched yourself. Lots of models and ad execs. 300 Lemoyne.

Le Grand Café. At 1720 rue St-Denis. Large, it's a two-floor jazz bar with tall glass doors to the street that are left open in the summer. Good live music.

Lola's. See the listing under Dining, above.

Lux. At 5220 boulevard St-Laurent. A funky, Paris-style complex with bar, restaurant, grocery, and bookstore with magazines from around the world. Open well past 3:00 A.M.

Moby Dick. Downtown at 1188 Sherbrooke Ouest; a

good and busy spot for conversation. Frequented by separated or recently divorced individuals.

Rising Sun. Slightly east of downtown, at 286 rue Ste-Catherine Ouest; good live jazz and blues.

Skala. A cheap drinking spot with terrace at 4869 avenue du Parc. Skala is favored by musicians, poets, anarchists, budding writers, and some elderly neighborhood types.

Thursday's. Downtown on 1449 rue Crescent. You'll find a cross-section of Montreal here, dominated by people from the advertising and fashion industries. The music is loud, and there is dancing and singles action. Thursday's is favored by the 35-plus crowd at night and by office workers of all ages between 5:00 and 7:00 P.M.

Spectrum. Bar–concert hall complex that books big-name touring music shows. Check newspaper listings for what's on. 318 rue Ste-Catherine Ouest.

Winnie's. Downtown at 1455 rue Crescent; a preppy Anglo crowd. Lots of wood, plants, and Old English prints. There is a deejay and dancing after happy hour.

Woody's Pub. Downtown (at 1234 Bishop); a large, generally crowded multi-bar place. Good English-style pub lunches. Dancing at night.

The Suburbs

If you get bored with city action, you can always head west into the suburbs to new places like **Cheers** (955 St-Jean North, Pointe Claire), whose shopping-mall location doesn't seem to deter hundreds of upwardly mobile and mostly Anglo drinkers, and **Quai Sera** (164 Ste-Anne Street, Ste-Anne de Bellevue), a waterfront dance bar that packs in a similar crowd—there is a small cover charge and men are required to wear a jacket. (Don't confuse the suburban Cheers with its parent bar downtown, which is popular mostly with recent teenyboppers.)

A visit to these bars could be preceded by a meal at a suburban restaurant:

Le Péché Mignon. The cuisine at this waterfront restaurant in Ste-Anne-de-Bellevue has touches of nouvelle—a trend that hasn't quite died in Montreal yet. Actually, its better elements—freshness and imagination—are retained. Portions, mercifully, are neither small nor overpowering.

In summer, ask for a table on the terrace that overlooks the boardwalk. Boats chug in and out of the narrow canal here; people promenade on the boardwalk. Try the snails, served partially concealed in scooped-out brussels sprouts, ringing a large plate covered with a sauce of cream, garlic, and parsley. Salmon marinated in citrus juices—in this case, grapefruit, orange, and a hint of lemon—is particularly delectable. For the main course, duck cooked two ways (thin slices of medium-rare breast of duck beside a succulent and whole leg covered in a traditional rich, dark brown sauce) is your best bet for dinner. Also try the fish and shrimp dishes. 132 Ste-Anne Street, St-Anne de Bellevue; Tel: 457-3584.

Le Vieux Kitzbuhel. This romantic restaurant, a branch of one in Montreal, is in an old mansion on Lake St. Louis in Ile Perrot (505 boulevard Perrot). Most of the six charming dining rooms have a view of the lake and of the garden sloping to it, with its white deck chairs and its wharf for the boat crowd.

There's a fair selection of veal, pork, chicken, and fish dishes, and, of course, homemade dumplings. Perhaps the most enticing feature of the menu is venison, flown in from Alberta. Other successful dishes include: a delicious Tyrolean wine soup—a heady concoction of wine, eggs, and cream with crisp croutons; venison pâté, fresh, rich and gamey; and medallions of venison, also very gamey and tender, served with a mound of good red cabbage and fresh baby dumplings. Tel: 453-5521.

Highway 20 West is the way to reach all these bars and restaurants. Take the Ste-Anne de Bellevue exit for Le Pêché Mignon, which is on the main drag of this little town, and for Quai Sera. The same highway also has an exit for St-Jean Boulevard in the municipality of Pointe Claire, where you'll find Cheers. Vieux Kitzbuhel is on an easy-to-find major street in Ile Perrot, the exit to which can also be found off Highway 20 West. The three exits are about a 30-minute drive from downtown Montreal.

—*Ashok Chandwani*

SHOPS AND SHOPPING

For years Montreal ruled as the unchallenged fashion capital of Canada. Factories and sweat shops along boulevard St-Laurent—an all-purpose thoroughfare that is, among other things, Montreal's answer to Manhattan's Seventh Avenue—produced the clothes worn by the rest of the country. The garment industry still accounts for 40 percent of the city's manufacturing jobs, but today Toronto can justifiably lay equal claim to the haute couture crown. Still, Montreal's long tradition, combined with its inhabitants' confident sense of style, has nurtured a thriving community of designers who sell their creations not only to large department stores but also from their own boutiques.

Many of the hottest design houses are clustered in Plateau Mont-Royal, an old residential and commercial district east of the mountain. **Parachute** (3526 St-Laurent) received wide attention a few seasons back when some of its flashy inventory graced Don Johnson, the fashionable police detective on *Miami Vice*. The trendsetting store, founded by British-born designer Nicola Pelly and Harry Parnass, a former professor of urban planning from California, is done in rough concrete for the floor, ceiling, and walls, and looks either half-empty or elegantly uncluttered depending on one's outlook (only 30 percent of the store is given over to clothing). The expensive, heavily textured silk, cotton, and woolen garments are displayed on sloping banks of stainless steel. "Stores like these are the salons of the 20th century," says Parnass, "a place where artists, writers, filmmakers, and other creative people congregate."

Known as Montreal's Soho area, upper St-Laurent now rivals St-Denis, downtown, and Laurier Ouest for choices in fashion, nightclubs, boutiques, and the rest. The eponymous owner of **Robert Krief** is the third generation of his family to work in leather. His welcoming shop is filled with jackets, trousers, skirts, and coats of supple leathers in 12 colors. Leather pants cost $340 CDN, a woman's short jacket $570. It's located next to his other boutique, **Paris, Texas**, a sports-clothing shop (5251 St-Laurent).

If prices are too much here, check out **Le Chateau**'s own label—knock-offs of the latest designer styles and retro fashions—at its two-floor boutique (5160 St-Laurent), or **Trois & Un** (at number 5129) for sportswear. Nearby **Luna** and **Le Lotus Blanc** have sensuously textured, lusciously colored cotton and rayon knit jerseywear. At **Double Vé** there is Annie Coriat-Ronsard sportswear and **Atout Fringues** has NafNaf Paris's latest casual wear.

Fashion for the home—whether avant-garde or retro—can also be found on St-Laurent. **Par le Trou de la Serrure** (at number 5101) combines the practical and the unusual in beautiful door and window hardware, while **Quartz** specializes in Eurostyle lighting, imported, and knock-off designs next door. For one-of-a-kind furniture finds from the 1930s through 1950s, head up to **M.A.D. objets de collection** at number 5330.

No imports darken the racks of **Revenge** (3852 St-Denis and 111 Laurier Ouest), which handles such Montreal couturiers as Maurice Ferland, Alain Thomas, and Jean-Claude Poitras, one of Quebec's hottest designers. Prices are somewhat lower than at Parachute. **Boutique Crise**, formerly on St-Denis, has joined the St-Laurent fashionables at number 3613. It still caters to a young, affluent clientele. A team of designers sells their own creations under the label Lou Gaeten.

In 1976 Ariane Carle switched from designing costumes for films to creating high-fashion knitwear. Her shop, **Les Tricots d'Ariane** (207 Laurier Ouest), stocks more than 50 styles of coordinated tops, skirts, pants, and jackets in basic colors, all in washable cotton-and-acrylic blends. Prices range from $32 to $325.

Hers is not the only "not-to-be-missed" boutique on Laurier Ouest, which has long catered to the carriage trade of **Outremont**—one of French Montreal's most elite neighborhoods. From St-Laurent to Côte Ste-Catherine the eight blocks of cafés, boutiques, galleries, and restaurants lining both sides of Laurier Ouest make this street a shopper's heaven. Home furnishings abound, from the latest wall coverings at **Griffe** (number 92) to ceramic tiles at **Ceramique Folco**, **Gres** (nearby at number 88). Eurostyle lamps and lighting fixtures are to be found at **Au Courant**. Close by are the French-Canadian pine antiques at **Boutique Confort** which vie with 21st-century accessories for bath, kitchen, office, and garden at **MDI** (at number 273). Siding with the nostalgic are **Cache-Cache**'s Victorian-inspired bed and table linens, plus unusual Third World handcrafted ceramics and pottery. Likewise, the unusual and the beautiful are to be found in the luxe tableware, glassware, dinnerware, kitchenware, and bathwear at **Maison d'Emilie** nearby. For the finest French bed and bath linens and accessories try **Décor Marie-Paule** (at number 1090).

For fashion, **Collections 24** (90 Laurier Ouest) has Canadian superstars Alfred Sung and Hilary Radley side by side with American designer Adrienne Vittadini and others. Like Robert Krief, **Carmen** (at number 265) designs leathers and knits, including outerwear, that give real meaning to the expression "wearable art." **L'Aventure pour Homme** and **L'Aventure pour Femme** are where you'll find Italian designer fashion favorites by Armani, Versace, Moschino and others. How to show off all this finery? Try on the precious and faux gems at **Cabochon** (number 207) and **Agatha Bijoux** (number 1054) jewelry boutiques.

St-Denis between Sherbrooke and Mont Royal is also worth a trip. Not only will you find bistros, bookstores, and galleries cheek-by-jowl (some of Montreal's finest) but you'll also find a plethora of Québeçois and international fashions for the body or the home. Le Château is here, as is one of **Thalie**'s boutiques for its designed-in-Quebec, made-in-Hong Kong, knitwear, offering well-made, distinctly styled, reasonably priced clothes for women and men. **Un Brin d'Elle** offers unusual sportif fashions by Maurice Ferland, Marcelle Danan, Maille à Partir, and others. For mad hatters of either sex, **Le Sieur Duluth chapeaux, bijoux et accessoires** is an absolute must. Most of the hats, jewelry, and accessories are designed in-house; custom orders are also accepted.

For the home, the offerings of boutiques such as Zone, Apres L'Eden, Bleu Nuit, Au Lit, Arthur Quentin, Crabtree & Evelyn, Aux Rêves de Morphée, and Chiquenaude (all clustered on St-Denis) range in style from English manor to French Château with stops in Italy and elsewhere. These emporiums offer a fabulous choice of bed, bath and table linens, upholstery fabrics, lace curtains by-the-yard, toiletries, stationery, kitchen, tabletop and dinner ware. The only problem will be trying to fit all those "must-haves" into your suitcase.

Shops in the bright, airy pedestrian corridors and spacious plazas of Montreal's *ville souterraine* (underground city) offer merchandise as stylish as the city itself. Place Ville-Marie contains some of Montreal's finest haute couture outlets. Along narrow la rue Elle (a pun, incidentally, on *la ruelle,* or alley) are 12 up-market boutiques that specialize in European imports. (**Mademoiselle Jacnel** also carries silk dresses by Jean-Claude Poitras.) **Lalla Fucci** sells clothes by Frank Usher of London and Parisian designer Anne-Marie Beretta. **Boutique Descamps**, just around the corner, is the only store in Montreal where you can find the entire line of bedding and accessories by the French design house Primrose Bordier. Around another corner in this elegant labyrinth of shops is **Davidoff**, a tobacconist specializing in Cuban cigars; a single Dom Perignon costs about $30.

At Place Bonaventure off Square Victoria, well-heeled office workers spend their lunch hours browsing in chic shops that line interior "streets" with names like Champs-Elysées and rue de Versailles. Shoe stores predominate, and a quick stroll past the shops here provides an overview of what's available all over the city. **Bally** has the best selection. The pricey **Boutique Fabrice** is the only clothing store in North America that stocks wool pants, sweaters, and other fashionable attire from Elge 4 of Paris. If marriage is in the offing, drop by a nearby bijouterie called **Edgar Charbonneau** to see the assortment of engagement and wedding rings. Most of the jewelry is produced in limited editions; customers can also commission their own one-of-a-kind creations.

A ride on the Metro west to Atwater Station and a short stroll through a pleasant underground corridor brings the intrepid shopper to Westmount Square, which contains some of the city's finest and most expensive fashions. **Boutique Chacok** features the styles of French designer Arlette Chacock, whose work seems inspired by boldly colored geometric and abstract patterns. **Lily Simon** sells more subdued styles from Sonia Rykiel and Claude Montana. Her boutique is one of Montreal socialites' favorites. For boots and bags, cross the corridor to **Quinto**, which offers such exotica as a python-skin purse from Italy and burlap-and-leather women's boots studded with rhinestones.

Back downtown, rue Peel is worth a visit for the boutiques at the **Les Cours Mont-Royal** shopping complex, which are as beautiful to look at as the fashions found within. Canadian superstar **Alfred Sung** has two boutiques here—the white-marbled salon featuring his day and evening wear, as well as his Club Monaco fashion emporium-cum-coffee-and-juice bar, featuring his sportswear labels. There are also boutiques filled with the finery of **Ferre**, **Armani**, and **Aquascutum of London** for the more traditionally inclined. For male trend-setters, there is **Lancia Uomo** for up-to-the-minute classic styles, while **Parachute** appeals to the minimalist man or woman. Challenging Parachute's mainly monochrome theme is fellow Canadian superstar Simon Chang's **La Cricca** boutique for women, where color runs riot from one end of the spectrum (and showroom) to the other.

It used to be that Montrealers really knew summer was in full swing when **Virlion** (2035 Crescent) held its annual outdoor lingerie fashion show. On a Friday in mid-July, weather permitting, models would glide about the stairs, landing, and sidewalk outside the store dressed in the shop's elegant inventory of silky teddies, lusty Merry Widows, and saucy corselets. A predictably large and appreciative audience gathered and, not surprisingly, local print and electronic-media reporters considered it a newsworthy event year after year. Alas, the shows are no more, and the boutique now displays its wares in a more conventional manner.

At **Il n'y a que deux**, also on Crescent, the high-price fashions (especially trendy woolens) of owners Carmen Michaud and Gordon Iaconetti are displayed in a minimalist setting in an airy, glassy trilevel store. But they are no longer the only ones catering to young-and-not-so-young fashion trendsetters. Marithé & François Girbaud's **Halles Capone** corner boutique (1370 Ste-Catherine Ouest), Zoo Option, and Grège Boutique (both on Crescent) bring the world's fashion luminaries to Montreal devotées. Grège, especially, leads the pack with clothes by Japanese superstars Yohji Yamamoto, Isey Miyake and Rei Kawakubo, as well as those by the newest darling of the international designer circuit, Italy's Romeo Gigli.

Up on Sherbrooke, carriage-trade discretion rules in expensive designer boutiques like Yves Saint Laurent and Giorgio Armani at Holt Renfrew, Lily Simon, and Sonia Rykiel, as well as Les Musts de Cartier and **Holt Renfrew**, where a black leather Gianfranco Ferre jacket with shocking pink lining costs $4,500.

In the heart of the central business district along rue Ste-Catherine, Montreal's major department stores are within a few blocks of each other. Although the stores carry much the same merchandise, **La Baie** (rue Ste-Catherine at Square Phillips) is the most stylish—it appeals to a young clientele and features prominent Quebec designers. **Eaton** (677 rue Ste-Catherine Ouest) sells a wide range of fashions and has boutiques specializing in Canadian designers. When you're ready for lunch, try the ninth-floor restaurant. The food is plain cafeteria, but the decor is modeled after the Art Deco dining room of the Ile de France, with 35-foot marble columns, alabaster vases, Monet grills, murals, and bas-reliefs.

Ogilvy (1307 rue Ste-Catherine Ouest) has shed its once conservative image, emerging as the peacock of Ste-Catherine. What began as a linen shop of Scottish origin in 1866 has been transformed into a magnificent department store, resplendent with jewel-like boutiques on every floor. Valentino, Joan and David, and Natori are here, as well as tweeds and smocked dresses for the more traditionally inclined. To reflect its rich heritage—the store has been a Montreal institution since it first opened—the cranberry-glass chandeliers, the sweeping staircase, and, best of all, the noon-hour ritual of a kilted bagpiper marching through the store have all been preserved.

Furs

Canada is the world's third-largest producer of furs (after the Soviet Union and the United States), and Montreal remains the country's fur capital after three centuries. The city's 200 fur-manufacturing firms are concentrated in a ten-block area in the center of the city. The annual Montreal International Fur Fair is the second most important show after the fur-fest in Frankfurt. The show is closed to the public, but serious buyers can visit such well-established salons as **Alexandor** (2025 de la Montagne), **Desjardins** (325 boulevard René Lévesque Est), and **Shuchat** (402 boulevard de Maisonneuve Ouest) to view Canada's forte, long-haired furs of beaver, raccoon, lynx, sable, and fox. Don't overlook **La Baie** (Square Phillips), whose fur-trading history dates back to 1670, when the Hudson Bay Company was founded by the famous duo of Montreal voyageurs and trappers Radisson and Grosseilliers. For the following 150 years, their company had a monopoly on the fur trade in Canada. While this is no longer the case, La Baie's furs still rank among the finest in the world. **Holt Renfrew** (1300 Sherbrooke) is also among the first-rank of fur salons. Originally Henderson, Holt and Renfrew Furriers, established in 1837, its furs have been worn by four generations of Britain's ruling class. (For Queen Elizabeth II's marriage to Prince Philip in 1947, Holt's gave her a custom-designed Labrador mink coat as a wedding gift.) Holt's also has Denmark's exclusive and expensive (but if you have to ask, you shouldn't buy) line of Birger Christensen furs.

Worth the trek is **Labelle Fourrure** (6570 rue St-Hubert). Coats, jackets, and stoles are priced from $2,000 to $50,000. Most are Canadian designs, but European houses are also represented.

Factory Outlets

In the past, a whiff of impropriety hung over shopping at factory outlets in Montreal. Manufacturers, understandably anxious about alienating retailers with discounted merchandise, opened their usually shabby premises for a couple of hours on Saturday mornings to a few select bargain hunters who knew the general manager and a password. The warehouses were run-down; elevators sometimes didn't work. Changing rooms, if any, were behind a curtain. These affairs were cash only, all sales final, and don't tell your friends. This is still the case at some wholesalers, but echoing the spirit of *glasnost* and with the institution of regular store hours, some outlets now get more traffic than stores in a suburban mall.

Most of the outlets are clustered in the Chabanel area west of boulevard St-Laurent in the north end of the city. Some are open 9:00 A.M. to 5:00 P.M. during the week, and from 8:00 A.M. to 1:00 P.M. on Saturdays; others are open only on Saturdays. **Aberdeen Clothing** (99 Chabanel Ouest, Suite 400) offers low prices on suits, dresses, blouses, and coats during regular shopping hours. Stylish leather jackets, clothes, and accessories as well as sportswear and shoes can also be found in factories at the following street addresses along Chabanel: 111, 125, 225, 333, and 555.

Specialty Shopping

Like any large center, Montreal has its share of specialty shops. **Robert Buckland Rare Carpets** (1451 Sherbrooke Ouest) is the city's only gallery devoted to antique carpets and rugs. The floor coverings come from private estates all over North America, and all date from before World War I.

In Vieux-Montréal is **Eole 2** (30 St-Paul Est), Montreal's only kite store. Named for the Greek god of the wind, the cheery shop is stocked with some 30 kinds of colorful kites, most designed by owner Jean Belanger and made on the premises. The most expensive item is the Giant Delta ($135); the most elaborate, a frail-looking Ghost Clipper Ship kite ($65), which takes more than 100 hours to build. The shop's other flying toys include boomerangs, Frisbees, and model airplanes.

As a curiosity, it's amusing to flip through the racks of outlandish outfits at **Joseph Ponton Costumes** (480 St-Francois-Xavier), even though most visitors probably won't return home with a kicky Julius Caesar ensemble or the $125 big-rabbit outfit. Founded in 1865 by brothers Joseph and Philippe Ponton, the store is still going strong, with some 10,000 costumes in stock for theatrical productions, New Year's parties, and Halloween (pumpkin and squash getups, vampire dentures).

The **Bead Emporium** (364 avenue Victoria, just south of

rue Sherbrooke in Westmount) has an astounding array of beads made of glass, ceramic, wood, metal, and even Plexiglas, along with necessities for do-it-yourself costume jewelry. The store also stocks jewelry from Africa and India.

Au Rêve de Morphée (4123 rue St-Denis, corner of Rachel) sells lace for curtains, tablecloths, and bed covers in thousands of patterns from France, Scotland, England, and Belgium. Handcrafted jewelry, semi-precious stones, fossils, and shells are exhibited and sold at **Le Nautilus** (in Les Cours Mont-Royal shopping complex and 4840 rue St-Denis). **Lawrmet** (5901 rue Sherbrooke Ouest, corner of Royal) sells everything that has anything to do with the game of darts, including carrying cases, dartboards, and the best brand-name projectiles.

Librairie Russell Books (275 rue St-Antoine Ouest, corner of Bleury) is perhaps the largest English-language bookstore in Montreal, with thousands of volumes lining the shelves and another million or so in storage. There are second-hand paperbacks, out-of-print books, and antiquarian volumes. The **Bibliomania Book Shop** (4685 avenue du Parc, corner of Villeneuve) sells antiquarian books dating back to 1660, and has a large selection of old magazines, prints, engravings, and sheet music. **Capitaine Québec** (5108 boulevard Decarie, corner of chemin Queen Mary) stocks eclectic collectibles, including comic books, fantasy games, obscure sci-fi books, and trading cards (sports, old movies, television).

Antiques

The section of rue Notre-Dame between rue Guy and avenue Atwater is called Attic Row because of its string of unpretentious antiques shops. **Portes & Vitraux Anciens du Grand Montreal** (1500 rue Notre-Dame) specializes in Canadian pine furniture and stained glass, while **Danielle J. Malynowsky Inc.** (1640 rue Notre-Dame) mingles Canadiana with Victorian and Chinese pieces. **Antiquitou** (2475 rue Notre-Dame) handles cash registers and old decoys. **Antiques Gisela** (1960 rue Notre-Dame) sells old toys, dolls, trains, and teddy bears. **G.M. Portal** (1894 rue Notre-Dame), **Antiques Landry** (1726 rue Notre-Dame), and **Sirois** (1646 rue Notre-Dame) deal mainly in oak and pine furniture.

To the northeast, in the Plateau Mont-Royal area, **Antiques Albert** (3762 boulevard St-Laurent) handles Victorian furniture, jewelry, and objets d'art, along with Art

Nouveau and Art Deco collectibles. You'll find antique watches, clocks, and other timepieces at **La Pendulerie Antique** (5037 rue St-Denis). **Galerie Leport-Tremblay** (3979 rue St-Denis) specializes in jewelry, vases, furniture, and curios dating from the turn of the century to 1950. In a variation on the antiques theme, **Maison l'Ami du Collectionneur** (111 rue St-Paul Ouest) in Vieux Montréal sells quality reproductions of 17th- and 18th-century Quebec furniture, all made by hand without nails.

Crafts

Vieux-Montréal is noted for its fine craft stores. In bold contrast to the *quartier*'s souvenir shops, which peddle pine carvings of *habitants* and mass-produced soapstone sculpture, these respected ateliers offer limited-edition, high-quality pottery, glass, and ceramics. A few of the best include **Centre de Céramique de Bonsecours** (444 St-Gabriel), generally considered the best craft gallery in the city; **Boutique L'Empreinte** (272 St-Paul Est), an artists' cooperative displaying a wide range of handcrafts; and **Le Guilde Graphique** (9 St-Paul Est), a frame shop that offers a well-chosen selection of contemporary prints and graphics.

Galleries

The galleries along Sherbrooke are among Canada's most prominent. **Galerie Walter Klinkhoff** (1200 rue Sherbrooke Ouest) is renowned for its contemporary Canadian art. **Polar Inuit Gallery** (1396 rue Sherbrooke Ouest) deals in soapstone sculpture from the North; **Eskimo Art** (1434 rue Sherbrooke Ouest) is the largest gallery in Canada devoted to Inuit art, and has an even wider selection of soapstone, whale bone, and ivory sculptures.

In front of **Galerie Dominion** (1438 rue Sherbrooke Ouest) stand Rodin's *Burgher of Calais* and Moore's *Upright Motive*. The four floors of the former gray-stone townhouse are crowded with the works of Old Masters and Canadian greats. Works by Ken Danby, Henri Masson, and Tony Onley are found in **Galerie Mihalis** (1500 rue Sherbrooke Ouest); **Galerie Atelier Lukacs** (1504 rue Sherbrooke Ouest) has a vast selection of paintings, sculptures, and drawings, featuring works by Lillian Broca, Peter Aitkens, and David Silverberg. Tiny **Galerie Amrad** (1522 rue Sherbrooke Ouest, corner of Guy) is Canada's only gallery devoted solely to African art.

Galerie Elca London (1616 rue Sherbrooke Ouest)

has a large collection of Eskimo and contemporary art. Downstairs at **Galerie Franklin Silverstone** (1618 rue Sherbrooke Ouest) is a showcase for contemporary ceramics, sculpture, and other mixed media including artisan handicrafts. Next-door **Galerie Samuel Lallouz** (1620 rue Sherbrooke Ouest) specializes in international contemporary artists with an emphasis on the avant-garde. Fabulous one-of-a-kind cut glass and ceramics, as well as futuristic jewelry, are found at **Galerie Elena Lee-Verre d'Art** (1518 rue Sherbrooke Est). If this becomes contemporary art overkill then retreat into the past at **Le Petit Musée** (1496 rue Sherbrooke Ouest), where ancient *objets* and *bijoux* from Egypt, Greece, and the Orient reveal their mysteries to the curious and the collector.

Farther afield, **Galerie Intercontinentale** (2158 rue Crescent) shimmers with exquisite glass objets d'art, sculpture, and vases crafted by French glassblower Robert Pierini. **Galerie Artes** (102 rue Laurier Ouest) specializes in limited-edition graphics—lithographs, woodcuts, etchings—by top Canadian and international artists.

—*David Dunbar and Mary Kelly*

THE PROVINCE OF QUEBEC

By David E. Scott

David E. Scott was born and raised in the province of Quebec, and returns frequently. He has been the travel editor of the London (Ontario) Free Press *for more than a decade.*

Canada's most culturally and historically interesting province is a vast territory, about one-sixth the total area of Canada, and larger than the combined areas of France, Spain, and West Germany. Included in that area is 71,000 square miles of fresh water. The northern three-quarters of Quebec is largely uninhabited and even unexplored, though much of it is known to contain enormous quantities of valuable minerals.

About 77 percent of Quebec's population of 6.5 million is concentrated in cities, and most of that is in Montreal (which has a population of more than two million) and its environs. Other urban-population pockets are in and around the cities of Hull (next to Ottawa), Quebec City, Sherbrooke, Laval, Longueuil, Verdun, and a number of cities and towns that surround Lac-St-Jean (St. John), source of the Saguenay River draining eastward into the St. Lawrence River north of Quebec City.

French is the mother tongue of more than 80 percent of Quebeckers, and outside Montreal that rises to 93 percent. One Quebecker in four speaks English in addition to French. The visitor who is unaware of these statistics can find himself in a lather when confronted by someone who, when asked for directions, for example, simply shrugs and walks away. Quite often the individual is walking away to fetch someone who has at least a smattering of English, but in remote areas off the established tourist tracks such individuals cannot always be found.

If you only know six (polite) French words, try to use them when you're in Quebec. If you don't know at least six French words (*bonjour, s'il vous plaît, où est*), you should learn them before visiting the province. If you don't speak or understand French, do not assume the chap from whom you are asking directions, ordering food, or trying to buy a souvenir speaks English and is snubbing you by refusing to do so. Here's where your pleasant smile pays off. After all, his life was going along just fine until you arrived and wanted something. For a friendly effort, he'll probably try to find someone who can speak English and help you out.

Most Quebec drivers are super macho and, unlike many of their neighbors in Ontario, know which is the passing lane of a four-lane highway. Be sure you do, too, or you may find a hood ornament stuck to the back of your car.

Many Quebec automobile drivers will display an intense determination not to be bested in a passing match, left behind in the dash for a tiny opening in traffic, or humbled by "*les spotteurs*," the Quebec provincial police. Should you be challenged for that tiny hole in the traffic, give way, even if you have the right of way. Console yourself with the fact that you're not backing down but just being a gracious guest in a foreign country.

Food and liquor are generally more expensive in Quebec than in other parts of Canada, but food is taken seriously. It is not unusual for the waitress at the humblest truck-stop restaurant to ask whether you want your hamburger cooked well, medium, or rare. Try to smile and laugh a lot while you're in Quebec. You'll notice that's what most of the natives do. You'll see more joie de vivre in Quebec than in any other part of North America.

MAJOR INTEREST

The Eastern Townships
Fishing

Winter sports
Summer resorts

St. Lawrence South Shore
Crafts

The Gaspé Peninsula
Seascapes and mountain scenery
Gaspé National Park in the mountains
Forillon National Park on the sea
Percé village for arts and fishing

The Magdalen Islands
Remoteness and tranquillity

The St. Lawrence Islands
Life in an old-fashioned style

St. Lawrence North Shore
Mountain scenery and rugged seascapes
Pointe-au-Pic summer resorts

The Laurentian Mountains
Ski resorts

For touristic purposes, Quebec comprises seven regions easily explored by the visitor. For internal political purposes, the province is divided into 18 touristic regions, some of which are almost inaccessible to the tourist except by chartered aircraft. In this guide the political boundaries have been ignored to simplify descriptions of the location of (and best routes through) the various geographic regions. The Magdalen Islands, included in this chapter, are somewhat difficult to reach, but the rewards to the visitor are great.

- **Eastern Townships.** This triangular area, south of the St. Lawrence River and north of the borders of the U.S. states of New York, New Hampshire, Vermont, and Maine, is rolling mixed farmland interrupted by small mountains of volcanic origin and dotted with lakes and laced by rivers and brooks. This is the area across the river from Montreal and Quebec City.
- **St. Lawrence South Shore.** South of the St. Lawrence River from Quebec City northeast to the beginning of the Gaspé Peninsula, this area lies between the Eastern Townships and the peninsula.

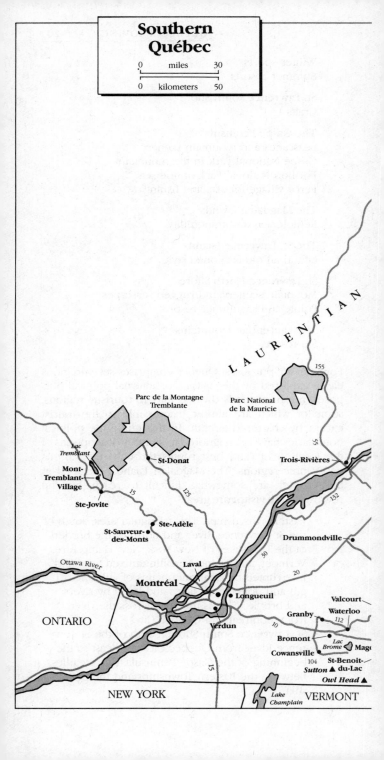

Southern Québec

```
0        miles        30
0        kilometers        50
```

LAURENTIAN

155

Parc de la Montagne
Tremblante

Parc National
de la Mauricie

55

*Lac
Tremblant*

St-Donat

Trois-Rivières

132

**Mont-
Tremblant-
Village**

Ste-Jovite

15

125

Ste-Adèle

**St-Sauveur-
des-Monts**

Drummondville

30

Ottawa River

20

Laval

Montréal

Longueuil

Valcourt

Granby

Waterloo

112

ONTARIO

Verdun

10

Bromont

*Lac
Brome*

Mago

Cowansville

**St-Benoit-
du-Lac**

104

Sutton ▲

15

Owl Head ▲

NEW YORK

*Lake
Champlain*

VERMONT

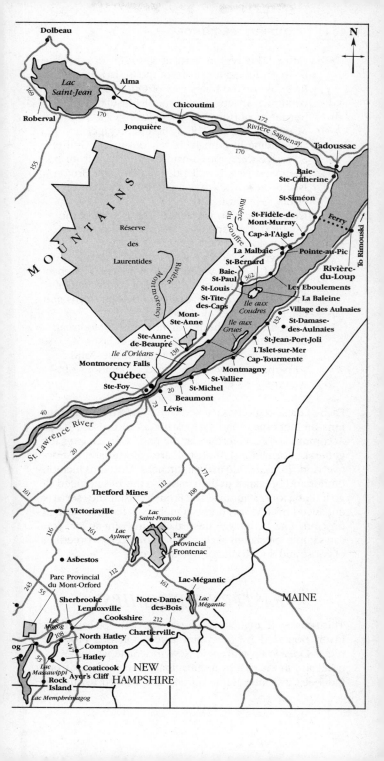

- **Gaspé**. This region starts at about Rivière-du-Loup on the south shore of the St. Lawrence River about 100 miles east of Quebec City, and continues around the Gaspé Peninsula to the border of northeastern New Brunswick.
- **Magdalen Islands**. This 12-island archipelago (Madeleine in French) is way out in the Gulf of St. Lawrence, approximately equidistant from southwest Newfoundland, western Cape Breton Island on Nova Scotia, and the north coast of Prince Edward Island.
- **Islands of the St. Lawrence**. The islands of the Upper St. Lawrence are Orléans, Coudres, and Grues—located near Quebec City.
- **St. Lawrence North Shore** is the Charlevoix area north of the St. Lawrence River between Quebec City and Tadoussac at the mouth of the Saguenay River, and north to Lac-St-Jean and the towns and cities that cluster along its shores.
- **Laurentians**. An hour's drive north of Montreal, this mountain range is riddled with lakes, streams, and family-owned inns, lodges, and re-sorts that have accommodated generations of winter-sports enthusiasts.

Each of these regions is packed with hundreds of different inns or "auberges" and various hotels and resorts. (See Accommodations Reference at the end of the chapter for general information.) Almost all are colorful and distinctive. And, all take pride in their kitchens. Most inns include dinner and breakfast in their rates, so there is no need to go looking for restaurants. The French cuisine they serve is enhanced by a "down home" Québecois flavor; in fact, at tiny inns like **L'Auberge des Falaises** in Point-au-Pic, you can sample specialties such as *sauvagine,* a cross breeding of goose and duck found only in this area.

EASTERN TOWNSHIPS

This roughly triangular area lies south of the St. Lawrence River, bounded by the point where Quebec Province meets Ontario Province and New York State west of Montreal, and in the east by an imaginary line southeast from Quebec City to the Maine border. The Eastern Townships cover about 5,000 square miles of hilly country dotted with lakes and laced by rivers and streams, and account for 10 percent of urbanized Quebec.

In the western one-third, north of the borders of the states of Vermont and New Hampshire, alluvial plains are interrupted by half a dozen volcanic peaks, the highest of which is Mont-Orford, scarcely a mountain at 2,860 feet.

The Eastern Townships are so named to distinguish them from the Western Townships, which are now in Ontario. The region is home to some 300,000 people, one-third of whom live in the city of Sherbrooke, and the balance in small towns or spread thinly across this vast area.

Until 1951 the area was known in French as Les Cantons de l'Est, but it's now called l'Estrie, a marriage of the words *est* (meaning east) and *patrie* (homeland).

The townships start less than an hour's drive east of Montreal with the flat farmland around Granby and Cowansville. A little farther east there is a mountainous region, part of the ancient Appalachian range. Sutton, Owl's Head, Bromont, and Orford are the highest peaks. At the feet of these small mountains are pretty lakes—Brome, Massawippi, Magog, Bowker, Memphremagog, Mégantic, Aylmer, Lyster, and St-François. Cruises are available on lakes Lyster, Mégantic, and Memphremagog. The lakes haven't been polluted by heavy industry or indiscriminate dumping, and most yield an astonishing variety of game fish.

The mountains draw skiers in the winter, hikers in the summer, and the lakes bring boaters, fishermen, and sunbathers from spring to autumn.

The city of **Sherbrooke** is called the Queen of the Eastern Townships. Around this industrial and commercial center are scores of villages, towns, and hamlets, many of whose names—now with French prefixes or suffixes attached—were assigned by the generations of Anglo-Saxon colonists who created homesteads and farms out of the primordial forests.

The 15 counties of the townships have names like Wolfe, Shefford, Stanstead, and Dorchester because they once were the exclusive preserve of Loyalists—English subjects who remained loyal to the British Crown and emigrated to Canada after the American Revolution. But French Canada's "revenge of the cradle" has since the early 1800s achieved a French-speaking majority in all the counties. It was a gradual takeover and one without the rancor that surfaced several decades ago, most noticeably in the West Montreal suburbs.

Names like Ste-Catherine-de-Hatley, Ste-Hilaire-de-Dorset and St-Jacques-de-Leeds recall the origins of the first settlers, few of whose descendants remain in this predominantly Francophone region.

French and English farmers have eked out their existences on this thin soil for generations, and each group has a healthy respect for the other. The movement to separate French Quebec from English Canada was never a highly emotional cause in these tranquil parts, where the Anglophone visitor will have little difficulty finding a native who speaks some English.

The western half of this region is the prettiest, reminding the visitor of England's Cotswolds, from which many original settlers came (though the townships are ten times the area of the Cotswolds). In the northwest, there are apple orchards and, as the land flattens to the east, fields of grain and corn.

In summer, five-star resorts around the major lakes offer excellent fishing and all water sports. Most have tennis courts and swimming pools and all are close to golf facilities. All major inns and resorts operate year-round, and in winter many of them cater to skiers and snowmobilers. Owners vie strenuously with each other to present the region's best table and you can expect to be served a memorable repast just about anywhere.

Some of the best of this region's year-round lodges and inns include **Le Manoir Hovey** and **Auberge Hatley Inn**, both in North Hatley; **Village Mont Orford** and **Domaine Avallon**, both in Magog; and **Residences Val Sutton** and **Village Archimede de Sutton**, both in Sutton. Alpine skiing is available at eight major centers in l'Estrie. Magog's **Station Touristique de Mont Orford** has added over $20 million worth of lift equipment and snow-making machines in the past five years.

All resorts have their own dining rooms, but visit North Hatley's **Le Manoir Hovey** or **Auberge Hatley Inn**, historic country inns, for some truly memorable dining fare. The former is a member of the prestigious, German-based Romatik Inn federation; the second has been accorded the Relais et Châteaux stamp of approval.

The Eastern Townships don't have a Niagara Falls or Rocky Mountains; nevertheless, bucolic scenes frequently await around the next curve of a secondary highway or gravel side road. Many of Quebec's remaining 150 covered wooden bridges are still in use here; there are elaborate Victorian mansions and wooden churches of graceful proportions; and meadows purple with clover roll down hillsides to twinkling rapids on a fast-flowing river.

There are some package holidays that enable the visitor to sample several different hotels. For winter, the packages are known as **ski inter-auberges**, and it's possible to cross-country ski from one inn to another and have your luggage sent along by vehicle. Farm lodgings are also available.

The hotels participating in the inter-auberge ski packages known as "Skiwippi" include the aforementioned Le Manoir Hovey and Auberge Hatley Inn as well as the **Ripplecove Inn** in Ayer's Cliff, situated in the middle of five major alpine ski centers. Any of the hotels can book your week package, which boasts 50 km (32 miles) of gorgeous Quebec countryside to ski across as well as gourmet Québecois dining in the winter wonderland of the Eastern Townships.

Snowmobilers will find over 2,000 km (1,250 miles) of trails beginning in Valcourt, the birthplace of Joseph-Armand Bombardier, the inventor of the snowmobile. Complete trail routes are available in the "Motoneig-Estrie" map available from the area's tourist information center.

Winter sports enthusiasts should write the Eastern Townships tourist bureau for up-to-date packages and prices on the various resorts. Association Touristique de l'Estrie, 2883, rue King West, Sherbrooke, Quebec, J1L 1C6. Tel: (819) 566-7404.

Around the Townships

A four-lane autoroute links Montreal with Sherbrooke, 144 km (90 miles) to the east. This is Highway 10, the fastest route for those visitors in a hurry to reach the heart of the townships and start their wanderings, but the real beauty of the townships lies north or south of this intrusion in the quiet landscape.

About 64 km (40 miles) east of Montreal, at **Granby**, there is a major zoo, with 350 species of animals as well as a reptile house. At Lac Boivin Nature Study Centre, also at Granby, there are more animals and a variety of interesting specimens of plant life and trees.

For those who know and love the drowsy communities of this region, their relative obscurity is a blessing. The winding secondary roads that link the towns and villages aren't crowded with tour buses and lines of vacationers' cars, and there aren't lines at the increasingly numerous excellent restaurants fashioned from gracious old homes by entrepreneurs who can work miracles over a cooking range.

Compared with what awaits the visitor in Gaspé and along either shore of the St. Lawrence River, none of the places we discuss below (in no particular route order) is cause for a visit on its own merits. But if you have opted to savor the rural loveliness of this area and find yourself near one of these places during your browsings, a certain town may justify the detour you may have to make to see it.

Waterloo, a dozen miles southeast of Granby, is renowned for its mushrooms, which you're likely to find in the stuffing of a duckling from nearby Brome Lake, the duck-breeding center of Canada. Waterloo has an unusual museum, **Musée Québecois de la Chasse**, which traces the history and techniques of hunting, and where you can have a meal highlighted by game dishes.

From **Magog**, a resort at the north end of Lac Memphremagog, which is shared by Quebec and Vermont, you can get a boat cruise on this cottage-and-forest-ringed lake. The cruise will take you past the Benedictine abbey at St-Benoit-du-Lac, a piece of Europe in the New World. The abbey's cheese, cider, and chocolate have earned a regional reputation and may be bought on the premises.

Parc du Mont-Orford is the home of an important art and cultural center where classical and jazz concerts are held during the summer season. If you're there on a clear day, take the ski lift to the top for an overview of the townships from the 2,860-foot-high summit.

North Hatley, at the north end of **Lac Massawippi**, is the prettiest of the townships' resort towns. Its beauty has attracted painters, writers, and artisans, whose works are available in local boutiques. Massawippi is only 12 miles long and a mile wide, but it offers up an inexhaustible supply of game fish and is said to contain 70 species. There's an English-language summer theater at **The Piggery**, and two of Quebec's best-known resorts are on Massawippi; **Hovey Manor** and **Hatley Inn** (Manoir Hovey and Auberge Hatley). Both carry the province's highest ratings in all categories and are favorite retreats of Quebec cabinet ministers.

While Sherbrooke is the Francophone cultural center of the townships, the village of Lennoxville, only 5 km (3 miles) south, is the English counterpart. Bishops University was started here in 1843 in buildings inspired by those at Oxford University, England. Just across the St. Francis River from the university complex is Bishops College School, founded in the same era and designed for the education of "the sons of English gentlemen."

Compton, Cookshire, Coaticook, Rock Island, Hatley, and Lac-Mégantic are other towns and villages with a slow pace and buildings that were erected as long ago as 1800. **Cookshire** is particularly attractive with its Balley and Pope houses built in 1800, the 1835 covered bridge, the 1864 Anglican church, and the 1868 post office. Rock Island has the Haskell Opera House, a scaled-down replica of the Old Boston Opera House built astride the Canada-U.S. border. Near Lac-Mégantic, from Notre-Dame-des-Bois you can drive to the 3,625-foot summit of Mont Mégantic, where an observatory contains the most powerful telescope in eastern North America.

Just south of Chartierville, on Highway 257 north of the New Hampshire border, is Quebec's **Magnetic Hill**. Like its famous counterpart near Moncton in New Brunswick, the phenomenon is simply an optical illusion. A visit to Quebec's Magnetic Hill is also a lesson in commercial promotion: Quebec's hill is not widely known beyond the immediate vicinity, yet its illusion is far more dramatic than that of the New Brunswick hill.

ST. LAWRENCE SOUTH SHORE

The stretch of St. Lawrence River southern shoreline from Quebec City northeast to Rimouski is included for the benefit of those who start their tour of the Gaspé Peninsula by car from Quebec City. Information on the first half of this section—from Quebec City to Rivière-du-Loup— will be of special interest for those who plan a St. Lawrence River loop: Quebec City to St-Siméon on the North Shore (see the section on North Shore below), cross the river by ferry to Rivière-du-Loup, and return to Quebec City on the South Shore. While the communities along this stretch of river have many points of interest for the visitor, the North Shore route is by far more physically attractive; it is mountainous and rugged, while the South Shore is flat and pastoral.

You'll make the best driving time along this section on the Trans-Canada Highway, Highway 20, but most of the attractions are to be found along Highway 132, which is closer to the river. Most towns along this stretch of the South Shore have at least a few fine old buildings carefully maintained or meticulously restored. In Lévis, a timber export center since 1810, there are three fine Victorian mansions on rue Wolfe (Nos. 2, 4, 6) and a magnificent view of Quebec City from **Terrasse de Lévis**.

At Pointe Lévis is **Fort No. 1**, a national historic park. The fort was built between 1865 and 1872 out of fear the Americans would attack Quebec using the railway linking the state of Maine to the city of Lévis. Fort No. 1 was one in a series of three separate forts making up part of the fortifications of Quebec City. The fort, of the Vauban type, was built behind considerable masses of earth.

Beaumont

The town of Beaumont has a beautiful 1821 mill, 20 historical homes of French inspiration, and a church with an interesting story. The first church was built in 1694, followed by the presbytery in 1722. A proclamation by General James Wolfe was pinned up by the British on the door of the present church, built in 1733. As soon as villagers had ripped it up, Wolfe's soldiers set fire to the church, but only the door would burn.

A mansard-type seigneurial mill here, perched on a cliff overlooking the Maillou waterfall, was first used as a carding mill; millstones and saws were later added so that grain and lumber could be processed. You can purchase muffins and bread made from flour milled on the premises of the three-story mill and baked in the traditional manner.

Behind the mill is a stairway leading to the river's edge near the ruins of another mill, where an archaeological dig is in progress. A video recording explains the history of the restoration and the findings from the digs being carried out on the sites of both mills. The mill is open from mid-June to the end of October, except Mondays.

The church in nearby St-Michel dates from 1858. At the entrance to the village (on your left) is a replica of the chapel at Lourdes. Restoration of the 1739 presbytery near the church has erased all traces of the English bombardment intended to force the inhabitants to accept the new regime after the fall of Quebec.

Just a few miles farther north on Highway 132 is St-Vallier and the **Musée des Voitures à Chevaux** (Horse-Drawn Carriage Museum). It has 65 summer and winter carriages and assorted equestrian accessories on display.

The next community, **Montmagny**, is one of the oldest on the South Shore. Masses of snow geese stop over here during their fall migration, and a snow goose festival is held October 15 to 25. At the Manoir Couillard-Dupuis, built in 1789, there is an exhibit about Grosse Ile.

About 10 miles northeast of Montmagny is the village of L'Islet-sur-Mer. It is nicknamed the "sailors' homeland" because sailors from here have served on every ocean of the world. On July 1, 1909, one of its most courageous sons, Captain Joseph-Elzear Bernier, took possession of the Arctic islands in the name of Canada, a feat recognized by a plaque on Melville Island there. The **Musée Maritime Bernier** (Bernier Maritime Museum), located in an old convent built in 1877, is the largest maritime museum in North America in terms of the size and quality of its collection.

St-Jean-Port-Joli

St-Jean-Port-Joli is Quebec's handcraft capital. Just outside the village is a mini-village of wood sculptors' workshops, the largest assembly of artisan-sculptors in the province. The wood-carving tradition was started around 1936 by the Bourgault family, but potters and weavers have also moved to the area. The 1779 church in the village is a classified cultural property. There is also a fine mill once owned by the Seigneurie de Philippe Aubert de Gaspé, and a stone home built for the English government as general headquarters of the militia.

There are two museums in town filled with the best examples of woodworking from the region, and another one with weaving looms, spinning wheels, dishware, and industrial and agricultural machinery.

Most of the shops selling wood carvings here also include an area in which the sculptors work. They're happy to chat with visitors as they work and answer any questions. The caliber of work varies from studio to studio and choosing the piece you want to take home can be difficult. Often, meeting and getting to know the sculptor helps make the decision easier and results in a work of art with a very personal connection.

A few miles east, in the **Village des Aulnaies**, is the oldest seigneurial concession on the South Shore from Montmagny to the Gulf of St. Lawrence. The manor, the communal mill, the miller's house, and the gardens are as they were in 1854 when the Neo-Classical manor house was built. The manor is surrounded by wide verandas bordered in frieze and well-kept gardens overlooking the river. Inside the manor, staff in period costume recall the era. The three-story gabled communal mill built of freestone has been restored, and visitors can purchase freshly milled flour and watch the trough of incoming water power the mill. The miller's house has been converted into a café-terrace where you can enjoy refreshments under huge oak trees. The estate is open daily from the last week of June through Labour Day.

Rivière-du-Loup (Wolf River) was founded in 1683. The town is shaped like an amphitheater on a rocky spur that advances to the St. Lawrence River. The city has a 90-foot waterfall within its limits, and it is an important junction point, being linked with St-Siméon on the North Shore by regular ferry service March 31 to January 2. For the next 104 km (65 miles) northeast to Rimouski, there is a procession of small villages and towns along the ever-widening St. Lawrence River. At Rivière-du-Loup, the river is about 12 miles wide; at Rimouski the width is 33 miles.

Rimouski, midway between Quebec City and Gaspé, is the last major city before the Gaspé loop. **Maison Lamontagne** here is one of the last examples of half-timbered houses left in Quebec; it is open daily from the last week in June to the end of the first week in September.

If you decide to stay the night before heading into the Gaspé region, there is a good range of affordable accommodation in the area and fine French dining is never far away. In Rimouski's **Auberge des Gouverneurs**, a 165-room château, fine dining is just down the hall, at the hotel dining room. Less grand lodging, which nonetheless offers a lovely river view, can be found at the **Motel Rimouski**.

THE GASPE PENINSULA

The Gaspé Peninsula is the portion of the province of Quebec that juts into the Gulf of St. Lawrence and lies between the St. Lawrence River to the north and the province of New Brunswick to the south. It is a hilly to mountainous area with well-forested slopes. The central portion is occupied by the Shickshock (pronounced sheek-shock) and Notre Dame mountain ranges, a continuation of the Appalachians, which rise in places to more than 4,000 feet and provide sensational spring heli-skiing (in which helicopters transport skiers to wilderness sites). The peninsula is more or less separated from the mainland of Quebec by the Matapédia River and Lake. The peninsula is 150 miles long and has 450 miles of coast along which a narrow fringe of population is spread in tiny fishing villages. The interior mountains are an obstacle to communication between the north and south coasts, and constitute a divide for the rivers flowing north into the St. Lawrence and south into Baie des Chaleurs.

A logical starting place for a tour of the Gaspé Peninsula is at Rimouski on the South Shore of the St. Lawrence River (for which see the end of the South Shore section above). You can fly to Rimouski, Mont Joli, or Matane and rent a car for your tour. If time is tight, you could also fly to the town of Gaspé and see the area's ultimate sights in one day. From Mont Joli you can do the Gaspé Peninsula circle tour in a rental car in two days, but forcing that pace through such spectacular scenery is ill advised. The tour merits a week at the very least, and to do it in less time is to miss too many memorable little restaurants, breathtaking vistas, and the experience of the people.

At any time of year, it's wise to have reservations along the way. Many motels are filled September to May by sales people and government officials, and in the summer months when those people don't travel in this region, more than a million others do. Another consideration when budgeting your time for a Gaspé tour is the weather. When an east wind blows in off the Gulf of St. Lawrence, the nasty weather can stay for days at a time. If you have some buffer time, you can use it by staying put wherever you are and catching up on your reading, visiting nearby museums, churches, or other attractions. When the weather clears, start moving again.

Yet another worthwhile thing to consider if you're bound to any Atlantic seacoast in summer is clothing. It's difficult when you're packing in sweltering heat even to think about warm and waterproof clothing, but you'd better have both with you on a trip around the Gaspé. The daytime highs inland can get as hot as they do anywhere else in eastern Canada, but it always cools at night, and the average temperatures are considerably lower than they are in Montreal or Quebec City.

The name Gaspé derives in one version from an Indian word meaning the end of the world, and historians should accept that because it's a far better name source than the alternative. Even today when you reach Gaspé it's not hard to imagine you have reached the end of the world . . . and who ever heard of Gaspar Corte-Real anyway?

Not only do you feel you've reached the end of the world at Gaspé, but you also soon realize you truly don't want to go back to the real world (unless you happen to come from a place with stunning seascape scenery and empty beaches, and where personal social status is earned by the cuisine you serve).

The Micmac Indians, called Indians of the Sea, have lived in the Gaspé Peninsula for more than 2,500 years. The first European settlers were Acadians, Loyalists, Bretons, Basques, English, Jersey, Irish, and Scottish. The diversity of these ethnic backgrounds may be seen today, expressed in everything from architecture to hair and skin coloration.

The Gaspé Peninsula is one of Canada's oldest tourist regions, but one known only by wealthy and adventurous North Americans until a couple of decades ago. They got here by boat or by risking their lives in automobiles on the narrow, washboard gravel roads that twisted up and down the frighteningly steep Shickshock mountainsides. To tour the Gaspé even in the 1950s was an adventure. You never knew when you might get stuck going up one of those incredibly steep hills after a rainstorm, and have to back all the way down again. After a couple of unsuccessful tries—each more scary than the previous—you'd have to call it quits and backtrack to the next settlement with a hotel or boardinghouse. You'd stay there until the road crews filled in the washouts and regraded the axle-deep washboard.

Nowadays a Gaspé tour is only an adventure in cuisine and scenery. The main highway around the coast is all

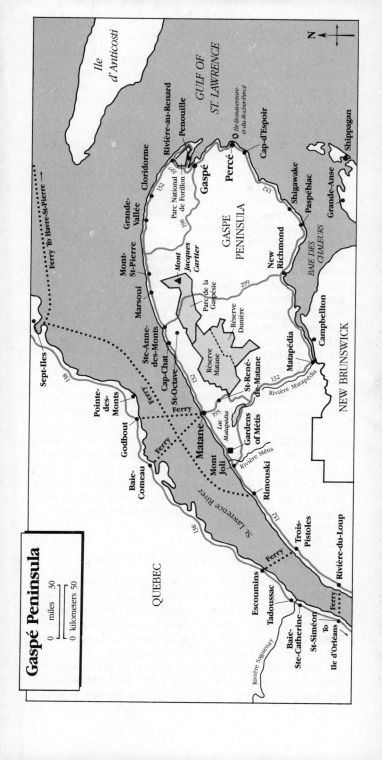

paved, and some sections are four lanes wide. Except in the most severe winter storms, people in the 600-mile-long string of settlements set their watches by the twice-daily Voyageur bus, which is their chief link with the other world.

Tourism is starting to become an important economic fact of life in the Gaspé, and the regional entrepreneurs have already done their homework in preparation for the new breed of visitor. Everything is organized: Hotel and motel prices and accommodation standards are set by the government; reservation systems are in place at all hotels; menus are bilingual; and most hotel rooms have color TV.

The hospitality factor has never needed brushing up on the peninsula. It has been a fact of life here since the area was settled in the late 1700s. Now that tourism is an industry and more and more visitors are crowding the highways and restaurants—to the inconvenience of the local residents—the same cheerful helpfulness is still available from fisherman to gas jockey, from restaurant waitress to lumberjack.

Everything that attracted those early tourist adventurers in the late 1800s is still here: the colorful frame houses overlook picture-postcard inlets from their perches on steep hillsides and capes; salmon rivers, gin-clear after tumbling down gravel beds from deep in the mountains, join the white-capped blue Atlantic in bays ringed by weatherbeaten fish shacks; sheltered coves are shot through with a hundred colors of paint on the fish and lobster boats, the lobster buoys, and the dories.

Should you start your Gaspé tour from Quebec City, take the Trans-Canada Highway (20) along the South Shore of the St. Lawrence. (For information on the portion of the trip from Quebec City to Rimouski, see the St. Lawrence South Shore section.)

The Peninsula's North Shore

Starting your Gaspé tour from Rimouski, you won't have to make any decisions about highway routes. It's Highway 132 from Rimouski east to Gaspé, from there to Matapédia at the New Brunswick border, and north again from Matapédia to Mont Joli on the St. Lawrence coast, just a few miles east of Rimouski, where you started.

The Gardens of Métis, about 40 km (25 miles) east of Rimouski, should not be missed if you are fond of flowers and landscaping. The property, also known as Villa

Reford, was owned by Lord Mount Stephen, the first president of the Canadian Pacific Railroad, who enjoyed salmon fishing in the Métis River and was part of the large English-speaking population who vacationed in family summer estates in and around this resort town.

Lord Stephen gave the estate to his niece Elsie Stephen Meighan Reford, who in 1928 transformed it into a magnificent British-style flower garden. Thanks to an exceptional micro-climate and abundant resources, flowers that could be found nowhere else in northern latitudes were soon blooming here. The 37-room summer "cottage" stands in the middle of the gardens and now houses a museum, restaurant, and craft shop. The gardens are open daily from mid-June to mid-September.

Matane, 48 km (30 miles) east of Métis, is the last ferry link to the North Shore (at either Baie Comeau or Godbout, at this point each more than 64 km/40 miles away across the St. Lawrence River). The ferry runs daily throughout the year. A side trip south on Highway 195 will take you to the covered bridges of St.-Jérôme-de-Matane and St-René-de-Matane.

About 16 km (10 miles) south of Cap-Chat—named for a rock resembling a crouching cat—is eastern North America's only helicopter ski site, at **St-Octave**. From March to the end of May, there are intermediate and expert runs on the immense stretches of snowfields in the Shickshock Mountains.

You're in the mountains now, and will be for the rest of the trip to Gaspé. The highway clings to the edges of some slopes and circles the base of cliffs at sea level. The St. Lawrence is salt water now, and has been since the east end of Ile d'Orléans. At times the highway may swing inland, climbing up over a steep granite headland before plunging down the other side to cross a stream or river flowing from deep in the mountains.

From Ste-Anne-des-Monts you can take Highway 299 south into **Gaspé National Park**, which contains Mont Jacques Cartier. The park, about 56 km (35 miles) south of Highway 132, is the only place in Quebec where you are likely to find moose, wood caribou, and Virginia deer all in the same territory, according to the levels of vegetation and climate. Accommodation is available at **Gîte du Mont-Albert**, a comfortable Quebec government-operated inn open only during the summer months.

About 32 km (20 miles) east of Ste-Anne-des-Monts on Highway 132, at Marsoui, there is a unique restaurant worth visiting—particularly if you have a healthy appetite for wholesome food. **La Cookerie** (The Cookery) isn't listed in any gourmet restaurant guides, and it isn't advertised on highway billboards. But anybody living along this stretch of the Gaspé coast can direct you to it. Drive slowly when you get near, because there's just a one-word sign outside the unprepossessing, weatherbeaten frame building. It says "Restaurant."

La Cookerie is on your right when you're driving toward Gaspé. It sits in a big gravel parking lot at the corner of the road that follows the Marsoui River inland to the mountains. The interior decor is early practical. Four long tables, covered with oilcloth and each seating a dozen at benches, fill the room. The unadorned wooden walls are painted white, and the linoleum-covered floor is spotless.

The places are all set, and on each table there are four or five pies and a plate of strawberry-jam tarts. The sugar bowl is a large enamel pot, and half a pound of butter sits on an enamel plate at each table. There's a menu on the wall, but a waitress comes to tell you the special of the day, which may cost $7.50. Often that's *cipaille* (pronounced sea-pie), a stew of chicken, beef, potato, carrot, turnip, and dumpling with a scoop of cole slaw on the side. A platter of thickly cut white bread arrives with the glass of water.

The size of the serving would buffalo a Weight-Watchers dropout. The entrée is followed by coffee and the baked goods. You just help yourself; if you want half a pie, you eat half a pie. If you want a sliver of each kind to establish a favorite, that's what you're expected to do—but don't miss the sugar pie, a local specialty.

La Cookerie is a wonderful holdover from another era. It was built decades ago for the employees of the local sawmill. When the noon whistle sounded, they'd head for La Cookerie, wash up in the long trough in a room outside the dining area, and tuck into the home-cooked food. The mill is closed now, but locals and knowledgeable travellers keep the place busy. It's open 6:00 A.M. to 8:00 P.M. seven days a week.

A dozen miles east of Marsoui—and where you'd least expect to find it—you'll run across the hang-gliding capital of eastern Canada. Just west of **Mont-St-Pierre** you'll come around a bend in the road and see a beautiful village site— a valley, plateau, mountain, and bay. If weather conditions are good, you'll see a number of gaily colored hang gliders floating through the sky. Take a side trip up Mont-St-Pierre to an altitude of 1,376 feet for a great panoramic view from any of the three glider-launching pads.

There's a covered bridge in Grande-Vallée, farther east from Mont-St-Pierre; a few miles along the road at Cloridorme, home of a major fishing cooperative, you'll see a series of long tables where cod is dried in the open air. These drying racks are called *vigneaux*. At Rivière-au-Renard, the industrial fish-processing center of the north shore of the peninsula, there's no admission charge to watch the processing of cod and turbot daily, when in season.

At this point, you can head south and inland and reach the town of Gaspé in about 32 km (20 miles), or you can stay on the coast and circle **Forillon National Park**, about twice that distance to Gaspé. The park boasts one of Canada's tallest lighthouses, a 121-foot-high historical monument built in 1858. For $1 you can climb to the top. The park contains three plant groups left over from the ice age: flora of the Penouille dunes; flora of the briny marshes in Penouille Bay; and the arctic and alpine flora of the cliffs. From May to October you can often spot a variety of whales from the clifftops, and gray and common seals can usually be seen disporting themselves close to shore. Free to wander through is a bunker built here during World War II as a lookout for the German submarines not infrequently reported in these waters.

Gaspé and Percé

Gaspé the town overlooks an immense natural harbor into which three celebrated salmon rivers empty: the Dartmouth, the York, and the St-Jean. The only wooden cathedral in North America is here, with a magnificent stained-glass window and fresco given by France in 1934 to commemorate the 400th anniversary of Jacques Cartier's arrival. Gaspé Museum is open daily throughout the summer, Monday through Friday the rest of the year; three of its rooms focus on the history of Gaspé.

The most spectacular sight on all the Gaspé tour lies 77 km (48 miles) farther south along the coast highway at **Percé**. You'll see Percé Rock long before you reach this picturesque fishing village: It looks like an enormous ocean liner aground, its bow facing the land. Waves have worn a hole through the rock near its "stern," and it's from that hole that the name Percé, or pierced, is drawn.

A free interpretation center at Percé will acquaint you with the heritage, history, and wildlife of the area. Naturalists are available to answer your questions. From Percé a number of entrepreneurs operate tours to and around Bonaventure Island, where puffins, terns, and cormorants nest in colonies of tens of thousands. Arrangements can be made for you to be left on the island and picked up later.

Percé is the real showplace of the Gaspé Peninsula, attracting artists, who claim the light is perfect, as well as nature lovers. This little fishing village has numerous gift shops, small museums, and art galleries.

There is an abundance of lodging in the Gaspé/Percé region, but try the **Hotel-Motel La Normandie**, a comfortable spot with a very good restaurant. The **Auberge du Gargantua et Motels**, open only during the summer season, is known for its fine food; seafood lovers should ask for the "catch of the day." Both places are at Percé.

If you decide to stay in Gaspé proper, head for the **Auberge des Commandants**, which offers splendid views of the bay and a discotheque to help work off the rich cooking from their dining room.

The Peninsula's South Shore

The balance of your tour around the south side of the Gaspé Peninsula will be along an ever-mellowing coastline, through fishing villages and towns that in some stretches seem to alternate between all-French and all-English.

There's a stop worth making at **Cap-d'Espoir**, about 22 km (14 miles) south of Percé. The Roman Catholic church here isn't the sort of building you'd reasonably expect to find in a region where the citizens traditionally have worked long and hard just to keep themselves alive. But when the parish decided to build a church in 1889 they decided they'd go for the works. The exterior is plain red brick, and there's a silvered spire and bell tower. On the outside, it isn't any different from a hundred other parish churches in rural Quebec. The attention and expense are revealed within.

The architecture is Roman-Corinthian; fluted white columns support the elaborately decorated arches of the 37-foot-high ceiling. The columns and ceiling are white and gold, and the gold, installed in 1912, is real. The pulpit and the doors into the sacristy behind the altar are priceless carved-wood artworks. A large mural by Quebec artist Charles Huot depicts the death of Saint Joseph, patron saint of the church. There are larger and more impressive cathedrals in many cities of the world, but the visitor cannot be prepared for what he will find inside this church.

Cap-d'Espoir, at the northeast entrance to Baie des Chaleurs, is sometimes marked on English maps as Cape Despair. Jacques Cartier called the place Cap-d'Espoir, or Cap-d'Espérance, meaning Cape Hope. In 1711 part of Admiral Sir Hovenden Walker's fleet was wrecked here, with the loss of all on board. The translation of Cap-d'Espoir, obviously, depends on whether one's background is French or English.

As your route swings south and gradually works westward, the terrain becomes less harsh and mountainous. Highway 132 will carry you from village to town to hamlet along the coast.

The land and seascapes become more pastoral as you approach the New Brunswick border at the mouth of the Matapédia River. There are some fine examples of early Victorian architecture in some of the coastal towns, and half a dozen small museums along the way. New Richmond, for example, founded by Loyalists, is remarkable for its Anglo-Saxon style of architecture. Large residences of the well-to-do are in the center of town, and the hillside farms are kept well back from the road by a tree-lined walk, as they are in Scotland.

From Matapédia, if you are returning to Quebec City, follow Highway 132 north up the Matapédia River valley. In just under 160 km (100 miles) you'll reach the St. Lawrence River at Mont Joli, about 365 km (228 miles) east of Quebec City.

THE MAGDALEN ISLANDS

You'll find the Magdalens marked on most maps and in most Province of Quebec tourism literature as Iles-de-la-Madeleine. They're an archipelago of 12 islands almost in the middle of the Gulf of St. Lawrence. The islands are 175 miles southeast of Gaspé, 70 miles northeast of Prince Edward Island, and 55 miles west of Cape Breton Island, Nova Scotia. A population of 14,000 on the seven inhabited islands prevents the Magdalens from being desert islands, but you don't have to drive far to lose sight of habitation and find your very own white sandy beach where you can make the first set of footprints since the last storm washed the beach clean. From the air, the islands appear emerald green and ringed in white, the color of 190 miles of sandy beaches. If the islands were about 2,000 miles south and had a few resort hotels and palm trees, they could give any Caribbean island fierce competition.

The charm of these islands is their remoteness from the hustle and bustle of mainland life. Only because they are far from the madding crowd, the beaches aren't littered with trash and jammed with vacationers frantically trying to see and do everything available during their seven- or 14-day vacation. About 20,000 visitors find their way here each summer, but the shortness of the islands' respite from the harsh weather of the rest of the year has discouraged big investors.

The largest hotel in the islands has only 56 units, the biggest dining spot can seat only 64, and there's a year-round pizza parlor that can seat 82. It's unlikely that any major hotel or motel chain will ever locate here, because they would have to pay off their investment on the proceeds of three summer months, and there's more money to be made more quickly almost anywhere else in southern Canada.

That economic fact makes the Maggies—as they're familiarly known—the almost exclusive vacation preserve of those who know where and when and how to make reservations for a hotel or motel room, a campsite, or one of the few chalets or houses for rent.

The craggy areas of coastline have been carved from grayish-red sandstone, gypsum, and other volcanic rock. Some of the ocher cliffs look as though a deranged giant sculptor had started his ultimate artistic masterpiece and abandoned the project partway through. Elsewhere, there are columns, tunnels, and caves gouged through the paths of least resistance by relentless winds and waves.

Everywhere there is wind. It averages 20 miles an hour, twice that of mainland Quebec. In summer the breezes can be welcome, when a hot sun bakes down on the bald hills, sand dunes, and blinding white beaches; in winter it tugs and howls at the gaily colored square-frame houses that are scattered across the landscape like a child's tantrum-tossed building blocks.

The wide expanses of open gulf water around the Maggies cause the near-constant winds, but they are also responsible for moderating temperatures, which from June to September average 10 to 27 degrees C (50 to 80 degrees F). In the winter, temperatures don't plunge so low as on the mainland. A lot of snow falls on the islands, but accumulation isn't a problem; most of it blows out to sea.

There are a few trees on the islands, but they're short and twisted. On rounded hills, cattle graze in summer beside small fields that grudgingly surrender hay, turnips, and potatoes. Wood is so scarce that the resourceful Madelinots have developed a kind of barn found nowhere else in the world. It is called a *baraque* and consists of four stout posts in a square supporting a four-sided roof that can be raised by ropes and pulleys as more hay is piled underneath. The roof is lowered as the hay is used.

The little houses of the Magdalens may appear to be distributed with as little planning and color as wind-driven confetti, but each faces the sea from which most families make their living. The season traditionally starts with the arrival of seal pups from the ice floes in March and April, and continues through the summer and fall with lobster, herring, cod, halibut, plaice, scallops, and mackerel. Most fishermen are grouped in cooperatives that sell to modern packing plants a snowball's toss from the docks where their wives, daughters, or girlfriends have the day's catch processed and frozen or canned within minutes of its leaving the boats.

Until a few decades ago, the population of the Maggies was about half French-speaking, mainly of Acadian background, and half English-speaking, mostly of Scottish descent. The population now is predominantly French-speaking, but those in tourism-related fields can and will manage some English. The few remaining English-speaking families are on tiny Ile d'Entrée and Grosse Ile.

Highway 199, a paved, two-lane highway, links the main islands, at times bisecting long spits of sand only a couple of hundred yards wide and frequented only by herons, cranes, and gulls. A dedicated sightseer could fully explore the main islands in two days. He'd drive about 320 km (200 miles), visit several churches and lighthouses, the windmill, a lobster- and fish-processing plant, a salt mine, and the Museum of the Sea at Havre Aubert. Near the museum is a Quebec government-supported handcraft center where artisans carve bowls and ashtrays from local stone, weave woolen goods, and sell paintings and photographs.

But somebody racing through the islands on a schedule like that would miss their greatest attraction: the lifestyle only now being nudged out of place by the 20th century; its man-made accoutrements; and the haunting beauty of those deserted, windswept dunes and beaches where the only sounds are those of wind and wave and the cries of wheeling gulls.

Hotel and motel accommodation on the islands is limited but relatively inexpensive. Don't expect color television in all rooms, or even your own bathroom *en suite*. Rooms are small, not air-conditioned, but spotlessly clean. At several small and unpretentious restaurants you'll be able to have fresh lobster or other seafood dishes at half mainland prices.

Two good spots to stay are the highly rated **Hôtel Château Madelinot** on Cap-aux-Meules, and the tiny (six-room) **Motel des Iles**, which may have the best auberge dining room on the Magdalens. For that indigenous island specialty known as "pot-en-pot," a tangy mixture of fish, seafood, and potatoes baked in a flaky pie crust, try **La Saline** on Havre-Aubert. On l'Ile du Havre, don't miss the seafood specials and mussel dishes at the aptly named **La Moulinère**.

Three airlines fly to the Maggies from Halifax, Charlottetown, and Gaspé. C.T.M.A. *Voyageur,* a freighter, makes one round trip per week from Montreal and can carry 15 passengers. There is daily ferry service from Souris, Prince Edward Island; the M. V. *Lucy Maud Montgomery* can take 90 cars and 300 passengers.

Reservations are not accepted for the trip out of Souris, and passengers board on a first-come, first-served basis. You can, and should, reserve at least seven days in advance for the return trip. Rates for the ferry are about $50 round trip per person, and about $100 round trip for an automobile. (See the Getting Around section at the end of this chapter; see also the chapter on Prince Edward Island.)

THE ISLANDS OF THE ST. LAWRENCE

There are three islands in the St. Lawrence River north and east of Quebec City where you can step back in time to another age. If you can overlook the rooftop television aerials and the automobile traffic, it isn't hard to imagine you've journeyed several centuries into the past.

The islands are Ile d'Orléans, Ile aux Coudres, and Ile aux Grues, and their residents enjoy a pace of life that's a whole lot slower than on the mainland. They have time to visit and gossip and make things with their hands. The housewives buy their bread from the baker, their meat from the butcher, and their fish from the fishmonger. Vegetables and fruit come from their own gardens in season, or from jars of preserves in the winter, because most homes have gardens out back and their owners have the time to keep them watered and weed-free.

Ile d'Orléans

Of the three islands, Ile d'Orléans, about eight miles northeast of Quebec City, has yielded most to modern times because it has been easily accessible by car across a suspension bridge (from near Montmorency on the North Shore) since 1935. Before the bridge all traffic came by ferryboat, and that inconvenience, plus the ferry toll, hampered the development of tourism.

Lack of a bridge for so long resulted in the islanders being called sorcerers, and today some islanders still refer proudly to themselves as "*sorciers.*" The sorcery rumor was started by French-Canadian mainlanders who were often puzzled by strange lights they saw flickering along the shore of the island at night. At a loss to explain the lights, they began to whisper among themselves that the island was inhabited by sorcerers. English Quebeckers who also saw the lights believed they were those of will-o'-the-wisps. There wasn't anything supernatural about the lights; the best explanation is that they were lanterns used by islanders to communicate with relatives or friends on the mainland.

After the bridge was built, it didn't take long for wealthy Quebeckers to decide the island's beauty made the commuting distance to downtown offices well worth while.

Many built homes on the north and west perimeters of the island, which afford an outlook across the St. Lawrence shipping lanes to the backdrop of Quebec City's Cape Diamond and the brooding Laurentian Mountains.

The island's population is now more than 6,000 and increasing, but the growth doesn't include any shopping centers and hotels springing up in the apple orchards and strawberry fields. In 1970 the provincial government declared the island a natural and historic *arrondissement,* or district. (Whereas in a park the government owns the land, in an *arrondissement* private ownership of the land remains but the government has a say in what is done with the land.)

Ile d'Orléans is elliptically shaped, 21 miles long and never more than about five miles wide. Chemin Royal (Royal Road), the paved road that skirts its shoreline, wanders through the island's six parishes. Farming is the traditional occupation, and the island's strawberries are known far and wide. Handcrafts are created in many homes—rag-rug weaving, wood carving, spinning, knitting, and crocheting.

There's a complete mix of architectural styles around the island, ranging from centuries-old stone churches and New England Victoriana to steep-roofed houses in gay colors with ski jump–shaped roofs and rows of dormer windows. The roofs are shaped like ski jumps so when snow slides off them in the winter it will not pile up against the first-floor windows. New homes are being built in the style of the *maison Canadienne* of the 1800s, many with two-car attached garages, two or three bedrooms, and most with split-fieldstone facing. The generations-old tiny roadside processional chapels and wayside crosses are maintained.

If you decide to spend a few days on the island, especially during the colorful fall season, book early at the small—only eight guest rooms—inn called the **Auberge Le Chaumonot**. It is both quaint and quiet. For a memorable meal, ask for patio seating outside the gorgeous stone restaurant called **Le Moulin Saint-Laurent**, a renovated mill that now serves the best of island seafood, wild goose, and beef dishes. A trio of troubadours strolls around the premises, entertaining diners with a combination of music and Gallic joie de vivre. Tel: (418) 829-3888.

Ile aux Coudres

Ile aux Coudres is smaller and even more slow-paced than Ile d'Orléans. It's about two miles offshore from Baie-St-Paul at the mouth of the Gouffre River, on the North Shore about 60 miles northwest of Quebec City. The island is served by a ferry that runs from the North Shore every hour in daylight, from St-Joseph-de-la-Rive at the base of the steep St. Lawrence shoreline that plunges down from Les Eboulements, a high cape with rounded peaks.

The island was named by Jacques Cartier in 1535 when he found quantities of hazelnuts growing there. A cross marks the location where the first Mass mentioned in Canadian history was celebrated by Cartier, on September 7, 1535. The three parishes each cluster around their church, and rotting *goélettes* (small wood boats) near rotting wharves tell the story of a once-flourishing coastal pulp-wood-transporting industry replaced by diesel trucks with the advent of improved and paved highways on the North Shore.

Handcrafts flourish on Ile aux Coudres, as do several resort hotels, but the baker still bakes crusty loaves each day, and social hour is at the post office each evening, when residents gather to get their mail brought over by boat from the evening North Shore railroad train.

There are about a dozen good auberges and motels on the island but there is only one that is operated year-round: the 98-room **Hotel Cap-aux-Pierres** in La Baleine, which comes highly rated and has a good dining room (the island is only 16 km/10 miles long, so it is easy to locate). There are other smaller inns, such as the **Motel Les Voitures d'Eau**, which, as its name implies, is situated on the coast with a wonderful view of the St. Lawrence. It is only open during the season.

A 32-km (20-mile)-long road around the perimeter of the island links the parishes of La Baleine (the whale), St-Bernard, and St-Louis. The island is almost wedge-shaped, about seven miles long, three miles wide at the west end, and tapering to a point at the northeast end. The north shore facing the mainland rises steeply from the ferry landing and continues into a plateau running the length of the island. Fields of potatoes or wildflowers slope off the St. Lawrence, accented by fir trees; tiny chapels and wayside crosses are found along the roadsides.

The south side of the island is a pebble beach that

makes for good picnicking with children—especially at low tide when they can find all manner of sea life under the seaweed in the tidal pools.

Ile aux Coudres has its legend too. Hundreds of years ago an earthquake caused a huge chunk of Les Eboulements escarpment to fall into the deep channel between Ile aux Coudres and the mainland, with considerable loss of life at an Indian village there. It is said that on a very still day you can see the remains of the Indian village on the bottom of the channel.

Ile aux Grues

This is the largest and only inhabited island of a 21-island archipelago off Montmagny on the South Shore of the St. Lawrence River about 35 miles northeast of Quebec City. The seven-mile-long island is linked by ferry, in season and depending on the tides, to Montmagny. Colonization started on the island in 1679, but in 1759 General James Wolfe's soldiers destroyed everything on the island. Prosperity gradually returned and the island found favor with those seeking peace and quiet. Today's visitors often bring their bicycles for a leisurely pedal, stopping at the cheese factory that sells its products on the premises.

There are now two inns on the island, the **Auberge de l'Oie Blanche** and **L'Auberge des Dunes**; both are quaint, nine-room establishments with fine dining. Room and board are also available at a historic manor at the tip of the island, the **McPherson Lemoyne Manor** (five rooms).

ST. LAWRENCE NORTH SHORE

The North Shore of the St. Lawrence River technically extends from Eastern Ontario to the Labrador coast, a distance of about 1,000 miles. The highway along that coast inches north and east, gradually linking communities previously accessible only by ship.

For many years Highway 138 reached only as far as Sept-Iles, about 960 km (600 miles) northeast of Montreal, but in recent years it has been extended another 208 km (130 miles) to Havre-St-Pierre. Beyond this point, the roads of coastal settlements that are still only reachable by air or water continue gradually to stretch out from each community, bringing closer the government and "outporter" dream of someday linking places like Blanc-Sablon— 400 km (250 miles) farther up the coast— to the rest of the mainland.

One of the most beautiful areas in this vast province of such widely diversified scenery is the 225-km (140-mile) stretch between Quebec City and Tadoussac. Highway 138 is paved, the formerly hair-raising mountain traverses have been tamed, and you could make the drive today in about four hours, including the ten-minute ferry crossing over the mouth of the Saguenay River from Baie-Ste-Catherine to Tadoussac.

Scenery buffs would have a tough time covering those 140 miles in two full days, and a keen sport fisherman would probably never get there at all. He'd have turned inland on one of the myriad pulp-logging roads of enormous Charlevoix County and angled himself to ecstatic exhaustion in the hundreds of brooks, lakes, and rivers, most of which abound with antagonistic speckled, brown, and rainbow trout.

If you have only a limited time to explore this very special province, consider first visiting Quebec City, described elsewhere in this guidebook, and then making a circle tour of the lower St. Lawrence. There are six "circle" tours available, because there are six ferry routes across the St. Lawrence River after you start driving east from Quebec City. Roll your own.

In a long—and frustrating—day, you could cover the shortest loop: Quebec City to St-Siméon on the North Shore, cross the river to Rivière-du-Loup, and return to Quebec City along the South Shore. That's a distance of about 375 km (235 miles), not counting the ferry trip. If you got an early start, you could also include Tadoussac, which would add another 64 km (40 miles) return trip from St-Siméon.

The frustration would result from not being able to stop and savor the sights and the country restaurants and *auberges* (inns). You would also have to forgo the opportunities of meeting, if only fleetingly, some of the friendly folk along the way, many of whom have a considerable command of English owing to contact during the past century with those English-speaking North Americans who have summered in these parts.

Along that route you will see roadside signs bearing the message "*compression*" with a pictograph of a car descending a 45-degree-angle hill. Take the warning seriously. It means use engine compression (low gear), and the warning should be heeded no matter how recently you've had your brakes relined.

Quebec City to Baie-St-Paul

Here's what you'd see on half the longest loop (the other half is included in the section on South Shore St. Lawrence): Leave Quebec City following signs for Highways 15A, 15B, 138, or Montmorency or Ste-Anne-de-Beaupré.

The many stalls and shops offering Quebec handcrafts that line the road east of Quebec City are well worth browsing through. The dyed sheep pelts in a kaleidoscope of colors, the home-woven rag rugs, the hand-knitted woolens, and beautifully detailed and expressive wood carvings are expensive but good value. They aren't turned out by machines. They require hours of patient work by skillful *habitants* whose families have handed down the tricks of the trade since they were brought to this country more than 300 years ago.

Watch for **Montmorency Falls**, on your left about 20 km (13 miles) east of Quebec City, a thundering cascade 112 feet higher than Niagara Falls and just as spectacular. There's ample free parking in a lot off the highway, from which you can walk to the base of the falls where the spray can take the sting out of a summer sunburn. Nearby at Ste-Anne-de-Beaupré is the shrine of Beaupré, Canada's answer to Lourdes, where generations of believers have been cured of various afflictions. Hundreds of discarded trusses, canes, braces, and crutches testify to miraculous cures. This has been a pilgrimage site since 1658, although the Neo-Romanesque basilica was only built in 1923.

From the same parking lot you can walk to the Cyclorama of Jerusalem, an astonishing reproduction of the Holy Land more than 44 feet high and about 350 feet wide, open daily from April to November. From Beaupré you can see the graceful, 5,700-foot suspension bridge to Ile d'Orléans (described in the section on the Islands of the St. Lawrence).

The highway climbs steeply from nearby St-Joachim up onto the back of the headland of **Cap-Tourmente**. A side trip off the highway brings you to the village of St-Tite-des-Caps, named because the village is behind the headlands (*caps*) from which you can enjoy a wide vista of the St. Lawrence River. St-Tite is the gateway to the Pendragon

Range of the Laurentian Mountains, which for the next 144 km (90 miles) rear up in granite headlands to heights of 4,000 feet above the St. Lawrence.

The headlands are separated by deep valleys carved over the centuries by rushing brooks. At the junction of each brook or small river with the St. Lawrence are villages or hamlets. Each has its wharf to which pulp logs were floated or trucked for loading onto *goélettes*. A few of these once-numerous quaint wooden boats still carry the logs from small ports to larger ones, where they are stockpiled for loading onto lake freighters bound for paper mills on the Great Lakes.

Baie-St-Paul is about 80 km (50 miles) east of Quebec City at the mouth of the Gouffre River, which has carved deeply into the Laurentian Mountains, carrying brown waters from the ancient forests. Generations of wood-carvers have passed on their skills in this valley, and most welcome visitors to their studios, knowing few can resist the local figures and faces and scenes they have captured in wood. The recently opened **Centre d'Art de Baie-Saint-Paul** is a two-level art gallery in which the works of local painters, sculptors, and tapestry weavers is displayed. There is no admission charge, but the number of browsers who leave without at least one purchase is small. Ile aux Coudres is off the mouth of the Gouffre, and described in the Islands of the St. Lawrence section.

Toward Tadoussac

There are two routes from Baie-St-Paul to La Malbaie. The best road, but least interesting, turns inland. The most scenic is the shore road, which climbs over a cape and then winds down to St-Joseph-de-la-Rive, climbs another cape to plunge again to the village of St-Irénée, and then makes another wild climb over another cape before winding down into **Pointe-au-Pic** near La Malbaie.

Pointe-au-Pic has been a summer vacationing spot for generations of wealthy North Americans. There are magnificent summer mansions here, the opulent stone fortress of the **Manoir Richelieu Hotel**, and two 18-hole golf courses with some of the most spectacular scenery in the world. The point abuts La Malbaie (meaning bad bay), so named by Champlain because the bay is deceptively shallow and has a rank smell at low tide due to sulfur deposits in the estuary of the Murray River, which flows into it.

If the Manoir Richelieu is a little grand for you, try

L'Auberge des Falaises, which is exemplary of Quebec country-style lodging. There are a dozen charming little rooms in the main house, which overlooks the town and bay area far below, and owner Denys Clouthier is currently building new apartment/condos on the same hill. The auberge is known throughout the region for its excellent kitchen, where the inventive chef creates delicacies such as smoked trout and salmon in the inn's own smokehouse, vinegars from Champagne and almonds, and even a surprisingly delicious onion jam! And, this is one of the very few spots in the world where you can taste a new creation known as the "sauvagine": a fowl that is part goose and part duck. It is raised only on the Ile d'Orleans, and is a treat reminiscent of chicken but with the texture of meat. Only in Quebec.

In the few miles between Pointe-au-Pic and **Cap-à-l'Aigle** there are more than a dozen of Canada's finest country inns. The cuisine at these inns is matched by only a few exceptional establishments in the rest of the province. In Pointe-au-Pic some of the best are: **Auberge Les Trois Canards et Motels, Auberge Au Petit Berger, Auberge Les Sources, Auberge La Maison Donohúe, Auberge La Petite Marmite**, and **Auberge Le Bel Arpent**. You won't go wrong staying at any of these inns. At Cap-à-l'Aigle don't miss a meal at either **La Pisonnière** or **Auberge des Peupliers**. They have 28 and 21 rooms respectively, and each room has a commanding view over the river and surrounding countryside from high atop the cape.

At the mouth of the Murray River at La Malbaie, about midway between Pointe-au-Pic and Cap-à-l'Aigle, you will see what looks like the carcass of a massive whale beached on its back, sun-bleached ribs reaching into the sky. This is the **Pelican**, a replica of a 17th-century warship that wrote a magnificent but little-known chapter in Canadian history. In 1697 her captain, Pierre LeMoyne, sailed the original 144-foot ship into Hudson Bay to take Port Nelson from the British. The Pelican was greeted by three British warships, but with typical Gallic insouciance she opened fire with her 44 guns. When the smoke had cleared, the Pelican has blasted the three British ships out of the water, but the Pelican was a loss as well. LeMoyne ran her aground on a shoal and abandoned her to the elements of those unhospitable shores.

Visitors are welcome at the building site and chances are that pipe-smoking history buff Francois Cordeau will be on the site to show you around and bring that naval battle alive in the telling. Cordeau has been on the building site from dawn to dusk since work started on the replica six years ago. The ship is being built from special timbers cut in the woods and hauled out by horses. Authentic 17th-century construction techniques are being used; the only concessions to this century are a sawmill and a crane. When the Pelican is launched in 1991 she'll carry three square-rigged masts and, after her shake-down, compete in the Tall Ships race and meeting in 1992 marking the 500th anniversary of the discovery of North America. After that she'll be used as a training ship for groups of up to 150 young Canadians who will crew her on promotional voyages to North American ports.

At St-Fidèle there's another choice of routes. The fastest turns inland, but the shore road will take you to two picture-postcard villages, each at the mouth of a small stream and between two high headlands.

St-Siméon is where you catch the modern ferry that sails frequently to Rivière-du-Loup on the South Shore. Another 20 miles downriver on the North Shore is Baie-Ste-Catherine, where you catch the free ferry across the Saguenay River to Tadoussac. The ferry operates so frequently there's no need to consult a schedule. At mid-point on the trip there's a splendid view up the river, whose banks are steep mountains that drop vertically into the river. Those white whales frisking around the ferry-boat are beluga whales. They average 13 feet in length and have no dorsal fin. If you're lucky you'll also see one or more of the grampus, or killer, whales. These reach a length of 60 feet and often come close to the ferryboat to sound. They don't belong here, but come down from the Arctic each summer to enjoy the best of saltwater and freshwater fish, both of which abound at the confluence of the rivers.

The Tadoussac Area

The town of Tadoussac gets its name from the Algonquin and means "breasts," with reference to the many rounded hills in the area. Although Tadoussac has been a vitally important Canadian seaport since the country was discovered, it has never grown larger than a small town of 1,000. Jacques Cartier came to Tadoussac in 1535, but it wasn't until 1600 that Pierre Chauvin built the first house in Canada there.

In 1615 the Recollect Jean Dolbeau started the first

mission to the Indians, which was taken over by the Jesuits in 1641. They built a stone church at Tadoussac, which was replaced by a wooden one in 1747 that is still standing. The sprawling, mansion-like 140-room frame **Hotel Tadoussac**, with its trademark red roof, dominates the face of the village above a curving sand beach. You may recognize it as the hotel used in the filming of *Hotel New Hampshire*. Yachts and pleasure craft are moored nearby, at a wharf at one end of the beach. Attractive native crafts are available from a cooperative artisans' outlet in front of the hotel. At Tadoussac you can go whale watching with a variety of entrepreneurs and get close-up views of up to ten species of whales, including the largest mammal living on this planet—the 95-foot, 140-ton blue whale.

Few Quebeckers are aware of it, but just a few miles east of Tadoussac is Canada's "other" desert. The Bald Head Hills near Brandon, Manitoba, are called Canada's only desert, but a century ago a vast sand dune extended from Tadoussac about ten miles east and inland. Time and man's persistence have shrunk the desert to only a few square miles. The desert doesn't have a name; it's referred to as **Moulin Beaude** (Beaude's Mill) after a mill that operated there decades ago and of which only traces remain.

Artists still haul their easels out to Moulin Beaude to capture scenes more reminiscent of Egypt than Canada, and the more intrepid take along old skis or toboggans to court sprains and nasty burns sliding down a 200-foot-high sand dune, across a narrow beach, and into the frigid St. Lawrence River.

From Tadoussac, you have an assortment of choices. You may return to St-Siméon and take the ferry to Rivière-du-Loup on the South Shore either to tour the Gaspé Peninsula or head west and return to Quebec City. Or you can take the highway north from Tadoussac or St-Siméon to the communities of Chicoutimi, Roberval, Jonquière, and Arvida around Lac-St-Jean, from which the Saguenay River runs. (There are outstanding trout streams in this area, such as the Ste. Marguerite.) Or you may continue northeast along the North Shore of the St. Lawrence River toward Sept-Iles (there are actually only six islands).

Toward Sept-Iles

The 416 km (260 miles) of Highway 138 between Tadoussac and Sept-Iles varies from rugged seascape to empty sandy beaches to long stretches of forest slashed by raging rivers that churn down from the mountains to the ever-widening St. Lawrence River. There are towns and villages along the river, many of them founded only within the past half century, although a lighthouse at **Pointe-des-Monts**—which houses a museum—was built in 1830. A restaurant now operates during summer in the former house of the lighthouse keeper.

Between Tadoussac and Sept-Iles there are four ferries crossing the St. Lawrence to the South Shore, so you don't have to retrace your steps if you found the drive boring. There are crossings from Escoumins to Trois-Pistoles; Baie Comeau or Godbout to Matane; and from Sept-Iles to Rimouski.

Nor do you have to stop at Sept-Iles. Highway 138 now continues another 208 km (130 miles) to Havre-St-Pierre, and from there you can take a ferry to **Anticosti Island** in the middle of the Gulf of St. Lawrence. The island is popular with sportsmen who hunt Virginia deer and fish for trout and salmon.

THE LAURENTIANS

"We soon found that the inhabitants were exclusively French-Canadians. In fact, we were in a foreign country, where the inhabitants uttered not one familiar sound to us." So wrote Henry David Thoreau about the Laurentian mountain region in 1866 in his classic, *A Yankee in Canada*. He continued, "I got home this Thursday evening having spent just one week in Quebec and travelled 1,100 miles. The whole expense of the journey . . . was $12.75."

Were Thoreau alive today, he wouldn't recognize this region of Quebec north and slightly west of Montreal, and his $12.75 might buy him a good lunch—but without wine.

The language has changed, too. Now it's called *hospitalité,* and it's spoken within earshot of all hotels, motels, ski lodges, and mountain ski lifts. Hospitality is a business here, and the beneficiaries pay for it. But there's a flair, or panache, and, yes, a joie de vivre that make it difficult to believe the waiters and waitresses, barmen, lift attendants, and bellboys aren't welcoming old friends to their personal playground.

There are extra gestures clearly not initiated by the thought of a possible tip, and extra services that follow a routine tip when a second tip obviously won't be immediately forthcoming. There's a lot of laughter and smiling: those holidaying, and those making it a holiday.

Wherever there is a hill in Quebec near a population center, there is a ski hill and a network of cross-country ski trails. But most of the centers have been modelled after those in the Laurentians.

The province's major centers, with vertical drop in feet after each, from east to west, are: **Le Massif**, near Baie-St-Paul east of Quebec City on the North Shore of the St. Lawrence River (2,500); **Mont-Ste-Anne**, immediately east of Quebec City (2,050); in the **Eastern Townships**, Orford (1,772), Owl's Head (1,770), Sutton (1,509), Bromont (1,328); north of Montreal near St-Donat, **Mont Garceau** and **Mont La Réserve** (both 1,000); and north of Ottawa-Hull in the Outaouais region, **Mont-Ste-Marie** (1,250).

But the Laurentians above all have been eastern Canada's ski center for generations—in fact the region has the largest single concentration of ski centers in North America, all within a 40-mile radius that starts a half hour north of Montreal and ends at Mont Tremblant. Within that area are 26 alpine centers and 46 cross-country centers with 1,864 miles of groomed cross-country trails. There are 285 downhill runs serviced by 90 lifts, from T-bars to quadruple-chairs.

Autoroute 15 runs north from Montreal, and 19 exits are marked to 26 major ski areas, each of which is served by lodges, inns, motels, and cabins, some of which are institutions more than a century old. All but four of the ski centers can guarantee good snow conditions because snowmaking equipment has been installed to build deep bases on the *pistes*. Ten of the centers offer night skiing.

Vertical drops at the 26 centers range from 328 feet at Côtes in Ste-Adèle to 2,132 feet at Mont Tremblant, a name that to many is synonymous with skiing the Laurentians.

The Mont Tremblant Area

Tremblant, the "trembling" giant to which the Indians attributed supernatural powers, rises behind the villages of St-Jovite and Mont Tremblant. From its summit at all seasons of the year there is a panoramic view of the surrounding forests, lakes, valleys, and villages. The mountain has something for every type of skier on its 30 runs through the forest.

This region has been a playground for more than a century; the focal point of **Cuttle's Tremblant Club** is a century-old log château overlooking Lake Tremblant. Cuttle's now has 35 rooms and more than 50 condos. **Gray Rocks Inn**, another Laurentian favorite, was developed in 1906 as a wilderness retreat. It began offering a mix of cross-country and downhill skiing in the late 1920s when guests slid along behind horse-drawn sleighs; a rope tow was installed in 1933.

The Mont Tremblant area really got onto the international ski map in 1939 when Philadelphia millionaire Joe Ryan founded **Mont Tremblant Lodge**. The resort fast became a favorite of American jet-setters who, because of World War II, could no longer ski in Europe's Alps. Long after the war was over Americans continued to return. Today, more than half the clientele of the area's lodges consists of Americans who pass the much higher peaks of New Hampshire and Vermont on their way to Quebec's Laurentians.

While Tremblant may be the biggest and best known, there are other very popular and well-known centers such as **St-Sauveur** at 700 feet, **Mont Blanc** at 1,000 feet, and **Gray Rocks** at 620 feet.

Even in a Quebec winter at its most vicious, the four-lane autoroute north from Montreal is almost always open and passable, and you can reach the first ski area in an hour—30 minutes in good weather. Exit 60 takes you to the **Valley of St-Sauveur**, where you have your choice of Mont Avila (623-foot vertical drop); Mont St-Sauveur (700-foot); Mont Habitant (548-foot); or Mont Christie (558-foot). Accommodation ranges from motels to auberges and condos, and in this one center alone there are more than 60 restaurants for après-ski fun along the main street of the village of **St-Sauveur-des-Monts**. Yes, there are discotheques too, because electronic amplification has long been a fact of life in Quebec.

During the past ski season, late 1988 to April of 1989, it was still possible to find hotel lodging for two at $15 a night, but in places like **Auberge Gray Rocks** the daily rate for two ranges from $267 to $675, including three meals a day, and that establishment's meals are gourmet. **Manoir Pinoteau**, a well-established and popular resort with all services and conveniences and excellent cuisine, ranges from $163 to $245 per couple per day without meals.

The Laurentian area on both sides of Autoroute 15, from 50 to 110 km (30 to about 70 miles) north of Montreal, is all-season resort country, but its prime seasons are autumn and winter. Though there are lakes and rivers for summer sport, they don't have the appeal of those of the more open Eastern Townships, or the rugged beauty of both shores of the St. Lawrence River and the Gaspé Peninsula.

In autumn, when the deciduous trees of the Laurentians turn color, the panoramas run a close second in spectacle to Ontario's Muskoka and Haliburton regions, or to the forests of Vermont and New Hampshire.

GETTING AROUND

The scenic charm and beauty of the province's countryside is best appreciated when driving your own vehicle—from bicycle to motorhome—so you can stop and browse in a little antiques shop or relax on the patio of the ivy-covered country auberge you just spotted while driving by. The Trans-Canada Highway (401 from Ontario) borders the St. Lawrence coast, but it is much more fun to explore the country roads.

By Bus and Train

The Bus Terminus in Quebec City is the hub of bus traffic to the far reaches of the region with connecting links at every little town and village throughout the province. The train is good for a direct transfer from Montreal to Quebec City but doesn't have the "off-the-beaten-track" connections of Voyageur, the major company servicing the province, or the smaller Autobus Dupont.

Bus Terminus. 255, boulevard Charest Est, Quebec. Tel: (418) 524-4692. *Train Information:* VIA Rail Canada, Gare du Palais, 450, rue Saint-Paul, Quebec; Tel. (418) 692-3940.

By Plane

As for flights, Air Canada uses the Quebec City Airport for its connecting routes (the other major carrier, Canadian Airlines, flies into Montreal), as well as many feeder airlines that service this huge province. Quebecair, Inter-Canadian, Air-Madeleine, and many charter airlines have flights into the interior, many to hidden fishing and hunting resorts.

By Boat

The most interesting mode of travel around Quebec is by the ferries throughout the St. Lawrence, from the cross-river ferry between Quebec and Lévis (Tel: 418-692-0550), the island ferry to Isle-aux-Grues from Montmagny (Tel: 418-248-3549), or the five-hour voyage to the Magdalen Islands from Prince Edward Island, which is actually closer to the Magdalens than any part of mainland Quebec.

The car ferry *Lucy Maud Montgomery* leaves Souris, P.E.I., from mid-June to mid-September at 2:00 P.M. (except Tuesdays) and departs Cap-aux-Meules, Magdalens, at 8:00 A.M. (Note: On Tuesdays, *Lucy* departs Souris at 2:00 A.M. and at 8:00 P.M. from Cap-aux-Meules.) *Information:* Cap-aux-Meules, Magdalens, Tel: (418) 986-6600; Souris, P.E.I., Tel: (902) 687-2181.

There is also a passenger/cargo vessel, the CTMA *Voyageur,* which makes a weekly trip from Montreal with a maximum of 15 passengers. For information: Montreal, Tel: (514) 866-8066 or Cap-aux-Meules, Tel: (418) 986-4224.

You can also cross the mouth of the St. Lawrence at its widest point, from Matane in the Gaspé to either Baie-Comeau or Godbout on the north shore of Manicouagan. The daily times vary during their June to September schedule, so check when you finalize your travel plans. Warning: The river here is unpredictable, so prepare for a possible rough crossing, especially later in the season. For information: Matane, Tel: (418) 562-2500; Baie-Comeau, Tel: (418) 296-2593; or Godbout, Tel: (418) 568-7575.

For complete information on the ever-changing schedules, check with the province's tourism offices prior to commencing your trip. Tourisme Quebec, Department of Tourism, C.P. 20,000, Quebec City, Quebec, G1K 7X2.

ACCOMMODATIONS REFERENCE

▶ **Auberge Au Petit Berger.** 1, Cote Bellevue, **Pointe-au-Pic**, Que. G0T 1M0. Tel: (418) 665-4428.

▶ **Auberge La Maison Donohue.** 145, rue Principale, **Point-au-Pic**, Que. G0T 1M0. Tel: (418) 665-4377.

▶ **Auberge de l'Oie Blanche.** Rue Principale, **Isle-aux-Grues**, Que. G0R 1P0. Tel: (418) 248-9080.

► **Auberge des Commandants**. 178, rue de la Reine, **Gaspé**, Que. G0C 1R0. Tel: (418) 368-3355.

► **Auberge des Dunes**. Rue Principal, **Isle-aux-Grues**, Que. G0R 1P0. Tel: (418) 248-0129.

► **Auberge des Falaises**. 18, chemin des Falaises, **Pointe-au-Pic**, Que. G0T 1M0. Tel: (418) 665-3731.

► **Auberge du Gargantua et Motels**. 222, Route de Failles, **Percé**, Que. G0C 2L0. Tel: (418) 782-2852.

► **Auberge des Gouverneurs**. 155, boulevard René Lepage East, **Rimouski**, Que. G5L 1P2. Tel: (418) 723-4422.

► **Auberge des Peupliers**. 381, rue Saint-Raphael, **Cap-à-l'Aigle**, Que. G0T 1B0. Tel: (418) 665-4423.

► **Auberge Gray Rocks**. P.O. Box 1000, **St-Jovite**, Que. J0T 2H0. Tel: (819) 425-2771.

► **Auberge Hatley Inn**. Route Magog, **North Hatley**, Que. J0B 2C0. Tel: (819) 842-2451.

► **Auberge La Petite Marmite**. 63, rue Principale, **Point-au-Pic**, Que. G0T 1M0. Tel: (418) 665-3583.

► **Auberge Le Bel Arpent**. 121, chemin des Falaises, **Point-au-Pic**, Que. G0T 1M0. Tel: (418) 665-4765.

► **Auberge Le Chaumonot**. 425, chemin Royal, **Saint-François**, l'Ile d'Orléans, Que. G0A 3S0. Tel: (418) 829-2735.

► **Auberge Les Sources**. 8, rue des Pins, **Pointe-au-Pic**, Que. G0T 1M0. Tel: (418) 665-6952.

► **Auberge Les Trois Canards et Motels**. 49, Cote Bellevue, **Pointe-au-Pic**, Que. G0T 1M0. Tel: (418) 665-3761.

► **Cuttle's Tremblant Club**. Chemin Lac-Tremblant Nord, **Mont Tremblant**, Que. J0T 1Z0. Tel: (819) 425-2731.

► **Domaine Avallon**. 897, rue Merry Nord, **Magog**, Que. J1H 5X7. Tel: (819) 847-3555.

► **Domaine Montjoye**. Highway 108, **North Hatley**, Que. J0B 2C0. Tel: (819) 842-8309.

► **Gîte du Mont-Albert**. Route 299, **Parc national de la Gaspesie**, Que. G0E 2G0. Tel: (418) 763-2288 or 763-2289.

► **Hôtel Cap-aux-Pierres**. 220, route Principale, **Ile-aux-Coudres**, Que. G0A 2A0. Tel: (418) 438-2711.

► **Hôtel Tadoussac**. 165, Bord de l'Eau, **Tadoussac**, Que. G0T 2A0. Tel: (418) 235-4421.

► **Hôtel Château Madelinot**. C.P. 44, **Cap-aux-Meules**, Que. G0B 1B0. Tel: (418) 986-3695.

► **Hôtel-Motel La Normandie**. 229, Route 132 West, **Percé**, Que. G0C 2L0. Tel: (418) 782-2112.

► **La Pinsonnière**. 124, rue Saint-Raphael, **Cap-à-l'Aigle**, Que. G0T 1B0. Tel: (418) 665-4431.

► **Le Manoir Hovey.** Chemin Hovey, **North Hatley**, Que. J0B 2C0. Tel: (819) 842-2421.

► **Manoir Pinoteau.** Lac Tremblant, **Mont-Tremblant**, Que. J0T 1Z0. Tel: (819) 425-2795.

► **Manoir Richelieu Hôtel.** 181, avenue Richelieu, **Pointe-au-Pic**, Que. G0T 1M0. Tel: (418) 665-3703.

► **McPherson Lemoyne Manor. Ile-aux-Grues**, Que. G0R 1P0. Tel: (418) 248-4536.

► **Mont-Tremblant Lodge.** Lac Tremblant, **Mont-Tremblant**, Que. J0T 1Z0. Tel: (819) 425-8711; in Canada, (800) 567-6761.

► **Motel des Iles.** C.P. 58, **Havre aux Maisons**, Que. G0B 1K0. Tel: (418) 969-2931.

► **Motel Rimouski.** 410, rue Saint-Germaine East, **Rimouski**, Que. G5L 1C7. Tel: (418) 723-9219.

► **Motel Les Voitures d'Eau.** 214, route Principale, **Ile-aux-Coudres**, Que. G0A 2A0. Tel: (418) 438-2208.

► **Residences Val Sutton.** 575, chemin Real, **Sutton**, Que. J0E 2K0. Tel: (514) 538-4444.

► **Ripplecove Inn.** 700 Ripplecove Road, **Ayer's Cliff**, Que. J0B 1C0. Tel: (819) 838-4296.

► **Saint-Louis-de-I'Ile-aux-Coudres.**   **Ile-aux-Coudres**, Que. G0A 1X0. Tel: (418) 438-2208.

► **Station Touristique du Mont Orford.** Orford Provincial Park, **Magog**, Que. Tel: (819) 843-6548.

► **Station de ski du Mont Sutton**, c/o Sutton Tourist Association, C.P. 418, **Sutton**, Que. J0E 2K0. Tel: (514) 538-2646.

► **Village Archimede de Sutton.** 110, rue Thibodeau, **Sutton**, Que. J0E 2K0. Tel: (514) 653-0982.

► **Village Mont Orford.** 5051, chemin du Parc, **Magog**, Que. J1X 3W8. Tel: (819) 847-2662.

Guides to each region that list accommodations are available through Tourisme Québec, C.P. (P.O. Box) 20,000, Quebec City, Quebec G1K 7X2; Tel: (514) 873-2015, or, toll-free from the eastern U.S., (800) 443-7000.

QUEBEC CITY

By Hazel Lowe

Hazel Lowe was travel editor of the Montreal Star *and associate travel editor of Montreal's* Gazette *before joining the Southam News feature service, for which she writes a weekly travel column. She lives in Montreal.*

Quebec City is the beguiling Old World city some travellers expect to find in Montreal when they visit that thoroughly modern international crossroads.

Unlike French Canada's financial hub, which recalls its colorful past in the few waterfront blocks of its historic *quartier,* the entire core of this provincial capital could pass for a postcard-pretty château town somewhere in France. At least, that's how Quebec City strikes most newcomers when they first enter the gates of the only walled city north of Mexico.

Snug within its gray-stone ramparts above the St. Lawrence River, still guarded by a fortified citadel, la Vieille Capitale maintains an 18th-century profile in the shadow of a multiturreted castle most travel-poster fanciers recognize at once as the baronial **Château Frontenac Hotel**. History buffs soon recognize other, older landmarks in a time warp of narrow streets that were planned more than 300 years ago. Lined with some of the oldest buildings in Canada, they still follow their original course through a historic district that UNESCO added to its World Heritage rolls in 1985. •

These days the time-worn thoroughfares of Old Quebec are convivial settings for bistros, boutiques, restau-

242

rants, and sidewalk cafés. They bustle with horse-drawn *calèche* traffic, sightseers, street artists, and weekday throngs of residents who refuse to abandon their small gem of a city to the tourist trade. It is their self-assured presence that dispels any notion of this city as a "living museum" kept alive only by travel literature. Quebec lives because its heritage-conscious population keeps it lively. Quebeckers frankly adore their unique, French-speaking hometown, and they cherish the "Cradle of New France" that Samuel de Champlain founded here in 1608.

MAJOR INTEREST

Vivid French colonial atmosphere
Dining

The Fortifications
Citadel
National Battlefields Park

Upper Town
Place d'Armes
Rue Ste-Anne shops and cafés
Rue St-Louis restaurants
Convent of the Ursulines
Dufferin Terrace river views

Lower Town
The Break-Neck Stairway
Place Royale colonial townscape
Maison Chevalier museum complex
The Royal Battery
River cruises
Quartier Petit-Champlain restaurants and shops
Vieux-Port shops and restaurants

New Quebec
Musée de Québec
Hôtel du Parlement

The story of Quebec is a tale of two cities. The 323-acre UNESCO preserve of Vieux-Québec (Old Quebec) includes the Upper Town and its fortifications, crowning a lofty promontory above Lower Town, which is the site of the first outpost Champlain and his doughty colonists settled between the waterfront and the sheer face of the cliff. The "new" city, beyond the 18th-century bastions, reaches out through its elegant residential neighbor-

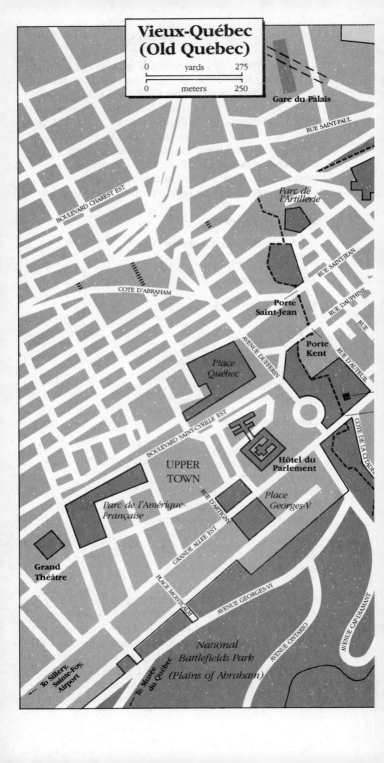

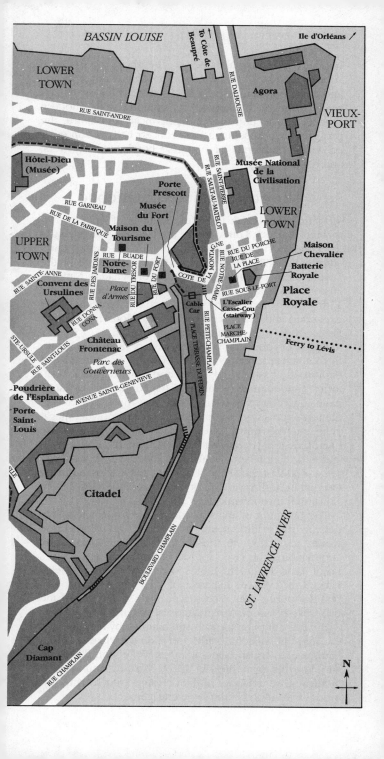

hoods and industrial zones to the shopping malls of suburbia, the provincial autoroute (highway) network, and the airport at nearby Sainte-Foy. Stretching out expansively from the old town's constraining walls, modern Quebec is the home of the provincial legislature, the provincial art museum, a civic concert hall, and an ever-growing community of high-rise hotels, office towers, and condominiums.

The Fortifications of Quebec

Most travellers catch their first glimpse of Upper Town through **Porte St-Louis**, where the Grande Allée changes its name to rue St-Louis. This noble Neo-Gothic entry (rebuilt in 1878) is one of the four remaining gates in the Fortifications of Quebec. Now part of Canada's National Historic Parks system, the walls were raised early in the 17th century during the French colonial regime, later expanded and reinforced by the victorious British after France ceded her colony to England in 1763.

Sightseers hooked on military history can follow a public footpath around the wall's three-mile circumference to explore the bastions, redoubts, and cannon-guarded batteries. Guided tours depart from the **Poudrière de l'Esplanade**, near Porte St-Louis, from May through October. Canada's parks system administers both the powder magazine and the military restorations at nearby **Parc de l'Artillerie**, on the wall's northwest ramparts, as reception and information centers. Artillery Park, where visitors can see a model of the city as it was in 1808, is closed during December and April. The powder magazine closes from November through mid-May.

The highlight of any wall tour is the star-shaped **Citadel**, on the critical southern flank of the old defense works. Crouched on the summit of Cap-Diamant and commanding the river approach, the home of Canada's Royal 22nd Regiment looms over **National Battlefields Park**. The 235-acre expanse of wooded parkland is a popular public area today, laced with scenic drives and pathways, blossoming with landscaped gardens.

But this clifftop plateau is still haunted by memories of Canada's most fateful battle. Here, on the Plains of Abraham, young British General James Wolfe won the day—and lost his own life—in 1759. Marquis Louis-Joseph Montcalm, commander of the defeated French army, was mortally wounded in the same engagement.

The Citadel is now as peaceful as the well-healed battleground and has been transformed into the city's most
impressive visitor attraction. Part of the 25-building complex, which is also the official Quebec residence of Canada's governor-general, is open to the public all year
(reservations are required December through February;
Tel: 418-648-3563 or 648-5234). A regimental museum
caters to guided-tour customers, and the glamorous "Van
Doos," spiffy in ceremonial red tunics and bearskin bus-
bies, change the guard and beat a daily retreat at 10:00
A.M. throughout the summer, weather permitting. Tattoo:
July and August, Tuesdays, Thursdays, Saturdays, and Sundays at 7:00 P.M., weather permitting.

Upper Town

Côte de la Citadelle links the Citadel to rue St-Louis, the
colorful Upper Town thoroughfare that follows the hillside down to **Place d'Armes**. Flanked by rues St-Louis, du
Trésor, Ste-Anne, and du Fort, this green fountain square,
shaded by stands of fine old trees, is still the heart of
Vieux-Québec's upper level. Cheerful against the somewhat intimidating backdrop of the Château Frontenac, the
little park is a favorite starting point for self-guided walking tours. Strollers can pick up complimentary brochures
and maps at the Maison du Tourisme, which faces the
square across rue Ste-Anne, and chart their own course.
    The busy pedestrian strip of **rue Ste-Anne**, lined with
restaurants, stores, and café terraces, crosses rue du
Trésor, a year-round rendezvous for street artists. Back
across Place d'Armes, Vieux-Québec's version of Restaurant Row follows **rue St-Louis** as it climbs toward the
street's namesake gate. It's hard to have an undistinguished meal here, where reliable establishments like **Le
Continental** (see Dining) were setting culinary standards
back in the 1950s. Rue St-Louis is the home address of
Aux Anciens Canadiens (Tel: 418-692-1627), a vintage
eating house dedicated to traditional Québecois cuisine.
If they reserve well in advance, local and visiting devotees
of *fèves au lard* (baked beans) and *tourtière* (meat pie)
can enjoy these local treats in the family homestead that
François Jaquet built to last forever in 1675.
    That was more than 30 years after the **Couvent des
Ursulines** was established around the corner on rue
Donnacona. The indomitable Ursuline sisters moved uptown in 1642 after enduring three bone-chilling winters

in primitive waterfront quarters. Part of the courtyard domain, where the good sisters presided over one of the first finishing schools for young ladies in North America, is now an endearing little museum crammed with period furniture, embroidered vestments, and memorabilia. The lovely convent chapel is open daily, spring through fall, and for Sunday Mass the rest of the year.

City explorers can look down on the riverside community from **Dufferin Terrace**, a breezy boardwalk promenade that follows the wall along the clifftop from Champlain's memorial statue opposite the Château Frontenac and Place d'Armes to the foot of the Citadel. The Victorian-era terrace, with its old-fashioned lamp standards and gazebo shelters, opens on Quebec's most memorable river view from the heights. From this fair-weather lookout (it's numbing in zero-degree weather), strollers can watch the oceangoing river traffic sail past the port below and on a clear day can see the Côte de Beaupré, Ile d'Orléans, and the south-shore countryside beyond Lévis on the opposite bank.

Lower Town

A funicular at the eastern end of Dufferin Terrace, where the founder's statue marks the site of 17th-century Fort St-Louis, rattles and creaks its way down to Lower Town. It's an interesting and mercifully brief ride for those who prefer the cable-car elevator to following the precipitous côte de la Montagne past Parc Montmorency and through recently rebuilt Porte Prescott, tracing a route Champlain cut into the cliffside more than three centuries ago. But passengers who ride the glass-walled car miss the adventure of descending the notorious *l'Escalier Casse-Cou* (Break-Neck Stairway) into the heart of Lower Town, where rue Sous-le-Fort meets rue Petit-Champlain. However, riders do disembark in the sturdy 17th-century house to which French explorer Louis Jolliet retired after discovering the Mississippi River.

Sadly, what could be a fascinating museum piece houses a glitzy souvenir shop, an unfortunate introduction to an otherwise beautifully restored historic district. Over the past 20 years the provincial government has invested millions in a project to keep the 17th and 18th centuries alive around **Place Royale**, where the first colonists staked a claim to a French empire in North America. A block away from rue Sous-le-Fort, this old economic crossroads of New France is the city's busiest tourist zone. But townspeople nonetheless live and work here in rehabilitated properties that authentically recapture a colonial townscape with sober gray-stone façades and high dormered rooflines. Guided and self-conducted walking tours of Quebec's birthplace begin at the information center on Place Royale, the colony's first marketplace and now the showcase of the restoration.

Surrounded by the private homes, business offices, cafés, and stores of the refurbished square, the stalwart little **church of Notre-Dame-des-Victoires** has dominated the old business district since 1688. Today it's part of the stage dressing for a festival of summertime entertainment, but it's also open for worship as well as sightseeing; Mass is still celebrated regularly at its unusual, castle-shaped altar. A historic collection of miniature sailing vessels hangs in the nave. Across the square, the **Maison des Vins** is open for 20th-century business in a building that the prosperous colonial merchant Lambert Dumont occupied 200 years ago.

Whether or not you are a connoisseur of the grape, you will probably enjoy visiting the Maison des Vins' minimuseum of rare vintage wines and wandering through the ancient cellar vaults, some of which predate the building. More than 1,000 different wines are for sale in this bountiful retail outlet—anything from an everyday table wine to a collector's item in the $700 range.

Close by, one of Place Royale's two interpretation centers traces "400 years of history" in the Fornel family's born-again town house on rue St-Pierre. A multimedia exhibit recalling New France as a trade center is located right on Place Royale. Both are open mid-June through September.

A stroll down rue Notre-Dame leads from Place Royale to rue Marché Champlain and a trio of substantial bourgeois homesteads that the master mason Pierre Renaud built for the Chevalier, Frérot, and Chenaye de la Garonne families in the 1750s. Impeccably restored, the **Maison Chevalier** complex features art and theme exhibitions mounted by the **Musée de la Civilisation**, a cultural center devoted to basic aspects of human behavior, which opened its new building on nearby rue Dalhousie in October 1988.

The triple-threat stately-home enclave was built within reassuring distance of the **Batterie Royale**, which defended the city during Wolfe's siege of Quebec. Lost for a couple of centuries under a welter of docks and warehouses, traces of the Royal Battery were resurrected in archaeological digs ten years ago at the juncture of rues Sous-le-Fort and St-Pierre. Today the born-again defense site is a small park, marked with interpretive signs and open free of charge every day from May through mid-October. The reconstruction, complete with cannon-flanked parapets and gun ports, overlooks the cruise-boat wharf off rue Dalhousie where M. V. *Louis-Jolliet* embarks on three daily cruises throughout the summer. Ninety-minute morning excursions cover the waterfront and harbor area. Two-hour afternoon voyages follow the St. Lawrence downstream as far as Montmorency Falls—one-and-a-half times the height of mighty Niagara—and around the shores of **Ile d'Orléans**, an island treasury of centuries-old farm villages, mills, and chapels, where strawberry fields share a designated historic district with an ever-growing community of summer residents. (See the Quebec Province chapter.)

First settled more than three centuries ago, this still-rural island wasn't linked to the mainland until 1935. Now the steel bridge off boulevard Ste-Anne, five miles east of Quebec City, provides easy access for visitors to the island's inns, restaurants, handcraft outlets, and roadside markets.

On summer evenings *Louis-Jolliet* makes three-hour voyages upriver to Cap-Rouge (no disembarkation), where the French attempted to establish their first colony in Quebec. Two other cruise companies, le Coudrier and Société Linnéenne du Québec Inc., chart a variety of cruises up and down the river and around the port area.

But photographers searching for the ultimate in dramatic shots of Quebec's skyline from the water can do just as well any day of the year (and less expensively) on the ferry to Lévis on the opposite shore. Whatever the season, the commuters' special departs every hour on the half hour from its dock opposite rue Dalhousie, near rue du Marché-Champlain, between 6:00 A.M. and 7:30 P.M. Evening crossings are less frequent but even more rewarding for vista fanciers. Depending on the weather, the trip takes about 15 minutes one way. Passengers who are not residents of the south-shore suburb rarely disembark at Lévis. However, dedicated history buffs may wish to visit the National Historic Park at Pointe Lévis, where British defense forces built a fort in 1865. Free guided tours of the park are offered from May to September, Wednesday through Sunday (Tel: 418-648-2470/2471/3564).

Lower Town explorers who admit they were born to shop can retrace their steps from the wharf to Place Royale or can climb one of the stairways linking the waterfront to the various levels of **Quartier Petit-Champlain**, as Quebeckers call the vintage section of Lower Town west of Place Royale. A bustling little neighborhood of specialty shops, restaurants, and snack bars is tucked into this once slummy area between boulevard Champlain and rue Petit-Champlain, where restoration projects have revived one of the oldest business districts in North America to its 17th-century heyday. Lined on either side with fashion boutiques, artisans' studios, and regional craft outlets, **rue Petit-Champlain** follows a picturesque course from the funicular terminal at the foot of the Break-Neck Stairway to its meeting with boulevard Champlain.

While shophounds consider Little Champlain their exclusive preserve, its best-known establishment is a *nouvelle* seafood restaurant founded by Serge Bruyère, one of Canada's most highly regarded chefs, who now presides over his prestigious uptown dining landmark, A la Table de Serge Bruyère. Housed unpretentiously in a centuries-old fieldstone building at the foot of the Break-Neck Stairway, **Le Marie-Clarisse** accommodates a faithful clientele of regulars in a cozy rustic-inn setting. Early-bird customers with reservations (Tel: 692-0857) occasionally get preferred seating—by the blazing hearth—if they arrive before the lunchtime crowd of Upper Town businesspeople and government officials. This local favorite is just as crowded at the dinner hour.

Lower Town extends eastward beyond its residential and business community to the **Vieux-Port** (Old Port), where Rivière St-Charles joins the St. Lawrence. The 80-acre riverfront complex includes shopping and dining facilities, a lock-serviced marina, sheltered promenades, and a huge open-air amphitheater Quebeckers refer to as the "Agora." The Canadian parks department administers a National Historic Park information center on rue St-André by the Bassin Louise marina, where four exhibition floors tell the salty story of Quebec's 19th-century port (closed December and January).

Vieux-Port really is a misnomer for this business, residential, recreation, and entertainment zone that the federal, provincial, and municipal governments are developing around Promenade de la Pointe-à-Carcy. Although the waterfront complex is steeped in maritime history, this oldest part of Quebec City's port has a brand-new look. Its aerial walkways are tomorrow-designed. Its interpretation center on Quais Renaud, housed in a former cement plant, has been refurbished in a cool, contemporary style, with glass-wall views of Lower Town and the river. In addition to the 6,000-seat Agora, there's a tent theater seating 1,000 and a café theater, as well as a farmers' market selling fresh local produce and flowers.

New Quebec

The 1800s ushered in a fortune-founding era, during which Quebec's Anglo-Scottish lumber barons and wealthy shipbuilders pushed the city limits beyond the western walls and toward the landed-gentry realms of **Sillery**, sitting pretty on the St. Lawrence shore between Parc du Bois de Boulogne and Sainte-Foy. Still an Anglo stronghold in a metropolitan region where 95 percent of the population speaks French, the old country-estate district is an attractive residential suburb today. Sillery is linked to the town-within-the-walls by chemin St-Louis, the western extension of the Grande Allée.

From Porte St-Louis, the **Grande Allée** sweeps grandly past avenue Dufferin, Parliament Hill, and the Hôtel du Parlement (Parliament Building), seat of Quebec's National Assembly, toward National Battlefields Park and the **Musée du Québec**. (Temporarily closed last December, the museum is scheduled to reopen in August 1990 after an eight-month expansion and development program.) This government-operated treasury of regional art, some of which dates back to the 17th century, is located at the western end of the park at 1 avenue Wolfe-Montcalm. It's only a short stroll from the Wolfe Monument, marking the spot where the British general died on September 13, 1759.

The Grande Allée begins (or ends) opposite the monument. Flanked by tall shade trees, sidewalk cafés, and the fashionable restaurants that have taken over blocks of dignified Victorian and Edwardian homes, this is Quebec's answer to the Champs-Elysées. Still residential on its western reaches, it channels Route 175 traffic in and out of the walled town through the oldest part of the new city. Indian braves followed this trail to the trading posts of "Kebec" centuries before the provincial legislature cast its graceful Second Empire shadow over Parliament Hill. Hôtel du Parlement has been a New Town presence at the corner of avenue Dufferin and the Grande Allée since the 1880s, and the Louvre-inspired quadrilateral building is open to the public most days of the year. Free guided tours are available (Tel: 643-7239).

More intriguing for people watchers with an eye for political power lunches, **Le Parlementaire** restaurant in Hôtel du Parlement is open to the general public for lunch and until 9:00 P.M. when the national assembly is in session. Outsiders can't make reservations at this palatial official dining room for members of the provincial government, and they often have a long wait before finding a table in this stately room. Still, the price is right, the menu is traditionally French, and many visitors find it interesting to dine in the precincts of power.

The home of Canada's oldest symphony orchestra is a close neighbor to the Parliament Building. Concert and theater lovers who can't make a performance at the **Grand Théâtre de Québec** (theatrical productions are presented only in French) can always drop by to admire Jordi Bonet's locally renowned mural and inspect the two auditoriums. Daily guided tours for groups are conducted through this performing-arts center at 269 boulevard St-Cyrille, two blocks north of Grande Allée. Reservations required (Tel: 643-4975).

GETTING AROUND

Quebec City is linked to the United States and the rest of Canada by major highways, but there is no scheduled international air service to the provincial capital. Air Canada, Québecair, and Nordair-Metro schedule frequent daily flights (35 minutes) to Quebec Airport at Sainte-Foy through Montreal's Dorval gateway.

Passengers can pick up rented cars at the Sainte-Foy terminal, a 20-minute drive from the city center. Taxi queues form just outside the airport building, where the Maple Leaf Tours shuttle bus that serves all Quebec's larger hotels meets incoming flights. The taxi ride to town costs about $16, the shuttle bus $6.75.

VIA Rail operates a four-times-daily, round-trip train connection (three and a half hours) between Montreal's Central Station and the Gare du Palais railway terminus on rue St-Paul, just beyond the walls. Voyageur Bus provides express service on the hour between Montreal (505 boulevard de Maisonneuve East) and the main Quebec

City depot on boulevard Charest. The 270-km (169-mile) bus trip takes three hours.

Travellers with a car should leave it in the hotel garage and explore this most walkable of capital cities on foot. City-operated and private parking lots are jammed throughout the tourist season, especially on weekends, and the local gendarmerie takes a dim view of violators in no-parking zones. The No. 11 city bus follows a direct route down Grande Allée from the Sainte-Foy motel strip to the center of Upper Town.

If you stop in at the Quebec City Region Tourism and Convention Bureau's information center on rue D'Auteuil, just east of Porte St-Louis, you can get the bureau's invaluable free guidebook to the city and region. Information officers are on hand to tell you anything you need to know about *calèche,* bus, and taxi tours; professionally guided walks; accommodations and restaurants; entertainment and shopping. The staff is bilingual, as is almost everyone else involved in city tourism. English-speaking visitors rarely encounter a language barrier in the heart of the tourist zone.

The Gray Line and four other companies operate year-round coach tours of the city. Spring through late fall, half- and full-day excursions are available to the shrine at Ste-Anne-de-Beaupré, Montmorency Falls, and the ancient farm villages of Ile d'Orléans. Mont-Ste-Anne, 38 km (24 miles) east of Quebec, near the shrine, is one of four ski-resort areas located within a 30-minute drive east or north of the city.

Quebec's best-publicized festival is its pre-Lent Mardi Gras, a wintry ten-day revel during which the most sophisticated Quebeckers lose their inhibitions in a whirl of sports events, parades, parties, and hoopla. But February visitors to the 33-year-old Carnaval de Québec really don't see the gracious old city at its best then, when it's overcrowded and overstimulated. Fun seekers who hope to meet Bonhomme Carnaval, the February festival's mascot snowman, should reserve accommodations well before Christmas.

ACCOMMODATIONS

The city's big new hotels all are located beyond the walls and at its motel community in Sainte-Foy—close to the airport, the Laval University campus, and the metropolitan area's two largest shopping malls. Accommodation *within* the fortifications is limited to small, old-fashioned hostelries and private guesthouses—with one outstanding exception.

The telephone area code for Quebec City is 418.

Within the Walls

Le Château Frontenac. Once they've laid eyes on it, few first-time visitors can resist the Neo-Renaissance appeal of this magnificent old Canadian Pacific structure. Certainly, it's hard to ignore, looming over Vieux-Québec like a ducal palace, its soaring towers, turrets, and spires dominating the skyline in all directions. It's hard, in fact, to compose a photograph of the historic *quartier* and its outskirts without including the famous verdigris rooftops.

The Canadian Pacific Railway raised the first wings of its stately home for discriminating travellers in 1893, adding the finishing flourish of a 17-story tower 30 years later, when guests still were more concerned with "*le bon ton*" than executive suites and gold keys. Unfortunately, some nitpickers today do carp about the lack of these computer-age amenities and the less-than-pristine condition of some guest units.

Admittedly, the hotel has been riding high on memories of the posh old days and a reputation it established more than half a century ago, but management is engaged in a massive, $50-million refurbishing project it expects to complete by 1991, by which time all rooms and suites will have been redecorated in the French Provincial style. Meanwhile, guests who book one of the choice river-view suites or romantic tower rooms are generally charmed by the ambience of the most expensive hotel in town. And the public rooms off the oak-panelled lobby are still impressive. The piano bar and the lounge next to the main dining room overlooking Dufferin Terrace are both popular rendezvous and Le Champlain, the hotel's main dining room, is the most elegant restaurant in town (see Dining section).

1 rue des Carrières, G1R 4P5; Tel: 692-3861 or, within the province, (800) 268-9420.

Hôtel Clarendon was Quebec's first "high-rise" hotel. Older even than its world-famous neighbor, the Frontenac, the 93-room landmark assumed a bold new Art Deco personality in the 1930s and decided to cling to a good thing. Convenient guest parking is available at the Hôtel de Ville garage across the street. Local diners swear by the hotel's **Charles Baillairgé Restaurant** and the innovative dinnertime offerings from chef Sonia Lefebvre's kitchen. Lunch in the same panelled and mirrored dining room is a disappointment. Still, it's an experience to visit Canada's oldest restaurant, which dates back to 1866 when the hotel was built.

In spite of its 50-year-old facelift, the hotel's guest units retain the slightly shabby but clean and comfortable atmosphere of an old-fashioned residential club, with narrow corridors and a décor leaning heavily on dark-colored plush. Management isn't planning to modernize again after a mere half century but the price ($169 for a suite, $109 for a double) is right and the Clarendon still has a faithful following.

57 rue Ste-Anne, G1R 3X4; Tel: 692-2480 or, within Quebec, (800) 361-6162; elsewhere in Canada, (800) 361-1155.

Hôtel Manoir Ste-Geneviève boasts a longer history than either of the above-mentioned hotels. Born at the height of the Victorian age, when British regiments garrisoned the Citadel, it was one of a row of town houses occupied by senior officers and their families.

Today the well-preserved relic of an imperial past represents the best of a unique Québecois tourist tradition. Old World, *pension*-style guesthouses really don't exist in the rest of Canada, but they flourish around Parc des Gouverneurs, where Mme. Marguerite Corriveau's impeccable little establishment looks across the green to the Château Frontenac. The Manoir attracts guests who prefer peaceful, homey surroundings to crowded hotel lobbies, and quiet comfort does indeed prevail *chez* Corriveau. Each of its nine spacious, high-ceilinged rooms is furnished and decorated individually, as they would be in a private home. (Compulsive housekeeper Corriveau has a passion for fresh paint, new wallpaper, new draperies.) All have private bathrooms and color TV, and two have adjoining (minuscule) kitchenettes. Prices are just over half the daily tariff at the Château—expensive enough, considering that none of the rooms has a phone and no meals are served. Even so, genial hostess Corriveau turns customers away from her fully booked house at the height of the season.

13 avenue Ste-Geneviève, G1R 4A7; Tel: 694-1666.

Hôtel au Château Fleur de Lys and **Le Château de Pierre** are two other avenue Ste-Geneviève properties worth considering if Mme. Corriveau can't accommodate. Both are less expensive and the Fleur de Lys, which has facilities for the handicapped, has won a Four Fleur de Lys rating from Quebec Tourism for "very good comfort."

Hôtel au Château Fleur de Lys. 15 avenue Ste-Geneviève, G1R 4A8; Tel: 694-1884.

Le Château de Pierre. 17 avenue Ste-Geneviève, G1R 4A8; Tel: 694-0429.

Around the corner on Place Terrasse Dufferin next door to the United States Consulate, **Château de la Terrasse** has been welcoming paying guests for the past quarter century. A former private home overlooking the Dufferin Terrace boardwalk and the river, this small, well-maintained 19th-century neighbor of the stately Château Frontenac has divided a four-story town house into 18 rooms, each with private bath, colored TV, and telephones, but no air conditioning. Guests pay a premium for river-view rooms at the front and for a suite with kitchenette, but the overall tariff is modest.

6 Place Terrasse Dufferin, G1R 4N5; Tel: 694-9472.

Manoir D'Auteuil, across rue D'Auteuil from the tourism and information center, is another popular small hotel of 17 rooms, all with private bath, TV and phone. Air conditioning isn't considered a necessary amenity in this moderately priced guest house but, like all the small properties mentioned above, the Manoir provides parking facilities for an additional fee.

49 rue D'Auteuil, G1R 4C2; Tel: 694-1173.

Outside the Walls

Hilton International Québec. Frequent business travellers who rely on guaranteed corporate comfort to make their day insist that this member of the Canadian Hilton group is the best hotel in town.

Conveniently situated near the Hôtel du Parlement, just west of the walls and only a five-minute walk from the city gates, the 500-room tower is linked to the convention center and opens into Place Québec's underground shopping world of 75 stores and services. The 17th and 18th floors are reserved for guests who pay executive-floor prices for extra pampering. Service throughout is cheerful and efficient. There is a pool and health club, and an attractively appointed restaurant, **Le Croquembroche**.

3 Place Québec, G1K 7M9; Tel: 647-2411 or (800) 361-7171.

Auberge des Gouverneurs (not to be confused with

the Sainte-Foy chain member on boulevard Laurier) is a provincial-government property, one of a Quebec-wide hotel group specializing in realistically priced hospitality. However, the per diem at the downtown Auberge is nearly as high as the nearby Hilton's, and newcomers who expect better things of a city-center hotel probably will feel they're paying plenty for their serviceable—but charmless—guest units.

Still, Auberge chain members don't make any claim to Grand Hotel status. The public areas were recently renovated, all the facilities are comfortable, and the outdoor and indoor pools are added attractions. The 379-room high-rise is favored by both business and leisure travellers because of its location convenient to both the old city and the new.

690 boulevard St-Cyrille Est (East), G1R 5A8; Tel: 647-1717 or (800) 463-2820 in Ontario, Quebec, Maritime; in U.S., (800) 624-2000.

Hôtel Loews Le Concorde made the Grande Allée scene 15 years ago, an unlikely space-age addition to a neighborhood steeped in 19th-century tradition. By now the geometric wedge of glass and concrete topped by a restaurant that looks much like an airport control tower is well grounded on Place Montcalm. Management has almost completed a floor-by-floor renovation; rooms and suites have been elegantly refurbished and the public areas on the lobby floor look brand-new.

Overlooking National Battlefields Park, Le Concorde boasts Quebec's only moveable feast in its revolving penthouse restaurant. The overall view of the city through the glass walls of L'Astral usually generates more enthusiasm than the buffet and *à la carte* menus. But guests award the hotel high marks for the generous size of its 425 rooms (all with river views) and for the honorary club membership they're entitled to when they check in during the winter: Facilities at the nearby Club des Employés Civils are open to all Le Concorde residents, including use of the health club, swimming pool, badminton and squash courts, and the curling rink. In summer, hotel guests are not permitted in the civil servants' club. They can, however, cool off in the hotel's heated outdoor pool next to the fourth-floor health club, a restful little retreat furnished with saunas, whirlpool, and Nautilus equipment.

1225 Place Montcalm, G1R 4W6; Tel: 647-2222 or (800) 463-5256 in Canada.

DINING

Secretly convinced they know more about good food and drink than their compatriots, Quebeckers admit the rest of the country is catching up to standards they set more than a century ago, when this was Canada's culinary capital. But they still feel Canada outside of Quebec has a long way to go. Meanwhile, they shrug off Toronto's self-conscious gourmandism and the number and variety of Montreal's fine restaurants. Civic boosters, to whom the art of dining is practically a religion, still claim Quebec City can count more *haute cuisine* establishments per capita than any large center in Canada and, perhaps, the United States.

Excellence isn't necessarily expensive in a town where even a modest meal is an occasion. Quebec has its share of fast-food emporiums and chain snack parlors and it is, of course, possible to order a disappointing dinner here, but the capital stakes its international reputation on the uniformly high quality of its restaurants, large and small. Many of the establishments with the priciest reputations offer a reasonable *table d'hôte* menu, especially at lunch-time. If you choose from the prix fixe selections you can avoid running up a budget-breaking tab. It's getting into the grape and the à la carte specialities that run up *l'addition*.

Quebec chefs and most Quebeckers subscribe to the principles of classic French cuisine, which is one reason diners won't find many first-rate ethnic restaurants here, although more appear within and without the walls every year. Innovators commanding the better kitchens have all embraced the philosophy of *nouvelle cuisine,* but most have taken a distinctive Québecois approach to the new school in their adaptation of regional produce.

A word to the hungry: No right-minded citizen hurries through lunch, which is a large, long meal in Quebec, almost as important as dinner. Early reservations for both meals are a must in the most popular restaurants, the majority of which stay open seven days a week during peak tourist periods. During the doldrum days, many close for lunch Mondays and Saturdays.

Within the Walls

When resident bons vivants want to celebrate a special occasion, and hang the expense, they call 692-3861 and book a table at **Le Champlain**. The Château Frontenac's main dining room has to be the most elegant restaurant in Quebec and certainly one of the most handsome in Canada. A kind of seigneurial serenity envelops this graceful, richly panelled room, with its majestic oak pillars and stenciled ceiling. Soothed by a harpist's serenade, diners relax in highbacked tapestry armchairs while they review chef André Butier's extensive menu. House specialties, which tend toward a conservative interpretation of traditional *haute* cookery, include sautéed sirloin steak in a sauce of cream and three varieties of cheese, thinly sliced duckling served pink and juicy in a delicate orange sauce, and heart of beef tenderloin enriched with truffles and a Madeira sauce. The hotel maintains a reliable cellar, service is calm and caring, and the general ambience is exactly what you would expect of a dignified, Old World dining room.

Across Place d'Armes, at the corner of rue du Fort, one of Upper Town's newer, niftier restaurants, **Gambrinus** (Tel: 692-5144), prepares seafood specialties in the *nouvelle* manner in a clubby hideaway under the Musée du Fort. The commercially operated sound-and-light museum has no connection with the restaurant downstairs, and it doesn't attract the same clientele. Bright young people about town congregate here for lunch at prices they can handle, and a mixed group of discriminating diners comes in the evening, which is pricier, but members of both sets consider themselves at home in this relative newcomer to the Old Town's established restaurant community.

Making its debut five years ago, Gambrinus opted for a contemporary decor as a change of pace from the rough stone walls, exposed brick, and crackling hearths most of its older neighbors favor. Bright floral tapestry, crisp café curtains, and green plants brighten a mellow background of mahogany panelling and polished brass. Although the split-level dining room is always crowded, it never seems so. Young chef Serge Gagné has an innovative way with seafood and a variety of veal dishes, not to mention his wicked chocolate-mousse *gâteau*.

An older snuggery, two blocks west along rue Ste-Anne, has been carrying on vivaciously at the same old stand on rue des Jardins for three decades. **Café de la Paix** (Tel: 692-1430) made a name for itself from the start as a noonday refuge for the legal fraternity from the old courthouse, who demanded excellence at fair prices.

Predictably, it soon came to the attention of travel writers and visiting celebrities. The cozy main-floor room drew hometown regulars as well, and old patrons are still charmed with the casual clutter of wine racks and hutches, the lamp-lit tables and Desrosier landscapes. By now the place is a tourist tradition, still amiable and unpretentious (owner Benito Terzini often regales guests with impromptu bursts of song), but the operation has expanded upward to a large, pastel-tinted second-floor room that lacks the country-auberge intimacy of the ground-floor café. Dinner prices on this upper level have soared as well. Beef Bourguignon, rack of lamb, quail in cherry sauce, seasonal game, and seafood are some of the house specialties.

Over on rue St-Louis's Restaurant Row, **La Caravelle** (Tel: 694-9022) clings to its 18th-century decor in a colonial setting of gray-stone walls and rustic furniture. A *chansonnier* performs through the dinner hour, when local customers mingle with visitors to enjoy traditional French cuisine and an interesting selection of Spanish dishes.

Up the street, **Restaurant Au Parmesan** (Tel: 692-0341) chooses to ignore the French, concentrating instead on robust Italian fare. Owner Luigi Leoni plays host nightly in a friendly, firelit room he's decorated with an eclectic collection of wine bottles. An in-house troubadour keeps the dinner hour lively.

The dean of rue St-Louis's Restaurant Row, **Le Continental** (Tel: 694-9995), has been perfecting its variations on the *haute cuisine* theme for more than 30 years. Two generations of the Sgobba family now reign over the kitchen and a quiet, formal dining room. It is patronized by longtime customers from government circles, as well as journalists, visiting dignitaries, and down-to-earth gourmets who like to eat well and reasonably.

Just around the corner on rue Ste-Ursule, a pretty hideaway called **Le Saint-Amour** (Tel: 694-0667) is light-years removed from the bonhomie of Restaurant Row. Romantic as a hearts-and-flowers valentine, the modish little salon that partners Jacques Fortier and chef Jean-Luc Boulay tucked into a restored Victorian town house ten years ago lives up to its loverly name in every seductive detail. The main dining room fairly blushes with tenderness—pink tablecloths, napkins, and walls, rosy candle glow, and rosy Renoir reproductions. A glass-enclosed dining terrace opens off the main room, adding a touch of hothouse green to the roseate *mise-en-scène*.

For all its sentimental staging, Le Saint-Amour couldn't

be more contemporary. It attracts a following of mostly young, worldly-wise patrons, the majority of them local devotees of Jean-Luc—with good reason. The master chef from Normandy adds other dimensions to the new school with his original, sometimes unorthodox, presentation of classic French dishes. His combination of rare beef fillet with a white sauce of Roquefort cheese, almonds, and hazelnuts has become a legend.

When expense-account hosts want to impress their clients, they introduce them to the joys of Serge Bruyère's table on rue St-Jean. The upper floors of the Livernois family's 1855 home, where Canada's first professional photographer practiced his art, now accommodates the best restaurant in Quebec City. All things considered, **A la Table de Serge Bruyère** (Tel: 694-0618) isn't expensive when compared with similar places in New York City or Montreal, but this isn't the spot for a folksy night out with the children.

The Lyon-born disciple of Paul Bocuse opened la Table nine years ago, when he bought the old building and divided it into three dining levels. The main-floor café, **A la Petite Table**, serves inexpensive lunches and afternoon tea. So does **La Serre**, a little glass-walled *salon du thé* and snackery that shares the ground floor complex with the **Le Petit Caveau** wine bar, Roger Geslin's confectionery corner of pastries and hand-dipped chocolates, and Bruyère's own gourmet shop of take-out delights. The upstairs floor is divided into two small dining parlors and a piano bar, the third floor into two private salons. In all, Chef Bruyère can serve no more than 50 customers at one time, so advance reservations are de rigueur.

Bruyère sets his tables formally, with peach-tinted linen, fresh flowers, and fine china and crystal against a contrasting background of exposed brick and stone. Prints and paintings soften the raw walls, and log fires burn on the hearths of both rooms, burnishing the chef's collection of copperware, adding wintertime warmth to the subdued lighting.

Winter or summer, Bruyère cossets his patrons with dishes like tender young Quebec lamb "with just a perfume of sweet garlic," a wreath of tiny pheasant slices in blueberry sauce, poached salmon in a delicate sabayon with black pepper, fresh scallops from the Iles de la Madeleine, and a "sausage" of salmon sauced with leek-flavored cream and white wine. A *table d'hôte* "Discovery" menu of eight courses is good value (under $50), but

Bruyère stocks one of the best cellars in Quebec City, and that's where the tab adds up.

Travel snobs turn up their noses at **Le Vendôme** (Tel: 692-0557) because it caters to large tour groups. But it would be a mistake to snub this senior citizen of Quebec's restaurant community. It's been open for business under the sign of the horsedrawn carriage for 36 years, clinging stubbornly to the slope of côte de la Montagne where the road tumbles down through Prescott Gate to Lower Town.

Le Vendôme is familiar territory to globe trotters who've happened upon its close relatives in France. They flourish throughout the country, in the back streets of Paris *arrondissements,* on the market squares of sleepy provincial towns, their prim lace curtains masking storefront windows and the cluster of white-clothed tables around a one-man bar.

Le Vendôme cherishes other mementos of its 1950s heyday too: murals of the Eiffel Tower and the Seine, a wainscoting of startling maroon tile, a hanging garden of ferns. Trendy it is not, and no one here is concerned with *nouvelle cuisine.* But the kitchen is concerned with such hearty, calorie-rich standbys as crusty onion soup gratinée, savory ragoûts, casseroles of chicken Bourguignon, succulent steaks, and Dover sole served with a simple lemon garnish and boned with surgical expertise. No frills, no kiwi fruit, no unpleasant surprises when the reasonable bill is presented. The restaurant was much cozier before new management extended a small café into a two-level dining hall, but lunch in the old front section—with a glimpse of river through the curtains—is still a nostalgic delight.

Outside the Walls

The latest In spot on Grande Allée's stylish restaurant strip is **Faubourg St-Honoré** (Tel: 529-0211), just opposite Loews Le Concorde. The St-Honoré set up shop here about eleven years ago as an up-market bistro with a café terrace and quickly developed into the trendsetters' oasis it is today. Now it's hard to edge through the door into a crowd that lines both street-level bars four-deep most early evenings of the week. But persevere. There's a winner upstairs. Just two years after it opened in 1985, the St-Honoré's chic second-floor restaurant won the provincial government's Mérite de la Restauration award.

That's easy to understand. Chef Mario Martel changes his

menu daily, and he brings verve and imagination to such game specialties as pheasant in ginger-and-honey sauce. He enhances fresh poached salmon with a cassis dressing, scallops with a blend of escargot and endive, and his presentation is a pleasure to behold. The *carte des vins* is longer than the somewhat limited *à la carte* menu. St-Honoré racks some outstanding Bordeaux and Burgundies in its lavish cellar, and customers who like to change wines with each course will approve of the wide choice of half-bottle options. The room's decor is as winning as Chef Martel's repertoire, a harmonious combination of warm mahogany panelling and cool etched glass, glowing in the soft light of hanging ceramic lanterns.

Auberge Louis Hébert (Tel: 525-7812) was a distinguished presence on Grande Allée long before the St-Honoré arrived. As advertised, it really is an inn, a small, European-style, private hotel of ten rooms, housed in one of the avenue's gracious old dwellings. However, the *auberge* is better known for its café terrace and restaurant than for its three floors of *pension* accommodations. Senior civil servants and power brokers from Parliament Hill tend to take over the dining room at lunchtime, but a mixed crowd of gastronomes reserves for dinner. Chef Hervé Tousin brings a *nouvelle cuisine* approach to a traditional French kitchen, locally renowned for seafood and gamey treats like wild boar, venison, and moose. Prices here vary considerably according to the choice of specialities and wines, but the *table d'hôte* menu is always manageable.

Just off the mainstream of Grande Allée, avenue Cartier turns north into the **Petit Quartier**, a fine food shopping center in a lively neighborhood of cafés, boutiques, and small-business firms, where adventurous chef Mario Bernardo is exploring new avenues of *cuisine légère*. Presiding over his voguish **Graffiti** restaurant (Tel: 529-4949) in the heart of the *quartier,* Bernardo "designs" meals that look as delectable as they taste. And aside from the odd experimental faux pas, his house specialties really are delicious, light, imaginative, and artistically presented. Best of all, it's easy to hold the dinner tab here to a reasonable level.

NIGHTLIFE

Quebec City doesn't indulge in the kind of after-dark recreation that travellers might expect of a popular tourist center. Conscious of its capital status, this seat of provincial government is a conservative town, given to sedate pleasures, never in competition with the freewheeling playground Montreal provides for visiting night owls.

Capital dwellers who aren't part of the government social circle consider an evening well spent at the Grand Théâtre. Once the season opens, sports-minded Quebeckers converge on the Coliseum at the suburban Exhibition Park to cheer the Nordiques on to higher National Hockey League heights. In summer the sidewalk cafés lining Grande Allée are the city's most popular rendezvous. The high-spirited enclave between Place Montcalm and Place Georges-V is transformed into one long block party by late afternoon when the terraces fronting Faubourg St-Honoré, Auberge Louis Hébert and Brandy start welcoming the pre-dinner crowd. The action goes on into the wee hours. Lingering over a long, candlelit dinner, humming along with the *chansonnier,* is a year-round diversion. Late-night revellers top off the evening at the Château Frontenac's piano bar (always sprightly) or watch the city lights from the revolving restaurant-bar atop Loews Le Concorde.

Discotheques are mainly for the young, although **Chez Raspoutine**, a Sainte-Foy disco bar at 2960 boulevard Laurier (Tel: 659-4318), caters to the 30-to-45 crowd. The house disco at **Loews Le Concorde** spans the generation gap as well. Newly renovated **Chez Dagobert** (Tel: 522-0393), the bright star of the Grande Allée constellation where *les gens huppés* congregate to see and be seen, devotes its second floor to a disco clientele in the 18–25 age category. Party people of all ages dance to live music downstairs. **Vogue** (Tel: 529-9973), on the corner of d'Artigny and Grande Allée, is another split-level fun emporium, with a café bar on the ground floor and a disco *en haut.* **Brandy Restaurant Bar** (Tel: 648-8739) is yet another Grand Allée hot spot whose regulars are convinced life ends at 35. Nearby **l'Express Minuit** (Tel: 529-7713) also caters to the young.

Back in the walled city where rue St-Jean winds down from its namesake gate, **Vendredi 13** (Tel: 692-1313) attracts young rockers, visiting and resident, to its boisterous disco bar. A few bright lights away, **l'Arlequin** (Tel: 694-1422) is the club for hard rock groupies. But *tout le monde* feels at home at **Merlin's** dancing bar (Tel: 529-9567) on avenue Cartier and its almost-next-door neighbor, **Le Turf** (Tel: 522-9955), a British-style pub where dancing is encouraged.

To accommodate the university set and its camp follow-ers, **Le Palladium Bar**, 2327 boulevard Versant Nord (Tel: 682-8783), opened last winter near Laval's Sainte-Foy cam-pus, with dancing room for 2,000. It's since become another one of the "in" places for disco devotees. **Beaugarte** (Tel: 659-2442), Sainte-Foy's upscale singles bar, is a pricy disco destination for mature table-hoppers of thirty-something who don't mind the trip out to boule-vard Laurier.

Although the last serious jazz club folded more than three years ago, groovers still gather at the Clarendon Hotel's art nouveau **Bar l'Emprise** (Tel: 692-2480) on rue Ste-Anne. The beat goes on from 11:00 P.M. to 3:00 A.M. seven nights a week. **Zanzibar** (Tel: 524-3321), just be-yond the walls on rue St-Jean, serves up nightly jazz the purists rate as "strictly granola" but it enjoys a devoted following. During Quebec City's annual summer jazz festi-val (usually from June 23 to July 2), the faithful gather at almost every bar, restaurant and available hall in town.

Pub life is something new and different in Vieux-Québec. Model versions of the British originals, local snuggeries are springing up all over town, purveying imported ales and Ye Olde England conviviality in the heart of Canada's French-speaking province. **Aviatic** (Tel: 522-3555), a clubby new pub-restaurant in the Gare du Palais railway terminus, specializes in imported beers. **Sherlock Holmes** (Tel: 529-9973), tucked away under Vogue on the corner of d'Artigny, is the latest newcomer to the Grande Allée bar community. A clone of London's late-lamented local of the same name, the veddy British Holmes is cosily at ease in its French milieu. **Thomas Dunn** (Tel: 692-4693), a rue St-Paul pub across from the rail station's surprisingly popular watering hole, also stocks imported ales. **L'Inox** (Tel: 692-2877) on the Vieux-Port's rue St-André, operates the only authentic brewery in Quebec City. Customers can watch three original brands brewed before their eyes and choose one to wash down the giant hot dogs the pub features as a house specialty.

SHOPS AND SHOPPING

Quebec doesn't pretend to be a shopper's paradise. Its six major shopping malls support 1,000 stores of all kinds, but a mall is a mall by any name, and visitors aren't likely to discover much in Place Québec's underground mart, Place Fleur de Lys and Place Laurier, that they can't find at home. Within the walls, côte de la Fabrique and rues Baude, Ste-Anne, and St-Jean are the main shopping avenues of the old commercial center around City Hall. Souvenir seekers can buy art hot off the easel in the mini-bohemia of rue du Trésor, where Quebec's indefatigable street artists display their canvases.

Rue Baude, at the bottom of the artists' lane, is the business address of **Holt Renfrew**, purveyor of furs and fashion to the carriage trade. One of a Canada-wide chain of exclusive clothing stores that a Montreal fur company launched in 1837, the Quebec branch carries designer-label imports and up-market merchandise for men and women. HR outposts are open in Place Sainte-Foy and the Château Frontenac. **La Maison Darlington** on the corner of rue Baude and rue du Fort expanded its long-established operation last year, the better to display its collection of imported woolens, tweeds, fine cashmeres, and hand-smocked dresses for little girls.

On rue St-Louis, **Les Trois Colombes** looks like a tourist trap from the outside, but once over the threshold shoppers discover a three-story treasury of hand-crafted collectibles from artisans' studios in Quebec, Newfoundland, New Brunswick, Nova Scotia, Ontario, and the Canadian North. Pottery, paintings, Eskimo art, and sculpture share shopping space here with exclusive designs in household accessories and fashion. Creative sweaters by Marilise Couture are one-of-a-kind confections in hand-woven mohair, handsomely combined with leather, silk, lace or fringe. But the big fashion item is the selection of reversible coats, each an original, designed and woven in mohair and wool by Lise Dupuis and her daughter. Spun in a rainbow of color combinations, each is hand-decorated with embroidery or appliqué work. Customers are guaranteed they'll never meet their double in a Dupuis creation.

On the threshold of the Vieux-Port, rue St-Paul is lined with antiques stores, but hopeful amateur collectors should remember that heirlooms from the seigneurial era—hand-carved armoires and four-posters, regional cottage furniture, and naïve religious statues—were snapped up by the professionals a generation ago. Genuine antiques are hard to find if you're a casual shopper. Still, rue St-Paul is a fascinating browsing territory for those who don't take their collecting too seriously. Up on rue Ste-Anne, **Aux Multiples** specializes in authentic (guaranteed) Québecois furniture, quilts, hooked rugs, woodwork, and other artifacts from a not-too-distant past. A branch gallery recently opened on rue Dalhousie opposite the Musée de la Civilisation in the Vieux-Port area.

Of all the city's shopping areas, Quartier Petit-Champlain in Lower Town is the most rewarding for out-of-towners. The *quartier*'s retail community is a co-operative association of owner-artisans who create most of the merchandise in their own ateliers or "import" collectibles from the studios of regional weavers, ceramists, and carvers.

Collectible Dolls

Michèle Prasil doesn't cater to the nursery set. The dolls for sale at **Le Fil du Temps** are works of art, each an original and designed for serious collectors who can afford to indulge their fancies. The Prasil studio on boulevard Champlain is a world of *poupées,* all dressed to the nines in hand-sewn garments: baby dolls, grandma dolls, Victorian belles, and disco swingers.

Clients can order replicas of their favorite person if nothing in the gallery collection suits them. Working from photographs, Michèle will create a reasonable facsimile of the real thing and dress it to order.

Fashion

Atelier La Pomme on rue Petit-Champlain is the place for couture leather. Here or at the nearby shop on boulevard Champlain, customers can choose from a high-fashion *prêt-à-porter* collection or order custom-designed jackets, skirts, dresses, pants, and accessories in the finest Argentine leathers. Practically everything in both stores is produced in the house studio, where La Pomme designers work with a rainbow of luscious colors in suede, pigskin, and silk-smooth leather. **Atelier Ibiza,** a few doors down the street, also specializes in fine leather, while **Peau sur Peau,** down the laneway staircase on the corner of Petit-Champlain and boulevard Champlain, offers "leather from head to foot" in high-style fashions for men and women.

Next door to La Pomme, **Les Vêteries-Blanc Mouton** creates fashion in wool, silk, mohair, and cotton. Big sellers here are comfortable, packable suits and dresses in hand-woven cotton, available in delicate pastels for summer and as resort wear, as well as citified color combinations in warm winter shades. Couture sweaters, beaded and embroidered for cocktail or *après-ski* occasions, can be created to order if nothing in the ready-made line appeals to you. The same is true for the heavier sports pull-ons that come with matching scarves and little caps. There is a good selection of sweaters for men too. Some of the combinations of color and material the shop's suppliers achieve are as unusual—and irresistible—as anything of the kind in the province.

Crafts

Le Jardin de l'Argile on rue Petit-Champlain is a souvenir shop with a difference, stocked with tasteful mementos of a Lower Town excursion, all in a reasonable price range. Owners Thérèse and Jacques Tessier have developed something of a following for their "Lorteau" figurines, schmaltzy-sweet but endearing little ceramic people captured in loving twosomes or dreamy solitude. The store carries regional pottery, carvings, wooden toys, and inexpensive take-home items like bottle corks with carved wooden faces and traditional "Gigueurs," loose-jointed wooden puppets that clog-dance on a string.

Pot-en-Ciel down the street takes Quebec crafts more seriously. The gallery shop displays and sells the works of more than a dozen artisans specializing in pottery, ceramics, sculpture, and carvings. Collectors of native crafts can find authentic Eskimo carvings (each piece guaranteed genuine and signed by the artist) at **l'Iroquois** on rue Sous-le-Fort, as well as signed prints by Arctic-zone artists. Unusual Indian handicrafts are a feature of the gallery collection which also includes a stock of inexpensive but attractive souvenir items.

Visitors who admire the traditional lace curtains framing the windows of so many farmhouses, country cottages, and picturesque cafés throughout Quebec can buy the same patterns by the yard at **boutique la Dentellière** on boulevard Champlain. This frothy little outlet for domestic and imported wares also sells ready-made curtains, tablecloths, boudoir frivolities, bathroom accessories, clothing, and a variety of lacy trimmings for all occasions.

Jewelry

Blanc d'Ivoire is one of the gems of Petit-Champlain's main shopping street. The small, unassuming studio-store is the workshop of creative young designer Dominique Audette. Her work, which includes originals in semiprecious stones, pearls, silver, and gold as well as the studio's hallmark ivory, is for sale (at astonishingly realistic prices) over the counter, but Audette has also established a market for one-of-a-kind pieces designed to order for individual customers.

OTTAWA

By Maura Giuliani

Maura Giuliani, a free-lance writer and editor for various publications and for the federal government, has lived in the Ottawa area for the last nine years.

Yes, it *is* the coldest national capital in the Western World (the worldwide title goes to Ulan Bator, Mongolia), but it is also possibly the most attractive. A relatively tiny city perched on the edge of the Ottawa River, Canada's capital is the perfect stopping point between Montreal and Toronto.

Its appeal lies in charms quite different from those of most urban centers. Ottawa is very much a "company town." Signs of federal occupancy are everywhere: in Gothic buildings, landscaped riverbanks, and fine museums. It is a place to put on walking shoes for perhaps two days and enjoy the benefits of federal government investment.

One of the nicest times to visit Ottawa is in mid-May, when the Festival of Spring celebrates the blooming of millions of tulips (a gift from Queen Juliana of the Netherlands—the queen and her family found refuge in Ottawa during World War II) massed in beds throughout the city. The flowering tulips are a hallmark of winter's demise here. The festival has grown over the years, and now includes fireworks, a flotilla on the canal, a marathon, and an ever-changing assortment of activities.

MAJOR INTEREST

Parliament Hill
Rideau Canal
Winterlude Festival

Ottawa is dominated by water routes, which divide and define the city. The Ottawa and Rideau rivers, as well as the Rideau Canal, are constant points of reference for inhabitants. The Ottawa River is the big one—a major waterway that offered early explorers access to the center of a new continent. In Quebec the river is known as the Outaouais, the name of a tribe of Algonquin Indians whose hunting area once spanned the stretch from the Ottawa River to Lake Superior. English settlers later changed the pronunciation to Ottawa, but both names are still in use by English and French Canadians.

Along this river, under the limestone cliffs on which Canada's parliamentary buildings now stand, passed missionaries and adventurers bound for the western wilderness. English and French explorers, Jesuits, and fur traders used the river from the early 1600s, but the United States was already an independent nation before this point on the Ottawa River became more than a temporary camping spot.

It was 1800, in fact, when an American from Massachusetts, Philemon Wright, trudged up the frozen river with five other families to establish a homestead on the north bank of the Ottawa River. He had been on the river the year before and recognized in the combination of dense forest and ample water power the elements of a profitable lumber trade. First called Wrightsville, then Hull, the settlement rapidly became a center for assembling rafts of white pine logs, which were sailed downstream to Montreal, then shipped to England.

Even in those days, before Canada had become a nation, its relationship with the United States was a constant political concern. After the War of 1812 the British were decidedly nervous about the St. Lawrence River being the only military supply route between Montreal and the province's strategic naval dockyards at Kingston on Lake Ontario. U.S. forts along the St. Lawrence east of the lake defended that border all too well, offering a constant threat to British gunboats and supply ships.

Westminster saw the Rideau River as a viable alternative to the St. Lawrence. Linked through a chain of lakes to

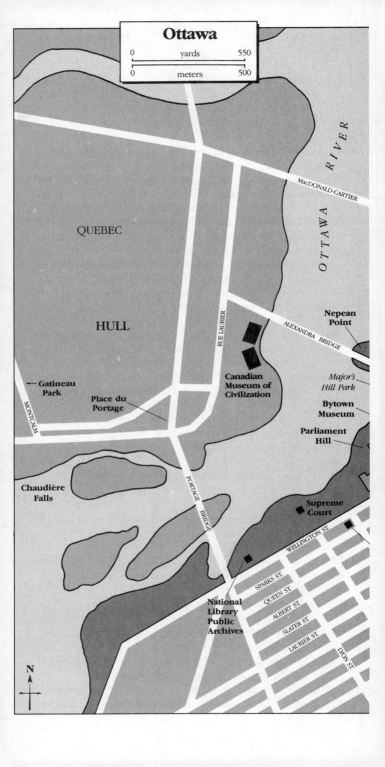

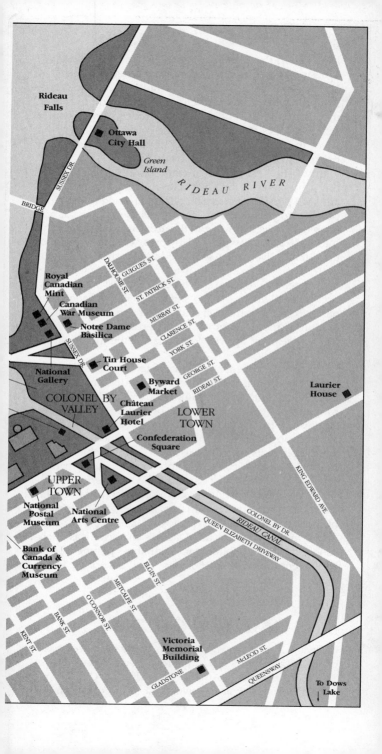

Lake Ontario, it promised safe passage from the east to Kingston. The British government committed itself to building a system that would include an entrance canal from the Ottawa River (to circumvent Chaudière Falls at the mouth of the Rideau) to the Rideau River, with a series of locks along the 125-mile route. A Colonel John By of the Royal Engineers was dispatched to Canada in the spring of 1826 to oversee construction.

It was the best thing that could have happened to the tiny settlement on the Ottawa River. Many of the military and civil personnel dispatched from England to build the canal were persuaded by land grants to stay in what was soon known as Bytown, and the area grew rapidly. By the mid 1830s, Wrightsville and Bytown were the center of the Ottawa River valley's squared-timber trade. Raftsmen found rowdy relaxation in Bytown on their way to Quebec, fostering the town's turbulent reputation—a reputation the settlement tried to shed in 1855 by changing its name from Bytown to Ottawa when it applied for consideration as the new capital of Upper and Lower Canada (upper meaning upriver, lower nearer the mouth of the St. Lawrence).

There were cogent arguments in favor of Ottawa as the provincial capital: Its distance from borders made it safe from hostile attack; communications with Montreal and Kingston were well developed by water; it was almost equidistant from Quebec and Toronto as well as being situated on the border of the two provinces; and—no mean point—its location was one of undeniable beauty. In 1858, Queen Victoria did appoint Ottawa permanent capital of the Province of Canada—and an American newspaper acknowledged the wisdom of the choice from the viewpoint of defense, noting that "invaders would inevitably be lost in the woods trying to find it."

Lost in the woods or not, Ottawa's character was established by that appointment. With the opening of the Parliament Buildings in 1866, the "civil" side of life in the new capital gained ground.

EXPLORING OTTAWA

Ottawa is a small town that breaks easily into three basic chunks: Upper Town, Lower Town, and Sussex Drive. The Rideau Canal has traditionally divided Ottawa into Upper Town and Lower Town. West of the canal, on the geographic high side, Upper Town is the area that belongs to government. Here the banks of the Ottawa River are limestone cliffs—the site originally of British military barracks and later of Canada's Parliament Buildings. East of the canal, below the cliffs, lived the lower orders. Enlisted men, canal laborers, and commercial elements—including Byward Market and a great many taverns—made up Lower Town. Running from Wellington Street along the Ottawa River to Rideau Falls, Sussex Drive connected the two areas and provided a conduit for incoming and outgoing shipments on the river. Everything merges near Confederation Square.

Upper Town

Confederation Square, more triangular than quadrilateral, with the National War Memorial to Canada's armed forces, is the pulse point of the city. From this junction of Ottawa's oldest streets—Wellington, Sparks, and Elgin—most points of interest are within easy walking distance. The urban area of Ottawa is compact, and driving and parking downtown offer more frustration than convenience. Taxis are easy to come by and, because of the short distances involved in the downtown core, are as practical as city buses. An alternative during the summer months is a shuttle bus service called Visibus that covers much of the area that is of interest to visitors. It trundles along Sussex Drive as far as the National Gallery and crosses the Ottawa River to the new Museum of Civilization in Hull. A flat rate of $2 gives you access for the day (9:00 A.M. to 6:00 P.M.) Details at the Visitors' Information Bureau.

A comprehensive Visitors' Information Bureau is located at 65 Elgin Street in the National Arts Centre facing Confederation Square. Check here for specifics on almost anything. Tour buses of the city run regularly from Confederation Square, but you can start on your own with Ottawa's raison d'être: the **Parliament Buildings**.

In front of Parliament's Centre Block an irresistible tourist attraction, the Changing of the Guard ceremony, takes place on the lawn every morning at 10:00 A.M. (from the last Sunday in June to Labour Day weekend). The scarlet coats and bearskins of the Governor General's Foot Guards set the tone for a tour of the site.

Before going inside, take a half hour to explore the grounds. A path behind "the hill" offers a spectacular view of the river (not to mention an assortment of statues). Guided tours through the buildings are available every day, but the best time to go is when Parliament is in session. (Parliament usually recesses for the summer months, Easter, and Christmas.) At two o'clock most afternoons you can watch the prime minister and his cabinet field questions from the "loyal opposition." A no-holds-barred confrontation, it's probably the best entertainment in town and worth the time spent standing in line to get into the public gallery. Question Period ends promptly at three, and its logical follow-up is formal tea at the Château Laurier, a five-minute walk down Wellington Street.

A Gothic delight of spires and towers, the **Château Laurier** was built about the same time as the Parliament Buildings (1916) and is typical of hotels constructed by the national railroads in their heyday—still a great place to stay, for comfort, location, and a sense of history. If you like odd spaces, ask for a turret room; otherwise, specify a room overlooking the river. One of the city's best handcraft shops, **Signatures**, is located on the first floor of the Château, with top-flight work by several local artisans in leather, glass, gold, and silk. Traditional British tea is served at the Château between 3:00 and 5:00 P.M. every day—finger sandwiches, cakes, and clotted cream included. Make a note, though, to go back to Parliament Hill in the evening (summer months) for a well-designed sound-and-light presentation on the lawn directly in front of Centre Block.

To gather in the remaining essence of government on Wellington Street, walk west from the Château past the parliamentary buildings themselves to the **Supreme Court of Canada Building**, the lobby and courtroom of which are open to the public on weekdays. The **National Library and Public Archives** are housed in the final building along Wellington; there are often exhibits on the first floor, which is open every day, but the library itself is strictly a reference facility.

The Bank of Canada, nearby on the south side of Wellington, is an architecturally interesting meld of two worlds: Modern glass towers flank the original bank building, in which an attractive **Currency Museum** now resides, enhanced by a soothingly lush garden. There is no admission charge at this museum, which holds the most complete collection of Canadian notes and coins in the world.

At this point you are very close to two reliable hotels: the

Delta Ottawa and the **Radisson Hotel**. Both offer predictable, comfortable accommodation at Ottawa's usual high prices. But another, untypical hotel lurks in this area. The tiny **Doral Inn** on Albert Street is a restored 1879 hostelry, where air conditioning and old-world ambience are attractively combined and rates are very moderate. A good Spanish restaurant, the **Costa Brava**, is a bonus if you stay here.

It isn't far back to Confederation Square, but instead of walking along Wellington take **Sparks Street**, which runs parallel to the south. The first pedestrian mall in Canada, Sparks Street is still a central shopping area. Check out **Canada's Four Corners** (at Sparks and Metcalfe) for traditional Canadian crafts. Another excellent spot is the **Snow Goose**, 83 Sparks Street, which houses a variety of native Canadian art and is a good source of Inuit (Eskimo) graphics.

Colonel By's Canal

It's impossible to ignore the **Rideau Canal** in Ottawa. From its beginnings in the Ottawa River, the Rideau Canal runs roughly south, bisecting the core of the city. Along both sides of the canal, between **Entrance Bay** (now called Colonel By Valley) and the point where it joins the Rideau River, are bicycle paths and parklands of which Ottawans make constant use. But start at the beginning: From Confederation Square, cross Wellington Street to the north side and the gully tucked in between Parliament Hill and the Château Laurier.

Mere feet from the centers of government and commerce, the Rideau Canal begins in this gully that has scarcely changed since the canal was completed in 1832. Here the Ottawa River, its limestone cliffs, and the first few Rideau locks seem isolated from the rest of the city. There is delight in just watching small boats being lifted up the canal in the locks, in seeing the old road that runs along the cliff wall, or in exploring the Commissariat.

The oldest surviving stone building in Ottawa, the Commissariat was built in 1827 as a military supply depot. Now the **Bytown Museum**, it houses a collection of artifacts from the city's earliest days.

On Wellington Street itself it's hard to avoid hawkers for canal tours. And why should you? The sight-seeing boats ply the canal all day, so choose a time when you're ready to relax and use an hour to see Ottawa from a watery vantage point. Or tour the same areas the way the locals do, by bicycle. Bikes are easily rented at the Château Laurier (by the hour or by the day). Although escorted tours are available, it's easy just to follow the bicycle paths going south beside the canal from the locks at Entrance Bay to **Dow's Lake** (about 6 miles round-trip). The necessities of life will all be at hand: A marina at Dow's Lake includes several restaurants—or you could save yourself for **The Ritz on the Canal**, located about halfway to Dow's Lake on the west side. The restaurant's setting is almost as good as the tiny, unorthodox pizzas that are its specialty.

Cycling along the canal in good weather, you will encounter Ottawans of all ages, bicycling, walking, or just sunning themselves on the grass. The city seems to live beside the canal all summer. In winter, the waterway takes on another life. The grass and bicycle paths are defeated by snow, but the canal itself is cleared to form the longest skating rink in the world. Ottawans love it! They skate to work during the week and skate with their families on weekends. Visitors have no excuses: Skates can be rented from kiosks at several points right on the canal ice. For ten days in February each year the canal becomes the focus for **Winterlude**, a festival of snow sculptures, harness racing, dog sledding, and general foolishness on ice. Lights line the canal and music plays for skaters, who turn up in the thousands.

Beside the canal, just below Confederation Square, stands the massive **National Arts Centre**, housing three performance halls where concerts, theater, and ballet are staged year-round. A pleasant restaurant, **Le Café**, is part of the complex, offering good food before or after a performance. During summer months Le Café spills out onto a canalside terrace and is a comfortable place to stop for a spritzer or a cup of tea.

Just around the corner, on Albert Street near Elgin, is the **Four Seasons Hotel**—an establishment with a reputation for especially good service. Cabinet ministers and senior bureaucrats are often seen here at breakfast and luncheon meetings.

Things change when you cross the canal from the west, including, quite often, the names of Ottawa's streets. Wellington, for example, becomes Rideau Street to the east of the bridge in front of Confederation Square. Easily seen from that bridge is the **Rideau Centre**, Ottawa's latest shopping facility. In true suburban tradition, it gathers together some 200-odd establishments, from boutiques to department stores to fast-food outlets, under one roof (good for a rainy or freezing day).

There are of course alternatives to eating in the shopping center. One unlikely corner hides an excellent restaurant, **Santé**, at 45 Rideau Street (near Sussex Drive) in a second-floor walk-up location. Those who make it up the stairs find good food (the chef is Trinidadian but the cuisine, which leans to tamarind and lemon grass, has Thai overtones) in comfortable surroundings. Inhabitants of the nearby parliamentary world know Santé; you'll need reservations (Tel: 232-7113).

Attached to the Rideau Centre is the new **Westin Hotel**. Well located and equipped with all modern amenities (including squash courts), it's another convenient place to stay, within easy reach of everything.

On the north side of Rideau Street, just behind the shopping behemoth, is the oldest—and one of the liveliest—parts of Ottawa.

Lower Town

Traditionally known as Lower Town, or the **Byward Market** area, this is the oldest part of Ottawa. The city's first houses—and taverns—were built here 150 years ago for the men who worked on the Rideau Canal. Bounded by Sussex Drive, Rideau Street, and St. Patrick Street, it's a compact area that has never lost its central role in Ottawa's commercial life, although it has moved up and down the social ladder over the years.

If Quebec lumbermen favored the bars of Lower Town in the mid-1800s, so do Ottawa's young professionals in the late 1980s. Lower Town is busy during the day, and just as busy at night. Much of the city's night life happens here (the rest of it is on Elgin Street, which runs south from Wellington Street), in wine bars (**Vine's**, at 54 York Street, is one of the best), pubs, and clubs like the **Rainbow Bistro** on 76 Murray Street. The sounds of rhythm-and-blues bands obscure conversation inside, and unless you get in early, the most you can hope for on a Saturday night is a bit of bar to lean against. The clubs all close at 1:00 A.M., but no need to despair: The bar crowd just moves over to Hull (about which more later).

The actual market still thrives. Many Ottawans shop here, particularly on weekends, in stores that specialize in cheeses, meats, fish, or fruits. During summer months local farmers set up stalls in the streets between the principal market buildings and offer fresh fruits, vegetables, and flowers.

Although the basic market function of the Byward area endures, it has been embroidered in recent years. Many of the older buildings now harbor chic boutiques as well as a variety of restaurants. This is a favorite haunt for locals on a Sunday. A stranger to the city might well presume that no one in Ottawa eats breakfast at home on weekends, the brunch habit is so prevalent here. Particularly during the summer, sidewalk cafés bulge on Sunday mornings. Byward Market is exempt from local bylaws that restrict Sunday store hours, so after brunch the logical thing here is to browse. Possibilities range from secondhand bookstores to designer clothing shops. One distinctively Canadian shop is **Suttles and Seawinds** (535 Sussex Drive), which sells handcrafted clothes from Nova Scotia.

Back lanes and small courtyards are part of the market area's ambience. A particularly charming, cobblestoned spot exists between Clarence and Murray streets: **Tin House Court**, which includes the façade of an old front wall affixed to the side of another stone building. The house from which the façade came was owned in the early 1900s by a city tinsmith named Foisy, and his skill at his trade is evident here. The **Courtyard Restaurant** (21 George Street) is a good Sunday brunch bet, with live classical music as part of the menu.

If you find yourself in Tin House Court, by the way, you won't be far from **Memories** (7 Clarence Street), a café infamous for desserts too good to pass up. The market area abounds in restaurants of every persuasion. From Tex-Mex to *nouvelle cuisine,* you'll find a quick or leisurely meal easy to locate. One that might—and shouldn't—escape you is the tiny café that is part of **Domus**, a kitchen-supply shop at 269 Dalhousie Street. This one is only open for lunch. For a special evening or lunch, **Le Jardin** (127 York Street) serves classic French food in a beautifully renovated old house. Or just wander until something strikes your fancy.

Any exploration of this basic part of Ottawa is incomplete without a walk down **St. Patrick Street**, where two original houses still stand. Typical of the small wood-frame homes once common in Lower Town, No. 138 dates back to 1850 and was the home for many years of Flavan Rochon, a wood-carver whose skills embellished the Library of Parliament. By the time of Confederation (1867) the more usual style of house was the one standing at 142 St. Patrick—three stories in stone, with a second-floor veranda.

Sussex Drive

Sussex Drive has been an impressive boulevard since Ottawa's pioneer beginnings. During the city's first century Sussex was a commercial center, lined with hardware and grocery stores, hotels and haberdashers. Running east and west, parallel to the Ottawa River, the street carried traffic to Queen's Wharf (long gone) and to the sawmills (equally extinct) at Rideau Falls, where the Rideau River empties into the Ottawa River. As river traffic gave way to road and rail, however, the street lost its status as a business thoroughfare.

In the early 1960s the federal government decided to preserve the old commercial structures on the east side of Sussex between George and St. Patrick streets, with the idea of creating a Confederation-period streetscape. Original façades were revived while interiors were gutted and rebuilt. Today these old buildings are thriving again and Sussex Drive is home to toney shops as well as being part of the well-used ceremonial route leading to Government House.

A walk along Sussex will be time-consuming, not because of the boulevard's length (from Confederation Square to Ottawa City Hall is just over a mile) but because there is so much worth seeing. The restored buildings in those blocks between George and St. Patrick streets will be on the right as you stroll down Sussex, but when you raise your eyes the spires of **Notre Dame Basilica** (Sussex Drive and St. Patrick Street) and the glass domes of the National Gallery dominate the skyline. The oldest church in the capital, and the heart of the Irish Catholic congregation in Lower Town, the basilica was consecrated in 1846.

Across the street, overlooking Nepean Point and the river, is the **National Gallery of Canada**. Designed by Moshe Safdie, it echoes in granite and glass the lines of the Parliamentary Library visible in the background. A stunning building, the new gallery offers first-rate exhibit spaces, restaurants, and quiet courtyards. Predictably, the National Gallery's collection of Canadian art is its strength, and while it offers a historical perspective, the gallery's best-known holdings are works by the Group of Seven. (See the Northern Ontario section below.) Just don't miss the reconstructed chapel from the Rideau Street Convent, an outstanding example of 19th-century French-Canadian architecture.

From the National Gallery site, you cannot miss the curved profile of the new **Canadian Museum of Civilization** on the opposite bank of the Ottawa River. If you're game, you can walk half a mile across the Interprovincial Bridge, or you can pick up the shuttle bus in front of the National Gallery.

This spanking new museum (opened in June 1989) is the work of Canadian architect Douglas Cardinal, who describes his design of curving walls and domed roofs as evocative of a Canadian landscape sculpted by the natural erosion of glaciers, wind, and water. State-of-the-art exhibits detailing human history in Canada abound, and the museum's world-famous collection of totem poles is reason enough for a visit.

The shuttle bus will return you to Sussex Drive, where there is more territory to explore (if you need a break first, there is a café and a restaurant at the Museum of Civilization). Just north of the National Gallery is the **Canadian War Museum**. Its collection includes not only the expected paraphernalia of conflict—torpedoes, tanks, and cannons—but more than 7,000 artworks that describe war through the eyes of artists from several countries.

Five minutes more down the road is the **Royal Canadian Mint**, adorned with turrets and battlements. Within its Gothic walls commemorative coins and medals, as well as the gold maple-leaf coins, are manufactured. Tours (by appointment; call 996-5393) are available year-round.

Continuing to walk east along Sussex, in ten minutes more you will reach Ottawa's City Hall on Green Island, where the Ottawa and Rideau rivers meet. There are often exhibits of works by local artists in the first-floor lobby. Across from City Hall are the Rideau Falls, flanked by a pleasant park. If you stop here and turn around, it will be an easy 20-minute walk back along Sussex Drive to Confederation Square.

To explore Sussex Drive farther to the east, a car or bicycle will be needed. Beyond City Hall, along the Sussex route, the diplomatic city emerges. The Department of External Affairs is housed in a multi-layered structure (tours available on weekdays) at 125 Sussex;

the French Embassy and the prime minister's residence (24 Sussex) both command attention, although neither is open to the public. At the end of Sussex (No. 1), about 3 miles from Confederation Square, is Rideau Hall, residence of the governor general. Superbly situated on 80-odd acres, the house and grounds may be seen only on tours (Tel: 998-7114).

Elsewhere in Ottawa

While the city is small, and does break into three basic units, there are a few things worth seeing that don't quite fit into this scheme. Because Ottawa is a national capital it enjoys a higher concentration of museums than most cities. They have a tendency to close on Mondays (check at the tourism information kiosk at the National Arts Centre, because some museums make exceptions during the summer months).

On the edge of the downtown core, on the corner of Metcalfe and McLeod streets (a 20-minute walk south from Confederation Square), is the **Museum of Natural Sciences** in the Victoria Memorial Building. The building itself is beautiful and was used to house Parliament when the Centre Block was destroyed by fire in 1916. Check out the plant gallery on the fourth floor.

Not a museum per se but an interesting Victorian house on public display is **Laurier House**, at 335 Laurier East (the canal divides Laurier Street into east and west). Formerly the residence of two Canadian prime ministers, Laurier House has several rooms furnished with period pieces.

The **National Aviation Museum** at Rockcliffe Airport has more than a hundred aircraft on display; the collection traces the progress of aircraft development from bamboo and balloon cloth structures.

HULL

Ottawa is located in the National Capital Region, an area that includes both Ottawa itself and, in Quebec on the north shore of the Ottawa River, Hull. Many Canadians would like to see the capital region become a distinct political unit (in a manner similar to the District of Columbia in the United States or to Canberra in Australia), but

Quebec has been reluctant to yield sovereignty over any of its territory.

Although linked by several bridges, the two cities are far from being integrated. Hull remains a French-speaking city and has retained its small-town, working-class character. Inhabitants of the two towns interact in two basic venues: as employees of federal government departments, some of which have been moved to Hull in recent years, and in Hull's late-night bars.

The Strip

When Ottawa's bars close at 1:00 A.M., serious revellers move across the bridges to Hull's **Promenade du Portage**. This main street sports a collection of bars and discos that stay open every night until 3:00 A.M. (and hardly warm up before 11:00 P.M.). The names of clubs along The Strip change frequently, but the general character of the area is very stable: The crowd is young, the music is loud, and the bouncers have no necks. Current lights along The Strip include J. R. Dallas (117 Promenade du Portage) and Zap (75 Promenade du Portage). The "older" crowd (read over 25) gravitates toward Chez Henri (179 Promenade du Portage), where the sound readings are a few decibels lower.

Food can also be found along The Strip. One tiny, inexpensive restaurant worth stopping at is **La Grenouille** (80 Promenade du Portage). The *table d'hôte* menu is limited, but the food is imaginatively and carefully prepared.

In fact, Hull has a number of good French restaurants. Among the best is the casual **Le Pied du Cochon** (248 Montcalm), which is located in the heart of a commercial area and justifies a detour. For a more formal atmosphere, the number-one spot in Hull is **Café Henry Burger** (69 rue Laurier). Go for the evening or schedule a long lunch—it will be expensive and memorable.

GATINEAU PARK

If you have a car, a 20-minute drive from Parliament Hill will bring you to the well-cared-for wilderness of Gatineau Park. Take Wellington Street west to the Portage Bridge and turn left at the first intersection in Hull (Taché

Boulevard). Follow Taché west for about a mile to the Gatineau Parkway, which is a righthand turn off Taché. Points of interest are marked by signs along the route. Some 88,000 acres belonging to the federal government, the park offers hiking trails, bikeways, and swimming in freshwater lakes. In the winter, superb cross-country skiing trails are maintained throughout the park, with cabins at which skiers may stop to warm up or cook lunch on wood stoves.

While you're in the park, stop at **Kingsmere**, the country estate of former Canadian prime minister William Mackenzie King. An eccentric man, King was given to trafficking with spiritual mediums and collecting "ruins," with which he festooned his estate. Among numerous bits and pieces gracefully scattered throughout the gardens are parts of the old Parliament Buildings that burned in 1916, and some Corinthian columns from a 19th-century bank building. A pleasant tearoom operates here during summer months.

GETTING AROUND

Ottawa has a newly renovated airport about 20 minutes' drive from Parliament Hill. City buses run every half hour between the terminal and downtown. Taxi fare to a downtown hotel from the airport will be about $18. An airport shuttlebus to several major hotels runs at half-hour intervals for $6 per ticket.

Despite Ottawa's location in the "central corridor" of Canadian passenger rail service, most Ottawans have a jaundiced view of train service. While several trains run daily between Ottawa and either Montreal or Toronto, they are frequently late—especially during the winter. The station is not downtown (it's located about 3 miles southwest of Parliament Hill), but it is linked to the city center by regular city bus service. Taxis are always available (the fare from downtown is about $8).

Canadian roads tend to run east and west. From Toronto, Highway 401 runs directly east, and you can cut north from 401 to Ottawa via either Highway 16 or 31. It's about a five-hour drive (450 km/280 miles).

From Montreal, there is also a divided highway (417), but it may rank as the most boring road on the North American continent. Your drive (192 km/120 miles) will be only a few minutes longer but it will be far more pleasant if you take Highway 17, which runs along the Ottawa River.

An intercity bus station is located on Catherine Street in Ottawa, with city bus stops close by.

Because so many of the reasons for visiting Ottawa are clustered in the downtown core, walking is the most practical way to see the city. A lack of adequate spaces has made parking a car in Ottawa both difficult and expensive. City bus service is extensive and reliable but operates on a strange, two-tier fare structure. During morning and evening rush hours (6:30 to 8:30 A.M. and 3:30 to 5:30 P.M.) it costs $1.70 to get on an Ottawa bus—the highest bus fares in Canada. At less busy times the fare is 85 cents. Unless you are going a considerable distance, a taxi will be far more convenient.

ACCOMMODATIONS REFERENCE

Hotels in Ottawa are expensive, but most offer substantial reductions on weekends. Check on available discounts when making reservations.

▶ **Château Laurier.** 1 Rideau Street, **Ottawa**, Ont. K1N 8S7. Tel: (613) 232-6411; in U.S., (800) 268-9143.

▶ **Delta Ottawa.** 361 Queen Street, **Ottawa**, Ont. K1R 7S9. Tel: (613) 238-6000; in U.S., (800) 268-1133.

▶ **Doral Inn.** 486 Albert Street, **Ottawa**, Ont. K1R 5B5. Tel: (613) 230-8055; in U.S., (800) 267-3344.

▶ **Four Seasons Hotel.** 150 Albert Street, **Ottawa**, Ont. K1P 5G2. Tel: (613) 238-1500; in U.S., (800) 332-3442; in Canada, (800) 268-6282.

▶ **Westin Hotel Ottawa.** 11 Colonel By Drive, **Ottawa**, Ont. K1N 9H4. Tel: (613) 560-7000; in U.S., (800) 582-6000.

▶ **Radisson Hotel.** 100 Kent Street, **Ottawa**, Ont. K1P 5R7. Tel: (613) 238-1122; in U.S., (800) 333-3333.

If bed and breakfast is a more appealing format, there are a number of guesthouses in Ottawa. A listing is available from Ottawa Bed and Breakfast, P.O. Box 4848, Station E, Ottawa, Ontario, K1S 5J1.

TORONTO

By Steve Veale

Steve Veale is a free-lance travel writer living in Toronto.
He contributes regularly to the Toronto Star, *the* Montreal
Gazette, Leisureways *magazine, and a number of news-*
papers in the United States, such as the Detroit Free Press
and the Buffalo News. *For almost a decade he was the*
promotion officer in the travel media department of the
Ontario government's Ministry of Tourism.

Toronto is a city that has finally shed its dull-duckling
image and turned into a rather glorious swan; gone are
the gawky days as a rather provincial British colony when
gray flannel was the the only fashion and roast beef the
only cuisine. Toronto, in fact, has become so chic and
trendy that a tourist who last visited in the early 1960s
would fail to recognize the place, both in style and spirit.
The changes have taken place with a vengeance, as if
Toronto is trying to make up for years lost while chained
in bondage to someone else's traditions.

And yet these changes, although they appeared to take
place overnight, have been the result of careful urban
planning. Toronto watched the blight that descended on
other North American cities in the 1950s and 1960s, when
the core areas slumped as everyone escaped to the suburbs. This city took the opposite tack; it revitalized and
rejuvenated its downtown (led by the huge Eaton Centre
shopping complex), rescuing it with elegant stores, luxurious condos, and renovated apartments, plus an explosion of restaurants, nightclubs, bars, theaters, and venues
for concerts and other performing arts—all of which
recaptured the downtown dwellers in record numbers.

Toronto today is a thriving city of business, from stock

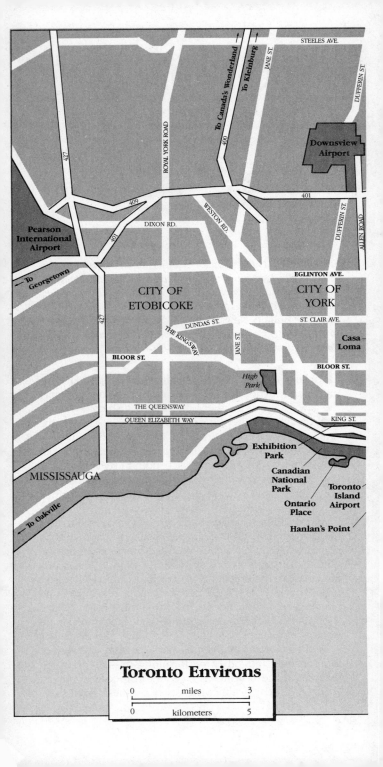

Toronto Environs

	miles	
0		3

	kilometers	
0		5

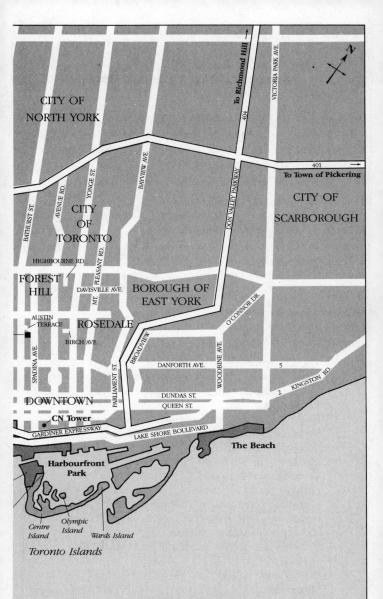

and bond trading to legal and government work to film and theater activity. It is also the safest and cleanest city of its size in North America.

Toronto is also a city under constant construction with the downtown landscape changing daily at the whim of major developers. Building landmarks are seemingly demolished overnight while others, phoenix-like, rise the following day to take their place. The city has been in a constant state of flux and change over the past decade. If you haven't been to Toronto for several years, many of your familiar landmarks—along with restaurants and bars—may have disappeared or been transformed into something else.

However, fair warning: Toronto has paid for its popularity with a steady climb in prices. It seems everyone wants to be here, whether to live or visit, and the soaring prices reflect what the market will bear—which seems to be quite a lot these days.

MAJOR INTEREST

The CN Tower
Harbourfront and the Toronto islands
Ontario Place
Casa Loma
Eaton Centre, huge downtown shopping mall
Yorkville shops, cafés, bars, nightclubs
Bloor Street's exclusive shopping
The Underground City
Canada's Wonderland
Ontario Science Centre
The Beach (swimming, shopping, cafés)
Performing arts: theater, concerts, opera, ballet, symphony, dance, cabaret
Festivals (Caravan, Caribana, Film Festival of Festivals)
Dining and nightlife
Shopping

(Note: Dining, nightlife, and shopping have been included because they have all become major activities for Torontonians over the past decade. There seems to be a great deal of disposable income in this city and much of it is spent on wining/dining/consumerism. Restaurants have become an evening's entertainment, not just an adjunct to a theater production, more bars spring up every week, and shopping has become almost a major sport thanks to the affluence of Toronto's citizens. Many Torontonians are engaged in rampant consumerism; simply wander through the Eaton Centre any Saturday afternoon to see them in action.)

Although Toronto has been hailed in recent years as "the North American city that works," the initial description of the settlement on the Lake Ontario shore was a far cry from this glowing assessment.

"The city's site was better calculated for a frog pond or a beaver meadow than for the residence of human beings," wrote John Graves Simcoe, the first lieutenant governor of Upper Canada, who discarded the original Turontu in favor of York, after the Duke of York, second son of the reigning monarch, George III. It is not known whether this rather ingratiating name change aided Simcoe's career.

The site soon became known affectionately, or disparagingly, as Muddy York by those who had to walk its streets. For a while the name Hogtown, proposed because of the increase in farmers' markets and livestock trading (today's St. Lawrence Market), seemed a viable alternative, but fortunately cooler heads prevailed, and in 1834 the official, final name for the growing community became the original Toronto.

The name itself stems from the similar sounding Huron word meaning "meeting or gathering place," thus making Toronto the world's first convention center. The French voyageurs were the first to meet with the native Indians and traded beads for furs at Fort Rouille, built on the site of the city's Exhibition Park, which is still the gathering place for annual fairs and sports events. When the British took over the area in 1788, the land was purchased from the Mississauga Indians for more beads, cloth, and blankets totaling about $1,700.

Contrary to Simcoe's pessimistic diaries, Toronto continued to grow and expand; by today's census it claims well over three million inhabitants in the metropolitan area (the city of Toronto proper has about 700,000). It remains the province's capital city, the financial center of the country, and it recently surpassed Montreal as the largest city in Canada. And, true to its roots, it has become one of the convention capitals of North America.

Today's inhabitants pronounce their city's name "Trawna," completely ignoring all the "Ohs" and the final

"T"; this is closer, perhaps, to the original Huron dialect, but it's a far cry from phonetic English.

For many years, the city was definitely Toronto the Good, a euphemistic add-on that translated as boring, dull, staid, or, as W. C. Fields once would have drawled, "I went to Toronto last Sunday; it was closed."

But things started to change following World War II with the wave of immigrants crashing onto the beaches of the New World: Italians, Chinese, Greeks, Japanese, Hungarians, Portuguese, Poles, and others, all combining to change the shape and flavor of the burgeoning community. In recent years people from the West Indies, East Indies, Pakistan, Vietnam, and elsewhere have increased the metropolitan census from about 750,000 in 1958 to today's total. The conservative WASPs and longtime Jewish population soon made room for a more international element. Witness the changing Jewish garment district of Spadina: Bagels and knishes have given way to egg rolls and noodles; Shopsy's deli to Peking Court. Toronto's business base also grew because of Canadian corporations' flight from French Separatist pressures in Montreal.

Toronto became not so much a melting pot as a mulligan stew, with a blend of ingredients—a touch of this culture, a pinch of that—that has created a spectacular mixture of sight and sound, color and style. And new arrivals daily add to the flavor of this multilingual metropolis.

Exploring Toronto

True to the cliché, Toronto really is a city of neighborhoods; areas that have nevertheless outgrown their boundaries and have stretched to blend in with another distinct culture. For example, the Fashion District along Spadina sells clothes and accessories. This runs into the Chinatown of Dundas Street West, which looks like a typical crowded street scene in Hong Kong. Yet, for a few blocks, you will be bewildered by the cultural mixture. A third-generation Russian/Polish/Armenian designs coats in one store while his neighbor, a recently arrived Chinese/Thai/Filipino teenager, creates some terrific wok concoction in the restaurant next door.

Though the nationalities do mix, there are various ethnic areas serving a particular food and fashion: the shmatte district of Spadina; the bright lights of Chinatown on Dundas West; the Portuguese market of Kensington; the Greek souvlaki along the Danforth; the Italian spumoni shops lining College Street; the monied mansions of conservative Rosedale and Forest Hill; the thousands of students throughout the Annex; the sandblasted-brick-house yuppies of Cabbagetown. The city often seems like a patchwork quilt of small neighborhoods threaded together by its diverse mix of people.

The laid-back yachting life of the harborfront segues into the concrete and steel of the city's Bay Street stockmarket area to the north; the boardwalk and racetrack of the Beach melds with the gritty and more industrial area of Queen Street; the Little Italy of College Street West soon meets the yuppified shopping section of **Bloor West Village**; the stately, century-old homes of the Annex turn into the chic condos of Yorkville, and the million-dollar mansions of Rosedale join the Greek tavernas when Bloor Street becomes the Danforth.

Each area is unique and proud to display its separate character; in fact most areas are well noted with street signs that state designations; College Street says "Little Italy" on all street signs; Dundas Street signs bear Chinese characters underneath; Cumberland Street is in the upscale Yorkville–Bloor shopping district; Queen's Quay West is Harbourfront; Greek letters underscore the Danforth signs; Spadina is brightly marked with a red "Fashion District" insignia, and so on. You know immediately which area of Toronto you are in.

The Annex, in the middle of the city, Forest Hill, just north, and Rosedale, east of center, are all residential areas, the latter claiming most of the city's mansions. Queen's Quay denotes the arts and crafts of Harbourfront and the three island yacht clubs; the Beach of eastern Queen Street is the boardwalk and trendy shops; **the Danforth** is crowded with Mediterranean restaurants.

Chinatown on Dundas West provides all the flair and food of the Orient, while Spadina's character mixes discount fashion with bagels and lox. Kensington Market, filled with kiosks and stalls and where you shop Saturday mornings for the freshest produce, could be a street bazaar in Portugal, whereas only the trendy and gold-card rich casually shop the designer labels in chic midtown Yorkville.

The formerly downtrodden **Cabbagetown** of north Parliament Street (so named because the poor Irish immigrants grew cabbage to eat instead of grass to mow in their front lawns) is now all sandblasted brick and cozy cafés, though it runs south into Regent Park, a poorer

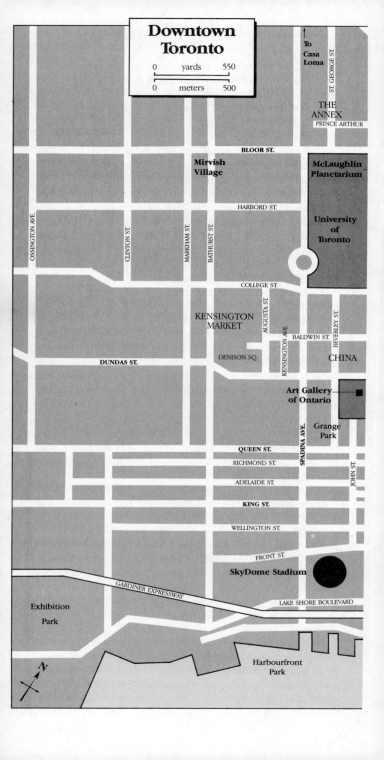

Downtown Toronto

0　　yards　　550
0　　meters　　500

To
Casa
Loma

ST. GEORGE ST.

THE
ANNEX

PRINCE ARTHUR

BLOOR ST.

**Mirvish
Village**

McLaughlin
Planetarium

HARBORD ST.

University
of
Toronto

OSSINGTON AVE.

CLINTON ST.

MARKHAM ST.

BATHURST ST.

COLLEGE ST.

KENSINGTON
MARKET

AUGUSTA ST.

KENSINGTON AVE.

BALDWIN ST.

BEVERLEY ST.

CHINA

DUNDAS ST.

DENISON SQ.

**Art Gallery
of Ontario**

SPADINA AVE.

Grange
Park

QUEEN ST.

RICHMOND ST.

JOHN ST.

ADELAIDE ST.

KING ST.

WELLINGTON ST.

FRONT ST.

SkyDome Stadium

GARDINER EXPRESSWAY

LAKE SHORE BOULEVARD

Exhibition
Park

N

Harbourfront
Park

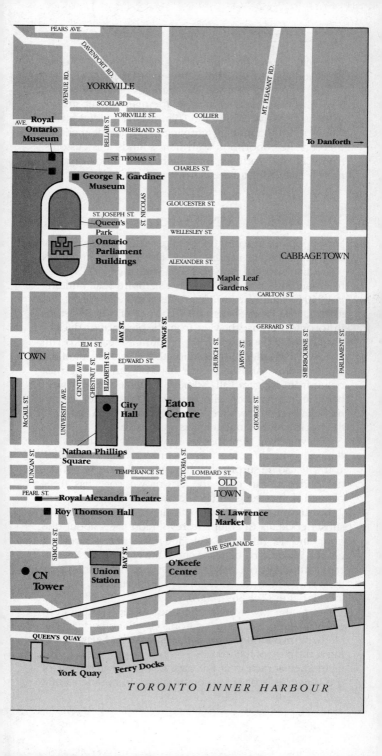

inner-city area of housing developments and street dere-
licts (not all of Toronto has been renovated).

The curse of Toronto's legendary blandness and
WASPism has been removed by the many ethnic groups
who have adopted the city. This mix has added a new
vitality to this continually growing city, where you enter a
different neighborhood with new sounds and customs,
from China to Portugal, from nightclubs to boardrooms,
merely by turning a street corner.

CN Tower

Most people visit Toronto for the permanent attractions of
the city, and there is none more noticeable than the CN
(Canadian National) Tower, at 1,815 feet the world's tallest
free-standing structure (New York's Empire State Building
is 1,250 feet and Paris's Eiffel Tower a mere 984 feet). The
tower, at 301 Front Street, should be one of your first stops
in Toronto, because the view from the observation deck or
the Top of Toronto revolving restaurant (seats 400) will
give you a wonderful orientation to the grid layout of the
city far below. And on a clear day you can see the mist
rising from Niagara Falls some 100 km (60 miles) away,
past the hundreds of sailboats and yachts in the Toronto
harbor (except in winter). The night view from Sparkles,
the world's highest nightclub, is impressive.

The view will demonstrate how easily the streets are
defined: everything in squares, perpendicular or parallel.
You will also be surprised at how green the city is; not just
the parkland but even the downtown core has trees
planted along streets and boulevards.

If you want to see the city spin around, book a table for
sunset cocktails (a complete revolution takes about one
hour and 12 minutes); Tel: 360-8500. For a revolving
dinner, it would be better to check the **Lighthouse Restaurant** at the lakefront Westin Hotel at One Harbour Square;
the view, while not so high, is still spectacular, and the
food is better (Tel: 869-1600).

Get to the tower early; the lines to the elevators can
easily take more than an hour on a clear summer day. The
Metro Convention Centre is the chrome-and-glass building at the base of the tower.

Another attraction at the base of the tower is **Tour of
the Universe**, a blast into outer space, compliments of a

flight simulator and visual special effects that will have you firmly convinced you have left this planet. An elevator takes you beneath the surface as you are led, by human guides and robots, through computerized passport controls and past video screens.

The newest attraction in the area, just beside the CN Tower, is the **SkyDome**, the world's first retractable domed stadium. This 56,000-seat homage to sport is the home of two of Toronto's major-league sports teams: baseball's Blue Jays and football's Argonauts. (Hockey's Maple Leafs will remain in the historic Maple Leaf Gardens at Carlton and Yonge streets, preferring ice to Astroturf.) The Sky-Dome, truly an engineering marvel, officially opened on June 3, 1989, while the first ballgame was played two days later (historic note: the home team lost!). The Dome could cover a 31-story building at center field and can rotate 180 degrees. Eventually there will be a 450-room hotel attached to the stadium, with 77 rooms overlooking the field (which will rent for $800 per day), an entertainment complex, and various restaurant and bar areas. The major problem will be traffic congestion. Take public transport, or, better still, walk to the game on one of Toronto's glorious summer days.

Harbourfront
and the Toronto Islands

For the past decade Toronto has been transforming a once dingy harbor area into a place that features arts and crafts, children's activities, theater, dance, films, as well as yacht basins, waterfront cafés, restaurants, and a lush two-mile waterfront promenade. The site quickly became popular for summer strolling, although in the past year the burgeoning condos have greatly increased the traffic and people density. York Quay (pronounced "key") Centre, however, remains true to its roots, with artists creating kiln-fired pottery and the like. The original "people place" is bordered on the east by the expensive shops of the **Queen's Quay Terminal Building**, actually a spectacular renovation of an old, unused grain terminal, and the **Hotel Admiral** on the west (this is one area where the council failed to stop developers).

Chips wagons selling fat french fries and hot dogs line the roadside (watch for the police giving them tickets for illegal vending), but if you want something more substantial, scenic, or alcoholic, check the outdoor lakefront café **Spinnakers** in the Terminal or the restaurants at Pier Four beside the Hotel Admiral.

For an escape to the island parkland, take the ferry from behind the Westin Hotel for a day of picnics, beach living, and swimming. You can rent bicycles, canoes, or rowboats on the connected islands (Ward's, Centre, Olympic, and Hanlan's Point). There are also three private yacht clubs on the island.

If you don't wish to spend the day on the islands, take one of several harbor tours through the interconnecting island lagoons with either Gray Line Boat Tours, 5 Queen's Quay West (Tel: 364-2412), or Toronto Harbour Tours, 145 Queen's Quay West (Tel: 869-1372). Tours depart hourly during the summer months.

Ontario Place

This amusement center at 955 Lake Shore Boulevard is likely the most popular spot on the waterfront, being the home of the original **IMAX film theater** with its six-story screen, the outdoor Forum concert stage, a separate children's island with winding water slide and huge wading pool, cafés, waterfront pubs, science exhibits, and starlight dancing. Ontario Place is a 96-acre park built on three man-made islands created, owned, and operated by the Ontario government.

The park is open from the third weekend in May to Labor Day in September; after a $5 admission fee most things are free, including the nightly concerts in the Forum, where entertainment ranges from Peter Allen to the Toronto Ballet. Ontario was the developer of the IMAX film system, and there are continuous shows in the 800-seat Cinesphere, a geodesic dome that seems to float on the waters of the lake.

The Cinesphere features several different films, about 40 minutes each, which have been specially produced to demonstrate the dizzying visual effects of IMAX. These effects range from silently soaring in a glider, zooming down a wooded ski slope or feeling the heat from within a northern Ontario forest fire. During the winter, Ontario Place presents its 70-mm film festival, with such visually striking films as (in previous years) *Apocalypse Now* and *Die Hard*.

There is also the **Trillium**, an upscale restaurant overlooking the water, which caters to local businessmen taking a break from the city's summer heat. In fact, on sunny afternoons you can often see them playing hooky, shoeless in their three-piece suits, navigating little paddleboats through the many canals.

The Trillium menu ranges from noontime hamburgers to dinner surf and turf; kids and families might want to try the waterfront Kelly's on the OP grounds.

City Hall
and Nathan Phillips Square

One of the major architectural attractions in Toronto is the City Hall on Nathan Phillips Square, which stands in striking contrast to the stately old headquarters just across the street, both opposite the Sheraton Centre. The huge arched towers of Finnish architect Viljo Revell opened in 1965 amid great controversy. Toronto the Good was shocked that the chosen structure didn't look like an official building should; it should look like, well, the old City Hall.

But when it officially opened, and the city wasn't destroyed in a flash of thunder and lightning, people started to realize they didn't have to appear old and stodgy. Buildings could be modern and inventive and still function properly. Since then, the look of Toronto has never been the same; old structures have learned to coexist in harmony with the latest in architectural design.

Eaton Centre and
the Underground City

If City Hall is the political mecca, then the Eaton Centre is absolute nirvana for consumers. Just steps east of City Hall, at the corner of Yonge Street, you enter the consumers' shrine, which has become a major visitor attraction as well. Hundreds of shops, restaurants, and pubs fill three floors all the way up to Dundas Street, a four-city-block area, where, like Alice's Restaurant, "you can get anything you want"—from fur coats to grocery greens, Canadian souvenir sweatshirts to deli delights, all in a vast complex based on the famed Galleria in Milan.

As you head south from the Dundas Street subway stop, this portion of the complex is actually Eaton's department store; six levels running the full consumer gamut from speciality food shops, casual and formal clothing, electronics, hardware and kitchen appliances. And when Eaton's ends, the individual shops of the Centre begin. This section of shops has only three levels, with the general rule of thumb being that the less expensive items (i.e., records, books, fast food alley) are located on the lower level while the quality and prices climb as you ascend the escalators (i.e., jewelry stores, exclusive clothing shops, full course dining). Coffee in the basement, cappuccino on the third level deck. And when you run out of Eaton Centre at the Queen Street subway, you segue into **Simpson's**, another vast consumer cornucopia. Simpson's wisely decided not to compete with the ultra-modern Centre but instead set about preserving the beauties of the past by spending millions cleaning and renovating their old downtown department store. Whether you wish to shop in space-age splendor or among the polished gargoyles of the past, you will find whatever you need between the two mega stores.

Dundas Street (the Atrium on Bay) is the farthest point north for Toronto's Underground City, which stretches from Front Street's Union Station at the south. Here are miles of bright, clean underground shopping; in fact, this is the world's largest subterranean complex, complete with green trees and waterfalls as well as restaurants, bars, banks, medical and dental offices, and 1,000 stores. This concourse is also a commuter's winter dream; you can drive to the GO train, arrive at Union Station, walk underground to one of the connecting office complexes, lunch, shop, entertain, and return to a suburban home without wearing an overcoat.

Spadina, Chinatown, and Kensington Market

For a complete change of pace, wander the streets and shop the stalls of three of the city's ethnic areas.

Spadina Avenue (pronounced "Spa-DINE-ah") used to be the Jewish garment and food district, but gradually, as the younger generation moved north in the city, the Chinese filled the vacant storefronts with noodle houses, vegetable stands, herbal medicine stores, and fashionable silk outlets. Around the cross streets of Dundas and Spadina, the two cultures now blend in consumer harmony. And though the debate still rages about where to go for a decent bagel (Montreal seems to have the edge on Toronto), there is no debate about the Oriental cuisine; culinary experts have proclaimed Toronto one of the best spots for Chinese food in North America. Try the second-story **Sai Woo** (no decor but wonderful food) on Dundas Street, or the acclaimed **Pink Pearl**, also on Dundas, for dim sum. Or visit one of the many nondescript, dingy-looking noodle houses; the worse the decor, usually the better the food.

West of Spadina along Dundas, turn right on Augusta Street and enter the back streets of Lisbon. This Portuguese market is the real thing: an Old World marketplace selling live chickens and fresh fish, fruits and vegetables, seeds and beans, delicious pastries and homemade sandwiches. **Kensington Market** runs north from Dundas to College Street and filters east to Spadina, mixing with the students of George Brown Community College. The market, especially on Saturday mornings (it's deserted on Sundays), is a shopper's and browser's delight, a crowded cacophony of haggling in Portuguese and English. This is a definite walking tour; besides, it's too crowded to drive through. Take a break at the outdoor patio of the **Abruzzi** for a tangy Portuguese-style coffee, an afternoon *cerveza*, or a platter of calamari.

Queen Street West

Wander south on Spadina a few blocks to Queen Street, and the scene changes again—to a more youthful, vibrant area (from University Avenue to Bathurst Street) that has become synonymous with the latest in music, style, and fashion in Toronto. This street is lined with tiny restaurants (Peter Pan, Queen Mother Café), sidewalk cafés, bookstores (lounging around Edwards Bookstore on Sundays is a favorite pastime for many), art galleries, secondhand clothing stores, often overpriced original-fashion boutiques, and, for some reason, dozens of electronics stores and low-priced furniture houses.

But the soul of Queen Street West is the music—whether the eclectic variety, from reggae to jazz, of the vanguard **BamBoo Club**, the country-and-western twang of the **Horseshoe Tavern**, or the driving rock sounds of the **Cameron**. The dance-palace/disco scene is ably represented by **The Big Bop**, at the corner of Queen and

Bathurst: two floors of earth-shaking music that draws long sidewalk lines every weekend.

This is Toronto's "bohemian village" area, filled with musicians, artists, and writers who help to propel the creative force of the city; you can feel at home here in your tweed jacket or dyed spiked hairdo.

For a contrast, take a drive or stroll through conservative **Rosedale** (take Sherbourne Street north of Bloor east) or **Forest Hill** (north of St. Clair Avenue, west of Yonge Street) for a taste of Toronto old money. Thinking of buying? Better have a million dollars or so to start. If you are exploring the area, don't dawdle in front of the mansions; the idle rich don't take kindly to people lurking on their sidewalks.

The Beach

On the other, eastern end of Queen Street, east of Woodbine Avenue, controversy long raged over whether the area should be known as "the Beach" or "the Beaches." Finally, an act of the city council opted for the singular form. Longtime residents were then able to rest easy. "Once a beacher, always a beacher" is the rallying cry for all those who live between Woodbine and the end of Queen at the trolley turnaround. This area is basically a small, thriving village, populated by older, longtime residents, up-and-coming yuppies, and some long-haired remnants of the 1960s. Some people literally never leave the confines of the Beach.

There are several miles of sand beach here bordering the cold waters of Lake Ontario (it doesn't matter that it is cold because often the posted signs say: "No swimming. Water pollution.") and a lovely boardwalk area filled with strollers, joggers, and bodies beautiful during the summer sun time. There are tennis courts and green picnic parks en route.

The area actually used to be a "resort" for people who lived in the city until finally the city sprawled out to meet the cottage boundaries. There are gorgeous old homes on either side of Queen Street, although rents soar on the south (water) side. Queen Street itself looks like a summer tourist town, complete with the functional grocery stores for the locals and trendy gift and clothing stores for the tourists. In summer, bathing suits on the main street seem to be de rigueur. The Beach is only a 20-minute

Queen Street trolley ride from the center of town, a quick yet crowded escape during the hot months.

For fast-food fare, try the great burgers and fries at **Licks**, consistently rated the best in the city; or the upscale **Summers** across the street, a renovated old bank building that still takes a great deal of your savings but does provide the interest of an inventive menu.

But perhaps the classic diner here is the **Garden Gate**, known to all as the "Goof." This is the definitive small-town Chinese restaurant: wonderful food, huge portions, low prices. It is also across the street from a grungy old repertory movie house called the Fox, right beside a laundromat. A "beacher" can put the wash in, have dinner at the Goof, switch to the dryer, watch a film for $2.00, pick up the laundry, and walk home, stopping for an ice cream cone on the way. A typical night in the Beach.

Another Beach contrast is the **Sunset Grill**, one of the best ever upscale greasy spoons with long weekend lines for their huge breakfasts (served all day), or the informal, tiny **Spiagga**, serving excellent Italian cuisine at the east end of Queen Street where the trolley loops at the end of the line.

Yorkville

The major downtown area, certainly for nightlife, bars, and restaurants (Bellair, Bemelman's, Remy's), and exclusive shopping (Holt Renfrew, Creed's, David's), and hotels (Windsor Arms, Four Seasons, Park Plaza), is the Yorkville–Bloor area, in the center of the city, just west of Yonge Street (pronounced "young"). This is chic and trendy at its finest: where you wear $200 jeans advertising someone else's name, and BMWs, Audis, Corvettes, and Cadillacs all jockey for the same illegal parking spots. (The police take great glee in towing cars off the streets every Friday and Saturday night, the theory being, if they have to work the weekend shift, anyone driving that type of car should pay for it.)

This area blooms with outdoor cafés and rooftop bars during the spring and summer, when Toronto comes out of winter hibernation; quite often lunch becomes dinner and rolls on into the night. The wining and dining establishments are filled with the rich and those hoping to be.

On warm summer weekend nights, both Yorkville and

Cumberland streets take on the atmosphere of a midway, with clowns, acrobats, street jugglers, and fortune tellers mixing with the bar and disco crowd.

Twenty years ago this exclusive area was a slum, a hangout for the new hippie generation, headquarters for the city's burgeoning folk-club and coffeehouse scene, and rife with marijuana. It was also filled every weekend night, mainly with parents looking for their runaway children. In one of life's wonderful poetic twists, those same "lost" children are now buying expense-account lunches and designer leather jackets here with their American Express gold cards.

Yorkville also plays host to the city's annual film festival, the **Festival of Festivals**, the world's largest public film festival. Every September, movie fans and some really big stars have ten days in which to pack in more than 250 movies from around the world: "gala" premieres from Hollywood, retrospectives, buried treasures, and the best of world cinema—shown in about ten different theaters in the Yorkville–Bloor area. Prices range from $250 for a gala pass (all gala films and parties) to a $65 daytime pass, good until 6:00 P.M.; Tel: 967-7371.

Casa Loma

If you want to tour old Toronto, there is no better spot than the city's famous 98-room castle, at 1 Austin Terrace, northwest of Yorkville. Erected in 1914 at a cost of more than three million dollars by Sir Henry Pellatt, Casa Loma would be impossible to build at today's rate of inflation.

Sir Henry actually had the castle shipped over from Scotland, brick by brick, and had it rebuilt, complete with secret passageways and hidden staircases. He even had carpeting put in the stables for his horses, which no doubt caused the cleaning staff no end of difficulties. The castle is truly a marvel, with its suits of armor, magnificent old pipe organ (conjuring up images of *The Phantom of the Opera*), turrets, and gargoyles.

It can be quite jarring while walking through normal city streets to look up and see this huge castle on a hill, out of place and time, a tribute to one man's obsession. Today the huge edifice is operated by the Kinsmen Club; it is open daily for tours and seems to be a popular spot for Saturday-night ballroom dancing and wedding receptions.

Museums and Galleries

Toronto has a goodly number of museums, from the majestic **Royal Ontario Museum** (the ROM), at the corner of Bloor and University, to the tiny **Museum of the History of Medicine**, just around the corner on Bloor Street West. The ROM is by far the largest, reopened recently after a two-year renovation. Renowned for its collection of Chinese antiquities, the ROM is also connected to the adjoining McLaughlin Planetarium, with its spectacular light show set to rock music, and has just joined forces with the **George R. Gardiner Museum** across the street, known for its delicate and colorful collections of ceramic art.

The **Art Gallery of Ontario** (AGO) holds the world's largest collection of Henry Moore pieces (look also for *The Archer* outside City Hall) as well as constantly changing touring shows. The AGO sits on the corner of Dundas Street West and Beverley, also serving as a cornerstone that unofficially marks this stretch of the city's Chinatown. For Canadian art at its best, visit the **McMichael Gallery Canadian Collection** at Kleinburg (about 30 km/18 miles north of Toronto; take Highway 400, then go west on Major Mackenzie Drive) for the famed colors of the Group of Seven, who painted the Canadian North early in this century.

There are two major areas for art galleries in Toronto: One is Yorkville, the second is on Queen Street West.

Serious collectors, however, would be well advised to contact **Libby's of Toronto** (Tel: 364-3730) for a gallery perusal or invitation to one of its art soirées. Libby's represents some of the best up-and-coming Canadian artists, as well as established painters, and representatives are available by appointment at their 463 King Street East gallery.

Performing Arts

Toronto has fast become an arts town: performing arts, visual arts, and the film arts. For instance, there are more theaters (over 40) in Toronto than in any city in North America, except for New York City—from the grandeur of the Royal Alex to the wooden benches at the Tarragon. Toronto is the home of the National Ballet Company, headed by Reid Maxwell; the Canadian Opera Company (COC), directed by Brian Dickie; and the renowned Toronto Symphony, conducted by Gunther Herbig (all three appointed within the last year).

Both the COC and the ballet use the 3,200-seat **O'Keefe Centre** (Yonge and Front streets) for their performances, as do most touring Broadway shows coming through town; many English-theater imports seem to play at the **Royal Alex** (perhaps because owner Ed Mirvish also owns the Old Vic in London), on King Street West, across from the visually striking and acoustically perfect **Roy Thomson Hall** (home of the symphony). The nearby Yonge Street **Pantages Theatre**, which recently underwent a multi-million dollar renovation, is currently home to *The Phantom of the Opera*. (The theater restoration was the brainchild of Toronto movie-mogul Garth Dabrinsky, father of the multi-screen cineplex theater.)

On any given night, there are dozens (hundreds, counting smaller cabaret and musical venues) of stage performances and musical concerts; check the three local papers (for entertainment, the *Toronto Star* is likely the best, followed by the *Toronto Sun* and the *Globe & Mail*) or the free *NOW* magazine, a weekly entertainment guide found on newsstands and in restaurants everywhere. The monthly *Toronto Life* and *TO* magazines are also at every newsstand.

For half-price tickets on the day of performance, visit the Five Star ticket booths on Yonge Street outside the Eaton Centre, just south of Dundas Street. The booth also provides a free magazine listing theater locations.

Festivals

There are more Italians in Toronto than in Milan; the Canadian city also has the second-largest Chinese population on the continent and more West Indians than anywhere else outside those sunny islands. The city recognizes these elements and celebrates them annually with various ethnic festivals, ranging from the mini–United Nations of Caravan and the colorful crowds of Caribana to the weekend Italian picnic on the Toronto islands.

For two weeks in June during **Caravan**, the more than 70 ethnic groups in Toronto set up their own pavilions throughout the city to introduce metropolitan residents to the finest from their native countries. Demonstrations include Ukrainian dancers, an Oriental tea ceremony, and Jamaican reggae. For a mere $10 you can buy a Caravan passport (which is stamped as you enter domain of each new country) for unlimited entry to dozens of buildings and tents during the annual June festival. You can also purchase individual tickets, but after three different pavilions you'll find you should have bought the passport. The location of each country is listed on maps at the Caravan office as well as in the daily newspapers. There can be long lines at the most popular pavilions, which change annually: Check the papers and listen to local gossip for the best ones this year.

The **Caribana** celebration started only a few years ago and already is host to half a million people during the first-weekend-in-August celebrations (the first Monday in August creates a long weekend for Canadians; all banks, government offices, and many stores are closed for Heritage Day). Caribana starts off with miles of parade through downtown (see local newspapers for parade times and routes) and usually ends near the Harbourfront area, where the party continues all weekend. Food wagons en route dispense roti and rice, and the police often turn a judicial eye should they spy an occasional bottle of a substance to be consumed only on licensed premises. Caribana is not just for the West Indian population; it appeals to all who enjoy the reggae beat of the islands. The festival is highlighted by the Miss Caribana Ball on Saturday night on the Toronto islands.

The "Miss Bikini of the Year" contest is the highlight of the annual Italian-language **CHIN Radio Station Picnic** on the Toronto islands every first weekend in July; advance newspaper photos of the contestants guarantee promotion for the picnic every year. The Italian community comes out in full force, hundreds of thousands, for this three-day celebration of their European background, complete with pasta, bocce balls, and (unofficial) competition of homemade vino.

There are numerous other ethnic celebrations constantly taking place throughout the year, from a Portuguese music festival in a Dundas Street park to a Greek Orthodox street parade along the Danforth. Toronto is proud of the many "new Canadians" who have chosen to live here yet take pride in remembering their native heritage, which has added so much to the heartbeat of the city.

Street Scenes at Night

There are thousands of restaurants, bars, and cafés across the city, but only certain places are automatically recognized by locals as a specific area where they can barhop. The most notorious scene is the **Eglinton Avenue** strip between Berlin on Yonge Street west to Mount Pleasant. The bars and clubs in this area have all sprouted in the last decade or so to accommodate the singles who live along the quiet streets in the residential houses and apartment buildings surrounding the bustling Eglington–Yonge corner.

The **Esplanade** area is also rife with bars, which have taken up residence in the old, now renovated, warehouses that face Front Street, bounded by Yonge Street (O'Keefe Centre) east to Jarvis Street and one block north to Wellington.

King Street West features the new Roy Thomson concert hall, home of the Toronto Symphony, just across the street from an old restored Victorian theater, the Royal Alexandra (or "Alex"), a 2,400-seat theater featuring Broadway tryouts or the Royal Shakespeare Company. Owner Ed Mirvish, who also runs the quaint, artistic area known as Mirvish Village behind his huge, garish Honest Ed's Discount Store on Bloor Street, manages a series of restaurants in the area seating thousands, featuring low-priced meals and acres of kitschy decor.

The trend setter for the area, **Joe Allen** (a New York–based bar known for its checkered tablecloths, sand-blasted brick walls, real burgers, and honest beer), recently decided not to remain in the shadow of the SkyDome along with the dozens of new bars and restaurants which have suddenly sprouted in each doorway. Joe Allen has closed its doors and will move to a new spot in the very near future. No plans have been announced yet but check the city phone book—wherever they move will likely be the next "hot spot" in the downtown core.

For details on places in these areas, see the Bars and Nightlife section below.

Canada's Wonderland

This is Toronto's four-month version of Disneyland, open from May to September, a theme park featuring three dozen different rides. For those more at home on terra firma, there is plenty of entertainment in this 370-acre park 30 km (18 miles) north of Toronto at Maple on Highway 400: a Broadway-style musical theater, an aquarium show, music performances, and plenty of restaurants. Connected with the park is the **Kingswood Music**

Theater, an outdoor, canopied concert stage that features musical acts; check the paper for daily performances and prices.

GETTING AROUND

Toronto has an international airport based at two terminals (with a third on the drawing board): Terminal One is the original airport; Terminal Two is the home of Air Canada, the national carrier, although some other airlines do use its services. When you book your ticket or confirm your flight out, check to determine which terminal you will be using. The official name for the airport is Pearson International (named after former Prime Minister Lester B. Pearson), but everyone still calls it Toronto International, or simply "the airport."

There is also the small Toronto Island Airport just off the harborfront area (at the base of Bathurst Street), which is mainly used for business commuter flights (for example, to Ottawa and Montreal) and STOL (short takeoff and landing) aircraft.

During peak times there is always a dearth of taxicabs at Toronto International; avoid arriving on a Sunday night if possible. The average price to downtown, which is approximately 30 km (18 miles) away, is about $25, including tip. Take a limousine instead; for some reason, the price is the same. Stands are found just outside each terminal building. The best public transit deal in town, however, is the Airport Bus from both terminals direct to the Royal York Hotel for a mere $7.

Toronto Transit Commission

The TTC is one of the fastest, cleanest, safest, and—most important—easiest transit systems in the world. Quite a claim, but true. Every year the subway/bus/trolley system wins awards for all these distinctions. (In fact, the transit system mirrors the city, causing no less a personage than the globe-trotting Renaissance man Peter Ustinov to remark that "Toronto is New York run by the Swiss.")

There are two main subway routes, the north-south Yonge Street line and the east-west Bloor line; the two meet at the corner of Yonge and Bloor, the crossroads of downtown Toronto. There are buses and trolley cars connecting with each subway stop; all you need is a transfer ticket (there are machines in the subways, or ask the driver aboard the bus system). You can literally go anywhere in the city via public transit—all for $1.10 per ticket; $8.00 for a book of eight tickets, or $46.00 for a monthly "metro pass."

There are free TTC Ride Guides available at every subway entrance, as well as enlarged maps of the entire system. The entrances are readily identifiable by the TTC logo.

For many years the old streetcars or trolleys, with their tracks imbedded in the roads and power wires overhead, formed the spine of the TTC; when it was suggested they be replaced with buses, there was a great hue and cry from the public to save their beloved and distinctive trolleys. So the TTC decided to order modern trolley cars instead, making Toronto one of the few North American cities still to run a viable, pollution-free trolley system. Watch for the new articulated (or "accordion") trolleys and buses: double cars holding up to 155 passengers, with flexible centers to accommodate the increased length.

In fact, one of the best ways to see downtown Toronto is on the special "Toronto by Trolley" tour, a 90-minute journey in a restored 1920 classic Peter Witt trolley car, from Cabbagetown to Chinatown, for $12.95 per adult ticket, $8 for children. Contact: Toronto Tours, 134 Jarvis Street, Toronto, M5B 2B5; Tel: 869-1372.

Construction is currently underway for a new light-rail transit line, which will service the growing Harbourfront area.

The TTC "GO" trains are the green and white, double-decker trains that bring daily commuters to the city core, extending from Oakville in the west to Pickering in the east, a route of some 68 km (41 miles). GO trains and buses also service 228 km of northern routes to Georgetown and Richmond Hill.

Taxis and Cars

Taxis are plentiful and readily available night or day. The rate set by the licensing commission is a flat rate of $1.70 for the first 350 meters (approximately ¼ mile) and $.25 for the next 350 meters, for one to four people. Waiting time costs $.25 for exactly 65 seconds.

There should be no problem in simply hailing a cab, especially in the downtown core, but if you need to call one, just check the yellow pages under "Taxicabs."

Drivers will find Toronto very easy to navigate: Everything is straight and perpendicular. Street maps are available at any tourist information booth or corner newsstand (*The Perly's Guide* is the most comprehensive). Some streets may occasionally fool you; for instance, University Avenue changes its name to Avenue Road north of Bloor Street; Bloor Street East becomes the Danforth across the viaduct; College is Carlton east of Yonge. There are some one-way streets downtown, off Yonge Street, and for a few blocks south of Dundas (Eaton Centre) you cannot make any turns off Yonge. But except for a few minor difficulties, Toronto is a very direct driving city.

Avoid Yonge Street south of Bloor in the summer months. This is a "cruising" strip (misnamed, because there is so much traffic you can hardly move), when Toronto shows a bit more of its true face to the world—a visage that mirrors nothing more than small-town Canada on Saturday night.

ACCOMMODATIONS
(The telephone area code for Toronto is 416.)

In Toronto, as in any major city bustling with over three million people, in a hotel you pay for what you get. Quite often, it seems, you pay for much more than you actually get, but that is the price of visiting a popular city filled with tourists, conventioneers, and travelling government and business executives. Since the government dropped the 7 percent room-accommodation tax, however, and because you are paying in Canadian currency, your bill may actually seem quite reasonable if you're from south of the Canada–United States border (for example, an $80 hotel room, as of press time, will translate to about $50 U.S.). And there still are other bargains to be found in the big city.

But whenever you decide to visit, call or write in advance and make a firm, cash-deposit or credit-card booking. If you don't during the summer's peak tourist season, with a possible convention of 10,000 delegates in town, you may find yourself sleeping on the boardwalk in Toronto's Beach area.

Bloor Street/Midtown Chic
The Windsor Arms. For many visiting celebrities and travelling businessmen, the Windsor Arms is the only place to stay; its four stories sit quietly on St. Thomas Street, just steps from the bustle of the trendy shops and bars of Bloor Street. There are only 81 rooms in this ivy-covered inn, each individually and tastefully decorated. Although there's no swimming pool or conference room,

there are four of the city's best restaurants, including the **Courtyard Café**, where folks come not only for fine dining but to see and be seen. Also, the "22," one of the city's "power" bars, plays host to various show-business personalities and deal makers.

The Windsor Arms is also one of only nine Canadian members of the prestigious Relais et Châteaux association, priding itself on "calm, comfort, and cuisine." The biggest surprise is the competitive price.

22 St. Thomas Street, M5S 2B9; Tel: 979-2341.

The Four Seasons. This glitzy gold and chrome, glass-and fern-decorated palace claims a landmark location at the beginning of the strip known as Yorkville, a stylish, expensive, and trendy enclave of restaurants and boutiques. Bring money, for both the area and hotel reflect an expensive and glamorous lifestyle. The street-level bars are excellent and pricey people-watching spots; Truffles and The Café rate among the city's best dining. The luxury of the rooms and quality of service should soften the inevitable blow of the bill. Voted one of the Leading Hotels of the World.

21 Avenue Road, M5R 2G1; Tel: 964-0411; in U.S., (800) 332-3442; in Canada, (800) 268-6282.

The Four Seasons also operates the **Inn on the Park**, a total luxury complex, from barbershops to bars, nightclubs, and restaurants, for those staying outside the downtown core. Because it borders greenbelt parkland, you can enjoy jogging trails or cross-country skiing. A resort within 15 minutes of downtown.

1100 Eglington Avenue East, M3C 1H8; Tel: 444-2561; in U.S., (800) 332-3442; in Canada, (800) 268-6282.

Park Plaza is across the street from the Four Seasons but a world away in style. More familiar than formal, the Park Plaza has long been known as one of the city's grand old hotels, where the "old family" clientele would dine every Sunday in the stately Prince Arthur Room. Regulars can always be found checking into the big, old-fashioned rooms, and locals frequent the rooftop bar with its city view. In recent years the hotel has been the September home of the city's ten-day film festival, listing everyone from Warren Beatty to Bette Midler as its guests.

4 Avenue Road, M5R 2E8; Tel: 924-5471; in U.S. and Canada, (800) 268-4927.

Brownstone Hotel. Located one block from Toronto's main cross streets, Bloor and Yonge (the center of the universe for many), the Brownstone is a tribute to an imaginative renovation team. This is the former Andore, (where rooms were often rented by the hour), now redone with polish, charm, and a good dining room/bar area. The rooms are clean and functional; the prices are surprisingly low for a good, centrally located downtown hotel.

15 Charles Street East, M4Y 1S1; Tel: 924-7381; in U.S. and Canada, (800) 263-7142.

Hotel Plaza II. It is easy to neglect this hotel, because it seems to blend into the Bay department-store shopping complex along Bloor Street, just east of Yonge. But it certainly is convenient to downtown shopping and bars, while also featuring some fine food in the Greenery, as well as good rates for its 256 rooms and extensive health-club facilities.

90 Bloor Street East, M4W 1A7; Tel: 961-8000; in U.S., (800) 323-7500; in Illinois, (800) 942-7400.

Sutton Place. Formerly a meeting place for Tory politicians, the Sutton Place now provides luxury living quarters for visiting movie stars, although lawyers, lobbyists, and legislators still visit because of its proximity to the government buildings. The millions spent on renovations are seen in the gilded lobby, dining, and bar areas (there is a great city view from the Stop 33 dining room), as well as in the rooms. It is a quality hotel (although rather formal and stiff); Lufthansa Airlines recently purchased the property as another link in their Kempinski chain.

955 Bay Street, M5S 2A2; Tel: 924-9221.

On the Waterfront
Harbour Castle Westin. This was the former Harbour Castle Hilton, which recently exchanged names with the downtown Westin, which is now the Hilton International Toronto—a confusing name flip-flop. Whatever its name, it still commands a magnificent harbor view from all of its 975 rooms. Featured dining includes the formal Chateauneuf and Poseidon rooms and the 36-story-high **Lighthouse Restaurant**, a definite highlight that revolves slowly and provides views around Toronto. Although inconvenient to the city core (taxis are plentiful here), the hotel has a complete range of amenities; ferries to the Toronto islands leave from the back door for a quick escape from the urban bustle.

One Harbour Square, M5J 1A6; Tel: 869-1600; in U.S. and Canada, (800) 228-3000.

Hotel Admiral. The newest brainchild of restaurateur

Walter Oster, this 157-room hotel boasts a fine kitchen as well as splendidly appointed rooms overlooking the yachts sailing the Harbourfront area. West of the Westin, it is even more inconvenient to downtown and crowded by condo construction, but it is well placed for a lovely walk along the clean, green waterfront area to the arts, crafts, and entertainment of the Harbourfront complex and upscale shopping at the Queen's Quay Terminal. There is a lovely fourth-floor outdoor pool area overlooking the harbor.

249 Queen's Quay West, M5J 2N5; Tel: 364-5444; in U.S. and Canada, (800) 387-1626.

Front Street to Midtown

Royal York. The grande dame of Toronto hotels, this 1,600-room mansion is still known as the largest hotel in the British Commonwealth; it is filled with restaurants and bars and is the home of the famed Imperial Room, the oldest continuously operating nightclub in North America, featuring acts as diverse as Peggy Lee and Anne Murray and female impersonator Craig Russell, who does both. The Royal York is the epitome of the term "faded elegance"; the rooms are fine, the service is okay, and the place is comfortable. A CP Railway hotel, it is located directly across the street from Union Station.

100 Front Street West, M5J 1E3; Tel: 368-2511; in U.S., (800) 828-7447; in Quebec and Ontario, (800) 268-9420; in the rest of Canada, (800) 268-9411.

Hotel Novotel. Located one street south of Front on the Esplanade at the corner of Yonge Street, is the 266-room Novotel, whose rather austere exterior hides a most pleasant lobby interior. The rooms are basic yet well-appointed and the rates very reasonable, especially considering the amenities—from spa facilities to fine dining in the Café Les Arcades. The location is another plus—immediately behind the O'Keefe Centre, bordering the bar-hopping strip of the Esplanade, and one block from the restaurants and nightlife along Front Street East. Also, it connects to the Gardiner Expressway for a quick getaway out of the city.

45 The Esplanade, M5E 1W2; Tel. 367-8900.

L'Hôtel. This glass-and-steel structure just west of the Royal York is connected to the huge Metro Convention Centre, so, obviously, a visitor will be deluged with conventioneers. The vast and somewhat austere lobby is often humanized by a formally attired duo playing classical piano and harp. The rooms are quite well done and the dining is very good, but you may get the feeling of being somewhat rushed because the next convention is due to check in soon.

225 Front Street West, M5V 2X3; Tel: 597-1400 or, in U.S. and Canada, (800) 268-9143.

Hotel Victoria. Recently resurrected from its rather seedy state, the Victoria is a little 42-room hotel that has gained new life with its improved decor, dining room menu, and comfortable lounge. The rooms are small but cozy, and the prices are reasonable. It is close to the Front Street theaters (the O'Keefe Centre and the St. Lawrence), the upscale bars of the Esplanade, and the St. Lawrence Market.

56 Yonge Street, M5E 1G7; Tel: 363-1666.

King Edward Hotel. Old World grandeur and style, with porters offering white-glove service and desk clerks resplendent in morning suits, the old King Eddy had fallen on hard times until England's Trusthouse Forte restored its former glory in 1979. (As you enter the luxurious lobby, try to determine which are the new pillars and which are the restored 85-year-old originals.) As for price, well, as the man said, if you have to ask. . . .

The various bars, especially the Consort Bar with its leather wingback chairs, are usually busy, and the excellent dining rooms of Chiaro's (pronounced with a "K") and Café Victoria are filled with old-establishment Toronto money and business executives. Bring an unlimited credit card; pure decadence.

37 King Street East, M5C 1E9; Tel: 863-9700. A double starts at $210; the Royal Suite, number 973, with five bedrooms, boardroom, and sunken living room, is $1,850 per night.

Sheraton Centre. Just across from City Hall on Queen Street West, this hotel is known for its many social and business functions. There are meeting rooms and exhibition halls galore, but there are also classy shops and cinemas (another link in the Underground City) and classier dining in the 42-story Russian Winter Palace. In between are good, functional rooms (1,399 of them) and bars and restaurants that won't break a holiday budget. Also, there is a tropical setting for a large indoor/outdoor pool area. Due to its location and size, the Sheraton is hard to miss, but just to assist the traveller the hotel is now outlined at night with a one-mile link of lights.

123 Queen Street West, M5H 2M9; Tel: 361-1000; in U.S. and Canada, (800) 325-3535.

Toronto Hilton International. The subject of a recent name change (see Westin), which is guaranteed to confuse the travelling public for some time, the Hilton is a good, functional hotel, with meeting rooms, designed for the expense-account business traveller. Dining in the lobby restaurant can be fun, with its cathedral-high ceilings, although you can opt for the downstairs Trader Vic's or the club-type atmosphere of the aptly named Barristers Lounge, frequented at lunchtime and after five by the city business types—since this is the heart of the legal/financial district. Most travelling guests tend to be from those professions as well.

145 Richmond Street West, M5H 3M6; Tel: 869-3456; in U.S. and Canada, (800) 445-8667.

The Westbury is a hotel that just hasn't kept up with the competition, but it still gets business thanks to its Yonge Street location, with a proximity to the Maple Leaf Gardens and CBC headquarters. The Westbury pioneered hotel dining in Toronto, and the main restaurant, Creightons, still serves a good meal, though not so imaginative as those from the new breed of Toronto chefs. The rooms are good, standard but comfortable, and the price is competitive.

475 Yonge Street, M4Y 1X7; Tel: 924-0611.

Delta's Chelsea Inn. Formerly known as an inexpensive downtown hotel, the Chelsea's prices have climbed along with its popularity. The 995 rooms enjoy a high occupancy rate, and the Chelsea Bun lounge (with some of the best Saturday afternoon jazz sessions) has a good local following as an after-five watering hole. The rooms are small but nice; some have kitchenettes. The pool and sauna areas are very popular with travelling families.

33 Gerrard Street West, M5G 1Z4; Tel: 595-1975; in U.S. and Canada, (800) 268-1133.

Downtown Holiday Inn. The hotel that advertises "no surprises" is a surprise, in that it is an upscale version of itself. Located downtown behind City Hall, the hotel offers well-appointed rooms, a friendly bar (Dewey, Secombe, and Howe—which sounds like an upscale law firm), pleasant dining, and both an indoor and outdoor pool, all for a moderate Holiday Inn price. And if you love Chinese food, you are only steps from the culinary delights and Oriental sights of the city's Chinatown on Dundas Street.

89 Chestnut Street, M5G 1R1; Tel: 977-0707; in U.S. and Canada, (800) 465-4329.

The **Chestnut Park Hotel** is the newest in the Carlton Hotel group (see following listing). Just across the street from the Holiday Inn, this recently-completed 26-story hotel packs in 522 rooms, a complete health club and gym, 20 meeting rooms, and a large ballroom. It pays tribute to the area with its China Grill Restaurant (which, however, serves a Continental menu and buffet) and the quite good Gallery Lounge with open-kitchen pasta bar and sushi counter. A great central location with the lights of Chinatown just outside your room.

108 Chestnut Street, M5G 1R3. Tel: 977-5000.

The **Carlton Inn** is just east of Yonge beside Maple Leaf Gardens, close to hockey games and concerts. Many rooms (536), but they are small. Indoor pools, sauna, good standard restaurants and bars; moderately priced.

30 Carlton Street, M5B 2E9; Tel: 977-6655; in U.S. and Canada, (800) 268-9076.

Bond Place. One block east of the Eaton Centre, an ideal spot for the visiting shopper. Small, comfortable rooms, with dining and lounges. The area is slightly seedy yet scenic, as some colorfully dressed women walk the streets.

65 Dundas Street East, M5B 2G8; Tel: 362-6061.

New downtown hotels under construction and due for occupancy sometime in 1990 include the latest—and apparently luxurious—Holiday Inn on Front Street West, within blocks of the CN Tower, Metro Convention Centre, and The SkyDome, and the city's first Hotel Inter-Continental, which is taking shape along the exclusive shopping section of expensive Bloor Street West and Avenue Road, with the frolic of Yorkville at its back door.

Something Different

The Bradgate Arms. Slightly off the beaten track, at Avenue Road and St. Clair Avenue, this hotel was created several years ago when two adjoining apartment buildings were enclosed under a glass dome and extensively renovated. The six-story lobby creates an airy effect; the former apartments now seem like small suites, complete with kitchen facilities. The hotel is bright, clean, and surprisingly inexpensive.

54 Foxbar Road, M4V 2G6; Tel: 968-1331.

Airport Hotels

Toronto's airport strip has an array of good hotels that are mainly used by airport personnel, late-arriving or early-departing travellers, business people, salesmen, and tourists who arrive in high season without advance bookings for a downtown hotel. Some have a full range of amenities, from nightclubs to swimming pools, while others offer basic accommodation and dining. The International Center, a huge exhibition hall close to the airport, also keeps the hotels in constant use. The largest with the most facilities are:

▶ **The Bristol Place**. 950 Dixon Road, M9W 5N4; Tel: 675-9444; in U.S. and Canada, (800) 268-4927.

▶ **Constellation**. 900 Dixon Road, M9W 1J7; Tel: 675-1500.

▶ Some others include the Airport Hilton, L4V 1N1, Tel: 677-9900, in U.S. and Canada, (800) 268-9275; the Best Western Carlton Place Hotel, M9W 6H5, Tel: 675-1234, in U.S. and Canada, (800) 528-1234; Howard Johnson, M9W 1J5, Tel: 675-6100, in U.S. and Canada, (800) 654-2000; and Holiday Inn, M9W 1J9, Tel: 675-7611, in U.S. and Canada, (800) 465-4329.

Executive Travel Apartments

Apartments for travelling couples, with or without children, and no limit (within reason) to the number of overnight guests, have also become popular with visitors. ETA has various locations throughout the city; for example, their recent addition in the Summit Apartments at King and Bathurst lists a fully equipped two-bedroom suite, with complete kitchen, maid service, exercise facilities, pool, sauna, and squash courts, plus 24-hour security. All accommodations are clean and well maintained. At a bit under $100 per night, a bargain, especially for families or groups intending to linger for the better part of a week.

1101 Bay Street, M5S 2W8; Tel: 923-3000.

Bed and Breakfast

For those who prefer to stay in a home atmosphere: **Metropolitan B & B Registry of Toronto**, 72 Lowther Avenue, Toronto, M5R 1C8. Tel: 964-2566. For $3.00 they will send you their booklet of listed homes. **Toronto Bed and Breakfast**, P.O. Box 74, Station M, Toronto, M6S 4T2. Tel: 233-3887. Rates are about $50 for a double room, including breakfast, in private homes.

The quality, of course, may vary. To be on the safe side, contact the very friendly Susan Oppenheim (her name means "open house") at the **Downtown Toronto Group of B & B Guest Houses** (P.O. Box 190, Station B, Toronto, M5T 2W1, Tel: 977-6841), whose organization provides large rooms in refurbished Victorian homes in the various residential areas throughout the city. A double starts at $50, including breakfast. If you need recommendations on restaurants or theater, just ask Susan.

There are complete listings of Toronto accommodations for every style and pocketbook, from deluxe suites to little self-contained units, available through the Metro Toronto Convention and Visitors Association, located at the Queen's Quay Terminal, 207 Queen's Quay West, P.O. Box 126, Toronto, M5J 1A7; Tel: 368-9990.

—*Steve Veale*

DINING

If we're talking about serious eating out, understand that Toronto dining shares in the general evolution of many—if not most—noncoastal North American cities. Pesto, garlic, mussels, calamari, satay, duck breast, goat's cheese, and the like have been well integrated into local menus; no longer do restaurants depend primarily on the stockyard. There's been an especially enormous increase in the popularity of fish. Even diner food tends to the leaner way. Grilling is probably the favorite way to cook. Franco/Italocized California is the ideal, followed by a certain ethnic mania largely directed toward Southeast Asian cuisine (China and Japan prepared local palates ages ago). Ethiopian and Mauritian creole also find a place. But there is surprisingly little *real* Mexican, and the Indian food is mostly Punjabi.

Since the local economy is prosperous, many Torontonians eat out as a matter of course—before the theater, to entertain, just for a change—and dress as they happen to be. Dining hours are fairly conventional, with most kitchens closing or closed by 10:00 P.M.; after that it's just snacks, though a few places serve meals up to about midnight. Most are completely dark on Sundays. The number of licensed dining establishments in the region, including pizza parlors and neighborhood eateries, is about 2,300. So which ones really matter?

The dining-out shift is from hotels (though some of their rooms do hold well) and elaborate steak/lobster baronies to small 40- to 50-seat restaurants. It's mainly in places like these that chefs in Toronto are trying to make a dashing name for themselves, in their quest to bring a signature to the anonymity of international cooking.

Another remarkable change is in the attitude toward the vocation of chef. It's no longer unusual for exceptionally bright engineering physicists to abandon promising careers and apprentice in a kitchen. For those who eat out, this is a fortunate condition, leading, of course, to a very welcome rise in the number of first-rate chef-owned restaurants—the pattern in France and Italy.

In general, Toronto's restaurants are much like its transportation system: dependable enough in attending to the basic requirements, often surprising in the method of delivery. Bad meals (or, at any rate, disgusting ones) are rare.

Service in Toronto restaurants is usually good—up to a point. Even in the most expensive places, where there is quite a bit of bowing and scraping, the saltcellar and pepper shaker may still be on the table when dessert is being served, or plonk may be served like expensive bubbly (or vice versa).

As for wines, local restaurant lists all too often rely on basic blends, but there are an increasing number that are breaking out of these unimaginative confines, almost always where the cooking is trying to do the same. Markups tend to represent greed; there's really no reason to go above 100 percent from cost price, especially for low-end, high-volume products in low-end, high-volume restaurants.

Summer is a beloved time of the year in Toronto, and many restaurants here make it a point of pride to have a suitable open-air area for consuming edibles and potables. Obviously, the most comfortable are away from noxious street fumes, preferably in a back enclosure shaded by trees.

All the major hotels have dining rooms; if we mention particular ones, it's because they are worthwhile for non-residents to consider.

Places discussed below without an indication of price level—subtle or otherwise—are moderate, which would mean $60–$85 for a meal for two, including wine, gratuity, and taxes.

Downtown/Harbourfront to King Street

The King Edward Hotel on King Street East has within its bosom the very expensive **Chiaro's** (pronounced with a "K"), all banker's gray, etched mirrors, Chippendale-style chairs (helps to keep the back poised), Chardin-like floral arrangements, and a Frenchified, nouvellish menu of toney stuff. Sometimes a piano/violin duo plays in the lobby, so its lovely music drifts in to reinforce the grandeur (otherwise, canned sounds). **Café Victoria** is its large-windowed and somewhat less expensive twin (side-street views), best for Sunday brunch, weekday lunch, and a novel pre-theater prix fixe that allows you to return for dessert after the performance. Afternoon tea is served in the lounge.

At its posterior are **Tom Jones**, a steakhouse with all the trimmings from shrimp cocktail and Black Forest cake to fawning service, and coolly minimalist **Nekah**, possibly Toronto's most exciting abode for the true *bec fin*. Nekah means "wild goose" in Ojibway, an indication that the game and the produce of (largely) Canada's waters are greatly esteemed for the table here. Only three set menus each night (one an abbreviation for theatergoers), with wines carefully matched to each exactly prepared dish. You must, however, value super-subtle food, and not care what it costs. A singular Sunday *dim sum* and other gustatory fêtes are occasional events. **Vines**, to the east of Nekah along Wellington Street, is a cellar seriously devoted to the grape (a good selection, and oftentimes a regional promotion); food is not so gravely considered here, but cold trout and cheese plates do duty. Neighboring Parisian-postered **Les Copains** introduces itself with a chocolate-dominated dessert table at the top end of a short flight of stairs from the street; it offers a contemporary French list.

Though quite different in style, **Shopsy's** and **Penelope** occupy the same office building opposite the O'Keefe (Yonge and Front streets) and St. Lawrence performing arts centers and share, so to speak, a street-side outdoor area: The first is a deli, with roots in what was once the populist Jewish quarter of tailors and furriers (Spadina) and aspirations to New Yorkese; the second tours Greek cuisine in a modern way, and its flaming *kefalotyri* cheese is fun to watch. Around the corner on lower Church Street, there is also a Greek menu at **Anesty's**, which manages a semblance of the Mediterranean in its converted warehouse space.

For Italian in the gilt manner, there's ample feeding at **Florentine Court** (97 Church Street), carefully managed by the same family for ages. **The Liberty**, immediately to the north, is for avid fans of roasted peppers, grilled food, and reproductions of *The New Yorker* covers and the Statue of Liberty. For Japanese you will probably enjoy **Nami**, at 55 Adelaide Street East, with its excellent *robata* counter in a most attractive, sophisticated, midnight-blue setting, and the plainer-looking and less expensive **Take-sushi**, particularly for sushi prepared in an entertaining way (22 Front Street West). The spacious **Abundance** at 81 Church Street has the carrot in a soup (glass-bowled) and a cake; you can eat outside if you want to.

La Maquette, in a historic 19th-century property, adjoins the Sculpture Garden and has views of St. James's Cathedral across King Street at Church—most advantageously appreciated over a Frenchified lunch from a second-floor conservatory abutment (or in summer on the patio underneath it). Summer, too, finds a fountain-centered back terrace at **Biagio** (157 King Street East), with the restaurant proper on the ground floor of Toronto's first public meeting place, St. Lawrence Hall, built in the 1850s. Intelligent cooking (risottos, much seafood) in the best Italian tradition; ditto service. Although a branch of an international chain, elegant **Bombay Palace** (71 Jarvis Street) shows lots of individuality, particularly at its buffet lunch. Around the corner from it, **Rodney's Oyster House** (209 Adelaide Street East) purveys the named bivalve and other notable shelled sea creatures (kept fresh in back-room holding tanks after their journey from the Maritimes) at a bar with a few tables in the plainest of basement areas; crowded at lunch, less so at night. An anonymous street frontage makes it hard to locate. Amazingly good, especially for the price.

The dining room at the Hotel Victoria (dubbed **56 Yonge** after the actual street number) deserves to be better known, for its comfortable space is home to both traditional and contemporary accents (there are wing chairs in the bar area), and its pre-theater prix fixe is a great convenience. On The Esplanade, **Café les Arcades**, seen through large semicircular windows under Novotel Hotel's evocative (of the Continent) loggia, is pleasant for a huge *salade niçoise* and other French budget familiars, though the decor itself seems as insubstantial as a Hollywood set.

Chanterelles is L'Hôtel's successful effort to provide

cosmopolitan luxe amid impressionistic oils, with seafoods and white meats prominent main dishes. Across the way, **Satay Garden** (146 Front Street West) is crowded, particularly at lunch, with seekers of Thai-inspired meals at popular prices. One block to the north, at the corner of Emily and Wellington, glass-fronted **Chez Max** continues the solid bourgeois cooking practiced when it was Maison Basque on Temperance Street; the menu's numerous regional dishes distinguish it from other local French *cartes*—Eve should put in another appearance for the remarkable Calvados-heated apple tart.

Down by the harbor, **Commodore's** at the Hotel Admiral has lovely views over the water to Hanlan's Point and the Island airport (where smaller aircraft take off and land), and a pricey menu of elaborated luxuries. The Harbour Castle Westin Hotel's *grande salle* **Châteauneuf** does not offer such aquatic views, but its kitchen and wine steward really understand the priorities of the very rich, who will find the contents of plate and cup visually satisfying enough. In between these two, in Queen's Quay Terminal, are **Pink Pearl Harbourfront** for decent dim sum and **Spinnakers** for afternoon tea or a drink at sundown. If you do take the ferry over to Centre Island, a nice place for an ice-cold beer or the informality of salads and pasta (to the right of the docks) is the **Island Paradise**; from here you can see the city's skyline, plus the aquatic comings and goings of amateur rowers and sailors, at temperatures at least ten degrees cooler than on the mainland.

A hangout for Bay Street (Toronto's Wall Street) appetites has long been on Adelaide Street West, at the very up-priced **Winston's**: in an Art Deco statement, there's beef and sole in ritzy abundance, with comparable wines. **Mövenpick Downtown**, around the corner on York, surprises right away by contradicting the rule that food found near hotels is usually routine. It has nice outside areas, both facing the street and in an inner court, breads and cakes baked on the premises, full breakfasts, buffets, and a solid wine list. Its Belle Terrasse is informal but not inexpensive; Rössli has the more expensive Swiss/Continental dishes of finesse. A hotel dining room that reveals accomplished cooking is **La Cour** at Hilton International Toronto. There's a sure-handedness in the preparation of even the most complex dishes, from seafood and game to sweets; the price is what you would expect to pay. The busy lobby abuts distractingly.

Simpson's, a grand—meaning real—department store opposite Old City Hall, has on its eighth floor the elegant **Arcadian Court**, where a pianist plays melodies beneath crystal chandeliers. Go for lunch, afternoon tea, and the buffet on Thursday and Friday evenings. Devotees should investigate the oysters shucked in the store's ground-floor café bar, **SRO. Senator**, a block north of St. Michael's Hospital on Victoria Street, goes all day long until the late hours, cheerfully combining diner fare with Thai-style chicken and chocolate bourbon cake. It has *the* local list of California wines. Much beloved by those from outside North America because it's so different for them.

King Street West/Theater and Concert Dining

It's westward-ho for the fastest-growing number of eating establishments, most of good quality, spurred on by assemblies for public entertainment (the most historic being the Edwardian Royal Alexandria Theatre, the most obvious, the SkyDome). Where there are circuses, there must be bread. **Telfer's**, which shares the King-Simcoe axis with Roy Thomson Hall, the mod-style home of the Toronto Symphony, wouldn't do violence to anyone who didn't like a garlic clove but does do updated North American favorites in a very comfortable beige/brass room; you can dance to soothing music, and there is an after-theater menu, too. Strung along Simcoe Street are **Simcoe** (jam-packed at lunch but quieter in the evening—just the way life is hereabouts), for earnest renderings of salmon and rack of lamb with modern gestures; and, side by side in well-appointed basements, **Shezan** and **Tidal Wave**. These two do, respectively, Indian and Japanese skillfully enough, and the latter's sushi bar incorporates a water passageway for little boats bearing the sea's morsels to those who ordered them.

Orso (106 John Street) and **La Fenice** do Italy proud: The first, à la New York, in an ex-Victorian farrier's, has a delightful second-floor patio, folkloric pottery, and trout and rappini doing their share to keep one and all happy, some nights unto the stroke of twelve; the second, à la Veneziana, in a designer's echo chamber, is the source of breathtaking risottos, an hors d'oeuvre trolley of flavorful simplicity, and olive oil–anointed grills of the freshest fish. Recently, **Valenzi** and **Primo Piano** (in the next block west of La Fenice) have joined these two in serving food of like style, in a bold or clean-cut setting. All are slightly expensive.

Located in two blocks between John and Spadina, Le Pigalle, Marcel's, and Julien do France proud, and comfortably. The waiters at lace-curtained **Le Pigalle** show real dash as they bring mussels in deeply herbal broth, and garlic-scented *frites* with grilled lamb chops from the rack; there is a nice back patio for those who don't like air conditioning. Upstairs, the servers at high-ceilinged **Marcel's** are a little more restrained, as they bring apéritifs from a list that matters—and also good edibles. The more expensive **Julien** is the right place to propose marriage or discuss some very hush-hush business deal, for if you say to the staff, "Keep away for twenty-three minutes, please," this will be done forthwith, and no muttering about it. Witty food and plenty of it—God bless Julien.

Hong Kong money is increasingly important in the business life of Toronto, so the newer Chinese restaurants must be sophisticated. **Hsin Kuang Seafood**, at the corner of King and John streets, has waitresses in silk *chi-paos* serving dum sum and other Cantonese and Szechuan dishes, in a glamorized heritage building. (An outlet at 324 Spadina Avenue is equally splendid.) **Soko**, at 325 King Street West, is one of the best for dim sum and for the flash of sizzling plates and complex sauces. Really clean and quiet, and the service is what is called French. With its slitted window of plastic-food replicas, **Yamase**, Soko's near neighbor, could be mistakenly judged ho-hum, set-menu Japanese; the approach here, however, is to serve an amazing range of appetizers and lesser-known dishes, including lots of salt-cooked food. Next door but one, **The Red Tomato** is for grazers seeking New York–style snacks (pizzas from a wood-burning oven, blackened fowl with salsa, gumbo—the list is long) at odd hours. Interesting combinations, good prices, but it can get noisy.

Filet of Sole, on Duncan Street (one of the boundaries of the Royal Alex's block), is a busy concourse at lunch and between 6:00 P.M. and curtain time. You may have to speak more forcefully than usual—the sound bounces around quite a bit in the big-windowed ex-warehouse—in the ordering of all manner of sea creatures (fried, steamed, broiled, or barbecued) and of wines whose prices show a praiseworthy restraint in markup. Down in a chaste basement room, **Raja Sahib** (254 Adelaide Street West) curries the essential flavors of Indian cooking, at modest prices.

Amsterdam (133 John Street) is full of metropolitan

razzmatazz, as befits a pub of vast expanse. The same can be said of **Rotterdam** (600 King Street West), its more westerly and also inexpensive sister enterprise of gleaming copper kettles. Food at both tends to strong flavors, and each has a boulevard area for the enjoyment of good weather.

Queen Street West

There are some serious gastronomic islets in this laid-back sea of spiked hair and uninhibited opinions on Queen West, generally between John and Spadina. Foremost and most expensive is **Le Bistingo**, where freshness and verve à la Française astound more often than not. Next (especially for price) is Monet-blue-cool **Beaujolais** around the corner on John, which introduced Toronto to the eggplant/goat's-cheese Oreo and the taste-it-all dessert ensemble, and **The Parrot**, ardent in the ways of Mediterranean flavors on contemporary foods, and concerned with the appropriateness of ingredients.

Le Sélect spills out onto Queen Street through windows folded back when the weather warrants. Its solid bistro menu speaks intriguingly with many foreign accents, and there's lots of merriment come Beaujolais nouveau time, when it's just a sea of blue suits and striped ties. Across the street at pine-pristine **Raclette**, wine is earnest business, its list running to 22 pages. The usual cheese/fondue dishes accompany, plus salmon and chicken in the contemporary mode.

Queen Street West is an area worth strolling, if the diversity of human interests or secondhand books and odd little edibles would make your day. At number 712, cheery **Vivi**'s sautéed eel in a basil coconut sauce would certainly fascinate; much else of its other fairly-priced Vietnamese fare might also do the same.

Chinatown/West of Yonge

Chinese immigrants and their descendants no longer restrict themselves to the Spadina/Dundas axis, so their restaurants are scattered throughout the metropolitan area, and the Vietnamese (mainly ethnic Chinese, though) have moved in to take their place. Still, enough Chinese establishments remain to give assurance that the district has not been misnamed. (Some stay open until quite late, and most are inexpensive.) Completely down-to-earth, **Lee Garden** (358 Spadina Avenue) is one of the best, and so vast is the selection of ingredients that almost any dish requested can be prepared—not that there's a dearth of offerings on the printed or wall menus. **Chinatown International** (421 Dundas Street West), more expensive, is best appreciated for its trolley-served dim sum. Behind a window of lacquered birds, **Kom Jug Yuen** (371 Spadina) simply buzzes with lots of budget-priced northern-style items. Near City Hall, **E-On** (56 Centre Avenue) provides dim sum straight from the kitchen and lurid-colored cakes, while **Yueh Tung** has a particularly fetching way with oysters in black bean sauce, served in a plain-Jane room at 111 Elizabeth Street. Although Cantonese-barbecue in decor, **Kam Wah** (149 Dundas Street West) offers a wide range of dishes, such as baked lobster and large platters of this and that in deft sauces, all just the ticket for repairing the tired being. A thrifty trinity.

Wah Sing is a real seafood treasure. It's one of several diverse restaurants along a short stretch of Baldwin Street, where you can also find meats and hot pots at the clean-cut **Eating Counter/Ohh Kitchen**, a multi-ingredient French-style menu at the moderately priced, antiques-filled **La Bodega**, and a forthright French menu at **Le Petit Gaston's** (its onion soup is a local legend). There is the vitamin-packed, mostly vegetarian fare at **Yofi's**; Caribbean ways of elaborate spicing and comforting portions at **Bahamian Kitchen**; and excellent little heart pleasers at **Kowloon Dim Sum**, which also has a regular, mainly Cantonese, menu.

Opposite the Art Gallery of Ontario are **Tall Poppies**, whose clever kitchen uses the market availability of fresh fish and meats to advantage in heartily sauced grills, and whose backyard offers a shady glen; and the ever-reliable **Mermaid**, which does seafood with a Danish accent in a nice formal style.

The Art Gallery of Ontario itself dispenses to the famished via the imaginatively named **The Restaurant**. It expands outdoors to a trellised area behind The Grange (the 19th-century gentlefolks' house that the gallery incorporates); most pleasant for a lunch of salads and light entrées. The appropriately monikered Village-by-the-Grange shelters **Young Lok Garden**, which has all-day, open-kitchen dim sum and dishes from several Chinese regions.

Slightly north of Dundas Street, along Elm, are the Thai-centered and expensive **Bangkok Garden**, complete with babbling brook and a menu representing all the cooking techniques of Asia; the best local Indian breads and such at **The Mogul**; high-quality grilled meats (forget almost everything else) and a late-night menu at **Barberian's**, in two pre-Confederation cottages filled with real and spurious Canadiana; and dependable **Old Angelo's**, advanced in years (60-odd) but modern in its Italian *cucina.*

Maple Leaf Gardens/East of Yonge

Maple Leaf Gardens accommodates thousands of events such as hockey games, track meets, Pavarotti recitals, rock concerts, and the like, and so has occasioned the establishment of places throughout the Yonge/Carlton/Church area to feed the multitudes. Most of them are ordinary (to be charitable) and a few worthy.

The Westbury Hotel's **Creighton's** is very formal, with a battalion of waiters to attend to every want, and is much appreciated for its game festival. The expensive **Carman's Club** (26 Alexander Street) is club in name only, for all are admitted, with steaks and some nice Greek-style go-withs. **George Bigliardi's** at 463 Church Street is another grand, comforting emporium for a favored cut of beef, this time Italian-accented.

Vagara Bistro, decorated like a sun porch, is an island of pasta-and-veal sanity at 475 Church Street in a *pazzo* district. Quality Inn Essex Park Hotel on seedy Jarvis Street, as functional as expected, has a gem in its **Essex Park Bistro**. Among its first and second courses, the surprise is the Calypso beat—limes, coriander, lemon, and bananas all give lustrous tones to red snapper and chicken.

Midtown Chic

There is a real clutch of major hotels in the vicinity of Bloor and Avenue Road, many with fine dining rooms. The **Prince Arthur Room** at the Park Plaza essays successfully both familiar and current styles, and with the formality that the setting deserves. Should the refurbishing of the nifty 18th-floor bar ever be finished, there are city views of capital interest to be had (over the Ontario Parliament Buildings, for instance). **Prego**, opposite the hotel on Renaissance Plaza, strives for modernity in the California way, using mock Chagallery to catch the eye.

The Windsor Arms Hotel is synonymous with the glamor of names and labels, so you ought not to be surprised to see Robert Redford and the like at **The Courtyard Café** supping on cuisine naturelle or more traditional pâté, *entrecôte,* and caloric sweets under a glassy roof; late-night orders are taken. The Windsor Arms's **Three Small Rooms** (moderate to very expensive) are collectively a wine cellar (and the hotel's list is magisterial), a grill room, and a room for high-falutin' cooking that is called simply The Restaurant.

Next door to the Windsor Arms, **Danish Food Centre** at Bloor and St. Thomas incorporates a ground-floor self-serve that is suitable for informal bites; the more expensive Copenhagen Room in the basement stresses blue cheese soup, roast duckling, red cabbage, aquavits, a Tuesday buffet, and other stately things of Denmark. (**Bemelmans** and **Bellair,** both off nearby Bellair Street on Cumberland and Bloor respectively, are Toronto landmarks. Known more for their bar scenes than for their cuisine, they are covered in Bars and Nightlife below.)

Noodles, at Bay and Bloor, for many years under the auspices of the Windsor Arms but now independent of it, was the first of the new-style Italian places in Toronto, with a daring delivery of pink neon and Milano-smart furnishings: The sun-dried tomato pizza and such remain, but now the emphasis is more on Italian regional dishes. **La Scala,** just down the street from Noodles on Bay, is mainly traditional Italian, in a like setting, with a serious wine list.

The Four Seasons Hotel, at Avenue Road and Yorkville, has the gravely baronial and expensive **Truffles,** from whose banquettes can be seen a passing parade of Eurodignitaries, usually dressed to the nines. There are some remarkable sauces for its luxurious fare.

Deep in the center of Hazelton Lanes boutiquedom is **Hazelton Club** (55 Avenue Road), with salads, pastas, and grills for lunch and views of an inner courtyard (used in the summer for open-sky eating; frozen over to become a skating rink in the winter). Yorkville Avenue and vicinity, east of Avenue Road, harbors a diversity of establishments. **Il Posto** cocoons those dining outside in the confines of shop-enclosed York Square; inside, it handles Northern Italian cuisine well enough in what feels like a swank club for residents of nearby ritzy condos. Mövenpick uptown's two restaurants, **La Pêcherie** and the more moderately priced **Bistretto** offer, respectively, seafood (mainly) from a chalkboard, done every which way, and the informality of mussels, *frites,* and the like—and until 1:00 A.M. most nights. **Karin** on parallel Scollard Street is refreshingly modern, serving grills, excellent ice cream, and nonroutine wines. Pretty **Le Trou Normand,** located in a cul-de-sac off Yorkville Avenue—so the cooking odors are pleasant on a summer's eve—has generously portioned, though expensive, regional French fare. **Zero** (as in aircraft, not valuation) surprises with budget Japanese, in severe surroundings, while **Siam** hides not its Thai intentions, doing a reasonable facsimile both in cooking and decor. **The Bottom Line** has a tiny dance floor and some sophisticated treatments for duck and lamb, yet maintains an unaffected air. For consuming Moroccan fare—and viewing belly dancers—while lolling on cushions, **The Sultan's Tent** is the place, with a tidy prix fixe only a few steps away on the west side of Bay Street.

Behind the Park Plaza on Prince Arthur Avenue, **Parioli** is luxe and glamor *à l'italienne,* and its desserts are appreciated by chocoholics. **Le Rendez-vous** inclines to Provence—and expertly so—as well as to calorie-rich opulence; impressive wine cellar, and suitable for Sunday brunch. Cumberland Street has it share of hooks for hungry passersby: photos of well-fed celebs dot the entranceway to **La Pergola**, which follows the old-fashioned Italian tradition (Venetian especially); try spacious and amiable **Shogun** for sushi-based set dinners, beauteous fruit plates, and gaudy cocktails; and its neighbor **Jacques' Omelettes** does that egg dish many, many ways—and with no onset of boredom—as well as serving a number of bourgeois dishes (there is a nice street view from its second-floor windows). Nearby **Dinah's Cupboard** is a wonderland for take-out and the most recherché of ingredients.

Auberge Gavroche (90 Avenue Road) couldn't be more gracious about serving its French food in a pleasant, made-over house: A reservation brings a card bearing your name in the loveliest calligraphy. Gorgeous desserts are served here, and a terrace at the street front is shared with **L'Entrecôte**, its relatively inexpensive upstairs prix-fixe bistro. A few doors away are white-stuccoed **La Ina** with a *tapas* bar, wood-burning oven (for roasting suckling pig), and Iberian wines, and **Sisi Trattoria** of the hearty Southern Italian style, so gusto is the prevailing mood.

Nearby **Pink Pearl** has all the smart accoutrements of the city restaurant; chopsticks on the table are the only indication that Cantonese and other regional dishes are the fare. There are two more restaurant stops on this block: **Arlequin** boldly courses through the Mediterranean, particularly Provence, with enormous panache, in a pretty little pink room at 134 Avenue Road. **Costa Basque**, a couple of doors down from Arlequin, looks hacienda-California, on many levels. Much seafood is served, influenced by Spain, and some Basque specialties. The titillating nude artwork at **Joso's** (202 Davenport Road), around the corner, cannot upstage the freshness of the fish offered, though the mega-garlicky black Sicilian spaghetti could. And within hailing distance (of a cab): **The Corner House** (501 Davenport Road), the made-over dwelling's five rooms the tableaux for a prix fixe of conservative (but not uninteresting) mien in the international mode—dover sole, lobster, beef Wellington; and **Indian Rice Factory** (414 Dupont Street), whose California-café exterior belies the verity of the Subcontinent on the plate; some seldom-seen preparations at Sunday brunch.

Metropolis (838 Yonge Street) is the pride and joy of those who think it's possible to have a distinctive Canadian cuisine: Here are local produce and products, used effectively and with sophistication. The room (looking a little shopworn, perhaps) leads to a back patio, and is mostly white itself (a black-etched skyline does relieve it a bit). Good wine list. On the other side of Yonge and up a block, **Saigon Star** (4 Collier Street) shows the importance of France in its Vietnamese cooking and does so in a respectable manner and setting.

Southward from Bloor, but not very far down, and just steps away from Yonge Street on Gloucester Street, is **Fenton's**, one of the very first Toronto restaurants to be liberated from the confines of steak/lobsterdom, to use flowers and greenery as part of the decor, and to import the exotic spices that have become the mark of local modern cooking. There are three venues for its wares (four, if you count the shop for take-out, cookbooks, and related cookery items): the expensive Garden, a bower that will cheer you up in any season; the equally expensive Front Room, with its warming woods and crackling fire; and Downstairs, where the informality extends slightly to the prices. All three share a magnificent wine list.

Sutton Place Hotel is very smart, and **Sanssouci**, its summery main dining room, follows suit: inventive, intricate cooking (but never silly), and a sommelier of renown. A nice place for afternoon tea. **Bistro 990**, across from the hotel, opens its French door out onto Bay, inviting passersby in for saddle of rabbit and grilled calves' kidneys with artichokes. It looks like a *Weinstube* (ochre vaulted ceiling, lots of wood trim) and, in fact, does have a good measure of wine. **The Vikings**, which has been around for ages, purveys the sort of food you would find on a well-run Scandinavian cruise ship. It's on St. Nicholas Street, where the first crossroad to the north is St. Joseph, an area of extant convents and seminaries, and site of **Bistro Bernard**, a blond-wood dispensary of fine wines, poached salmon, and cream-swirled veal ragout in the Swiss tradition.

Yonge Street, a manageable number of blocks north of Bloor, forms the western boundary of Rosedale, Toronto's earliest-established chic neighborhood and so has become the main street for feeding the inhabitants of this rarefied realm. This begins at tiny **La Bionda** (number 1017) with merry Cajun/California mixtures for escargots, scallops, and beef, and goes on to heart-throbbing modern Italianisms at supercharged **Cibo** (where the waiters treat women with matinee-idol manners), Grecized fresh fish grills in a marketlike setting at **Trata**, well-conceived modernity (Thai spicing practiced) at slim-dimensioned **Panache**, and more from the grill à la Italian-laundered Yankee at **Fred's Still Here** (the name indicating a stubbornness to survive). The nose first knows the superior worth of two attractive shops for take-out, or anything else to do with food: **David Wood** (number 1110) and **All The Best Breads** (number 1099). Informal **Tipplers**, a little beyond at number 1276, has an appealing range of wines by the glass or the bottle, in addition to seasonal foods treated very carefully. **Brownes Bistro**, on a near cross-street (4 Woodlawn Avenue), is where folk who don't want to cook tonight get glamorized sausage (lamb) with mashed spuds and pizza bread at close tables.

Eclectic and Ethnic

The expensive **Stelle** (807 Queen Street West) goes in for hybrid cooking—Thai spicing with rack of lamb, for example. This is quite a small room, in which white and corrugated iron siding predominate, so dress to contrast. **Lotus** carries market cooking to the extreme, shopping maybe twice a day, and the result is some astonishing Amero-Eurasian combinations that rival the gastronomic pleasures to be found at Nekah (downtown) and Pronto (see below). The room is an excessively plain storefront, but the restaurant, at 96 Tecumseth Street, is not cheap. **Palmerston**, at 488 College Street, has an agreeable back patio-cum-upper deck away from street discomfort in the summer, for seriously wrought urban nourishment (sorrel-decked duck liver in a warm salad; chèvre somewhere, of course; fab ice creams); it changes to simple barbecues (lamb burgers) at weekend brunch. Inside, the real treat for plutocrats is to get a seat by the open kitchen. **Renaissance Café** (509 Bloor Street West) is for unsolemn vegetarians, who might also like to sup multinational dishes on a sidewalk terrace; inexpensive. **Southern Accent** (595 Markham Street) approximates the sun-drenched coastal style of Louisiana in a storybook house and is a very professional and enjoyable operation, with a sidewalk patio. **Boulevard Café** will please the seeker of strong flavors, now and then Peruvian in inspiration, outside on the boulevard at 161 Harbord Street if the weather allows. There may be some interesting conversations to overhear as well.

Perched on the brow of a hill, **Scaramouche**, Benvenuto Place, just off Avenue Road, has a diamanté view of the downtown, fairly solid though expensive fare, a lounge for pasta and simple grills, and capital desserts. The dining room at the nearby **Bradgate Arms** on Foxbar Road is spacious and quiet; the service matches the up-market prices. **Centro** (2472 Yonge Street) *isn't* quiet, its Italo-California menu occasioning much interest from the Jaguar/BMW set. It looks like an expensive jeweler's from the outside, but it has, among other things, a wine library wherein shelves of bottles replace the books (you can imagine how extensive the offerings are, and the quality, and the expense).

Pronto, 692 Mount Pleasant Road, is the epitome of the modern up-market style in Toronto, a buzzing delight of theater and symphony—tastes and textures are the stars, though. It is not to be missed. **Furusato** (410 Bloor Street East) intrigues with its menu of Frapanese cooking, a meld of French and Japanese techniques and ingredients, which is served in a stark, black-dominated back room.

Philoxenia, as inexpensive as Pronto and Furusato are expensive, is an excellent introduction to the Greek food that is so characteristic of the Danforth (at No. 519), except that here it is remarkably light and digestible.

At Eglinton Avenue East and Leslie Street, the Inn on the Park's principal room, **Seasons**, is useful for the dormitory area of the eastern suburbs, with a wide-ranging menu of mods and trads in a classy setting. Ruling the York Mills/Don Mills crossroads, the Prince Hotel's **Le Continental** has dancing, classic cooking, a table-laden Sunday brunch, and views of a river valley

through huge windows. Both rooms are expensive.
Loons (2306 Queen Street East) hitchhikes around the
globe when composing its menu, and even has a daily
curry. There's some very clever cooking here and there's
also the boardwalk paralleling Lake Ontario to stroll
along, before or after dinner. This same great lake is
very much a part of the ambience at **The Guild Inn**, 201
Guildwood Parkway, Scarborough (too far for a taxi
from Toronto), whose unpretentious room has a menu
of smartly styled conservative dishes. Architectural odds
and ends from demolished buildings all over Toronto
populate the well-tended grounds.

Near Enough to the Airport

Babsi's is a two-room operation at 1731 Lake Shore Road
West, Mississauga, with a Swiss international hotel approach, lots of game, no dearth of good ingredients, and
attentive service. **Apricots** (52 Lake Shore Road East, Port
Credit), also expensive, has an imaginative, changing
menu and a summery room. Uncowered by its dreary
area, **Sammy's** (3409 Lake Shore Boulevard West) bifur-
cates its menu into familiar grillwork (with secret and
effective seasonings) and deft Louisiana cooking; a tropical theme is favored, even unto the drinks. **Rogues** is
located in a suburban shopping mall called Sherwood
Forest Village (1900 Dundas Street West, Mississauga)—
hence the restaurant's name—but it serves first-rate Italian food from an open kitchen. **Chez Marie** (485 Main
Street North, Brampton) is in an elegant wood-panelled
1930s mansion; spiffy food (rib-eye steak marinated in
spiced coffee), for which one pays a little more. **Café
Créole** (Skyline Hotel, 655 Dixon Road) is mainly a recreation of Cajun cooking at the height of its popularity,
but there are also international dishes. Jazz and freshly
shucked oysters also play a part.

—Joseph Hoare

BARS AND NIGHTLIFE

Like any city of more than three million people, Toronto
has a vast and varied social life that supports thousands of
meeting and greeting spots, from the friendly "neighborhood" to the ritzy on-the-town nightclub; the cut-off-jeans
crowd of the Balmy Arms to the tuxedoed swells of the
Imperial Room. In Toronto you will find the world's
highest dance floor; a bar where the Rolling Stones drop
in to play; a real English pub with imported beer and

barstools; North America's oldest dinner nightclub. Alas for movie trivia fans, the strip joint where the film *Flashdance* was born—Gimlet's—has fallen prey to the wrecker's ball.

There are comedy pubs, dinner theaters, jazz clubs galore (Toronto is known for its jazz spots), "down-home" Maritimer boot-stomping fiddle music, new-wave nightclubs, chic and trendy hot spots, palaces filled with thousands of dancing young people, bars for singles, sedate "businesspersons' " lounges, and clubs for those of alternative sexual lifestyles.

Most hotels have their own lounges, some a step above the average (for example, the Chelsea Bun of Delta's Chelsea, frequented by locals for good jazz), but we will concentrate mainly on the independent spots, both new and established, that will likely have the staying power to survive this trendy town of disposable bars.

The word "disco" seems to be dying here, if not stone cold dead, and though the former discos are still there, and likely play the same music, they are now known as "nightclubs." George Orwell would be pleased.

Yorkville

Home of the chic and trendy, and those wishing to be, this north midtown area (bordered by Bloor, Yonge, Avenue Road, and Davenport) contains some of Toronto's hottest partying grounds, with prices to match. The center is the **Bellair**, corner of Cumberland and Bellair, with a constantly crowded bar; drinking, dining, and dancing are on two levels. The food is surprisingly good and always inventive (unlike some spots that trade popularity for food quality). The glass panes are removed in summer, and café tables lining the sidewalks are filled in the afternoons by *nouveau riche* lady shoppers and later by evening revelers.

Farther down the street is the pub atmosphere of **Hemingway's**, much more casual yet just as crowded. This is an upscale burgers-and-beer bar, an informal and friendly oasis with a steady stream of regulars.

Around the corner on Yorkville proper (an expensive view can be had from the opulent ground-floor lounge of the Four Seasons Hotel) you can find such diverse spots as **Remy's** (check out their second-floor roof deck) or the back garden of **South Side Charlie's** off Old York Lane, a walkthrough connecting Cumberland and Yorkville. A block farther, amid all the sidewalk cafés, look for the

PWD sign (88 Yorkville Avenue) indicating a cozy cellar nightclub. Actually you can hear the sounds on the sidewalk—Latin, reggae, or r&b—as the 30-year-olds hang around the bar or hit the dance floor in this eclectic Art Deco room known for its funky sound.

Across the street is **Meyer's**: deli by day, jazz by night. Many people make this their last stop of the evening as they wander in for some great after-hours jazz or blues by the advertised headliners or at impromptu sessions by other musicians who have just dropped in from their regular gigs around town.

At the end of Yorkville, where it meets Yonge, is the **Copa**, a former warehouse that now can hold about 2,000 dancers and drinkers on two levels. It is a barn of a place, with a flashing light show and multi-screen videos. Surprisingly, the ages range from those who have just recently begun to drink legally (19) to three-piece business suit types. A deejay spins the sounds, though often a live band takes over; the cover charge varies.

Back on Bloor Street, check out the city's "power bar" at the Windsor Arms Hotel, 22 St. Thomas Street. The **"22"** is a piano lounge that attracts many show-biz types, who are either making deals or staying in the small, stately hotel (Katharine Hepburn to Mick Jagger). The summer patio evokes memories of a graceful French mansion, and yet "22" is just steps from the bustle of Bloor Street.

The scene changes dramatically just around the corner at **Bemelmans**, with its ultramodern chrome and brass. The bar area is filled from noon on, as are most of the restaurant tables (ask for the outdoor patio). Bemelmans remains open until after 3:00 A.M., and though you can't order alcohol after that hour, you can get a great eggs Benedict and cappuccino. The crowd is very much a "mixed bag," from punkers to businessmen, although you may notice a preponderance of good-looking males at the bar.

Queen Street West

From the glitz to the funk, Queen Street West (University to Bathurst, and slowly spreading) is an eclectic blend of artists, literati, and progressive music clubs. From the new-wave explosion of the **Rivoli** to the three-tiered disc jockey dancing of the multicolored **Big Bop** (with nightly lines), the keynote here is casual. The heart and soul of Queen Street West belongs to the **BamBoo**, in the center of the strip at 312 Queen West. So named for the former

"Wicker World" basket shop that it once was, the BamBoo refuses categorization, serving an excellent blend of Caribbean/Indonesian food, with nightly music specials from rock to reggae, fusion jazz to country blues. The cover charge varies with each act, but full houses emphasize that owners Patti Habib and Richard O'Brien always hit the right note.

Farther west is the **Horseshoe Tavern**, a 40-year-old Toronto rock mecca featuring mainstream local groups and legendary r&b masters. There is usually a cover, which obviously doesn't go toward improving the decor but is funneled into booking wonderful music; the decor itself is slightly seedy but down-home comfortable. Faded blue jeans mix with tuxedos that have escaped a stuffy party for the fun of the Horseshoe.

For truly seedy, you have to visit the **Cameron Public House** (408 Queen West), which has all the charm of a broken-down northern fishing lodge—until you order your first draft. The Cameron is like a crowded house party, the front room (with surprising ceiling frescoes) like a home kitchen, where people always seem to congregate and talk. The back room holds a tiny stage and a crush of standing people listening to good-time rock. The Cameron has its regulars, but if there is room they will gladly accept a guest.

The newest Queen West offerings are **X-Rays**, a rather stark-looking space (comedian Dan Ackroyd is a silent partner) that caters to the street's new-wave contingent, and **Stilife**, just south of Queen at the corner of Richmond and Duncan. It is easy to miss the place because the exterior says "warehouse"; the decor, however, screams ultra-chic. In fact, Stilife has been winning designer awards throughout North America. The interior is exotic yet comfortable, which also describes the clientele, who line up to pay a weekend cover of $10 for deejay dancing until 3:00 A.M. It is an experience just to see this club, but do get there early; entry is limited to 300 only. (Stilife serves dinner seven nights a week—with a bar menu—so get there before 9:00 P.M., order a fairly tasty dinner, and avoid the cover.)

Another recent spot just south of Queen is the basement-level **Tangerine**; a comfortable bar, liberal libations, spicy finger food (try the baked brie), steak and seafood dining for 130, and a mesmerizing fish-tank decor help the customer while away a pleasant evening. So do the music, lights, and dance floor, of course. Tangerine still has some growing pains, and it is difficult actually to locate the entrance at the corner of Richmond and Duncan streets (look for the Computer Connections business sign), but it is well worth the search. Closed Sundays.

King Street West

This area runs parallel (to the south) of Queen Street, separated only by two short blocks, but it might as well be a world away. This is an "uptown" area, as opposed to the funk of the Queen Street crowd, even though the main corner bar (King and John streets) is called **Downtown**, a large (holds about 400), fancy, and fun renovated warehouse with dancing at the front, a good restaurant in the back, and a regular deejay with weekend singers.

Although the vanguard of the King Street region, Joe Allen, has closed its doors, it is relocating, perhaps farther west on King. Manager John Maxwell hasn't announced the new location at this writing but loyal fans are just lying in wait for the rebirth. The Joe Allen group still runs **Orso**, its Italian dining cousin with a far-flung beer list, on the corner of John and Richmond streets.

Kitty-corner is the "brew pub" **Amsterdam**, where you can watch the staff creating the establishment's own beer and ale in the basement, then sample the wares upstairs in the bar with its four-story, cathedral-like ceiling. The dining is good, but most people come for the crowded bar scene, with outdoor seating jam-packed in summer. It is fun for a while, but the din created by the terminally trendy may force you to seek quieter drinking pastures. And though not quieter, you can have less pretentious fun at **Studebaker's**, a 1950s-style rock 'n' roll platter place around the corner on Pearl Street. And they do have a real Studebaker on display.

Since the announcement of the SkyDome site several years ago, new bars and restaurants have moved in and tried to establish loyal followings before the stadium's opening last spring. In the past year, however, everyone has tried to open something—bar, restaurant, deli, whatever—in the area. These places range from the huge **Loose Moose** on Adelaide Street, **Fred's Not Here** on King Street, **Don Cherry's Grapevine** (diehard sports fans only), and various others to service the sports and concert fans that pack the SkyDome most nights and weekends. Parking lot prices are appalling, so walk through town, take a cab, or catch the trolley.

The theater and music crowds frequenting the Royal

Alex or Roy Thomson Hall on King (and Simcoe) Street will often stop at one of Ed Mirvish's restaurants (they include **Ed's Warehouse**, **Ed's Seafood**, and **Ed's Chinese**— total seating of 3,000) or **Peter's Backyard**; although for a relaxed brandy, stop at the lounge of **Telfer's** on the corner, or stay longer for an excellent *après*-theater dinner.

Overlooking all of this—this being the entire city—is **Sparkles**, the world's highest nightclub and bar, in the CN Tower. The cover charge, which includes the elevator ride, is $5, and you can dance and drink 1,136 feet above the city lights. It has a great dance floor and light show, although the night view of the twinkling Toronto islands alone is well worth the ride up.

Esplanade and Front Street

This spiffed-up area just east of Yonge Street used to have old dingy warehouses but now contains several major theaters (the O'Keefe, St. Lawrence Center, Young People's Theater), the huge St. Lawrence Market, and many new offices—and, therefore, many new bars and restaurants. **Brandy's**, on the Esplanade, was the first in the area and remains the most popular; businessmen come for lunch and after work, then the evening dance crowd lines up every night. This is a comfortable bar during the day, with large wingback chairs, brass, and fern, although it is so crowded at night that the stylish patrons provide their own decor. The connecting **Scotland Yard** is another popular spot, with plenty of cranked-up music and a well-heeled crowd. (**Muddy York**, just across the street, only gets crowded when there's an overflow. Too bad, because it's a friendly bar, with dancing, and you can actually converse over the music.)

Around the corner at 85 Front Street East is **East 85th**, a rather laid-back r&b club serving good finger food and honest drinks and providing friendly music. Toronto's most sophisticated little jazz club is just across the street at **Café des Copains**: fine Continental dining upstairs and traditional jazz downstairs in the relaxed elegance of the basement.

Pat & Mario's, just steps east at Wellington and Church streets, is the premier singles bar in the area, with weekend crowds lining up to hit the fast-paced dance floor. The ages range from mid-20s upward. An older crowd than that found at **RPM**, a cavernous hall that packs in around 1,000 younger patrons most weekend nights. The deejay's selections echo throughout the two levels, and the $7 cover charge includes the daily buffet. It rocks on until 3:00 A.M., but is closed Tuesdays and Thursdays. RPM is at the bottom of Yonge Street, just east of the Toronto Star building (One Yonge Street) on Queen's Quay, which runs parallel to the waterfront.

The Beach

A ten-minute cab ride east will take you to the Beach, a two-mile strip of East Queen Street that seems like a little beach resort, an entity unto itself, independent of the nearby city with its gracious old houses, the boardwalk, the lake, and, of course, the beach. Along Queen Street East, however, you will find some good, friendly small-town bars, mainly frequented by residents. Several blocks along Queen Street east of Woodbine (the official start of the Beach) you will find **Lido**, which boasts a local crowd, but one geared to top-40 music on a video screen. There is no cover charge for the nightly deejay, nor for the live jazz groups on Sunday and Monday evenings. This is a 25- to 35-year-old crowd that likes to party. And eat: The roadhouse menu is a substantial one (with great combo baskets of shrimp and chicken), and you have to dance to work it all off. Lido has recently expanded, which has helped to decrease the waiting line outside. A stroll along Queen Street heading east will take you past various bars and casual dining spots: the **Beach Bar** with its side-street outdoor patio; the ever-popular **Scratch Daniels** filled with a slightly younger, rowdier set ordering pitchers of draft beer; the **Balmy Arms**, the quintessential "local" pub serving draft and darts; or the raucous music spilling out of **Quigley's**, **Babbage's**, or **Fitzgerald's**, all three oriented to local beach residents who range from upscale professionals to windsurfing jocks to long-haired sixties left-overs. Take note: **Fitzgerald's**, the last pub on the trolley line (one more street and you hit Scarborough) may have the best—and cheapest—chicken wings in town.

Yonge–Eglinton

North of Bloor, Eglinton Avenue east of Yonge to Mount Pleasant has long been known as the headquarters of Toronto's singles scene, where, for the past decade, bars and restaurants have sprung up to accommodate all the bachelors and bachelorettes who moved into the high-density housing area during the 1970s, before the city's expansions and when prices were much lower.

Take the subway to the Yonge–Eglinton station, then

spend the evening wandering. Starting at the corner of Yonge Street, check out **Berlin**, the newest dining/dancing nightclub in the area for people 25 and up. The music, supplied by BOB (Berlin's Own Band), usually attracts the 500-capacity crowd early, with anxious lines outside. Best to make dinner reservations to ensure a seat and avoid the cover charge. (For a different, though no less raucous, evening, the next-door **Duke of Kent** provides a typical English pub atmosphere, complete with imported beer, Cornish pasties, and a blend of United Kingdom accents.)

A block down Eglinton, you'll find one of the most popular singles bars in the city: **Earl's Tin Palace**. bustling bartenders and waitresses keep the upscale, trendy (no jeans, please) crowds happy. There are usually weekend lines, although if you go for dinner you'll avoid them.

Just around the corner on Mount Pleasant is a minor city legend, the **Chick n' Deli**, where aficionados can be assured of hearing some of the best jazz in North America. This is a cheery, unpretentious spot where you can see some of the jazz greats; it's especially pleasant on a rainy Sunday afternoon. And Chick n' also has some dynamite chicken wings. Very popular.

The Danforth

An old established area, the Danforth (this is actually Bloor Street East; the name changes over the Bloor viaduct, at Broadview) has long been known as the Greek ghetto, famous for some of the best Aegean food in North America (check out the Omonia, Ellas, the Odyssey, or some late-night souvlaki at Mr. Greek). However, a younger, yuppie group has been coming into the area, paving the way for more modern bars.

The newest is **Allen's**, an offshoot of the popular Joe Allen worldwide collection (New York, Los Angeles, London, Paris), a casually classy spot with dark wood design and deep blue interior. There is a burger bar as you enter, across from the bar, and a full kitchen for serving regular meals. As at its parent, there is a vast imported-beer list (try the malt *bière de garde* from France) and a wonderful back garden seating 100 under the old weeping willows. Toronto is the only city to have three establishments under the aegis of Joe Allen (yes, there is a real Joe Allen), which keeps proprietor John Maxwell very busy indeed. Located next to the Century Theatre at 143 Danforth.

Across the street at **Panama Joe's** (affectionately known

as PJ's) the scene is slightly more rowdy and louder, both from the crowd and the choices of the deejay. The building used to be an old movie theater, which has allowed the designer to be inventive and colorful, from the balconies to the Art Deco cornices. The over-25 crowd lines up each weekend; it's best to get there early for a table on the rooftop patio. And whatever your choice of libation, try the charcoal-cooked chicken satay or one of the stir-fried delicacies.

The Hargrave Exchange, just slightly east, is a perfect neighborhood local; the friendly staff seem to be on a first-name basis with most of the customers. Newcomers will feel at home very quickly among the casual crowd. Feel free to dawdle in the booths or join the ongoing dart tournament. And try their famous chicken wings (although only the brave order the "suicide" strength).

The largest area club is **Spectrum**, at 2714 Danforth, featuring the best light show in town: strobes, neon, and lasers. There is live entertainment on Thursdays only, while weekend dancing on the huge football-field-size dance floor goes on until 4:00 A.M. The second-floor dining room alone holds 200, and the over-25 crowd willingly lines up each weekend to pay the $7 cover charge after 9:00 P.M.; it's best to get there for dinner and stay for the light show. In a change of pace, Spectrum features ballroom dancing every Tuesday.

Other Entertainment

The above are only some of the bars, pubs, and night spots clustered in several popular—and populated—locations; there are countless more scattered throughout the city. Other recommended clubs would definitely include the r&b sounds of the **Bluenote**, on Pears Avenue (Avenue Road and Davenport); the rock at Spadina Avenue's **El Mocambo** (where the Rolling Stones dropped in one night for a surprise gig); the new-wave presentations of the "Izzy," the **Hotel Isabella**, on Jarvis Street North; the hot videos at the **Tasmania Ballroom**, at the bottom end of Jarvis; the reggae beat drifting from **Tiger's Coconut Grove** in the Kensington Market area.

Major dance nightclubs featuring deejays, current videos, and often live acts include **The Diamond**, on Sherbourne Street, **Krush**, on Kingston Road (north Beach area), and **Lee's Palace**, on Bloor Street West in the Annex area. After-hours (no alcohol after 1:00 A.M.) spots include the **Twilight Zone**, near the Richmond Street West's Bar

Tangerine, and St. Joseph Street's **Club Z**, near the busy nightlife corner of Yonge and Wellesley.

Dining entertainment is rampant in Toronto, from the first-class elegance of the Royal York's **Imperial Room** (Tony Bennett to Tina Turner) to dinner theater at **Garbo's** on Queen Street West, **His Majesty's Feast** down on the Lakeshore west, the **Limelight** on Yonge, just south of Davisville, or **Stagewest**, in the northern reaches of the city just south of Highway 401.

Comedy clubs include the world-famous Second City troupes at the **Old Firehall**, and **Harper's Night Magic**, both downtown on Lombard Street, **Yuk Yuk's** in York-ville, and **Arbuckles** on Front Street east of Yonge.

Toronto has other nocturnal pastimes, of course (it is not "Toronto the Good" all the time), and these might include visits to the **Brass Rail**, on Yonge just south of Bloor; **Cheaters**, at Yonge north of Davisville; or the **Filmore**, along Dundas East, for some research into the city's ecdysiasts, more commonly known as strippers.

As previously mentioned, check the local newspapers for the nightly entertainment scene. The most complete listing, however, can be found in the weekly tabloid *NOW*, which is available free at most restaurants and bars throughout the city.

Micro Breweries

A recent trend across Canada, from Vancouver to Nova Scotia, is the growth of micro breweries, breweries that produce a very limited quantity of highly select quality beer, ale, and lager. This is basically a cottage industry that now spans the country (although each brewery is indi-vidually owned); some seem to have sprung up as the result of a neighbor's basement homebrew that became so popular they built a little shop around it. Canadians have always had "the Big Three" beermeisters—Molson's, Labatt's, and Carling-O'Keefe—as well as the odd popular export such as New Brunswick's Moosehead brand, but other names such as Castle Brewing, Sleeman's, Les Brassauers du Nord, Okanagan Springs, and Ottawa Valley are popping up and finding regional acceptance across Canada.

Regular Canadian beer is stronger that American beer, yet weaker than many English brews. The microbeer boasts a more distinctive flavor, much more European in its outlook. One reason for this is that a batch of regular beer is brewed for three to five days, whereas the microbeer is brewed for a minimum of five *weeks* (usually seven before it is bottled). The micros use pure spring water as well, which helps create their own individual taste. Some brands seems so thick and rich on your tongue that you may want to chew them. For further information on the micro brewery phenomenon in Canada, consult expert Jake McKay, who produces the *Northern Brewer* magazine, which deals with all facts of the industry: 1561 Kingston Road, Scarborough, Ont. M1N 1R9; Tel: 699-6459.

Toronto is blessed (for beerdrinkers, that is) with four of these micro breweries: **Upper Canada** (the largest "micro" in the country), **Conners**, **Northern Algonquin**, and **Great Lakes**. All have free public tours and tastings, so if you are looking for something different to do on a rainy day (or a hot, sunny one for that matter) just give them a call.

Conners Brewing, 1335 Lawrence Avenue East; Tel: 449-6101.

Great Lakes, 155 Clark Avenue, Brampton; Tel: 451-0073.

Northern Algonquin, 550 Alden Road, Markham; Tel: 474-1179.

Upper Canada Breweries, 2 Atlantic Avenue; Tel: 534-9281.

—*Steve Veale*

SHOPS AND SHOPPING

The best buys in Toronto are those with a distinctly Canadian flavor: Eskimo carvings, an Ojibway quill basket, Mennonite and Amish quilts, early Canadian country-style pine furniture, Quebec folk art, a delicate hand-blown glass vase, a trendy outfit from one of Queen Street West's avant-garde designers.

By far the most interesting places to shop in Toronto are the neighborhoods that fan out from the city center: Bloor/Yorkville, Mirvish Village, The Kingsway, Bloor West Village, St. Clair West, the Danforth, the Beach, Queen Street West, Village by the Grange, Chinatown, Kensington Market, Harbourfront, and Yonge Street, Mount Pleasant, and Bayview from Davisville as far north as the city limits.

Bloor/Yorkville

Bloor/Yorkville, where Toronto's first coffeehouses and clubs (host to the likes of Gordon Lightfoot, Neil Young, and Joni Mitchell) have given way to extravagant renovations and elegant shops, is where you'll find Armani, Gucci, Valentino, and Saint Laurent along with a few others you may not have heard of. The latest entry in the opulence stakes is **Fetoun's**, 97 Scollard Street, a lavish four-story boutique featuring adventurous custom-made furs and spangled leathers with prices that make your knees shake. It's worth a visit just to see the raspberry-hued walls and the ornately decorated apartment on the third floor, complete with peach bedroom festooned in English lace, where pampered clients receive smoked salmon, caviar, and white wine to help them make up their minds. The Saudi-born owner and her husband also breed racehorses.

Hazelton Lanes, a mere stone's throw away, is Toronto's version of Rodeo Drive, a series of lanes winding in a figure eight around a skating rink in the winter, a garden restaurant in the summer. **Valencienne**, 25 Bloor Street West (upstairs), is a tiny hidden-away boutique that sells pure silk heirloom wedding dresses to princesses and movie stars. Prices are from $2,000 to $30,000.

Bloor West Village

Bloor West Village, one of the most pleasant places to shop in the city, was created by local ingenuity—it's a friendly, tree-lined part of Bloor Street, running from Jane to Runnymede, known for its meat markets, delis, pastry shops, flower stalls, and fashionable boutiques, steps away from High Park and easily accessible by subway.

The Kingsway

The Kingsway, slightly farther west along Bloor Street, extends from Prince Edward Drive to Montgomery Road. This upscale area is definitely worth a visit. Check out the **Lambton Mills Country Store** at 2940 Bloor Street West for unusual handmade dolls and keepsake boxes, and the **Keltic Touch** and the **Pant Bin**, at numbers 2998 and 3078 on the same street, for well-made clothing. **Side Step**, at 2988, is the place for low-priced linen clothes and hand-crafted leather belts, and an excellent book store, **The Bookmark**, is at 2 Jackson Avenue, around the corner from Bloor.

St. Clair Avenue West

St. Clair Avenue West, or Westclair, is known as Toronto's Little Italy. Italian designer clothes, linen and laces, leather and linguini, Pavarotti and Fellini are spoken here. Within these three blocks you'll find more than 40 shoe stores. Best buys are at **Venetian Shoes**, 1262 St. Clair Avenue West. You can see a lot of the neighborhood if you travel through on a St. Clair Avenue West streetcar; just be sure to get off to visit **Genesis** and **La Scala** (at 1188 and 1190 St. Clair Avenue West) for elegant Italian menswear and **Richard Babies Place Limited** at number 1242, the best place in town for designer children's wear. Cappuccino and espresso are always on the house in this neighborhood.

The Danforth

The Danforth, bounded by the Don Valley and Woodbine area to the east, might just for a minute remind you of Athens, with the smell of lamb roasting on a spit, the sound of bouzouki music, and the sight of all-night fruit markets. The oldest shops are the **Georgina Tea Room** (1918), where you get your tea leaves read, and **Thuna Herbalists** (1923)—both still going strong.

Chinatown and Kensington Market

Chinatown, bounded by Bay Street to the east, Spadina Avenue to the West, and College Street south to Dundas, is divided into old and new, a neighborhood of fish and meat stores, bakeries, herbalists, bookstores, discount clothing, crafts, discount art-supply stores like **Picasso's** and **Gwartz-man's**, and more than 100 restaurants. **Wing On Trading, Inc.**, 356 Spadina Road, is one of the oldest establishments, where you can find wooden ginger graters, handmade drums and flutes, paper kites, and the world's biggest umbrella, measuring 40 inches in diameter.

Kensington Market, bounded by Bathurst and Spadina, Dundas and College, with the main market streets being Augusta, Baldwin, and Kensington Avenue, is a jumble of noise, movement, and extraordinary smells. Everything is compact here, from the gaudy Portuguese hardware stores on Denison Square, to the endless stalls of fruit, vegetables, dried beans, fish, and cheese.

Mirvish Village

Mirvish Village, on Markham Street, is one block of reno-vated Victorian houses inhabited by artists, antiques deal-ers, booksellers, and discount design clothiers like **La Mode de Vija**. Mirvish Village was the brainchild of To-ronto's most famous entrepreneur, Ed Mirvish, who owns **Ed's Warehouse** (a bargain-basement store at the corner of Markham and Bathurst, with the world's biggest electric sign), and, downtown, the Royal Alexandra Theatre and surrounding restaurants.

The Beach

The Beach area is the city's earliest summer retreat; Queen Street East is just a few blocks from the lake, and home to some of the city's most interesting shops. It runs east from Woodbine as far as Victoria Park, and has everything from antique and junk stores to health and beauty emporiums and good secondhand bookstores. East to west: **The Animation Gallery**, 1977 Queen Street East, second floor, sells original hand-painted animation art, one of the fastest-appreciating art forms on the market. (Animation art has been featured in recent auctions held by Sotheby's and Christie's.) **Tambuli**, 1915 Queen Street East, sells church art, African masks, and Oriental rugs. **The Old Lamp Shop**, 1582 Queen Street East, is owned by antiques dealer Dominique Douillet, who restores and sells the elegant solid brass fixtures that graced the homes, businesses, and churches of turn-of-the-century Toronto. To add the right finishing touches to his lamps he has the largest selection of art-glass shades in Canada, many of them bearing the name of the famous Steuben glassworks, and a 1910 Art Nouveau lamp with stained-glass shade. Farther west is **Crème de la Crème**, 342 Queen Street East, which sells antique bathroom fixtures, and **Antiques in Time**, 173 Queen Street East, which has old clocks.

The Harbourfront

The Harbourfront runs along Queen's Quay directly at the lakefront and is a miracle of retrieved park space and warehouses, like Queen's Quay Terminal, that have been converted into a combination of galleries, shops, theaters, and living spaces. The Harbourfront is where you'll find **Harbourfront Antique Market**, a great place to browse for bargains on Sundays.

Queen Street West

Queen Street West, starting at McCaul Street and running west of Bathurst, may at first inspection seem intimidating, with all the Mohawk haircuts and new-wave youth, but it's also full of surprises and intriguing shops. Once it was the exclusive home of discount stores and jobbers; they now exist side by side with the boutiques, galleries, and bookstores that are the hallmark of the street. Over the stores, a good mix of students from the nearby Ontario College of Art, musicians, photographers, and young people are busy trying to find themselves. All the trendy young avant-garde Canadian designers are here: designers like **Ms. Emma,** 275 Queen Street West; Marilyn Brooks, Alfred Sung, and Pam Chorley at **Fashion Crimes,** 395 Queen Street West; the Bent Boys, Debra Kuchme, and Alexandra at **The Project Line;** Big Fish, Comrags, Zapata, Liz Lant, Lucas, and Tenzer at **Parade,** 557 Queen Street West; and Jean Claude Poitra and Philippe Ronsard at **The Atomic Age,** 350 Queen Street West—all are part of the Queen Street West scene. The area is a gold mine for vintage clothes with **Black Market** at 323A Queen Street West specializing in men's tuxedos from the 1940s and 1950s (popular with Toronto rock bands) and **English Eccentrics** at number 477. Farther west on the same street is **Romni Wools Ltd.** at number 475 for the best selection of yarns in town, **Nagash** at number 777 for unusual handmade leather goods, and artwork at number 670, **Algonquians Sweet Grass Gallery.**

If you explore the neighborhoods you'll find most of the interesting shopping, so we will zero in on the rest of the best shopping now by specialty.

Antiques

Doc John's Antique Doll Clinic, 194 Carlton Street East, is owned by John Hawkslaw, a pattern-maker who loves collecting old dolls. His oldest one dates from 1830. **Garden of Eden Antiques,** 2644 Danforth Avenue, is a bargain hunter's paradise crammed with beautiful merchandise, such as an unfinished pine occasional table for less than $100 and a stately 1930s sideboard for only $365. **Harbourfront Antique Market,** 222 Queen's Quay West, is billed as Canada's largest quality antiques market, open on Sundays. It has 70 permanent dealers, and another 200 dealers converge from all over the province on Sundays. **Linda Howard Antiques,** 581 Mount Pleasant, has a great supply of antique Mennonite and Amish quilts, early and contemporary Quebec folk art, decoys, wall hangings, hooked rugs, and early-Canadian pine furniture. **Sandy's Antiques,** 3130 Bathurst Street, is tucked away at the north end of Lawrence Plaza and up some nondescript stairs. Once you've arrived there's no mistaking the merchandise and good prices. The bargain here is the 50 to 60 percent discount on Birks estate sterling-silver flatware patterns as well as that on Wallace, International, Northumbria, and Jensen. The Royal Crown Derby china, crystal, cloisonné vases, tea sets, and trays make Sandy's a browser's paradise. **Somerville Antiques**, 606 Markham Street, has unusual items such as a Victorian croquet set, antique buttons, and ladies' fans.

Arts and Crafts

Indian Art. **Algonquians Sweet Grass Gallery**, 670 Queen Street West, Ojibway-owned, is an authentic native Indian art-and-crafts store (a rare find these days) featuring items selected with excellent taste: Indian carvings and prints, hand-sewn moccasins, beading, baskets made from porcupine quills, tamarack birds, birchbark bitings, duck decoys, and Cowichan sweaters from the West Coast.

Inuit Art. **The Guild Shop**, 140 Cumberland, has the best selection and prices for Inuit art. Owned and operated by the Ontario Craft Council, it is nonprofit, hence no hefty markup. A delightful little polar bear tapestry on a teal blue background by Veronica Manilak of Rankin Inlet is only $150, but you can go as high as $6,000 for a mother-and-child soapstone carving by Tutya Ikkidluts of Cape Dorset. **Fehely Fine Arts**, 45 Avenue Road, and **The Inuit Gallery of Eskimo Art**, 9 Prince Arthur, are commercial galleries with a good selection. Older pieces from the 1950s and 1960s are sometimes available at **Waddington McLean** auctions, 189 Queen Street East, held Wednesdays and Saturdays.

Crafts. **The Guild Shop** has top-quality Canadian crafts: leather, textile, glass, woodcarving, jewelry, pottery. **Bounty**, 235 Queen's Quay, also has superb examples of craftwork in all media by more than 120 artists, some of whom work in adjacent studios, open to the public, at the Harbourfront. **The Design Department Store**, Village by the Grange (entrance outside on McCaul Street), has carefully selected original designs in textile, ceramics, glass, wood, handmade paper, screen printing, toys, cards, jewelry, and clothing by students and graduates of the Ontario College of Art. **The Gardiner Museum Shop**, 111 Queen's Park (opposite the Royal Ontario Museum), has one-of-a-kind Canadian pottery pieces complementing the museum's outstanding collection of ceramic art. **Early Canadian Furniture Shops**, 8 Cumberland Street, has handcrafted pine and oak reproductions; requests for custom work are welcome.

Books

Toronto has a mind-boggling array of bookstores that reflect a certain eclecticism among its citizenry. The **Albert Britnell Book Store**, 765 Yonge Street, almost 100 years old, is the oldest in the city, still family owned and operated, and they say they will find any book in or out of print. **Ballenford Architectural Books**, 98 Scollard, has collector's items as well as contemporary books and exhibits of architectural drawings and models. **Broadway and Hollywood Books**, 17 Yorkville Avenue, has out-of-print and current books about stage and screen as well as some memorabilia. **Can-Do Bookstore**, 311 Queen Street West, is do-it-yourself heaven. Owner Stan Adelman, a Mr. Fix-It himself, claims to have more than 400 books on woodcarving alone.

Chapters, 2360 Yonge Street, is a bookstore, wine bar, and restaurant combo, with Monday night set aside for authors' readings. **David Mirvish Books on Art**, 596 Markham Street, has more than 40,000 titles (in and out of print), all valuable, in the heart of Mirvish Village. **Longhouse Book Shop Limited**, 626 Yonge Street, has only Canadian books, some 20,000 titles in stock, an excellent children's section, a Toronto section, native section, history, political science, and sociology. **Sleuth of Baker Street**, 1595 Bayview Avenue, has detective and spy thrillers as well as collectors' editions and a good selection of Sherlockiana. **That Other Bookstore**, 745 Queen Street West, is also a café. Owned by a former heroin addict turned drama therapist, the store's specialty is recovery and self-help books on every addiction, obsession, and unhealthy relationship known to man. **Theatrebooks**, 25 Bloor Street West (entrance on Balmuto Street, upstairs), specializes in theater, film, photography, and dance. **The Garden Bookstore**, 5 Yorkville Avenue, is Toronto's only bookstore devoted exclusively to gardening.

If you like quantity, **The World's Biggest Book Store**, at 20 Edward Street, one block north of the Eaton Centre, has 17 miles of bookshelves and more than one million books in stock. Its 55 specialty departments cover everything from accounting to zoology.

Antiquarian dealers of note are: Abelard Book Shop, 519 Queen Street West; About Books, 280 Queen Street West; Hugh Anson-Cartwright, 229 College Street, with a good selection of fine leather bindings; David Mason Books, 342 Queen Street West (second floor); Old Favorites Book Shop Ltd., 250 Adelaide Street West; Village Book Store, 239 Queen Street West; and Ten Editions, 698 Spadina Avenue, which has vintage sheet music as well as old books.

Chess Sets

The ROM (Royal Ontario Museum) Shop, 100 Queen's Park, has the best and most interesting selection in town; sets represent different cultures and historical periods, and prices are reasonable. There is a hand-carved, hand-painted wooden chess set of Russian Mongolian figures for $230, including board and case; another Russian set in walnut goes for $145; a Chinese carved marble set with ancient figures sells for $2,000, including the marble board. There is a Medieval set and an exact replica of the set used for the international chess tournaments every year; also hand-carved bone chess sets from $270 to $450 and a Viennese hand-carved rosewood set, including board and carrying case, for $135.

Children

La Petite Gaminerie, Hazelton Lanes, sells unusual designer clothes for children, mostly imported from France. Museum Children's Shop, 100 Queen's Park, is a gold mine of gift ideas for children. The biggest sellers are the plastic dinosaurs, accurately modelled on the museum's own collection; also dinosaur kits and wooden skeletal dinosaurs. Science City Inc. (Holt Renfrew Centre, lower level) is just the place for children with a scientific bent. Everything scientific and educational for all ages is here, from telescopes to chemistry sets. Science City has two more shops nearby for adults. The Children's Book Store, 604 Markham Street, boasts the world's largest selection of quality books, records, and tapes for children up to age 14, and a staff of helpful librarians and teachers. The Last Wound Up, 91 Cumberland Street, Yorkville, is strictly windup toys and music boxes for children and for adults who never grew up. The Toy Shop, 62 Cumberland Street, is two floors chock full of toys, books, and games from around the world. Touch the Sky, Inc., 836 Yonge Street and 207 Queen's Quay, is Canada's largest seller of kites, wind socks, wood chimes, mobiles, Frisbees, and hot-air balloons.

Clocks

Abernethy & Son, 3235 Yonge Street, is a father-and-son operation that grandfather started in Manchester, England. Each old clock is clearly dated, priced, and guaranteed for a year. There is a wide selection displayed from England and Scotland and a few early American clocks. The store has Long Case clocks, mantel clocks, and pocket watches (one in sterling silver circa 1750 was priced at $1,250). Prices range from $100 for an antique Victorian mantel clock to a William Cattell–built Marquetry Long Case clock circa 1664 for $30,000. Reproductions are also sold here.

Collectors

Toronto caters to collectors, with stores like **Autophile**, 1685 Bayview Avenue, which has miniature cars and a collection of motoring books; **Doc John's Antique Doll Clinic**, 194 Carlton Street East; **The Dolly Madison Co. Inc.**, 5336 Yonge Street, has a porcelain doll-making studio with finished dolls, kits, accessories, and collectible teddy bears; **Geomania**, Holt Renfrew Centre, lower level, a fascinating store with high-quality rocks, Mexican desert roses, rare butterflies, and a 380-million-year-old trilobite fossil from Morocco (which sells for $450). **George's Trains**, 510 Mount Pleasant, is Canada's biggest toy train store, with ready-made trains in all sizes as well as kits, collectible brass locomotives, and antiques. **Tall Ships**, 1545 Bayview Avenue: Owner Robert Jerred has a Royal Marine background and a fascination for all things nautical. You can find handcrafted scale-model ships, kits, nautical antiques, ships in a bottle, and nautical books.

Furs

Apart from pricey fur salons such as Holt Renfrew and Creeds, there are plenty of bargains on Spadina Avenue between King and Front streets at wholesale stores such as **Cosmopolitan Fur Co. Ltd.**, 204 Spadina Avenue, **House of Appel Fur Company**, 119 Spadina Avenue, **Leader Furs**, 330 Yonge Street, **Norman Rogul Fur Company Ltd.**, 480 Adelaide Street West, and **Paul Magder Furs**, 202 Spadina Avenue (more than 3,000 furs to choose from). The very best deal on furs is at **Formerly Yours**, a consignment shop at 1907 Avenue Road. Owner Nancy Gillick's in-laws are Montreal furriers who supply her with low-priced samples. She's been known to provide limousine service for out-of-town clients, who sometimes buy two or three coats at a time.

Gifts for Grandparents

Generations, 1695 Avenue Road. Systems analyst Erika Wybourn was frustrated because she couldn't find a suitable gift for her grandmother. She studied the market for three years before opening Generations, a little oasis for the elderly. There is a pot of coffee or tea waiting when you arrive and a comfortable bench. Merchandise includes reversible magnifiers with lights, nonskid slippers, touch-control lamp converters, large-faced playing cards, card holders and deck shufflers, pencils with grips for arthritic fingers, diabetic chocolates and jams, and a whole range of useful and attractive bathroom accessories.

Haute Dogs and Cats

Bowsers Boutique, 189 Highbourne Road, provides such necessities of a dog's life as silver dinner bowls, bow ties, hair bows, and designer leather coats with matching collars and leashes. For the truly serious-minded there are doggie life preservers, biscuits imported from Famous Fido's Deli in Chicago, dog beds custom-upholstered to match your living room, color intensifier shampoo to bring out Spot's shining highlights, and the Yuppy Puppy Treat Machine, a device with a bone-shaped handle for the dog to push so the treat comes out. Owner Eileen Wright outfits her clients in handknit sweaters, pink frilly dresses, or an English Lakeland coat. Grooming is available Mondays and Thursdays only. **Le Chaton**, 781 Queen Street East, has everything for cats from Sherlock Holmes deerstalker hats to jeweled gowns. You can also buy Siamese and Burmese kittens as well as a few other exotic breeds.

Jewelry

Emotional Outlet, 2487-½ Yonge Street, sells jewelry on consignment by Canadian designers at good prices. **Fortune's Fine Jewellery**, 1901 Avenue Road, is a new store with a talented designer, Michael S. de Costa, who handles everything from start to finish on the premises. **Harhay & McKay Jewellery**, the Holt Renfrew Centre, upper level, 50 Bloor Street West, is one of Canada's most progressive gallery shops, representing 16 artists who work in precious and not-so-precious materials. **The Jew-**

ellery Shop, Art Gallery of Ontario, 317 Dundas Street West, has a reputation for having the best hand-crafted sterling-silver jewelry by contemporary Canadian artists. **The Lapis Touch**, 80 Front Street East, is known for its unusual gold and silver jewelry designed with lapis lazuli from Afghanistan. Custom work is always welcome here.

Lace
Filigree Linens and Lace, 1210 Yonge Street, sells heirloom lace made up in sheets, pillowcases, curtains, bedspreads, and dress collars. **The Irish Shop**, Bloor Street West, also has old lace collars, accessories, and blouses.

Military Insignia and Miniatures
Toys for Big Boys, at Harbourfront Antique Market, has a wide range of militaria, including antique guns. **Labell's Toy Soldiers**, 100 Front Street West (Royal York Hotel, arcade level), sells a bewildering array of military miniatures perfect in every detail. You name it, Labell makes it: French cavalry figures, British soldiers from the Napoleonic Wars, Canadian soldiers from the War of 1812 to World War II, and Prussian hussars circa 1907. What better souvenir of Canada than a Mountie, on horseback or standing with a lance. The range is enormous, and the shop will sell you figures marching, running, firing, kneeling, even dying.

Museum Shops
ROM (Royal Ontario Museum), 100 Queen's Park, has three shops full of treasures and bargains. Best buys are the Portuguese ceramics, Thai tapestries, chess sets (some of which come in on consignment), and books. The tiny Reproduction Shop at the entrance has jewelry, scarves, pillowcases, and carved wooden wall decorations reproduced from the museum's collection.

Old Maps and Engravings
Beach Antique Maps and Prints, Harbourfront Antique Market, specializes in North American maps of the 18th and 19th centuries—at bargain prices. They also have a complete collection of Canadian and American landscapes from as little as $50 up to $1,000. **The Map Room** at Explorer House on Birch Street also has a good selection, but their prices are much higher.

Rare Musical Instruments

Remenyi House of Music, 210 Bloor Street West: Michael Remenyi is the third generation of a family-owned business, which started in Budapest in 1890 and travelled to Toronto in 1959. It's the only music store in Canada with a special harp salon. They specialize in antique instruments: stringed instruments, plucked instruments, brass, and woodwinds. The oldest instrument here is an early 17th-century violin. There is an artists' room in the basement where concert musicians come to practice when they're performing in Toronto.

Southpaws

The Sinister Shoppe (call 366-1790 for an appointment) has everything for left-handed people, including all kinds of kitchen supplies and instruction books on a wide range of subjects, from needlepoint to woodcarving.

Vintage Clothing

These are a few of the best places to find what your grandmother wore: **Black Market**, 323A Queen Street West, **Courage My Love**, 14 Kensington Street, **Divine Decadence**, 7 Charles Street West, and **Flying Down to Rio**, 614 Yonge Street.

—Sherry Boeckh

ONTARIO PROVINCE

By David E. Scott, Jean Danard,
and Steve Veale

*David E. Scott, the author of the Southwestern Ontario
section, also wrote the chapter on Quebec Province. Jean
Danard, who contributed the section on Muskoka and
Ontario's Near North, has lived in many parts of Ontario
and is now based in Toronto. She was travel and tourism editor of Canada's* Financial Post *before becoming a
free-lance writer. Steve Veale, the author of the Northern
Ontario and Eastern Ontario sections, also contributed
several sections on Toronto.*

Ontario is a vast province—not only to its north, up to
Hudson Bay, but east to west. It stretches from near
Montreal in the east to close to Winnipeg, Manitoba, in
the west. Down in the United States, this would be like a
single state with New York City at the east and Minneapolis, Minnesota, at the west.

An area this large—and diverse—will of course have
various regions, each offering a different experience to
visitors. For Ontario, that is first of all semi-urban *Southwestern Ontario,* the peninsula-like piece of land southwest of Toronto that is seemingly surrounded by the
Great Lakes.

Then there is the vacation cottage country just to the
north of Toronto and Lake Ontario: *Muskoka and the
Near North.* Next is *Eastern Ontario,* the water-oriented
stretch of land along the St. Lawrence River northeast of
Toronto and then inland and north to Ottawa. Finally, all
the rest: *Northern Ontario* (which might just as well be

called Western Ontario), the largely mountainous, distinctly non-urban area north of Lakes Huron and Superior.

SOUTHWESTERN ONTARIO

Southern Ontario is the commercial center of Canada, and the part of the country where business-oriented people will feel most at home. It is a region inhabited by merchants and wheeler-dealers. Nowhere is this more manifest than in the golden horseshoe, the nickname for the curve around the northwest end of Lake Ontario that runs from Oshawa in the east through Toronto to Hamilton in the west. Golden is not a reference to summer sunsets or autumn leaves in this the region where most of Canada's big business deals are struck. Golden refers instead to the costly mineral mined several hundred miles north of this area; its buying power is exchanged in tons of paper in the south, where money talks louder than in any other part of the Dominion.

It is not until you get about 80 km (50 miles) north of the Macdonald-Cartier Expressway (Highway 401)—the umbilical cord of southern Ontario's economy—that people generally are found to lead a more gentle lifestyle. Though some may resent to a degree the intrusion of strangers in their quiet communities, most will nonetheless pause to exchange greetings and comment on the weather.

The weather in Southwestern Ontario, in fact, is the despair of its forecasters. This region is almost an island, so winds coming to it across bodies of water pick up unpredictable amounts of precipitation. The region's southern shore is on Lake Erie; on the west it is separated from the state of Michigan by the Detroit River, the 460-square-mile Lake St. Clair, the St. Clair River, and Lake Huron, which wraps around the northern limit of Southwestern Ontario in the form of Georgian Bay. Even easterly winds blowing into Southwestern Ontario pass over Lake Ontario; those from the northeast cross Lake Simcoe, and east of that an area riddled with lakes and waterways.

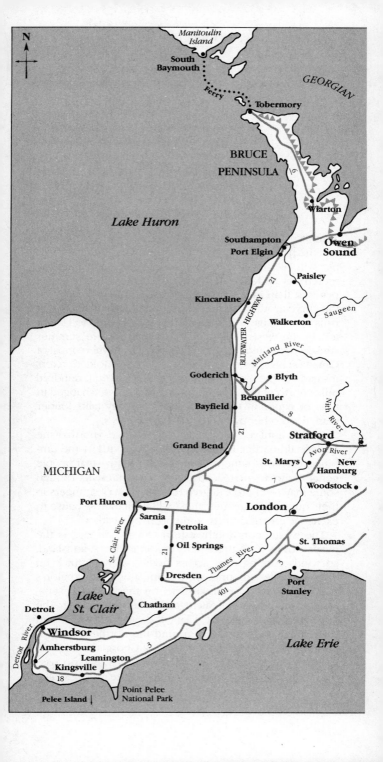

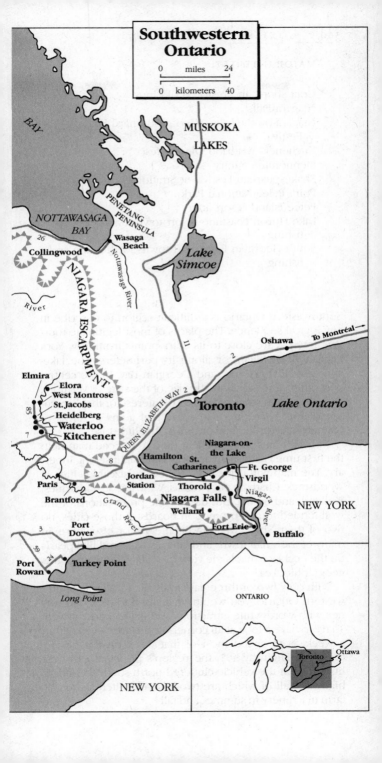

Southwestern Ontario

| 0 | miles | 24 |
| 0 | kilometers | 40 |

BAY

MUSKOKA LAKES

NOTTAWASAGA BAY

PENETANG PENINSULA

Wasaga Beach

Lake Simcoe

Collingwood

26

NIAGARA ESCARPMENT

Nottawasaga River

River

To Montréal

Oshawa

2

Elmira

Elora

West Montrose

St. Jacobs

Heidelberg

Waterloo

Kitchener

85

7

QUEEN ELIZABETH WAY

2

Toronto

Lake Ontario

Niagara-on-the Lake

Hamilton

St. Catharines

Ft. George

Virgil

8

Jordan Station

Thorold

Paris

2

Niagara Falls

Brantford

Grand River

Welland

Niagara River

NEW YORK

3

Port Dover

59

Fort Erie

Buffalo

Port Rowan

24

Turkey Point

Long Point

NEW YORK

ONTARIO

Toronto

Ottawa

MAJOR INTEREST

Craft shops and restored old inns
Niagara Falls
Niagara-on-the-Lake's George Bernard Shaw
    Festival
Kitchener–Waterloo Oktoberfest
Mennonite country
Shakespearean Festival at Stratford
Point Pelee National Park
Pelee Island resort area
Lake Huron coastline resort towns and deepwater
    fishing
South Georgian Bay resort towns for hunting and
    fishing

Southwestern Ontario is a difficult region to describe in any logical sequence. The places of most legitimate touristic interest are close to its entry points from New York State and Michigan, or along its perimeters—the lakeshores of Erie, Huron, and Georgian Bay. In the central part of this area, roughly the size of the state of Vermont, there are some scattered points of interest for the discerning visitor. There are also some real gems in terms of country inns for lodging or dining, but little else.

Nor will Ontario's excellent (and free) road map help the first-time visitor plan a worthwhile sight-seeing itinerary. The map will draw your eye to the sizeable cities of Woodstock, Chatham, St. Thomas, Windsor, St. Catharines, Welland, and Sarnia. But despite the protestations of the well-funded tourist-promotion boards of those cities, no two of them share what awaits the visitor elsewhere, in many of the small towns and villages scattered like pearls on the necklace that is the very irregular boundary of this geographic area.

With only two or three days available to sample Southwestern Ontario, you would be advised to pick one corner with worthwhile attractions and get to know it well. To try to have a look at all corners of the area, even within a week, is to spend most of that week on the heavily trafficked Highway 401, the region's principal east-west link, and on the vehicle-cluttered north-south secondary highways, all of which are two-lane and often shared by farm machinery in summer and fall.

THE NIAGARA FALLS AREA

The greatest concentration of attractions is in the extreme southeast of this region, on either side of Niagara Falls. The 35-mile length of Ontario's border with New York State has been showcased by the Niagara Parks Commission, a 103-year-old organization that operates on its own revenues and is not beholden to any political body for funds or direction.

The NPC has, over the years, acquired most of the riverfront property along the Niagara River, which it has turned into a long, narrow parkland where picnickers, cross-country skiers, bird watchers, and sunbathers are welcome at no charge. What used to be a six-month-long traffic snarl in the immediate area of the falls now won't frustrate the visitor, who can park in spacious lots and be taken to the falls on rubber-tired people movers.

Niagara Falls

The city of Niagara Falls has spent a lot of money cleaning up its core area, which used to be a glare of neon signs and tatty billboards directing the unwary to a variety of sleazy operations where they would be fleeced for tacky kitsch and served the kind of food that has incited prison riots. There still exist a number of questionable attractions for which admissions are charged, but most visitors with intelligence can easily determine what's worth shelling out a fistful of dollars to see.

The city's premier attraction is free, and each night throughout the year the three famous falls of Niagara are floodlit with moving colored lights, courtesy of the NPC. The falls should be seen both by day and by night. One of the best observation points for night viewing is from the dining room of the 50-story **Skylon Tower**. There you can have one of the best meals available in the city and area, and, as you enjoy it with a reasonably priced bottle of wine whose grapes were grown just down the road, the dining room slowly revolves 360 degrees.

That experience is doubly enjoyable from mid-November to mid-February, when the city is lighted by millions of colored lights as the owners of companies, hotels, private residences, and the other towers vie to outdo each other with variations on the Christmas-season lighting spectacle.

During cold winters, spray from the 162-foot-high Horseshoe Falls freezes on everything nearby, creating grotesquely attractive ice formations on trees, buildings, railings, lamp posts—and your car, if you've parked too close. Most years, ice cakes carried down the Niagara River from Lake Erie form a bridge across the river below the falls. Walking across the ice bridge was one of Niagara's winter tourist musts, until the bridge collapsed unexpectedly in 1912 and swept three visitors to their deaths.

Since the first European, Jesuit missionary Louis Hennepin saw Niagara Falls in 1678, the spectacle has drawn millions of tourists, and a considerable number of daredevils and suicides. A number of museums around the city attempt to chronicle the adventures of the six daredevils who have survived the plunge, those who have walked tightropes across the falls' face, and those who died in their escapade. No matter how carefully the various police forces patrol the falls area, an average of six bodies turn up each year in the giant whirlpool several miles below the falls.

(It isn't mentioned in any tourist literature, or by guides in and around the falls, but a word of warning is in order for those viewing the Horseshoe Falls from their closest edge on the Canadian side. Staring for any length of time at the smooth curve of water at the very lip of the falls can exert a magnetism—a fatal magnetism believed to have lured a number of people to their deaths. This observation point has recently been moved back a distance from the edge, and a higher fence has been erected.)

If you're going to enter any museum, make it the **Niagara Falls Museum**. It's North America's oldest and has a bit of everything—including seven authentic Egyptian mummies and the Daredevil Hall of Fame.

The visitor to Niagara Falls has shortchanged himself if he has not taken in the view from behind the falls and from below the falls on one of the **Maid of the Mist** sightseeing boats. The trip under the falls (Table Rock Scenic Tunnels) starts beneath Table Rock House, a limestone building near the lip of the Horseshoe Falls. Participants are outfitted with rubber boots, slickers, and hats, and then walk along a tunnel blasted through the rock behind the falls. There are openings in the tunnel through which you can see the wall of water roaring past and get a better idea of its volume and violence. There's also a viewing station halfway down the cliff; it is usually battered by heavy spray, a refreshing way to cool off on a hot summer day.

A short distance below the falls is a small pier from which sight-seeing boats take visitors up the Niagara Gorge to the base of the falls. The Maid of the Mist boats go as close to the base as they can—what appears as water directly in front of the wall of falling water is mostly air. Again, sightseers are dressed in rain gear against the capricious sheets of spray.

Yet another way to view the falls is by helicopter. The flight takes you across the giant whirlpool several miles downstream from the falls, and up the gorge of sheer rock cliffs to the falls. The final examination for the state of your heart is when the pilot banks the chopper around the lip of the Horseshoe Falls. It's one of those experiences you can carry to your grave.

Another thrill at Niagara is a trip across the **Giant Whirlpool** in the Spanish Aero Car. The whirlpool is several miles below the falls and is traversed by a large, open cable car that tends to swing and sway as it carries passengers on a round trip across the river at a dizzying height above the foam-flecked maelstrom below.

Though it may not be the "honeymoon capital" of the world any more, Niagara Falls still has hundreds of hotels, motels, cottages, and guest houses for honeymooners or anyone else. These range from the largest, the **Brock** and the **Foxhead**, with 238 and 400 rooms respectively, which are both connected to Maple Leaf Village, to the homier **Old Stone Inn** and **Holiday Inn by the Falls**, both near the Skylon Tower. You might even stay at the **Honeymoon City Motel**, next to the House of Frankenstein among the garish neon of Clifton Hill.

However, for all the accommodation in the Falls, it's best to go to one of the lovely inns on the lake, just down the parkway in Niagara-on-the-Lake. Book early; they are often filled with Shaw Festival theatergoers all summer long.

Niagara-on-the-Lake

From Niagara Falls you can drive south to **Fort Erie**, or north to Niagara-on-the-Lake. If time is short, skip the Fort Erie section, whose highlight in summer is a restored fort (originally built in 1764) facing Buffalo, with a military museum staffed by students dressed in period costume. Just outside Niagara-on-the-Lake is **Fort George** (1796), also facing New York State across the mouth of the Niagara River, and also staffed by students in period costume.

Niagara-on-the-Lake is a delight, although the reluctance by some of its influential residents (outside the retail sector) to share their lovely and historic town with the rest of the world makes for traffic snarls at the height of the summer-long tourist season, particularly on weekends. There isn't enough room for the invasion of motor coaches, motor homes, cars, and camper trucks to park along the streets of this community of 12,000 people, and the town has not seen fit to establish a parking lot outside town—because that would only encourage more visitors to come to the already crowded sidewalks, shops, restaurants, and pubs.

Theatergoers will know this village for the **George Bernard Shaw Festival**, the only professional theater company in the world devoted to the performance of the works of Shaw and his contemporaries. This cultural magnet had its humble origins in 1962 with underpaid thespians strutting the boards of an improvised stage in the old Victorian-era town hall.

The patrons were loyal, the stage drew increasingly impressive casts—Jessica Tandy, Paxton Whitehead, and Kate Reid, among others, have appeared here—and the festival now draws 290,000 people to a 16-year-old theater at the south edge of town. The brown brick building is mercifully shielded by landscaping and mature trees from the scenic Niagara Parkway drive, as its modern architectural style suits the town as gracefully as the Golden Arches at the north end of the community's main street.

The town's historic appearance is authentic. Niagara-on-the-Lake, known as Newark in 1792, was then site of the first parliament of the territory of Upper Canada. There are half a dozen excellent inns here, some of which were built for that purpose up to 150 years ago.

The relaxed, old-English atmosphere of the **Oban Inn** has been preserved with all modern conveniences, but book early; they have only 23 rooms and a permanent waiting list. It's also just steps from the local golf course. Avoid lunches at the Oban; while the food is good, they cater to crowded bus tours. **The Prince of Wales**, in the center of town, is a large luxury hotel with 104 rooms that are usually filled with theatergoers. This is the place to book a five-star dinner; they also serve a light piano bar buffet aprés-theatre. (For more casual dining, try the front porch of **The Buttery** across the street.) Another inn in the same $100-per-couple price range is the **Pillar and Post**. Its 91 well-appointed rooms are just a few blocks from the town square. Those seeking cozier, less expensive rooms might check out the 22-room **Moffat Inn**, the 9-room **Gate House**, or the 12-room **Angel Inn**. If you decide to visit the Angel, keep an eye out for the ghost who, according to legend, still wanders the halls at night.

A few miles upriver, in the quiet, historic village of Queenston, is the **South Landing Inn**. In the mid-1800s, when Queenston was a busy trans-shipment point on the Great Lakes, there were 13 inns here; The South Landing is the only one still in operation. Finally, the **Beacon Motor Inn**, 16 miles towards Toronto on the Queen Elizabeth Way, is a 58-unit motel offering excellent value, all services, and a regionally renowned nightly smorgasbord. All units and the dining room overlook Lake Ontario and the Toronto skyline.

From late summer to late autumn, the Niagara Peninsula is a cornucopia of fresh fruits and vegetables. There are fruit stands along all major highways, selling everything from fresh apple cider and grape juice to pumpkins and potatoes. The most comprehensive and freshest display you'll find on the peninsula is on Lincoln County Road 55, the route you'd take from Niagara-on-the-Lake to Thorold, the next major tourist attraction in the Niagara Peninsula. Just past the hamlet of Virgil, on the right and behind well-tended flower beds, you'll find **Harvest Barn Country Market**. This market stocks everything grown locally and imports other fruits and vegetables from around the world. There's a small bakery on the premises; tables are provided so you can dig right into the fresh produce, baked goods, and salads.

The town of **Thorold**, about 24 km (15 miles) south of Niagara-on-the-Lake, and a bit west of Niagara Falls, has only one feature to recommend it to the attention of visitors. The paper-mill town of 16,000 is on the **Welland Canal**, a 26-mile-long system of locks that raise ships 326.5 feet from Lake Ontario to Lake Erie. The 24-unit **Lock 7 Motel** at Thorold was built to overlook the final lock in the system. The motel is popular with ship watchers from April to the end of December, during which season about 4,000 ships—up to 730 feet in length—transit the lock right in front of the motel's picture windows. During shipping season, reservations are essential at this comfortable, family-owned motel, which serves only breakfast in its modest dining room.

The four-lane Queen Elizabeth Way (QEW) links the Niagara Peninsula with Highway 401, from which you can travel east to Toronto, or west to London and Windsor. Within this peninsula are the exceptions to the observation that most of Southwestern Ontario's points of touristic interest are around its perimeter.

Hamilton

This city of 300,000 is built under and upon an outcrop of the Niagara Escarpment west of Niagara Falls. It is the steel capital of Canada but, somewhat paradoxically, also home to a 2,500-acre botanical garden and an art gallery, the third largest in Ontario. Two museums are noteworthy: the Canadian Football Hall of Fame and Museum, which traces the 119-year history of the game in Canada, and the Canadian Warplane Heritage Museum, whose 35 aircraft are all capable of flying.

The city's foremost attraction is **Dundurn Castle**, the 19th-century, 35-room mansion of Sir Allan Napier McNab, prime minister of the United Provinces of Canada, 1854–1856. Just outside Hamilton (west off Highway 8, south of Cambridge, and well signposted) is **African Lion Safari**, a drive-through wildlife park with railway, cruise boat, petting area, and daily animal and bird shows. Excellent and reasonable lunches and dinners are available in a restored grist mill at nearby Ancaster; try to get a seat at the **Ancaster Old Mill** overlooking the dam and mill race.

There's a choice of accommodation in the downtown area, ranging from the sparkling new 300-room **Sheraton Hamilton** to the refurbished old-style luxury of the **Royal Connaught**. The food at **Vinton's Restaurant** in the Connaught gives it the edge.

Brantford

The man whose genius lets Brantford (west of Hamilton) call itself the Telephone City lived here with his family between 1870 and 1881, during which time he made the world's first long-distance telephone call from here to Paris, eight miles to the northwest.

The **Alexander Graham Bell Homestead** is a national historic site. About 90 percent of the period furnishings are original, but the instrument with which Bell made history is a replica; the original is in the United States. Next door to the Bell Homestead is the house of the Rev. Thomas Henderson, the first telephone business office in Canada, in which displays trace the evolution of the telephone from 1876 to the present.

The trek to **Paris**, following the route of the world's first long-distance telephone call, will be disappointing because the event is commemorated only by a plaque on a storefront, but just up the street from the plaque is a store that will make the detour to Paris worthwhile for shoppers. **John M. Hall's Linen Store** is like a living museum of a turn-of-the-century retail dry-goods establishment. The stock of quality linen and textile goods here draws a clientele from miles around.

Along the way to Paris is one of Ontario's finest restaurants, **The Olde School House Restaurant**. Steaks, salads, fish, and chops, some with a Greek flavor, are served in this turn-of-the-century schoolhouse, which hasn't lost its scholastic air. Be sure to finish up with a chocolate mouse—that's right, mouse. Paris, population 7,500, is at the confluence of the Nith and Grand rivers, just where each has carved a steep valley through the Niagara Escarpment. Paris is one of a number of Ontario communities calling itself "the prettiest town in Ontario," and it certainly is one of the beauty spots in Southwestern Ontario, a region that is alternately heavily populated or rolling farm country. The town has a dozen houses, two churches, and several walls built in cobblestone architecture—a rare building style in Canada—utilizing small, water-washed stones laid in horizontal rows.

THE KITCHENER–WATERLOO AREA
Kitchener–Waterloo

The twin cities of Kitchener and Waterloo, about 48 km (30 miles) northwest of Hamilton, are the gateway to Mennonite Country. For ten days in early to mid-October the cities, whose combined population is about 200,000, draw up to 600,000 people to **Oktoberfest**, a harvest blast floated on beer and held in 30 festival halls and tents, with related sporting events and a three-mile-long parade.

Of all the many farmers' markets in the province, Kitchener's is easily the most impressive. Four years ago it was incorporated into the vibrant new **Market Square**.

The complex is enclosed in green-tinted glass complete with clock tower and about 70 shops and boutiques. The square is connected by a glass-wrapped second-floor walkway to the **Valhalla Inn**, one of two properties in downtown Kitchener recommended as a base from which to explore this historic area of the province. The market's 100 vendors offer the usual meats, fish, and vegetables, as well as plants and a wide range of handcrafts. Hours are every Saturday from 5:00 A.M. to 2:00 P.M. and, from May to December, Wednesdays from 7:00 A.M. to 2:00 P.M.

Directly across the street from the Valhalla Inn is a glockenspiel that sounds daily at 12:15, 3:00, and 5:00 P.M. Immediately adjacent is the Kitchener Chamber of Commerce office, from which you can get detailed information about the attractions in the area. The **Walper Terrace Hotel** is one block north. After standing empty for several years, the 96-year-old, 115-room hotel has been completely restored to all its former elegance. Every original feature—from wooden trim moldings to carved marble pillars, from the ornate brass bannister of the main staircase to the Art Deco floor of the Terrace Café—has been faithfully refinished. The restored features have been pulled together by the skillful use of plush broadloom and pastel wallpapers and drapes. Each room has at least one piece of period cherry-wood furniture, along with the amenities you expect in a first-class hotel. Three restaurants and three lounges are available in-house. There's a mini-mall on the hotel's lower level with about a dozen shops.

Woodside National Historic Park in Kitchener is the boyhood home of William Lyon Mackenzie King, the tenth prime minister of Canada. The home is in a pleasant park setting and has been faithfully restored to the 1890s period. In Waterloo, which is really the northern extension of the city of Kitchener, is the **Seagram Museum**. The museum promotes the Seagram company product—alcoholic beverages—but explains the wine-and-spirits industry with artifacts from around the world. Open daily except Mondays.

St. Jacobs

St. Jacobs, about 24 km (15 miles) west of Kitchener and Waterloo, is at the heart of Ontario's Mennonite country. You'll first notice the extra-wide graveled shoulders of the secondary highways in the region, and before long you'll spot one or more of the black, horse-drawn buggies. You'll find after a short time in this region that you're not driving your car as fast as usual and that you've decided there's time for that second cup of coffee after lunch or dinner.

To watch the Mennonites go about their daily business is to watch a lifestyle from another era, the lifestyle of our forefathers, when life might have involved harder and longer physical work but was not as complicated, fast-paced, and downright hectic as it seems to be nowadays.

Benjamin's Restaurant and Inn is a great place for lunch or to stay overnight in one of the nine guest rooms in this recently reopened 1852-vintage inn. Kitty-corner in former grain storage silos from the old flour mill are **Village Silos**, now boutiques for local artisans and artists, where you can find almost any sort of craft or gift item. The **Jakobstettel Guest House** has 12 rooms in a turn-of-the-century red brick mansion on five landscaped acres, with swimming pool and clay tennis court.

In any direction from St. Jacobs are small villages, many with country inns where you can enjoy Mennonite cooking. The hitching rails in front of the stores in this area are not for effect; you'll see horses tethered, attached to the black carriages.

One of the best meals you'll find in the area is at the 151-year-old **Heidelberg Brewery and Restaurant** in the hamlet of the same name. Meals are served on nine-by-thirteen-inch platters; the ribs hang over the nine-inch side and a pigtail hangs over the 13-inch one. The Bavarian lager beer brewed and served here has a loyal local following. An adjoining 16-unit motel is in the $35-a-night range; the far-more-than-you-can-or-should-eat platters of food are under $10 a serving.

A few miles north of St. Jacobs is **Elmira**, another Mennonite town worth a visit. Shoppers can cross most souvenir and household items off their lists at **Brox's Olde Town Village Co. Ltd.**, a two-story emporium built of rough lumber and chockablock with interesting inventory.

West Montrose, just a speck on the map a half-dozen miles due east of Elmira, is a very special place for a picnic with goodies you bought at the Kitchener or Waterloo farmers' markets. Ontario's only covered bridge spans the Grand River here, and the scenery is bucolic. The lawns surrounding the approaches to the bridge are privately owned, but picnickers who respect the environment are welcome. The general store is renowned in the area for its ice cream cones, and also has an assortment of handcrafts in stock.

Elora

A few miles north of Elmira and West Montrose is the picture-postcard village of Elora. Pre-Confederation limestone buildings cluster around the banks of the Grand River as it froths through the jagged Elora Gorge. The village is anchored by an old grist mill turned swank hostelry with a deserved wide reputation for excellent Canadian and international cuisine: the Elora Mill.

The **Elora Mill** has 35 guest rooms in four original stone buildings. Each of the rooms is different in floor plan and decor, but all have period pine furniture and quilts handmade by area Mennonites. No room or hallway is without some section of original stonework or hand-hewn wooden beams. Just down the road is the **Desert Rose Inn**, which has five rooms set in a 122-year-old stone building.

Within the immediate vicinity of the mill there's a profusion of boutiques, pottery and antiques stores, and half a dozen European-style restaurants in original stone or frame buildings, most dating from the 1850s. The quiet, tree-lined streets invite strolling, and the boutiques invite browsing.

If the weather is on your side consider hiking the **Elora Gorge**, a pretty stretch of the Grand River with sheer limestone walls up to 100 feet high and trimmed with cedar trees. Pathways with sturdy guard rails follow the gorge walls. Do not attempt this hike in high-heeled or leather-soled shoes. The ground is often wet, and the trail is rough with loose gravel and sharp stones.

New Hamburg

About 24 km (15 miles) west of Kitchener, just off Highway 7, is the town of New Hamburg, which many travellers make the mistake of bypassing. The **Waterlot Inn** here overlooks a millpond off the Nith River, in a building erected by the local mill owner around 1846. The style defies simple description. Most of the brick building is Victorian, but a nonfunctional cupola adds an Italian flavor. The inn's restaurant enjoys a wide reputation for French cuisine and has earned numerous culinary awards. There are four dining rooms and a café patio-lounge. Try for a table overlooking the millpond and the beautiful lawns shaded by huge willows.

Three blocks from the heart of town is the **Selfhelp Crafts Canada** outlet, a Mennonite project to help Third World countries. The goods for sale at the center have been produced in 20 countries. The wood-carver, metal-worker, weaver, embroiderer, or jeweler sets the price for the article he or she has created. Selfhelp is a nonprofit program, and the only additions to the price at which the Third World producer sells his goods are the cost of transportation, customs, warehousing, and administration of the Selfhelp program, which has more than 100 outlets across Canada and the United States. The New Hamburg store, at 175 Waterloo Street, has brassware, hand-carved wooden articles, batik, jute mats, tooled leather, embroidered and handwoven linens, handcrafted greeting cards, baskets, wickerwork, jewelry, dolls, and toys. Next door, the Mennonites operate a used-clothing store, and on the other side of Selfhelp is **Riverside Brass**, a store that advertises its four rooms full of Canadian-made and imported brass items as the largest offering of brassware in Canada.

STRATFORD

From a modest but ambitious start in 1953, the **Stratford Shakespearean Festival** has become a major world theatrical event that draws more than 400,000 people annually to this city of 26,000 on the Avon River. Any physical resemblance to Stratford-upon-Avon in England is deliberate . . . and there are many.

The city now has three theaters. Festival Theatre, with its Shakespearean productions, is the major operation, but there are also the Avon Theatre and Third Stage, which offer music, opera, and contemporary drama. Tickets to Festival Theatre productions can be ordered through the box office; Tel: 519-273-1600.

Stratford's season is May 1 to mid-October. The city has more than 500 hotel and motel rooms to accommodate theatergoers, but there's one delightful inn right on the main street that is easily overlooked: **Bentley's Jester Arms Inn**, with 13 suites spread across parts of three buildings. Only four of the suites have windows facing outside; the other nine have skylights but are decorated so cleverly that it's some time before you notice your room has no windows. The suites used to be small apartments, and the kitchen equipment was left in each room. Most of the suites will sleep six (two people in a second-level loft). If you can't handle stairs, forget the Jester Arms. You have to climb 24 stairs to get to your room and another dozen to get to the second-level loft. Downstairs, there's a restaurant called **Bentley's**, serving lunch, afternoon tea (June through August), and dinner, and the inn has a delightful pub designed by someone who knows what an English pub ought to be like. Another good hotel, the 135-year-old **Queen's Inn**, reopened last year after a total renovation and rejuvenation. The 30 rooms and suites are elegantly decorated. The **Taylor and Bate Ltd. Brewing Pub** at street level revives a tradition started 155 years ago in St. Catharines by the owners' ancestors. The pub is a popular venue for locals and visitors, offering both bar stools and comfortable chairs.

Because of the large crowds the theaters draw to Stratford, the city has far more pubs and top-notch dining establishments than most cities of its size. Many stay open year-round. A handful of good pubs are within a few blocks of Jester Arms. At **Jay's** in the Albert Place Hotel you can have your drinks on sofas set around a blazing fire. **The Belfry**, above the also recommended **Church Restaurant**, is noted for its excellent, though expensive, food; the **Old English Parlor** is another fine pub. The younger set congregate at **Classics** or **Rumors**.

About ten miles west of Stratford, in the prosperous 19th-century town of **St. Marys**, is a well-preserved Victorian business district of limestone buildings, and another fine country inn, the **Westover Inn**, which opened in 1987. There are 22 bedrooms in three buildings—one used to be the dormitory when the estate was a Roman Catholic seminary—and the *nouvelle* cuisine here is gaining a dedicated following.

LONDON

This city of 285,000 people is almost exactly midway between Toronto and Windsor. Colonel John Graves Simcoe chose the site in 1792 for the future capital of Upper Canada, but he was subsequently overruled by a superior. It's nicknamed the Forest City because of the many venerable trees that shade its streets of stately homes.

Old money is alive and well here, and it shows. London is the chief metropolis of Western Ontario, a manufacturing, distributing, and financial center. There are more than 300 major industries in London, the head offices of two major life insurance companies and two trust companies, and the University of Western Ontario. There are no famous tourist attractions here, except perhaps for the city itself (and its architecturally striking art gallery, which offers a series of changing exhibitions); visitors delight in exploring London because it is so clean, well maintained, and riddled with lovely parks.

The city core is presently undergoing a major construction phase that will provide several downtown hotels and a convention center. The city's latest showpiece hotel is **The Sheraton Armouries**, a glass tower rising from the former armories building. For five-star comfort at a slower pace, consider the **Idlewyld**, a 112-year-old mansion turned into a 25-room hotel with all the comforts of home. The value in town is the 259-room **Briarwood Inn**, a modest and moderately-priced establishment.

A London restaurant that has endured more than a third of a century is the **Latin Quarter**. It's a New Orleans-style courtyard café with a casual atmosphere, wrought-iron, and gas lamps, and good food at reasonable prices. **Gabriele's** is good for European cuisine. For Eastern European cuisine try the **Marienbad Restaurant** or **Chaucer's Pub**. The food is Czechoslovakian and there's a central courtyard.

Second City is a comedy cabaret, with dinner if you wish. For especially good food with a view and service to match—tableside cooking, flaming desserts—book a table at **Michael's on the Thames**.

Just east of the city there's a pioneer village on the shores of Lake Fanshawe, a man-made lake for sailing, fishing, and swimming. The London International Air Show, held in early June for two days, has become one of the biggest air shows in North America, drawing the air forces of many countries and daily paid attendance of more than 25,000 spectators.

Port Stanley, south of London on Lake Erie, is one of London's summer playgrounds. A village of just under 2,000, it jumps in the summer and snoozes through the winter. There are half a dozen interesting retail outlets, one of which is **Kettle Creek Canvas Co.**, offering home-sewn 100 percent cotton fashions for men and women. During summer you can take a 45-minute trip to the hamlet of Union and back on antique cars of the Port Stanley Terminal Rail Inc., drawn by a steam locomotive. **Kettle Creek Inn** is an elegant ten-room hotel here with hospitable bar-lounge and superb cuisine served year-round—in fine weather, you can dine on an outdoor patio.

The Lake Erie Shore

Port Stanley is representative of the tiny ports, towns, and beaches that stretch along the northern shore of Lake Erie. If you leave Highway 401 and dawdle along the lakeshore of Southwest Ontario, you will find some great little fishing villages, sand beaches, and summer festivals. These towns include the resort beaches of **Long Point**, a sandy peninsula jutting some 40 miles into Lake Erie and the cottages and marinas of **Turkey Point** and **Port Rowan**.

The quintessential beach town, however, is **Port Dover**. This resort village comes alive in summer, as tourists and cottagers parade the boardwalk, line up to munch foot-long hot dogs and steamy french fries (chips) at the **Arbor** (a classic fastfood stand that is more than 60 years old), sprawl on the beach, or sip a libation on the deck at **Callahan's** lakefront restaurant.

A major fishing fleet sails from Port Dover, so there is fresh-caught fish daily. You can sample it at **Knechtel's** on the beach, but those who know go to the **Erie Beach Hotel** for platters of perch, shrimp, scallops, their special celery bread, and pitchers of various liquids to wash it all down. The place is always crowded and you might wait for up to an hour, but this is the best fresh fish you can get.

There are plenty of rental cottages in the area but if you stay at the Erie Beach you won't have to walk far after dinner.

THE WINDSOR AREA

Essex County, at the extreme western end of Southwestern Ontario, has some points of strong visitor interest. **Point Pelee National Park** reaches like a stout icicle into Lake Erie and is the southernmost tip of the Canadian mainland, on the same latitude as northern California. The 4,000 acres are a sandspit of marsh, trees, and grass.

The point is on the flyway for many species of birds, notably Canada geese, which migrate on north-south routes, as well as the monarch butterfly. There are an interpretation center, transit trains, nature trails, picnic grounds, and a mile of boardwalk through the marsh, with observation towers for birdwatchers. There are bicycle and canoe rentals and 14 miles of sandy beaches, but because of the delicate ecology camping is not permitted.

Motel accommodation is available in Leamington 10 km (six miles) north, but is usually fully booked well in advance of the butterfly and bird migrations. Try either the **Journey's End** or the **Pelee Motor Inn**. A few miles west of Leamington, near Kingsville, is the **Jack Miner Migratory Bird Foundation**. You can see the geese from the road, and the interior grounds are open to the public every day but Sunday from October 1 to April 10, except Christmas Day, Boxing Day, and New Year's Day.

Windsor, facing Detroit to the north across the Detroit River, is the nearest city for deluxe accommodations and other services. All guest and public room windows of the 22-story **Windsor Hilton** overlook the Detroit River, touted as the world's busiest inland waterway. The Automotive City, as Windsor is nicknamed, has done wonders cleaning up its formerly tatty, junk-littered waterfront, but there are not any other major tourist attractions. (The big draws are in and around Detroit.)

Pelee Island

Southwest of the tip of Point Pelee, halfway between Ontario and the state of Ohio, is Pelee Island (pronounced Pee-lee), the largest island in Lake Erie. It is reached by toll ferries from Leamington and Kingsville, Ontario, and Sandusky, Ohio. With the exception of Middle Island, which is negligible in size, Pelee Island is Canada's southernmost possession. It's a charming escape from either mainland.

Unpaved roads circle and cross the island, which is about eight miles long and four miles wide. In the entire road system there are only one stop sign and one speed-limit sign, because it's a laid-back sort of place where nobody is ever in a hurry. The island has several comfortable small hotels, like the **Westview** (open from May to November), but it is really cottage country for families from both mainlands.

Taxes are low because the municipality raises pheasants and charges wealthy hunters a stiff license fee for the right to shoot them in the autumn. The interior of the island is given over to the production of grapes for a local winery. You can take your car or rent a bicycle for touring (the island is flat). Whether walking or bicycling, be ready to receive—and return—friendly waves from the driver of almost every passing vehicle. Information on ferry sailings, fares, and reservations (which are strongly recommended for vehicles in summer) is available seven days a week by calling toll-free in the 519 calling area: (800) 265-5683, or (519) 724-2115.

Amherstburg

This town of 8,500 residents on the Detroit River about 29 km (18 miles) south of Windsor, has several points of historical interest, and a pleasant motel on the river with excellent dining facilities—**Duffy's Motor Inn**, where all rooms have a riverview. **Fort Malden National Historic Park**, first known as Fort Amherstburg, played an active role in the War of 1812–1814 and the Rebellion of 1837–1838. The 11-acre park includes remains of the original earthworks, a restored barracks, a military pensioner's cottage, two exhibit buildings, and picnic facilities.

The **North American Black Historical Museum** tells of daring escapes by U.S. slaves and the underground railway system many used to flee to freedom in Canada. An 1848-vintage church and log cabin contains artifacts from the slavery era. Photographs, crafts, and art displays trace the origins of black people from Africa through slavery to freedom and development in the Western Hemisphere; the museum is closed Mondays and Tuesdays.

Also of interest in Amherstburg is the **Park House**, originally built on the U.S. side of the Detroit River in 1796. The owner, a Loyalist who preferred not to leave his new home on the American side after the Revolution, dismantled it, floated the materials downriver, and reassembled the home at Amherstburg around 1799. The solid log home with clapboard siding and cedar-shake roof has been restored to depict the lifestyle of the Park family, which occupied it for years. An exhibit area contains pioneer artifacts. There are demonstrations of tinsmithing and of printing on a hand-operated press, the same press that turned out the first copies of the *Amherstburg Echo* weekly newspaper in 1874. From June 1 through August 31 the house is open daily; check the schedule for off-season hours.

Sarnia

This city of 50,000 faces Port Huron, Michigan, across the St. Clair River, which flows into Lake St. Clair on its way to Lake Erie. There are three points of interest near Sarnia: The first is **Oil Springs**, a hamlet of 630 people once known as the oil capital of Canada and the world. The Oil Museum of Canada here has working models of, and actual drill rigs from, North America's first commercial oil wells. The museum is open daily May through October, and from Monday to Friday the rest of the year.

When 19th-century drillers hit oil at Oil Springs, **Petrolia**, now a town of 4,500 people about 8 km (5 miles) north, became the world's first oil boom town. By 1890 it was the hub of an intercontinental refining empire. The world's first oil exchange was housed in a building that still stands today. **Petrolia Discovery** is a 60-acre, fully operational oil field looking and working as it did in the 1800s. Interpretive exhibits and a film describe the discovery and development of oil in the area. This display area is open daily from early May to late October. Petrolia itself is a pretty town with some fine Victorian architecture.

Dresden, about 35 km (22 miles) south of Petrolia, is the site of **Uncle Tom's Cabin**, a magnet for thousands of visitors annually. Uncle Tom's real name was the Rev. Josiah Henson, and he helped black slaves who escaped to Canada from the United States. His cabin and five other buildings are open seven days a week from May to the end of October. The tulipwood siding of the key building, Uncle Tom's Cabin, is well weathered after its 147 years of exposure to the elements. You can see the square-headed hand-made nails connecting the siding to the hand-hewn beams. The windows are of bubbly, wavy glass. Other buildings include an 1850s church, a house where newly arrived escaped slaves first savored their freedom, and a museum containing rare books and documents on the abolitionist era and about Uncle Tom. Scattered throughout the museum are balls-and-chains, head irons, slave whips, handcuffs, and clubs—graphic reminders of man's inhumanity slightly more than a century ago. An agricultural building contains early farming and logging equipment, farm wagons, and buggies.

An original smokehouse for curing meat was carved from a six-foot-thick sycamore, or buttonwood, tree.

THE LAKE HURON COASTLINE

Ontario's lower Lake Huron coastline stretches 218 miles, from Sarnia north to the tip of the Bruce Peninsula, which forms Georgian Bay on its east side. Much of the coastline is fine sandy beaches dotted with small summer resorts that draw mainly from neighboring Michigan and inland Ontario.

From south to north, the main resorts are strung along Highway 21, called the Bluewater Highway, which runs from Sarnia north to Southampton, where it turns east to the town of Owen Sound. Highway 6 runs north from this point up the Bruce Peninsula to Tobermory, which is linked by two large, modern ferries to South Baymouth on Manitoulin Island, a short cut to Northern Ontario from Southwestern Ontario. (See the Northern Ontario section for details on the ferries and the island.)

Grand Bend, up the coast from Sarnia, is one of the more popular resorts. In winter it has a population of 800; on summer weekends the beach and streets are choked with tens of thousands of people lured to the sand, the marinas, the hot-dog stands, and by all the other people to watch. Grand Bend also supports two straw-hat summer theaters, Huron Country Playhouse and Playhouse II, which offer cabaret theater from late June to early September. Grand Bend got a "new" resort last year. The **Oakwood Inn Resort, Golf and Country Club** was fully renovated and expanded into one of the finest all-inclusive resorts in the province. Its showpiece is a beautifully designed indoor swimming pool.

Bayfield, a community 29 km (18 miles) north of Grand Bend, is a pretty village of old-money summer cottages, with a main street lined with trendy boutiques in Victorian-era frame buildings. The **Little Inn of Bayfield** is an outstanding historic country inn in this picturesque village; its cuisine is popular with the yachting set that flocks to a modern marina in the mouth of the Bayfield River. While in Bayfield, be sure to have an order of some of the best french-fried potatoes found anywhere in the world. They're at the **Admiral Bayfield**, a walk-up window beside the **Albion Hotel** on the main street. The Admiral Bayfield serves only french fries and soft drinks to wash them down with. The Albion, a hostelry with loads of historic charm, is a great place for a lunch stop; their house pâté plate is the best in this part of Ontario.

With an uncharacteristic lack of diplomacy, Queen Elizabeth II once called **Goderich**, north of Bayfield, "the prettiest town in Canada," a claim that can be legitimately disputed by several dozen chambers of commerce. Notwithstanding, Goderich is certainly pretty, and its octagonal town green gives the town a one-of-a-kind center, with a handsome stone courthouse in the middle. The town of 7,500 residents sits atop a bluff overlooking the Maitland River and Goderich Harbour, the largest harbor on the Canadian side of Lake Huron. Ships load grain and salt, which is mined beneath the lake bed. Artifacts from Ontario pioneer life are assembled in the 20,000-piece **Huron County Pioneer Museum** collection. Over the past three years the museum's exhibit space has trebled, so allow at least two hours for an overview of this extensive collection, which includes a restored log cabin. Admission to this museum also gets you in to the **Huron County Marine Museum**, a collection of shipping artifacts and photographs housed in the former forward cabin of an old lake freighter down by the harbor.

The old Goderich jail is also octagonal. Properly known as Huron Historic Gaol, the 148-year-old building commands the finest building site in town, overlooking the harbor and the mouth of the Maitland River. A wander through the well-preserved facility prompts the visitor to reflect that crime levels might not have reached today's proportions had not so many improvements been made to North American jails over the years. The **Bedford Hotel**, anchoring one corner of the town's square, has recently been refurbished. The 93-year-old hotel combines the local watering hole, **The Duke of Bedford Cocktail Lounge**, with the upscale **Bruno's** across the hotel lobby. Bruno's is a ristorante by day with Italian cuisine and a New York-style nightclub by night. The hotel also has a traditional dining room which is bright and airy with a reasonably priced menu heavy on fresh lake fish and seafood.

Kincardine, a town of 6,000, also has its fine beach on Lake Huron, and attracts thousands in the summertime. Because there are so many year-round residents, the town doesn't have the carnival atmosphere you experience at Grand Bend.

Deepwater fishing charters in boats with all the latest

scientific gadgets for taking the guesswork—and sport—out of salmon fishing are available the length of the Lake Huron coastline, but the largest concentration of outfitters is in **Port Elgin**, a town of 6,000 north up the coast from this point. The electronics available to outwit fish are so baboon-proof that some outfitters advertise partial money-back guarantees if they're unable to get your hook into the mouth of a fish.

The Saugeen River flows into Lake Huron at **Southampton**, another small town on yet another fine sandy beach. This is also a reserved resort town where old money maintains all-season house-size cottages, and the tennis club has one of the largest membership rolls in Canada.

The town of **Tobermory**, at the tip of the Bruce Peninsula, is developing a substantial winter season with the increasing popularity of cross-country skiing and snowmobiling. There's such a large guaranteed annual snowfall that the Bruce Peninsula Snowmobile Trail Association maintains 1,000 miles of groomed snowmobile trails. Tobermory is also the terminal for the Chi-Cheemaun and Nindawayma car ferries to South Baymouth on Manitoulin Island off the Lake Huron north shore (see the Northern Ontario section below). **Wiarton**, at the foot of the peninsula and facing into Georgian Bay, recently earned the questionable distinction of Ontario's record for a year's snowfall—more than 20 feet. Prior to the enthusiasm for winter sports, the remote town of Tobermory came alive only during the short summer season, when visitors came to take glass-bottom-boat trips over some of the 19 shipwrecks in the area, and to visit the "flowerpots," island monoliths of stone carved by wind and waves. The clarity of the water of Lake Huron and Georgian Bay, and the profusion of shipwrecks, draws many scuba divers here.

INLAND FROM LAKE HURON

Inland from the Bluewater Highway between Goderich and Southampton is rolling farm country dotted by quiet, long-settled hamlets and villages. The region is carved by small rivers, many ideal for canoeing, and all excellent for fishing bass, trout, and salmon. Most towns in this area still have their downtown hotel, often a 150-year-old building of quarried stone where farmers and townsfolk socialize in Canada's answer to the rural British pub. Most of the hotels also rent rooms in the $25- to $45-per-night range. You'll get what you pay for at those prices, but it's still possible to get a clean, basic private room—usually with bathroom down the hall—from $25 a night. Several towns in this region rate brief mentions.

A few miles east of Goderich, an old stone mill on the Maitland River at Benmiller has been developed into a showcase rural retreat for the well-to-do. **Benmiller Inn** has modern, fully comfort-equipped rooms and suites overlooking the river or old stone buildings of the mill complex that have been lovingly restored. There are in-room wood-burning fireplaces, Jacuzzis, saunas, walking trails, an indoor pool, and a large international menu in the beautifully wrought dining room of the main mill building.

A few miles east of Benmiller, the village of **Blyth** has two major outlets for leather goods that draw customers from a wide radius. Blyth Festival Theatre specializes in recent Canadian theater from mid-June to mid-September. Lack of accommodation at any major facility nearby has inspired at least 30 country bed-and-breakfast operations in the immediate area. For information call Ontario Travel. Tel: (416) 965-4008 or (800) 266-3735.

Paisley, nicknamed Village of Bridges, has six inside the village limits that cross the four rivers converging here. Outfitter Ted Cowan, who makes his own canoes and a unique bent-shaft wooden paddle, will rent canoes for use on the **Saugeen River**, the best canoeing river in Southwestern Ontario. If you are planning to canoe the Saugeen, consider using the **Hartley House** in Walkerton as your base. These are not five-star digs, but at about $40 a night you're getting good value in this 127-year-old hotel with uneven floors and a lobby in which you can buy a good cigar, a bus ticket, or a tin of chewing tobacco. The hotel has an enthusiastic following in this small town of about 4,500 for its bargain-priced smorgasbords, and the owners make you feel as if you're a guest in a country home.

OWEN SOUND – NOTTAWASAGA BAY

The site of the town of **Owen Sound** is like a bowl with a wedge cut from it. The missing wedge is Owen Sound itself, the deep bay off the south end of Georgian Bay. The community rises on the sides of the bowl, overlooking the bay and the other sides. Geography makes it a compact site; its distance from any major city makes it a tightly knit community. This is fishing country year-round, hunting country in season, and when the ice is gone there's a variety of water for canoeing, sailing, and motorboating. A new hotel, **Inn on the Bay**, has 56 rooms and four suites, all overlooking the harbor. For dining at its finest try **Louis' Steak and Seafood House**, just east of the town center on Highway 26.

Collingwood is the highest section of the Niagara Escarpment and the ski center of Southwestern Ontario. Some summer attractions have been built to ease the overhead for the substantial accommodation inventory built for skiers. There's a 3,000-foot slide ride reached by the ski-hill chair lift, a water slide, and a tube ride (the last two only open in summer) 13 km (8 miles) west of the town of 12,000.

Wasaga Beach, a small resort town of 4,600, is built on a sandspit between Georgian Bay and the Nottawasaga River. Its nine-mile sweep of sandy beach draws cottagers and vacationers. There are two water theme parks with slides, bumper boats, and a wave pool. A new attraction at the edge of town is a theme park filled with scale replicas, carved from sand, of some of the wonders of the ancient world. Some of the most elegant motel rooms you'll find anywhere are available at the **Dyconia Resort Hotel** in Wasaga Beach. The motel has 32 rooms in a variety of shapes, styles, and sizes. All have wood-burning fireplaces and many have double Jacuzzi tubs.

MUSKOKA AND ONTARIO'S NEAR NORTH

Southern Ontario may be the industrial heartland of Canada, but in its hinterland most people seem to be in the business of having a good time. This part of the Laurentian Shield lying between Georgian Bay and the Ottawa River is the playground of the province. Many Americans and a few British discovered the holiday pleasures of this area more than a century ago, and in recent years Continental Europeans have also been coming on the scene.

Starting 60 to 90 miles north of Toronto or Hamilton, a spectacular lakeland spreads out, one that gets more wooded and less populated as you go north. The foliage and evergreen trees screen a vast array of inns, cottages, marinas, and all those facilities that—regardless of the time of year—make outdoor life so irresistible. Therefore, on weekends, particularly in summer, thousands of city people flee the concrete, and main highways that lead north are heavy with traffic as early as Friday noon.

MAJOR INTEREST

Lake resorts
Lake cruises and houseboat touring
Trent-Severn Waterway
Fishing, even in winter
Arts-and-crafts shows
Significant historical restorations
Fairs during fall foliage season
Canoeing and camping in Algonquin Park

Quiet retreats by lakes or streams are relatively easy to discover today, but think what this land must have been like in 1610, when the Huron Indians brought Etienne Brulé, then a lad of 16, from Québec to their village on Georgian Bay, to take the place of a young Indian sent to France by Samuel de Champlain.

The vacation pleasures of the lakes at the center of the Muskoka region—Rosseau, Joseph, and Muskoka—were discovered only in 1860 when two young men came from Toronto, hiking much of the way. They subsequently brought friends, and eventually many of them bought property on the islands. Much of the land bought then— even into the 1890s—has now been passed on to the third and fourth generations.

By the 1880s the area had become a magnet in summer for affluent families from the United States and England as well as southern Ontario. At first they came only to fish or escape hay fever, but that changed quickly, and soon many would come for two months, often with guests, taking the Muskoka Express from Toronto to Graven-hurst, a three- to five-hour train trip, before boarding a lake steamer to their cottages. Boating then took up much of their time.

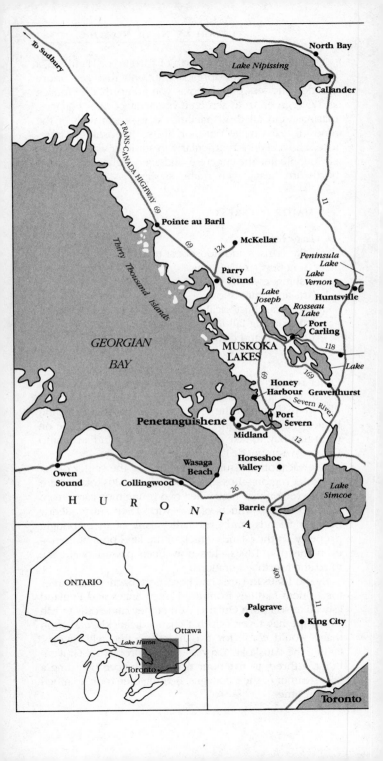

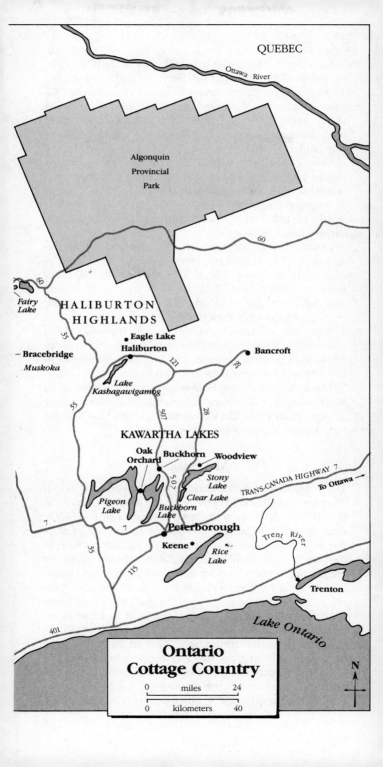

Ontario Cottage Country

In 1894 Toronto, with a population of 200,000, celebrated its 60th birthday. One February night that winter, 19 Muskoka property owners gathered in downtown Toronto to form the Muskoka Lakes Association. Today it has about 3,000 member families and a vigilant executive who make sure development does not spoil the Muskoka way of life.

Only two other Ontario areas were used as resorts before 1900: Georgian Bay's Thirty Thousand Islands and Stony Lake, one of the Kawartha Lakes used by the Indians as a natural "hospital." In the 1890s Toronto newspapers would be filled with news of summer activities at these various fashionable spots.

Ontario's near north has several large and distinct resort areas. The largest and most popular—as well as the oldest—is **Muskoka**, which, centered on the lakes of Rosseau, Joseph, and Muskoka, runs from Gravenhurst and the lower end of Georgian Bay to Huntsville in the north and **Algonquin Park** in the east.

Adjoining Muskoka's southern end is **Huronia**, which takes in the lower end of Georgian Bay west to Collingwood and, around Midland and Penetanguishene, contains the most historic sites in the province.

The lesser-developed **Haliburton** area, east of Muskoka and northeast of Lake Simcoe, abuts the southwest corner of Algonquin Park. **The Kawarthas** are just north of Peterborough, a town northeast of Toronto.

Muskoka

The small towns of **Bracebridge** and **Gravenhurst**, about 10 miles apart just off Highway 11, are the two main hubs in this area. Both lumbering communities in the 1860s, Bracebridge, now with 10,000 people and growing fast, is the more aggressive, actively courting industry as well as tourists. It is the municipal, judicial and health center for the district, home of the South Muskoka Memorial Hospital and Santa's Village, a children's amusement park. Cottagers on several lakes do most of their shopping here.

Gravenhurst, slightly smaller, revels in its location on Lakes Muskoka and Gull but also in its status as an artist's colony and cultural community. Many artists do live here (and elsewhere in Muskoka) and its opera house, built in 1901 with hammered-wood beams, attracts international artists. Gravenhurst is the home base for the Muskoka Festival, launched in 1973, which puts on Canadian plays, musicals, some children's theater, and a winter series. In summer, its productions also travel to Port Carling and occasionally to Huntsville, on Lake of Bays 30 miles north of Bracebridge. The festival is a training ground for young theater professionals and its Young Company performs at resorts, parks, and museums. Gravenhurst also has Music On the Barge, free concerts weekly by the side of Gull Lake, and both communities have a wealth of antiques and craft shows throughout the summer.

You can easily find the attractions that make people favor Muskoka. Some tourism associations here publish events booklets four times a year; you can find them in most stores, marinas, and even restaurants. Local papers and leaflets also list theater, arts-and-crafts shows, tours of artists' studios, and the like. In winter many carnivals take place.

Wherever there is a body of water, you are bound to find a cruise; information usually can be found at dockside and at the nearest lakeside town. Some operate only from late June to Labour Day, but others continue until mid-October. Overnight and longer cruises may be picked up in Gravenhurst.

The favorite on Muskoka lakes is the 99-passenger RMS *Segwun,* which is based in Gravenhurst and turned 100 years old in 1987. Sunset dinner cruises may sell out early. On Georgian Bay, where the Thirty Thousand Islands and rocky cliffs make the scenery more spectacular, there are many trips to choose from. Cruises leave from Penetanguishene, Midland, Honey Harbour, Parry Sound, even Pointe au Baril.

The biggest event in Muskoka is the **Antique Boat Show**, held in Port Carling on a July weekend. In recent years 150 boats, some from as far away as Florida, have been on display. Music lovers head for Parry Sound at the mid-point of Georgian Bay for the **Festival of the Sound**. For three weeks starting in mid-July visitors can enjoy chamber music interspersed with lighter fare, as well as cruises on the bay and nature walks.

Muskoka Resorts

Near Huntsville, on Peninsula Lake, is the **Deerhurst Inn and Country Club**, which dates to 1896, when an owner's grandfather opened the first small lodge in the area. Deerhurst now accommodates 600 people luxuriously in inn, condominium, and time-sharing units. Entertainment includes a Las Vegas-style show, other live entertainment, and dancing in the Piano Lounge and Four Winds disco. A giant sports complex has just opened with swimming, whirlpools, and tennis, squash and racquetball courts. A second 18-hole golf course will be ready for play by early summer. Another half-dozen resorts are close by.

Visitors to the three Muskoka lakes are more apt to stay in cottages that each year get more like second homes. But there are a few inns, a top-notch one on each lake.

On Lake Rosseau is **Windermere House**, a stately, pristine-white structure with a long second-story veranda overlooking a big, sloping lawn and a marina. It started as a simple fishing lodge in 1864 but developed into a haven for gentility. Now it has wider appeal. New owners recently modernized the property and made the menu more extravagant, but the old magic and impeccable service remain. Nightly entertainment ranges from Sunday-night live theater to big-band music on Saturdays.

Muskoka Sands Resort at the tip of Lake Muskoka also had a recent multimillion dollar makeover: This 33-year-old inn was gutted in 1987 and transformed into a resort having 48 units (62 bedrooms), six swimming pools, two squash and seven tennis courts. Facilities for golf and horseback riding are nearby and 102 spanking-new condominiums, with two to four bedrooms, sit on the property. Other activity centers on **The Boathouse** at dockside, painted in pastel hues, and its whirlpool bar. At night 200 people are often found in **Steamer Jake's**, the downstairs lounge built around a huge chunk of Muskoka granite.

If you want a quiet, restful time in Muskoka at a place where privacy is paramount and the food and wine exceptional, reserve a room (two have whirlpool baths) at **Sherwood Inn** on Lake Joseph. Rooms in the cottages under towering pines are chosen first.

Most tennis buffs have heard about Muskoka's **Inn and Tennis Club at Manitou**, considered one of the finest tennis camps in North America. Tucked away on a small lake near Parry Sound, it has 13 courts (one indoors) and usually one pro to every three players.

Antiques from England, France, and Hong Kong, as well as skylights, fireplaces, and private saunas, make this an elegant retreat, one that meets Relais & Châteaux standards, including cuisine prepared by a French chef.

The **Waltonian Inn** on Lake Nipissing, an hour's drive north of Huntsville, is outside Muskoka in the Near North region and worthy of note because of its winter specialty:

ice fishing in comfort. The inn has four heated and radio-equipped Bombardiers, each seating 12 people, to take guests to one of 35 ice huts, four to six people to a hut. Lunch is brought out at noon. Guests need to bring only a jacket and boots.

Huronia

The lower end of Georgian Bay from Owen Sound to Barrie, properly but seldom called Huronia, is quite separate. Only settlers were here when Muskoka was entertaining its first guests, but resort facilities are strictly 20th-century. Today Huronia is a burgeoning year-round vacationland with skiing in winter and beach life, water slides, golf, and the like in summer. An explosion of condominiums and town houses is now transforming parts of the area. In addition to attractive, sometimes even posh, living quarters, most resorts have every conceivable facility for the sports- and fitness-minded (all resorts mentioned below have a swimming pool, a whirlpool, and a sauna, for example). There is also a variety of good cafés and restaurants, some with entertainment. Wasaga Beach in Huronia, however, is Ontario's Coney Island.

Blue Mountain at Collingwood is the largest and most developed ski resort in the province, with 28 runs, 15 lifts including a high-speed quad chair, and computerized snowmaking. Cafés and bars abound—the newest is in the recently renovated Central Base Lodge. And with three slide rides and the 18-hole Monterra golf course (play out to the bay and back to the mountain) which opened in 1989, the resort is just as busy in summer.

Visitors can stay in the 103-room **Blue Mountain Inn** or in 250 two- and three-bedroom condominiums that owners make available. The knotty pine and copper lamps of the inn (which is also a conference center) give it a friendly, rustic ambience. Fitness facilities and racket sports get wide play here; five tennis courts are in the new recreation center.

Closer to Collingwood on the same highway is **Cranberry Inn Resort**, a more upscale operation with 112 rooms and 24 suites overlooking cedar woods. Guest rooms have pine furniture and big bathrooms. Also on the property are 625 condominiums, believed to be the largest cluster in Canada. The resort has 12 tennis courts (four indoor) as well as a marina on Georgian Bay and an 18-

hole golf course, both of which opened in 1988. Horse-back riding is available nearby in summer; skiing in winter.

Horseshoe Valley, a longtime ski mecca located 10 miles west of Barrie and an hour's drive from Toronto, is another developing prime resort in Huronia. In 1987 it opened the 104-room **Inn at Horseshoe** where parlor rooms and loft suites have queen- or king-size beds, cherrywood furniture, walk-in showers, and Jacuzzis. The six loft suites have two stories, a second TV and a skylight in the bedroom. They look over the valley and the 18th hole of the golf course opening late this year. The inn itself is an elegant set-up with fine dining overseen by an Austrian chef, piano bar, four pools including one for conversation, and a billiard table. A sports and leisure complex looks after fitness needs with a small gym and two squash courts; two tennis courts are outdoors. Some condominiums are in place here, including some for time-sharing, and there are plans for more.

The little neighboring towns of **Midland** and Penetanguishene (known as **Penetang**) in Huronia pin-point the most historic area of the province. Here, on the rim of Georgian Bay, Brulé learned Indian ways and, in 1649, the Iroquois murdered Jesuit missionaries. **Sainte-Marie among the Hurons**, three miles east of Midland on Highway 12, is a reconstructed mission where student guides, some in Jesuit garb, demonstrate the making of moccasins, square nails, and so on. A film of 17th-century pioneer life is also shown. On a hill on the north side of the highway is the **Martyrs' Shrine** to commemorate the slain Jesuits. Thousands of visitors and pilgrims flock here annually, one being Pope John Paul II in 1984.

Next to Sainte-Marie, the **Wye Marsh Wildlife Center** features a floating marsh boardwalk, canoe excursions, guided nature walks, and, in winter, cross-country skiing and snowshoeing. It is open year-round, while the other attractions operate only from mid-May to mid-October.

In Midland proper, off King Street in Little Lake Park, is the **Huronia Museum** which includes a full-scale replica of a 16th-century Huron Indian village. Ten miles to the west, in Penetang, is the **Historic Naval and Military Establishments** set up in 1814 to prevent Americans from disrupting a supply route to the upper lakes. The site has reconstructions of 15 buildings and impromptu play-acting by student guides.

Haliburton and
the Kawartha Lakes

East of Highway 11, which shoots straight north out of Toronto, and east of Lake Simcoe, are two smaller vacation areas: Haliburton and the Kawartha Lakes. These areas have many of the same features as the first two regions: rocks and hills, lakes, rivers, deep snow, a profusion of spring flowers, and the unforgettably brilliant color of autumn leaves; but they are separated from Muskoka and Huronia by a land rise that directs waters west to Georgian Bay and south into the Trent system—which flows into Lake Ontario.

The **Haliburton Highlands**, which claims 600 small lakes, snuggles into the southwest arms of Algonquin Park. In winter, snowmobilers and cross-country skiers flock to the area's extensive trails. The region is noted for the School of Fine Arts in **Haliburton**—a village with its own tartan—and many attractive small inns.

One retreat eagerly sought by young and sports-minded couples who appreciate good food, contemporary surroundings, and privacy is **Sir Sam's Inn**, the one-time country home of Sir Sam Hughes, Canada's minister of defense during World War I.

On the scene since 1984 but still little-known is the **Domain of Killien**, which accommodates 30 guests in cabins and a lodge on 5,000 acres of forest and lakeland. It is owned by a French count and his two stepsons, one of whom heads the four-man team of Cordon Bleu chefs. The resort attracts nature-lovers and those who seek peace, quiet, and good food. Rooms are simple but comfortable.

PineStone Inn, built in 1976 and still expanding, caters to businesspeople, with its executive chalets, suntan and exercise studios, jogging track, meeting rooms, golf, live entertainment—you name it.

A farm in 1918, the **Wig-a-mog Inn** on Lake Kashagawigamog is now a casual, family-style, country vacation spot that can keep 135 guests happy, some in cottages and poolside suites. The atmosphere is pleasant, the food is good, and the activities are endless any time of year.

PineStone and Wig-a-mog are two of ten resorts in this area that in 1983 developed a 150-mile linked trail for cross-country skiers. All now offer lodge-to-lodge skiing in January and February; guests ski with a guide while the luggage is driven in style. **Maple Sands Resort**, a small family-style inn in Haliburton that makes its own maple syrup, looks after the registrations.

Bancroft, outside this resort area, being considerably east of Haliburton (along Highways 121 and 28), is a mecca for rock hounds seeking semiprecious stones and rare minerals. Its annual five-day **Gemboree** is held in late July or early August.

Peterborough is the gateway to the **The Kawarthas**, whose many lakes are part of the Trent-Severn Waterway. This area was first explored by Champlain in 1615 and is now popular with boaters and fishermen. The **Trent–Severn Waterway** extends from Trenton on Lake Ontario to Port Severn on Georgian Bay, a distance of 240 miles through island-dotted lakes, sleepy rivers, a few small towns, and 45 locks.

Cruisers, sailboats, outboards, even canoes use the canal system but, in summer, the section east of Lake Simcoe sees a host of houseboats. The biggest fleet here—100 boats taken over from Three Buoys Houseboat Vacations—is now operated by **Go Vacations**, a specialist in managing recreational vehicles in North America and yachts in the Caribbean. On the Trent system, boats are picked up at Oak Orchard marina, at the Narrows between Buckhorn and Pigeon lakes.

Cruises take off from a couple of other spots. In Peterborough, two- and three-hour cruises in summer depart from the wharf behind the Holiday Inn on George Street, while the 54-passenger **Island Lass** has 30-mile cruises of Clear and Stony lakes, the latter known for clear, deep waters and hundreds of small islands. Departure is from Lock 27, 18 miles north of Peterborough on Highway 28.

On the north side of Stony is the **Viamede Hotel**, a lodge for fishermen and lumbermen in the 1860s that became a grand hotel in 1909 with long, sweeping verandas over the lake. Careful restoration of this old building in 1987 now offers 20th-century comfort, a long patio deck, and a dining room seating 125.

For the **Wildlife Art Festival** held in mid-August in the village of **Buckhorn** (on Highway 507 north of Peterborough), visitors come from as far away as Europe. At least 100 artists—printmakers, woodcarvers, painters— have works on sale, and other festivities precede the final big sale, tickets for which are sold out weeks in advance.

The **Gallery on the Lake,** just outside the village on 120 acres, is a hexagonal building of knotty pine showing the work of two dozen artists, some potters, and sculptors using wood, stone, and bronze. Behind the scenes in the same building is the Buckhorn School of Fine Art, offering instruction in various media. **Westwind Resort**, with 32 rooms and a large dining room overlooking Lower Buckhorn Lake, is a five-minute walk away.

Just south of Peterborough and a 90-minute drive from Toronto is **Elmhirst's**, a casual family resort on Rice Lake, mainly with cottage accommodation, each cottage with its own boat ramp. The resort has an air strip, its own air service, and a fly-in (accessible only by air) fishing camp to accommodate six people.

Algonquin Park

Algonquin Park's 2,900 square miles of unspoiled forests and streams were a source of inspiration for landscape artist Tom Thomson in the early 1900s. Today Algonquin Park offers the end of the rainbow for canoeists. Civilization—campgrounds, picnic sites, wilderness operators, and a few lodges—has penetrated its southwest corner; otherwise, except for the effects of acid rain, the wilderness park is unchanged since it opened in 1893. Moose, bear, wolves, and birds thrive here. Canoe routes web the park, and some hiking is possible, the Highland Trail being the most used.

One of the luxury resorts with Relais & Châteaux credentials is just off Highway 60, which, for 37 miles, cuts through the southwest corner of the park. **Arowhon Pines**, a rustic setup on its own lake, has every imaginable resort facility as well as magnificent food. Accommodation is in cabins with two to 12 bedrooms each.

Spas and Bed-and-Breakfast Homes

All over Ontario, but especially in tourist and resort areas, bed-and-breakfast homes have mushroomed in recent years. They are preferred by many visitors as much for the ambience and experience as the price. They may be lovely Victorian homes full of antiques, sit beside a lake, have a large garden or, as at **Pretty Valley Farm**, may be a log home with a valley view, whirlpool, pine-furnished rooms, and private baths.

The homes here are modeled after those in Europe. Some hosts may only have two or three rooms or may welcome guests only part of the year, but others make it a year-round affair and may even manage a registry of other homes. Very rarely is it a small inn where prices are at hotel levels, as is common in the United States. In all cases, rooms will have been specially prepared and are inspected regularly. Generally, full breakfasts are served. The handiest source of information is Patricia Wilson's *Ontario Bed & Breakfast Book* or Gerda Pantel's *Canadian Bed & Breakfast Guide*. Along with specific homes, both list reservation services such as **Country Host**. Others, such as the Muskoka Bed & Breakfast Association, can be tracked down through the local Chamber of Commerce or tourist office.

Spas are also getting more attention. The one in Muskoka is run by Eleanor Fulcher, an offshoot of her modeling agency in Toronto. Ten guests (women only) are accommodated in luxury at the **Eleanor Fulcher Spa** on the shores of Lake Muskoka, near Gravenhurst, for a week of fitness programs, massage therapy, and low-cal meals costing about $1,100. (This includes transportation to and from the Royal York Hotel in Toronto.)

Much larger and more lavish is the **King Ranch Health Spa and Fitness Resort** which opened in the fall of 1989 on 177 acres of rolling woodland and meadows about 20 miles north of Toronto. Modeled after Canyon Ranch in Arizona, it offers a full program of fitness and sports activities, services for stress reduction and nutrition counseling and rejuvenating body/beauty treatments. Three residences, accommodating 180 guests (120 rooms) in relaxing yet elegant comfort, connect to the club house where everyone relaxes, dines, and socializes. The gathering spot has meeting rooms, a den with music, a small movie theater, and a bar serving bottled spring and mineral waters from around the world. Seven-night all-inclusive packages in a double room cost $2,060 per person ($2,480 single) and include the use of spa and resort facilities as well as a choice of five personal spa treatments and two health/sports consultations. A service charge of 17 percent and a small government tax is added.

EASTERN ONTARIO

The drive from Toronto to Ottawa (on Highway 401 along Lake Ontario and the St. Lawrence River, then north just past Prescott on Highway 16) usually takes much longer than the allotted six hours. That's because the drive itself is a scenic one with some good explorations en route. Visitors can stop for a boat cruise through the beautiful Thousand Islands or a meandering excursion along the winding roads of Quinte's Isle. Eastern Ontario is an area of farmland and dairies, of country roads and interconnecting yachting canals, of historic military forts and modern-day ferry rides along the St. Lawrence River.

This is where Lake Ontario becomes the St. Lawrence River and huge freighters travel down to the Atlantic Ocean, sailing between two countries before starting their ocean crossing. Some ships are so large that passengers can almost touch the province of Ontario on one side and New York State on the other. (The St. Lawrence River is a perfect place to view the world's longest undefended border between two countries.) There are three bridges along the river that connect Ontario with New York State: between Ivy Lea in Canada and Watertown, Prescott and Ogdensburg, and Cornwall and Massena.

MAJOR INTEREST

Boat cruises through the Thousand Islands
Boldt Castle
Old Fort Henry in Kingston
Quinte's Isle
Antiques shopping

Although you can poke along the back roads of Eastern Ontario en route to Ottawa (just follow Highway 7 northeast from Peterborough) this is mainly just country living, farmlands and little towns along the road. It is in the little towns along this route—Marmora, Madoc, Tweed, Perth, and Smith Falls—that inveterate shoppers for "pre-loved" articles (including bona fide antiques, secondhand goods, and cute collectibles) will find various old, sometimes ramshackle, buildings piled with countless goodies from original turn-of-the-century oil lanterns to a Queen Elizabeth commemorative teaspoon. In antiques shopping one person's garbage is another's lifelong treasure. Every little town along this route has at least one such store; just ask directions from any of the locals as you pass through their town.

For those who wish to go farther afield in their search, there are many shops along the shores of the Ottawa River, which flows to the north of Eastern Ontario along the border with Quebec. In Pembroke alone (about 88 km/54 miles northwest of Ottawa) there is the **Quilter's Corner** (which sells not only quilts but fabric and instructions for do-it-yourselfers); **Heritage House** for fine crafts and stained glass; and **A and J Crafts** with a showroom of stoneware pottery that, according to the sign, is "open by chance or appointment."

Many Ontarians spend their summer vacations in this area taking their yachts, canoes, cruisers, or rented house boats through the Trent-Severn system of lakes and locks. (Houseboats can be rented from **Go Vacations**; see the Muskoka and Ontario's Near North chapter for information.) Thousands of pleasure boats travel the 385 kilometer waterway from the initial lock at Port Severn in Georgian Bay to the Trenton Lock near Trenton on Lake Ontario each year. Boaters can anchor their yachts for the evening and cook on board or pull their canoe onto shore, pitch a tent, and prepare a campfire for freshly caught fish. You pass through dozens of lakes—Couchiching, Simcoe, Scugog, Pigeon, Buckhorn—and can even spend the night at dockside resorts. These accommodations range from the old-world charm of the **Old Bridge Inn** at Young's Point to the more modern **Holiday Inn** on Peterborough's waterfront or the many inland campgrounds along the Trent-Severn.

In other words, this is a relaxing holiday cruise that can last one to two weeks—not to be taken if you are in a hurry. If, however, your time is limited, the scenic and varied drive from Toronto to Ottawa can be accomplished in as little as a day (although you will want to stay longer).

The Lake Ontario Shore

Most visitors prefer to drive from Toronto east along Lake Ontario and the St. Lawrence River without detouring into inland Eastern Ontario. And if you are seriously interested in your automobile (other than making sure it has enough gasoline and oil), your first stop after leaving Toronto should be the **Canadian Automotive Museum**, about 25 km (15 miles) northeast of Toronto at Oshawa, one of the main centers of the automobile industry in Canada. The museum, with over 80 antique vehicles plus related memorabilia dating from the beginning of the auto era, is at 99 Simcoe Street (north of Highway 401, take exit 417).

About 35 km (21 miles) farther north on Highway 401 are the neighboring towns of **Port Hope** and **Cobourg**. The towns have been called perfect lakeside towns, preserved in a bubble of century-old picture postcard serenity, with maple trees lining the sidewalks, 19th-century homes in pristine condition, and ornate stone churches coexisting with arts and crafts shops along the main streets. Many lakeside dwellers keep their boats tied up at backyard wharfs.

Surprisingly for towns this size, there are some good little restaurants, especially two in Port Hope that are housed in buildings from the past century. **The Carlyle** was originally built in 1857 as the Bank of Upper Canada, and the site of the **Greenwood Towers Inn** dates from 1877. Both feature good Continental cuisine at reasonable prices. The latter is actually on a wooded estate and has an inn of 48 rooms.

The beautiful sand beaches of **Quinte's Isle**, or Prince Edward County as the locals call it, can be reached by three main bridges off the mainland highway; at Carrying Place (Highway 33), Belleville (Highway 62), and Tyendinaga (Highway 49). This area, settled by the Empire Loyalists after the American Revolution, is still tinged with echoes of the pioneer past as museums, historical sites, and antiques shops are interspersed with roadside stands selling fresh fruit and vegetables.

Picton, with a population of 5,000, is the largest town in the area and the center for any local tourist information. After a drive through the wooded island countryside, head for the south-shore **Sandbanks and North Beach provincial parks**, where mountains of sand dunes ring the shore: an ideal spot for picnicking, swimming and camping.

If you don't feel like barbecuing your own hot dogs, stop at the stately gray-stone **Waring House Restaurant**, originally built in 1835 as a family home, now a restaurant specializing in European cuisine and fresh, home-baked breads and pastries. Try to visit for afternoon tea with fresh scones and jams.

There are many little motels, resorts, and bed-and-breakfast spots throughout Quinte's Isle. Check with the local tourism office or consider the **Isaiah Tubbs Inn & Resort** or the housekeeping cottages at the **Sandbanks Beach Resort.**

Kingston

The main city in Eastern Ontario is lakeside Kingston, situated at the northern end of Lake Ontario just as it narrows down to become the St. Lawrence River. **Old Fort Henry** here was originally built during the War of 1812 (and rebuilt in 1832) to repel the American invaders and to protect the Rideau Canal system at this strategic location. Daily tours of the fort are conducted from mid-June until Labour Day, with the sunset ceremonial retreat conducted Mondays, Wednesdays, and Saturdays, complete with precision military maneuvers, the fife and drum corp, and a fairly dramatic muzzle-loading cannon. The specially trained Fort Henry Guard are summer students chosen from Kingston's **Royal Military College** (Canada's version of West Point or Sandhurst), who maintain the 19th-century routine of the military fort. The college museum is situated in Canada's largest Martello tower and emphasizes the history of the college and its graduates.

Strategically located for defense, Kingston was actually the first capital of Canada (from 1841–1843) and the home of Sir John A. Macdonald, Canada's first prime minister. The area was settled in 1673 as a fur-trading station and quickly became a military stronghold. Kingston today retains its rich architectural and historical ties to the 19th century. For a good overview of the city there are daily summer tours, on the hour, that leave from Confederation Park across from City Hall.

Kingston truly is an aquatic-oriented city; many of the boat tours of the beautiful **Thousand Islands** that dot the St. Lawrence River originate here. The Ivy Lea Thousand Islands tour line features a replica of a double-decker paddlewheeler, while the *Wentworth Lady* has the intimacy and style of a 1950s cruise ship. The Kingston and Islands Boat Line Ltd. has two different cruises on its triple-decker *Island Queen* or a replica sidewheeler, the *Island Princess.* Prices range depending on the ship and cruise duration, but figure $5 to $7.50 per adult. To take a cruise just wander down to the main pier at the bottom of Ontario Street and choose a ship.

Instead of a three-hour cruise, you can opt for several days aboard the *MV Canadian Empress,* which has five different cruises including down river to Montreal and Quebec City. There are 32 staterooms on board, each with private washroom, dining areas, and ship's bar. Prices vary depending on the duration of the cruise, but an average cost is about $125 per day (including all meals). Contact the St. Lawrence Cruise Lines (Tel: 800-267-0960 from the U.S.; or direct in Ontario, Tel: 613-549-8091).

There is good accommodation in Kingston, ranging from hotels and motels to little guest houses, but your best choice is to stay on the very picturesque waterfront. Try the **Holiday Inn** or **Howard Johnson**, both good, with all the amenities and close to the boat lines. Request a lakefront view.

If you want a real view, however, check out the **Thousand Islands Skydeck** on Hill Island (below the Thousand Islands International Bridge). This 121-meter-high observatory provides a "clear day" visibility of almost 40 miles. If you care to sightsee longer, there is a licensed restaurant on the Skydeck.

And yes, as legend has it, the famous Thousand Island Salad Dressing was named for these islands. George Boldt, at one time the owner of New York's Waldorf Astoria hotel, was cruising in the area aboard his yacht when a steward served a new dressing with the salad. Boldt decided to use the dressing at his hotels and named it in honor of the beautiful area where it was first created.

If you take a Thousand Island cruise, and you should, make certain to take one that stops at **Boldt Castle**, perched atop a hill on Heart Island. As a tribute to his wife, the same George Boldt bought the island in 1899, had it reshaped in the form of a heart, and commenced to build a huge castle with materials from all over the world. When his wife suddenly died Boldt had already invested $2 million in his dream project, but he stopped work and left the shell there for tourists to wander through 90 years later.

The St. Lawrence River Area

A few miles north, farther down river (on the map it seems as though you are travelling up, but in navigational terms, it is down), is the little tourist village of **Gananoque**. Pronounced "gannon-ock-way," this is an Iroquois name that might mean "land sloping gently to the water."

This pretty little town is located in the center of the Thousand Islands region and operates its own boat line through the St. Lawrence; the Gananoque Boat Lines operates the world's largest aluminum vessels and carries up to 500 passengers on a three-hour cruise; lunch and dinner with bar facilities are available. (Before boarding the boat, however, check out the bargains in sweaters and handknitting yarns available at the **Gan Mill Outlet** in town.)

If you would rather dine on land than on a boat or skydeck, you will find Gananoque blessed with three historic inn/restaurants, rare for such a small town: **The Gananoque Inn**, the tiny **Grand McCammon Inn**, and the rather oddly named **Blinkbonnie Motor Lodge**. All three buildings are well over 100 years old, though thoroughly renovated, and each serves good fresh fish and Continental cuisine.

Something a little different for nautical fans—and the curious—is the non-denominational church service conducted every Sunday afternoon at nearby Half Moon Bay. The weekly lesson is delivered from a rock pulpit at the edge of a natural amphitheater and the congregation listens to the service from their boats.

Many drivers continue along Highway 401 through historic Brockville and Prescott and then turn up Highway 16 to Ottawa. However, carry on past the Prescott turnoff for a few miles to the town of Morrisburg and the nearby **Crysler's Farm Battlefield Park**, where there are modern conveniences such as an 18-hole golf course, riding corral, marina, theater playhouse, and a large recreational and swimming area. This seems a strange fate for the site of one of the most decisive battles in the War of 1812; as every student of Canadian history knows, Canada's defeat of the American army here was a turning point in the United States's attempt to conquer Canada. The actual site of the battle is now somewhere under the waters of the river, but when the shoreline was built up (so the story goes) the contractors used the original earth from the Crysler's Farm battleground. For diehard nationalists this is the equivalent of Canadian "holy soil," although no one has yet bottled it for sale in tourist shops.

From here you could either continue up Highway 401 to Cornwall, the easternmost city in Ontario, and then on to Montreal, or backtrack and then head north to Ottawa, a two-hour drive to the nation's capital and its Parliament Buildings, the National Arts Centre, and the new Canadian Museum of Civilization.

NORTHERN ONTARIO

Even most Ontarians believe they are in the "northland" when they drive 150 miles from Toronto to their Muskoka cottages. However, they have not yet begun to find north! The North is the country of inpenetrable forests, limitless rivers and rapids, lumbering brown bears and watchful majestic moose, the awesome scenery of Agawa Canyon and crashing whitecaps along the Lake Superior shoreline, or a quiet week on a remote fly-in fishing island with no other human being in sight. Ontario's North begins *above* Algonquin Park—which for many Ontarians is the limit of their north—and extends hundreds of miles north to Hudson Bay and as far west as Minnesota in the United States.

This is the North painted by the Group of Seven, Canadian artists who, in the first part of the century, captured the flaming leaves of autumn and the blue stillness of winter in the still unpopulated northern areas. (The Mc-Michael Gallery Canadian Collection of the Group of Seven at Kleinburg, just north of Toronto, will give the uninitiated a startling insight into the real "great white north.")

The predominant geographic feature of the landscape is the Precambrian, or Canadian, Shield: a rugged terrain of trees, rocks, and rivers—all natural elements that provide vast quantities of paper products, essential minerals, and water-power resources. The area is crisscrossed by 68,500 square miles of inland rivers and lakes (up to half a million; there are too many to accurately count or name); it is estimated that one-quarter of all fresh water in the world is found here.

The name Ontario itself stems from an old Iroquois word meaning "shining water." Or a Huron word meaning "beautiful lake." Or perhaps something from the Iroquois dialect meaning "rocks that stand by the lake," referring to the Niagara escarpment. In other words, no one quite knows; safe money would bet on the Iroquois, since by 1649 they had completely wiped out the Huron tribe.

The Ontario North is (to paraphrase a well-worn cliché) a great place to visit, but . . . not many people live there. Most of the province's nine million inhabitants cling resolutely to within a few hundred miles of the U.S. border. There are various reasons for this, from economics to weather. Northern residents will tell you, however, that it is a simple matter of gravity; everyone knows that cream rises to the top.

MAJOR INTEREST

Train tours of the interior, such as Agawa Canyon, Polar Bear Express
Indian pictographs
Visits to operating silver and gold mines
Amethyst mines
Fishing and hunting
Wilderness parks and camping
Northern wilderness scenery
Lodges and resorts

To explore the North, unless you are a dedicated wilderness expert who loves hiking and canoeing, you will use some main auto routes, such as the Trans-Canada Highway, as well as wilderness roads that will take you literally to the end of the line. There are, however, some interesting rail alternatives.

NORTHERN ONTARIO BY RAIL
VIA Passenger Rail

For many, this is the ideal method of seeing central and western Canada: sitting, chatting, sporadically reading, perhaps drowsing as the Canadian countryside flashes by, constantly changing as the inhospitable rocky cliffs of Lake Superior disappear during the night and become the flat morning wheat of the prairies, then the looming twilight of the Rockies. For this three-day trip to the West

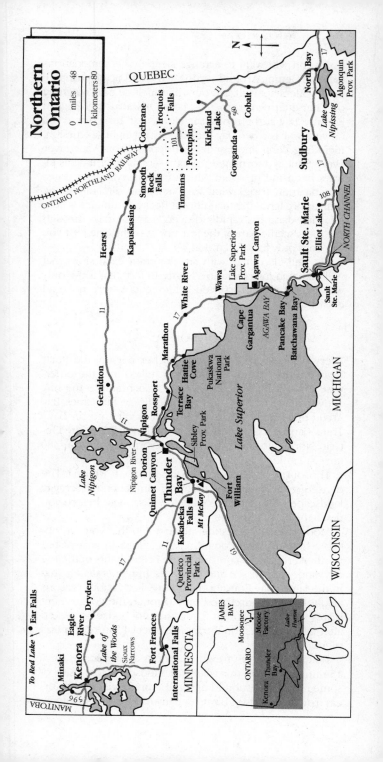

Coast you will want to arrange sleeper accommodations (see the Getting Around section at the end of the chapter).

VIA offers specialized tours that include seal watching off Charlottetown on the east coast or walrus sightings in Repulse Bay at the top of the Northwest Territories. The newest tour is a two-day "Rockies by Daylight" excursion, including Banff and Jasper, that departs from Vancouver every Sunday morning. (Daylight—or lack of it—has always been the problem with a regular, complete trans-Canada train trip; owing to scheduling difficulties, the train approaches the magnificent Rocky Mountains at sunset, then darkness rapidly descends as you pass through the most scenic part of the journey at night. The best you can do is pray for a full moon.)

VIA Rail also links with smaller train excursions that will take you into Ontario's North. In fact, that is the only way to see certain isolated settlements where no road exists.

Moosonee

Every day (except Friday), at $30 per person, the **Polar Bear Express** chugs 300 km (180 miles) into the otherwise inaccessible wilderness from Cochrane to the tiny native village of Moosonee on the lip of the James Bay Arctic tidewaters. (James Bay is a bay off Hudson Bay.) Trans-Canada VIA Rail passengers will transfer to the Ontario Northland Railway (ONR) at North Bay for the 380 km (240 miles) detour to Cochrane.

The journey is very picturesque, but the town isn't. The dense green forests and seemingly impenetrable craggy landscape thin out and completely disappear before you reach the tiny settlement.

Moosonee is interesting, however, in that you can observe how a native community functions in an isolated northern region in contrast to the bright lights of the big city; and you can see and purchase Indian crafts created in the James Bay Educational Centre. For various reasons alcohol can be purchased only through the government stores Monday through Thursday; no booze is served after 8:00 P.M., even on the motels' special Saturday "pizza night."

Board one of the freighter canoes at Moosonee for a 15-minute trip to the island of **Moose Factory**, site of some of the oldest buildings in the province; the explorers from the Hudson Bay Company had their first outpost here some 300 years ago. **St. Thomas Church**, a still active museum piece dating back to 1860, displays such unique items as moose-hide altar cloths, silk embroidery on white deerhide, and prayer books in the Cree language.

The James Bay Frontier Area is noted for fall-season duck and goose hunting; the most popular base, the **Hannah Bay Goose Camp**, rapidly books up in September and October, the only two months of its operation. Hunters should reserve a year in advance to be assured of some of the finest fowl hunting in Canada.

You can stay overnight at Moosonee at your choice of cinder-block–design motels (the **Moosonee Lodge** or the **Polar Bear Lodge**), although people may wonder about you if you do. You will certainly be a curiosity among the locals. The five-hour train stop should be enough.

The Agawa Canyon

The Agawa Canyon Train, like the Polar Bear Express, is the only way to see some of the most spectacular wilderness scenery in the world—and all from the comforts of a luxury passenger train. The one-day excursion on the Algoma Central Railway starts at Sault Ste. Marie (see below) and winds 200 km (120 miles) through luxuriant forests and over vertigo-inspiring railway trestles to a two-hour picnic stop (you can purchase a box lunch on the train) at the photographer's paradise known as the Agawa Canyon.

The canyon itself, designated a natural wilderness park, is maintained by the railways and cannot be reached by any other means. During the stop you can explore the canyon along various hiking trails, fish for trout in a nearby stream, or just admire the fjord-like beauty in the middle of northern nowhere.

A novice will soon learn that the train often stops along thick wilderness to pick up trappers, hikers, and occasionally a group with several canoes; the train is simply a rural version of an urban taxicab. People either flag it down or book a stop, arranging a specific time to meet the train following a week-long camping trip, for example.

The same ride from December to March (weekends only) becomes **The Snow Train**; it takes you along the same route, where you can experience the true winter wonderland found only in the great white north—but from the warmth and comfort of your passenger seat.

EXPLORING NORTHERN ONTARIO BY CAR

Just beyond Algonquin Park, the top of Ontario's "Near North," motorists will find Highways 11 and 17 meeting for an instant—at **North Bay**—then rebounding off each other in different directions. Highway 11 heads due north through Cobalt, Kirkland Lake, slowly curving left at Iroquois Falls, on to Kapuskasing, turning west by Hearst, through Geraldton, and dropping south to meet its former partner at Nipigon before going into Thunder Bay.

Highway 17 got the more popular and certainly much more picturesque southern route, following the Lake Superior shoreline west through Sudbury, turning north at Sault Ste. Marie, up through Wawa, White River, and tiny Rossport, to join 11 once again at the Nipigon River, one of the world's great fishing sites, and then, as with the northern route, going into Thunder Bay.

After Thunder Bay, Highway 17 continues west to Kenora and Lake of the Woods, then on to Winnipeg, Manitoba.

This is not only an area of rivers and forests but also the land of a million roadside motels, fishing camps, rustic resorts, and the occasional fancier hotel. There is no shortage of accommodation in this area; we mention a very few of the best or more interesting. However, you can always get a copy of the Ontario government's (free) accommodations guide before starting your trip (see "Getting Around" at the end of the chapter), or check the local tourist office.

Our exploration routes and descriptions assume that you will be travelling in season, not in winter or bordering months.

THE NORTHERN ROUTE
Mining Communities

The northern route of Highway 11 takes you into the much rougher, more rocky terrain of miners and engineers, the land of prospectors and boom towns that have gone bust. In fact, the town of **Cobalt** was born (or so the story goes) when in 1903 a frustrated blacksmith threw a hammer at an inquisitive fox that was spooking the horses. Apparently his anger affected his aim; he missed the animal and struck a mineral instead. Fred Larose's hammer chipped a rock and uncovered the world's richest silver vein.

Fred's hammer also produced one of the greatest mining stampedes in history, which led to the development of various other area communities such as Gowganda, Kirkland Lake, Iroquois Falls, and Porcupine. All of these towns have quieted down somewhat since their heady days of fast fortunes, although there are many old-timers around still panning for precious minerals and throwing hammers at rocks. Each community holds its own "Miners' Festival" at varying times throughout the summer months (check in advance for changeable dates) where grizzled prospectors will gladly spin tales of the olden golden years of fortune.

Kirkland Lake, one of the former boom towns, is the site of the elaborate Sir Harry Oakes Château, where displays include examples of prospecting, geology, mining, and material illustrating the personalities of the early prospectors who flocked into the region.

No one left such an indelible stamp on the mining communities as the château's former owner, Sir Harry Oakes, the epitome of a rough, bullheaded prospector. He made his fortune in the North, moved briefly to Niagara Falls, then continued his southern migration to the Bahamas. Never a lovable type, the often belligerent former miner was murdered by persons unknown in the 1940s in the Bahamas, a supposedly safe, easygoing country where he had fled to escape the dangers and cold of the North. (The famous murder was never officially solved.)

Farther along the highway you will see signs announcing your entry into **Timmins**, although it will be miles before you spot a settlement. Timmins, with a population of 45,000, actually has "city" boundaries of 1,260 square miles, thus living up to its claim as the "largest city in Canada."

The prospected gold at the turn of the century brought prosperity to the region, and the subsequent discovery of most of the world's supply of silver and zinc, making it one of the richest areas for mineral mining anywhere, ensured its future. There are tours of the various mines during the two summer months; the fascinating "underworld" operations are explained while you are some 3,500 feet beneath the earth's surface. (Timmins Chamber of Commerce; Tel: 705-264-4321.) Those with lung or heart conditions are advised to remain in the gift shop, or visit the Timmins Museum (open year-round), where the local mining history is explained.

Farther on, the little town of Cochrane is the start of the **Polar Bear Express**, the northland railway route "down" to the Arctic watershed communities of Moosonee and Moose Factory.

Paper Mills

There are several logging towns—Iroquois Falls, Smooth Rock, Kapuskasing, and Hearst (mainly French-speaking)—that feature public tours through their pulp and paper mills, the lifeblood industry of these northern communities. For example, the Abitibi Price company in **Iroquois Falls** arranges very popular plant tours during the summer months; hard hats (provided) are required as you are led through the papermaking process. Also, as a safety precaution, only small groups are allowed through. Although this may not sound exciting, it is: It's a fascinating look at an assembly line where huge trees are cut, folded, spindled, mutilated, stomped, mashed, and pressed into the miles of spinning paper rolls that eventually end up with the daily news stamped on it. (Iroquois Falls Chamber of Commerce; Tel: 705-232-4656.)

From here it is several hundred miles of straight highway flanked by dense forests and busy with many visiting rock hounds picking up the minerals, agate, fool's gold, and fossils that seem simply to be scattered around this mainly unpopulated stretch of road. The tall cliffs of **Nipigon** mark the end of the northern trail; here the two highways meet again for a joint run into Thunder Bay, the capital city of the Lakehead area.

THE SOUTHERN ROUTE
Sudbury

The highway into Sudbury is through a more populated area than the northern route and is a much more picturesque drive. Not that the city itself, the first center west from North Bay, can be described as pretty, but it has been improving. (One writer recently returned from the changing area and bemoaned the fact that "we can't use Sudbury jokes anymore; it looks too nice!")

Yet the area around the town is still the same lunar landscape that drew the American astronauts here to train for their moon missions. The pitted surface is believed to have been caused by a meteorite crash (almost two billion years ago), which brought with it mineral wealth including nickel, platinum, copper, gold, and cobalt. Sudbury is, in fact, known as the nickel capital of the world, a distinction noted with a 30-foot-high Canadian five-cent piece (four cents U.S.) prominently displayed near the highway.

It is somewhat ironic that this wilderness town has pollution rivaling smoggy Los Angeles, with the continuously operating smokestacks producing colorful hues from metal refining 24 hours a day. However, the city has been upgrading its image, one of the attempts being **Science North**, a hands-on science center exploring the natural wonders of physics and geology. There are also, of course, tours of the various mineral companies and mining museums, such as INCO and Falconbridge.

You might book at **Sheraton's Caswell Inn** and relax in its indoor pool and sauna (plus a good dining room) after a day of touring the mining area.

The Chi-Cheemaun Ferry

The bridge between Southwestern Ontario and the North is actually a boat. Or, to be more precise, a car ferry. This is the famed Chi-Cheemaun, a 140-vehicle, 638-passenger ferry that sails several times daily from the little mainland port of Tobermory at the northern tip of the Bruce Peninsula to the dock at South Baymouth on Manitoulin Island. Manitoulin lies off the coast of Northern Ontario halfway between Sudbury and Sault Ste. Marie. Last summer the Ontario Northland Marine Services (which operates the ferry service) decided that due to increased aqua traffic, they would add another ferry to the route. Nindawayma, or "the little sister" sails on the opposite time schedule from her big sea sister. You can now leave from either port every two hours instead of the normal four-hour wait. This is a slightly smaller version of the original well-known ferry and a welcome addition to relieve the lined-up summer crowds.

The Chi-Cheemaun, Ojibwa for "big canoe," makes the 1-hour-and-45-minute trip four times daily and is usually fully packed both coming and going. This is one of the most popular summer rides in Ontario. Tourists could always drive around Georgian Bay (through the "Near North"), but most would rather line up for the car ferry to Manitoulin Island.

The ferry has a 230-seat cafeteria, cocktail lounge, snack bar, and pleasant on-deck easy chairs. Rates range from $8.70 for one to $29 for a whole family (no maximum); car prices start at $18.50, and increase with the size of the vehicle. Bicycles are $3.70, while motorhomes may be $40.50. Reservations are available on early and late sailings only. (Chi-Cheemaun Ferry Service, Owen Sound; Tel: 519-596-2510.)

Manitoulin Island

Manitoulin Island is one of the great undiscovered and undeveloped tourist areas of the province; most visitors coming from the south simply leave the ferry at South Baymouth and drive straight across the island to the Little Current bridge linking Manitoulin to the Northern Ontario mainland. Unfortunately, they do not take time to dawdle and explore the world's largest freshwater island, with its quiet bays and inlets, sandy beaches, and tiny island villages. In fact, Providence Bay on the island's south side is billed as the longest sand beach in Canada.

Manitoulin is a sort of "middle earth," neither north nor south, but for the early natives, a place of dreams and legends. The Ojibwa saw Manitoulin as the home of the "Great Spirit" (nature and all its forces as represented in the spirit world as "manitous," and superior to all is the Great Spirit, the "Gitchi Manitou"). Since it is only fitting that this supreme being should live apart from others, what better place than a private island. Literally translated, Manitoulin means God's Island.

The 110-mile-long island itself boasts 1,000 miles of coastline and is dotted with little villages ranging from Little Current (1,500 people) to South Baymouth (62). There are seven different Indian reserves on the island, and several specialty stores, such as the **Perivale Gallery** in Spring Bay, sell some magnificent works of native art.

There are fishing charter boats available and some excellent yachting opportunities along the north channel; scuba divers will find some fascinating old shipwrecks along the north shore at Meldrum Bay.

There are few resort complexes or major hotels on the island (try the **Manitowaning Lodge** or **Silver Birches Resort**), for this is mainly a very relaxed retreat with various little "mom and pop" motel operations, house-keeping cabins, and fishing camps. Campers will do best to stay in the campgrounds beside the sand beach of Providence Bay.

The island's major attraction is the annual native "pow-wow" held every August 1 long weekend at the 30,000-acre Wikwemikong Indian Reserve on the eastern peninsula of the island. Native Indians come from across Canada and the U.S. for the four-day event, which features tribal folklore and customs, dancing, craft-making, and art. (Manitoulin Tourist Association, P.O. Box 119, Little Current, Ont. P0P 1R0. Tel: 705-368-3021.)

Elliott Lake, farther west of the road up from the Little Current bridge to Manitoulin Island on Lake Huron's North Channel, is billed as the uranium capital of the world, which was true until 1960, when the mineral bubble burst. It is still a well-planned community of 20,000, and recent developments have led to the reopening of some mines. Attend the annual Uranium Festival toward the end of June if you would like to experience some wild northern hospitality.

Sault Ste. Marie

Sault Ste. Marie, affectionately known as the "Soo," is the navigational gateway between Lake Superior and Lake Huron; the International Bridge across the St. Mary's River connects the city to its Michigan sister of the same name. The city of 85,000 is, for a bustling port and industrial town, surprisingly clean.

This is also the best place to watch the huge lake freighters pour through the lock system; better still, take the boat cruise of the Soo Lock System, a two-hour tour that leaves throughout the day (May to October) from the Norgoma Dock next to the Holiday Inn.

Displays at the Ermatinger House, the Sault Ste. Marie Museum, and the floating M.S. *Norgoma* detail the city's history, from its early founding in 1669 by a Jesuit priest, to the wild fur-trading days of the Hudson's Bay Company explorers, to the development of the area industries.

Sault Ste. Marie is also where you find the Algoma Central for the **Agawa Canyon Train** through the forests to the canyon (see the rail section, above).

Recommended accommodation here is the **Best Western Water Tower Inn**, complete with suites; prices are in the medium range. If you are taking the Algoma Central, tell them you are catching the 8:30 A.M. excursion for a confirmed wake-up call.

Heading North

It may feel as though you are leaving civilization as you head north from Sault Ste. Marie along the Lake Superior northern shoreline; until you reach Thunder Bay, some 500 miles away, there are only tiny towns (the largest, Wawa, has a population of 5,000), forests, parks, gorgeous scenery, and the loveliest deserted beaches you have ever seen—one of the many secrets of the North.

The little village of **Batchewana Bay**, about 80 km (50 miles) north of the Soo, is a pleasant place to explore the bays and beaches of the coast, but here perhaps a word of caution about Lake Superior: It is a cold lake and very unpredictable; exercise caution when fishing or canoeing, because even on a sunny day those calm waters can become turbulent whitecaps in minutes. (Canadian troubadour Gordon Lightfoot's song detailing the "Wreck of the Edmund Fitzgerald" is a true story; with no warning a storm materialized and crushed the ship and its entire crew.)

Indian Crafts

As you approach Pancake Bay north of the Soo you will see two stores located on the east side of the highway. Slow down, turn your steering wheel to the right, park and spend some browsing and buying time at the **Agawa Indian Crafts** and **The Canadian Carver**. Formerly across the road from each other, the two are now side by side to assist the consumer.

Proprietors June and Gerald Demers, who own both shops, have amassed in each store a collection of authentic native arts and crafts—such as Iroquois pottery, Micmac basketry, and Ojibway leatherwork—that adorn counters and walls (*without* the usual "Made in Korea" stickers). The shop is both an artisan's and consumer's dream. Look for the rough, hand-carved ceremonial masks, the visual interpretation of native deities.

Should hunger pangs strike about this time, look for the curiously named **Black Forest Motel** with its simple, homestyle restaurant. The name comes from the German-born owner who for 25 years has been serving generous platters of food and the best homemade sausage this side of Bavaria—and Lake Superior is just across the road.

If you will be camping, stock up on supplies at **Montreal River Harbour** (one of the very few inland deep-sea harbors in the world) before entering **Lake Superior Provincial Park**; the highway winds 90 km (56 miles) through the 580 square miles of wilderness park. Entry is free, but overnight campers must pay a site fee of $8.25 for main camping areas or $3 to camp along the interior hiking trails. Check out the little coves and beaches, particularly **Gargantua Bay**; follow the winding dirt road off Highway 17 to this lovely bay with a long sandy beach, picnic tables, and overnight facilities. It is a little-known spot that you might have all to yourself.

Most campers gather at the **Agawa Bay** campground, with its hiking and canoe routes, guided nature walks, and evening events in the park's amphitheater. This beach is rife with sparkling stones and gnarled pieces of driftwood, which are taken as souvenirs to be tumbled and shined, sanded and lacquered, eventually to appear as *objets d'art* on countless mantelpieces.

Longfellow's Hiawatha

The most fascinating feature of the park, however, is the centuries-old pictographs (archaeologists have discovered that Indians have been in the area for 11,000 years) carved into **Agawa Rock**, a cliff face rising some 75 feet above Lake Superior. These 30 Indian rock paintings are the basis for Longfellow's saga of Hiawatha, a poem learned by every North American child in public school. (Longfellow himself never did see the paintings but based his story on descriptions related by an explorer of the region.) This prehistoric depiction of a migration by canoe through the Lake Superior region, sculpted into stone and darkened with rust-colored iron-ore pigments, can be seen by anyone who wishes to climb the cliff, but those rocks can be wet and slippery, so wear good hiking shoes and exercise caution.

Wawa is "famed" for the 28-foot Goose statue (Wawa is Ojibway for "wild goose") housing a tourist information booth at its base; spend some time at nearby **Old Woman Bay**, a bit of the Bahamas in Ontario, where shallow sandy waters ensure bathtub-like temperatures in normally chilly Lake Superior (assuming you are travelling in summertime, of course). For accommodation, try the **Wawa**

Motor Lodge. There are units out front, but ask for one of the cabins, which are hidden from the road. These are log structures with cathedral-like ceilings, complete with kitchen and fireplace, and featuring dazzling northern sunsets from your back porch.

When you reach Marathon as you move westward, you may turn south on Highway 627 to the vast (714 square miles) **Pukaskwa National Park**. The area has some good wilderness walks and canoe routes, with some basic camping sites along the coastal trail. The purpose of the park is to preserve the geological Canadian Shield wilderness with its boreal forest. The park is also the southernmost range of a small woodland caribou herd; sit quietly by the shoreline at sunset and you may see one of these rare creatures. **Hattie Cove**, at the northern entrance, has a small campground, sandy beach, picnic areas, very cold water, and a boat launch.

The drive along the northern Lake Superior shore provides some magnificent wild scenery broken up by picturesque little lakeside towns and villages, such as Terrace Bay, Rossport, and the fishing center of Nipigon. Perhaps the best one to explore is **Rossport**, a little fishing village with a natural harbor and an archipelago of islands offshore, ideal for sailing and boating (you can charter craft at the government dock).

For overnight or a meal, try the **Rossport Inn**, a recently refurbished railway stopover built in 1884. There are six homey guest rooms (only $35 for a double), and the dining room features the local catch of the day. The inn has retained its rustic railway roots, with friendly northern hospitality.

The **Forget Me Not Gift Shop** in Rossport specializes in souvenirs that are a cut above the norm and feature the artisans of the North: everything from native pottery to hand-tooled leather goods. The shop also offers the best view of the town's picturesque harbor (in fact, so many people come to shop and stay for the view that owner Olav Sundland has a section of his yard marked "husbands' waiting area").

Non-fishermen may just pass through Nipigon—where our northern route on Highway 11 rejoins the southern route—but most travellers will be interested in the **Quimet Canyon**, farther on near the town of Dorion, a geological phenomenon similar to the Grand Canyon. Two miles long, more than 450 feet across, and 300 feet deep, the canyon was formed in prehistoric times by shifting glacial ice that ground out a huge depression in the rock; rare Arctic flora cover the canyon floor and cliffs. Much of the footpath around the canyon's rim is not protected by safety railing, so tread carefully.

There are several **amethyst mines** on the outskirts of Thunder Bay where you can hunt for rough specimens at open pit mines (paying by the pound as you leave) or buy jewelry and polished stones at the gift shop. Two sources are the Ontario Gem Amethyst Mine and the Amethyst Mine Panorama. This is the center of the world's amethyst supply, and you can literally pick the lavender and deep purple stones off the ground.

Just before Thunder Bay there is a bronze statue of Terry Fox, the 21-year-old athlete with an artificial leg who planned a run across the country, his "Marathon of Hope," to raise money for cancer research. It was at this halfway mark that his doctors convinced him to stop because the malignancy had spread; he was flown home to Vancouver, where he died soon after. It was Terry Fox who inspired wheelchair athlete Rick Hanson to undergo his two-year "Man in Motion" odyssey around the world.

Thunder Bay

The Indian origins of Thunder Bay start with the Sleeping Giant, the city's best-known natural landmark, which lies in the waters of the bay; from the town's harbor, some 25 km (15 miles) away, this piece of land looks like a huge man, arms across his chest, floating on the water. This is actually **Sibley Provincial Park**, where you can hike 7,000 feet above Lake Superior. Ojibway legend has it that the giant was once Nanibijou, or the Great Spirit, who lived on Mount McKay, which is today an Indian reserve. He protected his tribe, but he warned that they would perish and he would be turned into stone if the white man ever discovered their silver mine. Alas, he was betrayed, and as the invading ships came within sight, he created a storm that drowned them all. The next morning he had turned to stone and was left in the bay to guard the silver mine.

Thunder Bay (or T-Bay) is a sprawling amalgamation of two cities, Fort William and Port Arthur—a bustling seaport of 125,000 that annually stores over one billion bushels of wheat for shipment to the Canadian east. The early French explorers settled the area and used Fort William as the gateway to the fur-trading routes of the Northwest.

Old Fort William, an authentic reconstruction (the largest of its kind in North America), shows what the original settlement was like in the early 19th century. From May to September the fort is peopled by "residents" who carry on their daily business in period costume and speech. You can watch the blacksmith shoe horses, help make tallow candles, or attend a meeting of the town council.

The best way to see Thunder Bay is from the scenic lookout of **Mount McKay**, the Indian reservation (and also one of the area's four winter ski resorts), or on the cruise ship *Welcome* (leaving daily from the North Marina dock at the foot of Red River Road), which navigates among the Great Lake freighters in the harbor. Take a short drive west of town to the majestic **Kakabeka Falls**, the "Niagara of the North," for a picnic lunch beside the Kaministiquia River.

The area also has the largest Finnish population outside of Finland, supposedly because the early settlers found the rugged terrain much like their native country. Try the **Hoito Restaurant** (hidden away in a church basement on Bay Street) for some authentic Finnish food, or the **Kangas Sauna** on Oliver Road for true Nordic steam.

Since you may spend a few days in the area, you will be pleased to know that there is a full range of accommodation here other than the roadside-motel type of the past 500 miles to the east. Good accommodation and hotel dining can be found at the **Valhalla Inn**, the **Red Oak**, and the **Airlane**, all clustered near the junctions of Highways 11 and 17 and Arthur Street West; or the **Landmark Hotel** on the other side of town.

Uncle Frank's Supper Club on Highway 61 south, heading toward the ski hills, is a 1950s-style dining room, of faded elegance yet comfortable, with a wonderful fieldstone fireplace and serving huge 20-ounce porterhouse steaks. The **Neebing Roadhouse**, farther down the highway, with a glassed-in dining room overlooking the ski slopes, also has a casual country bar, which has become the definitive *après-ski* gathering place during the winter. (As mentioned, Thunder Bay has four ski areas within a 15-minute drive of the downtown area. They also boast "Big Thunder," the 90- and 70-meter ski jumps that annually host international competition.)

West of Thunder Bay is the land of seasonal summer resorts, sports lodges, and fly-in fishing outposts on any of the many thousands of lakes and rivers dotting the map. This time it is Highway 11 that takes the southern turn and runs along the tip of **Quetico Provincial Park**, a designated wilderness park with hiking and canoe routes (best to avoid May and June, when the dreaded black flies might carry you away).

Highway 11 meanders through the border town of Fort Francis, a popular U.S. crossing for vacationers coming through International Falls, Michigan, and then ends at Rainy River and the Minnesota border. The upper route, on Highway 17, will take you past the moose-hunting center of Dryden before reaching the magnificent Lake of the Woods resort area.

The town of **Dryden** lists a population of close to 6,000 and most of them owe their livelihood to the Canadian Pacific Forest Products Mills (formerly Great Lakes Paper). The mill presides over all in this town, announcing its presence with a constant haze of billowing smoke and—depending on the winds that day—a strong assault on the olfactory senses. Business at the moment is booming with a recent multi-million addition and in this age of factory lay-offs, an extra 150 workers. (Free tours—about 1½ hours in length—can be arranged by calling 807-223-9376 any weekday.)

Still, it is a pleasant little town, known for its hunting and fishing camps as much as its famous paper products. For local information, just look for the huge statue of "Max the Moose" located just outside the tourist bureau. Of particular interest for the uninitiated would be the MNR (the Ontario Ministry of Natural Resources) Northwestern Regional Fire Management Centre, which has the unenviable task of fighting forest fires for almost half of the province. You can arrange a tour (Tel: 807-937-4402) of this quite fascinating facility—it will ensure that you always make certain your campfire is stone cold before you leave the park.

Kenora

Once in this pretty little town, set your watch back one hour; you have driven so far you are in a different time zone—yet still in the province of Ontario.

This is now the **Lake of the Woods** area, a gorgeous landscape filled with thousands of lakes and coves all linked together in miles of waterway through forests and past cottages and camps. This is one of those regions on the globe that could vie for the title of "God's Country." There are probably more good fishing and hunting lodges in the Lake of the Woods area than anywhere in the world: literally hundreds of resorts specializing in fly-in fishing camps, native guides, and fall moose hunts. Fanciful names such as Red Indian Lodge or the Rod and Reel Resort in Sioux Narrows; Lindmeier's North Shore Lodge in Eagle River; Keyamawun Lodge on Red Lake; Long Legged Lake Resort on Ear Falls; and the aptly named Canadian Wilderness Camp near Kenora. (For how to get more information on these, see the Accommodations Reference section at the end of the chapter.)

A good vantage point for an overview of the entire area is from the tenth-floor dining room at the top of the **Inn of the Woods**, a circular hotel overlooking the boat-filled bay (the view, however, under a seemingly immutable Law of Travel, surpasses the cuisine). The best method for exploring the region is to rent a houseboat and dawdle around the beautiful lake system; check out Go Vacations (Tel: 800-387-3998 or 800-661-9558) or Houseboat Adventures (Tel: 807-468-3521).

Kenora, not to be outdone by Wawa with its Goose or Dryden with its Moose, boasts its own 20-foot roadside symbol. "Husky the Muskie," a huge statue of a jumping fish (a giant muskellunge) overlooks the bay of the town. And judging from an informal survey, Muskie is photographed by more tourists than the other two combined—there is something odder about a huge roadside fish standing on its tail than a moose or goose.

For the best steak ever (except for the one you cook on your own barbecue) visit the **Kenmore Hotel**. Don't let the rather seedy exterior fool you—or the interior, for that matter. After all, this is an unsophisticated little northern town. Just concentrate on your meal. Unfortunately, they will not divulge their secret, whether it is the aging process or seasoning, but the steaks are superb.

Perhaps as a reward for the long drive and the stays at the little roadside motels en route, you should visit **Minaki Lodge**, in the little fishing village of Minaki about 50 km (30 miles) north of Kenora, straight up Highway 596. This magnificent lodge of timber and stone, with its impressive cathedral ceiling, was built as a railway hotel, a midpoint lodge for travellers on a trans-Canada journey. Today, it is a rebuilt and refurbished grand hotel, with all-new guest rooms and fine dining, golf, tennis, boating, and fly-in fishing, managed for the Four Seasons (a Canadian chain that is known for its first-class properties) by the well-known Ontario resortier Michael Grise. Rates are surprisingly reasonable; the all-inclusive package (room, breakfast and dinner, all facilities) is a mere $325 per person for three days; $779 for a week.

As you backtrack and continue west on Highway 17, the roadside scenery, which has been lined with forests and rocks, becomes flatter, and the wooded areas much more sparse. By the time you reach the Trans-Canada Highway, or Highway 1 (more than 1,800 km/1,100 miles west of Toronto), which will stretch the rest of the way across the country to the British Columbia coast, the flat prairie will dominate the landscape and will do so for the next 1,000 miles. In fact, the scenery changes so dramatically when you reach the Manitoba border that that western province seems to be declaring its own identity, rejecting the wildness of Ontario's northland—filled with trees, rocks, and lakes—for the flat calm of golden prairie wheat.

GETTING AROUND

Muskoka and Ontario's Near North

To reach cottages or resorts, most people go by car, heading north up Highway 400 and then branching off on Highway 26 to Collingwood or Highway 11 to Muskoka. For the Kawarthas and Haliburton, the back roads are more scenic, but to save time go as far east as possible on Highway 401 before turning north.

Most people use Highway 35. This is the best exit for the Trent-Severn Waterway, the major portion of which is in the Kawarthas. Information on the system from most parts of North America can be obtained by telephoning Ontario Travel Information at (800) 268-3735. Alternately, contact the Friends of Trent-Severn, Box 572, Peterborough, Ont. K9J 6Z6; Tel: (705) 742-2251.

Driving time is short. From the north end of Toronto, it takes only two and a half hours to reach Huntsville in north Muskoka; one and a half hours to reach Collingwood in Huronia or Rice Lake in the lower Kawarthas. Haliburton is about a three-hour drive.

One train a day, except for Saturdays, leaves at noon heading north out of Toronto's Union Station, stopping at Gravenhurst and Huntsville. Another leaves daily at 9:25 P.M., making many stops on its way to northern Ontario. Book through VIA Rail in Canada or Amtrak in the United States.

Buses offer frequent, sometimes express, service on all well-travelled routes and serve all communities regularly.

Many resorts now will arrange pickup and return by air, usually from Toronto's Island Airport. From this point Air Muskoka (Tel: 705-687-6696) has flights daily to Muskoka Airport (located between Gravenhurst and Bracebridge).

Northern Ontario

The trans-Canada VIA Rail may not be on a par with the famed Orient Express, but then neither is the price. The basic rate between Toronto and Vancouver is $302 per person (coach seat); a roomette for one is an extra $190; a double bed, $400 a couple. The train is clean and comfortable; the roomettes are tiny (two seats facing each other during the day, a small bed at night), and food ranges from sterling-silver service to snack-bar menu.

You really should arrange for a roomette, or sleeper car. There is nothing worse than trying to doze in a train seat (except maybe a bus) as you spend three days crossing the country. The scenic glories are strained under these rather tiring conditions.

Most people board the train in Montreal or Toronto, although some start right at the East Coast (i.e., Halifax) for a full Canada tour. You can even board Amtrak at Penn Station in New York City and connect with a VIA train at the border. (VIA Rail, Passenger Services, Union Station, Front Street West, Toronto, M5S 1E6; Tel: 416-367-1925.) U.S. visitors can also check with their Amtrak representative; U.K. visitors with BritRail. Central information sources in Canada are **VIA Rail**, 2 Place Ville Marie, Suite 400, Montreal, Que. H3B 2G6; Tel: (514) 871-6000, or **VIA Rail**, 20 King Street West, Toronto, Ont. M5H 1C4; Tel: (416) 868-7211.

The Polar Bear Express

Book tickets through Ontario Northland Railway, 510 Main Street East, North Bay, Ont. P1B 8L3; Tel: (705) 472-4500, or Union Station in Toronto.

The Agawa Canyon Train

This train leaves from the ACR Mall station (Algoma Central Railway) on Bay Street in Sault Ste. Marie daily from June to October at 8:30 A.M. and returns by 5:00 P.M.; both cold and hot lunches are served; the fare is $35 round trip per adult. Book well in advance, especially if you're planning to travel during peak fall season, when you will experience the most brilliant autumn colors imaginable. Contact: Algoma Central Railway, 129 Bay Street, Sault Ste. Marie, Ont. P6A 1W7; Tel: (705) 254-4331.

ACCOMMODATIONS REFERENCE

Southwestern Ontario

▶ **Albion Hotel.** Main Street, Box 114, **Bayfield,** Ont. N0M 1G0. Tel: (519) 565-2443.

▶ **Angel Inn.** 224 Regent Street, **Niagara-on-the-Lake,** Ont. L0S 1J0. Tel: (416) 468-3411.

▶ **Beacon Motor Inn.** Box 70, **Jordan Station,** Ont. L0R 1S0. Tel: (416) 562-4155 or (800) 263-2442.

▶ **Bedford Hotel.** 92 Courthouse Square, **Goderich,** Ont. N7A 1M7. Tel: (519) 524-7337.

▶ **Benjamin's Restaurant & Inn.** 17 King Street, **St. Jacobs,** Ont. N0B 2N0. Tel: (519) 664-3731.

▶ **Benmiller Inn.** R.R. 4, **Goderich,** Ont. N7A 3Y1. Tel: (519) 524-2191 or (800) 265-1711 in Canada.

▶ **Bentley's Jester Arms Inn.** 107 Ontario Street, **Stratford,** Ont. N5A 3H1. Tel: (519) 271-1211.

▶ **Briarwood Inn.** 299 King Street, **London,** Ont. N6B 1S1. Tel: (519) 673-3300 or (800) 528-1234.

▶ **Brock Hotel.** 5685 Falls Avenue, **Niagara Falls,** Ont. L2E 6W7. Tel: (416) 374-4444.

▶ **Desert Rose Inn.** 60 Mill Street West, **Elora,** Ont. N0B 1S0. Tel: (519) 846-9600.

▶ **Duffy's Motor Inn.** 306 Dalhousie Street, **Amherstburg,** Ont. N9V 1X3. Tel: (519) 736-2101

▶ **Dyconia Resort Hotel.** 381 Mosley Street, **Wasaga Beach,** Ont. L0L 2P0. Tel: (705) 429-2000.

▶ **Elora Mill Inn.** 77 Mill Street West, **Elora,** Ont. N0B 1S0. Tel: (519) 846-5356.

▶ **Erie Beach.** Walker Street, **Port Dover,** Ont. N0A 1N0. Tel: (519) 583-1391.

▶ **Foxhead Hotel.** 5875 Falls Avenue, **Niagara Falls,** Ont. L2E 6W7. Tel: (416) 374-4444.

▶ **Gate House.** 142 Queen Street, **Niagara-on-the-Lake,** Ont. L0S 1J0. Tel: (416) 468-7201.

▶ **Hartley House Hotel.** 130 Durham Street East, Box 790, **Walkerton,** Ont. N0G 2V0. Tel: (519) 881-1040.

▶ **Holiday Inn by the Falls.** 5339 Murray Street, **Niagara Falls,** Ont. L2G 2J3. Tel: (416) 356-133 or (800) 263-9393.

▶ **Honeymoon City Motel.** 4943 Clifton Hill, **Niagara Falls**, Ont. L2G 3N5. Tel: (416) 357-4330.

▶ **Idlewyld Inn.** 36 Grant Avenue, **London**, Ont. N6C 1K8. Tel: (519) 433-2891.

▶ **Inn on the Bay.** 1800 2nd Avenue East, **Owen Sound**, Ont. N4K 5P1. Tel: (519) 371-9200.

▶ **Jakobstettel Guest House.** 16 Isabella Street, **St. Jacobs**, Ont. N0B 2N0. Tel: (519) 664-2208.

▶ **Journey's End Leamington.** 279 Erie Street South, **Leamington**, Ont. N8H 3C4. Tel: (519) 326-9071 or (800) 268-0405.

▶ **Kettle Creek Inn.** Main Street, **Port Stanley**, Ont. N0L 2A0. Tel: (519) 782-3388.

▶ **Little Inn of Bayfield.** Main Street, **Bayfield**, Ont. N0M 1G0. Tel: (519) 565-2611.

▶ **Lock 7 Motel.** 24 Chapel Street South, **Thorold**, Ont. L2V 2C6. Tel: (416) 227-6177.

▶ **Moffat Inn.** 60 Picton Street, **Niagara-on-the-Lake**, Ont. L0S 1J0. Tel: (416) 468-4116.

▶ **Oakwood Inn Resort, Golf and Country Club.** Box 400, **Grand Bend**, Ont. N0M 1T0. Tel: (519) 238-2324.

▶ **Oban Inn.** 160 Front Street, **Niagara-on-the-Lake**, Ont. L0S 1J0. Tel: (416) 468-2165.

▶ **Old Stone Inn.** 5425 Robinson Street, **Niagara Falls**, Ont. L2G 7L6. Tel: (416) 357-1234; in U.S. (800) CLARION; in Canada (800) 458-6262.

▶ **Pelee Motor Inn.** P.O. Box 616, **Leamington**, Ont. N8H 3X4. Tel: (519) 326-8647 or (800) 265-5329.

▶ **Pillar & Post Inn.** King & John Streets, **Niagara-on-the-Lake**, Ont. L0S 1J0. Tel: (416) 468-2123.

▶ **Prince of Wales.** 6 Picton Street, **Niagara-on-the-Lake**, Ont. L0S 1J0. Tel: (416) 468-3246.

▶ **Queen's Inn.** 161 Ontario Street, **Stratford**, Ont. N5A 3H3. Tel: (519) 271-1400.

▶ **Royal Connaught.** 112 King Street East, **Hamilton**, Ont. L8N 1A8. Tel: (416) 527-5071 or (800) 263-8558.

▶ **Sheraton Armouries.** 325 Dundas Street, **London**, Ont. N6B 1T9. Tel: (519) 679-6111.

▶ **Sheraton Hamilton.** 116 King Street West, **Hamilton**, Ont. L8P 4V3. Tel: (416) 529-5515 or (800) 325-3535.

▶ **South Landing Inn.** P.O. Box 269, 21 Front Street, **Queenston**, Ont. L0S 1L0 Tel: (416) 262-4634.

▶ **Valhalla Inn.** 105 King Street East, **Kitchener**, Ont. N2G 3W9. Tel: (519) 744-4141 or (800) 268-2500.

▶ **Walper Terrace Hotel.** 1 King Street West, **Kitchener,** Ont. N2G 1A1. Tel: (519) 745-4321.

▶ **Waterlot Inn.** 17 Huron Street, **New Hamburg,** Ont. N0B 2G0. Tel: (519) 662-2020.

▶ **Westover Inn.** 300 Thomas Street, P.O. Box 280, **St. Mary's,** Ont. N0M 2V0. Tel: (519) 284-2977.

▶ **Westview Tavern and Motel. Pelee Island,** Ont. N0R 1M0. Tel: (519) 724-2072.

▶ **Windsor Hilton.** 277 Riverside Drive West, **Windsor,** Ont. N9A 5K4. Tel: (519) 973-5555.

Muskoka and Ontario's Near North

▶ **Arowhon Pines.** Algonquin Park, **Huntsville,** Ont. P0A 1K0. Tel: (705) 633-5661 in summer; (416) 483-4393 in winter.

▶ **Blue Mountain Inn.** R. R. 3, **Collingwood,** Ont. L9Y 3Z2. Tel: (416) 869-3799 or (705) 445-0231.

▶ **Country Host.** R.R. 1 **Palgrave,** Ont. L0N 1P0. Tel: (519) 941-7633.

▶ **Cranberry Inn Resort.** Highway 26 West, **Collingwood,** Ont. L9Y 3Z4. Tel: (705) 445-6600 or (416) 962-7925.

▶ **Deerhurst Inn and Country Club.** R. R. 4, **Huntsville,** Ont. P0A 1K0. Tel: (705) 789-5543 or (800) 461-4393.

▶ **Domain of Killien.** Box 810, **Haliburton,** Ont. K0M 1S0. Tel: (705) 457-1556 or (800) 461-3400; Fax: (705) 457-3853.

▶ **Eleanor Fulcher Spa.** On **Lake Muskoka,** c/o Eaton Centre; 220 Yonge Street, Galleria Offices, Suite 215, P.O. Box 606, Toronto, Ont. M6C 1B8. Tel: (416) 979-7577.

▶ **Elmhirst's.** R. R. 1, **Keene,** Ont. K0L 2G0. Tel: (705) 295-4591.

▶ **Go Vacations.** 129 Carlingview Drive, **Rexdale,** Ont. M9W 5E7. Tel: (800) 661-9558 or (800) 387-3998.

▶ **The Inn and Tennis Club at Manitou. McKellar,** Ont. P0G 1C0. Tel: (705) 389-2790.

▶ **The Inn at Horseshoe.** R.R. 1, **Barrie,** Ont. L4M 4Y8. Tel: (705) 835-2790.

▶ **King Ranch.** R.R.2, **King City,** Ont. L0G 1K0. Tel: (416) 833-7721; Fax: (416) 833-2870.

▶ **Maple Sands Resort.** R.R. 1, **Haliburton,** Ont. K0M 1S0. Tel: (705) 754-2800 or (416) 281-3480.

▶ **Muskoka Sands Resort. Gravenhurst,** Ont. P0C 1G0. Tel: (705) 687-2233 or (800) 461-0236.

▶ **PineStone Inn. Haliburton,** Ont. K0M 1S0. Tel: (705) 457-1800 or (416) 423-2000.

▶ **Pretty River Valley Farm.** Box 254, **Collingwood,** Ont. L9Y 3Z5. Tel: (705) 445-7598.

▶ **Sherwood Inn.** P.O. Box 400, **Port Carling,** Ont. P0B 1J0. Tel: (705) 765-3131 or (800) 461-4233.

▶ **Sir Sam's Inn.** Eagle Lake Post Office, **Eagle Lake,** Ont. K0M 1M0. Tel: (705) 754-2188 or (416) 283-2080.

▶ **Viamede Resort.** Woodview P.O., **Woodview,** Ont. K0L 3E0. Tel: (705) 654-3344 or (800) 461-1946.

▶ **Waltonian Inn.** Lake Nipissing, R.R. 1, **Callander,** Ont. P0H 1H0. Tel: (705) 752-2060. Specializes in ice fishing.

▶ **Westwind Resort.** Box 91, **Buckhorn,** Ont. K0L 1J0. Tel: (705) 657-8095.

▶ **Wig-a-mog Inn.** R.R. 2, **Haliburton,** Ont. K0M 1S0. Tel: (705) 457-2000 or (416) 861-1358.

▶ **Windermere House. Windermere,** Muskoka, Ont. P0B 1P0. Tel: (705) 769-3611 or (800) 461-4283.

Eastern Ontario

▶ **Blinkbonnie Motor Lodge.** 50 Main Street, **Gananoque,** Ont. K7G 2L7. Tel: (613) 382-7272.

▶ **The Gananoque Inn.** 550 Stone Street South, **Gananoque,** Ont. K7G 2A8. Tel: (613) 382-2165.

▶ **Grand McCammon Inn.** 279 King Street West, **Gananoque,** Ont. K7G 2G7. Tel: (613) 382-3368.

▶ **Greenwood Towers Inn.** 162 Peter Street, **Port Hope,** Ont. L1A 3V9. Tel: (416) 885-7283.

▶ **Holiday Inn.** 1 Princess Street, **Kingston,** Ont. K7L 1A1. Tel: (613) 549-8400.

▶ **Holiday Inn.** 150 George Street, **Peterborough,** Ont. K9J 3G5. Tel: (705) 743-1122; in U.S. and Canada, (800) 465-4329; Fax: (705) 743-0033.

▶ **Howard Johnson.** 237 Ontario Street, **Kingston,** Ont. K7L 2Z4. Tel: (613) 549-6300.

▶ **Isaiah Tubbs Inn & Resort.** R.R. #1, **Picton,** Ont. K0K 2T0. Tel: (613) 393-5694.

▶ **Old Bridge Inn.** Young's Point, Ont. K0L 3T0. Tel: (705) 652-8507.

▶ **Sandbanks Beach Resort.** R.R. #1, **Picton,** Ont. K0K 2T0. Tel: (613) 393-3022.

Northern Ontario

▶ **Airlane.** 698 Arthur Street West, **Thunder Bay,** Ont. P7E 5R8. Tel: (807) 577-1181.

▶ **Best Western Water Tower Inn.** 360 Great Northern Road, **Sault Ste. Marie,** Ont. P6A 5N3. Tel: (705) 949-8111 or (800) 528-1234.

▶ **Hannah Bay Goose Camp.** c/o 195 Regina Street, **North Bay**, Ont. P1B 8L3. Tel: (705) 472-4500.

▶ **Inn of the Woods.** 470 First Avenue South, **Kenora**, Ont. P9N 1W5. Tel: (807) 468-5521.

▶ **Landmark Hotel.** 1010 Dawson, **Thunder Bay**, Ont. P7B SJ4. Tel: (807) 767-1681 or (800) 465-3950.

▶ **Manitowaning Lodge.** Box 160, **Manitowaning**, Ont. P0P 1N0. Tel: (705) 859-3136.

▶ **Minaki Lodge. Minaki**, Ontario P0X 1J0. Tel: (807) 224-4000 or (800) 465-3331.

▶ **Moosonee Lodge. Moosonee**, Ont. P0L 1Y0. Tel: (705) 336-2351.

▶ **Polar Bear Lodge. Moosonee**, Ont. P0L 1Y0. Tel: (705) 336-2345.

▶ **Red Oak Inn.** 555 Arthur Street West. **Thunder Bay**, Ont. P7E 5R5. Tel: (807) 577-8481 or (800) 267-7835.

▶ **Rossport Inn. Rossport**, Ont. P0T 2R0. Tel: (807) 824-3213.

▶ **Sheraton Caswell Inn.** 1696 Regent Street, **Sudbury**, Ont. P3E 3Z8. Tel: (705) 522-3000 or (800) 325-3535.

▶ **Silver Birches Resort.** R.R. 1, **Little Current**, Ont. P0P 1K0. Tel: (705) 368-2669.

▶ **Valhalla Inn.** 1 Valhalla Inn Road, **Thunder Bay**, Ont. P7E 6J1. Tel: (807) 577-1121 or (800) 268-2500.

▶ **Wawa Motor Lodge.** 100 Mission Road, **Wawa**, Ont. P0S 1K0. Tel: (705) 856-2278.

Fishing Lodges & Camps

There are hundreds of facilities not included here. For a complete listing, write for a free copy of the Northern Ontario book (also fishing, hunting, and boating) from Northern Ontario Tourist Outfitters Association (NOTO), P.O. Box 1140F, North Bay, Ont. P1B 8K4. Tel: (705) 472-5552.

There are also many cozy country inns dotted throughout the Ontario countryside for those who prefer more quiet charm than resort-style luxury. For bookings, or more information, contact **Barbara's Country Inns**, a most helpful reservation service at 121 Glen Road, Toronto, Ont. M4W 2W1. Tel: (416) 968-7590.

MANITOBA

By Lee Schacter

Lee Schacter was born in Manitoba and has lived there—currently in Winnipeg—all her life. She has written regularly for the Winnipeg Free Press *and has written scripts for the Manitoba Department of Education school broadcasts.*

Canada's "keystone province" is doubtless viewed by the uninitiated as a stretch of flat prairie, where there is nothing to do and nowhere to do it. They're totally wrong on both counts.

Geographically, Manitoba has prairies, parkland, forests, lakes, and hills. In the wooded areas, particularly in the north, there is some of the best hunting and fishing in Canada, as well as spectacular scenery. Manitoba even has the world's only human settlement where polar bears can be seen in their natural habitat: Churchill.

MAJOR INTEREST

Winnipeg
Museum of Man and Nature
Exchange District shopping and dining
River cruises
Assiniboia Downs horseracing
Folklorama festival
St. Boniface Museum

Elsewhere in Manitoba
Lower Fort Garry
Mennonite Heritage Village at Steinbach
Dauphin's Ukrainian Festival
Oak Hammock Marsh
Fishing in the north

Canoeing trips in the north
Whiteshell summer resort
Gimli summer resort
Rock hounding at Souris
Wasagaming summer resort
Spirit Sands desert
Polar bears and beluga whales at Churchill

WINNIPEG

Winnipeg, the capital of Manitoba, sits in proud isolation in the exact geographic center of the continent. Its closest big neighbor is Minneapolis, 750 km (450 miles) to the south. Winnipeg is a stable, busy city of 600,000 inhabitants, including members of some 30 ethnic groups—most of whom have arrived in the past 30 years.

Winnipeggers like their city, so they were not surprised when it received a three-star rating from Michelin. They like their city because it's not too big and not too small. A 35-minute drive gets them from one end of town to the other. The arts, in the form of symphony, theater, and dance, flourish here, and the streets are quite safe in most areas. In relation to a city like Toronto, the pace of life is leisurely.

Winnipeg's Rivers

The city is crisscrossed by rivers; the two greatest being the Red and the Assiniboine. The Red flows mainly through the northern part of the city, the Assiniboine through both the north and the south, and the two meet at The Forks, at Provencher and Water Street. Visitors can cruise these rivers on paddlewheel steamers; The *Paddlewheel Queen* and the *Paddlewheel Princess* cruise the Red River, and the *River Rouge* and *Lady Winnipeg* cruise both the Red and the Assiniboine, going through the city center. (The latter two sail from 312 Nairn Avenue; Tel: 669-2824, and the two former from the foot of the Provencher bridge at Water Street; Tel: 942-4500.) There's also *The Lord Selkirk,* one of the largest inland cruise ships on the continent (not a paddlewheel). It takes the visitor on a three-hour sail north and it also serves dockside buffets. It docks at the Redwood Bridge (Main Street at Redwood); Tel: 582-2331. These are lovely, cool outings for tired sightseers.

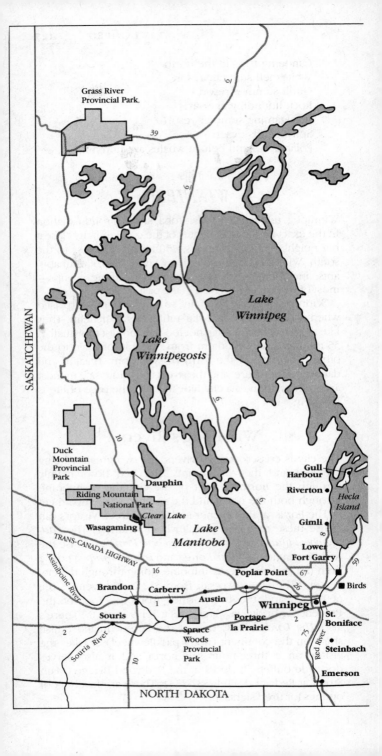

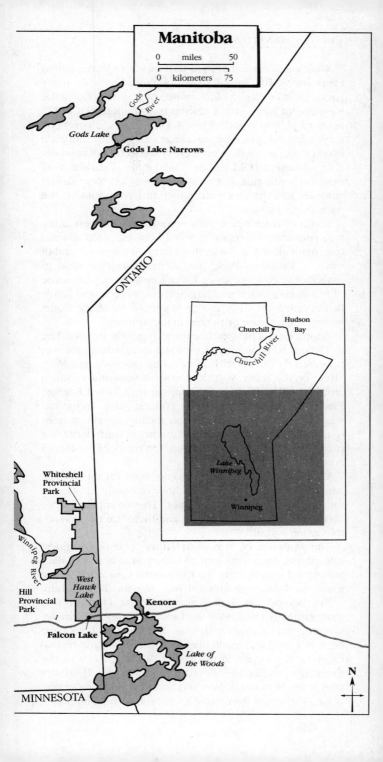

Winnipeg's city fathers saw to it that trees were planted everywhere. The air is free of pollution. There are many parks, most of them a block or two of greenery. But at the west end of Wellington Crescent is **Assiniboine Park**, 375 acres of rolling wooded lawns, picnic sites, a conservatory (a favorite place for weddings), and a zoo. There are even cricket grounds, where every weekend polite white-clad cricketers hold games. This peaceful park is very busy on weekends, but is never rowdy or noisy. In the summer months there are ballet and symphony in the park: free, of course.

South of Assiniboine Park is **Assiniboine Forest**, a nature preserve. There are rare wild flowers, wild animals (too many deer), and waterfowl here. At the north end of town is **Kildonan Park**, not as manicured or staid as Assiniboine Park but more like a forest. It contains some of Manitoba's oldest and largest trees, a creek, and lovely flower gardens. This is the home of Rainbow Stage, where musicals are presented in the summer.

Winnipeg is a flat city, like the vast prairie surrounding it. The city has one main downtown area, Portage Avenue, bounded by Memorial Boulevard on one side and Main Street on the other. Portage Avenue is now undergoing a face-lift, with a huge new shopping mall called **Portage Place**. The IMAX theater is in Portage Place, and it has what is called the finest motion picture system in existence. Films of extraordinary sharpness and clarity are projected on the gigantic screen, ten times larger than a conventional one.

Winnipeggers don't sit at home, even on the coldest winter days. In fact, perversely, they're out more often in the winter than in the summer. They complain more about the heat than the cold—and there are no mosquitoes when it's cold.

The **Museum of Man and Nature**, one of the finest interpretive museums in the country, stands at 555 Main Street, and beside it are the **Centennial Concert Hall**, the focus of Winnipeg's cultural life, and the **Planetarium**.

Just behind City Hall is the **Exchange District**. This interesting area was once the heart of Winnipeg's wholesale and manufacturing district. The old buildings have been restored and made over into fine stores and restaurants, facing a park in the center. Walking tours of the Exchange District are offered free by the city. The tours start at the Museum of Man and Nature and last about one hour. (Parks and Recreation Department; Tel: 986-6287.)

A new and exotic **Chinatown**, with restaurants, stores, and apartment blocks replacing run-down old buildings, is going up just past the Exchange District on King Street.

The trendiest area in the city is **Osborne Village**, a block-long street of clever little shops, restaurants (some with outdoor dining), and art galleries. This was once a tacky, run-down section of the city, and it took a great deal of courage for a few adventurous young entrepreneurs to open shops here. But the idea caught on, much to the surprise of Winnipeggers, who had been programmed for generations to shop downtown. Soon more shops opened: a kitchen shop, dress shops, a health-food store, a shop selling beautiful Icelandic sweaters and jackets, an art gallery. Now it's a great area for browsing even if you don't buy anything. You can stop for tea and scones at **The Tea Cozy**, 303-99 Osborne.

Corydon Avenue in staid River Heights at the south end of the city is the setting for more original shops, run by eager young businesspeople. Up until the early 1950s, River Heights was the almost exclusive domain of the city's well-to-do proper sort of people, but the barriers came down when people who didn't know they weren't supposed to be there moved in, plus people from the country, and those seeking well-kept homes in a quiet setting. Today, River Heights is a multi-ethnic district, with excellent schools, neighbors who mingle, a colorful Italian area, and the highest voter turnout in the city on any election day.

Elegant shops have opened up on Academy Road, which runs the length of the district: gift shops (the best is **A Touch of Class**), antiques stores, **The Paper Gallery**, where you can buy anything made of paper, expensive dress shops (**Sofia's**); you name it, it's here. Some of the shops have cutesy names, like Kitschy Kool and Boutique Monique, but the merchandise is superior, and so are the prices.

Winnipeg Theatre

Winnipeg has a number of small theaters. The **Gas Station Theatre** in Osborne Village carries productions by local and touring groups, and seats 232 people, a perfect size for shows which would not fill a large hall. There's modern dance, excellent children's shows, some experimental works, and standard drama. Tickets are not difficult to obtain, but it's a good idea to check with the box office beforehand. Tel: 284-5870 or 284-2757. The **Prairie Theatre Exchange**, in Portage Place, is big on plays that enlighten. That is, if you have the medium, send a message. But it does provide a forum for local playwrights. Tel: 942-5483. Probably the best of the small theaters, and the most professional, is **The Warehouse**, at 140 Rupert Avenue. They show alternative theater in a small house that seats 300 people on three sides of a floor-level stage, which brings the audience right into the play. Tel: 942-6537.

In July, there's **The Fringe Festival**, a binge of affordable theater, with touring companies from all over the globe playing in various parts of the city. For information, call The Warehouse box office.

One of Winnipeg's most popular attractions is racing at **Assiniboia Downs**. The track and grandstand facilities offer some of the best horse racing in the west, pari-mutuel betting, and a terraced dining room. (Located at 3975 Portage Avenue; public transportation available. Tel: 885-3330.)

Dining in Winnipeg

Winnipeg has more than 700 restaurants, and they range from the elegant and very expensive to family establishments. The latter are usually ethnic places, often small and inexpensive. (Visitors should know that Winnipeg restaurants tend to be closed in and dim; it's because there's no great scenery to look out on.)

Of Winnipeg's 50-plus Chinese restaurants, the best are **Marigold**, at 245 King Street in the heart of Chinatown (it has eight locations but this, the original, is still the best), and the **Foon Hai**, at 3-1855 Pembina Highway (in a small shopping mall opposite the Ramada Inn). At the Foon Hai, try the Mu Shu or the sizzling shrimps with black bean and garlic sauce. Winnipeg undoubtedly has the best Chinese restaurants in Canada. (Montreal and Toronto might argue the point, but a fact is a fact.) At the **India Gardens**, 764 McDermot (in the Exchange District), food is prepared as hot or as mild as you wish. **Homer's**, at 520 Ellice, is Greek. **Amici's**, at 326 Broadway, serves imaginative Italian food, heavy on the pastas and sauces. It is chic and expensive and is patronized by the young and prosperous. Reservations are a good idea; Tel: 943-4997. The same owner runs **Victor's**, a very expensive, standard Continental restaurant in Osborne Village.

For more ethnic fare try **Tropikis**, at 878 Ellice Avenue, for Caribbean food, cheap and wonderful (Tel: 788-4733); **Picasso's Seafood Restaurant**, at 615 Sargent Avenue, superb Portugese and Spanish meals (Tel: 775-2469); and **Monte Bello** for excellent and expensive Italian fare.' (It had better be good, with the large Italian community here.) Monte Bello is at 1480 Pembina Highway; Tel: 284-8402.

For those who want a bit more elegance there's **Du Bon Gout**, at 940 Corydon Avenue. It's a converted house run by two inspired amateurs. The food is spectacular—and so are the prices. Try the Veal Escalopes with smoked salmon and caper sauce, or the Bife a Portugais. For those who are of the opinion that the taste of chicken changes when different sauces surround it, the Stuffed Chicken Normandy should please. Along with Amici's, Du Bon Gout is rated one of the best restaurants in the city; Tel: 453-2291.

Now to the longest established ethnic restaurants here—the Jewish and Ukrainian. For these the visitor must drive to Winnipeg's **North End**. The North End is not merely a geographic location but a national institution. This was the area where immigrants from Eastern Europe, mostly Jews and Ukrainians, came in the early part of the century. Intensely ambitious, they expected their children to succeed in life, and succeed they did, to an astonishing degree. Many of them, like David Steinberg, are internationally known; others have achieved outstanding positions in law, medicine, and education in Canada. Countless books, plays, and songs have been written about Winnipeg's North End. Wherever ex-Northenders are, they carry that part of the city with them.

The Jews and Ukrainians have moved on, and a new wave of immigrants, mostly native Indians from Manitoba's reserves, now inhabit the North End. Winnipeg has the largest native population per capita of any North American city. (Los Angeles has the second.)

As to the restaurants in the North End: **Alycia's**, at 559 Cathedral Avenue, is a modest, family-run Ukrainian restaurant, where borscht, cabbage soup, holopchi, pirogi, and kielbasa are served. This is a very popular neighborhood place, small with reasonable prices. Reservations are advised; Tel: 586-9697.

For deli food, there's a trio of great places—**Garry's**, at 675 Jefferson (portions are enormous); **Oscar's**, at 1204 Main; and **Simon's**, at 1322 Main. Garry's has recently changed hands and the new owner is working hard to keep up with the competition—the three are in a perpetual contest to see which has the best corned beef and pastrami. Business people from all over the city come here for lunch.

Back downtown, there's **Rae and Jerry's**, at 1405 Portage Avenue, another Winnipeg institution. It's conservative and quiet, with food that's consistently good, especially the steaks and roast beef. It's a busy place, moderately expensive, with maternal waitresses who seem to have been there forever. Reservations are advised; Tel: 783-6155.

Finally, there's a bit of Olde England at **Jim's Fish & Chips**, a plain café at 1656 Portage Avenue that serves the best halibut in town. There is no ambience here, just good food. Jim's reputation has now spread throughout the city, so there's a steady trek of customers. Prices are very reasonable, and liquor is served. No reservations are taken, so be prepared to wait.

As for nightlife, the **Marble Club**, at 65 Rorie, and the **Night Moves**, a cabaret in Windsor Park Inn, at 1034 Elizabeth in St. Boniface, are extremely popular with young people. **Yuk Yuk's Komedy Kabaret** at 108 Osborne, or **Rumors Comedy Club** at 2025 Corydon, feature standup comics. Advance tickets are recommended at both clubs.

Accommodations in Winnipeg

(The telephone area code for Winnipeg is 204.)

Winnipeg has many hotels and motels, but most of the places where visitors can stay comfortably are in the downtown area. The few neighborhood hotels tend to be mere excuses to run a pub, and they are often noisy.

Close to the airport is the **International Inn**. This is a family-owned enterprise, and is a bustling, lively place with a warm atmosphere and all the amenities; indoor and outdoor pools and a professional dinner show in the Hollow Mug restaurant. The one drawback to the hotel is its distance from downtown, a 20-minute drive.

1808 Wellington Street, R3H 0G3; Tel: 786-4801 or (800) 528-1234.

The **Marlborough Inn** is a dignified structure with antique stonework and old-fashioned rooms. At one time this hotel was owned by a family who ran it on a very tight budget; now the purse strings have been loosened, giving the Marlborough a much more welcoming air. It also once had one of the worst restaurants in Winnipeg, where bookies would meet to take illegal bets. Now the restaurant is run by a remarkable woman and is a fine place to eat.

331 Smith Street R3B 2G9; Tel: 942-6411.

The **Relax Plaza Hotel** is your basic budget inn—new, clean, and adequate.

360 Colony, R3B 2P3; Tel: 786-7011.

For sheer posh there are the **Westin** and the **Sheraton**, both downtown, both expensive, and both catering to clients who want to be pampered. The Westin has a dinner theater called Chimes.

Westin, 2 Lombard Place, R3B 0Y5; Tel: 957-1350 or (800) 228-3000. Sheraton, 161 Donald Street, R3C 1M3; Tel: 942-5300 or (800) 325-3535.

The grande dame of hostelries, **The Hotel Fort Garry**, is in a class by itself. This regal hotel, where royalty once stayed, was built for the Canadian National Railway in the early part of the century and was then the epitome of elegance. When the railway was no longer able to support the hotel, it fell on bad times, with the city and environmental groups desperately trying to save it. It has now been named a heritage building, and by great good fortune bought by a gentleman who loves hotels. The Fort Garry has been repolished, refurbished, and updated without losing any of its previous grandeur.

1222 Broadway, R3C 0R3; Tel: 942-8251 or (800) 665-8088.

Shopping in Winnipeg

Favorite purchase items with visitors to Winnipeg are Hudson's Bay blankets and coats, made from thick pure wool for the past 300 years; Indian and Inuit artifacts; bone china; and woolens and furs. Go to **The Bay** for blankets and woolens; to **Birks** or **Breslauer and Warren**—two upscale jewelry stores—for china; for Inuit carvings and prints, try the **Crafts Guild of Manitoba**, an excellent shop run by volunteers, or the **Winnipeg Art Gallery**'s gift shop. Sheepskin coats and jackets are very popular because they're light and very warm. The best place to buy them is at **Lambskin Specialties**, 579 Selkirk Avenue in the North End (the store will even make them to order).

Winnipeg has many indoor shopping malls. The prettiest is **Polo Park** on Portage Avenue, recently renovated and now bright, airy, and lively. The best time to go is

Saturday afternoon, when what appears to be half the population of Winnipeg gathers there, especially the young.

St. Boniface

Across the Red River, south on Main Street over the Norwood Bridge, is St. Boniface, Winnipeg's French quarter, the largest French community in the West. When you cross into St. Boniface, a street becomes a *rue;* a road is a *chem;* "hello" becomes *bonjour.* Provencher is the main boulevard in St. Boniface, and here you can order croissants or frogs legs, buy a French-Canadian novel, and try out your French. You may be answered in English, because only a quarter of the population of 43,000 is French-speaking.

St. Boniface has a history dating back to 1738, when the explorer Sieur de la Vérendrye arrived. After him came four Grey Nuns from Montreal, and it was the convent built for them that later became the **Musée Saint-Boniface**. This, the oldest building in Winnipeg and the largest log construction in North America, contains an extensive collection of Métis artifacts, which vividly recall the early community.

In the early 19th century, the colony was predominantly Métis (French and Indian), and its leader was Louis Riel. In 1869 Riel led a rebellion resisting a takeover by Canada. Riel's rebellion came to an end when the region entered confederation. He fled to Saskatchewan, where he led an even bloodier rebellion, was captured, tried, and hanged in 1885. Riel has become a folk hero—plays are written about him and songs sung. His body was brought back from Saskatchewan and buried in the cemetery in front of St. Boniface Cathedral. A museum featuring French-Canadian artifacts sits beside the cemetery; nearby is St. Boniface College, the French campus of the University of Manitoba. The most exciting event in St. Boniface is the **Festival du Voyageur**, a weeklong carnival of fun in February.

There are a few excellent restaurants in St. Boniface that specialize in traditional French-Canadian fare. **La Vieille Gare**, at 630 Des Meurons, occupies a converted, elegantly appointed railway station built in 1914, and serves such specialties as châteaubriand, *canard à l'orange,* sole meuniere, or breast of capon in Champagne sauce (Tel: 237-7072). The **Red Lantern Steak House** at

302 Hamel Avenue is a cozy little restaurant that serves
such dishes as coquilles St. Jacques and *coq au vin* (Tel:
233-4841). **Le Beaujolais**, at 131 Provencher Boulevard,
serving traditional and nouvelle cuisine, is *haut ton* and
expensive. It's just a five-minute drive from downtown
(Tel: 237-6306). **Le Couscous**, at 135 Marion, is a bit of
Africa in St. Boniface, and features excellent northern
African food (Tel: 237-3775). Reservations are advised for
all of these restaurants.

French and English walking tours of St. Boniface start
from Taché Promenade, Taché Avenue at Cathedral Avenue; Tel: 233-4888.

THE RED RIVER BASIN

The Red River basin around Winnipeg is rich in history.
Here the Hudson's Bay and North West companies battled
for supremacy in the fur trade; Lord Selkirk brought his
settlers in the early 19th century; and Governor Robert
Semple and 20 settlers were massacred in 1816 by traders
of the North West Company.

Highway 238 follows the Red River north from Winnipeg. Scenic overlooks punctuate this lovely drive, on
which you will come to **Kennedy House**, built in 1866. A
glassed-in tea room overlooks English rock gardens.

Manitoba's fur-trading past is evoked in **Lower Fort
Garry**, the only original stone fur-trading fort still intact in
North America. Built in the early 1830s by Hudson's Bay
Company Governor George Simpson, it stands on the
banks of the Red River 20 miles north of Winnipeg. It was
never used for fighting but only to direct the affairs of the
company, and has been restored to its original character
by Parks Canada. It's easy to spend a whole day in this
fascinating place, where costumed animators give tours
and answer all questions. Visitors can reach the fort via
the scenic River Road Heritage Parkway, with its pretty
homes and the charming 19th-century St. Andrew's stone
church. The church, built in 1845, is still in use.

There's more history at **Ross House**, the first post office
west of the Great Lakes, built in 1854 by William Ross.
Located in Joe Zuken Heritage Park in Winnipeg, it's one
of the oldest examples of log-frame construction on the
prairies.

In the late 1800s many Mennonite people fled persecu-
tion in Europe and settled in southern Manitoba. **Stein-**

bach, 35 miles southeast of Winnipeg, was one of those early settlements. Today you can see the **Mennonite Heritage Village** there, a collection of authentic buildings, including a house-barn, a sod hut, a huge windmill, and a livery barn converted into a restaurant that serves Mennonite specialties.

Festivals

Every summer, from May to October, Manitoba is *en fête*. Every town and hamlet does its utmost to celebrate. It's good business, among other things. (When the town of Austin, population 400, draws 60,000 people to its four-day Threshermen's Reunion, that's good business.)

The best of these many festivals, **Folklorama**, takes place in August in Winnipeg. Put on by the city's 40 or more ethnic communities, it's a colorful and lively two-week celebration of the dances, music, arts, and food of each ethnic group.

The next biggest celebration is the **National Ukrainian Festival** near Dauphin, west of Lake Manitoba, which takes place during the long first weekend of August. It draws thousands of people from across the United States and Canada, and is so popular that rooms here are reserved a year in advance. There are stage shows at a 5,000-seat amphitheater on a hillside 10 km (6 miles) south of the town, with Cossack dancing and brilliant costumes, and, of course, authentic food and handicrafts. Dauphin, geared for its annual fiesta, has a number of motels. The one of choice is the **Rodeway Inn Motel**. Dauphin, incidentally, has a charming small museum, the **Fort Dauphin Museum**, a replica of a Northwest Territory trading post. It contains some ancient fossil remains that are the envy of large museums all over the country.

The mid-July **Winnipeg Folk Festival**, held at Birds Hill Park, on Highway 59, 25 km (15 miles) from Winnipeg, is a four-day feast of country, bluegrass, gospel, jazz, and old-time music. Musicians from all over North America perform at this festival, which is billed as a "gentle" experience (no alcohol or drugs are allowed). It's mainly attended by younger people, with a sprinkling of babies and older people, and it's very respectable. Birds Hill is a provincial park where Winnipeggers go to picnic in the summer and cross-country ski in the winter.

Bird-Watching

Manitoba is a bird watcher's paradise, and one of the best sites is right within the city of Winnipeg. The **Fort Whyte Centre for Environmental Education** is just a 25-minute drive from downtown at 1961 McCreary Road. Here 200 acres of land, reclaimed from a cement company's excavations, have been converted into one of the most diverse wildlife areas on the continent. The Waterfowl Gardens depict eight different wetland habitats in Manitoba, ranging from prairie potholes to the tundra of the far north, along with pinioned species of wild ducks indigenous to each type of environment. Self-guiding trails lead over a marsh; it's almost impossible to believe all this is within a big city, it's so quiet and restful.

Twenty miles north of Winnipeg, near Highway 67, is **Oak Hammock Marsh**, home of thousands of ducks, geese, and shorebirds. Fall is the best time to go, when the birds are migrating south, but summer is equally enjoyable. The serenity of the 8,646-acre marsh is soothing. There are a boardwalk and dikes to wander on, and you can drink the ice-cold artesian well water that flows into the marsh. Thousands of visitors, many of them highly experienced and travelled birders, visit Oak Hammock every year.

There is bird-watching throughout the province (**Churchill**—see below—is also famous worldwide, with some 200 species, including the rare Ross's gull), but the two spots mentioned above are the easiest to reach.

MANITOBA OUTSIDE THE WINNIPEG AREA
Farm Vacations

More than 50 farms throughout the province open their homes to visitors, who can choose from any number of activities or just relax and do nothing at all. Some farms specialize in hunting or horseback riding; others cater to seniors, children, or families. They all offer full room and board, separate accommodation in cottages, or trailer and tenting areas. Guests may eat all or some meals with the family, and are welcome to join the farm life. A booklet with rates and information is available from the Manitoba

Farm Vacations Association, 525 Kylemore Avenue, Winnipeg, Man. R3C 1B5; Tel: (204) 475-6624.

Fishing

Manitoba is a large province. It could easily accommodate North Dakota, Illinois, Iowa, and Wisconsin, with room left over for part of Rhode Island. In all these thousands of square miles, there are literally tens of thousands of lakes, which makes Manitoba an angler's paradise.

Fishing camps, ranging from deluxe to economy, cater to sporting types and provide boats, guides, and great fishing. Among the most popular areas are the Whiteshell Provincial Park in the south, where many Americans have summer homes; and in the far north, 300 km (175 miles) southeast of Hudson Bay, **Gods Lake** and **Gods River**. Gods Lake is large and cold, 400 square miles in area, surrounded by a wilderness of rock, streams, and northern conifers, conferring a solitude that is balm to the soul.

Because of the cold water—the ice does not melt until June—fish in Gods Lake are large and frisky. There are trout, walleye, whitefish, and northern pike, some tipping the scales at 20 pounds.

The four lodges in Gods Lake and one in Gods River have modern cabins, and provide all the amenities necessary in this part of the world. Of the four lodges in the area, two are excellent: the **Gods Country Lodge** and the **Gods Narrows Lodge**. The former has eight log cabins with showers, and meals are provided. There's a store that sells fishing licenses, and fishing gear. The latter lodge has six modern log cabins, also with showers, and again, meals are provided. **Schmerler's Gods Lake Lodge** is older, and it also has a store selling whatever is necessary for fishing. There's an unlicensed dining room. **Gods River Lodge** is run by an Indian tribe, and is in the process of being upgraded. At present there are four cabins with showers and an outcamp at Pine Rapids. You can hunt for waterfowl here. Only Gods Narrows Lodge is open year round; the others open in May or June, and close at the end of September. Each lodge has a landing strip, since they are accessible only by air. (Transportation is arranged by the lodges; see the Accommodations Reference section at the end of the chapter.) The few permanent inhabitants of this area are trappers who also work as guides at the fishing camps.

Canoeing

For canoeists there are several dozen identified **canoe routes**, a number of which are in southern Manitoba. One starts at Keewatin, Ontario, and goes down the Winnipeg River—the route of the historic fur brigade era, with spectacular wilderness scenery—to Lake Winnipeg, and then up the Red River to Winnipeg. In the north, there's the Land of Little Sticks route, a 2,000-mile marathon during the course of which the landscape changes from heavy forest to almost treeless tundra at Hudson Bay, with exit by chartered plane. (This route is for adventurous experts only.) Canoeists must use topographic maps, available at the Surveys and Mapping Branch, 1007 Century Street, Winnipeg, Man. R3H 0W4.

Touring Manitoba

Whiteshell Provincial Park, a 90-mile drive east of Winnipeg on Highway 1, is a good place to start an exploration of Manitoba. The Precambrian Shield here, the oldest rock in the world, is topped with pine and birch trees, ferns and wild roses, dozens of lakes (all cold), rivers, and rocky outcrops. The 1,000-square-mile park is green and still, and a woodsy smell hangs in the air. Just take along lots of mosquito repellent. **Falcon Lake** is one of the most popular areas in the park; it has a resort motel, marina, campgrounds, an 18-hole golf course, and beaches. There are more than two dozen lodges in the park where you can fish, swim, and go boating, among them the **Big Buffalo Resort** and the **Penguin Resort and Marina** at Falcon Lake. The Big Buffalo would be first choice. It has A-frame type cabins, with light housekeeping and showers. It is well maintained and comfortable. The second choice, the Penguin Resort, is older, but it too has pretty log cabins with light housekeeping, television, and showers or tubs. Neither resort has telephones, but who wants a telephone on a holiday anyway?

West Hawk Lake, with its icy waters and lovely surroundings, is a favorite with American visitors. The water is so clear, you can see to the bottom of the lake, once you have worked up the nerve to jump into it. The place to stay here is the **West Hawk Lake Resort**. These are individual cabins, and a good percentage of them are new. There is light housekeeping, and the newer cabins have televisions and are carpeted. They have either showers or tubs, and all the conveniences that are needed. Again, no phones.

As to where to eat in the Whiteshell, that presents a problem, because the restaurants cannot, in all honesty, be described as gourmet. However, the **Falcon Lake Golf Club** has a licensed dining room and the service is good. Also at Falcon Lake is **The Elnor,** which serves decent meals, and for snacking (sandwiches, hamburgers), there's the **Falcon's Nest Café.**

Gimli, 100 km (60 miles) north of Winnipeg on the western shore of Lake Winnipeg (take either Highway 8 or Highway 9), was settled by Icelanders in the mid-1800s. Now Gimli is a quiet, modest summer resort, and its blond, beautiful Icelandic youth are moving to Winnipeg—while Winnipeggers flock to Gimli in droves. Nothing is elaborate in Gimli, including restaurants, which are pleasantly passable, nothing more. The Bus Depot has good chips and hamburgers, the Falcon Café, decent sandwiches. Most cottage owners eat at home in Gimli.

As with restaurants, so with motels. The **Viking Motor Hotel** offers the best accommodations, clean rooms, and a good coffee shop.

Gimli may not offer great food or lodgings, but it has pure air, delicious drinking water, and a wonderful feeling of peace.

Another 50 miles north, on **Hecla Island,** is **Gull Harbour Resort,** offering solid luxury, for which you pay commensurately. Many people go there to rest and soak up the sun, but for the activity-prone there's golf on a spectacular course (the seventh-biggest on the continent) that has several fairways laid out along the shore of Lake Winnipeg, and there is tennis, sailing, windsurfing, and swimming. The cool breezes coming off Lake Winnipeg keep the temperatures here comfortable.

For something a little offbeat, head west from Winnipeg on the Trans-Canada Highway, past Headingley and the giant statue of the white horse beside the road (get a local resident to tell you the Indian legend behind the statue; it concerns a young Indian maiden whose soul passed into the horse's body). Turn north on Highway 26, past the gladioli farms, and on to Poplar Point, where you'll find **St. Anne's Anglican Church,** one of the oldest log churches still in use in western Canada.

Then drive west to **Fort la Reine Museum,** on the outskirts of Portage la Prairie. The original fort, built by the explorer Sieur de la Vérendrye in 1738, was his headquarters while he explored the territory. The present complex includes a trading post, a blacksmith's shop, and the 1882 official rail car of William Van Horne, builder of the Canadian Pacific Railroad. **Wayne's Café** in Portage la Prairie has surprisingly good hamburgers, sandwiches, and pies. For unusual accommodations, contact the **Pelechatys** who run a bed and breakfast (breakfast comes with Champagne) in their home, a structure of the Frank Lloyd Wright school.

Next, drive on to Austin and the Manitoba Agricultural Museum, an exhibit of antique farm machinery. Past Austin is Carberry, and here a change in the topography begins. The flat prairie gives way to softly rolling hills. At **Spruce Woods Provincial Park**, 16 km (10 miles) south of Carberry, is a desert, complete with sand dunes, reptiles (if you're lucky enough to spot one), and cacti. The dunes (known as Spirit Sands) are the remains of a huge delta of sand piled up during the Ice Age. They are extremely fragile, and visitors are not allowed to tramp over them, except on a self-guiding trail. Walking the desert takes about two hours, and when it's hot in the rest of Manitoba, it's even hotter here. But it's worth seeing a desert right in the middle of Canada.

If you decide to venture on, drive to Brandon, where there are three decent hotels—the **Victoria Inn**, the **Trails West Motor Hotel**, and the **Royal Oak Inn**. All have adequate dining rooms, the Victoria's being the best.

Brandon is Manitoba's second-largest city, with a population of 40,000. It's a very pretty place, with a small-town atmosphere but some sophistication. It has a good number of restaurants, a Sportsplex with an Olympic-sized swimming pool, and the B. J. Hales Museum, with mounted birds and mammals. On the whole, restaurants outside of Winnipeg leave a great deal to be desired, but Brandon has three good eating places, for which the traveller should be grateful. They are the **Skokonas Restaurant and Lounge** at 1011 Rosser Avenue, the **Colonial Inn** dining room at 1944 Queens Avenue, and **Churchill's**, in the Royal Oak Inn at 3130 Victoria Avenue. Skokonas is on a lower level, done up nicely with wood panelling, but, as with most Manitoba restaurants, dim. The steaks are good here (Brandon is a center for the cattle industry), and they do nice things with seafood. The Colonial Inn, with a standard motel dining room, has good food and delicious pastry. Churchill's has an ordinary menu, but it is done well. You don't have to get all gussied up to go to these restaurants, particularly in the motels— Brandonites certainly don't expect it. Skokonas is the only restaurant where you might be advised to make a reservation (Tel: 727-4395).

The next day, drive to **Souris**, 25 miles southwest of Brandon on Highway 2, a delightful town that has a core of Olde English cottages with names and lawns dressed up in masses of flowers. Even the fire hydrants are painted brilliant colors. The Souris River runs through the town, and over the river is the longest suspension foot bridge in Canada. It wobbles as you walk on it, but this one hasn't fallen down under the weight of a human being yet. There's another reason for going to Souris: It's the site of an agate pit that contains the largest variety of semiprecious stones on the continent. For a $4 fee you can grub around in the pit for as long as you want, and take out whatever stones you find.

Then head back to the Trans-Canada Highway and on to **Riding Mountain National Park**, where there are 75 cool lakes, dozens of nature trails through the woods, a resort town—**Wasagaming**—and unbelievably pure air. The park is on top of the Manitoba Escarpment and is an oasis of evergreen woods in the middle of a sea of rolling prairie. Just outside Wasagaming, which is on Clear Lake, is **Elkhorn Resort**. Elkhorn has luxury accommodations in a central lodge and in several chalets, in a lovely natural setting on a hilltop that looks down on rolling grassland, forest, and the resort's eight-hole golf course.

Churchill and Polar Bears

One of the last great wilderness adventures in the world is a trip to Churchill, the "polar bear capital of the world." It's also Canada's only inland seaport, and the feeding ground of beluga whales and the summer home of 200 species of migrating birds.

One thousand intrepid people live in Churchill, on the shore of the Hudson Bay, 1,600 km (1,000 miles) north of Winnipeg. They have to be intrepid to live so far from civilization. For nine months of the year this is a bleak and desolate area. For the other three months it is bearable. In the spring (late) and fall (early) the tundra is a blaze of color, covered with lichen and miniature shrubs and flowers. Ships from around the world take on grain in the harbor.

It's a lonely existence, and the residents here are a special breed—tough, skillful, hardy, and very independent. They cope with cold, with isolation, and with polar bears.

They've built themselves a complex that houses a high school, library, swimming pool, curling rink, and hockey arena. (You can't play hockey out of doors when it's 40 below.) They have a museum that has Inuit carvings and artifacts that are among the finest and oldest in the world.

The town is geared to tourists and to grain. Inuits who live in the region have seen their old way of life disappear under the onslaught of civilization, with very little to replace it. Some of them do Inuit sculptures and paintings that fetch very good prices in the south—that is, in Winnipeg. Inuit men also act as guides to tourists, who flock to Churchill by the thousands to see the polar bears and the beluga whales.

The best polar bear season is from early October to mid-November, and you can see the bears from the vantage point of a "tundra buggy," a bus chassis on huge tractor tires. The sight of the world's biggest land-dwelling carnivore a dozen feet away is an awesome one.

In summer the mouth of the Churchill River is the feeding ground of hundreds of white beluga whales, which can be seen from an open boat. These 12-foot relatives of the dolphin are gregarious and friendly, and have never been known to harm man or boat, though they may swim right alongside. It's fascinating to listen to their high-pitched tones as they call to one another.

People who come to Churchill to see the polar bears or the whales would be well advised to book with a tour. There are any number from Churchill, some for one day, some up to five days, and some overnight camping trips. **The Great Canadian Travel Company** and **Frontiers North** are two touring companies in Winnipeg that will arrange custom-made packages.

All of the touring companies in Churchill arrange both whale and polar bear sightings, and some do bird watching. **Churchill Wilderness Encounter**, led by Bonnie Chartier, a well-known birder, does all three. **Tundra Buggy Tours** is led by the man who designed the prototype for the tundra buggy. **Sea North Tours** received a grant in the past year to build a 40-foot boat for whale sightings. On this tour, hydrophones are put into the sea to magnify whale songs. (In Churchill, whales are called sea canaries.) An American, Dan Guravich from Mississippi, is famous for his work with, and photographs of, polar bears. He leads the **Victor Emmanuel Company**, and personally escorts all his tours. His photos of the bears can be seen in books and magazines.

Bookings for tours can be made with outfitters in Churchill, or personally with the companies:

- Churchill Wilderness Encounter. Box 9, Churchill, Man. R0B 0E0. Tel: (204) 675-2284.
- Frontiers North. 774 Bronx Avenue, Winnipeg, Man. R2K 4E9. Tel: (204) 663-1411.
- The Great Canadian Travel Company. 249 Bell Avenue, Winnipeg, Man. R2K 2M5. Tel: (204) 284-1580.
- Sea North Tours. 203 Laverendrye Avenue, Churchill, Man. R0B 0E0. Tel: (204) 675-2195.
- Tundra Buggy Tours. Box 662, Churchill, Man. R0B 0E0. Tel: (204) 675-2121.
- Victor Emmanuel Company. Box 891, Greenville, Mississippi, 38702. Tel: (601) 335-2444.

Across the river mouth is **Fort Prince of Wales**, a huge stone fort built by the Hudson's Bay Company in the 1700s to defend its fur trade interests in the New World. Three km (2 miles) upriver from the fort is Sloop's Cave, used by whalers and fur traders. Bird-watching is excellent throughout this region.

The only practical way to get to Churchill is by plane or train. For those to whom time is not of the essence, the train, VIA Rail, provides a luxurious trip with good food and comfortable sleeping quarters. The train leaves Winnipeg in late afternoon and arrives in Churchill at 7:00 A.M. A bus and guide will be waiting to escort VIA's passengers on a tour of the community and its surroundings. One VIA Rail tour includes a day trip by air to Eskimo Point in the Northwest Territories (weather permitting). Canadian Airlines International flies over hundreds of miles of lakes and forest, and finally tundra, en route to Churchill. This is truly *terra incognita*.

There are several nice places to stay in Churchill. After all, tourism is a big industry here. The **Seaport Hotel** and the **Tundra Inn** are both comfortable, clean, and have dining rooms. The **Polar Motel** will also do. All three places have cable and satellite television, bathtubs or showers, and airport limousines. Reservations should be made well in advance.

At night the skies over Churchill can put on the most brilliant display of aurora borealis seen anywhere in the world. The lights literally dance across the sky, outstripping the most spectacular fireworks or laser show.

"Primitive liberty, I have regained thee at last," said Chateaubriand, at the sight of the boundless North American wilderness. Churchill makes many a visitor feel the same way.

GETTING AROUND

From Winnipeg International Airport, visitors can rent a car, take a taxi, or use the airport limousines to get downtown. Four hotels—the International Inn, the Westin, the Charterhouse, and the Sheraton—have airport-shuttle bus service. Travellers arriving in Winnipeg by air should rent a car. Taking buses can be inconvenient, especially because the tourist sights are spread all over the city. The exception would be a bus tour offered by both Grey Line (Tel: 339-1696) and River Rouge (Tel: 669-2824) companies in red double-decker London buses.

To tour Manitoba outside Winnipeg, of course, demands a car, with the exception of Churchill; for VIA Rail information, see the Getting Around section for Ontario Province (or, for flights, check the Canadian Airlines International schedule).

ACCOMMODATIONS REFERENCE
(See also accommodations in the Winnipeg section.)

▶ **Bed-and-Breakfast Manitoba Limited.** 93 Healy Crescent, **Winnipeg**, Man. R2N 2S2. Tel: (204) 256-6151.

▶ **Big Buffalo Resort. Falcon Beach**, Man. R0E 0N0. Tel: (204) 349-2259.

▶ **Elkhorn Resort and Conference Centre.** Box 40, **Elkhorn**, Man. R0J 2H0. Tel: (204) 848-2802 or (204) 848-7606.

▶ **Gods Country Lodge. Gods River**, Man. R0B 0N0. Tel: (204) 335-2244.

▶ **Gods Lake Narrows Lodge. Gods Lake Narrows**, Man. R0B 0M0. Tel: (204) 335-2405.

▶ **Gods River Lodge. Gods River**, Man. R0B 0N0. Tel: (204) 335-2427/2333/2094; or c/o Paul Zanewich, P.O. Box 714, **Winnipeg**, Man. R3C 2K3. Tel: (204) 582-4937.

▶ **Gull Harbour Resort and Conference Centre.** Gen-

eral Delivery, **Riverton,** Man. R0C 2R0. Tel: (204) 475-2354
or (800) 442-0497 in Canada only.

▶ **Pelechaty's Red Roof House.** 102 First Street Southwest, **Portage La Prairie,** Man. R1N 1Y3. Tel: (204) 857-
7109.

▶ **Penguin Resort and Marina. Falcon Beach,** Man. R0E
0N0. Tel: (204) 349-2218.

▶ **Polar Motel.** 16 Franklin Street, Box 124, **Churchill,**
Man. R0B 0E0. Tel: (204) 675-8878.

▶ **Rodeway Inn Motel.** Highway 10, Box 602, **Dauphin,**
Man. R7N 2V4. Tel: (204) 638-5102.

▶ **Royal Oak Inn.** 3130 Victoria Avenue, Box 670, **Brandon,** Man. RZA 4Z7. Tel: (204) 728-5775 or, in Manitoba,
(800) 852-2709.

▶ **Schmerler's Gods Lake Lodge.** Box 1708, **Gimli,** Man.
R0C 1B0. Tel: (204) 642-5216.

▶ **Seaport Hotel.** Box 339, **Churchill,** Man. R0B 0E0. Tel:
(204) 675-8807.

▶ **Trails West Motor Hotel.** 210 18th Street, **North Brandon,** Man. R7E 5Z8. Tel: (204) 727-3800.

▶ **Tundra Inn.** 34 Franklin Street, Box 999, **Churchill,**
Man. R0B 0E0. Tel: (204) 675-8831 or (800) 661-1460.

▶ **The Victoria Inn.** 3550 Victoria Avenue West, P.O. Box
458, **Brandon,** Man. R7A 5Z4. Tel: (204) 725-1532 or (800)
852-2710 in Manitoba only.

▶ **Viking Motor Hotel.** Box 131, **Gimli,** Man. R0C 1B0.
Tel: (204) 642-5181.

▶ **West Hawk Lake Resort. West Hawk Lake,** Man. R0E
2H0. Tel: (204) 349-2244.

SASKATCHEWAN

By David Starre

David Starre, an avid outdoorsman and canoeist as well as a free-lance journalist and writer based in Saskatchewan, has travelled much of the Churchill River, and has lived in both northern and southern Saskatchewan.

Saskatchewan has two distinct regions, each with its own treasures to offer visitors. The southern two-thirds of the province is predominantly level plain broken by scattered ridges and valleys. Here, seemingly endless fields of wheat stretch north before giving way to the mixed woods of the province's central parklands. History draws many visitors to this region; the story of how the land was transformed from buffalo grass to wheat is a fascinating one that is retold through the province's many museums.

The northern one-third of Saskatchewan is dominated by hummocky, lake-studded terrain typical of the Canadian Shield. Sparsely populated, it primarily draws avid sportsfishermen, canoeists, and campers, who come to enjoy secluded waterways that have changed little since the days of settlement.

MAJOR INTEREST

Wilderness experiences
Fishing and canoeing

Regina
Royal Canadian Mounted Police Museum
Museum of Natural History

449

Buffalo Days country-and-western annual event
Saskatchewan Science Centre

Saskatoon
Saskatoon Western Development Museum
Mendel Art Gallery
Ukrainian Museum of Canada
Folkfest and Saskatoon Exhibition, annual events
Shakespeare on the Saskatchewan

Elsewhere in Saskatchewan
Moose Jaw, North Battleford, and Yorkton western
    development museums
National and provincial parks (especially Prince
    Albert National Park and Cypress Hills Provincial
    Park)
Lakes and rivers of the province's northern
    wilderness for canoeing and fishing
Big Valley Jamboree at Craven
Saskatchewan Handcraft Festival at Battleford
Community rodeos

Enter Saskatchewan along its east-west corridors, the
Trans-Canada and the Yellowhead highways, or venture
out from the province's two major cities, Regina (pronounced Ree-JI-neh) and Saskatoon, and you very
quickly discover that wheat is king here. Wheat fields are
everywhere—dusty gray to a deep black at seeding time,
rich green during the heat of summer, and ripe and
golden in the fall.

The prairies that these fields blanket are grand in their
immensity. Far horizons are seldom broken, and when
they are, it is usually by tall, brightly colored grain elevators. So it is understandable that a bread-basket image is
what most visitors carry away. It is an image that Saskatchewan people are proud of. Still, the traveller should know
that there is another, more subtle side to the province—
as Robert Moon writes in *This Is Saskatchewan!*

No, do not judge Saskatchewan by its prairies alone.
Go into the hills and at the top stand breathless from
the climb and the magnificence of what you have
seen. Dip down into the valleys and offer no struggle
as you succumb to the enchantment you find there.
Walk into its forests, climb over its northern rocks
and late at night listen to the lap of the lake waters. . . . Talk to its people and learn how closely men

are linked with this earth. Pause and listen to its lore and you will have as your reward as remarkable legends of strangeness and heroism as exists.

Moon's colorful words are sound advice on how to "do" Saskatchewan.

The Heritage

While little is known of Saskatchewan's inhabitants prior to historic times, there is evidence suggesting habitation more than 10,000 years ago. At the time of contact with early fur traders and explorers, Chipewyan Indians wintered in the northern fringes of Saskatchewan, moving out onto the tundra during the summer to hunt caribou. The Blackfoot and Assiniboine roamed the parklands and the plains, hunting the buffalo that provided both food and shelter. Later, migrant Cree pushed west, eventually becoming the dominant tribe. Some Cree adopted the ways of the Assiniboine and moved out onto the plains. Others moved north, deeper into the woods.

The first European to arrive on the prairies, in 1671, was Henry Kelsey, an employee of the Hudson's Bay Company sent inland to encourage distant Indians to make the long journey north for trade. What followed are stories of proud, noble Indians and their struggle to cope with change; of courageous voyageurs and the great rivalry between Bay men and the peddlers of the North West Company; of stouthearted Mounted Police red coats and the outlaws and whisky traders they were sent to tame; of rebellious Métis, under Louis Riel, and the army that marched west to defeat them; and of determined settlers who broke the sod and endured the drought and the Depression of the 1930s.

The Métis in Saskatchewan, a mixed culture of European and American Indian heritage, tell their story at Batoche National Historic Park, northeast of Saskatoon, and at Government House in Regina, the official residence of the lieutenant governor when the town was capital of the Northwest Territories. The play *The Trial of Louis Riel* is performed here three times weekly during July and August.

There is no one museum in Saskatchewan dedicated to the history of Saskatchewan's native Indians. Fortunately, that will change with the development of **Wanuskewin** (Cree for "living together") on the banks of the South

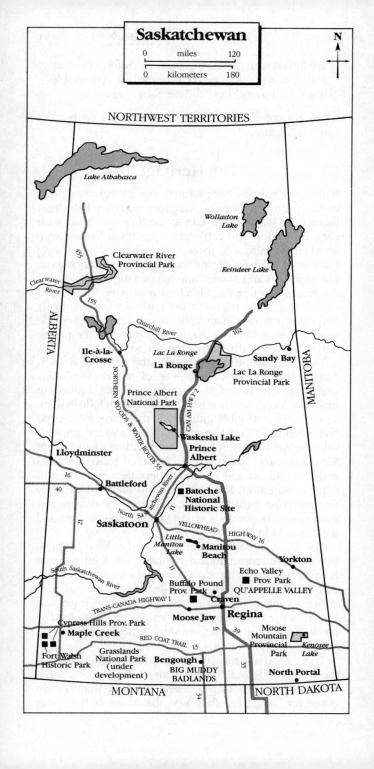

Saskatchewan River near Saskatoon. Archaeological studies at Wanuskewin have uncovered 19 prehistoric and
two historic sites. Included are a 1,500-year-old medicine
wheel, ancient tepee rings, and a natural buffalo pound.
While the site won't formally open until 1992, an interpretive officer has been hired and limited prearranged tours
are available. For more information contact the Meewasin
Valley Authority; Tel: (306) 665-6887.

Canada's acquisition of Hudson's Bay lands in 1870, the
arrival of the railroad, and the signing of Indian treaties
cleared a pathway for immigrants to head west. Even as
recently as 1885 there were only slightly more than
32,000 people living in what is now Saskatchewan; most
were Canadians born in settled regions to the east. Today
there are just over one million residents in Saskatchewan.
Its ethnic population is a mix of British, German, Ukrainian, Scandinavian, French, Native American, Dutch, Polish, Russian, and non-European cultures—in descending
order of population.

For early pioneers, starting out was a hard life at best,
especially for those with little money. Yet nowhere else in
Canada did so few people change a land so quickly as in
Saskatchewan—mostly through a cooperative spirit that
remains visible today in the friendly, helpful nature of the
province's citizens.

The story of development in Saskatchewan is told
through four branches of the **Western Development Museum**. Each branch of the museum has its own theme.
The story of the province's people is told at *Yorkton*. At
Moose Jaw, the theme is transportation. Here, a quick
look at the oxen-powered Red River cart, which brought
settlers west at what can best be deemed a steady pace of
15 miles a day, leaves modern-day travellers thankful for
progress. The museum's gem is its railway display. At
Saskatoon, visitors step out onto the streets of Boom
Town 1910. Agriculture is the theme of the museum at
Battleford, which boasts a living historical farm that
grows and harvests its crops using methods and machinery of the early 1900s. All four museum branches have
special events during the summer.

TWIN CITIES

Saskatchewan's two largest cities, Saskatoon and Regina,
serve as starting points for travel in the province. Saska-

toon only recently surpassed Regina in population; both are just over the 180,000 mark.

Ever since their beginnings the two cities have been in friendly rivalry with each other. Each competed for the right to become capital; Regina was the victor. Each competed for the University of Saskatchewan; Saskatoon won out. Regina created a man-made lake; Saskatoon built a mountain.

Regina

The founders of Regina had few ornaments from nature to work with. As Edward McCourt notes in his book *Saskatchewan,* the selection of a featureless creek crossing as capital of the Northwest, with the beautiful Qu'Appelle Valley only a short distance north, has been a puzzle to geographers and historians. In favor of the site was the fact that it was central to the southern plains and on the line surveyed for the Canadian Pacific Railroad. But, as McCourt suggests, the possibility of land holdings by certain influential individuals may have had more to do with it.

Originally called Pile O' Bones (after a pile of buffalo bones that lay along the banks of Wascana Creek), Regina was renamed by Princess Louise in 1882 in honor of her mother Queen Victoria. Ever since, Regina's citizens have worked hard to build a city worthy of its regal status. They dammed Wascana Creek to create a lake, and later 2,100 men enlarged the reservoir, dredging it with shovels and dump wagons. The dredgings were piled up to form islands in the enlarged waterbody. In 1908 workers started construction of Saskatchewan's Legislative Building, a grand center of government next to Wascana Park strongly reminiscent of the Palace of Versailles, and the city's most notable landmark.

A walk through **Wascana Centre** is a good place to start a tour of Regina. Attractions include the Saskatchewan Legislative Building, the Museum of Natural History, the Saskatchewan Science Centre, and the Norman MacKenzie Art Gallery. See the **Museum of Natural History** as a prelude to touring the province if starting out from Regina. Showcases in the museum's upper galleries introduce visitors to much of Saskatchewan's wildlife with dioramas depicting the animals in their natural habitat. A recently opened Earth Sciences Gallery on the lower level tells the story of how Saskatchewan evolved from temperate seas through the age of dinosaurs to the arrival of man. This new gallery is part of a three-phase, seven-year redevelopment of the museum. A native peoples gallery will be the next exhibit introduced. The **Saskatchewan Science Centre** is the park's newest attraction. It is housed in a wonderful old building that once operated as the city's main power station. Exhibits explore the human body, the living planet, astronomy, and geology. The **Norman Mackenzie Art Gallery** is in the process of moving to a new home within the park in the T. C. Douglas Building. Expanded quarters at the new location will enable the gallery to show off much more of its permanent exhibits. The gallery's collection ranges from Chinese and Egyptian antiquities to contemporary works by Canadian, American, and international artists. Gift shops are located at the museum, the art gallery, and at Wascana Place, which is the starting point for guided double-decker bus tours. The park marina provides a scenic spot to stop for lunch.

(For the Royal Canadian Mounted Police Museum in Regina, see the following section on the southern part of the province.)

Regina has its own symphony orchestra and active theater groups. The Saskatchewan Centre of the Arts, located in Wascana Park, has an excellent concert hall. Watch for venues at the Centre of the Arts and for annual summer events like **Buffalo Days**, a city exhibition with a country-and-western flavor.

The city's most luxurious hotels are located in its downtown core, with another grouping of good-quality accommodation located in the south along Albert Street, Regina's main north-south corridor. In the south, the **Landmark Inn** and the newly renovated **Regina Travelodge** are good-quality hotels of average price. Major hotels downtown include: the stately **Hotel Saskatchewan**, overlooking Victoria Park, the **Chelton Inn**, the **Regina Inn**, the **Sheraton Centre**, and the **Ramada Renaissance**. All are comparable when balancing quality and price. The Sheraton and the Ramada are the most expensive. The Travelodge and the Ramada both have impressive indoor waterslides that the kids will love.

These hotels are all a good choice for evening dining, especially **C. C. Lloyds** in the Chelton. Recommended places for lunch in the city's core include **Alfredo's Fresh Pasta and Grill** in the Scarth Street mall, **Bartleby's Dining Emporium** on Broad Street for steak and lobster, and

Mieka's on 11th Avenue, which serves both French and North American fare. For Japanese dining as authentic as you will find in Tokyo, try the **Neo Japonica** on Hamilton Street. **Roxy's Bistro** on 14th Street features innovative French cuisine; the **Cassa Ricci** on Broad Street has the best Italian food in town. For Continental fare, try the **Diplomat**, also on Broad Street, or **Upstairs Downstairs** just south of the downtown core on Smith Street. **Golf's Steak House** on Victoria street has great steaks. **Simply Delicious**, a small neighborhood restaurant on Victoria Street East is a must stop for apple pie and ice cream lovers.

To add entertainment to your meal try **Celebrations** on Albert Street North, a club that features a dinner theater in which the waitresses and waiters do double duty as actors, maintaining their characters while they serve you. Sometimes patrons also become part of the act. To round off the evening, head out to a country-and-western bar: The **Pump** on Victoria Street East is the most popular with the locals. You will find the younger crowd at the **Original California Club** in the Regina Inn and at **Hollywood's** on Albert Street North.

The Qu'Appelle Valley

Just north of Regina is the beautiful Qu'Appelle Valley. Formerly a glacial spillway, the steep valley now strings together a number of scenic parks and lakes, providing a dramatic departure from the plains above. Two provincial parks in the valley—Buffalo Pound, north of Moose Jaw, and Echo Valley, northeast of Regina—are recommended stops for campers. From a scenic point of view, a trip to Saskatchewan would not be complete without a drive through the valley. The Qu'Appelle is sandwiched between the Yellowhead and Trans-Canada highways, running in the same east-west direction. Watch for route signs and make sure to bring a camera and plenty of film, especially when the valley is lit up with the colors of fall.

A country-and-western festival in the Qu'Appelle at Craven is establishing quite a name for itself. Held in July, the **Big Valley Jamboree** annually attracts some 50,000 country-and-western fans from across the Canadian and American Midwest. They come to see some of the best American and Canadian performers in the business.

Visitors will find plenty of cowboys and cowgirls at the festival, and most people who attend own a Stetson or two that they dust off for the weekend. The festival attracts a mixture of young and old. Some come to picnic and others to party. Despite their differences, the two groups get along quite well. Camping is allowed here. Most people who do come bring along a motor home or a trailer, creating the biggest collection of campers on wheels to be seen anywhere. Bring lawn chairs.

Big Valley is also the site of a major rodeo held annually in August. There are *many* professional and amateur rodeos in Saskatchewan. Watch for small-town rodeos; they can be as entertaining as some of the larger city rodeos, if not more so—provided you don't mind rolling up your shirt sleeves and mingling with the locals.

Moose Jaw

A short drive west of Regina is Moose Jaw, a city noted for its past role as a hideaway for American gangsters. Rumor has it that Al Capone was among the number of shady visitors who once frequented the city. In addition to the branch of the Western Development Museum mentioned above, Moose Jaw is home to an excellent wild animal park and Canada's famous aerobatic team—the Snowbirds. The Canadian Forces Base at Moose Jaw is the Snowbirds' home, and they always put on a special performance for the hometown crowd at the Saskatchewan Air Show, held annually there in July.

Between Regina and Saskatoon is **Little Manitou Lake**, long known for the healing powers of its waters. Fed by deep springs, the lake has a mineral content similar to the Carlsbad Spa in Europe and a density greater than that of the Dead Sea. A heated mineral pool complex is located at Manitou Beach. The pool's soothing waters provide the perfect prescription for tired and stiff travellers, and a stop here is highly recommended.

Saskatoon

There is a story told about two travellers who had lost their way. Upon seeing a distant city, the driver stopped and asked a farmer working in his field where they were. "Saskatoon, Saskatchewan," the farmer replied. The slightly perturbed tourist went back to his car none the wiser. "I don't know where we are," he told his companion. "That farmer doesn't speak any English."

Both Saskatoon and Saskatchewan, like many place-names in the province, are Cree derivatives. Roughly translated, Saskatoon is what the Indians call a tasty purple berry found in abundance in Saskatchewan. Try some Saskatoon pie if you get the chance. (Saskatchewan is Cree for "the river that flows swiftly.")

Adorned by the South Saskatchewan River, Saskatoon came by its beauty much more easily than did Regina, and it is one of the prettiest cities in western Canada. There can be little doubt that the city's founders, teetotaling temperance colonists, would be proud of the city as it stands today, despite the fact that it is a far cry from what they had intended. The elbows bend as much here as anywhere else in Saskatchewan—if not more. For evidence of that, check out the country-and-western bars or the city's discos. The **Bar-K Ranch House** on 22nd Street West or the **Texas T** on 8th Street East are popular country-and-western bars.

It is the city's harmony with the South Saskatchewan River that gives Saskatoon its character. Presiding over the river is the **Hotel Bessborough**, one of the great Canadian château-style hotels and the city's most notable landmark. Also decorating the river are the gray-stone Gothic buildings of the University of Saskatchewan, the Mendel Art Gallery, and the Ukrainian Museum of Canada.

Attractions at the University of Saskatchewan include several science and archaeological museums, and the Diefenbaker Centre. John Diefenbaker was Canada's prime minister from 1957 to 1963. His popularity in Saskatchewan is made obvious by the fact that a number of his former abodes are now operated as tourist stops. They include his early homestead (which was moved to Regina's Wascana Park), his former law office in Wakaw, and the house he occupied while in Prince Albert (to the north of Saskatoon). Diefenbaker Centre doubles as a working archive and a museum that documents the "Chief's" career.

The **Mendel Art Gallery and Civic Conservatory** is situated on the west banks of the South Saskatchewan River in one of the most picturesque spots in the city. Opened in 1964, the gallery was named in honor of the late Fred Mendel, a prominent Saskatoon businessman who helped with its funding and who donated many Canadian works of art. An important part of the gallery's permanent collection are works by members of the

Group of Seven (see the Northern Ontario section) donated by the family of Fred Mendel in 1965. The museum is also a good place to see historical and contemporary Saskatchewan art.

The **Ukrainian Museum of Canada** showcases a culture that has contributed much to Canada's mosaic. The museum's focus is immigration, settlement, and community life on the prairies. Among its many artifacts is a collection of over 1,000 decorated Easter eggs, some brought to Canada by early immigrants. Easter eggs can be purchased in the museum gift shop.

Like Regina, Saskatoon has an active theater scene, its own symphony orchestra, and an excellent concert hall, which is located in Centennial Auditorium. Events to watch for include the increasingly popular Shakespeare on the Saskatchewan, the Saskatoon Jazz Festival, Saskatoon Exhibition, and Folkfest. **Folkfest**, held annually in August, is a celebration of the province's rich cultural heritage and features entertainment pavilions from around the world.

Shakespeare on the Saskatchewan features a different production annually. The outdoor play is performed downtown on the river bank, five nights a week, July through mid-August.

The **Saskatoon Exhibition**, a highlight of Saskatoon's summer for more than a century, has retained its pioneer flavor over the years. During the annual fair, the Saskatoon branch of the Western Development Museum features activities like butter and ice cream making and, at nearby Pioneer Circle, vintage farm machinery is brought back to life. A midway, an entertainment grandstand, chuckwagon races, and agricultural displays are among many other activities. Held annually the first week of July, the fair is kicked off by the Louis Riel Relay, a race that combines canoeing, horseback riding, and running.

Major hotels in Saskatoon are located in the downtown core, along Idylwyld Drive, the city's major north-south corridor, and near the airport in the northwest. Room rates and quality of accommodation are comparable to those in Regina. As in Regina, the more luxurious hotels are located downtown. Major downtown hotels include the majestic Hotel Bessborough, the **Sheraton Cavalier**, and the **Ramada Renaissance**. Ask for a room overlooking the river.

The **Holiday Inn** is conveniently located across from Centennial Auditorium and near the midtown shopping plaza, and is easily accessible from Idylwyld Drive. Hotels serving the airport include the **Saskatoon Inn** and the more economical **Relax Inn**.

All four downtown hotels have excellent dining. The Hotel Bessborough offers the best variety: You can choose from the Continental cuisine at **Aerials Cove**, the *teppanyaki*-style cooking of the **Samurai Japanese Restaurant**, or **Treetops**, a family-style eatery overlooking the courtyard. The best view from a restaurant in town is at **Villy's** atop the TD Bank Building. Fresh lobster and a variety of dishes served with European-style sauces are popular choices at this elegant dining spot.

A number of excellent restaurants are located outside the downtown core. **Cousin Nick's** on Grosvenor Avenue across from the Grosvenor Park Shopping Centre has great Greek food. **The Granary** on 8th Street East provides an ideal surrounding for Saskatchewan prime rib and has a well-stocked salad bar. At lunchtime, **Traeger's Fine Pastries and Tea Room** in the Cumberland Square Shopping Centre on 8th Street East and in the Paramount Fashion Centre on Second Avenue South is popular. **Lydia's** is a delightful European restaurant at Broadway Avenue and 11th Street.

Battleford, northwest of Saskatoon along the Yellowhead Highway, is home to the **Saskatchewan Handcraft Festival**. Featuring the exhibits of Saskatchewan's better-known craftspeople, the festival is one of the best places to seek quality handcrafts, including weavings, woodwork, pottery, stained glass, leather work, and Indian crafts. The festival is held annually in July. There is also a branch of the Western Development Museum here.

THE SOUTH

In July 1874 the first regiment of the North West Mounted Police began its historic march west to halt the whisky trade. Today in Saskatchewan two Mountie posts are still maintained as national historic parks: Fort Battleford in the northwest and Fort Walsh in the southwest.

Regina is the home of the RCMP's modern-day training base and its official museum. One of the most visited museums in Canada, the **Royal Canadian Mounted Police Museum** documents the force from its beginnings to the present day. It also provides a history of the northwestern frontier. Among exhibits are a beaded rifle case and tobacco pouch presented by Sitting Bull to Police Superintendent James Walsh. You will find the museum and training academy at the west central edge of Regina; turn west onto 11th Avenue from the Lewvan Expressway. Museum visitors should time their arrival with either the Sergeant Major's Parade, regularly held on weekdays at 12:50 P.M., or the force's Sunset Ceremonies, usually held on Tuesdays during the midsummer months at 6:45 P.M. Call the museum at (306) 780-5838 to confirm times.

Travellers can follow the force's route west by heading along the Red Coat Trail from Winnipeg, Manitoba, to Fort Mcleod, Alberta. Along the Saskatchewan portion are a number of attractions: Moose Mountain Provincial Park, the Big Muddy Badlands, Grasslands National Park, Fort Walsh National Historic Park, and Cypress Hills Provincial Park.

Moose Mountain Provincial Park, a poplar- and birch-covered plateau, is a favorite of local residents as well as visitors. It is located in the southeast corner of the province. Attractions within the park are its natural environment trails for hiking and horseback riding, a great golf course, and the waters of Kenosee Lake. Just outside the park near its entrance is a huge water-slide complex. One of the water-slide flumes is an eight-story free-fall; remember to cross your legs!

Kenosee Inn, in the park, is your best choice for accommodation. A new development, the 30-bedroom lodge has a full range of amenities, including a dining room and lounge and an indoor pool, sauna, and whirlpool. The inn also rents out two-bedroom, lodge-style units and cabins. For lunch or for evening dining try the golf-course clubhouse or the **Moose Head Inn** in the Kenosee townsite, a restaurant on one level and a nightclub on the next.

A haven for outlaws, the weathered buttes and eerie landscape of the **Big Muddy Valley** near Bengough once served as station number one on Butch Cassidy's Outlaw Trail between Canada and Mexico. Caves in the area are said to have provided hideaways for famous outlaws like Sam Kelley and Dutch Henry. The lawlessness began to decline with the arrival of the North West Mounted Police, who established a post there in 1902.

At this writing there are no public tours of the region.

Castle Butte, one of the valley's best-known landmarks, can be viewed from Highway 34 between Big Beaver and Bengough. A trail ride through the Big Muddy, held annually in late July, is a fascinating journey for visitors who can bring their own horses. Contact Donna Robinson for trail-ride information; Tel: (306) 268-4420.

Grasslands, one of Canada's newest national parks, is being developed to preserve the grandness of the Great Plains and to protect threatened inhabitants like the prairie falcon, the black-tailed prairie dog, and the prairie rattlesnake (perhaps the only resident of the province that won't greet you with a friendly handshake). The park is located near Val Marie in the southwest. Eerie badlands, Indian tepee rings, and historic trails are other notable features. An interpretive center is now in place at Val Marie but services for visitors are still limited. If you are interested in touring the region, take the guided tour offered by longtime resident Lise Perrault, who has plenty of stories to tell. Call the Parks Canada office at (306) 298-2257 or Lise Perrault at (306) 298-2241.

Cypress Hills near the southwestern corner of the province is one of 31 provincial parks in Saskatchewan, each with its own character. The Indians call the hills "Mun-a-tuk-gaw," the beautiful highlands. Left untouched by the last Ice Age, the highlands have a variety of flora and fauna not found elsewhere in the region, including the lodgepole pine that incorrectly give the hills their name. Rich in wildlife, the region was once a popular Indian hunting ground, and remains one of the best places in the province to see elk.

Cypress Four Seasons Resort, a new 36-unit hotel complex alongside Loch Leven on Highway 21 in the central block of the park, has all the amenities essential for a comfortable stay. It also rents out condominiums and cabins, the only other accommodations in the park besides the campgrounds.

At Cypress and at all of the province's major parks, it is essential to book ahead, especially during the summer months, when the parks become popular destinations for visitors and residents alike. In terms of setting and quality of accommodations, hotels in the parks are superior to those in nearby communities. On the average, you can expect to pay about $50 for one night's stay in a park, but cabins vary greatly in price, depending on how modern they are. Call Tourism Saskatchewan for information; Tel: (800) 667-7191.

THE NORTH

The great rivalry among fur traders stimulated competitive exploration and the establishment of many fur-trading posts from the South Saskatchewan River north. Many of these posts survived to develop into modern-day communities. Others have vanished into the woods from which they came.

The early voyageur routes are still in use. Now, however, the canoeists who ply their waters come for a different reason: some for the adventure and excitement of white water and wilderness; others for the recreation and relaxation that northern Saskatchewan's tranquil beauty provides. The province has documented more than 50 canoe routes. Several river systems rate among Canada's best canoeing waters; they include the section of the Churchill River that passes through Lac La Ronge Provincial Park (for the relatively inexperienced), and the section of the majestic river from Ile a la Crosse in the northwest to Sandy Bay in the northeast (for serious canoeists). Another challenging option is the Clearwater River.

The **Churchill River,** as it crosses Saskatchewan, is actually a series of elongated lakes interconnected by powerful rapids and waterfalls. Its shoreline and island mazes are a juxtaposition of rock knobs and ridges, boreal forest and muskeg. The **Clearwater River** is a more typical river trip. Along both systems, prehistoric pictographs can be found on rock outcrops, offering a mute record of earlier travellers who used the waterways. Travel on these routes is at your own risk—and there are no McDonald's restaurants along the way.

Freshwater fishing is northern Saskatchewan's premier attraction. Anglers from across North America head there each summer in search of trophy-size northern pike, walleye, lake trout, and Arctic grayling.

Close to 250 fly-in and drive-in outfitter camps cater to anglers as well as moose and black-bear hunters. **La Ronge**, in the north-central region of the province, is the departure point for many anglers. During the summer months, chartered floatplanes depart daily for secluded fishing camps.

Visitor accommodations range from luxurious and expensive lodges (by wilderness standards) to a most basic outpost cabin. You will probably be happiest with the ones that provide all the comforts of home, despite the extra cost. But no matter where anglers go here they will catch fish—especially when accompanied by an experienced native guide (provided at most lodges). At ease with the land, many of these guides still make their living from hunting, fishing, and trapping. And they seem to have a sixth sense when it comes to finding the best fishing spots. (Either that or they tell one another where the fish are biting.) For information on lodges call the Saskatchewan Outfitters Association "Fishing Line" at (306) 763-5434, or write for Saskatchewan Tourism's *Outdoor Adventure Guide,* Tourism Saskatchewan, 1919 Saskatchewan Ave., Regina, Sask. S4P 3V7; Tel: (800) 667-7191.

The town of **Prince Albert** is the gateway to northern Saskatchewan. A short distance north of the city lies **Prince Albert National Park**, perhaps the province's prettiest preserve, located in an area of transition between parkland and boreal forest. Wildlife in the park reflects the changing vegetation. Moose, wolves, and caribou stalk the northern forests; elk, deer, and badgers inhabit the aspen parkland. Bison roam freely in the park's southwest corner.

Waskesiu, a small resort town serving the park, offers a variety of recreational services with plenty of good-quality accommodations to choose from. Semi-modern cabins, hotels and motels, and condominium-style suites are available. Alongside the townsite is a popular beach, one of several in the park, a great golf course, and fully serviced campsites. (More primitive campsites are available in outlying areas.)

The **Lakeview Hotel** here is a good choice for full-service accommodation in terms of location and quality. The **Hawood Inn** has luxurious one- and two-bedroom suites with fireplaces. Both hotels have good quality dining rooms. For lunch try the golf-course clubhouse.

Many visitors to Prince Albert National Park make the long hike to Grey Owl's small log cabin deep in the backwoods on the shores of Ajawan Lake. It was here that Grey Owl—a trapper turned conservationist—lived, worked, wrote his popular books, and was finally buried. In the 1930s the colorful naturalist was heralded as Canada's, if not the world's, most celebrated spokesman for preserving the wilderness and its inhabitants. His image was tarnished somewhat when, upon his death, it was discovered that he was not the Indian he claimed to be but a white man born in Hastings, England. Despite this revelation, Grey Owl remains a folk hero in the eyes of many and will be long remembered for his message: "Remember you belong to nature, not it to you."

GETTING AROUND

Saskatchewan's two major airports are located in Saskatoon and Regina. Both cities are served by Canadian Airlines, Air Canada, and a regional carrier, Time Air. In Canada, flights to Saskatchewan depart daily from Halifax, Ottawa, Montreal, Toronto, and Winnipeg to the east and Vancouver, Calgary, and Edmonton to the west. In the United States, direct daily connections can be made through Minneapolis to Regina and Saskatoon as well as to provincial points north. Car-rental companies operate out of the province's major airports.

Regina is along VIA Rail's Winnipeg-to-Calgary route, and Saskatoon is along VIA's Winnipeg-to-Edmonton route. Greyhound operates similar bus routes along the Trans-Canada and Yellowhead highways. The Saskatchewan Transportation Company operates the major provincial bus line.

The Trans-Canada Highway (Highway 1) and the Yellowhead (Highway 16) are the province's two major east-west corridors. Other less direct routes offering a change of scenery include the Red Coat Trail (Highway 13) to the south and the Northern Woods and Water Route (Highway 55) to the north. North-south travellers can follow the CanAm International Highway—which follows a number of highways: 35, 39, 6, 3, 2, and 102—to La Ronge. This new route will eventually connect with El Paso, Texas.

Provincial information centers are located along the Yellowhead and Trans-Canada highways at entry points into the province and at North Portal along the North Dakota/Saskatchewan border. The province also operates a toll-free travel inquiry service. Call Tourism Saskatchewan: from Regina, (306) 787-2300; from Saskatchewan, (800) 667-7538; from other parts of Canada and the U.S., (800) 667-7191. The address is 1919 Saskatchewan Drive, Regina, Sask. S4P 3V7.

ACCOMMODATIONS REFERENCE

▶ **Hotel Bessborough.** 601 Spadina Crescent East, **Saskatoon**, Sask. S7K 3G8. Tel: (306) 244-5521 or (800) 667-8788; Telex: 074-2204.

▶ **Chelton Inn.** 1907 11th Avenue, **Regina**, Sask. S4P 0J2. Tel: (306) 569-4600 or (800) 667-9922; Telex: 071-2665.

▶ **Cypress Hills Four Seasons Resort.** Cypress Hills Provincial Park, Box 1480, **Maple Creek**, Sask. S0N 1N0. Tel: (306) 662-4477.

▶ **Hawood Inn.** Box 188, **Waskesiu Lake**, Sask. S0J 2Y0. Tel: (306) 663-5911.

▶ **Holiday Inn.** 90 22nd Street East, **Saskatoon**, Sask. S7K 3X6. Tel: (306) 244-2311 or (800) 465-4329; Fax: (306) 664-2234.

▶ **Kenosee Inn.** Moose Mountain Provincial Park, General Delivery, **Kenosee Lake**, Sask. S0C 2S0. Tel: (306) 577-2099.

▶ **Lakeview Hotel.** Prince Albert National Park, P.O. Box 26, **Waskesiu**, Sask. S0J 2Y0. Tel: (306) 663-5311.

▶ **Landmark Inn.** 4150 Albert Street South, **Regina**, Sask. S4S 3R8. Tel: (306) 586-5363 or (800) 667-8191.

▶ **Ramada Renaissance.** 1919 Saskatchewan Drive, **Regina**, Sask. S4P 4H0. Tel: (306) 525-5255 or (800) 667-0400.

▶ **Ramada Renaissance.** 405 20th Street East, **Saskatoon**, Sask. S7K 6X6. Tel: (306) 665-3322 or (800) 667-3020. Telex: 074-21569.

▶ **Regina Inn.** 1975 Broad Street, **Regina**, Sask. S4P 1Y2. Tel: (306) 525-6767, or (800) 667-5954; Fax: (306) 352-1858.

▶ **Regina Travelodge.** 4177 Albert Street, **Regina**, Sask. S4S 3R6. Tel: (306) 586-3443 or (800) 255-3050.

▶ **Relax Inn.** 102 Cardinal Crescent, **Saskatoon**, Sask. S7L 6H6. Tel: (306) 665-8121 or (800) 661-9563; Telex: 03-849331.

▶ **Hotel Saskatchewan.** 2125 Victoria Avenue, **Regina**, Sask. S4P 0S3. Tel: (306) 522-7691 or (800) 667-5828.

▶ **Saskatoon Inn.** 2002 Airport Drive, **Saskatoon**, Sask. S7L 6M4. Tel: (306) 242-1440 or (800) 667-8789.

▶ **Sheraton Cavalier.** 612 Spadina Crescent East, **Saskatoon**, Sask. S7K 3G9. Tel: (306) 652-6770 or (800) 325-3535; Telex: 074-2286.

▶ **Sheraton Centre.** 1818 Victoria Avenue, **Regina**, Sask. S4P 0R1. Tel: (306) 569-1666 or (800) 325-3535; Telex: 071-2606.

ALBERTA

By Roberta Walker

Roberta Walker worked for Macleans *and* Alberta Business *magazines and founded her own magazine for adventure travellers,* Real Travel. *A resident of Alberta for eleven years, she has walked, fished, and skied in most parts of the province.*

Since Alberta is barely a century old, its history is sparse and its cities are new, but the tradition of the frontier flourishes. The Rocky Mountains and Calgary's annual rodeo—the Stampede—are the province's main magnets for visitors wanting to explore the wilderness or relive the Wild West.

The mountain parks provide easy access to an extraordinary block of uninhabited wilderness. Horse-packing trips, climbing, canoeing, and hiking draw visitors to the mountains in the summer, while winter snows draw the skiers. Although the mountains are far from civilized in the urban sense, they have been hosts to tourists since the 1890s. Lodging ranges from turn-of-the-century resorts, which resemble castles more than hotels, to rustic cabins.

Most visitors enter and leave by air from Calgary or Edmonton, the capital city. Because the province's main attractions are huddled in the southwest corner, Calgary, affectionately known as Cowtown, is the closest gateway.

If Alberta is slim on history, it is heavy on paleontology and archaeology. Two sites containing dinosaur fossils and Indian artifacts are worth day trips from Calgary: The dinosaur park and the buffalo jump have joined Machu Picchu and the Parthenon as UNESCO World Heritage sites.

The northern region, beginning at Edmonton, attracts

467

hardy travellers to its three large rivers and Canada's largest park: Wood Buffalo. The country has abundant wildlife for sportsmen and observers alike, but travel in the north is time-consuming and inconvenient for the few tourist attractions it offers.

Although you could cram a visit to Calgary and the mountains into a week, two weeks gives you the necessary exploring time. A good tour of the province would begin with four days in and around Calgary, then three days in Banff and Lake Louise, followed by a day's drive up the Icefields Parkway to Jasper for three days. Then retrace your steps to Calgary.

First-time sightseers may want to enter or exit the province by taking the scenic train trip west from Calgary through Banff into British Columbia. Trains equipped with dome cars make this almost 24-hour run through the mountains daily. Although there is a train from Edmonton via Jasper to the coast, that trip is considerably less scenic. (See the Getting Around section at the end of this chapter for more information.)

Most of the province's alpine ski resorts are in the Calgary/Banff area, where there are six major downhill facilities within a two-hour radius. Jasper has excellent skiing but only one hill. All the ski areas have good restaurants and an ample selection of lodging, although many of the more rustic, cabin-like accommodations are closed in the winter.

MAJOR INTEREST

Hiking, trail riding, canoeing, mountain climbing
Skiing

Calgary
Devonian Gardens
Glenbow Museum
Heritage Park
1988 Olympic sites
Zoo
The Calgary Stampede

Day Trips from Calgary
Tyrrell Museum of Palaeontology
Head-Smashed-In Buffalo Jump
Prince of Wales Tea House

Banff
Cave and Basin
Banff Springs Hotel
Sunshine Village
Museums and galleries
Banff Centre
Sulphur Mountain Gondola

Lake Louise
Tea houses
Moraine Lake

Jasper
Maligne Lake

Edmonton
Festivals
Historic homes and museums
Muttart Conservatory
Old Strathcona district
West Edmonton Mall

In Alberta some of the plainest scenery in the world presses against some of the most spectacular; very recent human history is neighbor to the ancient remains of the dinosaur age, and a modern city overlooks the stupendous wilderness of the Rocky Mountains. This combination of wild scenery, history, and solitude has drawn visitors since the infancy of modern tourism.

The uninhabited wilderness, encompassing an area half the size of Denmark, isn't the least bit dented by the three million visitors a year who pass through it. The whole Rockies region is now prime bus-excursion territory for tourists from North America and Japan, but you can still hike for hours without seeing another soul.

Think of Alberta as an elongated rectangle trimmed by a spine of huge, rocky mountains on its long left side, and filled with grassland and a few people. By European standards, the population is sparse compared with the geography; Alberta could fit six Englands inside its provincial boundaries but accommodates one twenty-fifth of England's population.

Despite having half a million inhabitants each, Calgary and Edmonton are uncongested cities with the flavor of big small towns—and culturally one-dimensional, with the exception of their Chinatowns. The Chinese provided the labor force for the construction of the railroad in the

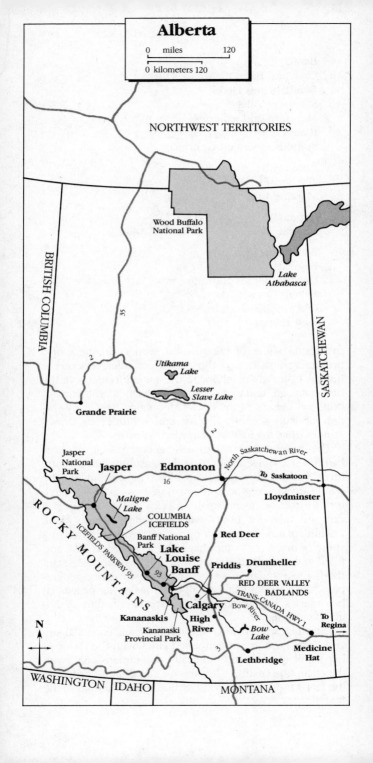

1860s, then settled in the west. Calgary's Chinatown is the second largest in the country.

Two centuries ago the prairies in the southeast were the domain of the buffalo, the Plains Indians, and the fur traders. One hundred years later the demise of the buffalo gave rise to ranching, and the Canadian Pacific Railway's transcontinental line opened Calgary as a shipping center and the mountains as a retreat for Europeans. Banff, located in the midst of the Rockies, became Canada's first national park in 1885; the Canadian Pacific Railway (CPR) built the castle-like Banff Springs Hotel in 1887 and Chateau Lake Louise in 1891, and the mountains were open for business.

Without the corporate push of the CPR, tourism in the Rockies wouldn't have charm or history. In 1886 Canadian Pacific executives were searching for a way to pay for their recently completed railroad. Witnessing the popularity of rugged trips to Switzerland, the CPR's general manager decided to capitalize on the Canadian wilderness by marketing it as a Swiss experience in the New World. Swiss guides were imported, and hotels were designed to civilize the wilds to European standards; the Rockies were promoted in those days as the Canadian Alps.

From the 1880s until the Roaring Twenties, resorts sprouted up throughout the region to play host to the Victorian adventurers who stayed for weeks to climb with Swiss guides, ride trails with cowboys, or soak up the mountain air. Things haven't changed much. The combination of comfort, accessibility, and rugged scenery that charmed the 19th-century visitor still draws people today.

SOUTHERN ALBERTA

Although most visitors come to Alberta to see the mountains, there are a couple of equally outstanding attractions in Calgary and southern Alberta. The Calgary Stampede is one of the major events on North America's rodeo circuit, while the dinosaur park and museum and the buffalo jump are exceptional archaeological sites.

Calgary

Calgary may push its cow town image, but visitors will see little of the heavy ranch influence. Instead they are met by an ultramodern skyline, good restaurants and theater, and a sophisticated oil business that left ranching in the dust commercially in the 1950s.

Calgary began life as Canada's first North West Mounted Police outpost, and "Calgary," which is Gaelic for "clear running water," aptly described the site of Fort Calgary, built on the banks of the Bow River in 1875. The only remaining building from Fort Calgary is the **Deane House**, built in 1896 by Captain R.B. Deane, commanding officer of the North West Mounted Police. Today it is a tea house serving lunch and high tea. The food is excellent and in the summer, salads are freshly picked from the garden on the grounds.

The city rises out of flat, bald prairie, and the river cutting through downtown is the only relief from an otherwise dull landscape. The completion of the Canadian Pacific Railway's transcontinental line through Calgary in 1886 breathed new life into the frontier town. Early Calgary was so saturated by the CPR that the city streets even bore the names of CPR executives until 1904. Good ranching and good transport made Calgary the hub of the Canadian meat business. Alberta beef still arouses provincial pride, and to show it off local restaurants offer 550-gram steaks. **Caesar's** and **Hy's** restaurants are located on 4th Avenue S.W., and compete for local business people seeking the best steaks in town. Although the food is western, country music and jeans would not be at home in these restaurants, which prefer candlelight, red velvet, business suits, and dresses.

In 1912 a sag in the ranching business prompted four local cattlemen to finance promoter Guy Weadlick in his Wild West show, the Stampede. Today, the **Calgary Stampede** draws a million spectators and revives Calgary's Wild West tradition for ten days each July. Horses appear downtown, and western dress and square dancing take over city street corners. Every shop sports western decor, and the city's restaurants and bars are jammed with merrymakers. The throngs of people are part of the fun, but be forewarned; hotels will be full, and you may have to wait for an hour or two to get into a bar with live country-and-western music.

The Stampede Grounds, located a few blocks south of downtown, are the main forum for festivities and the rodeo events. You can purchase tickets for each afternoon's rodeo (including bull riding, bucking bronc riding, and calf roping) in advance, but you can usually pick up last-minute seats at the Grand Stand box office located on the grounds. Even if you miss the rodeo, a trip to the grounds is an experience in itself: there are hundreds of displays, an amusement park, an Indian village with te-pees and dancing, and a shoot-out scene staged daily.

Corners of genuine cowboy culture persist beyond the Stampede, like at the **Riley & McCormick** western-wear shops in the 8th Avenue Mall and at the airport. Riley & McCormick have clothed cowboys since the turn of the century; they carry the essentials plus items such as hol-ster diaper pins for western babies. The **Ranchman's South** (on McLeod Trail) is a big barn of a bar with a large dance floor and top-notch country entertainment. Lo-cated in the south part of town, closer to ranch country, the bar is frequented by working cowboys. It has lots of color, including real saddle seats on the bar stools.

Heritage Park, located off 14th Street and Heritage Drive S.W., is an authentic re-creation of a prairie railroad town in pre-1915 Alberta. More than 100 buildings have been moved to the park from sites throughout the prov-ince and restored, including the homes of famous Calgar-ians. There are furnished homes, a newspaper office, and a church; visitors can sample goodies from the bakery, eat at the Wainwright Hotel, or ride on the steam engine.

The **Calgary Zoo**, the second largest in the country, is located along the Bow River in Calgary. If you don't mind an hour's walk along the riverside path, you can walk from downtown; otherwise, take the Light Rail Tran-sit train east, heading for Whitehorn. The zoo contains a Prehistoric Park, where life-sized replicas of the dino-saurs found in Alberta are displayed in their natural habitat.

In the winter, **Canada Olympic Park** offers beginners downhill skiing within the city limits. Advanced skiers will be bored unless they take a ride on the bobsled run, left over from the 1988 Winter Olympics. From top to bottom the bobsled run takes one minute and costs $100—an expensive minute, but survivors report the terror is worth it. The chicken start is lower and cheaper; only half the terror for half the price. Located on the west edge of town, the park was the site of the ski-jumping, bobsled, and luge events for the Olympics; site tours are given. The **Naturbahn** (natural luge) starting gate has been made into a tea house, commanding a view of the mountains and the entire park. It serves meals and high tea prepared by a European pastry chef in the summers, but is only open for Sunday brunch in the winter.

The **Palliser Hotel**, on 9th Avenue S.W., built in 1912, was Calgary's first skyscraper and remains the only hotel with any character. Located in the heart of downtown, it is the lodging choice for the prime minister and the royal family, and it is the traditional haunt of the ranching élite. Named after Captain John Palliser, who mapped the province for the Royal Geographic Society, the Palliser was one of four hotels built by the CPR to break up the journey for rail passengers travelling to the Rockies. Since dining cars were not a feature of early rail travel, these hotels gave guests a place to rest and eat amid the elegance of the era. The **Oak Room Bar**, a popular watering hole for downtown business people and visiting dignitaries, has the original chandeliers inspired by the German Renaissance. The **Rimrock** dining room is wallpapered with leather murals reflecting western life. Local favorites are clam chowder and crusty French bread, made in the hotel's original ovens. Within the last two years the public areas of the hotel have been restored to their turn-of-the-century grandeur, and many of the rooms have been refurbished. Try to get a room on the ninth or eleventh floor on the west side; these are the business or prestige rooms, and for the slight difference in price you will be treated to superb service and gorgeous rooms with a view of the mountains.

The **Westin** is a large, newly renovated hotel on 4th Avenue, offering that comfortable sameness of any modern first-class hotel. It is home to many visiting business people and their accompanying meetings, and contains the **Owl's Nest**, an outstanding formal dining room.

The **Sandman Inn** is the best of the moderately-priced downtown hotels in both facilities and location: It sits on the LRT line halfway between downtown and Kensington.

A short walk from the Westin, or from the Palliser for that matter, is the wonderful food of Chinatown (on Centre Street between 4th and 2nd Avenue S.W.). If you eat dim sum or Chinese brunch early Sunday morning at the **Silver Dragon** you could easily think you are in China because of the scarcity of westerners.

Another downtown breakfast spot, popular with those who can find it (334 Riverfront Avenue S.W. at Third Street), is the **1886 Café** housed in a homely little wooden building with an old sign saying Eau Clair and Bow River Lumber Co. It is indeed the former home of the company, built in 1886. There are no croissants at this place; the menu is strictly eggs, juice, whole-wheat toast, and award-winning coffee, with some distinct variations on eggs like a peaches-and-cottage-cheese omelette. Decorated with an eclectic assortment of antiques, the building is café upstairs and museum of Calgary city history downstairs. It is open for breakfast and lunch only.

East of the Palliser is the Glenbow Museum, and in the next block is the Calgary Centre for the Performing Arts. The **Glenbow Museum** has an excellent permanent collection of western Canadian art and artifacts, and realistic displays tracing western Canadian life from the fur trade to the oil boom. In addition, many international exhibitions stop at the Glenbow.

The new Calgary Centre, containing two theaters and a concert hall, features mainstream and offbeat entertainment both in music and drama; the quality, however, shows the inconsistency of youth. Theater buffs should try the **Lunchbox Theatre**. Buried in the Bow Valley Square office tower on 5th Avenue and 1st Street S.W., this casual theater fills with business people from 12:10 to 12:50. The Lunchbox, as the name implies, encourages you to eat during the compact performances of light musicals, mysteries, and the like. Arrive early; there are no reservations, and the Lunchbox often sells out.

The **Devonian Gardens** is an indoor subtropical garden with fountains and waterfalls. For downtown workers, this lunchtime spot is an oasis located in the Toronto Dominion Square shopping plaza (about two blocks from the Palliser). Farther down 8th Avenue, in the Penny Lane shopping center, a touch of Britain lives in **Canterbury's Bookstore**. Reminiscent of an English private library, the two-story bookstore has comfortable wingback chairs, a cappuccino bar, and a backdrop of classical music inviting you to linger over an extensive collection of books, including many on the history of Canada and Alberta. Across the hall is Canterbury's sister store, the **French Horn**, specializing in classical, jazz, and new-age music. Again the atmosphere is alluring, with a fireplace and comfortable antique chairs outfitted with headphones.

If you want to hear jazz and blues performers, go to the **King Edward Hotel** in the evening. The excellent entertainment compensates for the run-down decor and dubious location on 9th Avenue East.

For formal dining there is the **Chateaubriand**, one of Calgary's best French restaurants, at 823 14th Street N.W. at 8th Avenue. Although the linen tablecloths are loaded with silver cutlery, the Chateaubriand escapes pretentiousness with its warm service.

A Touch of Ginger (514 17th Avenue S.W. at 5th Street) is a small, elegant Vietnamese restaurant located in a renovated house. It adds gourmet touches to its excellent Vietnamese menu and makes some concessions to Western tastes with chocolate fondue supplied by local chocolatier Bernard Callebaut.

Da Guido's, one of many fine Italian restaurants in Little Italy, east of Centre Street and north of Memorial Drive, is small, dark, and very good. It is popular among provincial politicians.

The best people watching, boutique shopping, noshing, and designer coffee is found across the river from downtown in the **Kensington** area. This neighborhood, which begins at 10th Street and Kensington Road N.W., is loaded with interesting shopping, from locally designed clothes to Canadian crafts. The huge Galleria on Kensington Road sells work by Alberta artisans. The centerpiece of the neighborhood is the Plaza Theatre, featuring offbeat, foreign, and classic films.

Farther west on Kensington Road is the **Kensington Delicafé**, tucked into the tiny Recreation Center mall. This café has a casual atmosphere and terrific home-cooked meals that end with delicious desserts. It's open all day and has a steady flow of regular clientele. Folk and blues artists entertain here evenings after 9:00 P.M.

Day Trips from Calgary

Two UNESCO World Heritage sites preserving dinosaur fossils and Indian artifacts have recently opened museums and interpretive centers that document extinct creatures and lifestyles.

Only an hour-and-a-half drive northeast of Calgary, in the town of Drumheller, is the largest collection of dinosaur skeletons in the world. The **Tyrrell Museum of Palaeontology**, opened in 1986, contains 30 complete dinosaur skeletons and dozens of displays and minitheaters to lead visitors through the evolution of life. Allow yourself a minimum of two hours' viewing time, but the museum attracts hordes of visitors in the summer, so then you may want to add an additional hour to your schedule then. Drumheller has little to offer after museum hours, so plan to return to Calgary in the evening.

The drive to Drumheller passes through the **Red Deer Valley Badlands**, the great graveyard of the dinosaur age and home of the Hoodoos. Hoodoos are spires of rock saved from erosion by a hard sandstone cap. These strange hunks of landscape were feared by local Indians, who believed the Hoodoos to be petrified giants who came to life at night and hurled rocks at intruders.

Another day trip is a two-hour drive south of Calgary to the largest and best-preserved buffalo jump in North America. The drive takes you through empty prairie, but the mountain views to the west are inspiring. The Plains Indians got an edge on the buffalo by stampeding them over a cliff. The cliff, called a buffalo jump, was the centerpiece of the buffalo hunt.

Given the unappetizing name of **Head-Smashed-In Buffalo Jump**, this site was used for more than 5,600 years by the Plains Indians, and last used less than a century ago. The name describes the unfortunate fate of a young Piegan Blackfoot tribesman who was crushed to death while watching the buffalo jump 150 years ago.

The jump is a marvel of hunt engineering. Lanes 8 km (5 miles) long channeled the buffalo toward the 30-foot drop off the cliff. People stationed along the lanes waved buffalo hides to keep the herd in the lanes. Once the buffalo rushed off the cliff, the hunters finished them off with spears and arrows. An elaborate interpretive center, opened in 1987, presents a dramatic audiovisual reenactment of the hunt and contains displays of hunt artifacts.

If you need a spot of tea en route to the buffalo jump, or wish to spend an afternoon in ranching country, try the **Prince of Wales Tea House**, located west of High River. The tea house was the country retreat of King Edward VIII, who fell in love with Alberta ranching life during a visit to Canada. Edward owned the property for 42 years, but the simple life proved incompatible with Edward's other love, Wallis Simpson, so he sold the house. The house contains memorabilia, including photo albums of the prince and his family, and the staff is very knowledgeable about the house's history. Located on a working ranch, the hour-and-a-half drive to the tea house winds through spectacular ranching country toward the foothills of the Rockies, but don't make the drive unless you have reservations. (Tel: 403-395-2418.) Fortunately, there are good signs guiding you to this out-of-the-way spot, and you will be rewarded with a light lunch or high tea, complete with cucumber sandwiches on homemade buns and homemade sweets. To find it, head south from

Calgary on Highway 2 until you see a sign for the Prince of Wales Tea House, indicating a right turn, then follow the road for 23½ miles, watching for signs.

Calgary's ranching tradition has spawned a number of trail-riding outfits and guest ranches—24, to be exact—for people who want a more authentic Western experience. **Rafter Six Guest Ranch**, located in Seebe on the way to Banff, accommodates guests in a rustic, but far from shabby, three-story log lodge. Some of the other guest ranches are located south of Calgary in the foothills country more commonly associated with ranching. One such ranch is the **Homeplace Guest Ranch** in Priddis, which offers accommodation to just 12 guests in the main ranch house, year-round. Homesteaded in the early 1900s, the ranch's activities include trail-riding, pack trips, hiking, fishing, golfing, sleighrides, and cross-country skiing.

ROCKY MOUNTAIN REGION

Winter or summer, the mountains are a playground for outdoor pursuits or the pursuit of leisure. Within a two-hour drive west of Calgary there are six major ski resorts. Banff, Kananaskis, and Jasper all have championship golf courses. The entire mountain region is laced with hundreds of superb hiking trails that double as cross-country ski trails in the winter. The difficulty of choosing one is eased by numerous information booths staffed by knowledgeable people.

The ridge of huge, craggy peaks is visible as you leave the Calgary western city limits, and once you reach the parks you are surrounded by the rocky faces that enjoy only a couple of snow-free months a year.

Every hotel or restaurant in the area is dedicated to the setting; even gas-station coffee shops are bestowed with great views.

Kananaskis, the closest and least publicized park, was the one favored by former Premier Lougheed, who poured millions of provincial tax dollars into excellent facilities, not the least of which is Nakiska, site of the downhill events at the 1988 Winter Olympics. Although Kananaskis (pronounced Can-an-ass-kiss) has scenery equal to that of Banff, it doesn't have the fame, so the tour buses pass it by. There is no town, but there is a new hotel complex offering a variety of lodging, dining, and drinking spots. (See the Accommodations Reference section at the end of this chapter.) Even the campsites are first class; the **Mount Kidd** campsite takes reservations (Tel: 403-591-7700) and is equipped with tennis courts and a hot tub. The park begins immediately south of the Trans-Canada Highway to Banff, and the turnoff is well marked.

Banff National Park

An easy hour-and-a-half drive west from Calgary, **Banff** is the only real town in the park and, though small, offers all the amenities of a city, including theater and museums. Numerous restaurants, hotels, and designer shops are crammed into a five-block strip along Banff Avenue.

The town's location centered on the discovery of hot sulphur springs in 1887, which led to the creation of a European-type spa. The **Cave and Basin Spa** still exists, and the restoration of its outdoor pool retained the old design but improved the facilities. Another hot-spring spa sits on Sulphur Mountain.

The **Banff Springs Hotel**, nestled among huge mountains, was the largest hotel in the world when it was built in 1887. "The Springs," a castle-like structure that dominates the valley, has undergone numerous face-lifts to preserve her tarnished elegance. The mezzanine lounge, lined with large picture windows framing the mountains, can entice anyone to take a drink there in the afternoon.

Unfortunately, the charm of the public rooms does not extend to the bedrooms. If you have any doubt of the hotel's age, the clanging pipes and irregular heat will confirm it. The room prices may be the highest in town and the rooms a bit seedy, but the Old World glamour of this dowager resort makes up for her deficiencies. Also, it's the only true resort in town, with a superb golf course, tennis, swimming, stables, a variety of restaurants, and the lounge. Try to indulge in the Sunday brunch, which is not only gigantic, but superb: eggs Benedict perfectly cooked, smoked salmon, seafood salad, and fresh strawberry sorbet.

The romantic image of the hotel has earned the Springs a spot on Japanese television as a backdrop for soap operas. This publicity makes the Springs the lodging of choice for the Japanese tour groups that come to Banff each summer.

If you want to reach mountaintops without climbing, there are two gondola rides to get you there. One sits on

Sulphur Mountain, within view of the Banff Springs Hotel, while the other carries you to the Sunshine Village ski resort a few miles west of town. After the ski season closes, the gondola continues to carry hikers up the mountain to the year-round hotel at the top. The hotel's only outstanding attribute is its location. Even if you don't ski or hike, the gondola ride provides a great view and takes you to Alpine-type meadows.

Banff may be rustic, but you can find elegant French dining at the **Beaujolais**. The Beaujolais is the best restaurant in town, but you pay a premium for that pleasure. If you want something rustic and cheaper, go to the **Grizzly House**, located, as is the Beaujolais, on Banff Avenue. The atmosphere is reminiscent of a mountain guide's cabin, complete with animal heads and pelts; the specialties of the house are fondues and caribou, buffalo meat, or rattlesnake.

Despite Banff's wilderness bent, it has a strong cultural side. A fine-arts school, established in 1933, draws high-quality entertainment to the facilities at the Banff Centre. The Peter Whyte Gallery and the Luxton Museum expand on the region's history.

Lake Louise

Lake Louise, located half-an-hour's drive west of Banff, has no town to speak of but offers more spectacular scenery and more interesting accommodations than Banff. A small shopping center and a handful of ordinary restaurants and hotels constitute the village of Lake Louise, and there is little entertainment. The main attraction is the lake itself, originally named Emerald because of its brilliant color. It was renamed Louise after Queen Victoria's daughter.

The palatial **Chateau Lake Louise** sits at one end of the lake facing a huge glacier at the other end. The hotel, at 4,000 feet, was built in 1913 and is being completely renovated with a Bavarian motif. You have to pay an extra $50 to get a lakeview room, but the view is worth it. The older rooms may not have all the first-class touches but they are twice the size of the new ones, and those located on the third and fifth floor have lovely glass-enclosed balconies. Although the hotel is a prime stop for bus tours, you can escape the hordes in the **Edelweiss** dining room. The seating is set up for parties of two or four, with tables facing the lake. Continental cuisine, featuring venison, duck, and rabbit, is offered in a formal setting.

Many of the original hotels, camps, lodges, and tea houses built here by the CPR are still in use, accessible mainly by foot, horseback, or skis. Within a two-hour walk of Chateau Lake Louise are the tea houses built in 1923 at Lake Agnes and at the Plain of the Six Glaciers. Hikers who make the short but steep walk to the tea houses will be treated to bread, apple crisp, and tea, all made on wood-burning stoves.

Deer Lodge, located within sight of the chateau, was built as a trading post in 1923. Renovations have preserved the rustic dining room and huge stone fireplaces, but the rooms have been upgraded to resemble bedrooms in a home rather than a hotel. Be sure to ask for rooms in the new section, since not all rooms have been upgraded; the difference in price is worth it. The dining room serves excellent Continental cuisine, with homemade bread, and rivals the Post Hotel as the best restaurant in the area.

Moraine Lake, surrounded by ten peaks, is one of the area's most photogenic sites. It deserves its place on the Canadian 20-dollar bill. A short drive from Lake Louise, the Valley of the Ten Peaks has a tea house, built in 1906, and a few rustic bungalows collectively called **Moraine Lake Lodge**. It provides a good resting point to contemplate nature or a good starting point for many excellent hikes. The accommodation is primitive for the price, but you can't beat the view.

The **Post Hotel**, once a rustic log hotel, lost some of its rustic charm in recent renovations, but has been converted into an elegant first-class hotel with a rustic motif. Owned by the same people as the Beaujolais in Banff, the Post's original cabins and bar were built in 1942. The Post has been a favorite local eating spot for years.

Icefields Parkway

Originally constructed as a make-work project during the Depression, the Icefields Parkway (Highway 93) winds through 230 km (140 miles) of rugged glacier and mountain scenery. The road, completed in 1960, connects Lake Louise and Jasper, and gets its name from the chains of icefields lying parallel to the road. The glaciers are most visible at the Columbia Icefields located 60 miles south of Jasper. Here, the tongue of the glacier nearly touches the highway, and there is a hotel, an interpretive center, and guided tours to take you onto the surface of the glacier by Sno-Cat, but all the facilities are closed in the winter.

The only hotel on the highway with any character (and there are only three hotels at all) is **Num-Ti-Jah Lodge**. This small, wooden lodge, built on the shore of Bow Lake in 1939, was the setting for many Hollywood productions staged in the 1950s, particularly the Nelson Eddy Mountie movies. The rooms are primitive but comfortable, and the dining room has only average food, but the old-fashioned atmosphere redeems the place.

Jasper Park

Jasper Park, adjoining Banff Park's northern boundary, was established in 1907. Named after trapper Jasper Hawes, the park is located 362 km (220 miles) from Edmonton and 426 km (250 miles) from Calgary. The Jasper townsite evolved from the railroad business, not tourism, so it is less touristy than Banff, and there are a couple of great restaurants and hotels.

Many of the cabin accommodations, like **Becker's Roaring River Chalets** or **Tekarra Lodge**, are closed during the winter but are terrific places to stay in the summer. Private cabins, riverside locations outside of town, and excellent dining at Becker's and Tekarra make these a visitor's first choice, and they are popular, so reserve well ahead. **Jasper Park Lodge**, the Jasper equivalent of the Banff Springs, is an overpriced disappointment unless you stay in one of the cabins, which are well worth the difference in price. However, the lodge is the only resort with golf, a swimming pool, tennis, horseback riding, and the works (but eat in town). In town, the **Château Jasper** dining room is one of the best, featuring varied and creative Continental cuisine.

Maligne Lake, a one-hour drive from Jasper (easy to find if you drive; otherwise book bus ride and cruise at Maligne Tours in Jasper), is the second-largest glacial lake in the world. The two-hour boat cruise on the lake surrounded by mountain peaks is breathtaking.

EDMONTON

Edmonton, the capital and by far the oldest city in the province, is simply a government town spiced up by the presence of the world's largest shopping center. Edmonton owes its development to location: It is perched on top of the escarpment overlooking the North Saskatchewan River. The deep river valley divides the city and adds a hilly, scenic component to an otherwise flat landscape. Fort Edmonton was built in 1795 as a fur-trading post for the Hudson's Bay Company and later became a supply center for the north. Edmonton earned its reputation as the gateway to the north in 1898, when the Klondike gold rush drew thousands of gold seekers through Edmonton to the Yukon. Edmonton still holds the **Klondike Days** festival in July. Although people dress up in 1890s costumes and the festival is heavily promoted, some of Edmonton's newer festivals have eclipsed the Klondike Days in popularity.

Summer is the time to visit Edmonton because it is the season of long daylight hours and of festivals. The festivals begin July 1, when Edmonton becomes Jazz City, and its two-week-long jazz festival draws top musicians from across North America to perform in the city's clubs and bars. Klondike Days occurs during the last two weeks of July, followed by the **Heritage Festival** on the first weekend in August. This event, when ethnic groups gather to indulge in traditional dancing and food, draws a quarter of a million people.

The Edmonton **Folk Music Festival** takes place the second weekend in August. This outdoor festival, reminiscent of the 1960s, features a variety of music often not heard on the radio. For ten days in mid-August, the **Fringe Theatre Event** plays in the Old Strathcona area. An alternative theater event, the Fringe launches some 150 new productions in the city's 14 theaters.

Even when the Fringe festival is not on, **Strathcona** is the city's most interesting browsing area. Located on Whyte Avenue between 103rd and 106th streets, Strathcona's active historical society has restored many of the buildings to their turn-of-the-century grandeur. The **Strathcona Hotel** (1891) is a popular beer-drinking spot for university students, and Strathcona Square, developed in the Old Post Office Building, is filled with boutiques, galleries, and restaurants. South on 103rd Street is the **Cook County Saloon**, a western dance hall featuring country bands and Texas two-step lessons on Tuesdays and Thursdays.

Since there is no stately dowager of a hotel in Edmonton, the best downtown choices are the **Four Seasons** and the **Westin**. Both are excellent, modern first-class hotels in the heart of the shopping and entertainment district, within walking distance of the Citadel Theatre complex and the Edmonton Art Gallery. The Citadel and Shoctor theaters (located in the same complex) should not be overlooked, as they perform consistently fine work.

Some esoteric collections are housed in the city's smaller museums, which include Strathcona's model and toy museum, a police museum, and the Ukrainian Museum of Canada, which displays costumes and hand-painted Easter eggs. Ukrainians played a large role in the settlement of Edmonton and are still the dominant ethnic group.

Four huge glass pyramids, located in the river valley adjacent to downtown, are prominent and unusual landmarks. Built in 1976, the **Muttart Conservatory** houses a wide variety of plants, with each of three pyramids representing a different climatic zone—tropical, temperate, arid—and a special pyramid for unusual floral displays. It is like a plant museum because each of the plants is labelled with its name, along with a bit of plant history.

The Carvery dining room at the Westin is an elegant award-winning restaurant with prices to match. For colorful people watching in a coffeehouse atmosphere, the **Bistro Praha**, at 10168 100 A Street at 101st Avenue, is perfect. Popular with the after-theater crowd, as well as the onstage crowd and their fringe, the Bistro prepares an array of East European dishes and superb desserts. The food is obviously a hit because the menu hasn't changed in ten years. **La Boheme**, at 6427 112 Avenue, is a superb French restaurant and bed and breakfast, located in an elegant residential district. It occupies the main floor of the Gibbard Block, an apartment building built in 1912 and noted as the first in Edmonton to have hot water. Upstairs there are eight suites, newly renovated with antique decor. The main dining room, complete with lace curtains and tin roof, is the best choice in town.

Boccalino's, on Jasper Avenue, specializes in homemade pasta and home-brewed beer. Although large, Boccalino's is still intimate with its undoubtedly Italian decor. If you're interested in Chinese food, don't be deterred by the tattered exterior of the **Blue Willow**, at 11107 103rd Avenue, 111st Street. The National Hockey League players and other notorious appetites who frequent the place are a tribute to the great food. The **Sidetrack Café**, located near the railroad tracks at 10333 112th Street, 103rd Avenue, serves good food, but is best known for its international lineup of bands playing in the converted-warehouse setting. The music may run the gamut from blues to jazz to pop rock, but whatever the style, the quality is good.

Edmonton gained a place in the *Guinness Book of World Records* for the **West Edmonton Mall**, the largest shopping mall in the world. Don't let the crassness of this monster keep you away. Aside from the 800 stores, 100 restaurants, and 34 theaters, there is an NHL-sized ice rink where the Edmonton Oilers practice, recording studios where you can cut your own record, an indoor amusement park, a 5-acre water park with 22 water slides, and a wave pool complete with 7-foot waves. There is also an indoor lake with trained dolphins, submarine ride, and a replica of a Spanish galleon. West Edmonton Mall is as much an entertainment center as a shopping mall, and it is fun. The indoor lake would be at home in Hollywood, but the amusement park is getting a bit tattered.

GETTING AROUND

The Rockies region is packed with bus tours and tourists from June until September, so hotel reservations are a must. Even the campgrounds fill up by early afternoon. It is the same during the Christmas season, when Banff and Jasper hotels fill with skiers. The best time to visit the Rockies is late September and early October, during Indian summer. The days are still warm and the towns less crowded, so you have more choice of places to eat and sleep. It's also cheaper then, because some of the hotel rooms are discounted 30 to 40 percent. The only drawback may be snow if you decide to hike up to the higher elevations. The Stampede consumes Calgary in the first two weeks of July.

Dressing is tough even for the locals in Alberta because of the whimsical nature of the weather. Southern Alberta boasts chinooks, warm winds that within a matter of hours blow spring across the winter prairie. Temperatures may fluctuate by 20 degrees Celsius within a single day. In summer, Alberta generally has hot days and cool evenings that require slacks and a sweater.

Buses will take you from the airport to the major downtown hotels in either Calgary or Edmonton for one-third the price of a taxi, and many hotels offer complimentary shuttle-bus service. In Calgary the bus to downtown, the Airporter, charges $6 one way and $10 round trip. If you're arriving by VIA Rail, the national train service, you will be deposited downtown in either city

Edmonton's International Airport is located so far out of town that the price of a taxi to a downtown hotel would nearly equal a day's car rental. Since the attractions are not clustered downtown, a car is useful anyway. If you don't rent a car, stick to taxis for transport, because the public transportation is spotty—with the exception of the shuttle service to West Edmonton Mall offered by many of the hotels.

Calgary's new LRT train system will squire you around the city quickly and cheaply. Transit along the 7th Avenue strip downtown is free, but the "freebie" ends at City Hall Station heading south, before the Stampede Station. Calgary's grid system makes the city easy to navigate, and it is relatively uncongested for driving. The Trans-Canada Highway, which doubles as 16th Avenue N.W. within the city limits, is the main thoroughfare to the mountains. One main highway runs north-south to take you to the other attractions in the province, but posted directions to the highway from the city center are nonexistent, so a city map is essential.

For booking and complete information on the train trip mentioned earlier between Calgary and Vancouver, call VIA Rail at (514) 871-1331 or (800) 361-3677. The train leaves Calgary at 2:05 P.M. and arrives in Vancouver at 10:40 A.M. the next day; it leaves Vancouver at 3:10 P.M. and arrives in Calgary at 2:25 P.M. the next day (there is a one-hour time difference between Calgary and Vancouver). You can go one way, round trip, or get off anywhere you want; the train goes all the way to Montreal. The fare between Calgary and Vancouver as of this writing is $74 coach, one way. A roomette (sleeps one) is an additional $92. You should reserve at least one year in advance for the summer season, although bookings are taken an hour prior to departure with available seats. The extent of this service has recently been under government review, so be sure to check schedules and prices ahead of time.

There is a new service offered during the summer (May 24 until mid-October) catering to visitors who want to see the Rockies in the daylight. Although the scenery may be beautiful, the price is an outrageous $335 one way compared to the standard coach fare of $74. It does include one night's hotel and two days' worth of breakfasts and lunches. The trip is spectacular, but mountains do present some hazards, and train service can be interrupted by avalanches in the spring. Fall is a beautiful and less crowded time to take this trip. Although advance bookings are best—and some book one year in advance—a month or two advance planning would suffice.

ACCOMMODATIONS REFERENCE

▶ **Banff Springs Hotel.** Box 960, Spray Avenue, **Banff,** Alta. T0L 0C0. Tel: (403) 762-2211 or (800) 268-9411 in Canada. Book 6 months in advance.

▶ **Beckers Roaring River Chalets.** Box 579, **Jasper,** Alta. T0E 1E0. Tel: (403) 852-3779.

▶ **Chateau Lake Louise. Lake Louise,** Alta. T0L 1E0. Tel: (403) 522-3511 or (800) 268-9411 in Canada.

▶ **Deer Lodge.** Box 100, **Lake Louise,** Alta. T0L 1E0. Tel: (403) 522-3747 or (800) 661-1367.

▶ **The Four Seasons.** 10235 101st Street, **Edmonton,** Alta. T5J 3E9. Tel: (403) 428-7111 or (800) 268-6282.

▶ **Homeplace Guest Ranch.** Site 2, Box 6, R.R. 1, **Priddis,** Alta. T0L 1W0. Tel: (403) 931-3245.

▶ **Jasper Park Lodge. Jasper,** Alta. T0E 1E0. Tel: (403) 852-3301 or (800) 642-3817 in Canada.

▶ **Hotel Kananaskis. Kananaskis Village,** Alta. T0L 2H0. Tel: (403) 591-7711 or (800) 661-1581.

▶ **Kananaskis Inn. Kananaskis Village,** Alta. T0L 2H0. Tel: (403) 591-7500 or (800) 332-1013.

▶ **La Boheme.** 6427 112th Avenue, **Edmonton,** Alta. T5W 0N9. Tel: (409) 474-5693.

▶ **Lodge at Kananaskis. Kananaskis Village,** Alta. T0L 2H0. Tel: (403) 591-7711 or (800) 661-1581.

▶ **Moraine Lake Lodge.** Box 70, **Lake Louise,** Alta. T0L 1E0. Tel: (403) 522-3733.

▶ **Num-Ti-Jah Lodge.** Box 39, **Lake Louise,** Alta. T0L 1E0. Tel: Mobile Operator Calgary, ask for Num-Ti-Jah Lodge at 135-9002.

▶ **Palliser Hotel.** 133 9th Avenue S.W., **Calgary,** Alta. T2P 2M3. Tel: (403) 262-1234 or (800) 268-9411 in Canada.

▶ **Post Hotel.** Box 69, **Lake Louise,** Alta. T0L 1E0. Tel: (403) 522-3989.

▶ **Rafter Six Guest Ranch. Seebe,** Alta. T0L 1X0. Tel: (403) 673-3622 or 264-1251.

▶ **Sandman Inn.** 888 7th Avenue S.W., **Calgary,** Alta. T2P 3V3. Tel: (403) 237-8626 or (800) 225-6277 in Canada.

▶ **Tekarra Lodge.** Box 669, **Jasper,** Alta. T0E 1E0. Tel: (403) 852-3058.

▶ **Westin Hotel.** 320 4th Avenue S.W., **Calgary,** Alta. T2P 2S6. Tel: (403) 266-1611 or (800) 228-3000.

▶ **Westin Hotel.** 10135 100th Street, **Edmonton,** Alta. T5J 0N7. Tel: (403) 426-3636 or (800) 228-3000.

VANCOUVER
AND VICTORIA
By Garry Marchant

Garry Marchant lives in Vancouver and writes a monthly travel column for Vancouver Magazine *as well as articles on world travel for magazines throughout North America, Australia, Asia, and Europe.*

Few cities make such a powerful first impression on visitors as Vancouver. Lofty mountains, often blanketed by fresh snow, rise straight out of the ocean; blue inlets cut deep into the city center; and dense rain forests edge against the intruding high-rises. The sea air fairly sparkles, and when the breezes are right the natural perfume of fresh-cut cedar from the Fraser River mills scents the city.

The dramatic meeting of mountains, forests, and sea—and the gentle climate warmed by the Japan Current—shapes the local character, setting Vancouverites apart from other Canadians. No other major city lives so close to raw nature. From downtown high-rise towers of commerce, three-piece-uniformed stockbrokers and lawyers look out on tugboats hauling strings of barges loaded high with logs or wood chips and on floatplanes landing in the harbor, bringing lumberjacks, hunters, fishermen, and prospectors fresh from the bush.

On rugged Coast Range peaks, which are almost close enough to touch, eagles nest—and inexperienced city hikers often get lost overnight. Game wardens frequently have to chase bears away from suburban yards, and even in the crowded West End downtown residential area raccoon families saunter single file across trimmed lawns and terrorize local cats.

Outside of Victoria, Vancouver has Canada's finest climate. It *does* rain frequently in this West Coast marine climate, but even then the showers only serve to freshen the coast air. Despite its soggy reputation, Vancouver has less rain in June, July, and August than Edmonton, Winnipeg, Toronto, or Montreal.

Vancouverites (a Vancouverite is anyone who has been here more than a few months) boast of being able to swim and ski on the same day, although no one actually does. You can do much more; there are nine miles of public beach within the city limits, 18 public and seven private golf courses, 152 tennis courts, and miles of ocean, lakes, and rivers for canoeing, kayaking (ocean or white water), and water skiing. Alpine and cross-country ski slopes begin 20 minutes from the city center.

MAJOR INTEREST

Beautiful setting
West Coast good-living atmosphere
Gastown (historic buildings, shops, restaurants, people)
Granville Island (market, shops, theaters, restaurants)
Chinatown (restaurants, souvenir shops, exotica)
Stanley Park
Grouse Mountain by tramway

Day Trip to Victoria

Among Canadian cities, Vancouver is considered beautiful and fun-loving but somewhat frivolous. It is part of the Canadian mythology that many young prairie people yearn to escape the bitter winters and small-city life. The career-oriented ambitious types go to Toronto or Ottawa to become lawyers, accountants, advertising executives, or solemn civil servants. The romantics, the poets go west, searching for the good life, to survive however they can. This young city nurtures not just hedonists but confirmed oddballs. Easterners like to say that they tilted the country, and all the loose nuts rolled down to Vancouver. During the daft decade of the 1960s, the city had an official town fool, complete with court-jester cap-and-bells outfit. All forms of aberrant and extreme behavior,

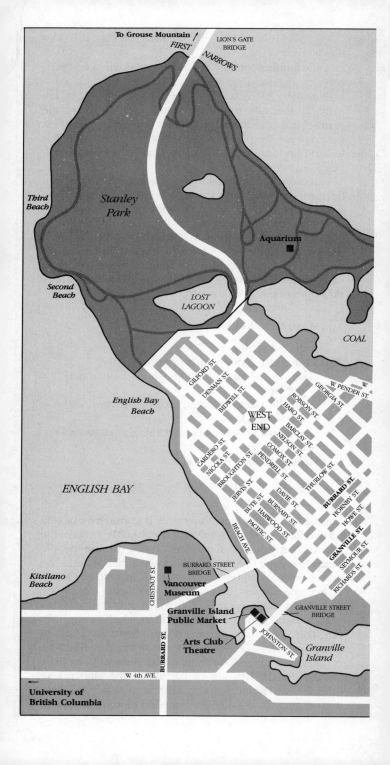

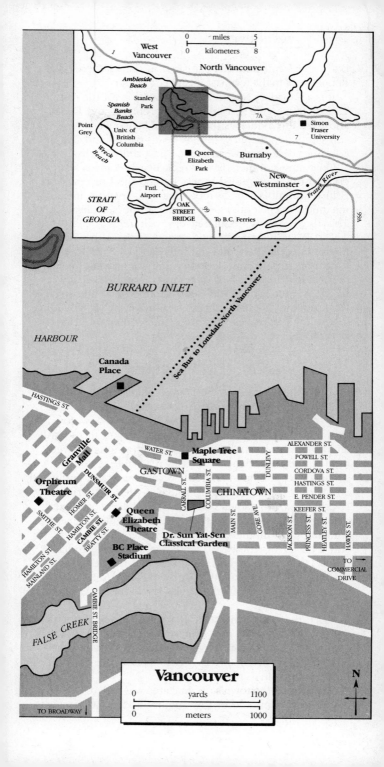

both social and political, start first in Canada here, take deeper root in the fertile soil, and last longer.

It is a Canadian New Year's Day tradition for the rest of Canada to snuggle sensibly before fireplaces and TV sets and gaze in wonder as thousands of Vancouver loonies, still steeped in the glow of New Year's parties and clad in costumes or formal wear, plunge into chilly English Bay.

On sunny summer days, **Wreck Beach**, Canada's largest, most famous nudist beach, behind the University of British Columbia, attracts more than 5,000 people, including nude beer vendors, in search of the seamless tan. This, too, is part of the Vancouver mystique.

The Polar Bear Swim and events such as the Fraser River Outhouse Race and the International Bathtub Race from Nanaimo across Georgia Strait confirm the image the rest of Canada has of Vancouver: That this is a city of flakes, a Lotus Land insufficiently imbued with the stern work ethic of Toronto, Ottawa, Hamilton, or Halifax. All this, of course, makes Vancouver entertaining for visitors as well.

Around in Vancouver

Canada's third-largest city, at 1.5 million people, is merely middle-sized by American or European standards. The "city" part is concentrated in the West End and downtown area, bordered by False Creek/English Bay to the south and Burrard Inlet to the north. Many attractions are free, or inexpensive, and most are easily reachable.

Vancouver can boast no noble beginnings, no Romulus and Remus mythology. On a Sunday in 1876, a garrulous riverboat captain named "Gassy Jack" Deighton paddled a dugout canoe away from the town of New Westminster, with his wife, mother-in-law, yellow dog, two hens, $6, and a barrel of whisky. He landed at a spot the Indians called Lucky Lucky, cracked the keg, and passed the cup around to workers from the nearby Hastings Mill. Appreciative mill workers built him a shack/saloon, and Vancouver was on its way.

When the Canadian Pacific Railway chose the spot as the terminal of the new transcontinental railway, the town's future was ensured. After the original shantytown burned down in 1886, new brick, stone, and cast-iron buildings rose in its place.

Gastown, as the town's original area was called, degenerated by the middle of this century as the city center moved west, and there was a move to tear it down. Instead, in the late 1970s the city restored the 19th-century buildings, laid brick sidewalks and streets, planted trees, and installed decorative street lights. The resulting heritage area has won a number of international design awards. Gastown is now a popular area of restaurants, bars, and shops from the chic to the tacky, selling antiques, totem poles, urban cowboy gear, and "Made in Hong Kong" moose-head ashtrays.

A statue of Gassy Jack atop a barrel now stands before the site of his first saloon, the Globe, on Maple Tree Square at the east end of Water Street. At the other end, the world's only steam-powered clock, built to cover a steam vent, cheerfully toots the Westminster Chimes on the hour. Place names such as Blood Alley and Gaoler's Mews remind us of rowdier, more colorful times.

Like Gastown, False Creek's **Granville Island**, between the Granville and Burrard bridges, was a grubby industrial area of factories, foundries, warehouses, shipyards, and railway sidings. In the 1970s, a time of awakening appreciation for the city's heritage, a major redevelopment began. Today, the rejuvenated island is a favorite recreation center that includes a houseboat community, theaters, the Emily Carr School of Art, art galleries, craft shops, bookstores, and equipment stores and chandlers for all the yachts moored here. An old warehouse has become a fashionable hotel, with a popular restaurant/club (see below).

The Granville Island Public Market, housed in a massive converted warehouse with a rough-edged decor of exposed pipes, beams, and tin sheeting, isn't the cheapest place to shop. However, its cheese merchants and butchers, its fresh seafood, pasta, and pâté sellers, and its craft shops provide such ambience and choice of goodies that no one minds the slightly higher prices. Granville Island even has its own micro brewery, which produces beer according to ancient Bavarian regulations.

Granville Island is a short taxi trip or, better still, a rowboat-sized ferry ride from the West End dock under the Burrard Street Bridge. (Parking is almost impossible.) The island is a perfect spot for an informal lunch, with a wide choice from the many takeout-food outlets (deli, Greek, fish and chips). Sit on the dock outside watching the fishing boats and yachts go by, or rent a rowboat, kayak, or sailboat and lunch on the water.

The heart of Vancouver is a peninsula surrounded by

English Bay, First Narrows, and Burrard Inlet. Stanley Park, with the Lions Gate Bridge crossing to the North Shore, occupies the northern half.

Extending from the park, the **West End** is one of Canada's most densely packed yet desirable residential areas. Here are many of the better hotels, restaurants, parks, and beaches as well as fashionable **Robson Street**. This once interesting ethnic strip, known also as Robsonstrasse, has been transformed into a row of expensive boutiques and cute restaurants.

Abutting the West End, the downtown core extends from **Burrard Street** ten blocks east to Beatty Street, and is filled with office towers, hotels, theaters, many (though certainly not all) of the good restaurants, and the nightlife.

Gastown, the original Vancouver, and Chinatown, are just east of downtown. Granville Island is southwest across False Creek under the Granville Street bridge.

To the north of this peninsula are the North Shore Mountains and suburbs, including the Grouse Mountain recreational area and parks and beaches. South, across the Burrard, Granville, and Cambie bridges, are residential areas, the university, several museums, and more beaches and parks.

East Side ethnic areas give way to suburbs such as Burnaby and New Westminster, which stretch out into Fraser Valley farming communities.

Ethnic neighborhoods are scattered loosely throughout the city, with the Greeks on West Broadway (toward the university), the Italians in East Vancouver, the East Indian community highly visible on south Main (toward the airport), and the Japanese (now mainly dispersed, except for the food stores and restaurants) east of Gastown along Powell Street. The borders are by no means fixed, and these areas are frequently filled with ethnic specialty shops and restaurants rather than residences.

Getting your bearings is easy in this city—provided visibility is good. Find the mountains, and you are facing north.

Vancouver's beaches are popular and crowded in summer, more for sunbathing, games (Frisbee, volleyball, wind-surfing), and people watching than swimming. The water is too cold even for locals, except for New Year's Day, when thousands traditionally join in the Polar Bear Swim. **Sunset**, **English Bay**, and **Second beaches**, stretching along the south of the city center peninsula to Stanley

Park, are popular with the urbanized West End residents and visitors from the downtown hotels.

Kitsilano Beach, across English Bay from the West End, is crowded with the young adults from that popular neighborhood. Farther west, near the university, **Spanish Banks**, with some of the best beaches, draws families, picnickers, and barbecuers. Farther west still, and the hardest to get to (snugly under the cliffs of the university), **Wreck Beach** is Canada's most famous public nudist assemblage, complete with unclothed beer and piña colada hawkers.

By contrast, West Vancouver's **Ambleside Beach** is the domain of fashionable matrons, their well-dressed progeny, and designer-accoutered joggers.

Vancouver was still just a big port and lumber town until after World War II. The major growth has been in the past few decades, so it is rare to meet a native-born Vancouverite in this community of newcomers. Most residents are refugees from the harsh winters of the rest of Canada, or immigrants from abroad.

Still, the city, supported by the mining and lumber industries, retains a certain pioneer air, aided by its proximity to sea and forest. Aside from natural resources, there is some manufacturing (high-tech electronics and computer software) and, of course, tourism.

Vancouver is more than just a pretty setting, though. In recent years, there has been a resurgence of interest in traditional native Indian arts and crafts. West Coast Indians were North America's greatest native artists, crafting totem poles, elaborate big houses, carved dishes, ceremonial masks, drums, rattles, and household items.

New totem poles have been raised in several parks and other public places in Vancouver and Victoria in recent years, and art shops stock masks, carvings, silver jewelry, and prints that they buy directly from native artists. Totem-pole carvers can be seen working in a number of places, including the Capilano Suspension Bridge in North Vancouver.

The University of British Columbia's **Museum of Anthropology**, a stylized version of an Indian big house set on cliffs overlooking the Pacific at the western end of the city, brings home the powerful feel of the highly developed West Coast native art. The huge concrete-and-glass building stores and displays some 20,000 artifacts, especially from the B.C. (British Columbia) coast. This is one of the world's most comprehensive collections of West Coast art, art that has been compared favorably with that of ancient Greece and Rome. The 46-foot-high windows in the Great Hall illuminate some of the grandest native pieces in existence, including towering totem poles, giant carved house-front figures, and feast dishes that resemble tub-size bowls on wheels. Next to the museum is a full-scale Indian big house and a group of contemporary totem poles. The university (for which see below) occupies a peninsula at the extreme west of the city, overlooking English Bay and Stanley Park to the north. From Granville Street downtown the number 10 bus goes directly to the university for $1.25—but avoid the morning rush hour when the buses are packed with students.

Vancouver is the terminus of both Canadian transcontinental railways and is the largest port in North America after New York City, shipping coal, grain, and forest products to the Orient. Turned resolutely toward the Pacific, this is perhaps the continent's most Asian city. Its large Chinatown is probably North America's most authentic, because of the influx of Hong Kong and Southeast Asian Chinese immigrants in the past decade.

The Ethnic Neighborhoods

Aside from the broader, cleaner streets, **Chinatown,** around Pender and Main streets, is remarkably like districts of Kowloon, Hong Kong; its stores overflow with Asian bric-a-brac and curios, accompanied by wailing Cantonese pop music, Peking opera. Chinese social clubs, movies, and newspapers abound, and its sidewalks are crowded with noisy shoppers. Fat, shiny-brown ducks hang from butcher-shop windows; boxes of such exotic vegetables as *bok choy* and *gai lan* clutter sidewalks.

Even the Eastern-influenced buildings, with moon doors and upturned tile roofs, the neon Chinese signs, and the pagoda-like telephone booths maintain the tone. According to *Ripley's Believe It or Not,* the world's narrowest building stands on 8 West Pender. It is two stories high, 96 feet long, and only 5 feet 10 inches wide.

Of recent interest is the new **Dr. Sun Yat-Sen Classical Garden,** the only one of its kind outside China. Artisans from the People's Republic modelled the classical garden at Pender and Carrall streets after that in the city of Suzhou during the Ming dynasty. Materials, tools, and techniques used were almost the same as for the original, and most of the material, including hand-fired roof tiles, carved wood-and-lattice windows, and limestone rocks, were shipped from China. The peaceful garden includes pavilions, covered walkways, terraces, lookout platforms, weathered limestone rocks, and reflecting pools.

Vancouver has the largest overseas community of South Asians (from India, Pakistan, and Sri Lanka—many by way of Uganda or Fiji) outside of London, and the largest Sikh community outside of India. Turbans and beards are commonplace in **Little India**, on South Main around 49th Street, an area powerfully evocative of the Indian subcontinent. In these few blocks are incense-scented sari shops, video stores advertising epic Indian movies, and restaurants serving India's Sovereign beer (brewed in Bangalore and sporting a likeness of Queen Victoria).

Alongside bolts of silver- or gold-threaded, hand-woven silk for saris is Indian costume jewelry: bangles, baubles, nose pins, five-finger rings, armlets, ankle bracelets with little tinkling bells, and toe rings. Food markets, fragrant with spices, sell subcontinental produce and fruits such as mangoes, jackfruit, and durians, along with papadums, jars of sauces, pickles, chutneys, henna, and anything else you might find in a well-stocked shop in India.

Other ethnic neighborhoods are scattered throughout the city, sought out by visitors after new taste sensations. The Japanese have been on East Powell Street since early in the century, and, although forcibly evicted during World War II, many have returned. In these two short blocks are Japanese restaurants, shops selling exquisite pottery and crafts, and fishmongers supplying the city's many sushi shops.

Greeks settled on Broadway, across English Bay from downtown, and Italians on Commercial Drive, in the East End about 3 km (2 miles) from the city center, and these areas are worth seeking out for the local grocery stores, coffee shops and, especially, fine, inexpensive restaurants.

East Hastings, an older area of shops, small department stores, and seafood cafés, separates Gastown and Chinatown and is ethnic, working-class Canada populated by husky, hairy loggers in red-plaid shirts and nail boots, fishermen and deckhands in bulky sweaters, and railway workers in denims. East Hastings, with its low-cost department stores, pawnshops, cheap hotels, beer joints, war-surplus stores, and greasy spoons, is another reminder of how close the city still is to its frontier origins.

Stanley Park

Stanley Park, North America's largest urban park (New Yorkers claim the same for Central Park), is a vital playground for outdoorsy Vancouverites. You can lose yourself (briefly) on the 22 miles of hiking trails and bicycle paths winding through the 1,000 acres of thick, broody rain forest.

The western tip of the downtown peninsula has beaches, bowling greens, cricket pitches, and tennis courts within walking distance of most major hotels. There is a zoo with polar bears, a miniature train that even adults can ride, totem poles, a Japanese monument, summertime cricket games, and outdoor theater. The seven-mile seawall is crowded even in winter with joggers, roller skaters, and bicyclists.

The **Stanley Park Aquarium**, Canada's largest, with more than 8,000 aquatic creatures, is also one of the largest in the world. It is best known for the dolphin and killer-whale displays of grace and power before spectators at the Max Bell Marine Centre, and for the comprehensive viewing galleries with large picture windows. The aquarium concentrates on marine and freshwater aquatic life of the North American west coast. Popular displays are the world-famous Pacific salmon sports fish, Arctic grayling, and several species of trout shown in their natural habitat. Depending on the season, the sharks, sawfish, and giant sea bass are fed on Wednesdays and Saturdays at about 1:00 P.M.; the sea otters and harbor seals, throughout the day.

Stanley is only one of 157 parks scattered throughout the city. Residents claim that there are actually thousands of parks, for Vancouverites are such ardent gardeners—a New York writer once commented—that the city looks like a seed catalog.

Elsewhere in Vancouver

For the greatest panorama of the city, take Canada's largest, most modern tramway 3,700 feet up **Grouse Mountain** to a restaurant, coffee shop, and, of course, ski slopes and hiking trails. For the Grouse Mountain Skyride, drive west on Georgia Street through Stanley Park and across the Lions Gate Bridge, turn right onto Marine Drive, then left onto Capilano Road. Follow the road to the base of the mountain, where there is parking.

Gamblers should head about 7 km (4 miles) east on Hastings to the local track, Exhibition Park, where, along with the many losers, there is a winner in every race.

The **University of British Columbia** campus, almost 1,000 acres of practically untouched forest on the tip of Point Grey at the western end of the city, is a popular hiking spot. The university welcomes visitors; information booths at all entrances provide maps and brochures. The main attractions, aside from the Museum of Anthropology discussed above, are the **Nitobe Memorial Gardens**, a traditional Japanese garden with a ceremonial tea house, an extensive rose garden, and the campus itself. The new University Endowment Lands Park, 1,700 acres of wilderness, is now officially protected from developers.

Despite its reputation, Vancouver is no cultural desert. You will find a dozen professional theater companies scattered throughout the city, two major universities (the other being Simon Fraser in nearby Burnaby, worth a look for its distinctive architecture), and the Vancouver Symphony Orchestra. The refurbished **Orpheum** on Granville Street, home to the VSO, is worth visiting for the elegant structure alone, especially in a town that is sadly lacking in fine old architecture. Most musical performances, from classical guitar to old-time jazz or grand musicals, are held in this ornately decorated theater, or in the larger, more modern Queen Elizabeth Theatre on Robson Street near the bus depot.

The Arts Club Theatre, with two locations on Granville Island, features fine contemporary productions, musical revues, and indigenous plays—a few of which make it to New York and London. Performing-arts patrons can dine at a Granville Island restaurant first, then enjoy the performance and drinks at the theater. Same-day half-price tickets for most performances are available at Front Row Center, 1025 Robson Street (cash only).

Eastern Canadians complain that it is pointless to make a business call to Vancouver after lunch on Friday, because the lazy hedonists will be gone for the weekend. True enough. On winter weekends most cars sprout rooftop ski racks like antlers on a rutting elk and join the stream out of the city to the slopes. And on warm Friday afternoons, a parade of sailboats, cruisers, fishing boats, kayaks, and canoes head out to sea past sunbathers on English Bay Beach.

For some ten days in mid-July, the **Vancouver Sea Festival** celebrates the city's maritime heritage with visits from U.S. Navy ships, a parade, salmon barbecues, and fireworks. Coinciding with the events, some 125 zany international competitors navigate the turbulent Georgia Strait from Nanaimo on Vancouver Island to Vancouver City in the Great International Bathtub Race.

At **Lonsdale Quay**, North Vancouver, where the Seabus docks, there are a number of modern, but unattractive commercial and residential buildings. However, the seaside walk to Sailor's Point park is pleasant, with scenic views of the city across the harbor. The busy quay is one of the city's most successful new Art Deco markets, with a variety of food stalls as well as produce, bakery goods, seafood, and handicrafts for sale.

There are some good restaurants on this side of the water, but not much nightlife.

GETTING AROUND

Vancouver is well connected to Europe, the United States, and Asia by a number of international airlines. More than a dozen airlines serve Vancouver International Airport, with the number growing every year. Air Canada, Canadian Air Lines International, and Wardair are the major Canadian carriers, with American, European, Asian, and domestic routes. American Airlines, Delta, United, and Continental serve the United States, with several connections a day to Seattle, San Francisco, Los Angeles, and Chicago. British Airways, Lufthansa, and KLM also fly to Europe, while Cathay Pacific, Japan Air Lines, Singapore Air Lines, Korean Airlines, Qantas, and Air New Zealand cross the Pacific.

Vancouver is the major departure point for cruise ships to Alaska. More than ten major lines, such as Princess, Holland America, Hapag-Lloyd Pacific, Sitmar, Costa, Cunard, Royal, Exploration, Admiral, and World Explorer, depart from the new **Canada Place cruise-ship terminal** for the coastal journey. Many tourists visit Vancouver for the first time while joining these cruises.

A number of small commuter airlines operate within B.C., some on floatplanes. Air B.C. has daily service from Coal Harbour downtown to Victoria's Inner Harbour. San

Juan Airlines connects Vancouver and Victoria with Seattle and waypoints. Small aircraft can be chartered for remote areas. Those flying private aircraft should contact the B.C. Aviation Council for information on some 374 land and water airports in the province and for practical trip-planning information. Write B.C. Aviation Council, 304-4160 Cowley Crescent, Vancouver International Airport (South), Richmond, B.C. V7B 1B8; Tel: (604) 278-9330.

Not everyone arrives by air. There is VIA Rail from the east, an excellent option for anyone eager to get the feel of the vast province, and major highways from the east and south. Vancouver is a three-and-a-half-hour drive from Seattle, and, except on summer and holiday weekends, when there are long lines, border crossings are a simple affair.

Those few who start their Canadian journey in Victoria can cross to Vancouver by BC Ferries (one hour and 40 minutes of stunning scenery through the Gulf Islands), fly city center to city center by Air B.C. floatplane, or take a helicopter. Any way you go, the scenic rewards are great.

From Vancouver's airport it is about a 25-minute taxi or bus connection to downtown hotels. Taxis should cost about $15 to $17. Airport Express buses cost $6.75 for adults. Most attractions, including Gastown and Stanley Park, are within walking distance or a short taxi ride from hotels. In summer there are horse-and-carriage rides and tours by antique cars.

The 400-passenger Seabus crosses from downtown to the North Shore suburbs, for an inexpensive sea view of the city. Tickets are $1.15, off-peak hours, and you can transfer onto buses at either end. The catamaran-hulled ferries leave the old Canadian Pacific Railway station in downtown Vancouver every 15 minutes for the 12-minute ride across Burrard Inlet to the North Shore.

It may be commonplace for people in large, older cities, but Vancouver has had its rapid transit system (the Skytrain) only since January 1986. Most of it operates above ground, so the half-hour trip between Vancouver and New Westminster is worth taking for the interesting perspective of the city and to see the old Expo grounds near False Creek and Chinatown. New Westminster, the former provincial capital on the banks of the Fraser River, about 30 minutes southeast of the city at the end of the Skytrain line, has an interesting and active public market and a pleasant riverside bar and restaurant. Vancouverites insist that they built the mass transit above ground not just because it was cheaper but because they did not want to deprive riders of the view.

ACCOMMODATIONS

(The area code for Vancouver and all of British Columbia is 604.)

Since the great building boom spurred by Expo 1986, Vancouver has been an excellent hotel city. Although the real bargains of post-Expo years, when hotels were running at low occupancies, are no longer so readily available, prices are still reasonable for a major city, and there is a wide choice, especially of first-class hotels. All of the top hotels are located within a few blocks of each other—an example of how compact this city is.

The stately **Hotel Vancouver,** the city's oldest quality hotel, is a great stone palace, a less elaborate version of the great Canadian Railways château style (such as Québec City's Château Frontenac and Victoria's Empress). Built in a modified 16th-century French Renaissance style, the hotel, with its steep verdigrised copper roof, decorative gargoyles, and exterior of the same stone used for the provincial legislative building in Victoria, stands out in a city not known for its architecture. Marble imported from Europe and the lavish use of exotic woods give the interior a palatial air. The lobby bar, adjacent to the Timber Club restaurant, is good for midday people watching. This is still one of the best places to stay in town, particularly on the Entree Silver and Deluxe Entree Gold floors.

900 West Georgia Street, V6C 2W6; Tel: 684-3131 or (800) 268-9143. (The hotel was recently purchased by C.P. Hotels, which has launched major renovations.)

The **Four Seasons,** part of the deluxe Canadian chain, is the best of the city's pre–building boom hotels. Large rooms, including a number of excellent suites, offer grand views from the higher floors, and the service is excellent. The spacious, airy **Garden Lounge,** a haven of tropical plants and splashing waterfalls, is one of the city's most popular hotel bars, and the **Chartwell Restaurant** has reaped a number of culinary awards. Shoppers have direct access to the hundreds of shops, department stores, and restaurants of the recently extended **Pacific Centre Mall.**

791 West Georgia Street, V6C 2T4; Tel: 689-9333; from Canada, (800) 268-6282; from the U.S., (800) 828-1188.

The **Wedgewood** is unique among the city's fine hostelries, the only major one not part of a chain. The owner gives the small hotel (94 rooms, including 29 suites and four penthouses; no pool) her personal touch, and the dedication shows. The Wedgewood has that intimate, friendly, old-European feel; here, the helpful staff quickly gets to know guests.

In the lobby and public rooms, antiques and original artworks accent gleaming brass, glass, marble, and polished woods. The bright, gardenlike **Bistro**'s tall Palladian windows look out on the glass and waterfalls of the courthouse complex across the street. Excellent for lunch.

845 Hornby Street, V6Z 1V1; Tel: 689-7777 or (800) 663-0666.

The new **Meridien** established itself as one of Vancouver's top inns within a few years of opening. The gracious European interior, decorated with marble and antiques, is appropriate for a member of the elegant Air France chain. The **Gerard Restaurant** rates as one of Vancouver's finest, and the pleasant bar, with its rich wood paneling, leather-button wing chairs, and stag horns on the walls, is reminiscent of a genteel British men's club. Rooms are large, and many have good views.

845 Burrard Street, V6Z 2K6; Tel: 682-5511 or (800) 543-4300.

Another successful newcomer, the **Pan Pacific**, is dramatically set on the water, overlooking the North Shore Mountains. Along with the billowing "sails" of the adjacent Canada Palace convention center and cruise-ship terminal, the great glass structure ranks as a symbol of the city.

The entrance, two escalator flights along an atrium to the lobby, gives a sense of West Coast spaciousness: They could raise a totem pole in there. While the hotel is aimed at the convention center and cruise-ship business, they have a number of suites designed for the luxury market. The **Pan Pacific Health Club** is one the best equipped and most modern in this town dedicated to fitness.

300-999 Canada Place, V6C 3B5; Tel: 662-8111 or (800) 663-1515.

In addition to these, Vancouver has many smaller, though very good, hotels. The old red brick, ivy-covered **Sylvia**, on English Bay adjacent to Stanley Park, is popular for both location and nostalgia. Watching the sunset over the freighters moored in the bay from the **Sylvia Bar** has long rated as one of the city's finest experiences. Unfortunately, they cut the bar in half to put in a forgettable restaurant. The Sylvia has added a new wing with more modern rooms, but many still prefer the original building.

1154 Gifford Street, V6G 2PG; Tel: 681-9321.

The **Pacific Palisades**, in the heart of the West End's chic shopping area and what is left of the old, European Robsonstrasse (Robson Street), is a favorite with long-term visitors. A former apartment block, the all-suites hotel is popular with Hollywood types—directors, technicians, cameramen, actors—filming here. A likely spot for discreet star-gazing.

1277 Robson Street, V6E 1C4; Tel: 688-0461 or (800) 663-1815.

In the same area, a number of once small, slightly worn West End hotels have been renovated in recent years, and now provide comfortable lodging for moderate prices. The three-story **Barclay Hotel** is conveniently located, pleasantly remodelled, and quiet with a congenial bar and surprisingly good restaurant for such a small hotel. Prices are particularly attractive off season (October 1 to May 31).

1348 Robson Street, V6E 1C5; Tel: (604) 688-8850.

A few hotels removed from the city center are worth considering. The **Granville Island Hotel**, a refurbished former warehouse south of downtown on what was an industrial island beneath the Granville Bridge, has a fine view of the cityscape across the water. The restaurant/nightclub **Pelican Bay** (alternatively, Pelvis Bay or Bay of Pigs) tends to the young and striving.

1235 Johnson Street, V6H 3R9; Tel: 683-7373 or (800) 663-1840.

The **Park Royal**, across Lions Gate Bridge, which connects the rest of the city with quiet and quaint West Vancouver, is suitable only for those with cars or a healthy budget for taxis. The ivy-covered Tudor building (just 30 rooms) is like an English country inn in a park setting. On the Capilano River a few minutes' walk from Ambleside Beach, one of Vancouver's finer suburbs with well-tended English country gardens, this is a pleasant retreat from the nearby city.

440 Clyde Street, V7T 2J7; Tel: 926-5511.

DINING

Longtime Vancouver residents recall the days, just a few short decades ago, when dining out was limited to steak and baked potato (with wine in a brown bag), or the number-seven special with egg rolls and fortune cookies in Chinatown. Although this is an exaggeration, the city's dining possibilities have developed remarkably in recent years, so much so that—in terms of variety at least—it leads the country, with due respect to Toronto.

This culinary range has been sparked by large-scale immigration and by the Vancouverites' determination to savor all of life's pleasures. A recent trend has been for many good restaurants to move away from the city center. While visitors can certainly eat and drink in style within walking distance of their downtown hotel, some of the city's interesting places now require a drive or taxi ride.

Vancouver is also part of the worldwide trend toward quality restaurants attached to hotels. The Meridien Hotel's **Gerard** (Tel: 682-5511), although a newcomer, is already established as one of the city's top French restaurants. The intimate dining room, done in soft pastels and gleaming in silver and crystal and starched linens, seats only about 30 diners. It is all very refined, a place to dress up and savor the Old World ambience (and don't forget the credit card or checkbook). Service has that Gallic flair, the seafood is good, and Gerard is particularly proud of its six-course specials.

Dining with a View

In a city so formed by its setting (and so chauvinistically loyal to it), dining with a view is important. The **Salmon House on the Hill**, 2229 Folkestone Way, West Vancouver, some distance from downtown, is dramatically situated on a mountainside facing the city to the south. The dining room is spacious and open, with West Coast cedar decor. It is especially pleasant to sit outside here on a sunny summer day. The salmon grilled over alder wood is succulent. The main complaint about this place (aside from its somewhat hard-to-reach location) is its popularity with tourists. Better reserve; Tel: 687-4400.

Bridges, on Granville Island, set between the Burrard and Granville bridges and overlooking the city across False Creek, is more conveniently located. Somewhat trendy, it is also a place to which locals take visitors to show off their city; the view is especially good from the top deck. The food, which comes from the sea, is also good. If you want the location without the food, there is a pub downstairs. In summer a restaurant appears on the dock, and diners laze away sunny afternoons in an atmosphere of fishing boats, sea gulls, and passing yachts.

Native Indian

Unique to this city is the **Quilicum**, 1724 Davie Street, near the Sylvia Hotel and Stanley Park, the only authentic West Coast native Indian restaurant in existence. Here is a truly not-to-be-missed Vancouver experience. Cedar-plank walkways along a floor of smooth, round stones pass between elevated eating platforms (with sunken areas for the legs, just like in Japanese restaurants aimed at foreigners). Original Indian artworks gracing the walls (masks, carvings, prints) are all for sale. The food, cooked over a fire at the end of the big house, includes such indigenous dishes as alder-wood-grilled salmon, caribou stew, grilled goat, rabbit, and *oolichan* (a small local fish). The place is run by native Indians, and the service is relaxed. Diners will have an unusual meal, a distinctive experience, and maybe purchase some interesting artwork.

French

The city has many wonderful French restaurants besides Gerard from which to chose. Although they vary in style of food, service, and decor, in terms of quality the differences are picayune; all are excellent.

For atmosphere as well as food, **La Côte d'Azur**, 1216 Robson Street, in the only remaining house in the row of newer buildings on Robson Street, has a dining room with tables around a wood-burning fireplace. In summer you can dine out on the veranda among potted geraniums and roses and overlook the passing show of power shoppers, punk rockers, perambulators, and dressed-to-be-seen West Enders.

Its worldly patrons (and there are many) say **Cafe de Paris**, at 751 Denman Street, is as authentic a bistro as you'll find on the continent, with plain, worn wooden floors, serviceable marble-topped tables, and black-clad French waiters in long white aprons. It is not just the atmosphere, but the fine cuisine that attracts the Francophiles. If you cannot stomach the *tripe a la Parisienne,* veal kidneys in porto sauce, or sweetbreads in heavy cream and calvados, there is simpler fare: pepper steaks, veal sauteed in Dijon mustard, rabbit, mussels, and several imaginative fish dishes (Tel: 687-1418).

The name of **Le Crocodile**, 818 Thurlow Street, comes from the owner/chef's favorite restaurant in his hometown of Strasbourg. This small West End establishment with a simple decor of sage-green walls hung with some decorative plates is cozy—and gets downright crowded with a full house of about 40 diners. On busy weekends, this is no place for an intimate, eyes-meeting-across-the-flickering-candlelight seduction dinner. But if you go to restaurants for the food, le Croc is well worth a visit. Besides regional specialties such as Alsatian onion pie, the menu lists a full range of Gallic offerings from duck pâté or smoked breasts of goose in a port sauce to pepper steaks, veal in tarragon sauce or roast lamb with basil sauce, and perhaps ending with pear poached in red wine—by which time the candles will have flickered away to a lump of wax (Tel: 669-4298).

Italian

For the finest in good—although not cheap—Italian food, head for the three restaurants in a row on Hornby Street about ten blocks south of the Vancouver Art Gallery and Hotel Vancouver, all owned by restaurateur Umberto Menghi. Each has its own speciality: **La Cantina** (Tel: 687-6621) for seafood; **Umberto's** (Tel: 687-6316), the original, for game; and **Il Giardino** (Tel: 669-2422), with an especially nice garden. A new Umberto project is the franchised **Umbertino's**, bright fast-food places serving inexpensive but good pasta. The Umbertino's on Robson is especially convenient for shoppers.

Not as toney as Umberto's places, **Il Corsaro**, 920 Commercial Drive (Tel: 255-1422), is out in Little Italy in the East End. For an informal dinner, the food is authentic and moderately priced. The decor in this sprawling place tends to gaudy: plaster arches and paintings-of-Venice style. The atmosphere is cheerful, unpretentious, and friendly.

Budget with Character

Vancouver has a number of budget restaurants that serve good food, often in interesting settings. The **Sapporo Ramen Shogun**, 518 Hornby Street, a short walk from Canada Place, is open only for lunch, and it is almost certain you will have to line up for its delicious servings of noodles, *gyoza* (Chinese dumplings), and rice dishes, in Tokyo style. Bamboo wall mats, traditional prints, and scurrying waitresses give this an authentic, efficient Japanese businessman's café feel. It is one of downtown Vancouver's great bargains.

The **Only Fish and Oyster Café** (20 East Hastings, on the edge of the East End) is an old Vancouver landmark, here since 1912 (which is almost forever in this new city). It has no toilets, no liquor license, no class: tiled walls and floor, linoleum floors, two tiny booths in the back, and everything is in beige and brown. Aside from a painting of the restaurant, the only decoration is a giant red fire extinguisher. You'll have to line up, even for the counter. The place is frequented by lawyers and stockbrokers, laborers and the literati—and all for good reason. The clam chowders, served out of pots as big as Douglas fir stumps, steamed clams, and the salmon, sole, halibut, and cod, as well as the jumbo shrimps in batter and oyster pepper stew, are all excellent. This is a terrific lunch spot but a bit too basic for dinner—and some visitors might not chose to be in the area after dark. Prices are higher than the lack of decor might suggest.

Far Eastern

Vancouver excels in Eastern-style restaurants, although the scene is as volatile as a Chinese chef's moods. Just a few years ago food lovers grumbled that the city had every kind of cuisine of the East except Thai. In not much more than a year, a dozen Thai places surfaced, most of them good. **The Thai House**, on the second floor of a building down a narrow alley off Robson Street near the Public Library, is most accessible to visitors. It is quite authentic, with Thai artwork on the walls. The service can be a little slow. The **Nakornthai Restaurant** at 1157 Davie Street is also centrally located, and Thai experts consider the food authentic, except for the Sunday buffet (Tel: 683-6621).

The more chauvinistic Vancouver gourmets claim, flatly, that their city has the finest Chinese food this side of the Pacific. Visitors from San Francisco or New York will likely disagree, but, arguments aside, you can dine well on almost any of the Middle Kingdom's cuisines here. (Not long ago, most restaurants were the garden-variety Cantonese, with a smattering of Mandarin. Now all are here, from Shanghainese to Szechuan and Chiu Chau; all that is lacking is a good, hearty snake-food place.)

For seafood (expensive), the downtown **Tsui Hang Village**, 615 Davie Street, serves excellent lobster in black bean or butter sauce as well as a whole range of finny dishes. With fish tanks all around, the atmosphere is quasi-aquarium; the place fills up on weekends, and it gets noisy—just the way the Chinese like it (Tel: 683-6868). For Szechuan food, the bright, airy **Grand View** at 60

West Broadway, about ten minutes from downtown, offers the city's finest. It is especially popular with the Chinese population, who go for the excellent noodle dishes and the great variety of highly spiced dishes.

With its Japanese population and its face to the sea, this port city has long had a smattering of good Japanese restaurants. The great increase of Japanese businessmen yearning for the familiar has led to numerous new establishments, most very good. The ever-popular **Kamei Sushi**, on the second floor of 811 Thurlow Street, is conveniently located just off Robson Street. Excellent lunch specials are served. You can sit at the counter and watch the sushi chef at work or get a private table behind the sliding paper screen. Prices are reasonable; it is advisable to book here in advance (Tel: 684-5767).

New Seoul, at Broadway and Commercial streets in the city's East End, away from the city center, is popular with the small but growing Korean population. The tatami rooms are actually Japanese, just as they are in good restaurants in Korea, so call it authentic. They have the standard Korean barbecues such as *kalbi* and *bulgogi,* marinated in garlic, sesame oil, chili peppers, and soy, which you cook yourself on a domed gas burner. An aromatic haze hangs in the air—and seeps into your clothes. The food and dining style seem to go down especially well in cold weather. Moderate prices; call to reserve, Tel: 872-1922.

Greek and Spanish

Of the many fine restaurants in the Greek district—Broadway south of the city center across the Burrard Bridge—**Orestes**, 3116 West Broadway, stands out, not just for the food (it is superb) but for the lively party atmosphere. This was one of the first Greek restaurants in Vancouver, popular with University of British Columbia students (the campus is nearby), who keep coming back after graduation. Food aside, this is a lively place; nooks and crannies spread over two floors and several rooms, and even open out onto the sidewalk on dry summer days. And Orestes is certainly friendly, especially later in the evening after the *ouzo* and *retsina* begin to flow. The world's only Greek singles' restaurant (Tel: 731-1461).

La Bodega, 1277 Howe Street (a 10- to 15-minute walk from most city-center hotels), a deservedly popular tapas bar, draws stockbrokers and punk rockers, Spanish language students, the theater set, and anyone who has ever discovered the place and makes it a regular hangout. It is not just the crispy, deep-fried calamari, the garlicky *patatas bravas,* the tender pork loin, or even the sizzling prawns in garlic. It is not even the lovingly made sangria or the baleful black bull staring from the wall, but the authentic Iberian atmosphere that makes this delightful, informal, and inexpensive bar/café one of the best in town (Tel: 684-3815).

Pub-like

Beer lovers will eventually find one of the three **Fogg n' Suds** that, despite the corny name, is a great place for a beer and burger-type lunch or dinner. Fogg claims to stock over 200 brands, Canada's largest collection, and takes the drinking of the amber nectar so seriously it has "passports" for the persistently experimental to keep records. The most accessible and pleasant Fogg is in an old West End brothel just off English Bay at 1215 Bidwell Street, with tables out on the sidewalk in summer.

For a pint and a pie (steak and kidney, sausage, Melton Mowbray) in an atmosphere that reasonably simulates an authentic British pub, the best places are the **Elephant and Castle**, 701 West Georgia Street, the **Rose and Thorn**, 757 Richards Street, and **Ten Sixty-Six**, at 1066 West Hastings Street.

NIGHTLIFE

Despite its fun-loving nature, Vancouver was not a great late-night town until recent years. It seemed as if all of those skiers and pleasure sailors needed a good night's rest and an early start to their play day. Evenings were lively enough, especially in the many fine restaurants, but the city closed too early for night owls. In the past decade or two that has changed, with a large number of nightclubs and dance spots opening (and some of them closing). Now, Vancouver by night is well served with coffee shops and music halls, comedy clubs, bars, and discos— as well as theater, opera, and symphony for the serious minded.

The city is North America's leading center for one popular form of dance. Its strippers have been celebrated internationally in film and song. Attractive young women perform at dozens of bars where there is no cover charge and drinks are standard prices. The most notable downtown venues are the Marble Arch on Richards and the Cecil, Austin, and Champagne Charlie's on Granville.

Dancing

Sophisticated revelers can wine, dine, and dance in style at the **Roof Restaurant and Lounge** atop the grand old Hotel Vancouver (900 West Georgia Street). In its previous form, as the Panorama Roof, this was a longtime favorite spot with Vancouverites, and locals again celebrate special occasions here. This is the only place of its kind in Vancouver, with live music (including big-band jazz) just right for dancing, views of the city (now slightly hemmed in by encroaching high-rises), and an elegant restaurant. You can spend your whole evening here, or move to more frenetic disco action. This is a somewhat dressy place, pricey, and perfect for over-40s and sophisticated younger people.

Most of Vancouver's good dance clubs are in a compact downtown area bordered by Smithe, Seymour, Pacific, and Beatty streets, so dedicated dancers can hit nearly a dozen of the city's most popular spots, all within walking distance of one another.

For several years **Richard's on Richards** (1036 Richards Street) has been the most popular club for the mid-20s and 30s (and the still-kicking 40s) set. You can spot it by the lines out the front door. Here is a club where singles meet other singles. It is upscale, noisy, with live top-40s bands, music videos, and a crowded dance floor. If you are lucky, you may get a seat in the mezzanine balcony to watch the action below.

Graceland (1250 Richards Street, entrance in an alley) is a newer alternative to Dick's on Dicks. West Coasters call this a "New York–style" club: warehouse-sized, with a large stage, some seats, lots of floor space, low light. It is definitely for the young—new wavers and ravers—with always something going on, from taped music to concerts featuring local or touring bands and even fashion shows.

Vancouver's dining and dancing spots are few but interesting. The **Soft Rock Café** in Kitsilano at 1925 North 4th Avenue, has something for just about everyone: dinner theater on Tuesdays, live jazz on Sundays, and top-40 bands weeknights, when the place is especially packed with the under-35 set. **Mulvaneys**, on Granville Island, is a bit unusual even for eclectic Vancouver. Named for a British Major Mulvaney, it leans toward a New Orleans theme with late 19th-century decor and Louisana fare: jambalaya, Cajun blackened redfish, Cajun lamb, gumbo soup, and grills. There is dancing on weekends, when the disc jockey plays top-40 music or tailors his selections to suit the crowd.

Music

A popular music place since the heady 1960s is the somewhat unusual **Classical Joint** (231 Carrall Street). It is unusual in that it has survived for 20 years in the same Gastown location and that it doesn't have a liquor license but still draws crowds to its live music, nightly, 8:30 P.M. to 2:00 A.M. Tuesday is jazz night.

Comedy

As in the rest of North America, comedy clubs have taken hold in Vancouver. Those who like to laugh, even if the humor is at times both off-color and off the mark, will spend a few happy hours in **Punchlines Comedy Theatre**, 21 Water Street in Gastown, the city's most established humor haven: movie-poster decor, scattered tables, and a stage with a stool and microphone where would-be Woody Allens will break you up or bomb out. The place is inexpensive and fun, even when the amateur comedians flop. Some good local talent, as well as frequent touring acts (Tel: 684-3015). **Yuk Yuk's** at 750 Pacific Street (Tel: 687-LAFF) also offers a wide range of humor, from giggles to belly laughs.

The Celtic School

The **Unicorn**, an "Irish singing pub" owned by the Rovers folk group, was such a huge hit at Expo '86—with long lines from midday to midnight—that they stayed on. Despite its inconvenient location at 770 Pacific (past the domed BC Place Stadium or the old Expo site), it still draws crowds who love the lively, loud, get-into-the-act brand of Irish folk music, a good basic menu, and reasonable prices. Get a cab out here if you are willing to squeeze around a table with other guests and sing along with the group.

The **Blarney Stone Inn** (216 Carrall Street), in the heart of Gastown, is an old-time favorite restaurant/cabaret for those who don't seem to care what music is trendy this season. There is a small cover charge unless you have dinner here. The menu offers standard meat-and-potato fare with some bows to the Gaelic (cock-a-leekie soup, Irish lamb stew, and salmon St. Patrick). Blarney Stone is a big, open, red-brick-and-solid-plank-tables kind of place that later in the evening settles in for lively, foot-stomping Irish music, sweet folk songs (alternating with standard rock and top-40s), and dancing. Some bands provide Canadian content as well, with "Farewell to Nova Scotia" and all 53 stanzas of "I'se the Boy That Built the Boat."

Quieter and more low-key, the **George V Pub**, at 801 West Georgia Street, in the high-ceilinged basement of the old Hotel Georgia downtown, gets lively at night when a kilt-clad singer belts out Scottish and Canadian folk songs. This relaxed, beer-drinking place, with standard British pub fare such as steak and kidney pie and bangers and mash, is popular for lunch.

Views

In this city that lives on its looks, a suitable end to an evening is a nightcap in a bar with a view. There are several in downtown hotels, all worth a drink for the lofty sight of the city lights coming on. From the Coast Plaza's (1733 Comox Street) 35th-floor **Humphrey's Restaurant** there are especially good views of the ocean, Stanley Park, and the houses climbing the North Shore mountains. The Sheraton Landmark's (1400 Robson Street) 42nd-floor revolving restaurant lounge, aptly named **Cloud Nine**, is the highest spot in town. Nurse a drink in this adult carousel and you will see the whole city and surroundings (including Mount Baker in Washington State by day) slip by.

For a ground-level view earlier in the evening, try for a window table at the bar of the **Sylvia Hotel** (1154 Gilford Street), one of old-time Vancouver's favorite haunts, on English Bay. A twilight drink while the sun slips behind freighters moored in the bay, the seawall joggers return home to rest, and the popcorn men pack up their red and orange carts, is one of this fortunate city's finest experiences.

SHOPS AND SHOPPING

Vancouver shopping is not just an excursion but an experience. Indeed, Vancouver's scope has stretched beyond the doldrums of dependable department stores to internationally acclaimed designer boutiques, lively public markets, British products, diverse ethnic areas, and fine contemporary and native artworks.

Omiyage

The Japanese, great gift givers, have a term for special souvenirs that typify countries visited: *omiyage*. Local *omiyage* here include such quality items as native Indian and Inuit handcrafts and carved B.C. jade.

In cobblestoned Gastown, Vancouver's historic birthplace, **Hill's Indian Crafts'** collection of Pacific Northwest Indian and Inuit art includes haunting carved masks and the famous handspun Cowichan sweaters made by that Vancouver Island tribe. In the adjacent alleyway, totempole carvers can sometimes be seen creating great cedar poles with small hand tools and equipment their forefathers predated: the chain saw. The nearby **Inuit Gallery** in a Gastown heritage building has among the finest collections of Inuit and Northwest Coast Indian artwork in Canada as well as Papua New Guinea works.

Among the numerous other native handcraft shops, three stand out. **Leona Lattimer**, at 1590 West 2nd Avenue adjacent to Granville Island, specializes in quality Northwest Coast Indian art. Native artisans can often be seen carving in the adjacent lot. The University of British Columbia's **Museum of Anthropology Shop** features silver jewelry, carved cedar masks, intricate woven baskets, and silkscreen prints. The museum is 20 minutes by car or bus to the city's West Side, but it is well worth the trip to see the award-winning architecture and exquisite native artworks.

The **Vancouver Museum and Planetarium Gift Shop**, just over the Burrard Street Bridge from downtown at 1100 Chestnut Street, has one of the largest collections of native art. On the long first weekend in July (Canada's national holiday) and three days in mid-November, you can see artists working in argillite, wood, silver, and gold. Crafts are discounted by ten percent.

A noteworthy newcomer to the Indian art scene is the **Gallery of Tribal Art** at 1521 West 8th Avenue, which features the best of B.C. and Papua New Guinea.

B.C. has the world's largest known jade deposits, ranging from the most common forest-green to pale green and black. The gem is used here to make exquisite jewelry, ornaments, and decorative tiles. Locally designed and crafted jade is available at **Sopel Jade Expressions**, 1572 West 4th Street, and **Jade World**, 1696 West 1st Avenue, near bustling Granville Island. At Jade World's studio you can see master carvers transform the raw product into finished art.

A leftover from Expo 86 is **Icicles** (3117 West Broadway), a store featuring goods and travel information from the Northwest Territories. This unusual boutique stocks such items as Arctic char, muskox, and Iqaluit whale tapestries.

Vancouver's proximity to the Pacific results in abundant fresh seafood, notably salmon, some of which is packed for travel. Recommended "seafood couriers" are **Jet Set Sam** at the airport, the **Lobster Man** on Granville Island, and the **Salmon Shop**, located at three public markets: Granville Island, Robson Street, and Lonsdale Quay.

Those interested in contemporary paintings by renowned Canadian and international artists should visit **Buschlen/Mowatt Fine Arts**, downtown at 111-1445 West Georgia Street. As well, the **Diane Farris Gallery** at 1565 West 7th Avenue is internationally acclaimed for its quality Canadian contemporary and folk art.

South Granville Street, between Broadway and about 15th Avenue, is the place to browse for art and antiques. Antique Row shops sell estate jewelry, silverware, and gorgeous period furnishings. On the city's West Side along 4th and 10th avenues, eclectic specialty shops sell such items as Southeast Asian artifacts, duvet covers, fitness togs, and brass and oak furnishings.

The **Made in British Columbia Shop** at 117 Water Street in Gastown is an amalgam of B.C. collectibles: tinned salmon in attractive cedar gift boxes, native carvings, jade and rhodonite sculptures, delicate hand-blown glass ornaments and marquetry wood plaques and boxes with Canada geese and killer whale designs.

Fashion

To climb British Columbia's lofty peaks and ford its rushing rivers you will need rugged outdoor gear. Two reputable outfitters are **Taiga**, at 1675 West 2nd Avenue near Granville Island, and **Coast Mountain Sports**, at 1828 West 4th Avenue, across the Burrard Street Bridge in Kitsilano. One of the better places to purchase ski clothing and equipment is **Can-Ski**, with four locations, including 569 Seymour Street downtown and Whistler Village. Ski rentals and repairs are also available.

The usual other designer boutiques (Ralph Lauren, Alfred Sung, and Rodier Paris) flourish mainly downtown on trendy Robson Street, in the **Pacific Centre**, and in the historic, arched-ceiling restorations of **The Landmark** and **The Sinclair Centre**.

Robson Street, which once housed small European bakeries and delis, has recently seen the decline of the deli and the rise of Art Deco designer shops, transforming Old World Continental to New World yuppie. Robson is still a pleasant place to stroll and people watch, with its cappuccino bars, trendy restaurants, and sidewalk flower stands.

Among Vancouver's numerous noteworthy furriers, the downtown **London Fur Salon** on 819 Hornby Street off Robson designs and fashions silky Canadian pelts right on the premises.

British Imports

Vancouver's ties with "old Blighty" are evident in tea vendors such as **Murchie's Tea & Coffee Ltd**. and numerous downtown tartan outlets—notably **House of McLaren, Edinburgh Tartan Shop** in Gastown, and **The Scotch Shop**. **Miller & Coe** on Hastings Street downtown has among the city's best selection of English bone china and crystal. To satisfy any yearnings for "the old country," **Marks & Spencer** department stores (downtown in the Pacific Centre and other shopping malls) have a good selection of St. Michael's clothing and specialty foods such as English-style bacon, kippers, toad-in-the-hole, and shortbreads.

Public Markets

Within the past decade, city planning has transformed some prime waterfront land from unsightly industry into attractive public markets such as **Granville Island**. The informal atmosphere here appeals to locals as well as tourists. While the covered markets overflow with fresh produce and local crafts, the scene outside includes lively street entertainers, cawing gulls, and myriad watercraft, from barges to kayaks. Granville Island's market is accessible by car or harbor ferries from downtown; the **Lonsdale Quay**, by car or Seabus from downtown across Burrard Inlet to North Vancouver; and the **Westminster Quay** by car or Skytrain from the city center southeast to New Westminster.

Richmond's attractive new **Bridgepoint Market** is easily accessible by bus or car. Head south over the Oak Street Bridge to the north end of Number 3 Road.

Ethnic Shopping

In Vancouver's ethnic cornucopia, its **Chinatown** is the second largest in North America after San Francisco's. Lively shops east of downtown along Pender Street, between Carrall and Gore, sell wicker products, china, celadon porcelain, teas, and exotic remedies from Kirin deer antlers to Korean red ginseng. **Ming Wo**, 23 East Pender Street, has among the city's best selection of cookware.

Tailors and dressmakers delight in **Little India**, some 20 minutes south of downtown at 49th Avenue and Main Street. There are large sari shops such as the **Guru Bazaar**, 6529 Main Street, which is a fantasyland of fabrics—bright bolts of silks and synthetics from India and Japan.

—Marnie Mitchell

DAY TRIP TO VICTORIA

To the rest of Canada, Victoria is "behind the tweed curtain." British Columbia's small (about 250,000 inhabitants) capital is certainly very British, and proud of it. Flower baskets hang from the lampposts, shops sell Harris tweed and Irish linen, and citizens play cricket and croquet. This charming city has a different feel from Vancouver. It is slower paced: relaxed, friendly, an island city. (There are duck-crossing signs at major streets.) Victoria retains its flavor of earlier times with its pleasant pubs, inns, and bed-and-breakfast places, its lack of high-rises, traffic, and crowds, and with its quiet, open spaces and many parks.

The city is worth much more than a day trip, but a day trip *is* possible from Vancouver by B.C. Ferries, the city-center-to-city-center Air B.C. floatplane, or by helicopter. (A day trip from Seattle is possible as well by a trip on the Victoria Clipper hovercraft or a cruise on the B.C. Stena Line.)

Despite its Union Jack image, Victoria is a curious mixture of British gentility and logger/frontier ruggedness, of high tea and draft beer. Here, *Town and Country* meets *Field and Stream*. This city of prim elderly ladies and dapper gentlemen close to forests and the sea is also a community of plaid-clad youth.

MAJOR INTEREST

Very British but with frontier contrast
Butchart Gardens
Parliament Buildings
Provincial Museum
Bastion Square Area (historical buildings)

Much older than Vancouver, the capital is a pleasant oasis of gentility. Established in 1843 as Fort Victoria, a Hudson Bay fur-trading post, it was the first European settlement on the island. The natural harbor at Esquimalt was the British Royal Navy's Pacific base for a time.

The city later thrived on lumbering, farming, fishing, and sealing. Now its industries include government and the armed forces (the Royal Roads Military College and a Canadian Navy base). Its equable climate, the country's balmiest, draws retirees from across Canada, giving Victoria its dichotomy of character, the genteel-among-the-rough-outdoorsy aspect.

A great outburst of creative energy in building, and a striving to emulate the European masters, gave Victoria its physical makeup. In just 35 years (1890 to 1925), the Parliament Buildings, Empress Hotel, Craigdarroch Castle, Hatley Park Castle (now the Royal Roads Military College), and Crystal Garden were built. Victoria developed its own distinctive style of architecture in the many stately residences that still stand.

Victoria is set on the Saanich Peninsula on southeast Vancouver Island (below the 49th parallel). It is an almost rural area of rocky bays and inlets, forested parks, small lakes, and a few low-lying hills.

Exploring Victoria

Victoria is best seen on foot. Downtown is a historical center of cobblestone streets, brick sidewalks, arcades, squares, and alleys. Street names such as Bastion Square, Trounce Alley, and Market Square are reminders that this was truly a Victorian colony. The old downtown area is a few square blocks that run from the Inner Harbour east to Blanshard Street. Places of historical interest extend from the Parliament Buildings about ten blocks north to Chinatown, Centennial Square, and City Hall.

The heart of Victoria is the Inner Harbour, busy with steamships and ferries from B.C. and Washington State, seaplanes from Vancouver and bush communities, and yachts from all over the world.

The stately, castlelike **Empress Hotel**, one of the great Canadian Pacific Railways château-style hotels, overlooks the Parliament Buildings and all the waterfront activity. The ivy-covered Empress, with its pinnacles and turrets and verdigrised roofs, fairly reeks of the British Empire. Rudyard Kipling, the old imperial apologist himself, stayed here, and must have felt at home among the lofty-ceilinged and columned grand lobby, the dark wood paneling, and the plush, richly appointed lounges, the clublike Bengal Room, and the former **Library Bar** (now a native art gallery) with its distinctive, ornate ceiling. Perhaps it was the Empress that inspired Kipling's comment at the turn of the century that Victoria had all the best of Bournemouth arranged around the Bay of Naples.

Tea time in the lobby, complete with scones, crumpets, clotted cream, cakes, and Empress Blend tea, is a must for visitors, even if it is somewhat contrived. The hotel was starting to show its age, but an extensive recent refurbishing has brought it back to its glory-days condition. To stay here is to partake of Victoria's history.

The proud, neo-Gothic provincial Parliament Buildings across the harbor, built of native granite and wood, were completed in 1897. The stately stone palatial structures sit on wide grounds dotted with statues of writers, philosophers, pioneers, and, of course, Queen Victoria. When the house is not sitting there are tours of the interiors, with their mosaic tile floors, intricate stained-glass windows, and "golden gates" leading to the marble-paneled legislative chambers.

During sessions, visitors can listen to the debates—in B.C. known more for acrimony than for subtle parliamentary repartee. At night the buildings are ablaze, like a fairyland castle, with thousands of light bulbs. (The first illumination of the exterior was on June 21, 1897, to commemorate Queen Victoria's Diamond Jubilee.)

Victoria has the three oldest standing houses in B.C., western Canada's oldest school building, and numerous heritage houses. Most of them are within walking distance of downtown. Maps and brochures are available from the efficient Victoria Visitors Bureau, on the harbor near the Empress.

The impressive **Royal British Columbia Museum**, between the Empress and the Parliament Buildings, gives a good sense of early B.C. Exhibits include a re-creation of a pioneer town, coal mine shaft, fish cannery, Peace River farm, and Captain Cook's private cabin aboard his ship *Discovery*. The third-floor gallery incorporates a complete Kwakiutl big house, with a full range of traditional housewares.

The forest of totem poles in **Thunderbird Park** outside the museum is perhaps the world's finest collection. An authentic hand-hewn replica of a Haida Indian big house, the traditional coast Indian dwelling, includes a studio. Inside, native artists carve full-scale totem poles, many of which are commissioned by heads of state, corporations, and cities around the world.

Many Eastern Canadians know British Columbia through the work of Emily Carr, one of Canada's finest artists, who painted rain forests, Indian totem poles, and villages. The house where she was raised, and later retired, still stands near downtown Victoria. The **Emily Carr Gallery**, 1107 Wharf Street, displays film presentations, manuscripts, and much original artwork of the dark, brooding forests she captured so well.

Butchart Gardens, 20 km (13 miles) from Victoria, on the road from the airport or Swartz Bay ferry terminal, is one important attraction that does require a car or an organized tour. This former limestone quarry, now 50 acres of elaborate gardens featuring many floral themes, is one of Victoria's prime attractions, drawing more than half a million visitors a year. Special events and fireworks displays are staged on summer evenings.

Shopping is a popular Victoria pastime and a very British experience. The **English Sweet Shop** on Yates sells English toffee, teas, biscuits, souvenirs, and china. **The Welsh Hand Loom** in Nootka Court and **Celtic Casuals** in Harbor Square both have fine Welsh tapestry, woolen clothing, and crafts of Wales. For fine quality native Indian handicrafts, Cowichan sweaters, jewelry, wood carvings, jade, and totem poles visit the **Indian Craft Shoppe** or **Cowichan Trading**, both on Government Street. **The Gallery of the Arctic** and **The Quest** are good for Canadiana, with limited-edition collector-quality Arctic prints and art and artifacts of the north, such as Inuit sculpture in stone and whalebone and stone-cut prints. The Quest has Cana-

dian handicrafts, pottery, prints, jade, and carved soapstone, and features exhibitions by national artists.

Staying in Victoria

Within the fairly limited downtown area are most of the
city's good hotels and inns. The **Holland House Inn**, just
two blocks from the Inner Harbor where ferries from the
U.S. dock, is a pleasant old street-corner building typical
of Victoria. Distinctive rooms in this small inn include
balconies, fireplaces, and four-poster beds.

Even closer to the harbor, the **Captain's Palace** provides accommodation in a three-story Victorian mansion
with crystal chandeliers, tapestries, stained glass windows
and doors, and rooms furnished with antiques.

The 12-room **Beaconsfield Inn**, in an English mansion
on a quiet street near Beaconsfield Park, includes a guest
library, conservatory/sunroom, gracious rooms with fireplaces and canopy beds, and a full breakfast every morning. By contrast, the **Laurel Point Inn** near the Parliament
Buildings is modern and features indoor/outdoor pools,
sauna, whirlpool, and tennis courts. As well, all rooms
have balconies with a harbor view.

Another modern hotel, the **Victoria Regent**, offers
apartment-style living with one- and two-bedroom suites,
some with Jacuzzis and fireplaces, and marina facilities
for visiting yachties.

Some rate city-center **Chateau Victoria** as the capital
city's top luxury hotel, with its pleasantly furnished rooms
with a view. The rooftop restaurant provides a bird's-eye
vista of Victoria and the harbor.

And of course there is the **Empress Hotel**, in a class by
itself. A Victoria landmark, the hotel is discussed above.

Dining and Entertainment
in Victoria

While big-city Vancouver wasn't looking, Victoria grew
into a sophisticated, cosmopolitan, and lively town. It is
no longer the fussy, stuffy little place of its reputation. For
the convenience of its many tourists and well-heeled
politicians, Victoria is unusually well served by good
restaurants and nightlife.

You can dine well, and savor history, at the **Latch**, the
old governor general's summer home in nearby Sidney

(about 60 km/35 miles north of Victoria on Highway 17, near the International Airport and the Swartz Bay Ferry terminal; a cab from the center of the city costs about $30). The custom in this fine log-and-natural-wood building with a number of rooms is to dine in one, move to the library for dessert, and finish with coffee in the sitting room.

Pagliacci's, or Pag's, open for lunch and dinner, is among the most popular dining spots in town, with consistently good food matched by a loud, lively atmosphere. It is centrally located on Broad Street, a block east of Harbour Square Mall. You will likely have to stand in line—and this is no place for an intimate candlelit evening. The **Herald Street Caffe** is also very popular with both young and old, formal and denim clad. Its atmosphere is bright and cheerful and the decor is Art Nouveau with contemporary paintings hanging on the walls. Lunch and dinner; Herald stays open late, and the mood can be very lively.

The Parrot House, on the top of Chateau Victoria, one of the best hotels, offers an outstanding panoramic view of this scenic seaside city.

Spinnakers' Brew Pub, across Johnson Bridge from the city center, is well worth the few minutes' drive. (Once you cross the bridge, turn left on Catherine Street. The pub is in a large, old waterfront building at the end of the road.) Spinnakers' started a trend in Canada, brewing its own beers and ales. Most of their brews are the flat, dull British-style, but there are some lively European-type lagers on tap. The fish and chips are unique. The halibut filet is coated with brewer's yeast and whipped egg-white batter. (The fries are too thick, however.) The spacious old brown wood place has a pleasant view across the harbor of the Parliament Buildings, the domed Empress Hotel, and floatplanes landing on the water. There is no reserved seating, so you have to hustle for a table by the window, and the kitchen runs out of specials such as the venison stew early.

If you do stay the night in Victoria, there is more to do than would be expected in a staid government town. **Harpo's Cabaret** (15 Bastion Square at Wharf Street) is a lively hot spot featuring music from reggae and African to rock and rhythm and blues. **Sweetwaters** at 27-560 Johnson Street serves up jazz to a youngish set.

The old **Oak Bay Beach Hotel**, located on the sea in a pleasant residential area east across the peninsula from the city center, is like an English Tudor country inn. The recently renovated rooms are large, many overlooking the Haro Strait, with the U.S.-Canadian border running mid-channel. **The Snug**, with its Olde English atmosphere of dark wood wainscoting, beams, and furniture, and leaded windows overlooking the sea, is an excellent choice for lunch even if you are not staying in this delightful inn. The lobby has a good, solid Edwardian ambience, with stuffed furniture, 14th-century antiques, and a fine 100-year-old piano that the resident pianist still plays.

The inn's 41-foot yacht, the *Mesouda,* makes sunset dinner and harbor lunch cruises, while the M.V. *Tasu* conducts daily salmon-fishing expeditions. In the summer they dock at the bottom of the garden. For hotel guests, cruise patrons, and those wishing high tea, the hotel provides a complimentary shuttle bus from anywhere in town.

GETTING AROUND

The easiest and cheapest way to get to Victoria from Vancouver is by Pacific Coach Lines from the downtown Vancouver bus depot ($16.50 one way). Buses board the ferry at Tsawwassen, south of Vancouver, and continue to downtown Victoria. The ferry crossing takes 1 hour 45 minutes, the whole trip about three-and-a-half hours. During the summer peak hours there are 16 scheduled crossings daily, from about 7:00 A.M. to 10:00 P.M. from either direction. Buses leave the station seventy minutes prior to the ferry departure.

You can also drive, although in peak seasons, especially during long weekends, there may be a several-hour wait for a place on the ferry, and you cannot reserve. Best check conditions ahead of time. B.C. ferry schedule information is available 24 hours a day by phoning (604) 685-1021 in Vancouver and (604) 656-0757 in Victoria. Fee for car and driver is $21.75 each way.

To reach the Victoria ferries from Vancouver, follow Oak Street south onto Highway 99 and turn right soon after the Dease Island Tunnel. The turnoff is well marked. Leaving Victoria, drive 32 km (19 miles) north on Highway 17 to the Swartz Bay Terminal.

Harbor-to-harbor Air B.C. floatplanes do the trip in 30 scenic minutes. In Vancouver, they depart from the Coal Harbor Terminal near the Bayshore Hotel (close to Stanley Park), landing in Victoria's Inner Harbor. Fares are

$152 round trip, but weekend fares are only about half that.

Helijet Airways flies jet helicopters from the heliport near the Seabus Terminal or the international airport in Vancouver to Ogden Point in downtown Victoria, a 30-minute trip. Excursion fares start from $99 round trip; Tel: 273-1414.

Several major airlines also connect Vancouver to Victoria, although this is not a practical alternative for a day trip.

The B.C. Stena Line operates round-trip daily cruises between Seattle and Victoria from May to October, with dining, licensed lounges, entertainment, casinos, duty-free gift shops, and so on. Reservations are advised for this 4½-hour journey. Tel: (604) 388-7397.

During the summer, the Blackball Transport operates four sailings daily aboard the M.V. *Coho* ferry between Victoria and Port Angeles, Washington. Sailing time is 1 hour 35 minutes. Tel: (206) 457-4491 or (604) 386-2202.

The 300-passenger *Victoria Clipper,* a water-jet-propelled catamaran, connects Victoria and Seattle in 2½ hours. Fares start at U.S.$33 one way, off season. Tel: (206) 448-5000, (604) 382-8100, or, in U.S., (800) 888-2535.

ACCOMMODATIONS REFERENCE

► **Beaconsfield Inn.** 998 Humboldt Street, **Victoria**, B.C. V8V 2Z8. Tel: (604) 384-4044.

► **Captain's Palace.** 309 Belleville Street, **Victoria**, B.C. V8V 1X2. Tel: (604) 388-9191.

► **Chateau Victoria.** 740 Burdett Avenue, **Victoria**, B.C. V8W 1B2. Tel: (604) 382-4221 or (800) 663-5891.

► **Empress Hotel.** 721 Government Street, **Victoria**, B.C. V8W 1W5. Tel: (604) 384-8111.

► **Holland House Inn.** 595 Michigan Street, **Victoria**, B.C. V8V 1S7. Tel: (604) 384-6644.

► **Laurel Point Inn.** 680 Montreal Street, **Victoria**, B.C. V8V 1Z8. Tel: (604) 386-8721 or (800) 663-7667.

► **Oak Bay Beach Hotel.** 1175 Beach Drive, **Victoria**, B.C. V8S 2N2. Tel: (604) 598-4556.

► **Victoria Regent.** 1234 Wharf Street, **Victoria**, B.C. V8W 3H9. Tel: (604) 386-2211.

BRITISH COLUMBIA

By Marnie Mitchell

*Marnie Mitchell, a Vancouver native, has worked in tour-
ism in the area for many years. She specializes in travel
writing for both trade and consumer magazines in Canada and abroad, and contributes a monthly shopping
column to* Key to Vancouver *magazine.*

While Canada's eastern provinces were busy forming
the Dominion of Canada in 1867, British Columbia, the
rugged renegade "out west," was busy with other affairs.
The newly colonized province was in the throes of a gold
rush. In fact, two of its towns were then the largest north
of San Francisco and west of Chicago.

Eventually the first transcontinental railroad linked the
last frontier to the rest of Canada, and British Columbia
("B.C."), somewhat reluctantly, joined confederation in
1871. But her stubborn pioneer spirit remains. The Rocky
Mountains, between B.C. and Alberta, are perhaps as
much a psychological divider as a geographic one, but
whatever the cause, B.C. is a strong-minded independent.

Easterners have long sought to make the paradisiacal
province their home, particularly the mild, Pacific port of
Vancouver, which they enviably call "Lotus Land." In fact,
the city is so inundated with newcomers it is unusual to
ferret out a native Vancouverite.

Most of the province's roughly three million people
live in the southwestern corner, in Vancouver and Victoria. Victoria, the provincial capital on Vancouver Island, is
very British, all tea and crumpets, brollies and double-

decker buses. Vancouver, the province's largest city, is a vibrant, cultural metropolis, yet it retains the air of a pioneer town. Indeed, the wilds are right on Vancouver's front doorstep—in several suburbs bears still wander into backyards and squirrels scamper into some West End condos.

B.C. looks more to the south than the east, and considers itself the California of Canada, for its ideas, entertainment, and attitudes. In recent years this notion has been strengthened by the influx of movie moguls, who have dubbed B.C. "Hollywood North."

Most visitors enter B.C. through Vancouver, the provincial gateway. After spending several days touring the city, the more adventurous head to the Island (meaning Vancouver Island), the Southwest, the Cariboo, or the Okanagan. These regions require several days each to tour adequately. Second-time visitors, or those with more time, head to the wilds of the north and then beyond to the Yukon and Alaska. Those arriving by car from Alberta can explore the Rockies on their way. Many first-timers and even repeat visitors take the comfortable trains: B.C. Rail and VIA Rail travel among the world's most spectacular scenery.

MAJOR INTEREST

Rugged mountain scenery
Hiking and canoeing
Salmon fishing
Cariboo Highway area
Rodeos and dude ranches
Skiing Whistler, the Okanagan, and the Rockies
Barkerville (excellent Provincial Heritage Park)
'Ksan historic Indian village
Exploring the many wilderness parks
The High Country
Okanagan vineyards

We cover the province starting from Vancouver (for which see the separate chapter on the city itself and on a day trip to Victoria), first with Vancouver Island to its west and then the Sunshine Coast to its immediate north and the Fraser Valley to the immediate east of Vancouver (both as "Southwest British Columbia"). Then we move up the Fraser Valley (it turns north at about Hope) along the Cariboo Highway, which is the main access to the province's

"Northwest"—the town of Prince George, across to the town of Prince Rupert on the coast, and the Queen Charlotte Islands off the coast.

The rest of the coverage picks up just north of the U.S. border in the High Country ("South-Central B.C.") and moves more or less east to the Okanagan; the Kootenay Mountains; and finally the Rockies and the Alberta border (Banff, Calgary, and Jasper are on the other side).

VANCOUVER ISLAND

Coddled at its south end by Washington's Olympic Peninsula across the Juan de Fuca Strait, Vancouver Island resembles a great berthing ship, a 12,000-square-mile landmass characterized by the craggy Coast Mountains, evergreen forests, and rolling farms inland. Although the Island lacks big-city sophistication, it charms visitors with a laid-back cordiality reflecting its logging, fishing, and mining heritages.

While Victoria, the provincial capital at the southern end of the Island, is decidedly British, numerous communities elsewhere have Indian names and cultural distinctions reflecting their heritage. Coastal villages and towns hug the eastern shore, while the mountainous west coast, with its vast, wind-shaped Pacific Rim National Park, is largely unpopulated.

Long before Captain Cook sailed in, the Kwakiutl, Nootka, and coastal Salish Indians shared the rich land and marine wealth of the largest and most diverse of North America's West Coast islands. Cook's arrival at Nootka Island in 1778 prompted further British, then Spanish, explorations.

Eventually Spain ceded her interests, and the British Hudson's Bay Company established Fort Victoria in 1843. Some 15 years later gold was discovered on the mainland at the Fraser River. Victoria, across the Strait of Georgia, became the supply hub and provincial capital—the latter a position it retained when British Columbia joined Canada in 1871.

The Island Coach Lines (Tel: 385-4411) serves all the major communities from Victoria to Port Hardy, but a private vehicle is needed to visit remote areas.

Allow a full day to visit **Botanical Beach**, a cluster of natural aquariums frequented by marine biologists, southwest of Victoria along Highway 14 past Sooke and Port

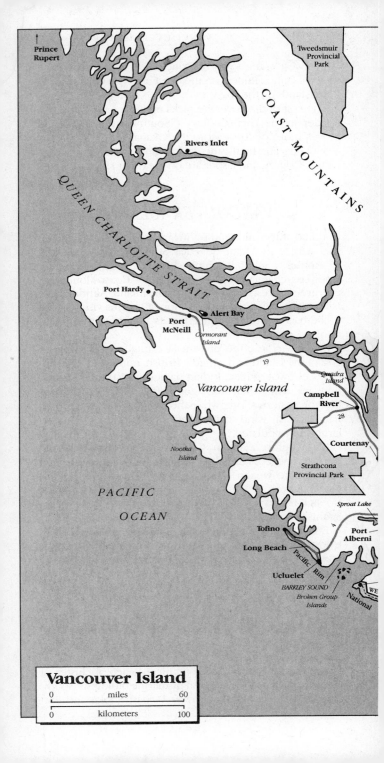

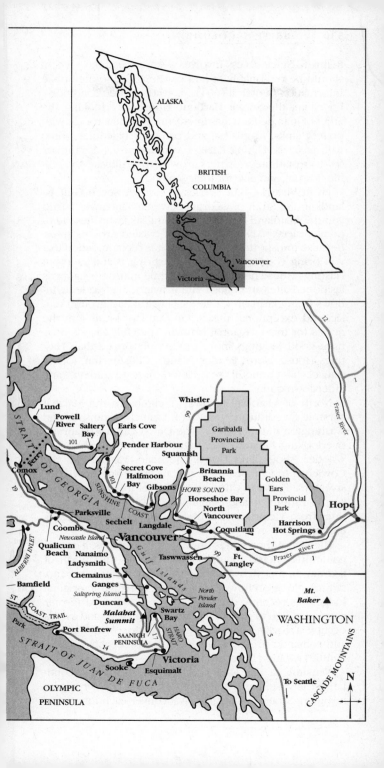

Renfrew. Since access involves a strenuous hike, visitors should be reasonably fit and phone ahead to the Sooke Information Center at (604) 642-6112 for tide conditions. En route, the **Sooke Harbour House**, overlooking the Strait of Juan de Fuca, has interesting sea-view rooms with pottery sinks, fireplaces, and patios or balconies, some with Jacuzzis. Dining here is as much visual as culinary art: Its restaurateur-owners grow herbs, cultivate 150 edible flowers, and dive for their seafood.

From Victoria, B.C. Ferries depart for seven **Gulf Islands** in the Strait of Georgia between Vancouver Island and the mainland. Artists and naturalists favor these temperate islets of Douglas firs and twisted arbutus trees. Because transportation is limited, it is recommended that you bring your own vehicle. **Saltspring Island**'s elegant **Hastings House** hotel, a former prime minister's haunt, is fashioned after an English Tudor manor, has leaded windows facing farm or sea views, classical background music, and exceptional meals. On Sundays locals join the guests for the substantial brunch. The Gulf Islands does have good lodgings more moderately priced than Hastings House. North Pender Island's **Cliffside Inn**, for instance, has tranquil sea views, fireside dining, and eiderdown quilts.

North of Victoria, Highway 1 climbs to the Malahat summit for dramatic views of Saanich Peninsula and Washington's Mount Baker. The **Dutch Latch Restaurant**, overlooking Finlayson Arm, also sells Delft pottery and wooden shoes, and Dutch chocolate. Farther on, the Cowichan Indians sell their famous heavy-knit **Cowichan sweaters**. Those not driving can travel this route on the scenic Esquimalt and Nanaimo Railway's **Malahat Dayliner** from Victoria to Courtenay, halfway up the island's east coast.

Highway 1 then winds north past **Chemainus**, a coastal community noted for its outdoor murals. Just north of Ladysmith, the highway leads to Yellow Point Road and, farther along, **Yellow Point Lodge**. When the original lodge was recently destroyed by fire, dedicated former patrons rallied to restore it. The new log lodge and cabins occupy a rocky peninsula, excellent for bird-watching and romantic strolls on quiet trails and beachfront. Few families vacation here, however.

Nanaimo, a deep-sea port and the island's second-largest city, sends daring "tubbers" 35 miles across the turbulent Strait of Georgia to Vancouver each July in the

Great International Bathtub Race. Most commuters prefer to take B.C. Ferries. The 1852 Hudson's Bay Company Bastion here is among the west's oldest remaining structures. Ferries for hikers (no cars permitted) leave regularly for Newcastle Island, a nature sanctuary with hiking trails, sandy beaches, and a heritage pavilion serving barbecued salmon.

North of Nanaimo, Highway 4 spurs west to Port Alberni. En route, in Coombs, goats graze on the marketplace roof; the 800-year-old Douglas firs in MacMillan Provincial Park resemble a vaulted cathedral. At Sproat Lake visitors can see the World War II Martin Mars water bombers used to fight forest fires.

In **Port Alberni**, noted for its exceptional salmon and steelhead fishing (also see Campbell River, below), Alberni Pacific Charters plies the local rivers in a unique flat-bottomed boat. Even amateur anglers are guaranteed a sizeable catch. In summer, the historic freighter M.V. *Lady Rose* transports mail, cargo, and passengers from Port Alberni through the Broken Group Islands in Barkley Sound to Ucluelet on the Pacific Ocean. Year-round cruises escort passengers through Alberni Inlet to Bamfield (south of Ucluelet), the northern end of the renowned **West Coast Trail**. This pre-1915 lifesaving trail was constructed to help shipwreck victims return to civilization. From May to September, stalwart souls hike the 48 miles from Port Renfrew on the island's southwestern edge north to Bamfield. In March and April, whale watching excursions depart from Bamfield and other coastal communities. Try Gulfstream II (Tel: 681-2915) or one of the companies advertising in the Vancouver newspapers.

Highway 4 continues west to Long Beach and the **Pacific Rim National Park**, where frequent torrents create hard sand beaches and cedar-scented rain forests. Here, naturalists seek teeming tide pools, seals, sea lions, myriad birds, and gray whales, often sighted on their spring and fall migrations. In summer, **Ucluelet**'s Wickaninnish Centre illustrates the ocean's indelible effect on the environment. The historic **Canadian Princess** steamship, which once plied the Inside Passage to Alaska, is now permanently moored in Ucluelet and operates as a resort hotel from March through September. Guests of the **Pacific Sands Beach Resort** near **Tofino** can watch seasonal storms or sunsets from cozy housekeeping units. Tofino's waterfront **Blue Heron Pub** has a post-and-beam interior and serves steaming local crab and clams. Nearby, the **Eagle Aerie Gallery**, set in a longhouse, displays the paintings of native artist Roy Henry Vickers, whose reverence for nature and the coast results in a powerful blend of contemporary and traditional imagery.

The Island's North

Back on the east coast, Highway 19 links the pleasant seaside towns of Parksville and Qualicum Beach, popular for beachcombing and water sports. The **Tigh-Na-Mara Resort** in Parksville is very West Coast in its seaside setting with woodland cottages. Forty-five miles north in Courtenay, the **Native Sons Hall Museum** of native art is well worth a visit. At Comox, near Courtenay on Highway 19 below Campbell River, a ferry crosses to Powell River on the Sunshine Coast on the mainland. Farther north is **Campbell River**, internationally renowned for its salmon fishing.

Campbell River vies with Port Alberni for the prestigious Salmon Fishing Capital of the World title. While the Campbell River Salmon Festival is held each first weekend in July, the annual Port Alberni Salmon Festival is held in the beginning of September.

From Campbell River a brief ferry ride leads to Quadra Island and the legendary **April Point Lodge**. From April to November this luxurious fishermen's mecca, on a secluded cove, arranges guides and equipment, even the freezing, smoking, and canning of your catch. The island's Kwakiutl Indian Museum and Cape Mudge petroglyphs are well worth a visit.

Strathcona, British Columbia's oldest provincial park, on Highway 28 west of Campbell River, is a wildlife sanctuary with an abundance of waterfalls, rivers, wilderness trails, alpine flowers, and tarns. The **Strathcona Park Lodge**, with its lakefront chalets, arranges adventure packages with canoeing, kayaking, hiking, mountaineering, and fishing. Winter guests can cross-country ski and snowshoe.

Few visitors will reach the northern community of **Alert Bay**, a living museum of Kwakiutl Indian culture accessible by Highway 19 up from Campbell River to Port McNeill and then by B.C. Ferries to Cormorant Island. Those who do will find the U'Mista Cultural Centre and the world's tallest totem pole.

In secluded Rivers Inlet, northeast of Vancouver Island on the mainland, the **Big Spring Resort** arranges all-inclusive, fly-in fishing packages during summer. Guests take a spectacular two-hour flight from Vancouver over coastal wilderness and pack little more than a toothbrush and a checkbook or credit card. The resort is as much a welcome retreat for busy executives as it is for world travellers.

At **Port Hardy,** about as far up-island as you can go, a chef in a kilt and tam prepares chicken and steaks over an open alder-wood fire at a restaurant called **Snuggles.** Port Hardy is the departure point for the scenic Inside Passage vehicular ferry to Prince Rupert up north on the mainland.

SOUTHWEST BRITISH COLUMBIA

Beyond Greater Vancouver, southwestern B.C. changes like a kaleidoscope. The Pacific Ocean shapes a jagged coast of coves, bays, and occasional beaches, surveyed by soaring eagles. Coastal mountains and rain forests gradually yield inland to verdant farmlands in the Fraser Valley. It is scenery that impresses even native British Columbians.

Howe Sound

On summer days the historic *Royal Hudson* steam train leaves North Vancouver for the Howe Sound fjords and **Squamish,** north of Vancouver. Sightseers can travel the five-and-a-half-hour round trip by train, or take the M.V. *Britannia* one-way and return by rail, which takes seven hours. Those driving to Squamish take the scenic Highway 99 north of Vancouver. En route is Britannia Beach, which once housed the British Empire's largest copper mine. Now, from May to September, the B.C. Museum of Mining conducts unique underground train trips and a historic village walking tour.

The mountains surrounding Squamish are excellent for outdoor recreation, particularly hiking and rock climbing. The experienced scale the great granite Stawamus Chief or hike Diamond Head and Black Tusk in **Garibaldi Provincial Park.** In summer, Alpine Adventure Tours (Tel: 604-932-2705) has exhilarating glacier flights. B.C. Rail and Maverick Coach Lines provide regular year-round service to Britannia, Squamish, and Whistler.

Some 75 miles north of Vancouver on Highway 99, past

Squamish, **Whistler/Blackcomb,** a prestigious four-season resort area best known for its skiing, has the longest lift-serviced vertical drop in North America. Collectively, the two mountains have 180 runs, groomed cross-country trails, even heli-skiing. In summer, when accommodation prices are drastically reduced, visitors can heli-hike, canoe, raft, horseback ride, or golf on an Arnold Palmer-designed course. Trendy **Whistler Village,** with its West Coast architecture, is a place to see and be seen. Although generally expensive, it is pleasant and social, with bars, bistros, and boutiques clustered cozily together. Street minstrels humor the crowds on summer weekends.

The newest addition to Canadian Pacific Hotels' prestigious line of chateau-style lodgings is its 350-room **Chateau Whistler Resort,** a year-round facility offering skiing, golf, and tennis. Adjacent to the hotel are high-speed chairlifts to Blackcomb and a new gondola to Whistler's 6000-foot peak. A long-standing favorite, the **Delta Mountain Inn** has indoor tennis, some in-room Jacuzzis, and a health club.

The Sunshine Coast

Across Howe Sound to the northwest the Sunshine Coast begins, with its quiet coves, bays, and windward arbutus trees. The gentle, unhurried lifestyle here lures fishermen, retirees, and logger poets. Visitors can spend one to several days touring by car, or take Maverick Coach Lines from Vancouver. B.C. Ferries has 40-minute sailings, year round, from West Vancouver's Horseshoe Bay to Langdale, the ferry terminal near Gibsons. From there, Highway 101 (the Pacific Coast Highway) winds north to Earls Cove, where another ferry serves Saltery Bay. This crossing allows motorists to continue up the 101 to **Powell River** (where ferries depart for Vancouver Island) and Lund, an isolated fishing village and terminus of the Pacific Coast Highway.

In Gibsons, near Langdale, where the lighthearted *Beachcombers* television series is filmed, visitors and locals appreciate the dramatic view of mountains and sea from **Gramma's Pub.** Gramma's also runs a beer-and-wine store and sells tongue-searing Portuguese sausage. Tiny shops in Gibsons sell local pottery and handwoven items.

Sechelt, with its fine, sandy beach, is noted for its

progressive Indian community, Canada's first to attain self-government. In summer visitors can watch artisans working in the carving shed, visit the community center with its impressive totem sentinels, and buy native crafts at the **Shadow Box Gallery**.

The **Wakefield Inn**, a favored watering hole near Sechelt, provides bed and breakfast in antique-furnished rooms overlooking the sea. There is Smuggler's Cove marine park and the **Jolly Roger Inn** on Secret Cove, with its typically Canadian West Coast wood paneling and vaulted, sky-lit ceilings. (Buccaneerish names flourish along the coast.) The comfortable **Lord Jim's Resort Hotel**, on scenic Halfmoon Bay with a fine view of twisted arbutus trees, has salmon-fishing charters year round.

Although moderate rainfall keeps it green, the Sunshine Coast receives 14 more sunny days a year than temperate Victoria. Numerous marine parks here attract boaters, fishermen, beachcombers, and divers. Scuba diving in the clear, protected waters south of **Pender Harbour** (rated among the world's best diving) and around Powell River reveals sea caves, enormous octopuses, reefs, and shipwrecks. **Lowe's Resort Motel** in nearby Madeira Park rents cottages, boats, and diving equipment.

The Lower Fraser River Area

East of Vancouver, Highway 7 meanders into the Fraser Valley farmlands, past tumbledown barns, grazing livestock, sawmills, tugs, and log booms along the lower Fraser River, which runs east-west here. Some 30 miles inland is **Fort Langley National Historic Park**, where the Crown Colony of British Columbia was established in 1858. Year round, this authentic reconstructed Hudson Bay depot employs park historians in period costume to regale visitors with tales of times past.

Farther on, **Harrison Hot Springs**, a small lakeside resort amid lofty mountains, is noted for its therapeutic public mineral pools. Locals regularly take the waters alongside world travellers. Cascade Bus Lines serves the village from Vancouver. The waterfront **Harrison Hot Springs Hotel** has heated indoor mineral pools, golf, boating, and tennis. The neighboring Bavarian-themed **Black Forest Steak and Schnitzel House** serves hearty German fare.

THE CARIBOO HIGHWAY
TO THE NORTHWEST

In the mid-1800s, determined prospectors from as far away as Oregon and California travelled to newly colonized British Columbia, up the relentless Fraser River from the Pacific Coast to Lillooet (the river comes down from the north past Lillooet and only turns west at about the latitude of Vancouver), then north to the Barkerville gold mines. The province's original Gold Rush Trail was once described as "utterly impassable for any animal but a man, goat, or dog."

Today's paved Cariboo Highway, or Route 97, passes historic mile-house communities where dude ranches and deluxe resorts have replaced prospectors' road-houses. Horses outnumber people on sprawling, sun-bleached ranchlands, and television-satellite dishes stand incongruously beside chicken coops and beehive barns. To the west of the turbulent Fraser, the landscape is high alpine with evergreen forests.

Visitors should allow several days to tour the area adequately. From North Vancouver, B.C. Rail's *Cariboo Dayliner* follows this scenic route on its run to Prince George in the north. Motorists can drive past Whistler, then take the spectacular, summer-only Duffey Lake Road to Lillooet. Or they can take the Trans-Canada Highway via Lytton.

In 1863, **Lillooet** prospered as Mile Zero on the Cariboo Highway, and was the second-largest town (after Barkerville) north of San Francisco. Now the past is revisited at the Lillooet Museum (open summers).

Some 130 km (80 miles) west of Lillooet, the new **Tyax Mountain Lake Resort** on Tyaughton Lake, the largest log structure on the West Coast, is noted for its cross-country and heli-skiing in winter, horseback riding and heli-hiking in summer. Non-motorists can take B.C. Rail to Lillooet, where the resort provides pick-up service.

Beyond Lillooet, some 40 miles northwest of 70 Mile House, the historic **Gang Ranch**, now B.C.'s largest, once paid its cowboys in beef and beans. Today, guests bunk in cowboy-style cabins and participate in ranch activities. To get there, drive north on Highway 97 some nine miles past Clinton. Here, the dirt Meadow Lake Road on your left continues another 50 miles to the ranch; Tel: (604) 459-7923 for details.

Unlike the Gang Ranch, **The Hills Health and Guest Ranch**, near the town of 100 Mile House, cleverly combines laid-back western hospitality with the elitist fitness craze. The spa features individual physical assessments and weight loss programs year round; horseback riding, fishing, and cross-country skiing are seasonal. North Vancouver's Sea to Sky Tours arranges rail and accommodation packages; Tel: (604) 984-2224 for details.

In winter the south-Cariboo area is dusted in powder snow, ideal for Nordic skiing through stands of birch and aspen. B.C.'s major cross-country ski center, the town of **100 Mile House**, has some 120 miles of machine-groomed trails concentrated around the Hills resort and the **108 Golf & Country Inn**. Guests of the 108 stay in an attractive wood-frame lodge overlooking a par-72, P.G.A.-approved golf course. Other summer activities include tennis, riding, and fishing.

The 30-mile Cariboo Marathon, the largest cross-country ski event in western Canada, attracts some 1,500 international competitors to 100 Mile House the first weekend in February.

Often, nothing disturbs the still lakes here in summer except a solitary boat or a flickering fish tail. Beyond 100 Mile House, Lac La Hache and Quesnel Lake are noted for kokanee salmon and rainbow trout, respectively. Outdoorsmen seek the many wilderness fly-in resorts, such as the remote **Stewart's Lodge and Camps** on Nimpo Lake. From May to October guests can stay in waterfront cabins and enjoy fly fishing and casting for rainbow trout in local lakes and streams. Transportation to the lodge can be arranged through Tweedsmuir Air Services (Tel: 604-742-3388).

Further east, the dusty, sprawling cowboy country at Williams Lake (north of 100 Mile House on the Cariboo Highway) breeds top rodeo athletes who compete with other Canadian and U.S. professionals in the acclaimed **Williams Lake Stampede**. The four-day event, held each first weekend in July, is Canada's largest rodeo after the Calgary Stampede.

Quesnel's **Billy Barker Days**, held each third weekend in July, is billed as more fun than the actual gold rush. Locals don period costumes for the gala parade, and there is gold panning, fireworks, and B.C.'s largest amateur rodeo.

Some 60 miles east of Quesnel (which is north of 100 Mile House) and the Cariboo Highway, **Barkerville** became "the largest town west of Chicago and north of San Francisco" in 1862 when Billy Barker, a wily Cornish prospector, hit the prospecting jackpot. In its heyday, the town yielded some $50 million in gold. In 1958 the government declared Barkerville a provincial historic park, restoring the many heritage buildings. In summer, lively, costumed orators and entertainers portray notorious citizens while the Theatre Royal presents bawdy musicals.

Just beyond, **Bowron Lake Provincial Park**'s 73-mile canoe circuit, once travelled by Indians and trappers, now lures international canoeists. The entire route takes six to ten days, revealing unspoiled vistas and seldom-seen wildlife. From May to October, **Becker's Canoe Outfitters and Lodge**, 72 miles east of Quesnel on Bowron Lake, provides canoes, camping, fishing equipment, and log cabins. **Pathways Tours** provides guided ten-day canoe packages from June through September (Tel: 604-263-1476). Non-motorists can take B.C. Rail or Greyhound bus to Quesnel, where Becker's provides pick-up service.

NORTHWEST BRITISH COLUMBIA

In the early 1900s, the B.C. artist Emily Carr painted powerful, haunting landscapes of the province's northwest rain forests and remote Indian villages. Her works are a significant portrayal of the vast, sparsely populated land known as Canada's gateway to the Yukon and Alaska. Although the few towns have grown substantially since Carr's time, they still thrive on forestry, mining, fishing— and the railroad that unites them.

To reach the central hub of **Prince George** on the upper Fraser River, visitors can take the Greyhound bus or B.C. Rail's spectacular 13-hour *Cariboo Dayliner* from Vancouver, or follow Highway 97 north from Cache Creek on the Trans-Canada Highway. From Prince George, VIA Rail hugs Yellowhead Highway 16 west to the coastal port of Prince Rupert.

Lacy aspens, sturdy spruce trees, and pulp incinerators, looking like huge inverted badminton birds, characterize the countryside surrounding Prince George, a fur-trading fort in 1807, now a rugged mill and railroad center. In summer the new Railway Museum (open weekdays) and the Northwood Pulp and Timber facility (which conducts

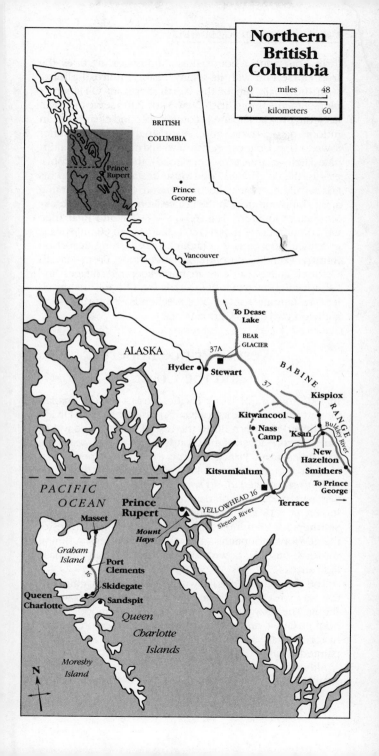

three-hour tours) honor these industries, as does the **Iron Horse Pub** with its grainy, historic railroad photos.

In the **Coast Inn of the North**, Sergeant O'Flaherty's pleasant sing-along "Irish New York Pub" serves its own tasty, dark brew. The inn is comfortable and clean, with an indoor pool, sauna, and, surprisingly in this frontier town, a fine Japanese restaurant. Six miles east on alternate Highway 16A (Giscome Road), the German proprietor of the celebrated **Log House Restaurant** displays his taxidermic trophies. Recommended big-game hunting and fishing outfitters in the Prince George area are: Rocky Mountain Outfitters, Tel: (604) 964-9186; and Bear Lake Guide outfitters, Tel: (604) 971-2220. Some 60 miles west of Prince George is the **Tachick Lake Fishing Resort** on Kenney Dam Road south of Vanderhoof. From May to October guests can stay in housekeeping cottages and fish for rainbow trout. But the big treat here is the excellent restaurant (only open weekends) featuring local game prepared by a German chef.

West to Prince Rupert and the Coast

In 1912 the Grand Trunk Pacific, the last leg of Canada's newest transcontinental railway, crossed the Great Divide and linked northern BC to the rest of Canada. Today, VIA Rail's *Skeena* (River of the Clouds) *Liner* winds west some 450 miles from Prince George to Prince Rupert. Pole-straight aspens, mirror lakes, and pulp mills gradually yield to sturdy cedar and spruce forests. The train leaves just past the break of day, at 6:15 A.M., and arrives in Rupert at 8:15 P.M. En route, passengers have a stop at **Smithers** for 25 minutes, enough time to take pictures of the glorious mountains and to stretch their legs. A dining car serves tasty, sit-down meals, or travellers can purchase light snacks

The Bavarian-themed town of Smithers (two-thirds of the way west) is noted for its cross-country and alpine skiing. The cozy **Hudson Bay Lodge** has an indoor whirlpool, a sauna, and a fireside lounge. Farther on are the historic 'Ksan and Kispiox Indian villages, frequently painted by artist Carr.

Although VIA Rail and Greyhound bus serve nearby New Hazelton, visitors need a car to see **'Ksan**, five miles north, set amid the rushing Bulkley River and the saw-tooth Babine Range—"The home of the quiet people." Seven tribal houses, guarded by cracked, graying totems, some more than 100 years old, preserve the Indian legacy. On-site carvers, using saws and tools their forefathers never had, infuse the air with a chopped-cedar scent. The 'Ksan Village and Gift Shop is open daily during summer and weekdays in winter.

Just beyond 'Ksan, Highway 37, then 37A, winds north to **Kitwancool**, a small Gitksan village with the world's oldest standing totem, called Hole-in-the-Ice. Some 100 miles farther is the glaciated, mountainous river port of **Stewart** that has appeared in several Hollywood movies, including *The Thing, The Ice Man, Bear Island,* and *Never Cry Wolf.* Transportation is by private vehicle or Seaport Limousine from **Terrace** (between New Hazelton and Prince Rupert). En route, wispy deciduous trees give way to substantial evergreens, and, nearing town, the enormous Bear Glacier extends its blue ice paw.

Neighboring **Hyder**, Alaska, is accessible by land only from Stewart. With the highest bar-per-capita ratio in the United States, the hamlet manages without law enforcement, local taxes, and Customs officials. In the raucous **Glacier Inn**, imbibers "get Hyderized" drinking Everclear, a 190-proof straight-grain Kentucky alcohol, with a water chaser. September visitors may see chum spawning in the nearby Salmon River, where gulls and bears enjoy the spoils.

Keen adventurers will continue north to **Dease Lake**—self-proclaimed "Jade Capital of the World"—and beyond to the Yukon and Alaska.

Others may return south toward Terrace on Highway 37 or on the rough but rewarding Nass logging road, past the 220-year-old Tseax Lava Flow, an eerie moonscape of lichen-covered rocks.

Terrace's Heritage Park, open in summer, displays several architecturally diverse log pioneer homes. Nearby, the **Northern Light Studio** sells quality native art, alder and yellow-cedar carvings, and B.C. jade. In an area synonymous with hunting, the **Bavarian Inn** restaurant features gourmet buffalo dishes and schnitzel and a Hunters' Den of stuffed wildlife. The towering cedar poles outside the Kitsumkalum Indian reserve at Terrace are the first to have been raised here in 150 years.

From Terrace to Prince Rupert on the coast, the Yellowhead Highway 16 and VIA Rail wind west along the Skeena River, through the mist-shrouded Coast Mountains and rain-soaked evergreens.

Prince Rupert

In Prince Rupert, where the Skeena meets the Pacific, few views can match that from the elegant **Crest Motor Hotel**. The Prince Charles Lounge here, with its warm brass, wood, and Scottish tartans, overlooks the Coast Mountains and tiny tugs pulling log booms 100 times their size. Whales migrate this way in spring, while seals and sea lions emerge year round.

A Cannery Row of weathered pilings and clustered fishing boats supports several good, uncommercialized seafood restaurants, such as **The Anchorage** and **Smiles** (the latter since World War II, and recommended in many food guides).

Prince Rupert's **Museum of Northern British Columbia** has a superb ethnographic collection of area artifacts. Outside, visitors can watch native artists at work in the carving shed. Nearby, the **North Pacific Cannery Village and Fishing Museum**, a National Historic Site, is probably the last remaining accessible cannery in North America. Machine shops, net lofts, canning lines, and hoists have been refurbished along the waterfront. The site is open from mid-May to mid-September. Those who are so inclined can rent rods and angle right from the dock.

B.C. Ferries' scenic 15-hour sailings back down to Vancouver Island are best in June and July, when there is extended daylight. The vehicular ferries make fewer trips in the off-season. On summer days and on weekends the rest of the year, a gondola climbs 1,850 feet from Prince Rupert to Mount Hays, overlooking the harbor, the Alaska Panhandle, and the Queen Charlotte Islands.

The Queen Charlotte Islands

These haunting, time-warped islands (six hours from Prince Rupert by B.C. Ferries) lure adventurous naturalists who seek the water-logged rain forests and ancient Haida totems eulogized by artist Carr. The fallen totems of Ninstints, declared by UNESCO a World Heritage site, are now protected in the federal government's **South Moresby National Park**.

The Queen Charlottes are a treasured wilderness,

steeped in Haida Indian culture, spectacular wildlife, and old-growth forests. Proud locals (the Haida here are politically and economically active) will gladly share a pint of good B.C. beer and tell a tale or two to those inclined to listen. While July and August are the warmest months here, April and May are the most exciting—grey whales feed along the coast and thousands of shorebirds dive for herring.

In summer, B.C. Ferries sail approximately five times weekly from Prince Rupert to Skidegate on Graham Island. There are fewer sailings the rest of the year. Canadian Airlines International flies daily into Sandspit, slightly south of Skidegate, on Moresby Island. Rental cars (a must) are available, along with float planes, helicopter tours, sailboats, power cruisers, and kayaks.

Lodgings once described as "worse than rustic" have been upgraded to "clean and charming." One new hostelry worth a mention is the **Spruce Point Bed and Breakfast**, an attractive, waterfront bed and breakfast in Queen Charlotte City near Skidegate. The cedar building has kayak rentals and is attached to a pottery studio. In Sandspit, the **Moresby Island Guest House** provides Continental breakfast and can arrange hunting and fishing expeditions. A pleasant local hangout is the waterfront pub in Port Clements on Graham Island, serving burgers and other standard grilled fare in a cozy, cedar atmosphere. More upscale is the **Café Gallery** farther north on the island in Masset. The café features European cuisine and fine seafood.

The **Queen Charlotte Museum** in Queen Charlotte City is a must, presided over by a great totem pole created by the renowned master carver Bill Reid. Inside is exquisite Haida art, notably the haunting masks once given to other museums, then returned to the Charlottes. Perhaps no group is better equipped to give insights into their rich ancestral past than the Haida Gwaii Watchmen who conduct trips to Ninstints and other remote areas. Tel: (604) 559-8225.

In Queen Charlotte City, Kallahin Travel Services is a one-stop-booking shop that can arrange accommodations, cars, and tours, and provides helpful advice year round. Tel: (604) 559-8455.

SOUTH-CENTRAL BRITISH COLUMBIA
The High Country

High Country, in the province's south-central region east of the Fraser Valley, is a vast jumble of sprawling cattle ranches, finger-like lakes, and immense mountains such as the Columbias and Monashees, protected in several wilderness parks.

The best way to explore is by car, allowing several days to see the sights at a leisurely pace. East out of Vancouver, Trans-Canada Highway 1 past Hope leads to the Hell's Gate Airtram, an exhilarating six-minute ride across the Fraser Canyon that operates from March through October. To the northeast are sun-parched grasslands and "a lake a day as long as you stay," as the area boasts. Tattoos and western gear constitute the dress code at **Coldwater Hotel** in Merritt, where pub patrons gustily chorus cowboy laments.

On Nicola Lake, the 82-year-old **Quilchena Hotel** started as a gold-rush packing company, then became a luxury retreat for the wealthy. From April to October guests stay in this somewhat worn but charming lodging with gurgling hot-water heaters, tiny, floral-papered rooms, and a bullet-scarred saloon bar.

Sagebrush scents the air and covers the hills at **Sundance**, among B.C.'s largest working cattle ranches, open March to October near Ashcroft. Here, authentic cowboys round up some 100 horses in spring and fall. Meat from the buffalo herd is frequently on the excellent menu. Reasonable rates include lodging, hefty meals, two daily horseback rides, and, in summer, tennis and swimming. Docile and spirited horses are matched with similarly disposed riders.

The **Ashcroft Manor Tea House**, a refurbished 1860s gold-rush lodge with century-old elm trees, is now used as a restaurant serving traditional teas from March to mid-November. Guests can shop for local art amid roadhouse relics. In summer, the excellent Ashcroft Museum displays several restored turn-of-the-century buildings.

The nearby town of **Kamloops**, Indian for "meeting of the waters," is named for the area's many lakes and rivers, popular with trout fishermen. Here, the paddlewheeler

Wanda Sue languorously plies the South Thompson River on summer days.

To the east on Trans-Canada Highway 1 is **Shuswap Lake**, a squiggly, H-shaped lake with some 600 navigable miles and numerous marine parks. It is ideal for canoeing, kayaking, and houseboating. In 1990 thousands of brilliant red sockeye salmon will surge through the nearby Adams River en route to spawning grounds. This is the culmination of a four-year cycle and crowds are sure to line the riverbanks in late September to late October to watch this extraordinary and emotional event. In **Sicamous**, Canada's self-proclaimed "Houseboat Capital," several companies rent the floating homes: Go Vacations, Tel: (800) 661-9558; and Waterway Houseboats, Tel: (604) 836-2505.

Near Alberta to the northeast the mountains rise abruptly beyond the "banana belt" of the Shuswap Lake district. Craggy, glaciated peaks, lofty meadows, and wilderness trails characterize **Glacier National Park** and **Mount Revelstoke National Park**, among the most dramatic scenery on the Trans-Canada Highway and VIA Rail's Canadian Pacific route.

Farther north, the view is equally impressive. Here, the Yellowhead Highway and VIA's Canadian National route climb past **Wells Gray Provincial Park** with its extinct volcanos, lava beds, and mineral springs. Near the Alberta border, both routes provide views of the 13,000-foot **Mount Robson**, the highest point in the Canadian Rockies, which the Indians named "Yuh-hai-has-hun," the Mountain of the Spiral Road. Farther along, across the Alberta border, is Jasper.

SOUTHEAST BRITISH COLUMBIA
The Okanagan

Anyone who has seen the popular movie *My American Cousin,* an impressionistic movie about innocent summer love, will recognize the Okanagan-Similkameen area below the High Country: dry, rolling sagebrush hills, lush orchards, and slender lakes. This sunny land lures the young, summer beach partiers, oenophiles gravitating to B.C.'s budding wine center, and sun-worshippers of all ages, drying bodies bludgeoned by rainy West Coast win-

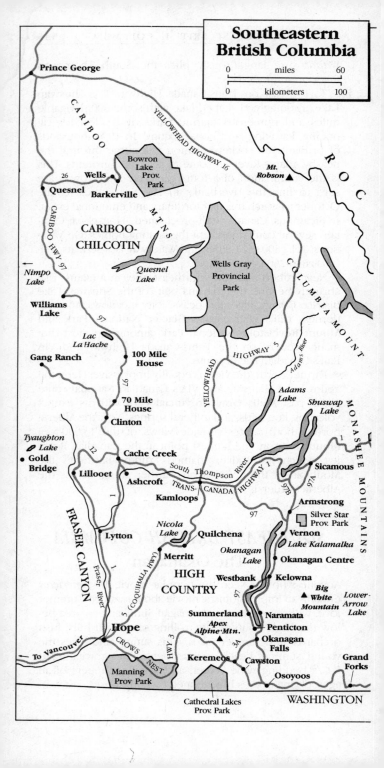

Southeastern British Columbia

miles 0 — 60

kilometers 0 — 100

Prince George

CARIBOO

YELLOWHEAD HIGHWAY 16

Mt. Robson ▲

ROC

26 Wells
Quesnel
Barkerville
Bowron Lake Prov. Park

CARIBOO-CHILCOTIN

MTNS

Quesnel Lake

Wells Gray Provincial Park

COLUMBIA MOUNT

← Nimpo Lake

CARIBOO HWY 97

Williams Lake

97

Lac La Hache

Gang Ranch

100 Mile House

97

HIGHWAY 5

YELLOWHEAD

Adams River

Adams Lake

Shuswap Lake

MONASHEE MOUNTAINS

70 Mile House

Clinton

Tyaughton Lake

Gold Bridge

12

Cache Creek

South Thompson River

1

Sicamous

Lillooet

Ashcroft

TRANS-CANADA HIGHWAY 1

97B

97A

Silver Star Prov. Park

Kamloops

Lytton

FRASER CANYON

Nicola Lake

Quilchena

97

Armstrong

Vernon

Lake Kalamalka

Okanagan Centre

1 (COQUIHALLA)

Fraser River

Merritt

HIGH COUNTRY

Okanagan Lake

Westbank

97

Kelowna

Big White Mountain ▲

Lower-Arrow Lake

5 (COQUIHALLA)

Summerland

Apex Alpine Mtn. ▲

Naramata

Penticton

Hope

← To Vancouver

CROWS

NEST

HWY 3

Okanagan Falls

3A

Manning Prov Park

Keremeos

Cawston

Osoyoos

Grand Forks

Cathedral Lakes Prov. Park

WASHINGTON

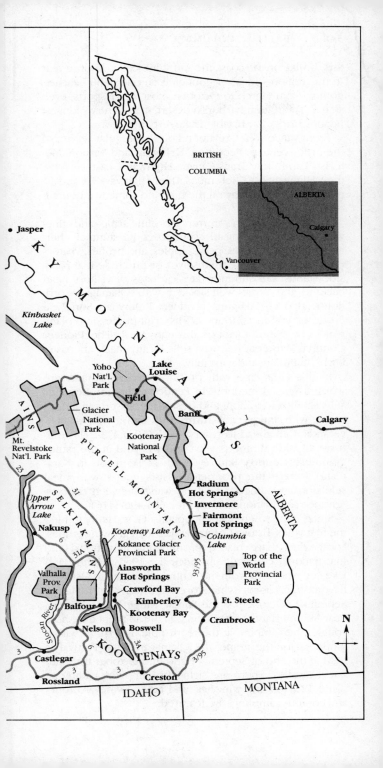

ters. Unlike on the coast, the sun shines 2,000 hours a year in this region—ideal for lounging on one of 30 beaches, golfing from March to October, most water sports, even skiing. The region harbors a desert, the country's longest floating bridge, and a fabled lake serpent.

From Vancouver, Greyhound bus has regular service to the major centers: **Penticton**, **Kelowna**, and **Vernon**. Motorists can follow Trans-Canada Highway 1 east to Hope, then Highway 3 to Keremeos, then Highways 3A and 97 north. Allow a full day on the bus, and some five hours if driving.

Abundant sunshine nurtures prolific fruits and vineyards. Delicate spring blossoms become summer cherries, apricots, peaches, pears, apples, and prunes. Visitors can pick the produce themselves or purchase it at roadside stands. On summer days carloads of visitors head back to the coast well-stocked with Okanagan (pronounced o-ka-NAH-gun) produce. Kelowna's Sun-Rype Products conducts tours of its fruit-processing plant, which is closed October through April. The **Pioneer Country Market** at Kelowna sells locally made antipasto, herbs, chutneys, and wine jelly.

In this area, ripe with produce, two restaurants are worth a special mention. In Penticton, **Granny Bogner's** sells schnitzel, salmon, and fresh fruit desserts in an old house with antique oak furnishings and a wrap-around veranda. Call ahead to reserve; Tel: (604) 493-2711. Intimate, fireside dining is what you will find at the rather grandiose **Country Squire** (north of Penticton in Naramata), where the proprietor assists guests with meal selection and diners take long walks between courses. Advance reservations a must (Tel: 604-496-5416).

Since 1899, when resident botanist G. W. Henry tended the first vines, British Columbia has been growing grapes. Local wines have placed prominently in national and international competitions since the 1960s. Hilltop and lakeside vineyards from the central Okanagan to Osoyoos have tasting rooms, wine stores, and tours from May to September/October. At the **Sumac Ridge Estate Winery**, near Summerland, visitors can golf the adjacent nine-hole course, then imbibe at the tenth hole. For those with a fondness for the grape, the Okanagan Wine Festival is held at the end of September and into October throughout the valley. There are stringent competitions among some 12 attending wineries, and guided vineyard tours and copious samplings are featured.

Among some 80 bed-and-breakfast establishments, one, the **Windmill**, eight miles east of Vernon, has rooms in an actual mill and serves homemade rolls and preserves. Canadian Pacific Hotel's luxurious **Lake Okanagan Resort**, 10 miles north of Kelowna on the opposite side of the lake, features tennis instruction on championship courts, golf on hilly terrain, horseback riding, and swimming from May to November.

As well as enjoying the fruits and the wines, visitors can take part in plenty of recreational pursuits. Extensive waterways are ideal for most aquatic sports, particularly fishing. Near Vernon, Kalamalka (Lake of Many Colors) yields plump kokanee salmon and trout. Trophy rainbow trout are the winter catch in **Lake Okanagan**, while smaller trout, whitefish, and burbot are hooked year round. Although never proved, a Disneyesque serpent, Ogopogo, is said to live in these waters. Tourism authorities will award $1 million worth of goods to anyone who can present evidence confirming its existence.

Houseboating is a pleasant way to see the lake and Canada's longest floating bridge, which links Kelowna and Westbank. Among numerous rental companies, Kelowna's **Shelter Bay Charters** (Tel: 604-769-4411) supplies luxurious, fully equipped Pleasurecrafts and "a complete selection of water toys." From here, the paddlewheeler M.V. *Fintry Queen* plies the waters on summer afternoons and evenings.

B.C.'s interior is as much a winter wonderland as it is a summer escape. Under usually fair skies, bronzed skiers tackle the dry, crisp snow on Kelowna's Big White, Penticton's Apex Alpine, and Vernon's Silver Star mountains. Non-skiers can spend the cold, clear winters ice skating, sleigh riding, and cross-country skiing.

Armstrong, north of Silver Star Mountain on Highway 97, is best known for its production of sharp cheddar cheese. During the summer the town's delightful Caravan Stage Company journeys in horse-drawn wagons, performing in the Okanagans' city and town parks.

While arid **Osoyoos** harbors a desert, with horned lizards, owls, and cactuses, **Cathedral Lakes Provincial Park**, south of Highway 3 near Keremeos, is the physical opposite, characterized by the awesome Cascade Mountains, alpine-type lakes, and geological grotesqueries.

From July to September, the secluded **Cathedral Lakes Resort** on Lake Quiniscoe offers wilderness packages (minimum stay two nights) and hiking trails for the moderately fit. Greyhound has daily bus service to Keremeos, from which the lodge can arrange pick-up. Motorists can follow Highway 3 to the Ashnola River Road and beyond to the base camp. Here, the lodge jeep will pick up—or energetic guests can hike the nine miles in.

The Kootenays

Southeastern B.C.'s Kootenays (east of the Okanagan area), where long, slender lakes flank the dramatic Selkirk Mountains, are an outdoor playland for mountain sports, golfing, and year-round bathing in natural hot springs. The region's beauty and generally amiable residents compensate for the occasional small-town rigidity.

In the late 1800s and into the 20th century, the Kootenays flourished with gold and silver mining. Today, silent ghost towns are eerie reminders of these lucrative times. Among the Kootenays' curiosities are wild whistling swans and the world's longest free ferry ride.

The easiest way to explore is by car, allowing a full day to drive from Vancouver via Hope and the Crowsnest Highway 3. Remnants of early-1900s Russian immigrant life is scattered throughout the farmlands surrounding Grand Forks and at Castlegar's Historic Doukhobor Village on the bank of the Columbia River. Traditional Russian black bread and steaming borscht are specialties in **The Doukhobor Restaurant** here.

In nearby **Rossland**, right near the U.S. border, turn-of-the-century mines produced 50 percent of British Columbia's gold. From May to October visitors to this southern mountain town can tour the Rossland Historical Museum and former Le Roi Gold Mine—the province's only hard-rock mine open for guided tours.

Some 50 miles northeast of here is **Nelson**, an architectural treasure trove of historic buildings set on the west arm of Kootenay Lake. Hollywood star Steve Martin perched on the roofs and swung from the rafters of several exquisite Victorian homes here while filming *Roxanne,* based on Edmund Rostand's classic, *Cyrano de Bergerac.* Self-guided walking tours pass some 350 provincially designated heritage buildings.

Motorists heading west on Highway 3A then north on Highway 6 into the Slocan Valley will pass the Valhalla Mountain Range and Slocan Lake. **Valhalla Provincial Park** has mountaineering, hiking, and remote beach camping. Alpine flowers here are at their best in August. The nearby **Sandon Ghost Town**, once a silver miner's El Dorado, now has little more than a summer museum. Further north, on Upper Arrow Lake, the **Nakusp Hot Springs** burbles among substantial cedars and lacy ferns. While the soaking pool is 112 degrees F the swimming pool is a mere 105.

Southwest of the hot springs on Highway 6 and 31A is **Kokanee Glacier Park**, from which the B.C.-brewed Kokanee beer derives its name. The park is noted for excellent hiking, ski touring, and trout and salmon fishing. Tucked under the mountains near the park are more effervescent mineral pools. The **Ainsworth Hot Springs Resort** overlooking Kootenay Lake has deluxe accommodations, golf, and a 95-degree F steam bath in a cave.

The ferry from Balfour across Kootenay Lake, the world's longest free ride, takes some 40 minutes, depending on which side you start from. On the Kootenay Bay side, while waiting to make a hole-in-one, golfers at the **Kokanee Springs Resort** have spectacular glacier views. The course is a championship 18 holes; lodging, from April to October, is in housekeeping chalets.

The Kootenay Skyway, the country's highest major thoroughfare, soars above Creston, where wild whistling swans nest in the protected **Creston Valley Wildlife Center**. Naturalists canoe or join forest and meadow walks and "marsh crawls."

The Rockies

In British Columbia's extreme southeast, the Purcell and Rocky mountains command the landscape as if demanding recognition. The Rockies, constituting the Great Divide between B.C. and Alberta, are showcased in two national parks on each provincial border. In B.C. they are Kootenay and Yoho. (Opposite them in Alberta are Banff, and farther north, Jasper National Park.) Superlative scenery aside, the region has all the recreational advantages of mountains: wilderness treks, downhill and heli-skiing, rafting, and observing wildlife. Craggy mountain men live here year round. Ardent skiers flock from the coast and the prairies at the first negotiable snowfall, and cameratoting tourists come to see the Rockies whenever they can.

The Trans-Canada Highway 1 and VIA Rail penetrate the area from either province. It takes some ten hours to drive from Vancouver, depending on the route taken. Greyhound buses stop at major centers.

This vast, rugged land was virtually impenetrable until the mid-1800s, when the Canadian Pacific Railroad first crossed the mountains, completing the last link in the country's transcontinental railway. In the southeastern town of **Cranbrook**, the railway museum houses the *Trans-Canada Limited,* a luxury 1929 train once owned by Canadian Pacific.

Nearby, **Fort Steele Provincial Heritage Park**, on Highway 93/95, is dwarfed by the Rockies. This site of B.C.'s first North West Mounted Police post has some 40 restorations, including the original officers' quarters and water tower. The park is open daily from May through October, with summer steam-train trips, vaudeville shows, and lively, staged street dramas.

Kimberley, Canada's highest city, perched in the Purcells, with its immense cuckoo clock, Der Platzl (people place), *lederhosen,* strudel, and schnitzel, has been called the most Bavarian village outside the Alps. Pizza and taco stands confirm that this is not Bavaria, however.

Top of the World Ranch, perched near the provincial park of the same name, is a down-to-basics working cattle ranch that accommodates guests year round in snug log cabins. There are breakfast rides, barbecues, campfires, and glimpses of wildlife and Canadian geese nesting in local lakes. Winter brings cross-country skiing, hay rides, and ice fishing.

Coddled by the mountains, Fairmont, Radium, and the lesser-known Lussier have year-round public hot springs. At the northern tip of Columbia Lake, **Fairmont Hot Springs Resort**, an attractive cedar lodge and woodland villas, has four odorless mineral pools that range in temperature from 35 to 45 degrees C. Since 1922 guests have been attracted to this mountain retreat for its two 18-hole golf courses, racquet sports, horseback riding, skiing, and a 6,000-foot runway minutes away. Some 10 miles north of Fairmont in Invermere is **Strand's Old House Restaurant**. This culinary hideaway serves pepper steaks, New Zealand spring lamb, venison, and savory homemade sauces to go with them in a historic 1912 building. Reservations are recommended in the summer; Tel: 604-342-6344.

Farther north, **Kootenay National Park** stretches some 65 miles along both sides of the Banff-Windermere Highway toward Alberta. Here glacial icefields plummet to valleys and chasms. Some 125 miles of hiking trails ascend the slopes for panorama gaping. Fall and winter provide some of the best wildlife viewing. Bighorn sheep, grizzlies, elk, wolves, coyotes, and the occasional moose can be seen.

Yoho (Cree for "how wonderful") gives a new meaning to the English word "pristine." In **Yoho National Park** more than 30 sawtooth peaks exceed 9,000 feet. Beneath them, near Field, the **Emerald Lake Lodge** was first opened in 1902 to serve wayfarers venturing into the Canadian Rockies. After extensive restoration, the exclusive resort reopened in 1986. The original hand-hewn lodge remains the dining and social center, while modern units have been built among the trees with lake and mountain views. It is wonderful.

GETTING AROUND

For details on getting to Vancouver, the area's main gateway, see the preceding chapter on Vancouver. Information on B.C. regions outside Vancouver is given throughout the text of this chapter.

For information on B.C. Ferries from Vancouver Island (Victoria and Nanaimo), see the Getting Around section at the end of the Vancouver chapter.

ACCOMMODATIONS REFERENCE

▶ **Ainsworth Hot Springs Resort.** Box 1268, **Ainsworth Hot Springs,** B.C. V0G 1A0. Tel: (604) 229-4212.

▶ **April Point Lodge.** Box 1, **Campbell River,** B.C. V9W 4Z9. Tel: (604) 285-2222 or (800) 663-5555.

▶ **Becker's Canoe Outfitters and Lodge.** Bowron Lake, Box 129, **Wells,** B.C. V0K 2R0. Tel: Wells radio operator (ask for Becker's Lodge) N698552.

▶ **Big Spring Fishing Resort. Rivers Inlet,** B.C. Reservations address: 204-1062 Austin Avenue, Coquitlam, B.C. V3K 3P3. Tel: (604) 939-2938 or in Canada and U.S., (800) 663-4400.

▶ **Canadian Princess Resort.** Box 939, **Ucluelet,** B.C. V0R 3A0. Tel: (604) 726-7771.

▶ **Cathedral Lakes Resort.** R.R. 1, **Cawston,** B.C. V0X 1C0. Tel: (604) 499-5848.

▶ **Chateau Whistler Resort.** P.O. Box 100, **Whistler,** B.C. V0M 1B0. Tel: (604) 938-8000.

▶ **Cliffside Inn.** Armadale Road, **North Pender Island,** B.C. V0N 2M0. Tel: (604) 629-6691.

▶ **Coast Inn of the North.** 770 Brunswick Street, **Prince George,** B.C. V2L 2C2. Tel: (604) 563-0121.

▶ **Crest Motor Hotel.** 222 1st Avenue West, Box 277, **Prince Rupert,** B.C. V8J 3P6. Tel: (604) 624-6771 or (800) 663-8150; Telex: 04-89145.

▶ **Delta Mountain Inn.** 4050 Whistler Way, P.O. Box 550, **Whistler,** B.C. V0N 1B0. Tel: (604) 932-1982.

▶ **Emerald Lake Lodge.** Box 10, **Field,** B.C. V0A 1G0. Tel: (604) 343-6321.

▶ **Fairmont Hot Springs Resort.** Box 10, **Fairmont Hot Springs,** B.C. V0B 1L0. Tel: (604) 345-6311.

▶ **Gang Ranch.** General Delivery, **Gang Ranch,** B.C. V0K 1N0. Tel: (604) 459-7923.

▶ **Harrison Hot Springs Hotel.** 100 Esplanade Avenue, **Harrison Hot Springs,** B.C. V0M 1K0. Tel: (604) 521-8888; (800) 663-2266 from Washington, Oregon, Idaho, Montana and British Columbia; and (800) 622-5736 from Seattle.

▶ **Hastings House.** Box 1110, 160 Upper Ganges, **Ganges,** B.C. V0S 1E0. Tel: (604) 537-2362.

▶ **The Hills Health and Guest Ranch.** 108 Ranch, Comp 26, 100 Mile House, **Cariboo,** B.C. V0K 2E0. Tel: (604) 791-5225.

▶ **Hudson Bay Lodge.** 3251 East Highway 16, P.O. Box 3636, **Smithers,** B.C. V0J 2N0. Tel: (604) 847-4581.

▶ **Jolly Roger Inn.** R.R. 1, **Halfmoon Bay,** Box 7, B.C. V0N 1Y0. Tel: (604) 885-7184 or (800) 663-0180 in Canada.

▶ **Kokanee Springs Golf Resort.** Box 49, **Crawford Bay,** B.C. V0B 1E0. Tel: (604) 227-9226.

▶ **Lake Okanagan Resort.** Westside Road, P.O. Box 1321, Station A, **Kelowna,** B.C. V1Y 7V8. Tel: (604) 769-3511.

▶ **Lord Jim's Resort Hotel.** Ole's Cove Road, R.R. 1, **Halfmoon Bay,** B.C. V0N 1Y0. Tel: (604) 885-7038; in Vancouver, 681-6168.

▶ **Lowe's Resort Motel and Campground.** Box 153, **Madeira Park,** B.C. V0N 2H0. Tel: (604) 883-2426.

▶ **Moresby Guest House.** 385 Alliford Bay Road, Box 485, **Sandspit,** Queen Charlotte Islands, B.C. V0T 1T0. Tel: (604) 637-5305.

▶ **108 Golf and Country Inn.** P.O. Box 2, R.R. 1, 100 Mile House, **Cariboo,** B.C. V0K 2E0. Tel: (604) 791-5211.

▶ **Pacific Sands Beach Resort.** Box 237, **Tofino,** B.C. V0R 2Z0. Tel: (604) 725-3322.

▶ **Quilchena Hotel. Quilchena,** B.C. V0E 2R0. Tel: (604) 378-2611.

▶ **Sooke Harbour House.** 1528 Whiffen Spit Road, R.R. 4, **Sooke,** B.C. V0S 1N0. Tel: (604) 642-3421.

▶ **Spruce Point Bed and Breakfast.** Box 735, **Queen**

Charlotte City, Queen Charlotte Islands, B.C. V0T 1S0. Tel: (604) 559-8234.

▶ **Stewart's Lodge and Camps.** Nimpo Lake Post Office, **Nimpo Lake**, B.C. V0L 1R0. Tel: (604) 742-3388.

▶ **Strathcona Park Lodge.** Box 2160, **Campbell River**, B.C. V9W 5C9. Tel: (604) 286-2008.

▶ **Sundance Guest Ranch.** P.O. Box 489 **Ashcroft**, B.C., V0K 1A0. Tel: (604) 453-2554.

▶ **Tachick Lake Resort.** Box 1112, **Vanderhoof**, B.C. V0J 3A0. Tel: (604) 567-4929.

▶ **Tigh-Na-Mara Resort Hotel.** R.R. 1, Site 114, Comp 16, **Parksville**, B.C. V0R 2S0. Tel: (604) 248-2072.

▶ **Top of the World Guest Ranch.** Box 29, **Fort Steele**, B.C. V0B 1N0. Tel: (604) 426-6306.

▶ **Tyax Mountain Lake Resort.** Tyaughton Lake Road, **Gold Bridge**, B.C., V0K 1P0. Tel: (604) 238-2221.

▶ **Wakefield Inn.** P.O. Box 490, **Sechelt**, B.C. V0N 3A0. Tel: (604) 885-7666.

▶ **The Windmill.** Site 19A, C2, R.R. 1, **Vernon**, B.C. V1T 6L4. Tel: (604) 549-2804.

▶ **Yellow Point Lodge.** R.R. 3, **Ladysmith**, B.C. V0R 2E0. Tel: (604) 245-7422.

THE NORTHWEST TERRITORIES AND THE YUKON

By John Goddard

John Goddard has travelled throughout Canada's north for the Canadian Press news agency as a reporter and photographer. Now based in Montreal, he is writing a book about the Lubicon Cree of northern Alberta.

THE NORTHWEST TERRITORIES

The Northwest Territories attract outdoors people who like to climb, fish, canoe, spot birds, track wild animals, or sit alone on a rock nurturing a sense of well-being. The place is unimaginably huge, covering almost one-third of Canada. Nobody tries to see it all in one trip. A good approach is to focus on a single objective: an activity or a geographical area.

It helps to know that there are two distinct geographic

regions, defined by the tree line, which runs on a diagonal from the Mackenzie Delta in the extreme northwest to Hudson Bay at Churchill, Manitoba, in the southeast. Everything above the line is treeless Arctic—traditional domain of the Inuit, formerly called Eskimos. Everything below the line is treed sub-Arctic—traditional domain of the Dene (DUH-neh), also called northern Athapaskan Indians.

It also helps to know that transportation routes tend to be north-south, connecting Baffin Island to Montreal, for example, and the Mackenzie Valley to Edmonton, Alberta. For travel planning, the territories comprise five areas: Baffin Island, the High Arctic, Keewatin, the Arctic Coast, and the Mackenzie Valley.

MAJOR INTEREST

Baffin Region
Cape Dorset artist cooperative
Kekerton historic whaling station
Auyuittuq glaciated wilderness park
Inuit camping at the floe edge
Nanisivik marathon run

The High Arctic
North Pole flights
Ellesmere Island wilderness park
Lake Hazen thermal oasis
Fort Conger historic camp
Polar Bear Pass naturalist site

The Keewatin
Baker Lake art
Throat singing
Inuit outpost camp
Thelon Game Sanctuary
Outings to view caribou, walrus, and whales
Wilderness canoeing

The Arctic Coast
Bathurst Inlet naturalist lodge
Flora and wildlife
Wilderness canoeing

Yellowknife and the Mackenzie Valley
Yellowknife and environs
Prince of Wales Northern Heritage Centre
Moraine Point Lodge

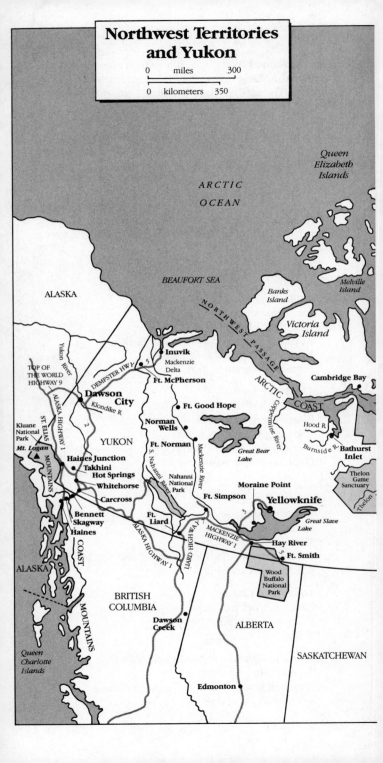

Fort Simpson
Nahanni National Park

Almost all parts of the Northwest Territories have become accessible to visitors in recent years through efforts of the territorial government. Standards for accommodations and meals in most settlements have risen by leaps and bounds, and services are offered almost everywhere to help you make the most of a trip. Prices are much higher than in southern Canada: up to $175 a night for room and board in an Arctic hostel. The best time to go is between mid-March, when the long days of sunlight begin and travelling conditions over ice and snow are still good, and late August, when summer wanes. The weather is highly changeable, demanding flexible schedules. Two pairs of sunglasses, warm clothing, and rugged footwear are essential for trips almost anywhere in the region. Credit cards and traveller's checks are not accepted in some outlying settlements, and cash is especially useful for buying items such as mukluks direct from a craftsperson. Maps and brochures, including the annual Explorers' Guide, can be requested from Travel Arctic, Government of N.W.T., Yellowknife, N.W.T. X1A 2L9; Tel: (403) 873-7200.

Northerners tend to like visitors and to view tourism as a pollution-free, renewable resource that creates such jobs as guiding and outfitting—jobs that utilize skills learned on the land and that are compatible with native ways of living.

Adapting traditional skills to a modern context is a broad-based, ongoing program in the territories, where nearly 60 percent of the people are native. Of the 52,000 people resident in the territories, 18,500 are Inuit, 11,500 Dene and Métis (mixed Dene and white blood), and 22,000 are grouped as "other." Representatives of all racial groups and geographic regions have been meeting for several years to develop new government structures for the territories, which, if adopted, would revolutionize the present colonial structure of government controlled by the federal powers in Ottawa. The proposal is much talked about across the north. It would divide the territories in half for more efficient administration: Nunavut in the east; Denendeh in the west. Draft constitutions for both new territories would guarantee native representation in the legislatures and would give native peoples power over areas of special concern, such as culture and wildlife protection. A remarkable aspect of the discussions has been the support of the white minority in promoting the native character of the territories, part of a general attitude the astute visitor is bound to notice: Despite a plethora of ethnic and regional differences, racism in the territories is minimal.

Archaeologists believe the Arctic regions were populated by a succession of migrating Inuit peoples from Asia over the past 4,000 years, each wave either dying out or being absorbed by the one that followed. Archaeologists call the earliest groups Independence I, pre-Dorset, Independence II, and Dorset. Collectively these cultures are known as the Arctic Small Tool tradition because of their common affinity for small stone scrapers, blades, and awls. Next came the Thule people, known for their whalebone houses, who are felt to be direct ancestors of the modern Inuit. Archaeological awareness is high in northern communities, thanks mostly to the Northern Cultural Heritage Project, which hires students from the region to work as junior archaeologists every summer in the High Arctic Islands.

The first known Europeans to become interested in the Arctic were British navigators looking for a northwest trading route to the Orient. Martin Frobisher arrived in 1576, followed by Henry Hudson, Robert Bylot, and William Baffin in the early 1600s. Not until 1905 was the Northwest Passage navigated successfully—by Roald Amundsen, a Norwegian—by which time the route held no commercial interest. During most of this century, many coastal Inuit were in contact with whaling vessels, whose crews exposed native people to fatal diseases but also introduced such innovations as tea, firearms, and iron cookware.

In the western sub-Arctic, early peoples are believed to have occupied the Mackenzie Valley for at least 10,000 years. They lived as small groups of nomadic hunters surviving on caribou, moose, beaver, rabbit, and fish. The five main groups of northern Dene today are the Loucheux (or Kutchin) in the extreme northwest, the Hare of Fort Good Hope, the large Slavey (or Slave) group south and west of Fort Norman, the Dogrib of Great Slave Lake, and the Chipewyans east of Great Slave Lake.

Fur traders from the rival Hudson's Bay and North West companies began penetrating the Mackenzie Valley overland in the late 1700s, setting up posts and engaging native peoples in the fur trade. The Hudson's Bay Company expanded to engage coastal Inuit groups in the early part of this century. Life gradually came to revolve around these posts, and to a large extent northern natives came to depend on fur sales for their livelihood. Profound changes in this status quo have occurred only recently. When fur prices fell in the 1950s, federal-government personnel arrived to distribute welfare funds, establish schools, and build houses. For the first time, native people moved into settlements on a large scale.

Although a few families continue to live full time on the land, settlements now characterize life in the territories. There are about 60 of them, widely dispersed. They differ in size, setting, and atmosphere, but they are alike in the way they function. The typical house is a prefabricated, pastel bungalow, although log houses are beginning to reappear in some Dene communities. Running water is uncommon; a water truck makes the rounds once or twice a week to fill a barrel or tank in each home. Small industries such as log milling and commercial char (trout) fishing have developed in some settlements, but most places have no economic base. The settlements are heavily subsidized, and almost all families take part of their living from the land. Even the most casual visitor is struck by the paraphernalia outside almost every home: snowmobiles, hide stretchers, animal-fur clothing, gasoline jugs, sleds, ropes, traps, and axes.

There are towns, too, in the Northwest Territories, the most important ones being Iqaluit on Baffin Island in the east, Inuvik near the Mackenzie River mouth in the northwest, and Yellowknife, the capital, on Great Slave Lake in the southwest.

THE BAFFIN REGION

The Viking adventurer Eric the Red is generally credited as the first white man to visit Baffin Island—at the farthest northeastern reach of Canada—late in the tenth century, but without leaving a lasting impression. The first well-documented visit was made in 1576 by English explorer Martin Frobisher, who had been looking for a northwest route to Cathay until rocks resembling gold quartz distracted him. He regrouped in England and returned to Baffin in 1578 with 15 ships full of settlers and supplies, intent on establishing a mining colony. The venture failed when the ore turned out to be iron pyrite.

Iqaluit

A town of 3,000 people, the capital of the Baffin region now stands near where Frobisher started to mine. It was founded as Frobisher Bay in 1914 by the Hudson's Bay Company, and renamed Iqaluit ("fish camp") in 1987, the Inuit word for the spot.

Few travellers make Iqaluit a primary destination, but it can make a worthwhile stopover before going on to places of greater interest. Its importance as a regional center dates from 1942, when the United States Air Force built an air base here. It was turned over to the Canadian armed forces after World War II. After the addition of a hospital and a regional Mountie headquarters, the community achieved town status in 1980. But the townsfolk had little to be proud of. Frobisher Bay had a reputation as an Arctic slum, a bad clash of southern and northern cultures. The subsequent growth of social services and a general maturing of the town now make it a comfortable and pleasant place to visit.

The Navigator Inn, the **Discovery Lodge Hotel**, and the **Frobisher Inn** all meet southern Canadian standards and include Arctic char, caribou, and Greenland shrimp on their dinner menus, as does the popular igloo-shaped restaurant **Komotiq**. The Frobisher Inn is not quite as new as the other two accommodations. Records and tapes of northern musicians such as Charlie Panigoniak and William Tagoona are available from the Hudson's Bay Company store. The hunters and trappers association runs an outlet at the airport, selling travel-packaged frozen char for departing visitors.

Whalebone homes built by the Thule people as much as 1,000 years ago can be visited by boat 20 minutes away at the **Qaummaarviit Historic Park**. Also of interest is the **Frobisher Bay Jewellery Shop**, a craft store that doubles as an experimental workshop for carvers, who are running out of their famous Baffin Island soapstone. Stones like Keewatin alabaster and Cape Dorset marble are being carved for the first time, with the help of such power tools as diamond-edged saws and air-driven hammers.

Cape Dorset

Scheduled flights travel twice weekly from Iqaluit to this settlement on the southwest extremity of Baffin Island, at the foot of the Kingnait mountain range. It is known for its gifted artists, foremost among them the carver and printmaker Kenojuak.

In 1953, after the market for white fox fur had collapsed, Canadian artist James Houston arrived under government auspices to develop Eskimo carving as a commercial enterprise, which met an overwhelmingly positive response in southern Canada and Europe. The Cape Dorset artists subsequently founded the West Baffin Eskimo Co-operative, and by 1959 it was turning out high-quality prints using techniques Houston had studied in Japan (techniques that have since spread to other communities). The co-op, which welcomes visitors, continues to be Cape Dorset's largest employer.

Dogsled trips and boat rides can be taken to the nesting grounds of the blue goose, in the **Dewy Soper Bird Sanctuary**, and to important archaeological sites. It was at Cape Dorset in 1925 that the archaeologist Diamond Jenness discovered the remains of an ancient Inuit people who inhabited the Arctic between 1000 B.C. and A.D. 1100. He called this the "Dorset culture," after Cape Dorset.

Pangnirtung

Scheduled flights from Iqaluit stop in Pangnirtung (population 1,000) three times a week, sometimes more often in summer. The settlement stands at the base of glaciated mountains on Baffin, north-northeast of Iqaluit, in a fjord off Cumberland Sound, which once teemed with bowhead whales. From the 1840s until about 1910 the area was chiefly a whaling center—at its peak, the most important one in the Arctic. White fox became valuable by 1921, when the Hudson's Bay Company built its trading post at Pangnirtung. Today, marine mammals and furbearers remain important to the subsistence of local residents. A thriving artist cooperative produces carvings, prints, tapestries, and also parkas. A $1 million visitors' center opened here in 1988, serving skiers and hikers bound for Auyuittuq National Park and helping others with trips to places like Kekerton.

Kekerton

Kekerton, on an island 30 miles south of Pangnirtung, opened in 1988 as the first historic park in the Northwest Territories. British whaler William Penny erected a station house on the site in 1857, quickly establishing it as the principal Arctic destination for British and American whalers. Their target was the magnificent bowhead whale, larger and heavier than a Greyhound bus. One whale could yield 150 barrels of oil, a major source of lighting and lubrication in Europe, and a ton of whalebone, which found countless uses in products requiring the flexibility now provided by plastics. Between 1820 and 1920 more than 18,000 bowheads were slain in the eastern Arctic; today only a few hundred remain. Kekerton is a monument to the majesty of the bowhead, the hardiness of the whalers, and the mingling of two starkly different whaling cultures—white and Inuit. It was also at Kekerton in 1883 that the pioneering German anthropologist Franz Boas formed his perspective on the equality of mankind. "I often ask myself," he wrote, "what advantages our 'good society' possesses over that of the 'savages,' and find, the more I see of their customs, that we have no right to look down upon them."

A boardwalk through Kekerton leads the visitor past whale-spotting lookouts, blubber-stripping sites, oil-rendering pots, Inuit houses, graveyards, and station-house foundations. To get there, visitors can hire a licensed Inuit guide through the Pangnirtung visitors' center; allow 12 hours for a round trip (by snowmobile in spring, by boat in summer).

Auyuittuq

Auyuittuq (oh-you-EE-too) National Park, north of Pangnirtung, boasts superlative ski touring and ski mountaineering. Downhill skiing is better in western Canada, but Auyuittuq, which is mostly glaciated by the Penny Ice Cap, offers the more thrilling, all-around wilderness experience. Skiers are completely isolated and must be self-sufficient. The best snow conditions are in April and May, but temperatures are usually more comfortable in summer. A popular though cruelly windy hiking route is the spectacular **Pangnirtung Pass** through the park between Pangnirtung and **Broughton Island**, a settlement of 440 people that has guest accommodations with meal service at the **Tulugak Co-op Hotel**; Broughton Island is served by scheduled flights from Pangnirtung and Iqaluit.

North Baffin

A unique and unforgettable northern experience is travelling in springtime to the floe edge, where land-fast ice meets open water. Groups of Inuit journey there to camp, hunt seals, and enjoy the 24-hour sunlight. At Pond Inlet and Igloolik, both north of the Arctic Circle, some outfitters and families are equipped to take visitors with them. The best time to go is usually late May and early June.

Pond Inlet (population 800) is a sheltered, scenic spot near the entrance to the Northwest Passage, with a sweeping view of the glaciated mountains of Bylot Island. It is an area rich in marine and bird life. Nearby, British whalers opened the Arctic whaling industry in 1820, killing bowheads by the hundreds for two decades before moving down to Cumberland Sound. A few whales are still around, and schools of single-tusk narwhals swim past in June or July—a phenomenon unique to north Baffin.

A modern, 16-room motel with a dining room, the **Sauniq Hotel**, opened in 1986; its management helps visitors hire outfitters for dog-team and snowmobile excursions to the floe edge, to char-fishing camps, and to the **Bylot Island** bird sanctuary. The best way to get there is a flight on First Air up the east coast from Iqaluit, rather than via Nanisivik, which is often fogged in.

Igloolik (population 850) is often praised for the strength and cohesiveness of its people. It has produced a number of political leaders, including Rhoda Inukshuk, past president of the Inuit political organization Inuit Taparitsat. It was also home during most of the 1970s to an eccentric American-born woman known simply as Georgia, who wrote pithy, lyric newspaper columns about Igloolik life, and later a book called *An Arctic Diary*.

After the last ice age the area around Igloolik, which is off the north end of the Melville Peninsula west of Baffin, became one of the first northern areas of human settlement. Archaeological evidence indicates that it has been occupied more or less continuously for the last 4,000 years. Besides looking at ancient campsites, visitors can become part of a living one. Outfitters are available for dogsled outings that can include camping in igloos and viewing walrus, seals, caribou, and polar bears. Regular flights reach Igloolik from Iqaluit and Resolute Bay.

Nanisivik (near the northern tip of Baffin Island) is a

lead/zinc mining settlement created in the mid-1970s, where on the longest day of the year—June 21—the Midnight Sun Marathon is held. A chartered jet full of runners arrives from Montreal two days early, weather permitting. The miners open their homes and communal dining hall to the visitors as part of annual town celebrations. Short-distance races are held the day before the marathon. The major race starts at the neighboring Inuit settlement of Arctic Bay (population 475).

THE HIGH ARCTIC

Resolute Bay (population 200) is the staging site for trips to the North Pole and the High Arctic Islands. It is found on Cornwallis Island facing the Northwest Passage and is named after H.M.S. *Resolute,* which was engaged in the search for the lost expedition of Sir John Franklin in 1850; later, wood from this ship was used to make a desk for U.S. President John F. Kennedy in the White House. The settlement began as an air base and weather station in 1947. An Inuit community was established in 1955, when the Canadian government moved several families from northern Quebec and Baffin Island to new hunting grounds here.

In a recent survey, Resolute Bay's weather ranked worst in the country for severity, discomfort, and gloominess, but a facility here for tourists ranks at the top for warmth, conviviality, and value for the money, drawing an adventurous, international clientele. Rates are less than $100 a day for room and board, the cheapest in the Arctic. Known officially as **High Arctic International Explorer Services Ltd.**, the combination tourist base and outfitting service is run by Bazel Jesudason, a former engineer from Madras, India, and his wife, Terry, a former kindergarten teacher from Trail, British Columbia. Anyone wishing to conquer the North Pole—whether by foot, motorcycle, dog team, or plane—talks to the Jesudasons first. Custom outings with Inuit guides, snowmobiles, and boats can be arranged, but it is better to join a scheduled group outing (5 to 11 days in duration and ranging in price from $760 to $3,000, not including airfare to Resolute Bay). The most adventurous expedition is by snowmobile-hauled sleds to **Grise Fiord** (population 114), Canada's northernmost Inuit community. Travellers camp on the sea ice, obtain their water by melting iceberg chunks, and are almost certain to see polar bears, musk-oxen, and caribou.

The High Arctic is unique for its starkness and sense of remoteness from civilization. Several dozen visitors a year pay up to $15,000 to fly to its northern extremity, the pole itself. Another highlight is northern **Ellesmere Island**, declared a national park reserve in 1986 and distinguished for its glaciated mountains. What scientists call a **thermal oasis**, an oddly warm, relatively lush valley, is located around Lake Hazen, the largest lake north of the Arctic Circle. **Fort Conger**, the historic camp on northeast Ellesmere from which U.S. Admiral Robert Peary launched his drive for the pole in 1909, is still largely intact and possible to visit by Twin Otter Airlines from either Iqaluit or Baffin Island. **Polar Bear Pass**, on Bathurst Island, is particularly rich in Arctic vegetation, birds, and wildlife. Three graves from Sir John Franklin's last expedition can still be seen on Beechy Island.

Resolute Bay is accessible from Montreal and Iqaluit in the east and from Edmonton and Yellowknife in the west, with flights three times a week in each direction.

THE KEEWATIN

Early fur-company explorers in the area west of Hudson Bay dubbed the area the Barren Lands for its lack of trees. Stories from the first half of this century link the name to starvation. John Hornby and his two companions exploring the Thelon River by canoe in 1926 were unable to find Beverly caribou—there were none there—and slowly starved to death over the winter. The caribou bypassed the Inuit in the 1940s and 1950s, bringing starvation to the area again, which Canadian writer Farley Mowat wrote about in *People of the Deer* and *The Desperate People*—two books still popular though not always accurate.

Rankin Inlet

The Inuit survived and now populate seven settlements in Keewatin, the largest of them being Rankin Inlet (population 1,400), established in 1955 on the west shore of Hudson Bay as a nickel mine. The mine closed after seven years, and Rankin Inlet endured trying times, but now it thrives as an administrative and servicing center. Attractions for visitors include the well-equipped

Siniktarvik Hotel and dining room, and a craft shop featuring *ulus* (Inuit knives), *kamiks* (Inuit boots), and ivory jewelry. Char-fishing trips by plane and freighter canoe and outings to the Marble Island whaling camps of the 1860s can be arranged at the Siniktarvik Hotel.

Baker Lake

One of the central attractions of Keewatin is Baker Lake (population 1,000), a vital community northwest of Rankin Inlet, known in art circles for its carvings and prints depicting the life and heritage of the caribou-hunting Inuit. In canoeing circles, it is known as the terminus of wilderness trips down the Thelon, Dubawnt, and Kazan rivers, all considered challenging for their remoteness and their harsh, changeable weather. In legal circles, Baker Lake is known as the hamlet that took a mining company to court and got a judgment in 1979 that reaffirmed the concept of aboriginal rights in Canadian law. The community is also known as the home of throat singers Emily Alerk and Lucy Kownak, masters of the art of manipulating the larynx to produce haunting, rhythmic sounds based on noises like the snap of a tent rope in the wind. Flights to Baker Lake are available from Rankin Inlet. Good accommodations and dining are available at the **Iglu Hotel**. Day trips can be taken to fishing spots, archaeological sites, and an Inuit outpost camp 20 miles from Baker Lake that is supported by the territorial tourism department. The **Thelon Game Sanctuary**, also accessible from Baker Lake, is a huge preserve for wide-ranging musk-oxen, caribou, and the Barren Ground grizzly.

Coral Harbour

Coral Harbour (population 475), although expensive to reach because of its remote location on Southampton Island in the north of the mouth of Hudson Bay, offers the chance to see beluga whales and walrus colonies. Highlights include archaeological remains 60 miles away (by boat) at **Native Point**, a sweeping ridge of land of whalebone houses and stone graves that was once home to perhaps a thousand Sallirmiut Inuit, who died out because of disease brought by European whalers in 1899. Coral Harbour can be reached by plane and boat from Rankin Inlet.

THE ARCTIC COAST

The mainland Arctic Coast was one of the last regions of the Northwest Territories to be explored, and it still is not heavily travelled. Botanists have recorded more than 1,100 varieties of plants in the region, and ornithologists have sighted some 180 bird species, many of which nest in the expansive **Queen Maud Gulf Bird Sanctuary**. Canoeists know the area for its four challenging wilderness rivers: the Back, Burnside, Coppermine, and Hood. Tour operators offer flying excursions of the region, lasting a weekend to a week, as well as hunts for polar bears and musk-oxen. Caribou hunts can be arranged through local hunters and trappers associations. Contact East Wind Arctic Tours and Outfitters, Box 2728, Yellowknife, N.W.T., X1A 2R1; Tel: (403) 873-2170.

Cambridge Bay (population 1,000) on Victoria Island due north of Regina, Saskatchewan, is the regional capital, distinguished by a co-op fish plant that processes 110,000 pounds of Arctic char a year. Lying half-sunken in the harbor can be seen the ship *Maud,* once used by Roald Amundsen and later sold to the Hudson's Bay Company. The settlement, served by scheduled flights from Edmonton and Yellowknife, acts as gateway to the six other settlements of the region.

A settlement of particular interest is **Bathurst Inlet**, which has been occupied by successive Inuit cultures for thousands of years. The small community here (population 60) is one of the few at which Inuit carry on much as they did before contact with whites. It has served as a trading post and mineral-exploration camp but has never developed into an established settlement. In 1969 the abandoned Hudson's Bay Company store and several other buildings were renovated by Glenn and Trish Warner of Yellowknife; from them they created the **Bathurst Inlet Lodge**, which has quickly acquired a reputation as a naturalists' haven that features Inuit help and a different Arctic scientist-in-residence every week. Sights include the local church, insulated with 300 caribou skins, and the thundering **Wilberforce Falls**, where Sir John Franklin once camped.

YELLOWKNIFE AND THE MACKENZIE VALLEY

Yellowknife, due north of Edmonton, Alberta, on the northern shore of Great Slave Lake, is a city of 12,000 people, two struggling gold mines, and three thriving governments—municipal, territorial, and federal—all paying generous travel and housing subsidies, and salaries that are generally higher than in southern Canada. It is a growing city, gradually replacing Edmonton as the gateway to the north. In Yellowknife the pioneering past imbues the pace of life, and the affluent present shows itself in worldly flourishes, like the cappuccino served at the **Float Base Bar** and the seafood crêpes at **Our Place Restaurant**. Hand-me-down shacks without running water fill the nooks and crannies of Old Town, while high-rise office and apartment buildings shape the skyline. The local population is a mix of old prospectors, dog mushers, miners, bush pilots, small-business people, architects, politicians, civil servants, and lawyers. The city possesses contrast, color, and a slightly invigorating tension in what might otherwise seem a dreary spot on the pre-Cambrian shield. Yellowknife is also the main crossroads for people from around the territories, including representatives on the Northwest Territories legislative council, whose 24 elected members debate in nine simultaneously interpreted languages. The council usually meets in February and October for two to four weeks at chambers in downtown Yellowknife.

The city got its name from a local Indian group, now extinct, the Yellowknives, so named because they were using utensils of yellowish metal when explorer Samuel Hearne encountered them in 1770. The metal was copper, but the name remained appropriate when gold quartz was discovered in 1896. Prospectors passed it up for the more accessible placer gold on the Klondike River in the Yukon, but they returned to erect a tent-and-shack city at Yellowknife in the 1930s, where they established mines and a respectable little town. A three-hour bus tour arranged through the visitors' center near City Hall covers most of the historic landmarks, including the stone monument honoring early bush pilots. A two-hour historical walking tour of the Old Town is outlined in the locally available pamphlet "Footloose in Yellowknife."

The three main downtown hotels (see Accommodations Reference at the end of the chapter) meet southern Canadian standards. They and the city's major restaurants regularly feature northern specialties, including Arctic char and whitefish—and sometimes musk-ox and caribou. In summer the refurbished, log-built **Wildcat Café** in Old Town is a must. In keeping with northern tradition, Yellowknife also has an active bar culture, offering many venues. No visit to Yellowknife is complete without a beer at the low-slung **Gold Range Hotel Bar**, with its crowded tables and country-rock bands.

The territorial museum, the **Prince of Wales Northern Heritage Centre**, stands at the edge of Frame Lake near downtown in a modern building designed by Vancouver architect Arthur Erickson. The exhibits, easily covered in half a day, document Yellowknife's beginnings and strongly emphasize the native culture and achievements in the north. One of the most striking exhibits is a moose-skin boat, built a few years ago under the museum's auspices by old-timers from the Dene settlement of Fort Norman. The mountain Dene of the area habitually built such boats in springtime to transport their winter fur catch to the trading post, and museum curators wanted one made before knowledge of how to do so was lost. The construction was fully documented in the films and still photographs that accompany the display. Lunch can be purchased in summer in a large skylit room upstairs.

A social highlight of the year is the Folk on the Rocks music festival at nearby Long Lake in July. Native crafts from throughout the territories are available at **Northern Images** in the Yellowknife Mall, and Dene products at **Treeline Trappings** on Franklin Avenue.

Activities outside Yellowknife abound: boat excursions on Great Slave Lake for an afternoon or several days; an evening drive by rented car along the Ingraham Trail for a meal at **Prelude Lake Lodge**; a trip by car and by three-quarter-mile footpath to Cameron Falls for a swim and picnic. Float planes are available for hire to outlying lakes and lodges.

Mackenzie Valley

The Dene settlements in the Mackenzie River Valley are not well equipped to receive vacationers, with the exception of **Fort Simpson**, west of Yellowknife, which has good accommodations (such as the **Fort Simpson Hotel**) and dining facilities, and to a lesser extent Fort Liard. Both are on the Liard Highway. The Mackenzie River itself runs north from the Great Slave Lake, past Fort Simpson, and into the Beaufort Sea. The Liard Highway, one of three routes entering the western territories, branches from the Alaska Highway at Fort Nelson in northern British Columbia and runs north through the Dene settlement of **Fort Liard** (population 400), known for its birch-bark baskets, past Nahanni National Park Reserve, and through Blackstone Park campgrounds to Fort Simpson (population 1,000), where the pope held mass for Canada's native peoples in 1987. An alternate route is the Mackenzie Highway from Alberta, through the towns of Fort Smith (population 2,500) and Hay River (population 3,000). Both highways lead to Yellowknife, although the route is cut during freezing and breakup every year at the Mackenzie River crossing. The third motor route into the territories is the Dempster Highway to Inuvik (covered in the Yukon section, below).

The Mackenzie region is great fishing country, and most of its lodges attract fishermen. The **Moraine Point Lodge** on Great Slave Lake, accessible from Yellowknife and Hay River, offers the kind of wilderness experience many travellers go to the High Arctic for. One of its owners is Yellowknife biologist Bill Carpenter, who during the 1970s was almost solely responsible for reintroducing purebred Canadian Arctic dogs to Inuit communities. The lodge's peak season is February to late spring, and activities include dog mushing, cross-country skiing, ice fishing, and the stalking of moose, caribou, wolves, and wood buffalo.

The Mackenzie region also attracts wilderness canoeists. The most popular river is the South Nahanni, in **Nahanni National Park Reserve**, recognized by UNESCO as a World Heritage site. It is memorable for the tumultuous Virginia Falls, narrow canyons, and stories of headless corpses, said to be those of prospectors seeking a lost gold mine.

THE YUKON

Tourism is the Yukon's number-one industry, founded on its majestic mountain wilderness and on fascination with the 1898 Klondike gold rush.

Unlike the Northwest Territories, the Yukon has roads—breathtakingly scenic roads—and is an ideal destination for owners of recreational vehicles. Motorists can reach the territory over Route 37, the Stewart-Cassiar Highway, through northwestern British Columbia, or over the more popular, better-serviced Alaska Highway, which officially begins at Dawson Creek, British Columbia, halfway up its eastern border with Alberta. Once in the Yukon, ambitious motorists can continue north all the way to the Mackenzie River mouth in the northwest corner of the Northwest Territories. They can also drive to Alaska, either along the foot of the St. Elias Mountains from Whitehorse through Haines Junction in the southwest corner of the Yukon, or west along the Top of the World Highway from Dawson City in west-central Yukon.

Scheduled ferries carrying passengers and vehicles connect Seattle, Vancouver, and Prince Rupert (on the coast of British Columbia) with the Alaskan ports of Haines and Skagway, both gateways to the Yukon. For airline passengers, there is jet service daily to Whitehorse from Vancouver and Edmonton.

Yukon visitors are well served between mid-May and mid-September by reception centers in the six main communities. Yukon Gold, a visitor radio station at 96.1 FM, broadcasts historical programs and news of special events from 9:00 A.M. to 9:00 P.M. daily. Free vacation catalogs and maps are available from Tourism Yukon, P.O. Box 2703, Whitehorse, Yukon, Y1A 2C6; Tel: (403) 667-5340.

MAJOR INTEREST

The White Pass & Yukon Railroad
Historic Skagway, Alaska
Chilkoot Trail
Whitehorse and environs
Cruises on the Yukon River
Carcross on the Tagish Loop

Historic Dawson City
Dempster Highway to Inuvik in the far north
Kluane National Park and St. Elias Mountains

A dour and determined Scot named Robert Campbell opened the Yukon to the British fur trade beginning in the early 1840s. He explored the Liard, Pelly, and Yukon rivers for the Hudson's Bay Company, which had been anxious about encroaching traders from what was then Russian-controlled Alaska.

Gold put the Yukon on the map. An Indian prospector from Carcross named Skookum Jim made the greatest gold strike in history on August 17, 1896, when he knelt for a drink of water in Rabbit Creek, a tributary of the Klondike River near the site of today's Dawson City. He ran to tell his partners, Tagish Charlie and George Carmack, that he had seen slabs of gold in the creek bed. "Then, as near as I can remember," Carmack, a white man originally from California, later recalled, "three full-grown men tried to see how big damn fools they could make of themselves. We did a dance ... composed of a Scotch hornpipe, Indian fox-trot, syncopated Irish jig, and a sort of a Siwash hula-hula." They renamed the creek Bonanza and set off the Klondike gold rush.

Tens of thousands of people headed north, most of them by steamer up the British Columbia coast to Skagway, Alaska, and over the rugged Coast Mountains by foot and mule through either the White Pass or the even tougher Chilkoot Pass. Long lines of humanity from horizon to horizon, bent double under their supplies, negotiated the mountains and floated down a series of rivers and lakes to the mud flats where Dawson was fast expanding at the confluence of the Klondike and Yukon rivers. One of the most outstanding personages of the day was Sam Steele, superintendent of the North West Mounted Police. He and 100 men imposed safety regulations and civil law, staking the territory for Canada and ensuring a certain orderliness in the gold rush.

The next stampede was by the U.S. Army in 1942. The American military feared invasion from Japan via Alaska and, to head it off, built the Alaska Highway in nine months, from Dawson Creek, British Columbia, through the southern Yukon to Fairbanks, Alaska. "The Road to Tokyo," as the soldiers called it, was 1,500 miles of track through virgin sub-Arctic wilderness. Whitehorse, along the route, was transformed almost overnight from a town of 500 people to a construction hub for 30,000 workers. The Japanese never came.

By 1982 all of the Yukon's major mines had closed because of low prices for zinc, lead, silver, and copper (some of the mines have since reopened, and the economy is stable). The main challenge to Yukoners now is to create a social system that attains the difficult balance of economic growth, wilderness preservation, and the rebuilding of the native community after the disruptions of the gold rush and the highway boom. Of the 27,000 people resident in the territory, about 6,000 are native. The Council for Yukon Indians has been engaged in aboriginal-rights talks with the federal and Yukon governments for several years, hoping a settlement will bring more political clout and economic opportunities to the native people, and benefits to the Yukon as a whole.

The White Pass & Yukon Railroad

The train through the historic White Pass from Skagway, Alaska, is a spectacular way to enter the Yukon, and offers an almost mandatory sidetrip for visitors arriving from other directions. Passengers ride in luxurious old parlor cars along a narrow-gauge line built between 1898 and 1900 to ease travel over one of the most treacherous segments of the route to the gold fields.

The trip begins in Skagway, climbing through panoramic vistas past Bridal Falls and over Deadhorse Gulch, where 3,000 packhorses and mules died under the ruthless ambitions of gold stampeders. The train continues to White Pass Summit, 2,865 feet above sea level near the Canada–U.S. border, then descends the other side to Fraser, British Columbia. From there, passengers have a choice. They can ride the train back to Skagway, or continue by bus to Carcross and Whitehorse, the Yukon capital. The Skagway round trip takes just under three hours, and runs twice daily between the third week of May and the third week of September. The trip between Skagway and Whitehorse takes six and a half hours, available once daily from either direction.

The railway also serves hikers of the popular **Chilkoot Trail**, which begins near Skagway and rises over the Chilkoot Pass to Bennett, British Columbia. The spectacular trail was carved by gold stampeders before the railway was finished and takes about four days to cover. From

Lake Bennett, the train takes hikers to Fraser to board the train back to Skagway or the bus to Whitehorse.

Skagway, Alaska

Skagway is the northernmost port on Alaska's Inside Passage. It evolved from a camp with a single log cabin in 1897 to a staging center for thousands of gold seekers one year later. Soon known as the toughest town in America, it came under the control of a bland, smiling hooligan named Soapy Smith, who prospered through gambling, prostitution, hijacking, theft, and murder before finally being gunned down on the Skagway docks. Today Skagway's carefully renovated buildings and boardwalks give travellers a flavor of gold-rush days.

Skagway is also a starting point for the White Pass & Yukon Railroad and the **Golden Circle Route**, one of the north's most scenic and historic drives, covering 360 miles via Carcross and Whitehorse to Haines Junction and down to Haines, Alaska. Among the attractions are the White Pass summit and Deadhorse Gulch.

Whitehorse

Whitehorse, in the southwestern part of the Yukon, north of Skagway, began as a staging ground for gold seekers emerging through the White Pass to descend the Yukon River to the Klondike, and the spirit of '98 lives on. With a population of 19,000, Whitehorse is the largest urban center in the Canadian north. It is also the Yukon's capital and a crossroads for travellers between Alaska, British Columbia, historic Dawson City, and Inuvik, in the Northwest Territories at the mouth of the Mackenzie.

From early June to mid-September there are nightly performances of the Frantic Follies at the **Westmark Whitehorse Hotel**, featuring skits and cancan dancing reminiscent of gold-rush times. A two-hour boat cruise can be taken through **Miles Canyon**, once dangerous rapids; and dinner cruises on the Yukon River are offered when the riverboat M.V. *Anna Maria* is in town. The S.S. *Klondike* stern-wheeler, launched in 1937, is on display near downtown and creates a focus for Yukon River history. The Yukon Historical and Museums Association offers free guided walking tours of downtown Whitehorse, guided bus tours are available, and the Yukon Conservation Society provides guided nature walks in the area. The **MacBride Museum** is worth visiting for its gold-rush collection and stuffed Yukon animals.

Outside of town there are opportunities to pan for gold, ride horses, swim in the **Takhini Hotspring**, and eat fresh barbecued salmon during readings from the works of Robert Service, a historic figure whose legacy is difficult to avoid here. Service is celebrated as the Bard of the Klondike for his entertaining, if not particularly literary, poems such as "The Law of the Yukon," "The Shooting of Dan McGrew," and "The Cremation of Sam McGee."

The 60-foot twin-deck *Anna Maria* also makes six scheduled round trips on the Yukon River to Dawson City (four days downriver to Dawson, five-day return). A one-way trip is 460 miles and evokes the heyday of Yukon River travel. For information and reservations: Karpes and Pugh Yukon River Trading Company Ltd., P.O. Box 4220, Whitehorse, Yukon, Y1A 4S3; Tel: (403) 667-2873.

Full details on how to enjoy the Yukon capital and its surroundings are available at the Whitehorse Visitor Reception Centre, 302 Steele Street, one block north of Main Street (Tel: 403-667-2915). The center is open from 8:00 A.M. to 8:00 P.M., between mid-May and mid-September, providing information on shopping, accommodations, restaurants, and local events. (We list some good accommodations at the end of the chapter.) An audiovisual show, *Faces of the Yukon,* describes the Alaska Highway, the Dempster Highway, Dawson City, and other highlights. Work by Yukon artists is on display in the foyer.

Carcross

An easy side trip from Whitehorse is the **Tagish Loop**: south to Carcross, east to the Alaska Highway, and back to Whitehorse, a round trip of 100 miles through the scenic lake district of southern Yukon, easily covered in an afternoon. Carcross (population 150) is dominated by the Matthew Watson General Store, established in 1911, and the Caribou Hotel, opened during the 1898 gold rush. An old steamboat and tiny locomotive are on display, but of greater historical significance are the graves in the overgrown cemetery, of Skookum Jim, Tagish Charlie, and George Carmack—discoverers of the Klondike goldfields.

Dawson City

Re-creating for visitors some idea of the place as it existed in gold-rush days, the Canadian parks system has done much to restore some of the luster of Dawson City (population 1,500; in west-central Yukon) claimed by time and shifting permafrost. Local characters colorfully play out personal myths in prospector hats and dungarees. Commemorative stamps can be purchased at a post office dating from 1901; the Gaslight Follies revue is staged nightly at the reconstructed Palace Grand Theatre; gambling is legal at Diamond Tooth Gertie's Gambling Hall; period fashions are on sale at the historic Madame Tremblay's Store; and readings from his works are held at Robert Service's old cabin. A cabin that was once home to American writer Jack London is also open to visitors, but, oddly, another historic building has been overlooked by Parks Canada. It stands near the Service cabin—paint peeling, boardwalk overgrown, the only hint of its significance a sign saying "Berton home." It is the boyhood home of author and broadcaster Pierre Berton, one of Canada's most prolific writers and the son of an 1898 stampeder. Berton's mother, Laura, wrote the book *I Married the Klondike*—based mostly on her years in this house.

Among the annual special events in Dawson City is the Commissioner's Ball in June, when the head of the Yukon government throws a dance at the Palace Grand Theatre, to which revellers come in period dress; visitors and many of the Yukon's leading citizens attend. Discovery Days in mid-August marks Skookum Jim's historic find with a parade, canoe races, and dances. The Great Klondike Outhouse Race through town in early September features a bizarre competition of outhouses on wheels.

Hotels are varied and plentiful. Four main ones are listed at the end of this chapter.

Beginning near Dawson City, the all-weather, gravel-surfaced **Dempster Highway** runs 448 miles north through sub-Arctic bush and over Arctic tundra to Inuvik, in the Northwest Territories. It offers spectacular, wide-open scenery but is not a road for amateurs: There is only one service stop in the 300 miles between Dawson City and the Dene settlement of Fort McPherson (population 700) in the Northwest Territories.

Inuvik (population 3,200) was built in 1954 as a regional government center and developed during the

1970s into a supply base for oil exploration in the Beaufort Sea. Development of offshore reserves is on hold pending a change in world oil prices, but Inuvik nevertheless remains a lively town—especially in the 24-hour daylight during summer—of trappers, pilots, scientists, and entrepreneurs. Good accommodations and dining are available, as well as services to explore the sprawling, labyrinthine Mackenzie River Delta. The leading hotels are the **Finto Inn** and the **Eskimo Inn**.

Kluane National Park

Kluane is a wilderness park embracing the St. Elias Mountains and Canada's highest peak, Mount Logan (19,850 feet). Moose, grizzly bears, mountain goats, Dall sheep, and caribou roam here unthreatened by hunters, and 150 species of birds have been recorded, including the rare peregrine falcon. Conditions and regulations for serious adventurers are rigorous, but casual visitors have easy access to day trails, one of the most memorable being the hike up Sheep Mountain near Haines Junction, where hikers can approach to within a few yards of docile, big-horned Dall sheep.

GETTING AROUND

Transportation routes to the North tend to be north-south. Montreal and Ottawa serve the Baffin region with direct flights to Iqaluit. Flights from Ottawa continue up the west coast of Baffin Island, while flights from Montreal continue to Resolute Bay, sometimes with stops at Hall Beach on the Melville Peninsula, or Nanisivik at the north end of Baffin Island. All settlements of the region can be reached by regularly scheduled flights, the main jump-off points being Iqaluit and Resolute Bay.

Direct flights from Winnipeg, Manitoba, serve Rankin Inlet, capital of Keewatin, and regularly scheduled flights from Rankin Inlet serve the other Keewatin communities. In an exception to the north-south rule, Rankin Inlet can also be reached directly from Iqaluit in the east and Yellowknife in the west.

Edmonton serves the Mackenzie River Valley and western Arctic with direct flights to Yellowknife. Passengers from Edmonton can also reach Fort Smith, Hay River, Fort Simpson, Norman Wells, Inuvik, Cambridge Bay, and Resolute Bay without changing planes. Regional centers are: Yellowknife, serving the Great Slave area, the Mackenzie

River, and Arctic Coast; Norman Wells, serving nearby Mackenzie River communities; Inuvik, serving the western Arctic; and Cambridge Bay, local jump-off to the Arctic Coast communities.

Edmonton and Vancouver serve Whitehorse, in the Yukon, with some flights connecting to Dawson City and to Inuvik in the Mackenzie Delta.

Dozens of package tours originate from Montreal, Ottawa, Toronto, Winnipeg, Edmonton, Vancouver, Seattle, and all northern regional centers. Some of them cover giant swaths of territory, others are locally oriented. A complete list of tour operators and outfitters for the Northwest Territories is available from: TravelArctic, Government of the Northwest Territories, Yellowknife, N.W.T., X1A 2L9 (Tel: 403-873-7200). For similar information on the Yukon, write: Tourism Yukon, P.O. Box 2703, Whitehorse, Yukon, Y1A 2C6 (Tel: 403-667-5340).

ACCOMMODATIONS REFERENCE

Accommodations standards in the North have changed dramatically for the better in recent years. They meet southern standards in Iqaluit, Yellowknife, Fort Smith, Hay River, Inuvik, Whitehorse, and Dawson City, and serve visitors well in intermediate-size centers such as Pangnirtung, Cape Dorset, Pond Inlet, Resolute Bay, Rankin Inlet, Baker Lake, and Fort Simpson. In outlying settlements, services generally diminish with the size of population. Visitors can be asked to double up, and cooking tends to be simple—circumstances that can generate camaraderie and enhance a visit.

▶ **Auyuittuq Lodge. Pangnirtung**, N.W.T. X0A 0R0. Tel: (819) 473-8955.

▶ **Baker Lake Lodge. Baker Lake**, N.W.T. X0C 0A0. Tel: (819) 793-2905.

▶ **Bathurst Inlet Lodge.** Box 820, **Yellowknife**, N.W.T. X1A 2T2. Tel: (403) 873-2595.

▶ **Discovery Inn.** Box 784, **Yellowknife**, N.W.T. X1A 2N6. Tel: (403) 873-4151.

▶ **Discovery Lodge Hotel.** Box 387, **Iqaluit**, N.W.T. X0A 0H0. Tel: (819) 979-4433.

▶ **Downtown Hotel.** Box 780, **Dawson City**, Yukon Y0B 1G0. Tel: (403) 993-5346.

▶ **Edgewater Hotel.** 101 Main Street, **Whitehorse**, Yukon Y1A 2A7. Tel: (403) 667-2572.

▶ **Eldorado Hotel.** P.O. Box 338, **Dawson City**, Yukon Y0B 1G0. Tel: (403) 993-5451.

► **Eskimo Inn.** P.O. Box 1740, **Inuvik,** N.W.T. X0E 0T0. Tel: (403) 979-2801.

► **Esunqarq Motel.** Katudgevik Co-op, **Coral Harbour,** N.W.T. X0C 0C0. Tel: (819) 925-9969 or 925-9926.

► **Explorer Hotel.** Postal Service 7000, **Yellowknife,** N.W.T. X1A 2R3. Tel: (403) 873-3531.

► **Finto Inn.** P.O. Box 1925, **Inuvik,** N.W.T. X0E 0T0. Tel: (403) 979-2647.

► **Fort Simpson Hotel.** Box 248, **Fort Simpson,** N.W.T. X0E 0N0. Tel: (403) 695-2201.

► **Frobisher Inn.** Box 610, **Iqaluit,** N.W.T. X0A 0H0. Tel: (819) 979-5241 or (800) 263-6425.

► **Gold Rush Inn.** 411 Main Street, **Whitehorse,** Yukon Y1A 2B6. Tel: (403) 668-4500.

► **Grise Fiord Lodge. Grise Fiord,** N.W.T. X0A 0J0. Tel: (819) 980-9913.

► **Iglu Hotel. Baker Lake,** N.W.T. X0C 0A0. Tel: (819) 793-2801.

► **Ikaluktutiak Cambridge Bay Hotel.** Box 38, **Cambridge Bay,** N.W.T. X0E 0C0. Tel: (403) 983-2215 or 983-2201.

► **International Explorer's Home.** Box 200, **Resolute Bay,** N.W.T. X0A 0V0. Tel: (819) 252-3875. This is the headquarters for High Arctic International Explorer Services Ltd.

► **Keewatin Guest Lodge.** Box 20, **Rankin Inlet,** N.W.T. X0C 0G0. Tel: (819) 645-2402.

► **Kingnait Inn. Cape Dorset,** N.W.T. X0A 0C0. Tel: (819) 897-8863 or 897-8847.

► **Leonie's Place. Coral Harbour,** N.W.T. X0C 0C0. Tel: (819) 925-9751 or 925-8810.

► **Midnight Sun Hotel.** Box 840, **Dawson City,** Yukon Y0B 1G0. Tel: (403) 993-5495.

► **Moraine Point Lodge.** Box 2882, **Yellowknife,** N.W.T. X1A 2R2. Tel: (413) 920-4542 or (413) 873-8249.

► **Narwhal Arctic Services.** c/o Gord Stewart, Box 88, **Resolute Bay,** N.W.T. X0A 0V0. Tel: (819) 252-3968.

► **The Navigator Inn.** Box 158, **Iqaluit,** N.W.T. X0A 0H0. Tel: (819) 979-6201.

► **Sauniq Hotel.** Toonoonik Sahoonik Co-op, **Pond Inlet,** N.W.T. X0A 0S0. Tel: (819) 899-8928.

► **Siniktarvik, Rankin Inlet Lodge.** Box 190, **Rankin Inlet,** N.W.T. X0C 0G0. Tel: (819) 645-2807.

► **Tujormivik Hotel. Igloolik,** N.W.T. X0A 0L0. Tel: (819) 934-8814.

▶ **Tulugak Co-op Hotel.** Broughton Island, N.W.T. X0A 0B0. Tel: (819) 927-8932.

▶ **Westmark Whitehorse Hotel.** Box 4250, Second Avenue and Wood Street, **Whitehorse**, Yukon Y1A 3T3. Tel: (403) 668-4700.

▶ **Westmark Inn.** Box 420, **Dawson City**, Yukon Y0B 1G0. Tel: (403) 993-5542.

▶ **Westmark Klondike.** 2288 Second Avenue, **Whitehorse**, Yukon Y1A 1C8. Tel: (403) 668-4747.

▶ **Yellowknife Inn.** Box 490, **Yellowknife**, N.W.T. X1A 2N4. Tel: (403) 873-2601.

CHRONOLOGY OF THE HISTORY OF CANADA

- **A.D. 986**: Bjarni Herjolfsson, sailing from Iceland, misses Greenland and sights the Canadian coast.
- **1000**: Leif Eriksson heads expedition to Vinland (L'Anse aux Meadows, Newfoundland).
- **1497**: John Cabot discovers Canada's east coast—and all its fish.
- **1504**: St. John's, Newfoundland, established as base for English fisheries.
- **1534**: Jacques Cartier lands at Gaspé, in Quebec, and claims land for France.
- **1535**: Cartier sails up St. Lawrence to Hochelaga, now Montreal. Names Canada with Indian word for a settlement: "Kannata."
- **1577**: Martin Frobisher reaches Hudson Strait.
- **1583**: Humphrey Gilbert claims Newfoundland for Britain even though fishing vessels are also there from France, Spain, and Portugal.
- **1605**: Port Royal (Annapolis, Nova Scotia) established by Sieur de Monts and Samuel de Champlain.
- **1608**: Champlain founds Quebec and starts eight-year sporadic exploration of interior, reaching Georgian Bay.
- **1610**: Etienne Brulé sent to Huron village on Georgian Bay in exchange for an Indian going to France. Henry Hudson discovers Hudson Bay.
- **1616**: Indian schools set up at Tadoussac and Trois Rivières.
- **1617**: The first Quebec colonist—apothecary Louis Hébert—arrives from Nova Scotia.

- **1639**: Hôtel Dieu, the first hospital, opens at Quebec.
- **1642**: Ville Marie, later Montreal, founded by Maisonneuve.
- **1649**: Martyrdom of Jesuit missionaries Jean de Brébeuf and Gabriel Lalemant and destruction of their mission. Groseilliers and his young brother-in-law, Radisson, reach Lake Superior and return with 60 canoes full of beaver pelts.
- **1666**: Jean Talon, the colony's first business manager, arrives in Quebec and takes census: 3,215 Europeans, including two married couples under the age of 15.
- **1668**: Groseilliers leaves England for Hudson Bay, returning in 1669 with pelts worth £19,000.
- **1670**: With this success, the Hudson's Bay Company is founded by Prince Rupert with title over the entire watershed.
- **1672**: Frontenac appointed governor of New France; builds Fort Frontenac on site of present Kingston, Ontario.
- **1678**: Niagara Falls has first white visitor: Father Jean-Louis Hennepin.
- **1713**: France surrenders to England any claim to Hudson Bay region, Newfoundland, and Acadia (now part of Nova Scotia).
- **1714**: Louis XIV orders building of Louisbourg fortress.
- **1734**: First road opens between Quebec and Montreal.
- **1745**: Fort Rouille (Toronto) built to stop smuggling to English colonies.
- **1749**: Halifax founded with 2,500 settlers; St. Paul's Anglican Church built.
- **1755**: Nova Scotia expels Acadians not swearing allegiance to Britain.
- **1758**: Louisbourg falls to the British.
- **1759**: General Wolfe defeats Marquis de Montcalm on Plains of Abraham.
- **1763**: France and Spain cede to Britain all North American territory east of Mississippi except St. Pierre and Miquelon.
- **1774**: Quebec Act sets up nonrepresentative government and allows freedom of worship (has been called the Magna Carta of French Canada). The Act irritates New England colonists.

- **1775**: Outbreak of the American Revolution; the siege of Quebec City.
- **1778**: Captain Cook lands on Vancouver Island and claims the Pacific coast for Britain.
- **1783–1784**: Immigration of United Empire Loyalists to New Brunswick, along St. Lawrence, Niagara and Detroit rivers, and Bay of Quinte.
- **1789**: Sir Alexander Mackenzie reaches Beaufort Sea by following the river that is to bear his name.
- **1793**: Importation of slaves into Upper Canada forbidden.
- **1803**: Using rags, first paper mill established near Lachute, Quebec.
- **1807**: David Thompson, noted mapmaker, crosses Rockies; Simon Fraser travels 800 miles from source of Fraser River to Pacific.
- **1811**: In Eastern Ontario John McIntosh finds and transplants apple tree from which his son Allan later develops the McIntosh apple. Red River Settlement, first in Western Canada, founded by Lord Selkirk with 12,000 Irish and Scottish pioneers.
- **1812**: Americans declare war against Britain and are defeated at Detroit and Niagara by troops led by Sir Isaac Brock.
- **1813**: To warn of another American attack at Niagara, Laura Secord walks 19 miles through dense bush with her cow.
- **1824**: First medical school in Canada opens in Montreal, later part of McGill University.
- **1829**: Welland and Lachine canals open.
- **1832**: Opening of Rideau Canal links Lake Ontario to Ottawa River.
- **1837**: Rebellion in Lower Canada and Upper Canada against ruling establishments. Lord Durham dispatched as governor.
- **1839**: Durham's report criticizes the ruling cliques and recommends self-government and union of two Canadas.
- **1841**: First meeting of Parliament of Canada at Kingston.
- **1844**: Charles Fenerty in Nova Scotia discovers how to make paper from ground wood pulp. George Brown, at 26, publishes first issue of *Toronto Globe* as a weekly Liberal paper; it goes daily in 1853.
- **1846**: Irish-born Reverend William King from the

U.S. sets up Elgin Settlement for escaped slaves in Kent County.

- **1847**: Lord Elgin arrives as governor-general, with instructions to give responsible government a fair trial.
- **1857**: Queen Victoria chooses Bytown (Ottawa) as capital of Canada.
- **1858**: Gold found in Fraser River Valley (British Columbia).
- **1859**: Tariffs set up so manufacturers can compete abroad.
- **1864**: Fathers of Confederation meet at Charlottetown, Prince Edward Island, October 10–27, and in London, December 4, to pass resolutions for British North America Act.
- **1866–1867**: Fenian raids (militant Irish-Americans angry with Britain).
- **1867**: On July 1, Nova Scotia, New Brunswick, Quebec, and Ontario unite to become Dominion of Canada, with Sir John A. Macdonald the first prime minister. Toronto schoolteacher Alexander Muir writes patriotic song "Maple Leaf Forever" for his pupils and, for $30, has 1,000 copies printed. It is soon pirated by a music publisher. Indian game of field lacrosse becomes Canada's national game by law. It still is.
- **1869**: Outbreak of Red River Rebellion, uprising of the Métis in West under Louis Riel. After second rebellion in 1885, Riel executed and becomes hero. (See the Manitoba and Saskatchewan chapters.)
- **1875**: Supreme Court established.
- **1885**: Last spike driven for Canadian Pacific's transcontinental railway.
- **1896**: Gold found in the Klondike.
- **1900**: Economy of Canada booming; thousands of Europeans accept offer of free land.
- **1901**: Marconi receives first transatlantic wireless message at St. John's, Newfoundland.
- **1903**: Fred LaRose, blacksmith, accidentally finds rich silver deposit in Cobalt, Ontario, and starts a mining stampede.
- **1909**: First flight in Canada of heavier-than-air machine under its own power: McCurdy's Silver Dart.
- **1914**: Discovery of oil at Turner Valley, near Calgary.

- **1917**: Women get the vote in federal elections. Income tax introduced as "temporary" wartime measure. Collision of munitions and supply ships in Halifax harbor creates an explosion that kills 2,000 and injures 9,000 people.
- **1923**: The world's first hockey broadcast made by Foster Hewitt in Toronto from a telephone booth.
- **1926**: Prime Minister Mackenzie King at Imperial Conference in London asks that Canada be independent; Balfour Declaration recognizes autonomy for all Dominions. This becomes law in 1931 with passing of Statute of Westminster.
- **1934**: Dionne quintuplets, first to survive more than a few hours, born near Callander, Ontario.
- **1938**: At Kingston, Ontario, Prime Minister King greets Franklin Roosevelt, the first U.S. president to visit Canada.
- **1947**: Oil is discovered at Leduc, Alberta.
- **1949**: Newfoundland becomes tenth province of Canada.
- **1961**: National program for health insurance goes into effect.
- **1965**: The red maple leaf becomes official flag.
- **1967**: On July 7, French President Charles de Gaulle visits Montreal and declares: "Vive le Québec libre!"
- **1969**: Parliament decides Canada should change to metric system of weights and measures.
- **1970**: FLQ (Front de Libération Québecois) kidnaps Pierre Laporte, Quebec minister of labor, and leaves his dead body in trunk of car; War Measures Act declared and 500 people arrested.
- **1976**: Montreal hosts summer Olympic games, Canada's first. Led by René Lévesque, the Parti Québecois, which advocates independence for Quebec, wins a majority in the National Assembly. In the 1980 referendum, 60 percent of Quebeckers vote to remain in Canada.
- **1978**: Spanish galleons dating to 16th century discovered in icy waters off Red Bay, Labrador.
- **1982**: Canada gains new Constitution, the Charter of Rights and Freedoms.
- **1986**: Expo 86 in Vancouver, British Columbia, attracts 22 million visitors.

- **1988**: Winter Olympics held at Calgary.
- **1989**: On January 1, the Free Trade Agreement with the United States, which was signed in 1988, becomes law. By 1998, all tariffs between the two countries are to be phased out.

—Jean Danard

INDEX

FOR THE BEST IN PAPERBACKS, LOOK FOR THE

In every corner of the world, on every subject under the sun, Penguin represents quality and variety—the very best in publishing today.

For complete information about books available from Penguin—including Pelicans, Puffins, Peregrines, and Penguin Classics—and how to order them, write to us at the appropriate address below. Please note that for copyright reasons the selection of books varies from country to country.

In the United Kingdom: For a complete list of books available from Penguin in the U.K., please write to *Dept E.P., Penguin Books Ltd, Harmondsworth, Middlesex, UB7 0DA.*

In the United States: For a complete list of books available from Penguin in the U.S., please write to *Dept BA, Penguin*, Box 120, Bergenfield, New Jersey 07621-0120.

In Canada: For a complete list of books available from Penguin in Canada, please write to *Penguin Books Ltd, 2801 John Street, Markham, Ontario L3R 1B4.*

In Australia: For a complete list of books available from Penguin in Australia, please write to the *Marketing Department, Penguin Books Ltd, P.O. Box 257, Ringwood, Victoria 3134.*

In New Zealand: For a complete list of books available from Penguin in New Zealand, please write to the *Marketing Department, Penguin Books (NZ) Ltd, Private Bag, Takapuna, Auckland 9.*

In India: For a complete list of books available from Penguin, please write to *Penguin Overseas Ltd, 706 Eros Apartments, 56 Nehru Place, New Delhi, 110019.*

In Holland: For a complete list of books available from Penguin in Holland, please write to *Penguin Books Nederland B.V., Postbus 195, NL-1380AD Weesp, Netherlands.*

In Germany: For a complete list of books available from Penguin, please write to *Penguin Books Ltd, Friedrichstrasse 10-12, D-6000 Frankfurt Main I, Federal Republic of Germany.*

In Spain: For a complete list of books available from Penguin in Spain, please write to *Longman, Penguin España, Calle San Nicolas 15, E-28013 Madrid, Spain.*

In Japan: For a complete list of books available from Penguin in Japan, please write to *Longman Penguin Japan Co Ltd, Yamaguchi Building, 2-12-9 Kanda Jimbocho, Chiyoda-Ku, Tokyo 101, Japan.*